BLOOD
THE OMNIBUS

WELCOME TO THE world of Blood Bowl – football played fantasy-style, where teams can be human, orcs and ogres, and players are as likely to throw a goblin as a ball! It's a brutal game full of grid-iron grit where the referees are as tooled up as the players and life and death hangs on the application of a magic sponge. These three stories follow the career of Dunk Hoffnung, as he works his way up from unemployed adventurer to star player with the Bad Bay Hackers. Sport in Warhammer has never been such fun!

More Blood Bowl by Matt Forbeck

(Book 4) RUMBLE IN THE JUNGLE

BLOOD BOWL
THE OMNIBUS

Matt Forbeck

A Black Library Publication.

Blood Bowl copyright © 2005, Games Workshop Ltd
Dead Ball copyright © 2005, Games Workshop Ltd
Death Match copyright © 2006, Games Workshop Ltd
This omnibus edition published in Great Britain in 2007 by
BL Publishing,
Games Workshop Ltd.,
Willow Road, Nottingham,
NG7 2WS, UK.

10 9 8 7 6 5 4 3 2 1

Cover illustration by Philip Sibbering.

A CIP record for this book is available from the British Library.

ISBN 13: 978 1 84416 515 5
ISBN 10: 1 84416 515 9

Distributed in the US by Simon & Schuster
1230 Avenue of the Americas, New York, NY 10020, US.

See the Black Library on the Internet at
www.blacklibrary.com

Find out more about the world of Blood Bowl at
www.specialist-games.com/bloodbowl

'Hi there, sports fans, and welcome to the Blood Bowl for tonight's contest. You join us here with a capacity crowd, packed with members of every race from across the known world, all howling like banshees in anticipation of tonight's game. Oh, and yes there are some banshees... Well, kick-off is in about two pages' time, so we've just got time to go over to your commentator for tonight, Jim Johnson, for a recap on the rules of the game before battle commences. Good evening, Jim!'

'Thank you, Bob! Well, good evening and boy, are you folks in for some great sporting entertainment. First of all though, for those of you at home who are unfamiliar with the rules, here's how the game is played.

'Blood Bowl is an epic conflict between two teams of heavily armed and quite insane warriors. Players pass, throw and run with the ball, attempting to get it to the other end of the field, the end zone. Of course, the other team must try and stop them, and recover the ball for their side. If a team gets the ball over the line into the opponents' end zone it's called a touchdown; the team that scores the most touchdowns by the end of the match wins the game. Of course, it's not always as simple as that...'

CONTENTS

AUTHOR INTRODUCTION

I LOVE BLOOD BOWL.

I first played the game with one of my college roommates, Bryan Winter, back in 1989. He worked for a game store and had a copy of the second edition, the one with the Astrogranite board. We pummelled each other's teams up and down that board and had a fantastic time.

That's one of the reasons I asked about a job in Games Workshop's Design Studio when I was in the UK on a student work visa back in 1989. I wanted to see Europe after I graduated from college but didn't have enough money to just travel. In all of Europe, only the UK both participated in the work visa program and used a language I spoke.

That September, I took a one-way flight to London and landed with $600 in my pocket and almost everything I owned in a pair of duffel bags. I didn't know a soul in the entire country. The Wednesday morning I landed in London, I phoned up the Design Studio in Nottingham and arranged for a job interview.

I showed up for the interview in a suit and tie, which – as you know if you've ever visited any game company's offices – made me embarrassingly overdressed. I thought the interview went well, but I didn't realize (and wouldn't know until years later) that I was up against two others who'd applied for the same job. At the end of the day, they gave me an editing test and asked me to complete it over the weekend.

They asked me if I knew proper British editing marks. Nodding, I lied to say I knew the American version, but I was confident I could pick up the UK version fast. When I got back to London, I went straight to the nearest bookshop, just off

Piccadilly Circus, and bought a Queen's English dictionary that contained a list of standard editing marks in the back.

I returned to the Design Studio on Monday with my duffel bags on my back. I handed over the redlined test and explained that if a job was offered to me that day I'd be thrilled. Otherwise, my father's friend's boss's daughter lived in Oxford and would likely offer me a couch to sleep on until I could manage to find a bartending gig.

Fortunately, I got the job.

I worked at the Design Studio until February, when my visa was about to expire. Phil Gallagher, who ran the studio at the time, offered me a full-time job, but my girlfriend at the time wanted me back home. I had to make a huge decision.

I followed my heart and went back to the States. That girl is now my wife of 15 years and the mother of our five children. Clearly, I chose well.

Still, I made some wonderful friends in my short but intense time at Games Workshop, including my co-workers: Rick and Lindsey Priestley, Marc Gascoigne, Andy Jones, Graeme Davis, Richard Halliwell, Jervis Johnson, Robin Dews, Nigel Stillman, Andy Warwick, John Blanche, Alan Merrett, Paul Bonner, Bob Naismith, Mike McVey, and many more. My roommate in Nottingham, Bill – you know him as William – King, became one of my best friends ever, so much so that we've crossed oceans for many visits, including attending each other's weddings.

After I got back to the States, I had the privilege of helping develop *The Blood Bowl Player's Companion*, which – not so coincidentally – featured more American Football-style rules for the game. I played the game a few more times over the years, but eventually I moved on to other things. After all, I had a burgeoning career as a freelance game designer to develop

Still, I kept in touch with some of the people I'd known at the Design Studio. I had nothing but fond memories of that time and those people, and given any chance to meet up at a convention or elsewhere, I happily took it.

Then, in 2004, my old friend Marc Gascoigne asked me to pitch him some ideas for novels for the Black Library. I rushed a dozen out to him. He wrote back to say he especially liked one, the one I'd thrown in as more of a joke than anything else because who would expect that anyone would ever really want to publish novels about that game I'd loved so much.

He wanted *Blood Bowl* novels – a trilogy no less.

I was thrilled. I'd desperately wanted to write these books. I just never had guessed that Marc and my editor Christian Dunn would give me a shot at them. It had all come full circle.

Blood Bowl brought me to Games Workshop, and it brought me back too. It's the game that keeps on giving. Christian's moved on to Solaris Books, but now I get to work with Lindsey Priestley again instead. Look for the fourth book in the trilogy (as Douglas Adams used to refer to his now-classic *Hitchhiker's Guide to the Galaxy* series) – *Rumble in the Jungle* – on shelves soon.

So, enjoy the adventures of Dunk Hoffnung and his maddeningly warped and dysfunctional families, both on the field and off. They and the game they love have brought me a lot of happiness over the years, a wealth of wonderful times with friends and stories to tell. I hope you get a kick out of them too.

Matt Forbeck
July 2007

BLOOD BOWL

Dunk Hoffnung hated his life, or what little he thought might be left of it. He hadn't always felt this way. In his youth, in Altdorf, he'd led the kind of sheltered life that only wealth and privilege could provide. As the eldest heir to the massive Hoffnung fortune, he'd lived far above the squalor of the ghettoes of his hometown. Back then, he'd been mostly and happily ignorant of the kind of existence the vast bulk of the population scratched out in the shadow of his family's towering keep.

Then everything had gone wrong.

'No one ever made a fortune without making a few enemies,' Dunk's father, Lügner, liked to say. He'd repeated it often enough that Dunk felt comfortable ignoring it. After all, he'd reached twenty-three years of age without ever having tripped over that particular dictum. Then it reached out and bloodied his nose.

So, scant months after his family's fall from grace, Dunk found himself clambering up the side of the forsaken pile of rubble called Mount Schimäre, bent on doing something to redeem his name and, by some extension on which he wasn't quite clear, that of his family.

Here in the Grey Mountains, right on the edge of the Empire and more than a hundred miles from his old life, the sky looked different, colder somehow, more distant. It was still all part of the same world though. Perhaps it was he that had changed.

Dunk was still tall, graceful and strong; the benefits of the best trainers in the arts of war and athletics that his family's gold crowns could buy. His hair was jet black, and he'd had to have it cropped short to keep it from snarling and falling into his eyes. He'd lost his fine silver combs along with everything else when his family had been run out of their home. His eyes were still the penetrating silver of a bright, full moon. They saw the same things as before, but the man behind them had changed.

Dunk's boot slipped on the gravel of the trail up to the creature's lair, snapping him out of his thoughts. Self-pity would do him no good here. No matter how much he might think he deserved death, he was determined to make the dragon at least work for it.

The people of Dörfchen had warned him against taking this path. 'Fear not, good people,' he'd told them. 'By tonight, you will no longer shiver in the shadows of the foul beast that has terrorised your hamlet for so long.'

They'd just laughed and sent him on his way. At the town's only public house, the Crooked Arrow, they'd been happy to tip a pint or three in his direction for his efforts. Old Gastwirt, the innkeeper, had even stood Dunk the price of a bottle of brandy as a sign of support. 'You can pay me for it when you return,' he'd said.

The inn's common room had fallen uncomfortably silent at those words. Gastwirt's own laugh had caught in his throat, but he'd still managed to hand Dunk the earthenware bottle with the red wax seal still intact over the cork.

Dunk had made good use of the bottle on the road to the dragon's cave. The spirits tasted like they'd been fermented in casks tainted with warpstone, the shards of coagulated Chaos that spawned the mutants that were rumoured to teem beneath the streets of the Empire's cities. Even the smell of the stuff made his head swim, but Dunk needed something to stoke the guttering fires of his courage. In that respect, the foul liquid served all too well.

Dunk hadn't realised how much he'd had to drink until the trail into the mountains had become so bad that he'd had to dismount from Pferd, his faithful stallion, a fine beast with a coat and mane as black as Dunk's hair and a cantankerous attitude to match. Only two steps out of his stirrups, the hopeful hero found the earth tilting under his feet, sending him tumbling back down the slope until he lodged in a gnarled buckthorn bush that brought him sharply to his senses.

Now, here, only steps away from the steaming mouth of the dragon's cave, Dunk's head started swimming again. His heart hammered so hard that he was amazed that it didn't knock against the inside of his armour's shimmering breastplate, announcing his presence to the creature within. His hand went to the hilt of his sword, and the earthenware bottle clanked against it, causing him to jump.

Dunk looked down at his hand as if the bottle had suddenly grown out of it. Then he pulled the cork from it again with his teeth and took one last belt for good measure. As he did, he wondered if the beast he sought could spit gouts of fire from its gullet. At that moment, Dunk felt maybe he could match that feat.

Dunk pressed the cork back into the bottle and put it down at his feet. If he survived the day, he promised himself to finish it in the victory celebration the grateful people of Dörfchen would no doubt throw for him. Otherwise, he hoped the next worthy hero who happened along might use it to toast his memory.

Finally faced with the objective of his quest, the lair of the beast whose blood he hoped to spill and thereby wash clean his sins, Dunk drew his sword and opened his mouth to speak. Though before a sound escaped his lips, he stopped cold.

Try as he might, Dunk could not think of what to do. The honourable thing, from the heroic stories on which he'd been weaned, would be to announce his presence and call the dread beast forth to impale itself on his blade. That had been what he'd intended to do once he first heard of this damnable creature, but in the clarity of the moment – such clarity as he could find with his head swimming as it was – that seemed like nothing less than sheer folly.

'Perhaps I should poke around a bit first,' Dunk said to himself, louder than he'd intended. When no winged fury came screaming out of the cave to answer his slip, he nodded to himself and crept forward as quietly as he could.

Dunk's armour clinked and clanked so much as he moved that he felt he might as well be wearing a set of cymbals, to announce him like a visitor to a foreign court. The old stories he had once been so fond of, no matter how foolish they seemed now as he peered into the darkening cave, told of the deep slumbers in which dragons waited between snacking on their yearly virgins, and he fervently hoped that at least this part of the tales might be true.

As Dunk shuffled further into the cave, he realised that he had forgotten to bring something with him to light his way. He had some torches back in his saddlebags, but those were with Pferd.

Dunk gazed behind him to the west and saw the sun dipping toward the canopy of the wide forest beyond. He knew that if he went back for a torch it would be pitch black before he could return to the cave. While the thought of putting off his destiny for another day appealed to him, he couldn't bear the thought of returning to the Crooked Arrow to spend the night. He feared that the tales the townspeople would surely repeat about the dragon would force his will from him for good and send him off to another part of the Empire in search of easier means of penance.

Instead, Dunk sheathed his sword, trotted back to the earthenware bottle, and snatched it up. Then he removed the red silk scarf he'd worn around his neck every day since young Lady Helgreta Brecher had given it to him nearly a year ago. At the time, he'd treasured the gift from his betrothed as his most valued possession. Now, his arranged marriage was nothing more than a bittersweet memory and the scarf was little more than a reminder of how far he'd fallen. It was only fitting then, that it help light the path to his redemption.

Dunk uncorked the bottle and stuffed the end of the scarf into it with the barest tinge of regret. The contrast between the finery of the scarf and the crudity of its new home struck him as appropriate, although he couldn't say how. Then he pulled his tinderbox from his pocket and struck a fire on the scarf's free end.

Carrying the makeshift light high in his left hand, Dunk drew his sword again with his right. As he entered the cave, the light from his bottle-lamp showed that the interior cavern was much larger than its mouth implied. It seemed to go back and down forever, disappearing into blackness beyond his light's reach.

The wind whistling past him like something alive, Dunk moved further into the cave. When he realised he couldn't see the walls to either side of him, he started to panic. He clink-clanked as quietly as he could over to his right until he reached the comfort of the wall there, then walked along again, hugging it close.

As Dunk crept further into the cave, the sound of the wind breathing through the cave's mouth fell behind him. He found the silence strangely comforting, although the nothingness it implied put him on edge. Where was the pile of gold and gems on which the great beast had made its bed? Or maybe that part of the stories was wrong too. But where was the beast itself?

Perhaps the dragon was out hunting, terrorizing another village elsewhere in the mountains. Could it be plotting evil ends with some fiend of Chaos in the Forest of Shadows that lay on the other side of these rough, high peaks?

It was then that Dunk tripped over the pile of bones.

He'd thought the first of them was some kind of rippling formation in the rocks, possibly formed by the heat of the dragon's fiery breath over the centuries. He'd stepped right on them, and they rolled beneath his feet like the smoothed logs on which the young Dunk once watched dwarf labourers draw battered ships out of the River Reik and into Altdorf's legendary dry-docks. He spilled forward and found himself unable to control his fall, rolling along on more and more of the brownish, flesh-stripped things until he came to a clattering halt in a heap of skeletal remains in which he could have buried a mountain bear.

Dunk thrashed about in the mound of bones for a moment, crunching them under his armoured bulk. It flashed through his head that the bones were alive, grabbing at him, trying to pull him down to share their communal grave. When he finally stopped smashing them down though, he realised the only threat they posed to him was that he might stab himself on one of the broken ends he'd created.

Throughout the fall, Dunk had managed to keep aloft his left arm and hold on to his makeshift torch. He'd dropped his blade some-where in the process, but was pleased that he had held on to the bottle-lamp so well. He could use that to find the sword, but if he'd kept the sword instead of the light he might never have been able to find his way out of the cave.

Dunk cursed his luck as he scrambled to his feet, shards of bone falling from his armour.

'Only I could find the lair of a missing dragon,' he said. As the words left his lips, relief washed over him. He'd done his duty, faced up to his fears, and everything had come out all right. He was still alive.

Dunk wasn't sure just how he felt about that. He'd been robbed of a chance to earn fortune and glory, after all, but the thought that he'd traded that for a reprieve from all-but-certain death tempered his regret.

He brought the light closer to the bones. There had to be dozens of skeletons here, representing most of the peoples of the Old World. Many of them clearly had once belonged to humans. Others dis-played the short, stout frame of dwarfs, and a few more were even smaller, either those of halflings or – the thought made Dunk shud-der – children. One set of long, thin bones convinced him that the dragon must have once made a rare snack of a wood elf too. He pulled his sword from beneath its delicate ribcage.

Something grated on Dunk's nerves, and for a while he blamed it on the bones arrayed around him. He imagined the voices of all these doomed souls crying out to him for vengeance, and he grimaced at the thought that he had no idea where to find their killer.

The silence of the cave finally grabbed Dunk's attention. The noise from the wind had stopped.

Unnerved, Dunk stepped from the rattling pile of bones and made his way back towards the exit. As he drew closer, he grew concerned. The day's dying light that had streamed in through the cave's mouth wasn't where he thought it should be. Had his sense of direction become confused by his spill? He considered going back and trying to retrace his steps again when he saw the darkness shift before him.

Dunk's breath caught in his chest. He realised that one problem with wandering through a dark cave with a light was that creatures could see you long before you could see them.

The hissing noise that stabbed from the darkened region between Dunk and the exit nearly made him leap from his armour. The serpentine head that followed it, striking into the glow of his bottle-lamp's light, shocked him in a different way. The head was long and thin, mounted on a snakelike neck, but he had expected something much larger. He almost giggled in relief.

Before he could finish his thought, an angry bleat filled the cave. A goat? In here? Had the dragon been out hunting and brought back the poor beast for its evening's repast? Dunk saw the outline of the billy goat's horns stretching out on the edge of the darkness. It wasn't a fair damsel, he knew, but he could still hope to save it from joining the other bones in the back of the cave. Here, at last, was a chance for him to do someone – or rather something – some good.

Dunk's hopes for gratitude vanished like an arrow fired into the night when a deep growl reverberated throughout the cave. He snapped his head about, searching for the source of this new threat. Then the face of a lion poked into the light next to the serpent's head, on the other side from the goat.

The configuration of faces confused Dunk, and he stood stock still, staring at them as though they were a living puzzle that would somehow solve itself. And then it did.

The creature moved forward towards the would-be hero, into the makeshift lamp's light as it guttered in the face of its three breathing heads. Its leonine front paws scraped at the cave's rocky floor, as if it were sharpening the wicked claws before launching an attack. It unfurled its greasy, bat-like wings, which were wide enough to fill the cavern, brushing them against the opposing walls. Its tail, like something that should have been attached to a gargantuan scorpion, curled forward between the wings, small flashes on the tip convincing Dunk that even this appendage had eyes. As its three heads, and its tail, glared at the intrepid fool who had dared invade its home, the chimera clopped and scraped its hoofed hindquarters like a bull preparing to charge.

Dunk edged backwards as the creature came towards him, but it matched him step for step. As he moved, he spoke. 'I'm terribly sorry,' he said to the creature, hoping it might somehow be able to understand him. 'I was looking for a dragon.'

The goat-head snorted.

'You come from Dörfchen,' the snake-head hissed. It spoke the Reikspiel tongue of the Empire flawlessly, although with an oddly familiar accent that Dunk identified as hailing from distant Kislev.

The lion-head uttered a curious growl. 'You're earrrrly,' it said.

Dunk could have sworn the lion-head smiled. 'You... you were expecting me?' he stammered. He hefted his sword, testing its weight, just as he had before every sparring match against his trainers back in Altdorf. He'd never been in a real, to-the-death fight and he hoped they'd taught him well. This time there would be no mercy, he was sure, only blood.

'Our last sssacrifissse was not ssso long ago,' said the snake-head.

'It's a booonus,' the goat-head said. 'Our reputation groooows.'

'Yessss,' the snake-head said. 'It drawsss usss fresssh victimsss.'

'Frrresh meat!' the lion-head said.

'Ah,' Dunk said. He had wondered why the villagers had been so eager to point out the location of this 'dragon's' lair to him. Old Gastwirt had even offered to draw him a map. Now it was clear. They depended on foolhardy heroes like himself to find their way up here regularly to make their regular 'sacrifices' to their local menace. In return, the creature left the hamlet alone. No wonder they'd been so friendly and free with such a total stranger.

'I'm afraid there's been a mistake,' Dunk said as his heart sunk into his boots. 'I wasn't sent up here as your next meal.'

'Explaaain!' the goat-head said. The lion-head snapped its jaws to punctuate the demand.

Dunk swallowed hard. 'The kind and dedicated people of Dörfchen,' he said, 'fear that you might be... tiring of your standard fare. They sent me up here to take your order for your upcoming repast.'

The three heads looked at each other, mystified.

Dunk continued, amazed that he could still speak and stunned at the words escaping his lips. 'Would you prefer a virgin of some sort? Or perhaps a nice little goblin? I'm told we might even be able to procure a few snotlings, or perhaps a little gnoblar to chew on?'

Three sets of eyes narrowed at Dunk. As the light from his bottle-lamp began to die, he noticed that all six orbs glowed green with the crazed light of Chaos.

'Of... of course, you can just stick with your standards.'

The lion licked its muzzle with a black, forked tongue.

'I really do recommend the snotling though,' Dunk said softly. 'It's much tastier than the hu-human.' His voice trailed off as he finished.

'Posssssibly,' the serpent-head said as it weaved hypnotically back and forth, like a snake trying to turn the tables on an unwary charmer.

'But you'rrre herrre,' the lion-head growled.

'Nooow,' the goat-head bleated. With that, the great beast slouched forward.

As the lion-head leaped out towards Dunk, he slashed at it with his blade. The never-bloodied edge cut through the creature's mane and trailed a splatter of blood in its wake. The lion-head yowled in pain and surprise, and the goat squealed in protest.

Emboldened by his success, Dunk brought his sword back for another swing. As he bought the blade forward, though, the snake-head darted out and struck the weapon from his hand. It sailed off behind him, and he heard it land clattering in the pile of what little was left of the chimera's past victims. Dunk gawked for a moment at his empty hand, sure that his bones would soon join the others.

The trio of heads loosed terrifying laughs. The cacophony startled Dunk into action. He gripped hold of the only thing he had left, the barely burning bottle-lamp, and hurled it at the creature with all his might.

The earthenware bottle smashed into the creature right where its three heads met. Its noxious contents splashed across the chimera's chest and necks, and burst into flames. The blaze blossomed against the chimera, and the three heads screamed in an unholy choir of fury and fear.

Dunk glanced back over his shoulder to where his sword had gone spinning away, but the back of the cave was shrouded in utter darkness. He'd have a better chance of finding a wishbone than his blade in that mess. Turning back towards the chimera, which was trying to beat out the flames engulfing each of the heads by banging them against each other, he realised there was only one way out of the cave: past that burning beast.

With a strength fortified by desperation, Dunk lowered his shoulder and charged directly at the monster. 'Keep low and move *through* your foe,' he heard Lehrer say, the old trainer's voice echoing in his head. 'The low man has control.'

Only this wasn't a man that Dunk faced but a beast three times his size. Still, he hoped, the same principle should apply.

The fire had blinded the chimera, and it was turning away towards the cave's entrance when Dunk barrelled into it. He caught it directly below one of its wings and knocked it sprawling into one of the cavern walls. Without stopping, he spun away from the creature, flinging himself around the beast and past it toward the twilight sky beyond.

Dunk was giddy with glee as he sprinted for the exit. If this experience had proved one thing to him, it was that he wasn't ready to die quite yet, especially if it meant becoming a twisted abomination's next meal.

As Dunk reached for freedom, though, something hard and sharp slammed into his back, its meaty tip stabbing through his armour and into the flesh beneath. Lights flashing before his eyes, Dunk tumbled forward, out of the cave, letting the force of the blow push him further from his foe.

When he finally came to a stop, Dunk scrambled to his feet and whipped about, fearful that the winged beast would come roaring out of the cave after him. From the trio of screams emanating from the flickering lights still flashing from the cavern mouth, he guessed that the beast was too busy saving its own life at the moment to finish taking his.

Dunk's left arm was numb from the shoulder down and hung limp in its socket like a piece of meat. For a moment, he feared the blow might have severed the limb, but he checked with his good hand, and it was still there. He was wondering what was wrong with it when the numbness started to fade, only to be replaced with the excruciating sensation of a thousand fire ants biting into his wounded arm. His stomach flipped about like a dying fish pulled from its cool river home and slapped down on the cruel wood of a sun-warmed dock. He bent over and retched.

Wiping the remnants of his last meal from his mouth and soaked in the stench of the Dörfchen liquor that had tasted like embalming fluid as it erupted from his gullet, Dunk realised what had been done to him. Angry and nearly blind, the chimera had lashed out at him with its two-eyed tail and stung him with its venomous barb. He had escaped its lair, but it seemed that he could not outrun the effects of its wrath.

'Never let it be said that I didn't flee with the best of them,' Dunk said to himself as he stumbled down the mountainside, wondering how he was going to be able to find his black horse as the last rays of daylight raced from the sky.

WHEN DUNK CAME to, he found himself lying over the saddle of his horse, which was standing outside the Crooked Arrow. The night was fully dark now, although a light burned inside the place, visible through the cracks in the thick, but poorly fitted shutters that covered a window in the upper floor of the grey-plastered building.

Dunk slid from the back of Pferd and shook his head to clear the sheets of cobwebs that he felt had accumulated there. The brisk night air bit into his face and whistled through the hole in the back of his armour, poking him awake. He tested his arm and found that although it still hurt he could move it once again. The fire ants had apparently fled for a more hospitable home, one that didn't have a chimera angry at it.

Dunk tripped forward and steadied himself against the inn's scarred oaken door. It was quiet inside and dark but for the light above. It must have been late, the regulars had long since gone to bed. He knocked on the door and waited, listening.

In the room above, he heard a pair of voices, a man and a woman, arguing in hushed tones. Then the light went out.

Dunk knocked on the door again, louder this time. Only the crickets in the distance answered. He looked up and down the wide, unpaved road. The few other shops and houses that lined what could only charitably be called the centre of the hamlet were all dark too. The people who resided within them, resting easily in the shadow of the monster-infested mountain, another 'sacrifice' – Dunk, in this case – having recently been sent off to placate the neighbouring beast.

This time, Dunk banged on the door with all his might, his mailed fists making dents in the already battered, ironbound planks. 'Open up!' he shouted at the top of his lungs. 'Open up, *now*!'

He'd been trying to help these ungrateful bastards, and they'd as good as sent him to a certain death. Somebody was going to pay.

'Go away!' a voice rasped down from above. Dunk looked up to see Gastwirt leaning out through the now-open shutters, his long hair like strings of greasy white cotton and his flimsy nightshirt, which barely covered his massive gut, fluttering in the breeze. 'We're closed for the night!'

'You'll open up for me, damn you!' Dunk shouted up at the innkeeper, shaking his fist at the bewildered old man. 'After what I've been through, I've earned the right to a warm bed tonight.'

Gastwirt squinted down at Dunk and then ducked back inside for a moment. When he reappeared, he held a lantern high in one arm, and he peered down again to see who might be so bold as to make such demands. 'You!' the innkeeper said, recoiling in horror as he recognised Dunk's face. 'You're supposed to be dead!'

'And you're supposed to be an innkeeper!' Dunk shouted back at Gastwirt. 'Let me in, and give me a bed. I'm hurt!' He rubbed his shoulder as he said this, wondering just how bad it was.

Gastwirt peered down at Dunk, suspicion etched on his doughy face. 'How do I know you're not a ghost come back for your revenge on our fair town?' he asked. 'No one else has ever returned from the creature's cave alive.'

Dunk pulled off his right gauntlet and flung it at the innkeeper. The metal glove smacked Gastwirt right in his bulbous nose and then dropped back down to the ground where Dunk retrieved it.

'Could a ghost do that?' Dunk asked as the innkeeper howled in protest.

At that moment, the front door creaked open. Dunk stared into the darkness beyond, ready for a guard of some sort to spring from the shadows. He looked down and saw the small figure standing there framed in the doorway, barefooted, dressed in a grimy, once-white nightshirt and holding a small oil lamp.

For an instant, Dunk thought that the newcomer was a child with dark and curly hair, perhaps a son or grandson of Gastwirt's, who'd been roused by the arguing. Then he noticed the traces of stubble on the little person's chin and the wrinkles around his wide smile and dancing grey eyes.

'Now, son, I ask you, is that any way to make a reasonable request of your host?' the halfling said.

'Morr's icy breath!' the innkeeper cursed above. 'What are you–' He leaned further out the window until he could see the halfling waving up at him from the inn's threshold.

'Shut that door!' Gastwirt shouted before he disappeared back into the his bedchamber, slamming the shutters closed behind him as he went.

The halfling held out a hand of greeting towards Dunk and waved for him to come inside. 'I'd hurry yourself in here quickly, son, before that walrus makes his way down those stairs. He'll double bar the door for sure.'

Dunk reached back and wound Pferd's reins around the hitching post outside the inn, then slipped in past the halfling while nodding his thanks.

'I'm glad someone around here understands hospitality,' he said. He stuck out his hand at the halfling. 'I'm Dunk.'

'Slogo Fullbelly,' the halfling said, his hand almost disappearing within Dunk's much larger mitt.

'Slick, you stinking bastard!' Gastwirt howled as he slipped down the last few stairs and fell onto his rump in the back of the room.

'Slick, to my friends,' the Halfling said in a confidential tone.

The innkeeper leaped to his feet far quicker than Dunk would have guessed the man's bulk could allow. 'You've no friends here, you sawed-off con artist,' Gastwirt said, shaking a finger at Slick.

Dunk stepped between the innkeeper and the halfling before Gastwirt could wrap his thick paws around the little one. 'He did me a good turn when you refused,' he said to the innkeeper.

Gastwirt looked up at Dunk, just a hint of green haloing his face. 'I don't open the door for anyone I don't know after dark,' he said. 'Not when I've sent everyone else home.'

Dunk stepped closer and glared down into the shorter man's watery blue eyes. 'I met you earlier today.'

'And sallied off to certain death, just like all the others, sure that providence and your own sheer arrogance would let you rule the day, to kill–' The innkeeper cut himself short. 'By the gods' grace and mercy,' he said in awe, 'did you actually *kill* the beast?'

Dunk grimaced, suddenly aware of how much his shoulder still hurt. 'I made it back alive, but not unscathed.'

'Ooh,' Slick said from behind Dunk. The would-be hero turned and saw Slick standing on a nearby table, peering at his back. 'That's a mighty nasty-looking hole you have in your armour there, son,' he said.

'It's nothing…' Dunk started to say, but he couldn't bring himself to finish. 'It hurts like blazes,' he conceded.

'Allow me,' Slick said, reaching up to unfasten the buckles that held Dunk's breastplate and backplate in place.

'You can't do that here!' Gastwirt complained. 'I can't have wounded strangers stumbling into my place in the middle of the night.'

Dunk growled at the man, then reached over and snatched a long, sharp spear from where it hung over the massive mantel in the room. He shoved its wicked, barbed tip towards the innkeeper and growled again, the pain from his sudden movements tainting his wordless threat with a dose of desperation.

'I think, kind sir,' Slick said to the innkeeper gravely, 'that you'd better make friends with this man quickly if you don't wish to find yourself thrown out of your own establishment.'

Gastwirt looked up into Dunk's pained eyes. The warrior could see the thoughts whirring through the man's brain as he weighed the risks of the various avenues of action open to him. Then the innkeeper's shoulders sagged in resignation.

'All right,' said Gastwirt as he padded towards the open door and shoved it shut, then dropped two bars of solid, ironbound oak behind it. 'Let's be quick about this.' The innkeeper returned, firing up a lantern that hung from the ceiling in the centre of the room.

'Sit down, son,' Slick said to Dunk, 'and I'll have a look at that trouble of yours.'

Dunk slumped in the chair nearest the table on which the halfling still stood. He yanked his breastplate and chestplate off with one hand, but when it came to slipping out of the mail shirt, he found it hurt too much. With a wave from Slick, Gastwirt ambled over and helped the halfling pull the damaged, bloodied armour off, as well as the undershirt beneath it.

The innkeeper gasped in horror at the sight of the puncture wound in Dunk's back. Slick just clucked his tongue and ordered Gastwirt to hustle off to the kitchen and bring back a bucket of water and some clean rags. 'It's not as bad as it looks,' Slick told Dunk. 'I've seen far worse.'

'Are you a physician?'

The halfling chuckled. 'Hardly, son. I'm a Blood Bowl player's agent.'

Dunk turned and gave Slick an appraising look. 'For which team?' he asked.

'I work for my player,' Slick said. 'Negotiate his contracts, defend his honour, get him as much time on the pitch as I can, for the most pay. Some agents handle a handful of different players all at once, but I prefer to concentrate on one star player at a time. That kind of dedication to personal service makes all the difference.'

'Who's your player?'

Slick looked over to where the dying embers still glowed soft and red in the inn's fireplace. 'I've had a lot of them over the years.'

'Who is it now?'

Gastwirt burst back into the room right then, half a bucket of sloshing water in one hand and a fistful of grey, threadbare rags in the other. He set the things down on the table next to Slick, who took one of the rags and dipped it into the bucket.

As the halfling gently rubbed the wet rag around the area of Dunk's wound, cleaning the blood away, he said, 'Let's just say I'm between clients at the moment. Blood Bowl is a dangerous game.'

'I've never seen a match.' Dunk suspected that Slick was talking so much just to distract him from how much the rag stung. Either way, he was willing to go along with it.

'Really?' Gastwirt said in excited disbelief. 'If I'd lived in a big city, I'd go to the matches every week.'

'I've never much seen the point of it,' Dunk said, gritting his teeth as Slick rubbed more water into the wound. 'A bunch of grown people – or dwarfs, or elves, or orcs, or ogres or worse – chasing a football around a field? Why bother?'

'Because,' Slick said as he dried Dunk's shoulder and wrapped it with another rag, 'it pays better than thievery.' As he finished up, he patted Dunk on the shoulder and handed him back his bloodstained undershirt. 'Besides, people who go off looking to pick fights with dragons shouldn't speak ill of the career choices of others.'

'I'll take that under consideration,' Dunk said.

'You're a lucky man,' Slick said as he slid down off the table and picked up his candle from where he'd left it. 'The poison of a sting like that can be fatal.'

As the words left Slick's mouth, Dunk's head started to spin again. 'I just wish I was dead.'

'Let's get this boy a bed,' Slick said to Gastwirt.

'Right away,' the innkeeper nodded. He led Dunk to a door in the back corner of the common room. It opened onto a private quarters little larger than one of the closets in the family keep in which Dunk had grown up. A bed of straw lay scattered in the far corner. The young warrior stumbled over to it and lay down his head. He was asleep before the innkeeper shut the door.

Dunk awoke at dawn to what sounded like a gang of angry giants tearing the roof off of the building. Still shirtless, he leapt to his feet and cast about for his sword for a moment before he remembered that he'd left it in the chimera's cave. A banging at the door brought his attention slamming back from last night to the present.

'Hey, hero!' Gastwirt said through the thin planks of the door. 'If you want to make a name for yourself, now's the time!'

As Dunk shoved on his boots and tossed on a shirt, the innkeeper threw open the door. 'No time for modesty,' Gastwirt scowled. 'Your Chaos-damned doom followed you here, and if you don't go out to meet it, it'll tear the town apart trying to find you.'

For a moment, Dunk didn't understand the man's words, but then a roaring, hissing, bleating yowl rattled the ramshackle shutters strung across the cramped room's lopsided window. The young man's eyes felt like they might spring from his head as he stared out of the window and then back at the white-faced innkeeper.

'The chimera is here?' Dunk asked, the thought gluing his feet to the rough worn floor.

'Got it in one,' Gastwirt said with a pitiless smirk. 'And it wants your head.'

'How do you know that?' the shocked Dunk asked.

The strange choir of angry voices outside changed from howls to shouts, and Dunk could make out its chorus. 'The hero!' it said. 'Bring us his head!'

Dunk glanced around him. No blade, not even a knife. He thought of running, but he knew he'd never outpace the winged beast. Pferd might be able to outrun the creature, but the last Dunk had seen of his horse it had been hitched out in front of the inn, in the open, a ripe target on which a mad monster could unleash its wrath.

The innkeeper was right. He was doomed.

Gastwirt reached out and grabbed Dunk by the shoulder, his injured one, which felt like a lance rammed through the warrior's arm. He cried out in protest and shrugged free, but the innkeeper just grabbed his other arm instead.

'Your hand put this wheel in motion,' Gastwirt snarled at Dunk. 'You placed your bet, and now it's time to pay up.'

Slick stepped in from the hallway and slipped in between the two men. 'You can't send him out there,' the halfling said. 'That beast will rip him apart.'

The innkeeper's hand let go as Dunk wrested his other arm away. Gastwirt leaned down to shout into Slick's face. 'This bastard you've befriended went out last night and enraged that carnivorous creature. If we don't give it what it wants, it'll kill us all!'

Slick nodded as he considered this for a moment. Then he turned back to Dunk and said, 'He's got a point, son. Sorry about all this, but you'd better go.'

'What?' Dunk said. As he spoke, something heavy crashed onto the inn's roof, and dust and clods of dirt cascaded down from the ceiling. 'I'm not going out to face that thing.'

Dunk turned to Gastwirt. 'You and your friends sent me off to die. You can all rot!'

Slick patted Dunk on the back of his leg. 'Come now, son, there's no reason for us *all* to die, right?' His tone sounded as if he were trying to convince Dunk to take a walk with him in the rain. 'There's no way for you to get away from that beast, so you might as well go face up to it like a man. Think of the children.'

'What children?' Dunk asked, goggling at the halfling.

Slick shrugged. 'It's a town. There have to be children here, right?' He looked to Gastwirt for some help.

'Loads of children,' the innkeeper said. 'Normally you can't walk around here without tripping over them. They're orphans, too, the whole lot of them. A pitiful bunch to be sure.'

Dunk snarled at the blatant lies. Still, he thought, there did have to be some innocents in this town, and he couldn't be the cause of their deaths.

'Fine,' he said. 'I'll go. Wish me luck, you cowards.'

Slick clapped Dunk on the back of his thigh and favoured him with a rueful smile. 'A man like you has no need for luck, son. Just go out there and face your fate.'

The chimera cried out for Dunk again. Shaking his head, the young warrior shoved past the halfling and pushed the innkeeper out of his way. He wasn't doing anyone any good stuck in this room, least of all Pferd.

As Dunk stormed into the inn's empty common room, he heard the innkeeper behind him quietly say, 'Ten crowns says that beast eats him for breakfast.'

'You, sir,' Slick said, 'have yourself a bet.'

Dunk didn't know why the halfling would be willing to wager on him. He would have bet against himself if there had been any way to collect. Still, the thought that someone – anyone – had any kind of confidence in him encouraged him.

When the building's shutters rattled again with the chimera's roar and the beating of its wings, Dunk knew, however, that confidence wouldn't get him far. 'Can you at least loan me a blade?' he called back at the innkeeper. He turned to see Gastwirt and Slick had followed him from the room, perhaps eager for the show soon to come.

The innkeeper, mindful of his bet, Dunk suspected, just shook his head. Slick, on the other hand, disappeared behind the bar that ran along the room's north wall. A moment later, something long and sharp came flying over the bar to stab into the floor near Dunk's feet.

'Every barman has one,' the halfling said as he rematerialised from behind the bar.

Dunk pulled the weapon from the floor and examined it. The sword was short, about half the length of his own blade, and it looked as if it had been used more often as a kitchen utensil than a weapon. Still, it beat using his bare hands. He hefted the thing in his hand and headed for the door.

Pferd stood there in the early morning light, straight, tall, and unperturbed. The black horse's reins remained wrapped around the hitching post. He whinnied a short greeting to Dunk but showed no signs of fear, as if the creature still whirling somewhere overhead was little more than a sparrow with a poor attitude.

Dunk remembered how he had chosen Pferd for his own. One night, a fire had broken out in his family's stables. Trapped, some of the horses had panicked and run deeper into the flames. They had all perished, but Pferd had stood his ground until the guards rescued him. He alone had survived.

'That's the horse I want, father,' the young Dunk had said the next day. 'That's a beast you can count on.' He had not once regretted making the request.

Scanning the skies above as he left the shelter of the inn, Dunk slashed out with his borrowed blade to cut loose Pferd's reins. The blade bounced off the hitching post, leaving the leather leads intact, the weapon's edge too dull to split them.

Dunk cursed as he reached out and loosed Pferd's reins with his other hand. 'Where is that thing, boy?' he asked. The horse didn't respond.

As he moved past Pferd and into the open street, Dunk used the sword to shade his eyes as he searched for the chimera among the low, dark clouds scattered by the stiff breeze that swept down from the mountains that day. He saw nothing up there, not even a lone bird. Dunk allowed himself a moment of hope that the creature had tired of hunting for him here and had flown off for other parts, but he quickly quashed it. Hope made a man lose focus, he knew, and that could be fatal.

'You'll need this, son!' Slick shouted from the doorway of the inn.

Dunk glared over at the halfling to see him wrestling with the sharp end of the massive spear that had hung over the mantel in the inn's common room, dragging the bulk of its length behind him. 'Get back in there,' Dunk ordered Slick as he dashed over and snatched the spear from him. 'That thing could snap you up without stopping to chew.'

'You're welcome!' Slick said, the sly grin never leaving his face. 'I hope you're better with a spear than you are at expressing your gratitude.'

Dunk started to come up with a snappy reply, but a loud noise from down the street saved him from having to make the effort. He whipped his head around to see the chimera pulling a holy icon from the steeple of the local temple. A man in red, priestly robes dashed out of the place, a gaggle of worshippers hot on his heels, all screeching louder than even the chimera above them. The heavy, stone icon crashed to the ground behind them as they raced up the street.

'You!' the priest said, pointing a thick finger at Dunk. The man's corpulent face was red with the exertion of having managed to dash from the church before all of his followers, despite the fact he'd been standing at the altar in front of them. His round blue eyes glared at Dunk from under bushy, white eyebrows. 'This is all your fault!'

'Sod off!' Dunk spat. He'd had enough of priests for a lifetime. He gave the gods their due, of course, but he had little time for the parasites who fed off the reputations of their chosen deities by purporting to bring their messages to the masses.

The priest's face flushed even redder, and Dunk thought, perhaps even hoped, that the man might keel over right there with a stopped heart. Instead, the priest waved his terrified congregation after him, saying, 'That's who the beast wants, dead or alive! Let's give him to it!'

As the priest charged at Dunk, the young warrior swung around the dull end of the spear and caught the holy man squarely in the chin. The priest collapsed in his robes like an item of laundry falling from a washing line. The others behind their religious leader froze in their tracks.

Dunk brought the sharp end of the spear around to bear on the handful of temple-goers staring at him. He didn't want to hurt them, but he feared they didn't share the same concern for him. The best way to end this altercation would be to stop it now. 'All right,' he snarled at those facing him, his voice dripping with menace. 'Who's next?'

'We are!' the chimera yowled in a trio of unnatural voices. Still atop the temple, it spread its bat-like wings wide and launched itself straight at Dunk, its paws and hooves ready to pummel and pound the young warrior into the dirt.

Dunk dived to the left as the creature came at him and it sailed harmlessly overhead, the tips of its claws finding no mark. It squawked in frustration as it curled back up into the open sky. The townspeople looked up after the thing, then looked at each other and scattered, each racing for a different hiding place, hoping that the chimera would choose to chase easier prey.

The priest scrambled to his feet, blood trickling from his mouth, the same colour as his robes. He glared at Dunk and yelled, 'Kill the stranger!'

It was only when the priest looked around to see who would follow him that he realised he was alone. His eyes narrowed on the tip of the spear which Dunk pointed at him, and then he too turned and fled straight back down the street.

Dunk loosed a mean laugh until he saw the chimera's winged shape swing around towards him at the end of the street. The beast rolled into position and hung in the sky for just a moment before plummeting into a dive straight down the length of the road.

Dunk's first instinct was to simply jump into a building. He noticed that Gastwirt had shut his inn's front door behind him, leaving Slick pounding desperately from the outside in an effort to get back in.

As Dunk looked about for another path of escape, he noticed that the chimera's angle of dive would take it down far short of his position. For a moment, he thought the creature had misjudged the distance or simply wanted to skim the edge of the earth and rip him from below, but then he saw its real target: the priest.

The holy man realised this at about the same time Dunk did. He turned around immediately and started sprinting back in Dunk's direction.

The priest glanced left and right madly, snapping his head all about. His parishioners had not only abandoned him, they'd locked their doors behind them. No matter where he turned, there was no help to be had.

Dunk hated to see a man cry like the priest – who wailed in desperate terror. He hefted the mighty spear that Slick had given him and took careful aim. It was heavy but well balanced. With luck, it would fly straight and true.

'No!' Slick said as he tried to crush himself into the narrow shelter offered by the frame of the inn's door. 'Don't do it, son! That priest is dead anyway! Save yourself!'

Dunk snorted to himself, not sparing a second to glance back at the halfling. His target zoomed toward him at top speed. Armed only with the spear, he was only going to get one chance at this.

Dunk cocked back his arm, his shoulder flexing against the strain. Then he stepped forward and hurled the spear with all his might.

The chimera bore down on the priest mercilessly, all three of its heads reaching for the man at once, their jaws thrown wide open to expose gaping maws, each filled with a set of vicious teeth or fangs.

The priest screamed, offering up a quick prayer for mercy from the gods.

Dunk's spear shot forth and stabbed into the snake-head, straight through its fanged mouth. It rammed up through the roof of the thing's mouth and pierced its brain from below. It kept going until the thickening shaft caught in the snake-head's skull.

At that point, the spear's momentum snapped back hard against the chimera's own, whipping the creature's middle head back and up along its serpentine neck. The creature went tumbling backward over itself, the spear pulling it along until it embedded itself in the compacted dirt of the street, pinning the creature there by its killed head.

The priest looked up from where he had fallen to his knees in the final moments of the chimera's pursuit, ready to make peace with the gods and plead for guidance into the afterlife. He saw nothing but open sky above him, and turned back to see the chimera pinned in the middle of the street like some massive insect in a particularly horrid collection.

'Praise the gods!' the priest said. 'They have saved us all! Thanks be to them in their wondrous wisdom!'

'How's that?' Dunk said.

The priest looked back to where the unarmed warrior stood in the street, naked to the waist. He tried to speak, but no words escaped his lips.

'*I* saved you,' Dunk said. Behind the priest, the chimera's remaining heads roared and bleated in fury and frustration. 'Kill you aaall!' The goat-head said as the lion-head loosed another blood-curdling cry.

The sight of the wounded beast seemed to bring the priest back to himself, and he fixed Dunk in a baleful glare. 'That creature,' he said, 'would never have bothered us if not for your interference.'

Dunk couldn't believe his ears. He shook his head as if to clear out the lies. 'You told me it was a dragon! A weak and old dragon! You sent me to my death!'

The priest snarled back at the young warrior. 'Your arrogance sent you on your path.' A cold laugh escaped him. 'You think you would have done any better against a dragon?'

Dunk gritted his teeth in frustration. 'I just saved your entire town from a menace that has plagued it for generations. The least you owe me is your thanks.'

'Really?' the priest said. 'We should thank you for destroying the balance of power in this region?'

Dunk gaped at the godly man.

'That creature you just maimed, is the most powerful in the area. While we lived in its shadow, it kept us safe from threats of all sorts: brigands, carrion, orcs, even real dragons. Now, here we are, exposed to the world around us and every horrible thing in it. You've just destroyed this town.'

Dunk fell to one knee and put his head in his hands. The man's words were madness, he knew, but they were the last thing he'd expected. He'd slain the beast, hadn't he? Where was the glory? As for fortune, the only thing he'd seen in the creature's cave had been mounds of bones. Dunk supposed that a chimera had little use for diamonds and gold.

Where had it all gone wrong?

A small hand came down on Dunk's shoulder. He turned to see Slick looking him square in the eye. At this level, the Halfling didn't look nearly so much like a child.

'That's gratitude for you, son,' Slick said. 'But it gets worse.'

Dunk shook his head at the halfling. None of this made any sense to him.

'How?' he said. He'd thought it was a rhetorical question.

Slick nodded down the street. Dunk looked up to see the towns-people poking their heads out of their homes, spotting the still-howling chimera, and then pointing their fingers at Dunk. He couldn't hear their words, but he didn't care for the tone of their voices.

'Son,' Slick said, 'don't stick around to find out.'

It was almost dark before Dunk dismounted from Pferd and set up camp for the night. There were no other inns in this part of the Grey Mountains, not this close to the Axe Bite Pass that led through the highest peaks on its way to distant Bretonnia. It was not a safe place for lone travellers at night, but Dunk was sure that Dörfchen would have been even less hospitable.

Dunk was still stunned at how the people of that ill-fated and ungrateful town had responded to how he'd saved them from the monstrous beast that had fed upon their populace – and good-hearted strangers, it seemed – for untold years. He knew that there were bad people in the world, the near-destruction of his family in Altdorf bore stark testimony to that, he just hadn't realised *everyone* was that way.

Everyone but me, he thought. He had suspected that the citizens of Altdorf, corrupted by living in the very heart of the Empire, in the actual seat of the Emperor's power, were perhaps a special case. Those raised in such an environment could fall so easily into crime and violence, just like his younger brother Dirk.

Like many in Altdorf, though, Dunk had fancied that the people of the country, were blessed with a simpler outlook on the world, one that made them more kindly and innocent. To find out he'd been so wrong was yet another blow to his already fragile view of the world.

When Dunk heard a set of hooves clip-clopping up the mountain trail, his heart leapt into his throat. He'd been a fool to start a fire here, it seemed, but he'd been cold and hungry and too depressed about the state of the world to worry about things like brigands or worse. He hadn't seen another person since he'd left Dörfchen and so had tossed caution to the wind.

Dunk drew his long hunting knife, the only weapon he had left on him after losing his sword in the chimera's cave. He had thought about circling around town and going back for it, but the thought of the chimera freeing itself and coming home to find him in its lair once again had kept him out.

Dunk glanced around but quickly saw there was no place for him to hide. The mountain sloped away sharply from the wide trail, both up and down, but no trees grew on this rocky terrain, only a feeble bush or two, hanging on to this small strip of level ground as best it could.

Dunk stood and held his knife before him, putting the fire between him and whatever was trotting up the trail toward him. It was a moment before the rider drew close enough for Dunk to be able to pick its shape out of the surrounding darkness. It was waving at him.

'Hallo!' the rider called. Slick Fullbelly, dressed in a dark green cloak and a suit of golden-brown tweed that barely contained his eponymous gut, and riding a small, dirt-coloured pony built like a barrel. Slick smiled broadly towards the fire and the young man that stood behind it. 'I was hoping that it would be you!' He showed all his teeth.

Dunk strode around the fire, sheathing his knife as he did. The halfling was many things, but not, he hoped, a threat. He beckoned Slick to come and join him by the fire.

Slick drove his tubby pony up to the edge of the fire where it ground to a halt. He looked as though he would have had to split his legs exactly apart to fit them around the creature. The saddle sat on the pony's back like a child's cap on the head of an ogre. It seemed the only thing keeping it in place was the way the saddle was strapped tightly enough to cause the pony's fattened flesh to bulge around it on all sides. While this might have seemed cruel with another mount, the pony just took it in stride, its natural cushioning protecting it from any discomfort.

Slick slid from the pony's back as if dismounting from a boulder. Then he turned to Dunk with a grin. 'It's good to see you again, son. I was afraid you'd gotten away from me,' he said.

Dunk motioned for the halfling to sit down on a patch of ground near the fire. 'You're not after me, too, are you?' he asked. He eyed Slick warily despite himself.

The halfling laughed. 'I don't think so,' he said, a merry twinkle in his eye. 'At least not for killing Dörfchen's murderous town mascot. That thing needed to be shown the door a long time ago.'

Dunk sat down a quarter of the way around the fire from Slick. He had a bit of bacon he'd cooked up still in the pan, soaking in its own hardening grease. He offered this to the halfling without a word.

Slick took the pan and said, 'My undying thanks.' With that, he pulled a fork from the pocket of his waistcoat and set to work on the lukewarm food. He stuffed bite after bite into his mouth, seeming to take special delight in the bits to which large dollops of the coagulated fat had attached themselves.

'I've already eaten, of course,' Slick said between mouthfuls, 'but there's always room for bacon. When you're on the road like this, you never know when you might be able to eat well again, so I prefer to travel like a camel with what I need most already inside of me.'

From what Dunk could see, Slick was prepared to last through at least a month of short rations without undue suffering.

'What is it you want?' Dunk said.

The halfling stopped chewing for a moment as his eyes flew wide. When he resumed, he grinned around the fat stuffed into his cheeks. 'More suspicious already,' he said. 'I like that.

'You know I saw you yesterday in the inn. I thought about warning you about the creature in that cave, but I could see you wouldn't have any of that. You were bent on killing that 'dragon' you'd been hunting for, and little things like the truth weren't going to get in your way.'

'Hey,' Dunk started to protest.

'Oh,' said Slick, waving off the young man's concerns, 'don't think bad of yourself for it. I've seen this happen lots of times before. You're a young man, you have something to prove, you think you can make yourself into a hero. You think other people will respond to that and treat you with courtesy and respect, adoration, even love. But it just doesn't work that way, son.'

Dunk stared at the halfling, amazed. It was if Slick could see right into his heart. 'How can you be so sure?' the young hopeful asked.

'Because,' Slick said, as seriously as if announcing the death of his parents, 'I've been there.'

Dunk smiled softly in spite of himself. 'You were a hero?' he asked. 'Did you slay many dragons?'

'Now see here,' Slick said, as indignantly as he could around the fist-sized ball of lard squished in his cheek. 'It's not all about killing giant, flying lizards now, is it? Not all heroes are murderers, you know.'

Dunk's face flushed with his shame. 'I'm sorry,' he muttered.

The smile came back to Slick's greasy lips as if it had just passed behind a cloud for a moment. 'Don't fret about it, son. People make that sort of mistake about me all the time. They think just because I'm a halfling I can't make any sort of contribution to society other than keeping any plate in front of me clean.'

Dunk looked down at the pan to see that Slick had certainly polished its surface spotless. The halfling didn't miss a beat though.

'But I gave up all that hero nonsense long ago,' he said, waving his fork at Dunk before licking it clean and sticking it back into his pocket.

'Nonsense?' Dunk said. 'What's wrong with being a hero?'

Slick snorted. 'Nothing,' he said, 'if you don't mind a life filled with poverty, fear, and death. Most folks prefer the status quo, even if they're living next door to a monster that might make off with their children at any moment. Sure, it's a horrible thing, but who knows what else worse might be out there? Better the daemon you know.'

Dunk shook his head. 'I can't believe that,' he said. 'Can people really be so cynical? What about improving your lot and that of your neighbours?'

'Like you did in Dörfchen today? You saw how grateful they were about that. You're lucky you got out when you did. When Old Gastwirt told the townsfolk I'd given you that spear, they nearly lynched me on the spot. If the chimera hadn't gotten up and bitten the baker nearly in half at that point, I think they'd have had me.'

'The creature killed someone?' Dunk's heart sunk with these words. He'd hoped he'd put an end to the creature's reign of terror for good.

Slick nodded. 'He wouldn't have, of course, if they hadn't freed him.'

Dunk goggled at this. 'They did what?'

The halfling smiled as he picked a piece of bacon from between his teeth with a small sliver of steel he'd pulled from another pocket in his waistcoat. 'The fools freed him. The priest gathered together a group of men, and they went out to where the thing was staked down and pulled the spear out. They thought they could get the creature back to its cave and let it heal up so it could "protect them from the power vacuum" you were bent on creating.'

'And it repaid them by killing the baker?'

Slick sighed bitterly, the humour draining from him.

'He wasn't much of a man, a bit too slow of foot, for one, which is what did him in, but he made the best pies in the Reikland.'

After a long silence, Slick pointed his toothpick at Dunk and said, 'It makes my point, though, you see. Being a hero is a sucker's game.'

Dunk gazed upwards into the brilliant stars shining in the Old World sky. They were just the same as they'd always been for him, every day of his life, but today they seemed more distant and cold. As a child, when Lehrer had tried to explain the nature of the constellations to him, the ancient patterns had transformed themselves into creatures from the myths and legends he so loved. Now, they were just stars again.

'Now, Blood Bowl,' Slick said, stabbing with his toothpick for emphasis, '*that* is a game.'

Dunk scoffed at the mention of the blood sport. He knew all about Blood Bowl, the insane game in which two teams faced off against each other in some mad abstraction of a real battle. Instead of killing each other to the last foe, though, they had to move a ball, sometimes covered with fang-sharp spikes, past the other team's side of the field, into its 'End Zone', scoring a touchdown. The team with the most touchdowns after an hour of sometimes-murderous play won the match.

'I hate it,' Dunk said, trying to keep his voice even.

Slick's eyes grew wide and as round as his cheeks. 'Hate it? How can you hate it? It's the greatest thing to happen to sport – ever! Maybe even to civilization itself.'

Dunk nearly succeeded in stopping himself from sneering. 'Or it's the worst. It's a bunch of thugs standing toe-to-toe and beating each other mercilessly for the enjoyment of others. The football is only a pretext for the violence. They might as well smash it flat and be honest about how the bloodshed is the only thing that keeps people coming back.'

Slick smiled with the vision that flashed in his head. 'I actually saw that happen once, in an Orland Raiders game. They were playing the Oldheim Ogres, and the ogres forgot they were in the middle of a match. The Raiders lost five players before the referees got things under control again.'

'That's horrible!' Dunk said, shuddering with revulsion.

'Hey, son,' Slick said seriously, 'you're the one that wants to be the hero. How do you think most heroes make their names around here?' The halfling waited for a moment, but Dunk didn't answer, too astonished that someone would actually defend this monstrous game; and so eloquently.

'They kill things,' Slick said. 'Sometimes they kill "monsters". Other times it's their own kind. At least on the Blood Bowl pitch, there are rules.'

'That no one pays attention to,' Dunk countered. 'I've seen bar brawls with more respect for life.'

Slick smirked. 'You're confusing rules with lives. Hitting someone hard in the middle of the match isn't just legal, it's encouraged. If you can knock a foe out of the game, so much the better for you and your team.'

'But the players cheat all the time!' Dunk said. He couldn't believe he was having this conversation with a halfling here in the middle of the Grey Mountains. He'd left Altdorf behind so he could get away from such things, and now it seemed that they'd followed him into the wilderness. Perhaps he'd been wrong to head into the Reikland. Maybe the Middle Mountains would have been better.

'That's all part of the game,' Slick said. 'It's only cheating if you get caught. Then there are penalties.'

'If you haven't paid off the referees.'

Slick grinned at that. 'The other team can always try to buy the refs too. It all balances out in the end.'

'It's all about murderous greed and filthy gold.'

'And mindless violence,' Slick said. 'Don't forget the mindless violence.'

'Exactly!' Dunk said. 'It's just like, like…'

'Like real life,' the halfling finished, 'only more so. It's brilliant.'

Dunk hung his head and fell silent.

After a while, Slick spoke. In a tentative voice, he said, 'The best part about it is that you're perfect for it.'

Dunk's head snapped up. He glared at the halfling as if he'd cursed him and said, 'What are you babbling about?'

Slick grimaced, as if being forced to bring up an unpleasant topic for the sake of a good friend. 'Well, think about it. You're young, strong, and obviously trained for battle. You'd be wonderful at it.'

Dunk shook his head, perhaps more emphatically than he would have liked. 'You're talking madness.'

'Am I? I watched you fight that chimera. I saw you throw that spear straight down its gullet. You're a natural thrower if ever I've seen one. The best I've ever seen.' Slick saw the earnest doubt on Dunk's face and added, 'I swear in Nuffle's name.'

'Nuffle? The god of Blood Bowl?'

Slick nodded, 'As revealed to us in the sacred texts handed down by the first Sacred Commissioner Roze-El.'

Dunk held back a deep frown. 'That god means nothing to me.'

Slick showed a greasy grin. 'Then you're just going to have to trust me.'

'You're an agent,' Dunk said, edging his way back to where he'd been sitting by the fire. 'No one trusts an agent.'

'Not bad,' Slick snorted. 'You're not as clean-cut ignorant as you come off.'

Dunk started to say something, but the halfling cut him off.

'But then again, no one could be, right?'

Dunk held up a finger to interrupt. When he had Slick's attention, he spoke. 'Is that why you followed me here? To recruit me into playing Blood Bowl?'

The knowing smile slid from the halfling's fat face. He stared into Dunk's eyes for a moment before saying anything. Dunk suddenly felt like a particularly tasty pastry in the halfling's favourite bakery.

'I'll come clean with you, son,' Slick said. 'The answer is yes.'

He held up his hands before Dunk could protest.

'I didn't come to Dörfchen looking for you. I wasn't looking for anyone in particular, just looking for someone special, if you know what I mean. There's a team I work with that's desperate for some new blood, including a good thrower: the Bad Bay Hackers.'

'I don't recognise the name.'

'I thought you didn't follow the game.'

'I hate the game, but that doesn't mean I can get away from it.'

'Well said,' Slick nodded. 'Anyhow, these guys are from just north of Marienburg and they're a group of up and comers, just the hungry sort who require the services of someone like me.'

Dunk rocked back, holding his legs to his chest. 'How's that?' he asked. 'You don't look like much of a player.'

Slick almost choked on his laugh. 'Hardly, son. But I can find them players, fresh blood from the corners of the world they don't know much about yet. Sure, they could trade for better players, but they'd have to give up their own talent – what there is of it – for that. Better to go out and find some raw rookies and mould them into the kind of players they need.

'That's where you come in.'

'Forget it.' Dunk leaned forward and spat into the fire, which sputtered at his insult.

'But, son,' Slick said. 'It's everything you want: gold and glory. This is the way heroes are made these days.'

'I'm not interested.'

Slick nodded. 'Let me ask you a question. Do you know who Grimwold Grimbreath is?'

Dunk pouted but he played along with the halfling's game, waiting to see where it headed. 'Captain of the Dwarf Giants.'

'Hubris Rakarth?'

'The Darkside Cowboys.'

'Hugo von Irongrad?'

'The Impaler? He's with the Champions of Death.'

'Schlitz "Malty" Likker?'

'The Chaos All-Stars. What's the point of all this?'

Slick's smiled split his doughy face. 'Name me the last person to kill a dragon, in the last five years.'

Dunk opened his mouth, but nothing came out.

'The last ten?'

'There was that dragon terrorising the Border Princes, Blazebelly the Devourer.'

Slick nodded. 'But who killed him?'

Try as he might, Dunk couldn't answer.

'Gold and glory, son. If you want it, the best way is by playing Blood Bowl. And I can help.'

Dunk felt his will wavering. Slick added one more thing, softly.

'I know about the Hoffnungs, son. I know all about your family's downfall and what part you played in it.'

Dunk's breath caught in his chest. 'How?'

Slick smiled ruefully. 'I'm always on the lookout for new talent, son. Sometimes recruiting players means having leverage on them.'

'Including blackmail?' Dunk said. The thought that Slick knew of his shame and would expose it to the world drove him nearly to despair. He considered throttling the little agent right there and then, but he couldn't bring himself to do it.

'I prefer "strategic bargaining positioning",' Slick said.

Dunk felt disgusted. He hated the halfling and everything he'd said, but he hated himself even more. Hearing that Blood Bowl was the best way to make money and a name for yourself in today's world wasn't the worst part of it. *That* was the fact that Dunk had been trying to convince himself was otherwise for months. The day's events had overcome his last arguments, and the threat of public disgrace pushed him right over the top. There was for him, it seemed, only one path left.

'All right,' Dunk said to the halfling through gritted teeth. 'I'll do it. On one condition.' His stomach flipped over as he spoke. He'd hoped that he would never have to sink so low that playing Blood Bowl looked like moving up, but here he was. He'd just make the best of it. Maybe there was room for real heroes in this game too – even if he doubted it himself.

'What's that?' Slick tried to suppress his toothy joy, but failed utterly.

'Tell me who killed Blazebelly the Devourer.'

Slick shook his head sadly before he answered. 'No one, son. He killed all comers.'

THE NEXT MORNING, Dunk awakened to the smell of frying bacon. He sat up to find Slick spearing fresh-cooked strips of meat and stuffing them into his mouth. The halfling waved at him as he rubbed the sleep from his eyes.

'Morning, son!' Slick said. 'You looked so peaceful there, I didn't want to wake you.'

'So you just pillaged my saddlebags instead.' Dunk shot Pferd an evil look. The horse had been trained to avoid strangers, but apparently it had decided Slick qualified as a friend. Dunk himself wasn't so sure he was ready to apply that label to the halfling.

'I prefer to think of it as "sharing",' Slick said amiably. 'After all, we're going to be spending a lot of time together.'

Dunk grunted as he got to his feet. 'I thought you were supposed to be making me rich and famous.'

Slick stabbed through three pieces of bacon and offered them to Dunk as he stepped forward. 'You expect a lot overnight,' Slick said. 'I like high aspirations. I have them for you myself.'

'Before we go too much further down this road,' Dunk said in as businesslike a fashion as he could muster, 'I have some questions.' Although Dunk's father had kept most matters of the family business from him in his youth, he had picked up some of his father's style. He knew how to handle himself in a negotiation, or so he liked to think.

'Of course, son. I'd be surprised if you didn't.'

'First, what are you paid?'

Slick smiled. 'Right! Gold before glory it is then. That's an easy one – you don't pay me a thing.'

Dunk smiled right back at the halfling, hoping he didn't look as nervous as he suddenly felt. 'You'll be my agent out of the goodness of your heart?'

'In a sense, yes,' Slick said. 'More to the point, I handle all negotiations and collections of your remuneration. When you are paid, I take a small and reasonable percentage for myself off the top and pass on the vast bulk of your earnings to you entirely untouched.'

'And how much of a percentage am I to pay you?'

Slick waved off the question. 'Son, with my experience and expertise, I'll make you so much more money than you'd make on your own that it's more like your employers end up paying me to help you.'

'Uh-huh,' Dunk said, unimpressed. 'How much?'

The halfling swallowed. 'Ten per cent.' He held up a hand. 'Before you object, I'll have you know that's entirely reasonable. Some of the other agents in the business charge up to half as much again for half the service.'

It was Dunk's turn to smile faintly. 'That's fine.' He knew from watching his father that such a percentage was customary. The only trick was making sure the halfling's fingers weren't so sticky that he took more than his share, but that was a problem for another time.

'Next: where are we going?'

'Again,' Slick smiled, 'an easy one: we're off to Magritta, where the upcoming *Spike! Magazine* Tournament is to be held at the end of the month.'

'Magritta?' Dunk's face fell. 'I thought you said the Hackers were from Bad Bay.'

'They are, and that's where I've just come from. Pegleg is desperate for new players, so I've been trailing along in their wake, looking for just the right person.' The halfling fixed Dunk in a hungry tiger's gaze. 'Lucky me.'

'Who's Pegleg?'

'Captain Pegleg Haken is the team's coach, an ex-pirate who lost both a leg and a hand at sea.'

'Sounds like a tough customer.'

'You'd have to ask the sea creature that ate those missing parts.'

'So why Magritta?'

Slick finished off the last of the bacon and started packing up. Dunk considered complaining about the meagre portion of the breakfast he'd been served, but didn't want the halfling dipping into his stores again. If they were going to Magritta, the supplies would have to last them at least until they reached Bretonnia. After that, they'd have to cross all of that nation and most of the Estalian Kingdoms too, which meant either an ocean voyage, a trip through the distant Irrana Mountains, or a long trek around them.

'The Hackers need new players, and that's where they're holding their try-outs.'

'Isn't that cutting it a bit close to the time of the tournament?' Dunk started helping Slick pack everything up.

'Welcome to the world of Blood Bowl, son. More teams lose out at tournaments from a lack of healthy players than on the pitch. They're disqualified before they face even their first opponent. You're only allowed sixteen players on a roster, but you need to be able to put at least eleven players on the field. That doesn't leave much room for error, given the injury rates in this game.'

Dunk stopped checking Pferd's saddlebags to stare at the halfling. 'Just how dangerous is this?'

Slick frowned. 'Haven't you ever seen a game?'

Dunk shook his head. 'Most of what I know comes from my little brother Dirk. He always loved Blood Bowl.'

'Well, good on him, then,' Slick said, the frown still marring his chubby cheeks. 'I don't want to lie to you, son. This is a dangerous game. People get maimed or killed all the time. It's part of the sport.'

Dunk nodded solemnly, not meeting the halfling's eyes. 'I knew I didn't like it for a reason.'

'Don' t worry about it, son. A brave lad like you can handle it. It's not any more dangerous than poking around in a chimera's lair by yourself.'

Dunk flexed his injured shoulder as he mounted Pferd. 'I wasn't too fond about how that worked out either.'

Slick scurried atop his four-legged barrel of a pony. 'Gold and glory,' he called after Dunk as he prodded its back to keep up with Pferd. 'You won't find that in a cave!'

THE TRAIL THROUGH the Grey Mountains was uneventful. As they rode down out of the range, the stark beauty of the mountains clashed with the lush green of the fertile plains beyond. Dunk stared out at it wordlessly for hours while Slick prattled on.

The halfling, it seemed, could hold forth on any subject endlessly. Slick was prepared to opine at length no matter what the topic or how little he knew about it, even in the absence of any rejoinders from Dunk.

At first it annoyed Dunk, but once he got used to it, he found he almost liked it. He'd grown up in a busy household. There was rarely a dull moment in the family's keep. Over the past months Dunk had led a solitary life, as he'd never been able to find himself the crew of stalwart companions he'd always romantically imagined would join him in pursuit of fame and fortune. The rank cowardice of others hadn't stopped him, of course, but he had missed the sound of another person's voice.

Slick supplied that in spades.

'Where to from here?' Dunk asked, cutting-off the halfling in mid-sentence. He had no idea what Slick had been babbling about anyway.

'Straight for Bordeleaux,' Slick said, pointing directly toward the setting sun. 'Right on the shore of the Great Western Ocean. Pegleg took the Hackers by sea to Magritta, sailing through the Middle Sea and down around Bretonnia and Estalia to where Magritta sits on the Southern Sea. If we hustle, we can meet the boat at Bordeleaux and hitch a ride for the rest of the journey.'

'And if we miss them?'

Slick dug his heels into his pony, sending the rotund creature cantering forward just a bit faster. 'Best not to let such issues arise,' he called back over his shoulder at Dunk.

THE DUO'S TRAIL led them through the most fertile of Bretonnia's lands, the farmland that sprawled between the River Grismerie and the River Morceaux. These were names that figured large in the legends Dunk loved. As they rode along, his mind wandered back over the exploits of Sir Leonid d'Quenelles and the brave pack of fighting souls he'd led into battle after battle.

In Dunk's youth, he'd hoped that he would one day find himself following in the footsteps of his heroes, at least metaphorically. He never imagined he'd actually follow their geographical paths.

The people of the Two Rivers Basin, as they sometimes called themselves, were friendly enough. The sight of a warrior like Dunk often put them on the defence, but Slick's charisma put them at ease soon enough. No one could possibly see the little person perched on his enormously fat steed as a threat, and anyone who travelled with such a happy creature couldn't be all bad, it seemed.

WHEN THE PAIR finally reached Bordeleaux, they'd been riding hard for over a week and had put over five hundred miles behind them. And Dunk was thoroughly sick of his travelling companion.

'Are we there yet?' Dunk asked for what must have been the hundredth time.

The testy tone of Slick's response suggested that he was ready to expand the size of his circle of friends, too. 'Not quite,' the halfling said, taking a swig from the seemingly bottomless wineskin he kept with him at all times. He'd taken every opportunity to refill it along the trail, and there had been plenty. The vineyards of Bretonnia were widely acknowledged to be among the finest in the worlds, with most of the vintners' production flowing into Bordeleaux to be shipped throughout the Old World and beyond.

'I've gotten you to the big city,' the halfling said, spreading his arms out toward the sprawl of buildings, streets, towers, and even castles that comprised Bordeleaux. 'Isn't that enough?'

Below them, the River Morceaux cut a line through the centre of the city, passing through the last of the series of locks that allowed barges and smaller ships to roam the river's upper reaches. At the last of these, the river spilled beneath the Bordeleaux Bridge. It stretched across the watery span in the shadow of the Governor's Palace and the Bordeleaux Fortress, the two largest and most magnificent structures that Dunk had seen outside of Altdorf. They stabbed into the midday sun as if to grasp that fiery orb, and the lesser buildings around them looked as if they hoped to push them to succeed in their ancient competition.

'I thought we were heading for Magritta,' Dunk said.

'There's time enough for that, son,' Slick said as he slung his wine-skin into its home over his back. 'We may have a few days yet before the *Sea Chariot* arrives, possibly a week or more.'

'Or we might not,' Dunk said. 'I'd rather we got to the docks and asked after the ship before we settled in somewhere.'

'Of course,' Slick nodded, shading his eyes with his hand as he scanned the shores below. In the distance, a cluster of seagoing ships gathered on the south bank of the river, just to the west of the massive bridge. Their sails fluttered in the same easterly breeze that ruffled through Dunk's hair. 'But there's little chance they beat us here. They would have had to make – oh, burnt beef!'

Dunk stared in the same direction as Slick, craning his neck toward the docks on the river's other side. 'What's wrong?'

'They *are* here,' Slick said, grimacing. 'They must have found a tail-wind straight from the Realms of Chaos.'

The halfling pointed toward the docks. 'You see that cutter there, the one with the green and gold flag?'

Dunk squinted down into the distance and spied a dark, little ship moored between a pair of frigates. It bore a single mast, rigged fore and aft, set back toward the rear of the ship. Its headsails fluttered into the wind as the sailors below hauled them into the breeze. The banner that flew from the top of the mast bore a trio of white swords forming a massive H, emphasized by a pine-green block H underlying them, all centred on a field of brightest yellow.

'It's the Hackers all right,' Dunk said, panic creeping into his voice. 'It looks like they're getting ready to set sail.'

Dunk turned to Slick to ask what they should do, but the halfling had already given his pony, which Dunk now knew was known fondly as Kegger, his heels. The round and graceless halfling bounced along atop the galloping butterball at top speed, his legs in his stirrups the only thing keeping him from flying off like a shot from a cannon.

Dunk spurred Pferd after the halfling and quickly caught up with him. 'Go – on – with – out – me!' Slick hollered, his voice jerking with every bounce on Kegger's back. 'I'll – catch – up!'

Dunk nodded and gave Pferd his head. The stallion charged forward through the congested streets of Bordeleaux, people scattering out of his way, warned by Pferd's galloping hooves and Dunk's desperate cries.

As Dunk reached the docks, he shouted for the ship to stop. He could see that the sailors had yet to cast off the mooring lines, but it would only be a matter of moments before they did.

'Ahoy, the ship!' he cried. When he saw scores of heads turn his way from dozens of ships, he changed his call. 'Ahoy, *Sea Chariot*!' he called at the top of his lungs. 'Ahoy!'

It hadn't occurred to Dunk that as much as he and Slick wanted to get to the *Sea Chariot* before it set sail, there were others who would prefer they didn't. That's why the pile of barrels that rolled in front of him was such a surprise. The large kegs of wine were waiting to be loaded onto a nearby sea barge for transport along the coast, but someone cut them loose directly into Dunk's path.

Pferd reared back and nearly threw Dunk as he tried to avoid being crushed under the heavy barrels. Somehow the young warrior managed to hold on until Pferd brought all four hooves safely back down on to the wooden docks.

'That's far enough, I think,' a voice came from the other side of the barrels.

'Do yourself a favour and forget about that ship,' called another.

A pair of mostly toothless, half-shaven faces peered over the top of the impromptu barrier and grinned at Dunk. 'A team like that's got no place for you, mate,' the uglier one said. The duo waved their longshoremen's crating hooks meaningfully.

Dunk snarled and ran Pferd back along the docks the way he'd come. When Slick spotted him, the halfling howled, 'The – other – way!'

Dunk ignored him as he spun his mount back about and spurred him on toward the barrels that blocked his way to the *Sea Chariot*. With a final burst of speed, Pferd leapt up and just cleared the top of the barrels. He would have clipped the heads of the two dockworkers, but they threw themselves to the decking as the horse bounded through the air.

Past the barrels, Dunk rode up to the *Sea Chariot*, crying, 'Hold! Hold!'

The sailors with the mooring lines in their hands looked toward the bridge for direction. There, standing just before the hatch to the captain's quarters, stood a tall, proud man. Beneath his golden tricorn hat trimmed in forest green, his long dark hair cascaded in curls onto the shoulders of his long, crimson coat, which he wore open over a ruffled white shirt and black leggings. His face might once have been handsome, in more carefree days but now it wore openly the burden of his responsibilities, marring his once-charming features. Where his right leg had once been, he now stood upon a steel-shod shaft of wood running from the knee down. A viciously shaped and sharpened hook stabbed from his left sleeve where his hand had once been. This was no doubt Captain Pegleg Haken, in what was left of his flesh.

Pegleg's eyebrows curled at the sight of the young man on the ebony horse racing towards his ship, and he stroked the end of his greasy, black goatee with his good hand. He waved his hook at the sailors at the mooring lines and said calmly, 'Belay casting off yet, dogs. Let's see how this plays out.'

Relieved, Dunk called up to Pegleg. 'My thanks. Hold but a minute more until I can find–'

Dunk turned to see the two dockworkers now accosting Slick. The halfling had tried to work Kegger around the barrier of barrels, but the pair of thugs had easily intercepted him.

'We're not letting another one get past us, mate,' Dunk heard one of them say to Slick.

'We might have to slit your throat just to make an example of you,' the other growled. 'After all, we have a reputation to uphold round these parts, don't we?'

'Back off of him,' Dunk said as he rode up behind the two men. He reined Pferd to a halt and slid from his saddle in one smooth motion, landing before the thugs as they turned to face him.

'Right,' the uglier one said, a gap-toothed grin on his face. 'Looks like this is our lucky day, don't it?'

'Got that right,' the less ugly one said, swinging his hook before him, taking cuts out of the air at every turn. 'This one's head will make a right fine trophy, won't it?'

'Run!' Slick shouted as he and Kegger scrabbled for the safety of the other side of the barrels. 'Get on the ship! I'll catch up with you in Magritta!'

'See,' the ugly one said to his friend. 'I told you this was one of them, didn't I?'

'That you did,' said the other. 'I owe you a pint.' He crept toward Dunk, his crate-hook before him and a wicked grin on his face. 'We can pay for it with what we take from his corpse, can't we?'

Dunk reached for his sword, and realised once again that it wasn't there. He'd had cause to regret this many times since leaving his blade back in the chimera's cavern but particularly now. He grabbed his hunting knife instead.

As the less-ugly thug lashed out at Dunk with his hook, the young warrior stepped inside the man's reach and grabbed his arm, causing the murderous tip of the hook to sail wide. Then Dunk slashed out with his knife and felt its glistening blade part the thug's throat, separating it from his chin.

As the first thug's life spilled from his throat, Dunk swung the dying man's now-flaccid arm wide toward his uglier friend. The errant hook slapped into the man's head, point first, embedding itself in his grimy skull. The thug's eyes rolled back up into his head as he staggered backwards and fell, nothing but the whites staring back at the young warrior who had dispatched him so easily into the afterlife.

Dunk stepped back to witness his handiwork. Both of his assailants lay dead at his feet, the blood from the first one's throat forming a rapidly spreading pool that lapped at the young warrior's scuffed boots. Neither even twitched.

A round of applause burst out from the deck of the *Sea Chariot*. Dunk looked back to see the crowd of people arrayed on the cutter baying their approval of his lethal skills.

'You, young sir,' Pegleg called out to Dunk, 'are welcome to come aboard.' He turned to his first mate, a tall, buff sailor with chocolate-coloured skin. 'Get us underway as soon as that man, the halfling, and their mounts are aboard.' With that, he entered his quarters and shut the door behind him.

Dunk glanced over at Slick, who gave him a big, grinning thumbs up. 'Wonderful work, son!' he said. 'What a great way of displaying your considerable talents. Sometimes a little showboating really pays off.'

Dunk smiled weakly as he looked down at the two corpses whose blood stained his boots. He'd never killed anyone before, he realised.

All those countless hours of training, of sparring with Lehrer, with Dirk, with anyone else he could find, they'd all paid off. He just wasn't sure he liked what they'd bought.

THE FIRST MATE welcomed Dunk and Slick aboard as they led their mounts up the gangplank. 'The name is Cavre,' he said, pronouncing it 'carve'.

'Good to see you again, Fullbelly,' he said to Slick, as he shook his hand. The halfling's hand disappeared inside Cavre's massive grip. 'Who's your friend?'

'Permit me to introduce Dunk Hoffnung,' Slick said, 'a talented young player with plenty of promise. One of the best natural throwers I've ever seen.'

'That's high praise,' Cavre said as he shook Dunk's hand. Despite the man's obvious age – he was greying at the temples and his hands and arms bore many small scars – his hands were as soft and warm as a newborn's belly.

'Not *the* Cavre,' Dunk said respectfully. The tall man laughed, and it was a sound that brought a smile to the lips of all that heard it.

'I thought you didn't follow the game,' Slick said to Dunk.

'Even I've heard of one of the greatest blitzers in the game.'

Cavre blushed, his skin turning even darker. 'You flatter me, Mr. Hoffnung. I just move the ball down the field.'

'Which is more than most players can say,' Slick said.

'There's no trick to it,' Carve said. 'Just do what you're supposed to do, and do it well.'

Dunk handed Pferd's reins to a square-jawed man with short, dark hair and a black strip of a tattoo that wrapped around his head and covered his eyes. A blond-haired man with a similar tattoo took Kegger's reins and they led the mounts into the ship's hold.

'We don't normally take animals on board,' Cavre explained, 'but Mr. Fullbelly has a special arrangement with the captain.'

Slick grinned. 'See, son, the sort of crowd you fall in with can colour your fate.'

'For good or bad,' a voice growled from behind Dunk.

The young warrior turned to see a tall, broad man glowering at him. He was about Dunk's height, but broader across the shoulders. The sides of his head were shaved, but he'd grown long what was left so that it pulled back from his widow's peak to a long warrior's braid threaded through with bits of steel wire. He smiled, and Dunk saw that he'd filed each of his teeth to a dangerous point. He seemed like a walking shark.

'The name's Kur Ritternacht,' the man said as he tried to crush Dunk's hand in a vicelike grip. The young warrior gave back as good as he got, refusing to squirm in Kur's gaze.

'Never heard of you,' Dunk said. 'But then I only know of the *star* players.'

Kur released Dunk's hand, and the young warrior breathed a private sigh of relief. 'Don't worry, kid,' he said. 'I don't play for the *fans*.' His emphasis on the last word left no doubt that he considered Dunk to be a member of this lowly class, something unworthy of his attention. He turned his back on Dunk and walked away.

'Don't let him rattle you, son,' Slick said, patting Dunk on the back of his leg. 'He's just worried for his job.'

'How's that?' Dunk asked as he watched Kur shove sailors out of his way as he went to recline in a hammock set up near the ship's bow.

'He's the Hackers' starting thrower… for now.'

Dunk looked down at the halfling grinning up and him and felt a shiver run up his spine.

'Don't let him rattle you, Mr. Hoffnung,' Cavre said.

Dunk smiled at the man. 'You can call me Dunk, please.'

Cavre smiled and shook his head. 'Thanks, but no.'

'I'd feel more comfortable if you did. Only my old teacher called me Mr. Hoffnung.'

'And why is that, do you think?' Cavre asked. He raised his eyebrows and waited for the answer.

'I took it as a sign of respect,' Dunk answered, just a bit confused.

'And did you father's other employees call you Mr. Hoffnung?'

Dunk thought about that for a moment. 'No, actually, none of them. They reserved that name for my father.'

'Do you know why?'

Dunk shook his head. He had a few ideas, but he somehow knew that none of them would match up with what Cavre would tell him.

'First names are something to be shared with your peers.' Cavre smiled and then snapped a salute at Dunk before returning to his duties on the ship.

Dunk and Slick strolled over to the ship's railing so they could watch the towering buildings of Bordeleaux recede as they moved further down the river and towards the sea. The midday sun shone down on them brightly, bouncing off their red tiled roofs and piercing the smoke rising from the tall chimneys spotted throughout the town.

'Well, we're here, son,' the halfling said. 'That was the first part. Now all we have to do is complete the second.'

After a long moment, Dunk prompted Slick to continue. 'Which is?'

'To make the team, of course. Once we reach Magritta, Pegleg will set up a quick and dirty training camp and host try-outs. It'll be up to you to outshine the others. Those who do will find themselves filling out the Hackers' roster. The rest just get to go home.'

Dunk turned around and leaned his back against the railing. He scanned the people around him, many of them working the ship's rigging or helping guide it through this narrowest part of the navigable portion of the river as the *Sea Chariot* raced toward the sea. Others sat by themselves or stood gazing back at the city they'd left. A few exercised in ways that were designed more to impress the observer than condition the participant.

'How many spots are there?' Dunk asked.

'Now that's thinking,' Slick said, turning to follow Dunk's gaze. 'I like to see that in my players.'

'How many?'

'Assuming there haven't been any injuries or desertions since I left Pegleg in Bad Bay, there were twelve active players on the team. That leaves four spots to fill.'

'Who's on the team already?'

'You already met Cavre and Kur. The two men who took our mounts, those were the Waltheim brothers, Andreas and Otto. Otto's a catcher and Andreas is a blitzer. You see that woman over there?'

Dunk followed Slick's finger over to where a tall, androgynous figure swung high in the ship's rigging. The blond-haired woman swung from rope to rope, working like a spider in its web, as if she was as at home there as anywhere else in the world.

'That's Gigia Mardretti, the other catcher. Her lover is the man in the crow's nest, Cristophe Baldurson, one of the linemen.'

Dunk craned his neck back to see a small, stocky man scouting out toward the horizon and shouting orders to the bridge below.

'The man at the ship's wheel, that's Percival Smythe, a good bloke if a bit smug in his position. He's the other, other catcher.'

Slick swung his attention back toward the lower part of the ship's rigging, where men worked the sails, unfurling them into the wind where they billowed taut and tall. 'That lot there are the rest of the linemen: Kai Albrecht, Lars Engelhard, Karsten Klemmer, Henrik Karlmann. Kai and Lars have the dark hair, although Lars has thirty pounds on Kai. Karsten has the dark blond hair, and Henrik's the one with the white-blond locks.'

It struck Dunk as funny that Slick would refer to these men by the colour of their hair. They were uniformly the toughest group of people he'd ever seen. He supposed, however, that the hair was what set them apart from each other. They must have heard Slick mentioning their names, but they went about their business like trained professionals. They had no time for a hopeful rookie and his pint-sized agent.

Dunk counted up the names quickly, then glanced at Slick. 'That's only eleven,' he said to the halfling. 'You said there were twelve.'

Almost as if prompted, the hatch through which Dunk and Slick's mounts had been taken into the hold flung open, and a large humanoid creature stalked out. He stood somewhere over eight feet tall and had to have weighed in at nearly four hundred pounds. Great tusks jutted out from his lower jaw, lending a hungry look to the already monstrous face lurking below his bald and polished pate. Despite his size, his dark eyes seemed beady, set deep into his craggy face above a broken nose that featured a golden ring large enough to serve a bracelet for Dunk.

Someone in the bow of the ship screamed. A low rumble escaped the ogre's chest, and it took Dunk a moment to recognise it as laughter.

'Dunk Hoffnung,' Slick said out of the side of his mouth, never taking his eyes from the massive creature approaching them, 'meet M'Grash K'Thragsh.'

Dunk's breath caught in his chest. The ogre before him seemed like something out of a child's nightmare, so large and impossibly ugly that he could only have been excavated from the darkest fears buried in that child's mind. Its breath smelled like it had been chewing on rotting meat and gargling sour goat's milk.

Strangely, it was smiling.

Stunned, Dunk's first inclination was to reach once again for his nonexistent sword. Instead, he stuck out his hand and said, 'Well met, M'Grash.'

The ogre looked down at Dunk's hand, and thunder rumbled in his chest. He reached and took hold of the young warrior's hand with surprising gentleness. Though when he shook it, Dunk feared his arm might separate at the elbow.

'Name?' M'Grash said.

Dunk couldn't tell if the ogre was greeting him or threatening him. He had no social points of reference for this kind of meeting. In a flash, he decided to remain friendly and calm. Any other route, including leaping over the ship's railing – which he considered for a moment – seemed sure to end in a terribly painful demise.

'I am Dunkel Hoffnung, from Altdorf, the capital city of the Empire.'

A thick smile spread across the ogre's face. M'Grash's mouth was wide enough that Dunk was sure he could stuff his whole head into it. He hoped that no similar idea was passing through the ogre's mind at the moment.

'Dunkel,' M'Grash said, the name rolling around on his tongue like a side of beef, sounding suddenly all too small in that massive mouth.

'My friends call me Dunk,' the young warrior said, realizing then that M'Grash still held his hand in its massive mitt. He carefully extricated it from a grip he was sure could crush his comparatively tiny bones.

'Dunkel,' M'Grash repeated. 'You are Dunkel.'

'Um, yes,' Dunk said. 'That's fine. Call me what you like. I'd like to be your friend.'

A gurgling noise erupted from next to Dunk, and he looked down to see Slick looking as if he'd choked on his favourite kind of candy. The wide-eyed halfling gazed up at him and shook his head back and forth as he whispered, 'Oh, no, no, no, no, no.'

Before Dunk could ask what Slick was warning him against, he heard M'Grash rumble in childlike delight, 'Friend?'

Dunk snapped his head back around to look into the ogre's gleeful eyes. The young warrior knew only one thing at that moment; that he should do whatever he could to avoid disappointing M'Grash. Tentatively, carefully, he nodded, bracing himself for whatever might happen next.

'Friend!' M'Grash howled at the top of his capacious lungs. 'Friend!'

The ogre gathered up Dunk in his arms and gave him the bear hug of his life. The air rushed out of his lungs, and for a moment Dunk flashed back to an incident in the play yard of his family keep when his entire class had piled upon him during playtime. Crushed beneath so many bodies, he had wondered if he would ever be able to breathe again.

This was worse.

It only lasted for a moment more before M'Grash let go. 'Friend!' he roared again. This time, he tossed Dunk into the air and caught him in his outstretched arms. 'My friend!'

When M'Grash brought Dunk back within arm's reach, the young warrior grabbed on to the creature and embraced his massive neck with all his might. 'That's right!' he said. 'I'm your friend for life!'

'For life!' M'Grash said, returning the hug, much to Dunk's despair. As the air rushed from his lungs again, he thought to himself, at least I'm not being tossed in the air.

An instant later, Dunk found himself standing on the ship's deck again, right before the massive creature. Without moving his hands, he mentally checked through his body, searching for any broken bones or otherwise permanent damage. Other than a few possible bruises, he thought he'd live.

'My friend Dunkel!' The ogre's grin was terrifying. Dunk was afraid he'd made the creature so happy he'd keel over dead right there.

'Mr. K'Thragsh!' Cavre's voice rang out from the bridge. 'That will be enough.'

It was if a storm cloud had opened up over the ogre's head. As Dunk looked up at the creature, it seemed almost possible that he was large enough to demand his own weather. M'Grash's face fell, and his bottom lip shot out in a pout that looked like it could have beaten Dunk senseless.

'About your duties, please, Mr. K'Thragsh,' Cavre said. 'I'm pleased you've made a new friend, but we depend on your abilities to get us to sea.'

M'Grash's lip pulled at least halfway back in, and his eyes brightened. 'Bye, friend!' he said to Dunk before turning away and stomping up toward the bridge.

'By my grandmother's best buttered biscuits,' Slick said, 'I thought you'd made your last friend ever for a moment there.' He scanned Dunk over, checking for injuries. 'You need to be more careful with ogres.'

Dunk nodded, still stunned by the encounter. 'Who was that?' he said, his voice distant, as if just waking from a dream.'

'M'Grash is the Hackers' best blitzer. Pegleg found him in the forests around Middenheim. He lived with a family of loggers there who'd taken him in as an infant. Apparently the locals killed his family but couldn't bear to put the sword to a newborn.'

'But he's an ogre,' Dunk said quietly, almost ashamed of the words as they left his mouth. 'I mean, don't ogres normally eat people?'

Slick nodded. 'Most do, but M'Grash's upbringing changed that. He eats a lot, but humans, elves, halflings, and the like are not on the menu.'

Dunk shook his head to clear the cobwebs. It was as if his mind had left him during his meeting with M'Grash, keeping him from screaming out loud in absolute terror. Now it came smashing back into his brain.

'Is he dangerous?'

'Very,' Slick said. 'But he treasures his friends. Congratulations for making it on to that tiny list.'

'Really?' Dunk said, slumping against the ship's rail as the cutter found its way to deeper water. Its sails snapped briskly as it the wind pulled it to the west and the open sea beyond. 'He seemed friendly enough to have an army on his side.'

Slick smirked. 'Most folks don't respond so well to an ogre's greeting, son.'

Dunk breathed in big gulps of the salt-tinged air. He'd never been on the ocean before, and never on a sailing ship so large. The barges that crawled up and down the Talabec and the Stir as they met at Altdorf to form the mighty Reik might have been larger, but they couldn't rely on something as capricious as the wind to move them toward their goals. The whole day seemed painted with a thick coat of the surreal, and he feared life would only get stranger as the days rolled on.

'Who are those others at the bow?' Dunk asked, hoping to take his mind off what had just happened.

Slick looked over at the three men sitting together at the bow of the ship, almost in the shadow of Kur's hammock, as if he were an altar at which they worshipped. They wore their dark hair wild and greasy, and they seemed to be missing most of their teeth. They chatted with each other furtively, their eyes darting about the rest of the ship. The largest of them, a bear of a man who now seemed tiny compared to M'Grash – Dunk hoped the rest of the Blood Bowl league wasn't filled with creatures like that – glared over at Dunk and flashed him a sneer filled with golden teeth.

'Those are the other hopefuls, I suspect,' said Slick. 'Once we get to Magritta, Pegleg will hold team tryouts. Bloodweiser Beer is sponsoring the event, so they'll have plenty more give it a try once we get there. I'd guess that lot signed on back in Bordeleaux.'

'What makes you say that?' Dunk asked, still just a bit fuzzy headed.

'For one, they're Bretonnian for sure. Just listen to those mealy-mouthed accents. More importantly, though, do they remind you of anyone?'

Dunk stared at the men for a moment. The gold-toothed one spat back in his direction. Then it dawned on Dunk, as cold as a wintry dip in the Reik. 'Do all the dockworkers in Bordeleaux look so much alike?' he asked, not sure what the best answer would be.

'Only when they're brothers or cousins.' Slick shook his head. 'Blood Bowl is a deadly game, on the pitch and off. Those ruthless buggers we met on the dock didn't attack us at random. They wanted to thin out the competition for their friends here.'

'But won't there be a lot more hopefuls in Magritta?'

'I said they were ruthless, son, not smart.'

Dunk lay his head back against the railing and looked up at the open, blue sky. 'What have you gotten me in to, Slick?' he asked.

'Just settle back,' the halfling said. 'We have a long trip still ahead of us.'

* * *

DUNK AWOKE THAT night with a knife against his neck and a garlic-coated voice hissing in his ear. He knew who it was, at least within a group of three people, before he heard the words. 'You killed my brother, and now you're going to die.'

Most of the Hackers had gone below decks after sunset. Their berths were down there, as was the galley. Cavre had brought Dunk and Slick a bowl of passable stew each and handed out the same to the trio at the ship's bow. 'Recruits sleep on deck, Mr. Hoffnung,' he'd said. 'When you make the team, you'll find yourself below.'

'When?'

Cavre had just smiled and then disappeared through the hatch again.

'The agents sleep up here too?' Dunk had asked Slick.

The halfling had looked up from his bowl of stew, already over half in his belly. 'You see any other agents around here, son?'

Dunk had made a show of looking around, but he had known the answer. 'Nope.'

'Blood Bowl teams don't care much for agents. We're more what they like to call a "necessary evil". We bring them the best talent, but we also make sure they pay the best rates for it.'

'So you're sleeping up here?'

Slick grinned as he finished up his stew and set his bowl aside. 'I wouldn't trust my neck down there.'

Now it was Dunk's neck on the line. Without thinking, he brought up his hand to grab at his attacker's knife arm. The assassin pulled back and brought his knife down at Dunk's chest instead, intending to plunge his blade deep into the young warrior's heart.

The point of the blade glanced off the breastplate under Dunk's shirt.

You think I should take it off, Dunk had asked Slick. We're on a boat after all.

Not tonight, son, Slick had said as he laid his head down on the deck and closed his eyes. Better to get the lay of the land before you let down your guard. Besides, if you get tossed overboard in the middle of the sea, you'd be better off getting dragged to the bottom before the sharks got you.

Slick had snickered at that, making Dunk think the halfling had intended it as a joke. However, when he thought of Pegleg, it didn't seem all that funny.

Dunk slid from under his attacker and let out a yell for help. He couldn't see much in the darkness. The ship sailed along under a sliver of a moon, the pilot able to pick out the coastline several miles to port, but Cavre had said the captain didn't like to attract attention at night. That sort of thing could be fatal out here, so they ran without out lights instead.

The lookout in the crow's nest heard Dunk's cry and opened his hooded lantern, shining it down on the deck below, catching the young warrior in the light.

Dunk glanced back, and his assailant – one of the recruits from the bow of the ship – tackled him. Dunk slammed back an elbow and felt it smash into the man's cheek, the bone cracking from the force.

Still in the man's grip, Dunk wrenched himself about and found the man about to drive the knife down at him again. This time the attacker aimed for Dunk's eyes with a two-fisted stab straight down.

Dunk reached up with both hands and caught his attacker by the wrists, stopping the point of the knife bare inches from his hose. The man grunted with fury and strained to bring the knife down further. He was strong, maybe stronger than Dunk, and in his position he could bring all his weight to bear. Slowly, inexorably, the point of the knife drove lower and lower, glinting in the lookout's lamplight, as well as that of a beam piercing the night from the cutter's bridge.

Dunk pressed up against his attacker's arms with all his might. He tried to wriggle left and right, but the assailant held him fast with his legs. There was nowhere to go.

Dunk howled in frustration. Then suddenly the attacker was gone, hauled up into the night. The lights followed the man, and Dunk saw him thrashing about as he dangled precariously in M'Grash's grip.

The ogre held the panicked man at arm's length and roared at him. 'Don't hurt my friend!'

The terrified assassin brought his knife around to stab it into M'Grash's neck. The ogre didn't see the attack coming, and Dunk feared the killer might fell even the massive creature with a well-placed blow.

'Get rid of him, M'Grash!' he shouted.

The ogre swept his arm out and back, then hurled the assassin into the black waters beyond the ship's rail. He screamed the entire way as he arced through the night air until crashing through the waves into the deep below.

The attacker's two friends dashed forward from their spot at the bow, their rapiers drawn, and thirsty for the ogre's blood. Although he knew it was foolhardy, Dunk pulled out his hunting knife and stood with M'Grash, ready to take on the duo if they pressed the issue.

The gold-toothed man lashed out, but Dunk leaned back, just out of reach, and the sharpened blade whizzed bloodlessly by. 'That's three lives you owe me now,' the man hissed in his Bretonnian accent.

'What in Nuffle's name is going on?' a voice shouted from behind Dunk. He glanced over his shoulder to see Cavre storming towards him and the others, four of the team's linemen behind him, each bearing a long knife. 'Stand down!' he said. 'All of you!'

M'Grash fell to his knees instantly. Even in this position, he looked down at everyone else on the ship.

The two attackers immediately started in with their lies. 'This man threatened us, and when Patric tried to defend himself, he had his pet ogre here throw him overboard!'

Off in the distance, somewhere in the water behind the ship, Dunk could hear a voice calling out for help. It was barely loud enough to hear already, but he knew the man was shouting as loudly as his lungs would let him. He started to say something, but Cavre cut him off.

'Shut your mouths, all of you!' The blitzer turned to the ogre. 'Is that what happened?'

M'Grash shook his head so violently that Dunk feared his eyes might fly from their sockets. 'Dunk in trouble. I help.'

'Their friend tried to knife me in the night. He could have killed me if M'Grash hadn't stopped him. When he tried to stab M'Grash too, he threw the man overboard.'

Cavre shaded his eyes against the light and looked up at the crow's nest. 'Is that how it happened?'

A voice Dunk recognised as Kai's called down. 'Who would you trust?' Cavre opened his mouth to respond, but Kai cut him off. 'M'Grash's pal there has it right, as far as I saw.'

Cavre glared at the gold-toothed man and his companion. 'Mr. Jacques Broussard and Mr. Luc Broussard, is it?' he said. The men nodded sullenly. 'Surrender your blades, all of them. There will be no killing here. You save that for the field.'

The men hesitated for a moment, then complied. The first only had his sword and a knife. Luc, the one with the golden teeth, removed three other blades secreted about his body and handed them to Cavre. The blitzer weighed them in his wide, soft hands for a moment, then threw them overboard.

Jacques began to protest but Cavre cut him short. 'You're lucky that's not you, Mr. Broussard. Now shut up and go back to where you were. If there's another disturbance, I'll have you thrown to the bottom of Manann's watery kingdom, and you can search for your lost weapons there.'

The two men slunk back towards the bow of the ship without another word. The looks they shot back at Dunk felt like they might set his clothes afire. When Slick slapped him on the back of his thigh, he nearly jumped from his skin.

'That pair won't be giving you any more trouble for the rest of the trip, son,' the halfling said. 'Just leave them a wide berth.'

Dunk turned to Cavre and shook the man's hand. 'Thank you, sir, for seeing through their lies.'

The blitzer grimaced. 'I wasn't doing you any favours, Mr. Hoffnung. There may be some rivalry between those who wish to join the Hackers, but I won't permit that to spill blood on this trip. Once we get to shore, though, you're on your own.'

Dunk nodded. 'I understand.' He hesitated a moment before continuing. 'Can I ask you one more question?'

'Go ahead, Mr. Hoffnung.'

'What about the man overboard?' Dunk pointed back behind the ship, from where he could still just barely hear his attacker's forlorn cries.

Cavre's face turned even more serious now. 'For what he did, Mr. Hoffnung, I'd have had him thrown overboard. M'Grash here just saved me the trouble.'

With that, Cavre turned and led the linemen with him back down the hatch.

FIVE DAYS LATER, the ship pulled into the wide and sheltered Bay of Quietude, around which sprawled Magritta, perhaps the busiest port city in all of the Old World and certainly the busiest Dunk had ever seen. Dunk and Slick stood at the port rail as the ship slipped into the harbour and found itself a mooring at the pier. By now, the sun was high enough to splash the city with sunlight.

Guards in each of the two fortresses capping the twin horns of the bay waved down at the *Sea Chariot* as it found its way to the sheltered waters. They bellowed at the sight of the Hackers' banner, some of them starting in with a rousing chorus of 'Here we go, here we go, here we go!'

With the *Spike! Magazine* tournament about to begin, it seemed that Blood Bowl fever had infected the entire town. Dunk was just glad to get a friendly response from the watchers in the towers. The catapults and trebuchets trained toward the bay made it clear that unwelcome guests would not enter so easily.

Other than Bordeleaux, Dunk had never been in a seaport before, and Magritta was as different from the Bretonnian town as Altdorf itself. The salty waters of the bay lapped right up against the docks that lined the edges of the city. From that buttressed border of wood and stone, the streets wound their way up into the hills that overlooked the water until they terminated in a tall stone wall that lined the natural ridge encompassing the bay.

'Is it safe for us to be here?' asked Dunk, suspicious of every new town after his reception in the previous two.

'Very,' Cavre said over Dunk's shoulder. 'With *Spike! Magazine* holding its tournament here, there won't be any trouble. No one would dare, it's worth too much to them and losing the tournament would half cripple this place.'

'It's all about the crowns,' Slick said, a faraway look in his eyes. Dunk imagined he could see the reflections of those gold coins spinning in the halfling's pupils. 'The tournaments bring a huge number of visitors to the region with coins to toss around like confetti. Plus, there are the sponsors: Bloodweiser and the like. Not to mention the Cabalvision rights. I hear the new Wolf Network – you know, Ruprect Murdark's group – won the rights this year to bring their camras to the field.'

'Camras?' Dunk had avoided most exposure to Blood Bowl throughout his life. Given his brother's passion for the game, it hadn't been easy, but he'd managed it.

'Enchanted boxes with a spirit trapped inside of them. The box is formed so the spirit has to look out through the glass lens on the front of it at all times. Back when there was an NAF–'

'A what?'

'The Nuffle Amorica Football league? The original league founded by Commissioner Roze-El back in 2409?'

'That's a hundred and fifty years ago, a bit before my time.'

'It didn't dissolve until 2489.'

'Still.' Dunk waved his hands at himself.

'Wait.' Slick narrowed his eyes at the young man. 'Just how old are you? I can never tell with humans. Never mind! Don't answer that. I'm sure I don't want to know. It'll just make me feel older than I want to be. Where was I?'

'Crowns. Camras. The NAF.'

Slick brightened. 'Right! The various broadcasting companies hire wizards to use the Cabalvision spell to broadcast whatever the spirits in the camras see. Some people pay to have these appear directly in their minds. Others prefer to watch them in their crystal balls. Some of the best pubs have dozens of them, some larger than a wagon wheel, showing all the games played around the Old World at once.'

'My family had one of those. I never knew how it worked.'

'Other people use their Daemonic Vision Renderers to keep the broadcasts around so they can play them back later. These have the games broadcast into the head of an entrapped daemon, which is ensorcelled into having to play back the games it's seen at the owner's request. Of course, most daemons have tiny brains, so they can only remember so many different games at once.'

'You're kidding,' Dunk said.

'Pegleg's got one in his cabin. That's why he never comes out during the whole trip. He locks himself in there to study the games – both ours and those of our likely opponents – picking out their weaknesses and protecting our own.'

Dunk shook his head. 'Amazing. All this over some game.'

Cavre spoke up as the ship slipped into its slot in the docks. 'It's not just *some* game, Mr. Hoffnung. It's the greatest game ever.'

SLICK WOKE UP Dunk at the crack of dawn the next morning. The Hackers had been the first Blood Bowl team to arrive in town, even though the games were due to start in only two days.

'Travelling to these games is expensive,' Slick explained as Dunk ate his breakfast and got ready for practice. 'Most teams like to cut their trips as short as possible. No other Blood Bowl games are played in the region the week before the tournament. Everyone wants to be healthy for their shot at one of the four big cups.'

'There are four of these things?'

'There are lots of these things, if by "things" you mean 'tournaments.' There's probably a Blood Bowl game going on somewhere on any given day of the year, and there are tournaments every month. The big four – the Majors – those each only happen once a year.

'Your timing couldn't be better, son, for starting out a career. The *Spike! Magazine* tournament is the first of the Majors. From there, it's the Dungeonbowl, a series of games played in underground stadiums, but you need to be sponsored by one of the Schools of Magic to enter that, so the Hackers won't be in that this year. After that is the Chaos Cup, which is just as crazy as it sounds. It all culminates in the Blood Bowl, the greatest tournament capped by the greatest championship game of the year.'

'I thought the game was called Blood Bowl.'

'Technically, it's Nuffle Amorica Football, or just Nuffle, but most people just call it after the most important match. 'Blood Bowl' just has a much better ring to it than NAF, don't you think?'

Dunk just shook his head. 'All those games, all the blood. How does anyone survive a full season?'

'Son,' Slick said, patting Dunk on the back. 'You'd better just concentrate on surviving the tryouts.'

THE HACKERS HAD set up camp in an open area on the western shore of the bay. The tents stood on the dry part of the beach, and the gentle lapping of the waves lulled the team to sleep at night.

During the day, the team and its coaching staff assembled on a level grassy field between the beach and the great wall that ran between the city proper and the westernmost of the two fortresses that guarded the entrance to the bay. A score of hopefuls showed up for the try-outs on the first day, lured by the chance to play in one of the Majors, even for a relatively new team like the Hackers.

Slick informed Dunk that the current odds against the Hackers winning the tournament were 40 to 1 against.

'How many teams are entered?' Dunk asked

'It varies from year to year. It's somewhere in the hundreds.'

Dunk's jaw dropped.

'Son,' Slick said, 'the Majors are big. Humongous. Wait until you wander into town and see the tens of thousands of fans there. How do you think the teams can afford to pay the players so much gold?'

Dunk shook his head. 'How do they whittle so many teams down? Do some of them not have to play in the first round?'

'Sometimes I forget how little you know about the game,' Slick laughed. 'The first round doesn't have any eliminations. The teams play as many games as they like against as many opponents as they like, although you can only play the same team once. If you win, you get a point.

'At the end of the first week, the teams with the top four number of points scored enter the semi-finals. The winners of those games face off in the finals, and the winner of that game is the champion. The runner-up gets 100,000 crowns, and the team that wins first place gets 200,000 crowns and the *Spike! Magazine* trophy; a mithril spike held in the fist of a gilded gauntlet.'

Dunk whistled. 'Do the players see any of that?'

Slick raised an eyebrow at the young warrior. 'Is that a hero's first concern?'

'Isn't it a Blood Bowl player's?'

'Right you are, son!' the halfling said, slapping Dunk on the back and then looking him in the face. 'Ah, I've never been prouder.'

Dunk almost thought he saw a tear start to form in Slick's eye, but the halfling started talking again, breaking the sentimental mood. 'Some players get bonuses if their team wins a big tournament. It depends on the team and the deal that the player strikes with the team.'

The halfling's grin set Dunk's teeth on edge, as Slick hooked his thumbs into his ever-straining braces and said, 'That's where I come in.'

Dunk stood up. Having come from wealth and been sheltered by it, the topic always made him uncomfortable. He knew that he needed to make a fortune somehow to help restore his family's name and to make up for the horrible mistake he'd made to trigger his family's fall in the first place. He was going to have to get over his embarrassment at talk of money for this to work at all. While he didn't always like Slick, he was thankful that he'd found him. The halfling would give him just the kind of help he needed – or so he hoped.

'Right!' Slick said. 'It's time to report in for practice. You're going to have to look sharp. I did a bit of scouting around last night, and there's a lot more competition for those spots than we saw on the *Sea Chariot.*'

The two emerged from the shelter of their tent and trotted over to the practice field. Along the way, Dunk stopped to check on Pferd. The stallion had survived the ocean voyage well, but Dunk could tell he was anxious to stretch his legs. He'd have to take him for a ride later.

'How many?' Dunk asked.

'At least two score,' Slick answered, his tone flat and business-like.

Dunk nearly tripped over his own feet. 'More than forty?' he grimaced. 'Vying for how many spots?'

'There are four open slots.'

Dunk ran his hand through his hair. 'I didn't think there would be so many.'

'Don't worry about it, son,' Slick said. 'It doesn't matter if there are four or four hundred. You've got the talent to be the best.'

'But I don't have the first clue about what I'm doing.'

'Again,' Slick said with that grin that made Dunk shudder, 'that's where I come in. Stop for a moment, and I'll tell you what you need to know.'

Dunk nodded. 'We don't have much time.'

'It's all right,' Slick said, flipping a hand at Dunk. 'I won't get into things like throwing team-mates or avoiding chainsaws or Dwarf Death-Rollers. I'll just cover the basics.

'Blood Bowl is played on a field or "pitch" a hundred paces long by sixty wide. At each end of the pitch, there's an "end zone". The idea of the game is to take the football and get it into your opponent's end zone by any means available, and score a touchdown.

'Each game starts with a coin toss. The winner chooses to kick off the ball or receive. If the ball goes out of bounds, the fans just throw it back in, and the game keeps going. It only stops for a touchdown. Then the team that scored kicks off to the other team, and it all starts over again.

'There are two thirty-minute halves with a twenty-minute break between. When the clock runs out, the team with the most touchdowns wins the game.'

Dunk listened intently throughout. 'That doesn't sound so hard to follow.'

'It's not,' Slick said. 'That's what makes it so popular. Even goblins can manage it. There's all sorts of fun stuff I'm leaving out, of course, like how to best cheat and how to bribe the referees but we'll have plenty of time to get to that once you make the team. The only real rule you need to remember is this: no weapons allowed.'

Dunk cocked his head at the halfling. 'I thought you said something about chainsaws and Dwarf Death-Rollers.'

Slick nodded. 'All that and more. I said they're against the rules. I didn't say you wouldn't see them.

'Blood Bowl is, at its core, an abstraction of the battles and wars that rage across these lands every day. As the saying goes, "all's fair in war".'

'That's "love and war," I think,' Dunk said.

'You don't say?' Slick said, seemingly genuinely surprised. 'I can't say I know much about love, son, but I'll teach you everything I can about this kind of war.'

As Dunk and Slick finally topped the rise from the beach to the level area that served as the Hackers' practice field, they saw nearly fifty hopefuls lined up along the edge of the field, waiting for Pegleg to speak to them. Slick slapped Dunk on the leg and the young warrior raced over and fell into line.

Dunk gazed along the line to check out the competition. There were humans from all walks of life and many lands around the Old World and beyond. Magritta was the crossroads of this part of the globe, and it showed in the faces of these people. There were blond-haired, axe-bearing warriors from Norsca, who wore their locks in long, complex braids under their horned helmets; olive-skinned dandies in turbans and colourful robes from Araby; even more exotic people with straight, black hair under wide, conical hats from far-off Cathay; nearly black-skinned hopefuls from the distant South Lands; and many more souls from Estalia, Tilea, Bretonnia, Kislev, and even Dunk's own home: the Empire.

Dunk noticed that all of the hopefuls were humans, not an elf, dwarf, or halfling among them, much less a goblin or an orc. In fact, of the Hackers' current players, there was only one nonhuman face among them: M'Grash. Dunk wondered how an exception to the (perhaps unspoken) rule had been made for the ogre, although he could certainly see how such a creature would be a tremendous asset to any team. Most of them were men, of course, although a few women stood out in the group, clearly ready to grind into the dirt any man who might question their abilities.

Before Dunk could think more about this, Cavre stepped up before the line and called the hopefuls to attention.

'Pardon me, kind ladies and sirs!' the dark-skinned man shouted. The chatter in the line fell silent. 'My name is Rhett Cavre. I'm not only the assistant coach here but also the starting blitzer, unless one of you thinks you're good enough to take my job.'

Nervous laughter rippled through the line at that.

'Welcome to the Hackers' boot camp, and good luck. I hope to get to know you over the next two days and maybe even play with the best of you in the tournament. As we run you through our drills and test your skills and abilities, I want you to remember the one rule we enforce above all others with the Hackers: always listen to your coach!'

Cavre turned to the side, sweeping his arms wide toward Pegleg. 'With that in mind, allow me to introduce the coach of the Bad Bay Hackers: Captain Pegleg Haken.'

Pegleg, still dressed in his captain's uniform, limped his way towards the line, step-tap, step-tap, step-tap. When he reached Cavre, he took off his sword belt and scabbarded cutlass and handed them to the star blitzer. Then, still without saying a word, he glared up and down the line, scanning the motley faces he found there. Then he drew a deep breath and spoke.

'I've never seen such a sorry lot of losers!' Pegleg growled with the voice of a drill sergeant and the attitude of a daemon. 'You stupid sods came here because you want a chance to risk your lives for a bit of glory and gold. You are idiots! Blood Bowl is a hard game for hard people. If you want to earn some money by fighting, try something safer… like joining your local *army!* At least they feed you for free there!'

Pegleg bowed his head and shook it, his black curls bouncing beneath his bright-yellow tricorn hat. 'The life expectancy of the average Blood Bowl player is measured not in seasons, but games. I'm sure that some of you have families back home that care about you, friends that wouldn't mind seeing you again while you're still breathing, maybe even a lover that hopes to hold you in her arms again.'

He looked up from under the brim of his hat. 'The best advice I can give you is to leave. Now.'

A pair of brothers from Tilea, standing next to Dunk, looked at each other and started to weep. As one, they broke from the line and raced for the beach and the safety of the streets of Magritta beyond. Five others calved off from the line and chased after the others. One of the dandies from Araby joined them, wailing the entire way.

Pegleg glared at the remaining hopefuls until the cries of the cowards faded into the distance. 'Anyone else?' he said.

Dunk felt his foot start to step forward, but he pressed it down into the soft earth instead. He hadn't come all this way to give up now. Blood Bowl couldn't be any more dangerous than fighting dragons. Or a chimera. Could it?

'Now that those weak-livered pansies are gone, we can get down to business,' Pegleg growled as he paced back and forth along the line of hopefuls. Step-tap, step-tap, step-tap. He waved his hook as he spoke, often coming within bare inches of a hopeful's face. No one dared to flinch.

'Give me fifty laps around the pitch!' Pegleg roared. 'Now!'

BY THE END of the first day of the two-day boot camp, Dunk wished he was dead. He was sure that it would hurt less. When he sat down in his tent that night, every inch of him seemed to be sore and bruised.

'You think this is bad,' Slick said. 'Wait until you wake up tomorrow.'

The first day had been all about testing the hopefuls' raw abilities, as well as their limits. Pegleg and Cavre had run them through drill after drill: races, obstacle courses, tackling, throwing, catching, and more.

It was clear that Dunk would never be the blitzer Cavre was. He didn't have a head for tackling, and nearly half of the others were able to outrace him in a dead sprint. Perhaps he'd be best as a lineman or a catcher, although Slick was pushing him to try for thrower.

'Blitzers are often the team captains and the top-paid players,' the halfling said, 'but sadly that's not where your talents lie. Throwers are the next best.'

'Won't I just end up playing behind Kur?' Dunk asked. 'I don't think he's going anywhere soon.'

'Even the toughest players get hurt sometimes. It's inevitable. That's why they have backups. Sooner or later, those players get their chance on the pitch, often in the most important parts of the game.

'Besides, if you shoot for thrower and fall short, Pegleg can always make you a lineman instead. Aim high, son.'

'You think I can make thrower?' Dunk tried to keep the need out of his voice, but feared the halfling could hear it.

Slick patted the young warrior on the back. 'I could feed you a line of lies, son, but you'd see right through that. I'll be honest with you: I don't know. You have all the raw talent you need, but your lack of Blood Bowl skills could haunt you.'

Dunk knew what Slick meant. He'd been trained with the sword, the knife, the bow, the spear, to be a warrior, not a Blood Bowl player. While the skills needed for both overlapped, they weren't identical.

'Still,' the halfling said softly, 'I've never seen someone with an arm like yours. The way you brought down that chimera? Simply stunning.'

'It was a lucky shot,' Dunk said as he lay back on his cot.

'Then be as lucky as you can,' Slick said as sleep reached out and surrounded him like a dozen linemen and beat him unconscious.

'AWAKE, YOU ROTTERS!' Pegleg's voice shouted, waking Dunk from his dreams, seemingly only a moment after he lay down his head. 'Awake! The last of you buggers out of his tent gets cut right now!'

Dunk rolled out of his cot and stumbled out of the tent, still in the same clothes he'd been wearing yesterday. He'd been too tired to change into a nightshirt. He ran a hand over his face and another through his hair as he raced to the impromptu line forming in front of Cavre as Pegleg stormed through the camp, hollering at the top of his capacious lungs.

A dozen others joined Dunk immediately, and another few trickled in soon after, moving slowly and groaning from having to stretch their tortured muscles with such little notice.

Dunk's whole body was sore from his head to his toes, but it wasn't as bad as he'd feared. Back home, Lehrer's training program had kept him in decent shape, and the long journey to Magritta hadn't afforded him much opportunity to grow soft. Still, he'd worked himself as hard as he ever had yesterday, and he felt it.

After a full pass through the camp, Pegleg limped over to stand next to Cavre and survey the line. Of the forty or so hopefuls that had stuck around through the training yesterday, only twenty stood in the line now.

'Mr. Cavre,' Pegleg snarled. 'I told you this was a sorry lot.'

'I didn't disagree with you, captain.'

'Where are the rest of them?'

'I'll check, captain.'

'No.' Pegleg held Cavre back with his gleaming hook. 'I'll rouse them myself.'

The pirate-coach stalked through the camp, peering into the tents. Those nearest to the line were all empty, their former occupants staring back at Pegleg from the line. Dunk's tent was further back, closer to the sea.

Pegleg came to a tent and stopped. 'Wu Chen!' he shouted. 'This isn't a brothel in Cathay! Get out here.'

As the silence from the tent grew longer, Pegleg's face grew redder. With a horrible snarl, the pirate raised his hook high and brought it down, ripping through the fabric of the tent. 'I said *get out here!*' he raged. 'You *worthless–*'

Pegleg cut himself short as his hook tangled in the cloth. He tugged at it, trying to free his arm, but he only wound himself in further. With a mighty, two-handed wrench, the stakes holding down the tent gave, and Pegleg cascaded backward, the whole of the tent coming with him, entangling him in its cloth and its lines.

'Mr. Cavre!' Pegleg shouted as he fell backward, wrapped in the remains of the tent tighter than any mummy. The players, whose half of the camp lay on the other side of the bonfire in the middle of the camp, started to laugh as their leader's tent-packaged body began to roll toward the sea.

'Mr. Cavre!' Pegleg shrieked as he heard the lapping of the waves and realised the extent of his plight.

The blitzer was already on his way. 'Mr. K'Thragsh!' he shouted as he sprinted toward the captain. 'A hand if you will!'

The ogre burst out of the pack of players and dashed toward Pegleg as he rolled toward the waters of the bay, screaming, 'Mr. Cavre!'

The captain's struggles only made his situation worse. If he'd have stayed still, he probably wouldn't have continued to roll down the gentle slope toward the sea. As it was, he fought and clawed away with his hook like a cornered wildcat. At one point, he managed to tear the fabric from in front of his face. The sight of the approaching water snatched a horrifying scream from his chest, which was cut off when he rolled over on his face again.

Despite M'Grash's long-legged stride, Cavre reached the captain first and stopped him from rolling further. He stopped the man just before the high-tide mark, much to the captain's delight. However, before Pegleg could offer his thanks, M'Grash picked him up and dangled him from the end of his outstretched limb like a prize fish he'd just managed to haul to shore.

'Get me away from the water!' Pegleg bellowed. The ogre nearly dropped him in shock, but the creature managed to recover himself and carried the captain back toward the bonfire pit, still held in front of him like a newsworthy catch.

Before M'Grash got too far, Pegleg's struggles bore fruit. The tent-trap he found himself in finally gave way entirely, and he plummeted from the ogre's grasp, crashing to the ground. M'Grash blushed red as he stared at the ragged remnants of the tent, still hanging in his hand.

The players burst out in howls of laughter, which were only made worse when Pegleg tripped over his good leg as he tried to stand up. Some of the hopefuls joined in too, although quietly. The last thing any of them needed was Pegleg mad at them.

The captain finally leapt to his peg and shook the tent's lines off of his leg. 'What are you all laughing at?' he snarled at the players. The uproar only got louder.

Pegleg stormed over to the players, his hook held out and high, ready to impale the first person he met. But before he could exact his revenge, Cavre's voice rang out.

'Captain!' he said. 'We have a problem!'

Pegleg stopped so hard, he drove his peg halfway into the beach's sand. 'It had better be good, Mr. Cavre!' he said, his face as crimson as his coat.

'It's murder, captain,' Cavre said. 'Murder!'

Even as far away as Dunk was, he could see the body lying in the spot left bare by Pegleg's destruction of the tent. It was Wu Chen's.

Pegleg rushed over to the corpse and cursed. Holding the curved end of his hook against his forehead, he said something quiet and respectful over the body. As he finished, he looked up and gasped.

'Quick, Mr. Cavre,' he said, 'check the other tents.'

Dunk's stomach fell into his boots. He and the other hopefuls watched from the line in detached horror as Cavre and Pegleg went through each of the tents, pulling back their flaps one by one. One by one, they discovered a full score of dead hopefuls, each cut down in their prime.

The other players came over from their side of the camp to help. They hauled the bodies from the tents and stacked them up near the fire pit, one at a time. Dunk tried to go down to help too, but Cavre pointed him back toward the line. 'This isn't something for the hopefuls to help with, Mr. Hoffnung,' he said.

'Why not?' Dunk asked. He'd trained with each of the victims yesterday, and he wanted to do what little he could for them.

'Tell him, Mr. Fullbelly,' Cavre said to Slick before returning to his grisly work.

The halfling took Slick by the leg and guided him back to the line. 'Think about it, son,' he said softly. 'Who stands the most to gain from all this?'

As Dunk returned to his place, he glanced up and down the line at the faces of the other hopefuls. 'We do,' he said with a grimace.

It took the Hackers the better part of an hour to pick through the place. Once all the bodies were accounted for, Pegleg looked up at the line of hopefuls. 'We don't have time for this, Mr. Cavre.'

'Aye, captain,' the blitzer said. Then he raced up to where the hopefuls still stood and said, 'You lot are with me. We have a long day ahead of us, and a few deaths never stopped a game of Blood Bowl.'

10

THAT DAY'S TRAINING was even worse than the first. This time around, Cavre fitted each of the players with a spare set of armour before practice began.

Dunk was amazed at the sophistication of the armour. Unlike the stuff he'd worn before, which was fashioned for the rigors of battle, this sort of armour was designed for the weaponless head-knocking and unarmed combat of Blood Bowl. It featured massive spaulders – Slick called them 'shoulder pads' – which were made as much for knocking down other players as for protection.

Dunk also wore a helmet that featured a wrought-iron grill over the face to protect his eyes from probing fingers, or so it seemed. Unlike traditional helmets, though, this one featured padding on the inside to protect the skull from the regular blows rained down on it by opposing players. It was painted in a loud yellow and featured the three crossed swords on a green background that comprised the Hackers' logo.

Overall, the armour fit tighter than Dunk was used to, and featured more padding underneath. It was built for speed as well as protection, to allow the wearer to run as well as survive an attack. The armour of the linemen and blitzers was just a bit heavier than that of the throwers and catchers, whose smaller shoulder pads were built so they could easily lift their arms over their heads.

The helmet, the shoulder pads, the gauntlets and even the knee and elbow pads featured sharp sets of spikes that would quickly make a mess of unprotected flesh. Their presence explained the amazing number of small dents found on most of the sets of practice armour loaned out to the hopefuls.

After getting fitted with the equipment, the hopefuls played a loose scrimmage against each other, mostly just running through a set of plays over and over again. The hopefuls lined up against each other and tried to accomplish whatever goals Cavre set for them, which ranged from successfully throwing the ball to running the ball through a phalanx of linemen. Dunk found himself in a set of thrower's armour, ready to throw the ball downfield, towards the opposing team's end zone at a moment's notice.

Dunk decided he liked being a thrower for more than just the gold and glory that Slick had mentioned. When you had the ball in the game, there wasn't much more frightening than realising that everyone on the opposing team hoped to crush you far enough into the turf that you couldn't get up without a group of helpers armed with a set of trusty shovels.

When most players had the ball, there was little they could (or at least should) do but run for the end zone and hope to find some daylight along the way. Throwers, though, could scramble around as much as they liked until they found someone downfield (closer to the end zone) to chuck the ball at. Some of the balls they worked with were spiked too, which made catching the ball a bit more of an adventure, but all of the catchers did their best, even when their efforts drew their own blood. They all wanted to make an impression, and not of the full body-in-the-turf variety.

At midday, Cavre called a break for lunch, and the hopefuls joined the team members around the fire pit for more of the team's traditional stew. This always seemed to be made of some mixture of cheese, beer, and some sort of unidentifiable meat. Dunk had already had more than his fill of the stuff aboard the *Sea Chariot*, but after a day and a half of Blood Bowl tryouts it tasted like the finest of meals ever served in his family's keep back in Altdorf.

The spirits were high among the hopefuls, although the players were more subdued. During the middle of the meal, Pegleg, who had been wandering around the camp all morning, came by and whispered something in Cavre's ear. The two men were on the other side of the fire pit, and try as he might Dunk couldn't hear a thing they said to each other. For a moment, he thought they might be looking at him, but it happened so quickly he told himself it was his imagination.

In the afternoon, the hopefuls played a full scrimmage game against the players. The professionals whipped the amateurs like orc stepchildren. Several of the hopefuls limped off the field, or were carried off, injured. Those who were left grinned openly. It left them fewer competitors for the four spots available on the team.

'You're doing great, son,' Slick said during a break in the action. 'There's really only one person you have to beat for that thrower spot.'

'I know,' Dunk said, as he tossed back a tanker of water, swished it around in his mouth, and spat it out. 'Luc,' he said, as he glared over at the Bretonnian with the golden teeth.

Luc noticed Dunk looking at him and stalked over toward the young warrior, his lip curled in a savage sneer, exposing his fake, yellow teeth. 'Give up now and leave, Imperial. I'm the Hacker's next thrower.'

'Save it for someone who hasn't seen you piss yourself in front of M'Grash,' Slick said, stepping between the two.

Luc looked down at the tubby halfling and laughed. 'Still letting others do your fighting for you?' he said to Dunk. 'On the pitch, it'll be just you and me.'

TIME IN THE scrimmage was winding down. Cavre had been swapping Luc and Dunk out for the thrower's position the whole game. Luc had made a few fine throws, but he'd also hurled three interceptions. The professionals mostly had their way with the hopefuls, as was to be expected. They were eager to take the newcomers down a peg or two, and it caused some of the amateurs to become frustrated and make even worse mistakes.

Dunk was used to this kind of pressure. Back in Altdorf, Lehrer had arranged for him to spar against only the best in the Empire, and the opponents received bonuses if they beat the young warrior. Dunk had taken many losses at the hands of Lehrer's friends, but over time he'd become a better swordsman for it.

After the professionals scored yet another touchdown, the hopefuls lined up to receive the kick-off once again. Dunk was way back with Luc, who stood on the other side of the field from him.

Cavre kept time on a stopwatch. Before the kick-off, he looked at it and said, 'This will be the last chance. The next touchdown ends the game.'

Dunk rubbed his hands together and waited for the kick. It sailed down the field, over the heads of most of the players and angled right for him. He stretched out his arms and caught it with both hands, just as Cavre had taught him.

Dunk knew exactly what he wanted to do as soon as he got the ball. The trick was finding enough time to pull it off. He looked down the field and saw the professional linemen charging straight toward him. Meanwhile, their catchers hung back to cover the amateur catchers racing for the end zone.

Dunk tucked the ball under his arm and dashed off to his left, toward where Luc was standing. 'Block for me!' he said to the Bretonnian.

'Of course,' Luc said, venom dripping from his tongue. He stepped forward to put himself between Dunk and the oncoming linemen. Then, at the last second, he dove to the side, letting the professionals past.

Dunk was not only ready for this, he'd planned for it. With the professionals charging for Luc, he'd feinted moving behind the traitor and then dashed back to the right.

The professionals weren't fooled for long though. Karsten and Henrik swerved past Luc and chased right after Dunk. The young warrior gazed downfield, hoping that one of the catchers had managed to get open. He saw a young man from Albion, Simon Sherwood, racing for the right corner of the end zone and waving his arms wildly.

Dunk heard Karsten and Henrik's boots stamping across the field behind him, growing closer with every step. It was now or never.

Dunk cocked back his arm and put everything he had into hurling the football down the field. The worst part was concentrating hard enough to ignore the sound of the two stocky linemen stormed up behind him. As he released the ball, they hit him as one, knocking him flying to the turf.

Still under the two linemen, Dunk craned his neck to the left and stared downfield. Through all of the players now charging back down toward the other end of the field, he could see the corner of the end zone he'd targeted, and Simon sprinting toward it at top speed. The only player between Simon and the ball was the terrifyingly tall M'Grash, but when he looked up to see where the ball was, he hesitated, tripped, and fell. The ball arced down out of the sky as if it were skating down a rainbow, and landed right in Simon's outstretched hands.

Pegleg let loose a blast on his referee's whistle and threw his hand and hook in the air, signalling a touchdown and the end of the game.

The amateurs went wild, shouting and screaming as if they'd just won the Blood Bowl itself. Some of them raced back, grabbed Dunk and hoisted him upon their shoulders so they could parade him around the field. The professionals stood back and watched the whole thing, smiling unabashedly at the hopefuls' joy in the game.

'Not bad, Mr. Hoffnung,' Cavre said to him as Dunk was carried past. 'Your team lost 5 to 1, but that was a fine play.'

Dunk grinned widely and glanced over at Slick. The halfling tossed him a thumbs-up.

When the celebrating died down, Cavre called out. 'Congratulations to the prospects for a game well played. You can't fault your enthusiasm.'

A round of cheers went up from the professionals, who seemed pleased to have such a solid group of hopefuls trying to join their team. They and the prospects gathered closer to Cavre to listen as he spoke.

'As you know,' the blitzer said, 'we have only four spots available on our team. I wish that we had more, but those are the rules. Those of you who don't make it, don't be discouraged. The way this game is played, there are more openings on many teams every week, and we're sure to have more by the time this tournament is over.'

The gathered crowed laughed nervously at that.

'So, as soon as Captain Haken gets here, we can get on with… ah, there he is!' Cavre pointed to his right, and the crowd assembled around him parted to let Pegleg through.

The look on the captain's face was dead serious, and the smiles left the faces of all those who saw him. He limped through the crowd and said, 'A moment of your time, Mr. Cavre.'

The blitzer excused himself, and he and the captain walked off toward the city's wall and spoke in hushed voices.

'What do you think they're on about?' Simon asked Dunk. The two had been shoved together ever since the big play.

'I don't know,' Dunk said.

'My guess,' said Milo Hoffstetter, the hulk of a man from Middenheim who'd been campaigning hard for the blitzer spot, 'is they figured out who the killer is.'

Dunk felt someone tugging at his shoulder. He looked down to see Slick trying to pull him from the crowd. 'What is it?' Dunk asked.

'I need to talk with you,' Slick said.

'What about?'

'Now, son.'

Dunk looked around and realised everyone else was watching him and Slick. He shrugged at them. 'He's not really my father, you know.'

The players all shook with laughter at that. Meanwhile, Dunk slipped away from them and after Slick.

'What is it?' he asked the halfling. He'd never seen Slick so agitated. His colour was a bit off and Dunk thought he could see him sweating, something Slick had confessed to hating so much that he would only consider it in life or death circumstances. 'They're just about to announce who made the team,' Dunk said, hoping that would cheer him up.

'That's the least of our concerns,' Slick said.

These words stunned Dunk. He'd never known the halfling to put anything above Blood Bowl. For the past few weeks, preparing Dunk to make the team had been the only thing that Slick had concerned himself with.

'You're scaring me.'

Slick looked up into Dunk's eyes, searching there for something. 'No,' he said, almost to himself. 'You didn't do it, did you? You don't have it in you.'

'What in Morr's secret names are you talking about?' Dunk's heart had just about stopped. He was so focused on Slick, he didn't hear the step-tap, step-tap, step-tap behind him until a gleaming hook fell on his shoulder.

'Mr. Hoffnung,' Pegleg said.

Dunk whirled about to face the captain. As he did, the hook sliced through the shoulder of his shirt and drew blood from his skin. 'What is it?' he asked. He saw the captain, Cavre, and everyone else in the camp all around him now, all eyes intently on him.

Pegleg reached into his long, crimson coat and drew out something bound in a white cloth. As he unwrapped it between his hand and hook, a long knife with a serrated edge appeared. It was covered with blood from end to end.

'This is the blade that killed all those hopeful souls in the dark of night,' the captain said, like a judge intoning a life sentence. 'I found it in your tent.'

11

THE CROWD SURGED around Dunk, and he suddenly found it hard to breathe. 'You can't be serious,' he said, trying to stay calm. 'I didn't do this! I wouldn't!'

Pegleg held the knife in his hands as if gauging its weight. 'That may well be, Mr. Hoffnung,' he said, his eyes never wavering from Dunk's. 'But this is a hard game for hard people, and some of them will do anything to get their first team contract. I've seen men do worse for gold, to be sure.'

'Pegleg,' Slick said. 'Captain. I'll vouch for this boy's character. I slept in his tent all night and didn't hear a thing.'

The captain gave the halfling a mirthless smile. 'I know you'll understand, Mr. Fullbelly, that I can't really take the word of a man's agent. Your bias here is clear.'

'But, Captain–'

Pegleg cut off Slick's words with a wave of his hook. Then he gazed at Dunk again. The young warrior thought he saw a hint of sadness in the man's eyes.

'I didn't do it,' Dunk said again. Even as the words left his lips, he could see that they were falling on deaf ears.

'Some coaches,' Pegleg said, 'would appreciate your drive. Anyone willing to kill a dozen people in cold blood could be a real asset on a Blood Bowl team.'

Dunk started to relax a bit, but then he saw Pegleg hand the blood-ied blade to Cavre and begin fingering his hook.

'Others would kill you on the spot, cut you into pieces, and throw those into the sea.'

Dunk swallowed hard at that and quickly assessed the crowd. He was outnumbered nearly thirty to one, and he didn't have a weapon at hand. The Blood Bowl regulations had forbidden him from bring-ing even his knife onto the field.

The looks on the faces around him ranged from anger to disbelief. Two of the hopefuls, though, were grinning: Luc and Jacques. Were they just happy to see him go, or was there something more damning behind those hateful smiles?

'So,' Dunk said, summoning up every bit of courage he had and wondering if he could outrun everyone else here. He was sure that Cavre could catch him in a straight sprint, but if he kicked the blitzer in the knee before taking off he might have a chance.

'So,' he repeated again, looking straight into Pegleg's eyes, 'what do *you* plan to do with me?'

Pegleg grimaced for a moment, then waved off in the direction of the tents full of the dead. 'Those people knew what the risks were when they tried out for the team. If they didn't die in the camp here, there was a good chance they'd have never made it past their third game.'

The captain stared hard at Dunk. 'However,' he said. 'I can't have myself and every other member of this team fearing every moment for their lives. Cutthroats can't go around cutting the throats of their own kind.'

Dunk didn't like where this was heading. 'So?' he said.

'So, you're off the team.'

Most of the people in the crowd gasped. Luc and Jacques snorted out hard, mean laughs. Cavre frowned. Dunk saw tears welling up in M'Grash's eyes. Slick all but wept.

'I was never on it.' Dunk feared he was pointing out the obvious.

'You would have been,' said Pegleg, 'if not for this.'

Slick wailed openly at this, and he somehow found himself in the arms of M'Grash, who cradled the halfling in his monstrous arms like a fussing baby as he stifled his own sobs. Dunk started to say some-thing to Pegleg. He thought that he should make some kind of a speech to punctuate a grand exit. Instead he just said, 'Fine,' turned, and left.

'It's NOT OVER, son,' Slick said. The halfling's eyes were dry now, although the smoke in the pub, a dark, cheap place known as the Bad Water, irritated them something fierce. The place was packed wall to wall with Blood Bowl fans in town for the tournament. 'The Hackers were just our first option, not our last. Look at it this way. We got a free ride to Magritta out of them!'

The thought did little to comfort Dunk, try as he might. 'I'm not sure I'm cut out for Blood Bowl,' he said.

Slick, who was more than a little drunk at the moment, slapped a hand on his chest in shock. 'Not cut out for Blood Bowl?' he gasped. 'You, son, are the most natural talent I've ever seen in this game, maybe that the game itself has ever seen. If not for this dirty trick some scoundrel played to keep you off the team, you'd have been a definite. You'd have gotten the top starting salary, to boot.'

With that, Slick's eyes began to tear up again, and Dunk felt obliged to reach over and pat the halfling on the back. This kind gesture nearly knocked the imbalanced Slick off his extra-high barstool.

Dunk reached over to steady Slick and his stool. When he had succeeded, he noticed that someone was standing behind him and watching him. He turned to see an attractive young woman with long, auburn hair and dark black eyes that seemed to suck in everything they saw.

'Can I help you, my lady?' Dunk said in a tone that purposefully betrayed the fact that the answer to this question should only be 'no'.

'Are you Dunkel Hoffnung?' the woman said with a twinkle in her eye and a half-smile on her ruby-painted lips.

'Who's asking?' Slick said, instantly seeming sober now that he had something to take his mind off the events of the day.

'Lästiges Weibchen,' the woman said, 'on special assignment from *Spike! Magazine*.'

Slick stood up on his barstool to seem as tall as possible. It wobbled under him a bit, but he was able to right it without help from Dunk. 'You hear that, son? *Spike! Magazine* is on to you already. I told you that you were fated for great things in this game.'

'Interesting things, for sure,' Lästiges said, keeping her eyes drilled to Dunk.

'What's special about your assignment?' Dunk asked, returning the reporter's gaze without flinching.

'Have you ever heard of Dirk Heldmann?' This wasn't a question, Dunk knew.

'Who hasn't?' Slick answered. He looked over at Dunk. 'The team captain of the Reikland Reavers. They haven't had a blitzer that good since Griff Oberwald's playing days. That's the problem with human teams,' he said to Lästiges as an aside. 'Too short-lived to ever build a real dynasty.'

'Your name,' Dunk said to the woman. '"Weibchen." That's from Marienburg, isn't it?'

'You should know, Mr. *Hoffnung*,' Lästiges said through gritted teeth.

Dunk shook his head. 'We don't want to talk to her, Slick,' he said. 'She's nothing but trouble.'

'How *dare* you?' Lästiges said, her dark eyes flashing. 'After what your family did to mine–'

Dunk turned his back on the woman and picked up his stein of Killer Genuine Draft. 'It was business,' he said, 'and it was before my time.'

Lästiges ground out a little growl. 'Well, if you won't talk with me, I'm sure Dirk Heldmann will. *Spike! Magazine* is dying to know what the Reavers' top scorer thinks about his big brother being accused of murder.'

'Khaine's bloody teeth!' Slick said, turning to Dunk. 'Dirk Heldmann is your brother?'

Dunk slammed back what was left of his beer and turned back to talk to Slick and Lästiges, his eyes glowering at her. 'When he announced he was going to take up Blood Bowl, our parents disowned him. He changed his name before his first game.'

'Word is your family sent him off to play Blood Bowl for his own safety,' Lästiges said with a vicious grin. 'After they imploded in such a terrible mess, anyone could understand why he'd want it that way.'

Dunk considered throwing his beer at the woman, but his stein was empty. He signalled the bartender for another in case the urge struck him again.

'Nice to see the press is as fair and impartial with Blood Bowl as it is with real news,' Dunk said. 'I don't have anything to say to you.' The bartender slipped over another stein with the initials KGD chiselled on it in what were obviously supposed to be dwarf runes. It was a fairly drunk dwarf responsible for these runes, though. 'I think you should leave.'

'Really?' Lästiges said with mock surprise. 'After what's been happening with you lately, I thought you might want all the friends you can get.'

Dunk frowned. 'I've been banned from the team. What else can they do to me?'

Lästiges threw back her head and laughed. 'You see those two over there?' she asked, tossing her lustrous hair toward a far corner of the pub where two people sat, dressed in black robes. One was the shortest elf that Dunk had ever seen – thin and pale, with white-blond hair and proud, angular features – but a foot shorter than most other elves. The other was the tallest dwarf Dunk had ever seen; stocky and swarthy, with soot-black hair and a rough-hewn face, but a foot taller than most other dwarves.

In fact, the two were nearly identical in stature so that Dunk had the strange impression they were twins. Their uniform dress – dark robes sashed with red ropes and featuring a frothing Wolf embroidered across their chests – only emphasised the effect.

'Who are they?' Dunk asked, feigning indifference. As he spoke, he knew that the duo was aware he was talking about them, even if they were too far away to hear his words.

'GWs,' Slick said in what he seemed to think was a hushed whisper, although in his drunkenness it was more like a soft shout. 'Game Wizards. They work for the Cabalvision networks to keep the teams in line.' He pointed unsubtly at the wizards' uniforms. 'Those two must be here for Wolf Sports.'

'Are they the law around here?' Dunk was confused. What business was it of these people what happened in the Hackers' camp?

Lästiges giggled. On anyone else, this might have seemed cute, but with her it was clearly meant to be cruel. 'Oh, they're much worse. The Cabalvision networks make a fortune with these tournaments, and it's their job to make sure no one damages the rating with silly things like, oh, I don't know – *murdering a dozen of your fellow prospects.*'

Dunk tried to feign indifference and change the subject. 'Slick,' he said, 'do you know anywhere around here I can find myself a good blade? I feel naked without a proper sword on my hip.'

Slick pulled his attention away from the GWs slowly. 'Wha? Oh, yeah, son. We'll see what we can do about that. First thing tomorrow.'

'I've done what I can to help here,' Lästiges said merrily. 'I'd like to interview you sometime later, Dunk, maybe when you're a bit more available. Perhaps we could do you and your brother at the same time.'

Dunk stared into his stein. 'I haven't seen my brother in three years.'

'All the better,' Lästiges said. 'I just love family reunions, especially under such happy circumstances.'

Dunk gripped the handle of his stein and tried to convince himself the beer in it would be better in his belly than all over the reporter. When he looked over his shoulder to gauge the distance to his target, she was gone. He glanced at the door across the crowded room and saw her disappearing into Magritta's early dusk.

'Do I have to worry about the law in Magritta?' Dunk asked Slick.

'Ordinarily, yes,' the halfling said. 'But this is during one of the four Major Tournaments. The prince of Magritta doesn't want any major disruptions during this event. It brings a lot of crowns into the city's coffers and, by extension, into his. He's usually happy to leave things to the Game Wizards instead.'

'How much do I have to worry about them?' Dunk tried to keep his voice steady.

'Not too much, I'd say, son.'

'How's that?' Dunk shot a look at the halfling and saw him gazing toward the exit.

'They're on their way out of here right now.'

Dunk screwed up his face for a moment as he tried to figure out what was going on. He thought these Game Wizards would at least want to question him. Maybe Lästiges was leading them on to their next 'suspect' instead.

'Whew!' a voice said from behind Dunk and Slick. 'I thought those two would never leave.'

THE YOUNG WARRIOR and the halfling turned toward the voice as one. There they saw a greasy creature with wide, green eyes and a long, wide nose with a wart on each side of it. Oily wisps of colourless hair swept aimlessly over his sunburned scalp and weeping patches of acne covered his pustuled face. He extended his hand to Dunk and then to Slick, who shook it, mostly because they were too stunned by the man to think better of the gesture.

'Name's Gunther the Gobbo,' the man said. His high-pitched voice seemed to be always on the verge of breaking into a mad cackle. 'I've come to talk with your boy here. I understand he's quite a… talent.'

Dunk nodded queasily. Slick spoke up, eager as a stray dog presented with a plate of raw beef. 'You have that right. He's the best young recruit I've ever seen, and I've seen them all for the past fifty years. Take my word for it, this kid's bound for the Hall of Fame.'

Gunther nodded excitedly. The way his head bobbed, Dunk wasn't sure it was properly attached to his neck. 'Great, great! That's just what I hear.' Then Gunther's tone lowered into a comic imitation of conspiratorial. 'I also hear you had some problems today, perhaps of your own creation.'

'I didn't kill all those people!' Dunk shouted. He'd had enough of the accusations, especially from people he'd just met.

The entire room fell silent, and all eyes snapped over to Dunk.

'Of course, you didn't, son,' Slick said awkwardly. 'It was a bloody war, and I'm sure you only killed a small percentage of them.'

The room burst into laughter, and the patrons and staff went back to their own conversations.

'Well played,' Gunther said to Slick, oozing sick admiration. 'Just the kind of person I'd like to be in business with.'

'What are you selling?' Dunk asked.

'Ha!' Gunther said. 'That's funny, kid. You must be new around here. I'm not *selling*. I'm *buying*.'

Dunk shot Slick a what's-he-talking-about look. The halfling, still standing on his barstool, put an arm around the young warrior as he spoke.

'Gunther the Gobbo here, he's one of the biggest bookmakers in the Old World. He takes bets from all comers, sets the odds, then pays the winners and collects from the losers. Best of all Gunther here has set himself up as an odds making expert on Cabalvision too.'

'I used to appear on CBS, but Wolf Sports just picked me up,' Gunther said as he flashed Dunk a smile that reminded him of the chimera.

'CBS?' Dunk asked Slick.

'Crystal Ball Service. One of the Cabalvision networks. It conjures images into crystal balls around the Old World rather than popping them into the minds of subscribers.' The halfling pointed out the large, glassy balls hanging over the bar and in various corners of the pub. They were dark and cloudy now, but Dunk suspected that was because no games were being played at the moment.

'So, kid,' Gunther said, barely catching the drool from his chin with a red velvet handkerchief that looked like it had been trapped in such service for years. 'Aren't you going to ask me what I'm buying?'

Dunk looked Gunther up and down again, then shook his head. 'No.'

The young warrior had expected the bookie's face to fall, but Gunther's grin just widened, and his handkerchief lost its battle with the drool for a moment. 'C'mon, kid, all the rookies are shy the first time they meet me. Don't you sweat it. Ask me.'

Dunk started to shake his head again, but Slick interrupted. 'Tell him,' the halfling said.

Gunther slapped Slick on the back and nearly knocked him from his barstool. Trying to right himself, the halfling lurched backward and fell neatly behind the bar.

'Oi!' the burly bartender said as he snatched Slick up and shoved him back onto his stool. The back of the halfling's green jacket was soaked with some strange mixture that smelled flammable. 'I've warned you before about trying to sneak back here for a drink!'

'You must have me mixed up with someone else,' Slick said, as politely as he could, trying to press his curly hair back into place. His voice squeaked like that of a talking mouse. 'I've never been here before.'

The bartender, a dark-haired man with a bushy moustache and a tattooed goatee glared at Slick for a moment before tossing a bar rag at him in disgust. 'Right!' he said as he went back to serving drinks to a pack of skaven – walking ratmen – at the other end of the bar. 'You half-pints all look the same to me,' he muttered.

Slick dried his hair off with the bar rag, then looked at it in disgust and tossed it back over his shoulder. 'You were saying?' he asked Gunther.

'I heard about your problems earlier today,' the bookie said. 'I can help.'

'News travels fast,' Dunk said, instantly suspicious.

'How?' asked Slick, ignoring Dunk.

Gunther leaned in towards them, and whispered low enough that only they could hear. 'I can get your boy here on the team of your choice.'

'How's that?' Dunk asked.

Slick put a hand on the young warrior's chest. 'Now, son. When someone of the Gobbo's stature offers to lend you a hand, the polite thing to do is accept.'

Gunther gave Slick an unintentionally horrible toothy grin. Things were caught in there that were rotted worse than the teeth that held them. The stench caused Dunk to reel back. He took another pull from his stein to kill the smell.

'You're a creature I can do business with,' Gunther said to Slick, and the two grinned at each other like cats about to split a wounded eagle.

'How can you deliver on a promise like that?' Dunk asked. He ignored the dirty look Slick shot him.

Gunther narrowed his eyes at Dunk. 'Let's just say that in my line of work a lot of people end up owing me favours.'

'What's the catch?' Dunk asked, returning Gunther's glare.

The bookie's face broke into a smile again. 'No catch, kid. Just a couple of friends doing each other favours.'

'We're not friends.'

'Everyone has to start somewhere, son,' Slick said. 'We haven't known each other all that long ourselves.'

'We haven't done him any favours.'

'Not yet,' said Gunther, a knowing look in his eyes, 'but someday, when I need one, you will.'

Dunk nodded. 'You fix the games you take bets on.'

Slick slapped a hand over Dunk's mouth. 'Son!' he said in a mixture of exasperation and shame. 'Don't you talk like that to our new friend.'

'*Your* new friend,' Dunk said as he pulled the halfling's tiny hand from his face.

'Any team you like,' Gunther said. 'Interested in playing for the Reavers? I can make it happen.'

'Not interested.'

Slick gasped in heartbreaking disappointment.

'Okay, kid,' Gunther said. 'Have it your way, the hard way. Those people who aren't my friends sometimes find it extra hard to win a spot on a team.'

'Is that a threat?' a voice from behind Dunk said. The young warrior had been so focused on Gunther that he hadn't heard the speaker come up behind him.

Dunk spun about on his stool, and there stood his brother Dirk. Dunk often marvelled that they had both come from the same set of parents. Where Dunk was broad and dark, Dirk was lithe and light. The younger Hoffman stood an inch or two taller than Dunk but weighed twenty pounds less. Under his straight, white-blond hair, his bright blue eyes glared straight past Dunk and down at Gunther.

'No!' Gunther said, back-pedalling a step or two. 'Of course not. I don't work that way, Dirk, you know that.'

Dirk nodded. 'I know exactly how you work, Gunther, so I'm going to warn you once: leave this man alone.'

Gunther regained some of his composure at this. 'Look here,' he said. 'The kid is an adult. He can make up his own mind.'

Dirk turned toward Dunk, finally looking him in the eye. 'Do you want anything from the Gobbo?' he asked. As he spoke, he shook his head no.

Dunk hadn't seen his brother in three years. He'd left long before the family had fallen apart, and never looked back. This had left Dunk alone to handle the Hoffnung clan's catastrophic implosion. Despite this, he found himself glad to see his brother again. He had a few more scars and looked older than the years should have made him, but it was still Dirk for sure.

Dunk shook his head in tandem with his brother. 'No,' he said.

'You heard him, Gunther,' Dirk said, turning back toward the bookie. 'Decision's made. Respect it.'

The Gobbo looked up at the two men, then flashed a wink at Slick. 'No problem, Dirk. Always happy to do a favour for you.'

'It's not a favour,' Dirk said darkly. 'It's an order.'

Gunther held up his hands in mock surrender, but he looked at Dunk before he turned to leave. 'That's okay,' he said. 'There are lots more where you came from – wherever that is.'

The three watched the Gobbo leave. Dunk watched Slick dab at his eyes with his sleeve, then turn toward Dirk and offer his hand.

'So you're Dunk's brother,' the halfling said evenly. 'I should have known.'

Dirk shook Slick's hand. 'I don't tell *all* the family secrets.'

'You didn't have to do that,' Dunk said, jerking a thumb at the door through which the Gobbo had disappeared. As he spoke, he felt his resentment toward his brother rising in his chest.

'We're brothers,' Dirk said. 'Only *I* get to abuse you, and you didn't seem to be handling it so well yourself.'

Dunk stepped off his barstool and stood nose to nose with Dirk. 'I can manage. I did just fine without you for the past three years.'

An icy smirk spread across Dirk's battle-scarred face. 'That's not what I heard from Lehrer.'

Dunk's face flushed with shame. He bowed his head to hunt for some self-control as he felt his fist clenching. Another comment like that from Dirk, and it would find itself flying toward his face all on its own.

'Aren't you going to introduce us?'

The melodious voice sounded out of place here in the Bad Water, like a morning dove singing against the background of a catfight. Dunk raised his head to see its owner, and his breath left him.

'My apologies,' Dirk said to Dunk, although the young warrior still ignored him. 'This is my team-mate, Spinne Schönheit. Spinne, this is my older brother Dunk.'

Spinne stood as tall as Dunk, although that was due to the high-heeled leather boots that stretched up to the back of her knees. Her long, strawberry blonde hair cascaded past her shoulders, where it was caught in a single, thick braid intertwined with ribbons of silver and gold. Her wide blue-grey eyes transfixed Dunk, holding him paralysed in their bright gaze. The words that fell from her wide, sensual lips each seemed so precious that Dunk wanted to hunt down each one and cage it forever.

'My pleasure,' Spinne said in a voice as smooth as a fine chocolate liqueur. 'You never mentioned you had a brother,' she said to Dirk, never taking her eyes off Dunk. 'Is it Dunk Heldmann then?'

Dunk found he could not reply.

'Hoffnung, actually,' Dirk said. 'Heldmann is my game name.'

Spinne smiled softly at this, and Dunk felt his heart would melt and run out through his boots.

'Have you come to see Dirk play?'

When Dunk didn't reply, Slick leapt into the gap. 'Actually,' he said, sticking out his hand for Spinne, 'he's here to play. I'm Slick Fullbelly, esquire, his agent.'

Spinne gave Slick her hand, and he bent over it brushing it gently with his lips. She giggled at that. Dunk had never been jealous of the halfling before, but now he ached with it.

'You?' Dirk stuck in at Dunk, his jaw gaping wide. 'Really?'

'What team are you with?' Spinne asked. Dirk stared at his brother at this, evidently interested in the answer too.

'None at the moment, I'm afraid,' Slick said with open regret. 'If you'd asked me this morning, I'd have said we'd be with the Hackers for sure, but an unfortunate event and an unjust accusation seem to have precluded that.'

'The Bad Bay Hackers?' Dirk said, still gaping at his older brother. 'I heard half their recruits were murdered this–' He cut himself off as he goggled at Dunk. 'That was… that *couldn't* have been… you?'

Spinne flashed a wide, perfect, ruby-lipped smile hungry enough to devour a dragon whole. 'I respect a man who goes for what he wants.'

'Well,' Dunk started, too stunned to be half as articulate as he wanted, 'it wasn't really like that.'

'I can't believe my ears,' Dirk said, holding his head with both hands. 'After what Lehrer told me, I thought you'd sunk as low as you could, but murdering people to get on a Blood Bowl team? That's, well, that's impossible, isn't it?'

Dunk suddenly remembered how angry he was with his brother. 'How would you know?' he asked. 'Where have you been for the past three years? Out chasing after glory and gold! Where were you when I needed you?'

Dirk's demeanour turned glacier-cold. 'I could ask the same of you, brother.'

Seeing red, Dunk smashed his stein down on the top of the bar. Beer and shards of pottery splattered everywhere. 'That's it!' he roared at his brother.

Dirk's fist flashed out and flattened Dunk's nose, sending him sprawling back along the bar and into the pack of skaven. The ratmen scattered before the much-larger man, drawing their knives as they went.

Dirk drew his blade and leapt to stand over his fallen brother, who sat covered in sawdust and the skavens' spilled cider. 'Back off!' he said to the ratmen, who chattered at him through their six-inch-long front teeth. 'No one harms him but me!'

A blade sang out from someone standing just inside the nearby doorway and slapped Dirk's sword away. The skaven skittered away, looking for some sort of hole in which to hide.

Dirk brought his blade back around to where it clashed against the newcomer's. 'What is it you want?' he snarled at the dark-skinned man.

Cavre glared steadily over their crossed swords. 'I need to talk with your brother, Mr. Heldmann,' he said to Dirk, never taking his eyes from Dunk's. 'If that's not too much to ask.'

Dunk had never been in Pegleg's tent before. The coach didn't fraternize much with his players, let alone lowly prospects. It was taller and better appointed than any other tent in the Hackers' camp, floored with wooden planks that Dunk suspected had been taken from the deck of the *Sea Chariot*, perhaps directly from the captain's own quarters. A large crystal ball sat in the centre of a large, oaken desk, the surface of which was carved with letters, lines and figures Dunk could not decipher.

'I suppose you're wondering why you're here, Mr. Hoffnung,' the coach said. He sat in a chair behind the desk, and as he spoke he scratched something in the desk's top.

Dunk sat in a small folding chair opposite Pegleg. Staring up at the grim look in the ex-pirate's eyes, he had no doubt why he was here. Only the solemn vow Cavre had given to Dirk that Dunk would not be harmed kept him from fleeing into the darkness right then and there. That, and the fact that Cavre stood directly behind him and would probably put him down at the first false move he made.

The young warrior realised that Pegleg was waiting for an answer. He shook his head. 'No, sir,' he said sullenly.

From under his brilliant yellow tricorn, Pegleg shot his first mate a concerned look. 'Cavre? Have you already informed Mr. Hoffnung of this evening's events and how they are entwined with his eventual fate?'

'Not a word, captain.'

Pegleg narrowed his eyes at Dunk. 'You are aware of the murders, then?'

Dunk nodded slowly, confused. 'That's why you cut me from the team this afternoon,' he said. 'Despite the fact I had nothing to do with them.'

A smile tickled at the edge of Pegleg's mouth. 'I see, Mr. Hoffnung. You continue to maintain your innocence then?'

Dunk nodded as if nothing could be more evident.

'Then I suppose you had nothing to do with this evening's killings either?'

Dunk froze, stunned. 'What?'

Cavre spoke. 'Sometime shortly after sundown, Andreas and Otto went to collect our newest players for a celebration. They found Mr. Sherwood and Mr. Reyes in fine condition. Sadly, the same could not be said of the Broussard brothers.'

Dunk felt the beer in his stomach start to creep its way up his gullet.

'What was wrong with them?' he asked. He forgot to supply any honorific when addressing Pegleg, but the coach ignored it.

'Why, Mr. Hoffnung, they were dead, of course.'

Using his good hand, Pegleg reached down and pulled something bundled in a crimson cloth from a drawer in his desk. He tossed it on to the desk and peeled back the fabric with his hook so deftly that Dunk suspected he could fillet a fish with its tip.

It was the same knife Pegleg had found in Dunk's tent before.

'They were killed with this.'

Dunk gasped for air. 'Don't tell me you found that in my tent again.'

'No, Mr. Hoffnung,' Pegleg said flatly. 'It was sticking out of Luc Broussard's right eye.'

Dunk's head reeled. He found it hard to focus, but he couldn't pull his eyes away from the freshly bloodied knife. He clamped down hard on his rising stomach, afraid that everything he'd put into it since that morning would come spraying onto the coach's precious floor.

Instead, out came a rousing, tent-shuddering belch.

Dunk looked up sheepishly at Pegleg and then back at Cavre, who both stared at Dunk as if he'd grown a second head. 'Um,' he said, 'excuse me?'

Cavre just shook his head at Dunk, while Pegleg seemed to be sniggering behind the hook he raised to his face.

'Well,' Pegleg said once he'd regained his composure, 'on that auspicious note, I'd like to inform you of your new status, Mr. Hoffnung.'

Dunk repressed a shiver, although whether of anger or fear he could not tell. 'You can't think I had anything to do with this,' he said.

Pegleg shook his big, tricorn hat. 'No,' he said. 'Several people placed you in the Bad Water from when you left here until Mr. Cavre brought you to me. You're off the,' he looked at the sharp, shining device in place of his missing hand, then cleared his throat, 'hook… so to speak.'

Dunk slumped back in the folding chair, astonished at the heights and depths of his day. Then he sat bolt upright again. 'What about the other killings?' he said. 'Do you still think I had something to do with those?'

Pegleg shook his head. 'We never did, Mr. Hoffnung. The attempt to frame you by placing the murder weapon in your tent was far too obvious. You may not be a great Blood Bowl player yet, but you're hardly a fool.'

'Then why did you cut me from the–? Oh.' This line of questions led Dunk to an answer he didn't particularly like.

Pegleg shook his head again. 'You're a fine player, Mr. Hoffnung, and I'd be pleased to offer you a spot on our team, but I hoped to play along with the killer long enough for me to be able to learn who he was. In all honesty, I suspected the Broussard brothers, but these most recent events seem to have taken them out of the running.'

'Unless they killed themselves out of guilt, captain,' Cavre said.

Pegleg chortled at that. 'Very good, Mr. Cavre. I'll admit I hadn't thought of that. Very good!'

Dunk stared at Pegleg, afraid that he might for a moment be serious. The captain saw the look and waved it off.

'This is all beside the point, of course. The fact is that we have two more people dead, leaving us once more short-handed on this team. Those are spots we need to fill.'

It finally dawned on Dunk why he was here. 'You want me to play for the Bad Bay Hackers?' It was a question less of curiosity than astonishment.

'Didn't I just say that, Mr. Hoffnung?' Pegleg looked over Dunk's shoulder at Cavre. 'Well, didn't I?'

'Not in so many words, captain,' the blitzer said.

Pegleg harrumphed. 'I supposed I'll have to be a bit more direct about it then. Mr. Hoffnung?' He looked Dunk straight in the eye and pointed at him with the curve of his hook. 'I'd like to offer you a position as our backup thrower. Are you interested?'

A strange mélange of emotions washed over Dunk. This was why he was here in Magritta, right? To try out for the Hackers, to launch his Blood Bowl career. At the same time, he couldn't get his father's disparaging attitude about the game out of his head. His parents had disowned his brother over playing the game, after all. That was hardly a concern these days, but it still gave Dunk pause.

'Yes!' Slick's voice shouted from outside the tent. The halfling stormed in through the closed flaps, barely disturbing them as he passed, and stabbed an index finger toward Pegleg's face. 'He'll take it!'

All eyes in the tent turned toward Slick and he suddenly realised he'd become the centre of attention. He blushed with a sheepish grin, then spoke more calmly to Pegleg. 'Assuming we can come to a mutually beneficial agreement, Captain Haken, of course.'

'Of course,' Pegleg replied, rolling his eyes.

Cavre came around from behind Dunk and walked over to a locked cabinet against the right wall. He produced a key and opened it, then extracted a large, tall bottle wrapped in woven strands of something that looked like straw to Dunk's eyes. He placed it on the table, next to the bloody knife, along with a pair of crystal glasses.

'A drink of Stoutfellow's finest to seal the deal?' Pegleg said to Slick.

'Let's start with a toast to celebrate our mutual recognition of our desire to work together,' the halfling said, 'and we can work our way up from there.'

Cavre took Dunk by the elbow and led him from the tent.

'Don't worry yourself, son,' Slick said as Cavre escorted Dunk away. 'By the time I work out your deal with this scallywag, he'll have promised us his hook and an option on his leg – the good one!'

BACK IN THE Bad Water, Cavre raised a drink to Dunk. 'Here's to the game,' he said to the rookie as they clinked their steins together. 'May you leave it better off than you found it.'

Dunk drank deeply from his KGD, then wiped his mouth and smiled at Cavre. 'Are you talking about me or the game there?' he asked.

Cavre smiled. 'The toast doesn't say, does it, Mr. Hoffnung? That's what makes it such a good toast. Congratulations.'

Dunk smiled. He hated the circumstances under which he'd come to his new position – if he even had it yet, although he trusted Slick to take care of that – but he found himself pleased to be in it. For tonight, at least, he was ready to let his ambivalence drain away so that he could enjoy the moment for the magical thing it was.

Dunk knew that thousands of people, maybe millions, would kill to be able to play Blood Bowl professionally. *And somebody did*, he thought, which gave him pause. He shoved that aside with the rest of his doubts though. He hadn't killed those people, and it seemed that Pegleg and Cavre finally believed him. That was enough for now.

Dunk let the joy of his good fortune, or fate, as the case may have been, flow over him. Doing this had to beat chasing after dragons, and it was far enough away from Altdorf that he might even be able to forget what had happened to his family back there and what he'd had to do with it. He drank deeply from his stein, then slammed it back down and ordered another.

SEVERAL STEINS LATER, the world seemed a much friendlier place to Dunk. He clapped Cavre on the back and said. 'I'm just thrilled to be able to work with you.'

Cavre smiled patiently at the rookie. 'So you keep telling me, Mr. Hoffnung.'

'We're team-mates now,' Dunk said. 'You can drop the 'mister' bit. Call me Dunk.'

Cavre shook his head. 'I work with a lot of people, Mr. Hoffnung. On a Blood Bowl team, they tend to come and go like grist on a mill-stone. Only a rare few do I ever call by name.'

'But I'll be the thrower,' Dunk said, the drink making him a bit more distressed by Cavre's cavalier attitude than he normally would allow. 'You're the blitzer. Those are the team's top two positions. We'll have a natural bond.'

Cavre snorted softly as he raised his stein to his lips. When he brought it down, he gazed at Dunk with his dark, brown eyes that seemed like they'd maybe seen too much over the years for their own good. 'Sometimes it works like that,' he said, 'true. But not always. I've been working with Mr. Ritternacht for two years now, and there's no such bond there.'

Dunk's heart sank. If Kur hadn't been able to inspire any kind of respect in Cavre in years of trying, what hope did Dunk have? On the other hand, Kur didn't seem like the kind of person who cared to try for such things. That lifted Dunk's spirits for a moment.

'And you're still just the back-up thrower, Mr. Hoffnung,' Cavre pointed out.

Dunk's spirits sank again. He took another belt of his KGD.

'So, sailor, what does a girl have to do around here to get a guy to buy her a drink?'

Dunk looked up to see Spinne on his other side, away from Cavre. She smiled at him, but he couldn't move his tongue, maybe *because* of that smile.

A mug full of mulled wine slid down the bar and skidded to a half in front of Spinne. Dunk looked down at it as if it had been conjured from thin air. Then he glanced back at the bartender and caught his eye. 'Put that on my tab,' he croaked out.

'It looks like you're celebrating,' Spinne said as she brought the mulled wine to her soft lips. Dunk found himself just as jealous of the mug as he had been of Slick earlier.

'Mr. Hoffnung here has just been offered a position with the Hack-ers,' Cavre offered from over Dunk's shoulder.

Spinne smiled. 'Congratulations!' she said, clinking her mug against Dunk's stein. He almost dropped his beer, but he managed to rally enough to join her in her toast.

'What position will you be playing?' Spinne asked.

'Thrower,' Dunk said.

'Behind Kur?'

Dunk nodded. 'For now.'

Spinne laughed. 'That's confidence for you,' she said to Cavre over Dunk's shoulder. 'Don't you find a rookie's ambitions amazing?'

'Not anymore, Spinne.'

She looked back at Dunk. 'He's just flattering me. He remembers back when I was a rookie too. I had so much to learn, didn't I?'

Dunk nodded. 'I suppose I do too.'

'More than you know, my Dunkel,' Spinne said. 'More than you know.'

'My brother used to call me that,' Dunk said. 'Do you know where he is?' He craned his neck around, suspicious that Dirk was watching him, frozen like a deer in the bright light of Spinne's attention.

'I don't have any idea,' she said. 'Is it important? Oh, you'd like to share your news with him, right?'

Dunk shook his head. The last thing he needed right now was a conversation with Dirk. He was feeling good, and he knew that would bring him crashing back down to the dirt.

'We're not together, you know,' Spinne said. 'Your brother and I. He likes to give people that impression sometimes.'

'I had that impression.' Dunk's day had just gotten even better.

'Sometimes I let people think that. You wouldn't think it would be hard to keep men away from me, would you?'

Dunk smiled, boggled by the insanity of the question. 'Is that a joke?' he asked, looking her up and down. 'I think you'd need an army – or at least a good set of linemen.'

Spinne frowned. 'I'm not some kind of princess. I'm a Blood Bowl player.'

'And one of the best around,' Carve said. Dunk turned as he heard the man's stool push back from the bar.

'I'm going to call it a night,' the blitzer said. 'I'd love to be able to help Mr. Hoffnung here celebrate his impending contract all night long, but we aren't in Magritta for pleasure.'

'Right!' Dunk said. 'I can go back with you. Is there some kind of curfew?'

'Yes,' Cavre laughed. 'But it only applies to players.'

'But…' Dunk was confused.

'Have you signed a contract yet, Mr. Hoffnung?' Cavre asked, still smiling.

'No, but I'm sure that–'

Cavre cut Dunk off with a wave of his legendary hands. 'Then your time is still your own. This is the last night that may be true for a while, Mr. Hoffnung. I suggest you enjoy it.'

With that, Cavre snapped off a quick salute and took his leave. Dunk turned back to Spinne, who seemed to be standing closer to him than before.

'Well,' he said, 'it seems I'm on my own for celebrating my good news. Would you care to join me?'

'Haven't I already?' Spinne smiled at him with dreamy eyes.

'So,' Dunk asked, 'what do you suggest a young rookie do with his last night of freedom?'

As Spinne leaned in and pressed her breathtakingly soft lips against his, she said, 'Oh, can't we think of something?'

THE NEXT MORNING, Dunk slunk back to the Hackers' camp in the cold light of early dawn. His head pounded like a dwarf jackhammer any time he bent over, which he'd done in Spinne's room to grab his pants before she hustled him out the door. He hadn't bent over since, but his head was still spinning with the events of the night before. To be cleared of murder and then to be offered a position with the Hackers was amazing enough, but to then bed the beautiful Spinne was too much for his brain to handle, as evidenced by the fact that it seemed ready to spin out of his skull at a moment's notice.

'Ah!' Slick shouted as Dunk tried to sneak into his tent. 'There you are! Cavre told me you might be out late celebrating your last night as a civilian, but I didn't imagine it would be *all* night. I didn't think you had it in you.'

Dunk winced at the noise of the halfling's voice and held his ears. It conveniently allowed him to hold his head together at the same time.

'Oh,' Slick said, a bit more softly this time. 'I see you're paying the price for your pleasure last night,' he chuckled. 'Thank Nuffle you won't be playing today.'

'How's that?' Dunk said, surprised at how relieved he was by this bit of news. Then his relief morphed to concern. 'We didn't make a deal?'

Slick feigned shock at the rookie's words. 'Do you really think I would let Pegleg go to sleep last night before he made us an offer we just couldn't refuse?'

Dunk's headache eased at this. 'So we have a contract?'

Slick's grin showed all the teeth in his chubby mouth. 'It's all ready for your signing. We just need to go over to Pegleg's tent to get your ink on it.'

'How much are we talking about here?' This morning, Dunk had realised he'd spent just about every last crown he had on his celebration. Buying a round for the bar had been a lot more expensive than he'd imagined. It had cost him even more, in terms of his health, when everyone in the bar tried to return the favour to him. If Spinne hadn't taken him out of the Bad Water when she had, he might have woken up under one of the pub's tables, or maybe lying out on the docks with his head hanging over the edge of a pier.

'Seventy,' Slick said proudly.

'Seventy crowns per game?' Dunk said, nodding his approval. 'Not bad. Depending on how often we play, I might be able to send up to half that home.'

Slick snorted. 'That's not quite it.'

'Seventy per month then?' Dunk said, creasing his brow. 'That's still workable, I suppose.'

'Not per month,' Slick said, a mysterious smile still plastered across his face. 'That's per year.'

'Per year?' Dunk said, frowning now. 'I thought Blood Bowl players made real money. That's less than six crowns a month. It's liveable, but I could make more money as a ratcatcher in Altdorf. Of course, that's one of the most dangerous jobs in the Empire, shy of dragon-hunting or, I thought, playing Blood Bowl, so it doesn't pay too bad. Have you ever looked down in those sewers? I think I'd need more than–'

'Son,' Slick said. 'That's seventy *thousand* per year.'

Dunk's hangover vanished.

'You're – Slick, my head must be fuzzier than I knew. I thought you just said 'Seventy thousand crowns a year.''

The halfling nodded, his grin wider than ever, so wide he started to jump up and down to spread it further. Dunk grabbed his tiny hands and started jumping with him. The two hooted and hollered until Dunk was sure they must have woken up everyone else in the camp.

'And that's before your part of each game's take,' Slick said.

'There's more?' Dunk said, still stunned by the initial number.

'Every game a team plays comes with a purse put up by the sponsors. For non-tournament games, it's not always all that much, a few score crowns each for the winners, a little less for the losers. For any of the Four Majors, though, it can be as much as another thousand apiece.'

'Let's go!' Dunk said, already halfway out the tent.

'Wait!' Slick said, panic nearly stealing his voice.

'What's wrong?' Dunk said.

'It's better to stay cool about these things, at least in front of your coach,' Slick said. 'You don't want them thinking they paid too much for you.'

'Right,' Dunk nodded. 'Right. Stay cool.' He found that he couldn't strip the grin from his face though. 'How am I doing?'

Slick reached up and smacked Dunk on the side of the head. His hangover came ringing back in, hungry for revenge.

'Hey!' Dunk protested, grimacing in pain.

'There,' Slick said. 'Now you look cool.'

'Thanks!' Dunk said as he aimed a fist at Slick's head, but the halfling capered out of the way.

When the pair reached Pegleg's tent, the coach called for them to come in before they even announced themselves.

'How did you know it was us, sir?' Dunk asked.

Pegleg squinted at Dunk as if perhaps regretting his decision to sign the man to a contract, no matter how much he might need him. 'It's a small camp,' he said at last. 'I heard you whooping in your tent from here. I assume Slick told you about our agreement.'

Dunk nodded.

'Excellent, Mr. Hoffnung. Then, if you're amenable to that arrangement, all we need is your signature here.' Pegleg took two pieces of parchment from the centre drawer of his desk and slipped them across the surface to Dunk. With his hook, he pushed a quill pen and a pot of the best ink from Cathay after it. 'Take your time and read it if you like.'

Dunk did. If there was one thing he'd learned from his family, it was how important it was to read something before you signed it. There were two identical copies of the contract, which was surprisingly short and simple, and the deal seemed more than fair to him.

'I thought it would be as long as a book of spells,' Dunk said, signing his name next to Captain Haken's on the bottom of both of the documents.

'They used to be,' Pegleg said, 'but we don't hire Blood Bowl players based on their intelligence. Many of them can't even read. We try to make it as easy as possible.'

Pegleg took one of the contracts back from Dunk and gave the rookie the other. He slid his contract back into the desk, then rose and offered Dunk his hand. Dunk took it and shook it firmly.

'Welcome aboard, Mr. Hoffnung,' Pegleg said. 'May you have a long and exciting career.'

'Thanks, coach!' Dunk said. He surprised himself by how much he loved calling someone that. 'I'm ready for duty. When's the next practice?'

Pegleg allowed himself a small smile. 'No practice today, Mr. Hoffnung. At noon, we have our first game of the playoffs, against the Darkside Cowboys. It's going to be a long week, with games every other day, but not for you.'

'Excuse me, coach?' Dunk said, suddenly concerned. 'Why not?'

'Regulations state that a player cannot take part in a game until twenty-four hours after he's been hired. It helps keep teams from trading ringers in and out at the last second.'

'Doesn't that happen all the time anyhow?' Slick asked. 'It's a dirty game. Why start playing clean now?'

Pegleg smirked. 'Normally I'm not so circumspect about such things, as you well know, Mr. Fullbelly. However, the murders garnered the attention of the Game Wizards, so we're not able to be so careless with the rules as we might like.' He turned to Dunk. 'You'll be eligible to play during our next game in two days. In the meantime, I have an assignment of vital importance for you that, coincidentally, will keep you from the arena today.'

'What's that, coach?' Dunk said eagerly.

'The rest of us will be in the arena,' Pegleg said. 'We need someone to guard the camp.'

OFF IN THE distance, from the stands of the Bay Water Bowl in the heart of Magritta, the crowd roared for what Dunk could only assume was another touchdown for somebody. He hoped the Hackers had scored, but he had no way to know. Pegleg had refused to activate his crystal ball for this game, insisting that Dunk patrol the camp instead. 'Otherwise, you'll be stuck in here watching the game, Mr. Hoffnung, while someone robs us blind.'

Dunk had to admit that he probably would have found it hard to pull himself away from watching the game via Cabalvision. He'd seen precious few games in his life and never watched one all the way through. Now it looked like that might not happen until his first game as a professional player, and the thought made him nervous.

To take the edge off his nerves, Dunk took to pacing around the camp with Slick. This not only helped him walk off his excess energy, but it also meant he was doing a good job at the task Pegleg had set for him.

'It's important you keep Pegleg happy,' Slick told Dunk. 'While we have a great deal with him, he can fire you at a moment's notice.'

'And then I'm out in the cold?'

'He still has to pay you for the month after you're fired, unless you take up with another team, of course. Then you're on your own.'

'But I don't want to do that. I like the Hackers.'

Slick looked up at the rookie. 'What would you do if someone offered you more money, son? A lot more?'

'Sign up with them for *next* season, or ask to be traded.'

Slick smiled wanly and shook his head at Dunk. 'That, son, is why you have me to handle the deals around here. It's not all that simple.'

Dunk glared down at the halfling. 'You can't make another deal without my say-so though, right?'

Slick nodded. 'I need your mark on the bottom of the contract, don't I?'

'Always looking out for me, right?'

'I'm not the only one,' Slick said as they strolled along. 'You might want to extend some gratitude toward your brother.'

Dunk froze in his tracks and frowned. 'For running out on our family when we needed him most?'

Slick shook his head. 'I don't know the details of all that, son. Not any more than Dirk told me, at least.'

'Dirk…?' Dunk cocked his head at Slick. 'He… he told you about my family?'

The halfling nodded sheepishly. 'You don't think I was wandering through Dörfchen on a whim? That would have been an amazing coincidence. '

Dunk stared at Slick. 'Dirk told you where to find me?' He felt like he might start to choke. His voice grew more strained as he spoke. 'He told… he told you about what happened with our family? He gave you what you needed to blackmail me into playing Blood Bowl?'

Slick put up his hands to calm the young man down. 'He was only looking out for you, son. He'd heard you'd set off to slay dragons. He was concerned for your life.'

'Blood Bowl is safer?'

Slick summoned up a wide grin. 'It pays far better.'

Dunk jammed the heels of his hands into his eyes. He wanted to throttle the halfling and then hunt Dirk down and do the same for him. His brain felt like it might burst out through his eardrums first.

Dunk pulled his hands from his face and roared at Slick in heart-rending frustration. The halfling flinched away and tumbled onto his back, raising his arms to fend off Dunk's attack.

Dunk glared down at the halfling lying there in the ground, defenceless against him. He could have gutted him with his bare hands. He could have broken his neck with a single twist, but he couldn't bring himself to do it. He threw back his head to roar again when he spied the far-off entrance to Pegleg's tent moving. He immediately fell silent and pulled Slick to his feet. 'Did you see that?' he asked the halfling.

'If you mean how you knocked me into the beach, then yes, I got that,' Slick said, spitting out a mouthful of sand.

'Someone's in Pegleg's tent.'

The halfling sat up and joined Dunk in peering around the edge of their tent. 'Are you sure?' he asked.

Dunk nodded, his anger fading away. 'I saw the flap of his tent moving, and there's no breeze in the air today.'

'Maybe Pegleg came back for something he forgot.'

'In the middle of a game?'

Dunk grimaced and drew the sword that Pegleg had given him. 'We can't have you guarding the camp with that little snotling-sticker of yours,' he'd said.

When Dunk had first pulled the blade, he'd been astonished at its sharpness and balance. It was as if it had been forged for his hand. 'It's marvellous,' he'd said to Pegleg. 'I can't thank you enough for it.'

'No,' the coach had said, 'but you can pay me. It's coming out of your first month's salary.'

'Will I have anything left?' Dunk had asked, just a bit worried.

Pegleg had narrowed his eyes at the rookie. 'Mr. Hoffnung, are you sure your agent fully explained to you the exorbitant amount of gold I'm paying you?'

The blade felt just as good now as it had before, and its heft in his hand gave Dunk a shot of confidence. 'I'm going in,' he said.

'Good on you, son,' said Slick. 'I'll stay out here to sound the alarm if you don't come out in five minutes.'

Dunk glared at Slick. 'How very brave of you.'

The halfling shrugged. 'I'm an agent, not a player.'

Dunk patted Slick on the head and then took off for Pegleg's tent at a dead sprint. When he reached the tent's door flap, he charged right through, his sword in front of him.

There, behind Pegleg's desk, stood a middle-aged man dressed entirely in robes of a dark, midnight blue, trimmed with bluish-white piping that seemed to glow against the bulk of the cloth. The man was tall and gaunt with a wispy white beard. His hair, if he had any, was covered entirely by a silver skullcap that approximated the outlines of a taut widow's peak that came to a point in the centre of his forehead. His bright green, watery eyes glared out at Dunk with a hatred the young man had rarely seen, and the man's lips trembled nervously as he spoke.

'L... leave now,' the man said, shutting the drawers of Pegleg's desk that he'd been rummaging through, 'and I will not feed your s... soul to the Blood God Khorne.'

'You're sure that's not "K... Khorne"?' Dunk said as he came at the man, his blade before him, ready to strike.

'Everyone's a c… comedian,' the man said with disgust. He turned toward the dressing screen in the back of Pegleg's tent. 'Stony, please remove this man.'

The hairs on the backs of Dunk's arms and neck stood on end as the dark-skinned creature crept around the edge of the screen. It was no taller than Dunk, except for the twisted horns curling atop its head and its wide, bat-like, claw-tipped wings that scraped against the tent's walls and ceiling as it moved forward on goat legs. It flexed its thick muscles as its full-crimson eyes, which seemed to be filled with blood, rested on Dunk, and a set of savage talons popped from the tips of its fingers.

'Yes, Zauberer,' the creature rasped, its voice like metal on stone.

'That's "master" to you, gargoyle,' the man said menacingly. Then he pointed to Dunk. 'Kill him. Permanently. Now.'

DUNK LEAPT AT the daemon, his sword flashing out before him. The wizard, if that's what Zauberer was, fell back out of the way, clutching some papers in his grasp.

Dunk's sword slashed across the gargoyle's chest, biting through its thick skin and drawing blood. The sight brought a smile to the rookie's face. If the thing had been made entirely of stone, this would have been a short and fatal fight – for him. As it was, he thought he still stood a chance.

The gargoyle bellowed in pain. The closest thing Dunk had ever heard was as a child when he'd seen a man get his arm caught in a mill. The combination of the man's screams and the sound of living bone being ground to dust had set his teeth on edge in the exact same way.

The gargoyle jumped into the air on its backward-folding legs and launched itself at Dunk. It slammed into him painfully and the two went soaring back through the tent's front flap and into the open area beyond.

Caught in the gargoyle's granite grip, Dunk struggled to catch his breath. As he did, he smashed the pommel of his sword into the creature's face, drawing both blood and a sinister cackle from the thing's battered mouth. He lashed out again and his blade sliced through the edge of one of the gargoyle's grey, leathery wings.

The daemon howled in rage and shoved Dunk away from it, sending him tumbling back over himself until he came to a stop near the now-cold fire pit in the middle of the camp. When the rookie managed to recover his feet, the daemon was nowhere to be seen. The wizard, on the other hand, was sprinting along the beach, back toward the distant docks of Magritta.

His sword still in hand, Dunk burst out of the camp after the wizard. Zauberer's speed was no match for the rookie's, and soon Dunk was close enough to hear the wizard's laboured wheezing as he tried futilely to outrace him.

'Dunk!' Slick shouted from somewhere back in the camp. 'Look out! Above you!'

Dunk cursed himself for being so foolish. Of course, that's where the gargoyle had gone. He'd taken his focus off of the greater threat in this fight, and now he would pay for it, possibly with his life.

The gargoyle slammed into Dunk from behind, hard. Instead of sprawling along the wet sand of the beach, though, Dunk found himself being lifted into the air with the fervent beating of the creature's leathery wings.

The rookie wrenched himself around in the daemon's rough-hided arms as they climbed higher and higher into the air. Dunk looked back to see the waters of the bay growing further away by the second.

The gargoyle bared its teeth at Dunk, its face only inches from his. It was a moment before Dunk realised the creature was smiling.

Dunk smashed the creature in the face again, but it just kept smiling at him, unaffected by the blow and uncaring about the blood that it brought forth.

Dunk raised his right arm as high as he could and slashed at the creature's wings. His blade sliced straight through the top angle of one of the wings, and it collapsed instantly, unable to hold the air any longer.

This elicited a stony screech from the gargoyle as it flopped lower, struggling to keep aloft with only a single working wing. 'We are over the water,' it said in its metal-on-stone voice. 'You will kill us both!'

It was Dunk's turn to smile as he angled a blow at the creature's other wing. '*I* can swim,' he said.

The blade cut deep into the wing, and it parted like a torn sail. The gargoyle and Dunk plummeted out of the air as if struck by a boulder from one of the trebuchets mounted on the fortresses at the tips of the bay's horns.

Dunk smashed the creature in the face again as they fell and pushed away hard. The gargoyle's arms let him loose as it began to flap them as well in a vain attempt to keep itself in the air. He kicked away from it and arced into a long, curving dive, tossing the blade clear. The last thing he needed was to impale himself on it when he hit the water.

Dunk hoped the water would be deep enough where he landed.

The rookie pierced the surface of the bay like a giant bird of prey going after a fishy meal. The waters were cool, and the shock of hitting them nearly drove the air from his lungs. He curved himself about as his momentum tried to carry him deeper, letting the water sluicing around his body bring him parallel with the bay's sandy bottom then push him back toward the surface.

When Dunk's momentum finally ran out, he kicked hard and climbed his way back to the surface as fast as he could, his arms and lungs protesting at the effort. He could see the light of the sun high overhead through the water above him. All he had to do now was reach the unfiltered light before he ran out of air.

A moment later, Dunk's head broke the surface. He nearly choked while gasping in the sweet-tasting air. His lungs filled again, he glanced about for the shoreand then made a beeline for the nearest beach.

When Dunk finally found sand beneath his feet again, he looked back at the bay behind him that had almost become his unmarked grave. The well-named Bay of Quietude was as calm as it ever was, except for the ripples his own movements threw across its surface.

'By Nuffle's horny helmet, son,' Slick said as he raced up to the rookie. 'That was amazing! I've never seen anything like it.'

'Just.' Dunk stopped for a moment to hack a few dregs of water out of his lungs. 'Just doing my job.'

Slick scratched his chin with a fat finger at that. 'I'd say this is beyond the call of duty. Perhaps we can put in for hazard pay?'

At that moment, the waters behind the pair erupted, and the gargoyle flung itself into the air again. It let loose a horrifying screech that put gooseflesh all along Dunk's waterlogged skin. Then, glaring down at Dunk with its blood-red orbs, it faded away in the light of the merciful sun.

Dunk slumped back down on the beach stripping off his wet clothes until he was barefoot and naked to the waist. 'I think the players got off easiest today,' he said. A moment later, a roar went up from the distant stadium again.

'We can but hope, son,' Slick said. 'We can but hope.'

IN DRY CLOTHES once more, Dunk, who was sore over every inch of his body from his spectacular dive, stood with Slick in Pegleg's tent. 'What do you think this Zauberer was after?' the rookie asked.

'I don't know,' Slick said, who seemed spooked to be in a tent where a daemon had recently slouched. 'And I don't care. We got rid of him, didn't we? There should be a bonus in it for us. Guard duty's supposed to be little more than busy work. It's not meant to be life threatening.'

Dunk ignored the halfling. 'He had something in his hands when he left, a sheaf of papers.'

'Contracts maybe?' Slick offered. 'Perhaps he works for another team and wants to know what Pegleg is paying his players.'

'Why would that be important?' Dunk asked.

Slick smiled, finally back on ground familiar to him. 'Lots of teams like to try to poach the best players from each other. To do that properly, the more you know about your targets the easier it is. After all, it's hard for a team to outbid your current salary if they don't know what it is.'

'I suppose,' Dunk said, not entirely agreeing with the halfling. 'Wouldn't it be easier to just ask? If most players are as greedy as you imply, they'd be happy to let prospective teams know their asking price.'

Slick nodded. 'But lots of players lie about that. For one, it's a matter of pride. Everyone wants to be known as the player with the highest price tag.'

"That gives new meaning to "most valuable player".'

'For two,' Slick continued, 'players would love to get an offer that's substantially above what they're really making. With the real numbers in hand, a coach only has to offer the least amount necessary. While negotiating, it puts him in a real position of strength.'

'I'll take your word for it,' Dunk said.

Far outside the tent, the crowd in the stadium roared again.

'I hope that's good news,' Slick said. 'We could use some right now.'

'Too bad,' a gruff voice said, just before its owner entered the tent. 'Gotcha bad news right here.'

The intruder stood nearly eight feet tall and seemed nearly as broad across. He had to bend over to fit into the tent, scraping the tops of his pointed, bark-coloured ears on the canvas ceiling. His thick arms were long enough that they almost dragged to his feet. Sharp tusks rose from the bottom, lantern-shaped jaw of his savage-cut mouth, and their tips scraped raw patches on either side of his flat, upturned, almost piggish nose, which squatted just under his beady, black eyes set wide apart in his ham of a face.

'Skragger,' Slick whispered. In the silence of the tent, it sounded like a cannon's shot.

'You can't be in here,' Dunk said to the black orc.

The creature was dressed in filthy but stylish Orcidas clothing, and a thick, gold ring pierced the centre of his nose, almost daring someone to try leading him around by it. A small tuft of salt-and-pepper hair jutted from the top of his head, and Dunk was struck by the wrinkles on the creature's face. Most orcs died young. Skragger was unarmed it seemed, but so, Dunk remembered, was he.

Skragger's long, right arm reach out and smacked Dunk to the ground. It came so fast, he almost didn't see it.

'Nuff from you,' the massive orc said. 'Talk,' he said jabbing his chest with a black-nailed finger. Then he pointed at Dunk. 'Listen.'

Dunk scrambled to his feet and nodded, his cheek still stinging from where the orc had hit him.

'Dunk Hoffnung?' Skragger said, pointing at Slick. The halfling's eyes sprang wide as he squeaked and gestured toward the rookie instead.

Skragger turned toward Dunk, a satisfied smile on his horrible face. 'Dirk yer brother?'

Dunk nodded silently as he tried to scan the room. Pegleg had to have another weapon in here somewhere. He considered diving under the tent's back wall and taking his chances with outrunning the black orc. Skragger might once have been able to chase Dunk down, but it didn't seem that the years had been kind to him. Still, that would mean leaving Slick behind to the black orc's nonexistent mercies, and Dunk couldn't bring himself to risk that.

'Wuz Orland Raiders blitzer,' Skragger said, pointing at himself now. 'My record: Most Touchdowns in a Year.' The creature pronounced the last words carefully and proudly, something the rookie wouldn't have guessed the orc was capable of.

Dunk nodded. 'Congratulations,' he said earnestly.

Another scabby orc paw snapped away from Skragger's side and slapped him to the ground.

'Don't innerupt,' Skragger growled.

The rookie nodded, silently this time, as he crawled back to his feet. Now both of his cheeks burned. At least it seemed that the black orc was more interested in talk than murder.

'Yer Dirk could break record.' Skragger frowned, exposing all of his lower row of yellowed, broken teeth. 'That can't happen.'

'Really?' Dunk said, pride in his brother unexpectedly welling in his heart. He glanced at Slick and asked, 'Dirk could do that?'

Slick nodded at Dunk from where he cowered behind Pegleg's bed. 'He's off to a great start. He almost managed it last year. He only fell five touchdowns shy.'

'*Too* close!' Skragger snarled. He aimed a blow at Slick but only succeeded in knocking a post off of Pegleg's bed, the top of which was carved in the shape of a human skull. It fell next to Slick's feet, a none-too-subtle warning as to Skragger's intent.

'Tell Dirk, back off,' the orc continued. 'Breaks *my* record, Skragger breaks him.' With that, he drew up both arms and brought them down, smashing Pegleg's thick, oaken desk in two. 'Break you too.'

Dunk looked at the splintered remains of the desk at his feet, then back up at Skragger. 'I'll let him know.'

Skragger guffawed rough and low at this. As he did, he pulled a grimy shred of parchment from the pocket of his greasy Orcidas sweatpants. From his other pocket, he pulled out a short pencil that was far too small for his massive hands. He licked the tip with a tongue as rough as sandpaper, set it to the parchment and crossed out something with a single line. Then he looked around.

'Which team?' Skragger said.

Dunk cringed as he leaned just a little over the edge of the destroyed table and said. 'I'm sorry. I don't understand.'

Skragger grimaced in anger, and Dunk braced for another smack. 'Which team owns thizzere camp?'

'Ah,' Dunk said, brightening at the ease of the question, although he didn't quite understand the motivation behind it. 'The Bad Bay Hackers.'

Skragger glared down at his list for a moment, then scowled and took out a tiny pair of wire-rimmed glasses that he perched on his nose. 'Hrm,' he said. 'Ritternacht still with ya?'

'Kur?' Dunk said, smiling. 'He's the starting thrower.'

Another slap sent Dunk reeling backwards, slipping under the back flap of the tent and tumbling into the sand. As the rookie lay there on the beach, feeling his jaw to see if it was broken, he saw the tip of a pencil appear at the top of the tent's rear flap. It tore downward in a smooth, steady move, parting the fabric neatly in two.

Skragger stepped through the new-made gap. 'That warning fer Dirk?' he said. 'Goes fer Kur too.'

With that, the black orc crossed another name off his list and then strode off toward Magritta's docks. Somewhere in the distance, a crowd roared again.

'As a guard, you make a wonderful thrower, Mr. Hoffnung,' Pegleg said after Dunk explained to him everything that had happened that afternoon. 'Wizards, daemons, and a black orc blitzer too?'

'I know it seems too insane to believe,' Dunk started.

'I coach a Blood Bowl team,' Pegleg said evenly as he stirred around in the remains of his desk with his hook. 'There are few things too insane for me to believe.'

Dunk hung his head. 'I'm sorry, coach,' he said. 'I did the best I could.'

Pegleg waited a moment before responding. 'It's not your fault, Mr. Hoffnung. It seems fate has it in for us today.'

'Speaking of which,' Dunk said, 'how did the game go?'

Pegleg frowned. 'We lost,' he said. 'Get out.'

'I'd like to warn my brother that his life is in danger,' Dunk said.

Pegleg rubbed the arc of his hook on his head, letting the touch of the metal cool his brow. 'Permission denied, Mr. Hoffnung. You can tell him in two days. The Reavers are next up on our dance card.'

Dunk nodded. 'What about Kur?'

'That,' Pegleg said, 'had better come from me. After the game Kur played today, though, I'd say that Skragger's record is in no danger from that quarter.'

'Okay, but–'

'Dismissed, Mr. Hoffnung.'

OVER THE NEXT two days, many of Dunk's new team-mates wanted to ask him about what had happened at the camp while they'd been at the game. He told the story over and over again, keeping as best he could to the facts as he knew them. He figured that anyone on the team deserved to know what was happening with the team. After the murders during and after the try-outs, it was clear that something dangerous was happening around the team, and the incidents during the game only amplified that feeling.

'Daemons, you say?' asked M'Grash. The ogre had taken a distinct liking to Dunk, and he felt obliged to cultivate it, not least because he'd rather have M'Grash on his side than against him.

The ogre had a certain childlike, uncomplicated quality about him that Dunk admired. He was a simple creature of simple needs, and playing for the Hackers met most of them nicely. For all that, he was lonely.

'People afraid of me,' the ogre said, 'but me not bad.'

This came shortly after Dunk had witness M'Grash tear the top off a barrel of beer with his teeth. The two had settled down for a drink afterward and were now commiserating over draughts of Killer.

'Me no daemon though,' M'Grash said. 'Don't like daemons.'

Dunk smiled as he picked a splinter out of his stein. 'I can understand that. I don't like them much either.'

'Daemons kill people.' The gigantic creature shuddered, and Dunk felt a strange urge to put his arm around him and tell him it would be all right.

'Some do,' Dunk said. 'But I don't think you'd have been in any danger from this daemon, big guy. Even with his wings he wasn't half your size.'

'Little daemon?' M'Grash brightened at this.

'Compared to you,' Dunk said, raising his drink to the ogre, 'yes. Much littler.'

'Not afraid of little daemons,' M'Grash said. He rested the heel of his hand on one of Dunk's shoulders, and his fingers reached all the way to the other shoulder. 'Keep Dunkle safe from daemons.'

'I'll drink to that,' Dunk said, tapping his stein against M'Grash's half-empty barrel. And they did.

THE NIGHT BEFORE the next game, Dunk found himself sitting at the bar of the Bad Water again. He tried to tell himself that he wasn't there just hoping that Spinne would show up, but he soon admitted he was only trying to fool himself. He'd tried to stop by the Reavers' camp earlier, ostensibly to warn Dirk about the threat from Skragger, but he'd been turned away as soon as he identified himself as a member of the Hackers. Apparently visits from family were okay, but not from players on opposing teams.

Calling the Reavers' compound a 'camp' was a bit of misnomer. The place had a practice field like the one the Hackers used, but it was marked off with proper lines for the boundaries and every ten yards along the field. A host of guards patrolled the place around the clock. Of course, they didn't have much to worry about there, as the Reavers didn't sleep in tents nearby their field. Instead, they had reserved every room in the Casa Grande, the best-appointed inn in all of Magritta. Only the prince's castle had better accommodations, it was said.

The guards at the hotel had turned Dunk away too, but he'd left a message for Dirk, asking him to meet him at the Bad Water. He'd done the same for Spinne as well.

Dunk signalled for the bartender to bring him another pint of Killer. The rookie hadn't had much money to spend since he'd left his family's home many months before, and he was enjoying being able to not worry about it so much. He promised himself that he wouldn't be buying a round for the bar that night, but just before the place closed he ended up doing just that.

Dirk and Spinne never showed.

THE DAY OF Dunk's first game dawned bright and painfully early for the young man. His head felt as if M'Grash had decided to stuff it with cotton and use it for a pillow. Fortunately, as the day wore on Dunk felt better and better, and by the time the game rolled around he was ready to play.

Of course, as a new recruit and the backup thrower behind Kur Ritternacht, Dunk quickly discovered that he couldn't expect much playing time. Kur himself made this clear when he looked at Dunk after the pre-game workout and said, 'Make yourself useful, boy. Get me some water.'

Dunk looked the older thrower in the eyes, unblinking. 'I'm your backup, not your waterboy.'

Kur sneered. 'I was giving you a chance to get more exercise in another role. Something other than bench-warmer.'

Dunk raised his eyebrows at this. 'Kur,' he said, 'I'm just keeping it warm for you.'

Kur sneered as he headed into the locker room to suit up.

PEGLEG ORDERED EVERYONE to get into their full armour, even the backups like Dunk. They might not see any time on the field during the game, but they had to be ready at a moment's notice to hit the turf when needed.

The armour Dunk wore was heavy when he lifted it up, but once he had it strapped on properly it was amazingly easy to handle. The colours were just like that of the Hackers' helmet he'd worn during tryouts: green and gold.

'These are the "away team" colours, son,' Slick explained as he tried to help Dunk get the straps adjusted properly. 'Forest green shirt and bright gold pants, with all armour colour-coordinated to where it's placed. Your shoulder pads are green, for instance, while your kneepads are yellow.'

'Do we have 'home team' colours too?' Dunk asked.

Slick nodded. 'The home team is usually the highest seeded team in any particular game. "Seeds" are rankings given to the participating teams based upon who the host committee thinks are more likely to win the tournament. The other side is then the visiting team.'

'What are the Reavers seeded?' Dunk asked.

'First, although there's some argument about that. Some folks thought that honour should have gone to Khorne's Killers. With luck, we won't end up playing them. When you run up against a bunch of warpstone-tainted mutants whose only binding trait is their insane worship of a violent blood god, you can lose even if you win, if you know what I mean.'

'And what are we ranked?' Dunk asked, trying to change the subject.

'Two hundred and third.' Slick waited a moment before continuing. 'Out of about two hundred and fifty.'

'That doesn't seem good,' Dunk said. 'Are we that bad?'

'Now that you're on the team?' Slick said with forced merriment. 'Of course not.'

Dunk frowned.

'Seriously, son. We only had twelve players going into this tournament. Some people didn't even think the Hackers would survive the long journey from Bad Bay, what with Pegleg's fear of water and all.

'His what?' Slick ducked under Dunk's rotating shoulder pad. 'I thought he was a pirate.'

'Word is he was but that it ended badly. He's hated the water ever since. Given a choice, he stays dry at all times. He doesn't even drink water! Sticks entirely to burgundy wine.'

Dunk groaned. 'He doesn't even face the bay during training, does he? He always stands with his back to the water. Why would he ever travel by sea?'

Slick snorted. 'It's not that he likes to. It's just the fastest way to get to someplace like Magritta. You noticed he never came out of his cabin the entire trip.'

'I thought he was studying games on his crystal ball.'

'Oh, he does that too,' Slick said. 'It's one of the reasons he's such a great coach. He turns his weaknesses into strengths. He has to focus on those games to distract himself from his fears, and it drives him to be the best coach he can. I've never seen someone with as much of a command of the game as Pegleg.'

'I wonder what it was that turned him against the sea like that?'

'The man's missing a hand and the better part of a leg, son. Let your imagination run wild.'

Dunk fell silent for a while and let Slick work on all of the straps he was wearing. 'Do we ever play games at home?' he said, after a pause.

'You would, if the Hackers had a home stadium to play at. Like most teams, these days, they play games at stadiums owned by the cities who play host. This place, for instance,' he said, 'belongs to Magritta.'

'They don't have a home base at all? Do they just travel all year long?'

'Mostly. In between the Majors, if they can't find a game along the way, they sometimes hole up in Bad Bay. There's a field there they use for practice, although there aren't any stands. It doesn't make for much of a home field advantage, and its hard to sell tickets to it, so the Hackers spend most of their time on the road instead, pursuing the larger purses offered for games in better venues.'

'It sounds like a hard life,' Dunk said.

Slick nodded as he finished with the final strap. 'It's our life now.'

AT GAME TIME, the team lined up at the exit from the locker room, ready to race out on to the field. Pegleg stood at the ironbound oaken door and doffed his hat. It was the first time Dunk had ever seen him without it. He was amazed to see that Pegleg's long, curly hair was in fact a wig that was attached to the tricorn hat. Underneath it, he was as bald as a dragon's egg.

Just because the hair was missing, though, didn't mean Pegleg's scalp was unadorned. A tattoo of a snake wound up from under his collar and leapt onto his skull where it spread out like a hooded cobra to cover the whole of his naked pate. The eyes of the cobra were a bloody red and the fangs that pointed down toward Pegleg's shining eyes glistened with venom. Or was it sweat? Dunk couldn't tell.

The thought of venom sent his thoughts careening back to his experience with the chimera and how sick its sting had made him. He'd come a long way from that cave in the Grey Mountains in only a few weeks.

'Listen up, you scurvy dogs!' Pegleg began, shattering Dunk's reverie. 'This is our first game with our full complement of new players. That means we've finally got a chance!

'I want you to hit the Reavers with everything you've got. There is no such thing as "dirty play" in this game. The only crime is getting caught! And I've made a contribution to the Referees' Widows and Orphans Fund to guarantee the zebras won't be watching us too closely.'

The team laughed evilly at that. Dunk was a bit too horrified to say anything.

'Your first job is to get the ball into the end zone. Your second job is to stop the Reavers from doing the same. Use any means at your disposal to accomplish these lofty goals. Kick, bite, smash, punch, even *kill* if you have to. It's not necessary, of course, but if you can make sure a Reaver won't be coming back for the rest of the game, then more power to you!'

At first, Dunk's thoughts went to Dirk and Spinne. They were among his targets, his and the rest of his team's. Suddenly, he wasn't so sure about his contract anymore. Then he realised that all of the Reavers would be coming after him and the rest of his team with the same murderous abandon. Then he was absolutely positive he'd made a mistake.

Pegleg continued unabated, his voice building from simple menace to a bloodthirsty crescendo.

'Now, go out there and tear the Reavers limb from limb! Make them sorry they even woke up today! Make their mothers sorry for having them!

'GO OUT THERE AND WIN THIS THRICE-DAMNED GAME!'

The rest of the team roared in approval, and their coach threw open the door to the playing field. They charged out n single file, and as they left the tunnel from the locker room and hit the sunlit field, the crowd let loose a deafening, thunderous noise that shook the supports of the stadium until the entire ground threatened to come crumbling down into the field after the players.

'What,' Dunk asked himself as he followed the others on to what he now could only think of as the killing ground, 'have I gotten myself in to?'

17

IF THE NOISE from the crowd deafened Dunk from inside the locker room, it stunned him once he reached the dugout, a stone-lined pit that sat on the edge of the field, between the stadium's seats and the game's sidelines. The tunnel from the locker room came out in the middle of the dugout and stretched twenty yards in either direction, giving members of the team and staff plenty of room to move about, as well as a rat's-eye view of the action.

Dunk was glad that he had been the last through the door. When he stepped into the dugout, he stood frozen in his boots. He'd seen games on Cabalvision before but only through a crystal ball. He'd never even been in the stands for a game, and to now be here with tens of thousands of fans cheering and booing all at once over-whelmed him. He thought that perhaps dragon slaying wasn't such a bad career choice after all.

'Keep moving, son!' Slick shouted up at Dunk.

The rookie looked down at the halfling, who he could barely hear over the roaring crowd. It was like standing in the ancient market in Altdorf when the Emperor's entourage marched through. The raw emotion in the place was both humbling and moving. Although one part of Dunk wanted to turn and run, another part needed nothing more than to charge out on to that field and give the fans the kind of game they so desperately wanted.

'Keep moving!' Slick yelled again, giving Dunk a push in the back of the legs this time. 'Go find your seat!'

Dazed, Dunk gazed around the dugout. Over to the left, he spotted Guillermo Reyes, Milo Hoffstetter, Simon Sherwood and Kai Albrecht sitting on a bench. They were still in their armour, but they'd taken their helmets off to get a better look at the field. Risers lifted the bench to put them at eye-level with the players.

A thick, brick wall behind these players, with a bit of a roof slanting over them, protected them from the fans to their rear. That didn't stop the crazed spectators from throwing all manner of things down at the dugout. As Dunk walked over to join the others, dozens of steins shattered on the dugout's roof, spattering beer, ale, and some worse things all about the place. He flinched at the sound of the first few, but they soon faded into the background, suffocated by the rest of the racket.

The starting players had already raced on to the field, which seemed to be what had caused the crowd to go from simply excited to entirely insane. The two teams met in the centre of the field, on which someone had emblazoned a beautiful blue and white crest showing a sailing ship on calm seas against a yellow field shaped like a shield.

'That's the Oliveri family crest,' Slick said from behind Dunk. 'They've ruled Magritta for over fifty years.'

The rookie turned, surprised to see the halfling there. Slick shrugged at him. 'It's the safest place I could think of. You don't think I'm going to wait in the camp after what happened during the last game?'

Dunk smiled, happy to have a familiar face around. 'What's happening out there?' he asked.

As he spoke, a voice thundered out over the stadium, louder than Dunk could have imagined. It even drowned out the roaring for a moment.

'Now, please welcome today's home team, the Reikland Reavers!'

'That's the Preternatural Announcement system,' Slick shouted into Dunk's ear over the resultant bellow from the crowd as the Reavers' starting players took the field. 'That's Bob Bifford's voice. He's been doing these games for years. Keeps bouncing back and forth between Cabalvision networks to whichever one has the contract this year.'

'Isn't he a vampire?' Dunk asked. Even he'd heard of Bob Bifford and his partner Jim Johnson, who Dunk knew was an ogre like M'Grash. 'How does he do this during the day?'

'Sun Protection Fetish,' Slick said. 'How do you think guys like Hugo "the Impaler" von Irongrad ever manage to play day games? They keep their SPF on them at all times.'

'Even at night?'

'You never know when a team wizard might conjure up some magical daylight.'

Dunk nodded at that. 'Why don't we have a team wizard?'

Slick rubbed his fingers together. 'Too much gold. Pegleg's saving his wizard budget for the semi-finals, if we make it.'

The Reavers stormed toward the centre of the field, chanting, 'Em-pe-ror! Em-pe-ror!' As Altdorf's best and brightest team, they had the favour of their nation's ruler, and they dedicated every game to him as a matter of course.

Among the Reavers, Dunk spotted Spinne and Dirk at the front of the pack. Like the other Reavers, they wore war paint on their faces, visible even under their helmets. Dunk noticed that everyone seemed to have black stripes painted under their eyes and white strips across their noses.

'What's all that for?' Dunk asked Kai, waving a hand over his face. He noticed that the lineman bore those same stripes.

Kai smiled at the rookie's naiveté. 'The black lines help keep the sun from reflecting off your face and into your eyes.'

Dunk nodded at that. 'And the white stripes?'

Kai pulled the strip off his nose and held it out for Dunk to see. It looked like a stiff, little board, but it was sticky on the side to be pressed against the nose. 'The Snot Stoppers are new. They bear a small enchantment designed to open up your sinuses so you can breathe better. It's supposed to enhance athletic ability.'

Dunk squinted at the thing as Kai put it back on his face. 'Does it work?'

Kai frowned. 'I don't know. I wear it because it helps me smell players coming at me from ten yards away. Those undead and goblin teams really stink!'

Bob Bifford's voice rang out over the PA system again. 'And heeeere we go! The teams meet in the centre of the field for the coin toss. As the captain of the visiting team, Kur Ritternacht will call it in the air.'

Dunk watched as the referee – a mean-looking, dark-skinned elf with a crimson crest of hair, dressed in a shirt with vertical black-and-white stripes – pulled out a large gold coin and spoke to Kur. 'Orcs or Eagles?' he hissed. Without waiting for an answer, he flipped the coin in the air.

'Orcs!' Kur shouted.

The coin fell to the ground and bounced high on the stony surface. When it rolled to a stop, the referee shouted out 'Orcs it is!'

Kur muttered something to the referee, who then tossed the ball to Dirk.

'The Hackers win the toss and elect to receive. The Reavers take the east end of the field and set up to receive the ball,' Bob's voice said.

'What's this made out of?' Dunk said, pointing at the field. 'I've never seen a coin bounce like that before.'

'Go ahead and touch it,' Slick said.

Dunk slipped off the bench and reached out from the dugout to lay a hand on the field. It was rough and tough like stone, but it gave and rebounded like flesh. If it had been warm, Dunk might have thought it was living. He picked at it with one of the spikes that jutted from the knuckles of his fingerless gauntlets, and a small chunk came free. When Dunk looked back at the material, though, he couldn't find where the chunk had come from. It was if the stuff had somehow managed to heal.

A stein of ale smashed against his shoulder pad, and Dunk – realizing he wasn't wearing his helmet – slipped back into the dugout before someone in the crowd developed better aim.

'It's called Astrogranite,' Slick said as Dunk took his spot on the bench again. 'Its as tough as stone, only better. Low maintenance too.'

Without warning, the crowd started to groan in a low-pitched tone. Dunk looked out to see the Reavers' kicker getting ready to boot the ball downfield. As the kicker got closer to the ball, the pitch of the crowd's inharmonious moan rose until it transformed into a screech as the kicker sent the ball sailing west.

The ball came right down toward Cavre, who caught it neatly and began dashing east, toward the Reavers' end zone. The game was on.

Dunk spent the first half of the game sitting next to the other 'scrubs', as Kai called all the players on the bench. 'Because we're the ones called in to clean things up after someone's blood has been spilled.'

'Being a backup is not so bad,' Guillermo said. 'You get to sit here on the sidelines where it's safe. You get paid the same no matter if you play or not. And you get great seats to watch the game.'

'Why did you try out for the team if you don't want to play?' Milo asked.

'My brothers bet me that I wouldn't do it,' Guillermo grinned. 'They scraped together ten crowns that said I'd wash out before the cuts. I'll do just about anything to win a bet with my brothers.'

'Including signing up to play a ridiculously dangerous game?' Simon said. The way he shivered as he spoke told Dunk that Simon was starting to regret having made the same decision himself.

'Well,' Guillermo smiled in his warm, Estalian way, 'I thought I'd just decline the offer if it came, but when Coach Pegleg sat me down to explain the terms, I just couldn't refuse.'

Dunk nodded. He knew exactly what Guillermo meant. This wasn't the career of dragon slaying he'd set out for when he left town, and he was a bit concerned how anyone from his family – well, besides Dirk, of course – would react when they saw him on the field. But the gold took the sting right out of that.

Bob's voice belted out over the crowd noise, which had finally died down a bit, although it sometimes crested like one of the monstrous waves in the Sea of Claws, on which Dunk's family had vacationed every year.

'Rhett "the Rocket" Cavre receives the ball and launches himself downfield. The Reavers' linemen charge forward to stop him, but the Hackers set up a nice line of blockers to give their star player some protection.'

'This is exactly the kind of thing the Hackers need to do to win this game,' Jim said. 'The Reavers outmatch the Hackers at just about every position, so the Hackers must play together as a team to have a prayer. Coaching will be the key here.'

'True enough, Jim, but what about the new recruits the Hackers just picked up only two days ago? Do you think they've had time to integrate with the others and gel into the kind of lean, mean, bruising machine they have to be to prevent a repeat of that gut-wrenching loss against the Darkside Cowboys?'

'Gut-*spilling*, you mean!' I haven't seen that much blood on the ground since your last family dinner!'

'Stop it, you big lug. You're making me drool!' Bob said. Dunk could hear him licking his lips.

'Oh! Cavre pitches the ball back to the Hackers' starting thrower, Ritternacht, the third-leading thrower in the league last year. Ritternacht drops back into open territory and pumps a fake. Then he sees an open man downfield and lets it rip!'

'Look at that ball sail along!' said Jim. 'It's heading right for the end zone!'

'Wait a minute! Dirk "the Hero" Heldmann has an angle on it. He leaps up and… yes! Intercepted!'

The crowd went nuts, and Dunk could barely hear the announcers as he watched the drama play out on the field.

Dirk took off with the ball, running towards the south side of the field to gather some room. Then, still charging at top speed, he hurled it straight down the field and into the end zone.

'Spinne "the Black Widow" Schönheit reaches up with those long, lovely arms of hers and hauls the ball in, dodging a last-second dive from Karsten "the Killer" Klemmer. Triple K goes wide and into the stands while Schönheit executes a victory dance in the end zone. Touchdown!'

'That's not the only thing being executed, Bob. It looks like those fans are playing wishbones with Triple K's legs!'

Dunk stood up, but he couldn't see Karsten anywhere. It was if the carnivorous crowd had swallowed him whole. From the sounds of it, they were chewing him up pretty badly.

A moment later, the crowd spat Karsten back into the end zone. Spinne pirouetted over to the injured player and spiked the ball down into his face. It stuck in his open-faced helmet, right between the top ridge and his single chin bar.

The Reavers charged back to their end of the field, leaving the Hackers to lick their wounds. A team of litter bearers raced out to collect Karsten and cart him off the field. They deposited the man in the Hackers' dugout, and Dunk could see blood trickling from a half dozen wounds in Karsten's exposed flesh.

'That took all of one minute,' Pegleg snarled, checking the green and gold pocket watch he'd pulled from his crimson coat as the game began. He'd been pacing up and down through the dugout since, watching the clock almost as much as the game. He looked over at the bench and sighed.

'It's going to be a damned long day.'

FROM WHERE HE stood at the edge of the field, Pegleg looked at his bench. His gaze sliced through each of the players, evaluating them one by one.

Dunk felt Pegleg consider him for a moment and then move on, and he couldn't tell if he was relieved or disappointed. The other scrubs sat frozen stiff, afraid to attract their coach's attention with the slightest movement. Beside him, Dunk could hear Simon whispering a mantra over and over again: 'Don't pick me. Don't pick me. Don't pick me.'

Dunk looked up at Pegleg and saw the coach glaring down at him, a pitiless smile on his face. 'Mr. Hoffnung,' Pegleg said, pointing his hook at the rookie. 'You're in.'

Dunk surprised himself by leaping up and darting out of the dugout to stand next to Pegleg. 'Who am I in for, coach?' he asked.

Pegleg lowered his head and rubbed his eyes with his good hand. A low moan emanated from the other side of the dugout where an apothecary, a tall thin man wearing a grimy, once-white coat and a pair of magnifying glasses over his eyes, was working on Karsten.

'No leeches!' the lineman screamed. 'No leeches!'

'It's that or the bone drill,' the apothecary wheezed. As he spoke, he put down the slimy green things flopping about in his fists and picked up a vicious-shaped metal device. As he spun its handle, the blood-caked tip whirred and clacked. Dunk had never heard such a horrible threat.

'Leeches!' Karsten said. 'By Nuffle's dirty cleats, I'll take my chances with the leeches!'

'But Karsten's a lineman,' Dunk said. 'I'm a thrower. What about Guillermo?' The rookie looked back over his shoulder to see the new lineman drawing a finger under his throat at Dunk. He wasn't sure if Guillermo meant for him to be quiet or that the lineman wanted to kill him. Maybe both.

'You're my man, Mr. Hoffnung,' Pegleg said. 'Don't question my judgment – ever.'

'Aye, coach,' Dunk said with a snappy salute.

Pegleg glared at the rookie as if he couldn't tell if the salute was in mockery or earnest. Then he looked out at the field and said, 'No matter. Make your peace with Nuffle, Mr. Hoffnung, and welcome to your first game of Blood Bowl.'

Armed with some hurried instructions from his coach, Dunk strapped on his helmet and charged out on to the field. The crowd cheered as he raced toward his designated spot, right near the midfield line. Dunk raised his hands in the air to encourage them.

'What do you think you're doing?' Dirk said, standing opposite from Dunk across the line.

'Working the crowd!' Dunk said. 'Blood Bowl's a game that's larger than life. I'm giving them what they want.' He raised his arms again, and the cheering grew.

'Listen to them go!' Dunk said. As he spoke, he spotted Spinne standing several yards back and caught her eye. She smiled at him and blew him a kiss. He caught it in both hands and raised it into the air like a trophy before bringing it back down to stuff into his mouth. The crowed loved it.

'Do you hear what they're saying?' Dirk asked.

Dunk stopped pandering to the stands for a moment and listened carefully. It took him a moment, but he managed to pick some words out of the roar, two words that the fans kept chanting. When he realised what they were, he blanched.

'Fresh meat! Fresh meat! Fresh meat!'

Then the crowd began its collective low groan again, signifying the upcoming kick-off. As the sound grew louder and higher, Dirk beckoned Dunk with a crooked finger, saying something.

'What's that again?' Dunk asked as he leaned forward, cocking his head toward his brother.

The screaming of the crowd reached a crescendo as Dirk shouted at Dunk. 'Remember when you knocked me out of that window when we were kids?'

Dunk nodded. He'd been ashamed of that incident since the day it had happened. Dirk had fallen from the keep's east tower and nearly been killed. Only the intercession of the best apothecary in town had saved the young boy's life. It had been an accident, but the blame for it fell squarely on Dunk's shoulders.

Dirk flashed Dunk an evil grin, then lowered his shoulder and slammed his spiked pad into Dunk, knocking him flying backward to the ground. Dunk's head hit the ground, and stars zoomed past his eyes. The next thing he knew, he felt Dirk's boots stomp on his chest as the Reaver blitzer literally ran right over him.

'Now we're even!' Dirk shouted back as he charged down the field, after the ball.

Dunk crawled to his feet and shook his head. It felt like his brain was loose. The world swam around him, threatening to pitch him off its edge.

The rookie clung to what Pegleg had told him, and he started running toward the end zone.

'Your brother is going to knock you flat,' Pegleg had said.

'No he won't, coach,' Dunk had said, bouncing up and down as he surveyed the field. 'I can take him.'

Pegleg had grabbed the faceguard on Dunk's helmet and wrenched the rookie's head around until they were looking eye to eye. It had hurt, but Dunk hadn't said a word, his tongue catching in his mouth.

'You're going to let him,' Pegleg had said. 'Then you're going to get up and run for the end zone for all you're worth.'

'Which one?'

'Theirs,' Pegleg had said, pointing in the direction the rest of the Hackers were already facing.

'Got it, coach. See, I always get those mixed up, whose end zone is whose. Is yours the one you're defending or the one you're attacking. I can never–'

'Go. That. Way.' Pegleg stabbed his hook toward the Reavers' end zone to punctuate each word. Then he brought the hook around to come up under the chin trap of Dunk's helmet. The sharp tip had caught Dunk right in the fleshy part of his neck there. A single sharp jab could have shoved the hook up into Dunk's mouth so that Pegleg could lead him around by his jawbone.

'Don't disappoint me,' Pegleg had said. Although he'd only whispered, Dunk had heard him as clearly as if everyone else in the stadium had been struck dumb.

All this in mind, Dunk sprinted as hard as he could toward the Reavers' end zone, struggling to clear his head as he ran.

'This time, Kur Ritternacht fields the ball directly,' Bob's voice said. 'He gets some good blocking from the Hackers' linemen and moves the ball forward. K'Thragsh, the only nonhuman player on the field, opens up a hole for him, and he dashes through it.'

'Yes!' said Jim's voice. '"Monster" M'Grash K'Thragsh was one of the Hackers' standouts last year, and a play like that really shows you why. That's the sort of player you can build a team around – or destroy another team with!'

As Dunk ran, he heard someone else pounding after him. He glanced over his shoulder and saw Spinne racing towards him. He had the angle on her to the end zone and he knew he'd get there first. He winked at her, then looked up past her toward the sky.

There, hovering in the air like some great bird of prey, hung the football. It paused for a moment at the top of its arc, then came plummeting back to earth. As it approached, it seemed to move faster, and Dunk realised he'd have to run as fast as he could to catch it.

His eyes still on the ball, Dunk sprinted for the end zone and a date with the ball for which he could not be late. As the ball closed the last few yards toward their mutual meeting spot, he stretched out his arms as far as they could go. The ball landed hard in his fingertips, hard enough to break them, or so it felt. He grabbed at the ball as it were life itself and pulled it in hard to his chest, where he cradled it like an infant.

Dunk hit the ground and rolled hard, keeping himself wrapped around the ball, protecting it from the Astrogranite, which was not as forgiving as he'd hoped. As his momentum faded, he rolled neatly out of his tuck and to his feet. He held the ball high over his head in a moment of pure triumph, and roared along with the crowd.

'Amazing!' Bob's voice said. 'Hoffnung, the rookie phenom from Altdorf, scores a touchdown in his first minute of play!'

The moment was cut short, though, when someone hit Dunk from behind and drove him into the stands.

'Ooh!' said Jim's voice. 'Apparently Dunk's not as much of a lover as a fighter. Lady Schönheit there just made him pay so much for his score that he'll be making equal monthly instalments for the next three years!'

The fans, some of who were more frightening than the players, grabbed Dunk with their meaty paws and greasy claws and passed him bodily up toward the top of the arena. Someone ripped the ball from his hand and bit it in half with his frothing teeth; a rabid dwarf, from the look of him, with a chain that hung between his pierced ear and nose. His face and the shaved sides of his head were tattooed, except where a thin dorsal fin of hair stabbed up from the top, dyed a glaring orange.

Dunk was just happy the dwarf had gone for the football instead of his arm. He looked back down to where he'd come from and saw Spinne waving at him and blowing a good-bye kiss.

'I'll be right back!' he shouted down at her.

The fans around him burst out laughing at this and practically hurled him towards the top of the stadium. As Dunk kept moving up and up, he recalled that the edge of the stadium stood two or three stories above the ground, maybe more, and the crowd was hauling him straight toward that edge without any sign of stopping.

'Ah,' Bob's voice said, 'it looks like Magritta's infamous Dead End Zoners have decided to commemorate the rookie's amazing achievement with a trip on the Bay Water Bowl's express escalator to the afterlife.'

'No!' Dunk shouted as he flung himself about, trying to find a handhold on someone or something, anything to bring this deadly trip to a stop. He scored purchase on a snotling, but when he pulled at it, the tiny goblin simply leapt atop his chest and starting spitting in his face.

'It's sad,' Jim's voice said, his tone betraying that he felt anything but grief, 'to see such a promising career cut so short. This has to be some kind of record: first and last touchdown scored in under a minute!'

Dunk flung the snotling away, and the creature landed in a mob of fans watching him be hauled away, chanting, 'Over! Over! Over!' Someone smacked the hapless snotling into the air again, and the creature began a long circuit around the stadium, bouncing about like some kind of fleshy beach ball.

Dunk had other worries though, as he could not find a way to slow his progress toward his first and surely final attempt at flight. He thrashed about as best he could, but the fans passed him along by the spikes on his armour, holding him fast. The straps that Slick had done such a good job of tightening now trapped him inside his prickly shell, and there was no escape from it.

When Dunk reached the edge of the stadium, he flung out his arms to grab at the wall, his final chance of escaping this predicament, even if it meant brawling his way back to the field from the cheap seats on down. The fans were ready for this trick though. (It frightened Dunk to consider how many times they'd pulled this off, they executed it – and possibly him – so well.) They hoisted him high into the air and pitched him far out over the stadium's rear wall.

'Say so long to Dunk Hoffnung, you fanatics!' Bob's voice said.

'See ya!' the crowd answered as one, drowning out Dunk's screams as he fell flailing toward the ground far below.

When Dunk woke up, he hurt so badly he assumed he was dead. At first, he assumed the nauseating way the world rocked beneath him convinced him he'd sustained a horrible head injury. Then he smelled the tang of salt in the air, and he realised he was on a ship.

Dunk had never been below deck on the *Sea Chariot* before, but he imagined this was exactly what it would be like. He groaned as the ship crossed a particularly choppy section of sea, forcing him to feel the size and shape of his stomach in a way he never had before.

Slick was at his side in an instant. 'Nuffle's bloody balls, you're awake,' the halfling breathed. He reached out with a cool, damp cloth and laid it across Dunk's brow, which seemed to help stave off the nausea, at least for the moment. 'I thought we'd lost you for good.'

Dunk's stomach turned, and he sat up, fighting back his body's demand to vomit. Slick shoved a bucket in front of him, and Dunk clutched it like a poor man clinging to his last crown.

'Me too,' Dunk said. 'What happened?'

Slick grimaced. 'The crowd grabbed you and tossed you over the top of the stadium.'

Dunk rubbed his aching head. His hand ached too, as did his arm and every other part of his body. 'I remember that part,' he said. 'What happened after that?'

'The referee called a penalty.'

'That's good.'

'Against you.'

'What?' Dunk said. His head felt like it might explode.

'He called it excessive celebration, you jumping over the edge of the stadium like that.'

Dunk wanted to let his jaw drop, but he was sure whatever was in his stomach would come storming out after that, so he grimaced instead. 'I did not jump over that edge. I was thrown!'

Slick nodded. 'I know, son, as did everyone else in the stadium, but the fans liked the call so much it was bound to stand.'

'How could a referee make a call like that?'

Slick patted Dunk on the knee as if the rookie was a small child. 'How does any referee make a call in a gold-infested game like Blood Bowl?'

'Are you saying he was bribed?'

'Yes,' Slick nodded, 'and by both sides too. Apparently the Reavers have deeper pockets than ours, although I suppose that's no surprise.'

Dunk slumped back in his bed. 'At least I scored a touchdown.'

Slick stayed silent.

'I said, at least I scored a touchdown.'

'Yes, son, about that.'

Dunk sat up again, too agitated to think about his stomach any more. 'Don't tell me the ref negated the touchdown too.'

'He tried to.' Slick's toothy grin put Dunk's mind more at ease. 'The fans didn't like that at all though. It's one thing to buy a ref. It's another to make it so obvious.

'Also, people just loved the style you showed by rolling up into that triumphant stand. That and feeling sorry for you for being thrown over the edge of the stadium caused a bit of a riot.'

'Really?' Dunk smiled in spite of himself.

'They stormed the field and grabbed the ref. Then they sent him up after you. Sadly for him, they didn't give him the easy route.'

Dunk's jaw did drop this time. 'They sent me by the easy route?'

'You're still here, aren't you?'

Dunk rubbed his head again. 'I'm not so sure.'

'It turns out there's a series of awnings tiered below the spot where you were tossed over. You hit every one of them. Tore through most of them, but they slowed you down enough so when you hit that sausage on a stick vendor, it was not so bad.'

'Not so bad?' Dunk said softly. 'How long have I been out?'

'Three days.'

'*Three days!*' Dunk could not wrap his aching head around that concept. 'I thought you said it wasn't so bad?'

'Well, the fall wasn't so bad. The sausage vendor, though, he wasn't happy about how you destroyed his cart. He beat you senseless. It took three of our linemen to pull him off of you.'

Dunk let his head sink into his hands. So much for his great debut. Could he ever recover from this?

'Where are we now?' Dunk asked.

'The *Sea Chariot*,' Slick said. 'You're in what passes for a sickbay around here. It's mid-afternoon. Everyone else is above deck.'

'What happened to the tournament?'

'We lost, Mr. Hoffnung!' Pegleg swept into the cramped little room and glared down at the rookie. 'In no small part, the blame for that gets laid at your feet. Too busy celebrating after your first touchdown to worry about the lady Reaver coming up behind you? That was a *rookie* mistake.'

'I'm a rookie,' Dunk offered.

'That's not good enough, Mr. Hoffnung,' Pegleg said as he shoved his hook into Dunk's face. The rookie froze, afraid that the thing's vicious tip might accidentally catch his nose. 'Not *nearly* good enough. I don't pay you a ludicrous amount of money to make mistakes, rookie or otherwise. I pay you to *win games!*'

'What happened to the game?' Dunk asked, hoping to change the subject. As he spoke, though, it occurred to him that this might be the exact wrong subject to change to.

Pegleg spat on the floor. 'A tie,' he said, as if someone had just suggested he trade in his hook for a bouquet of wilted roses. 'The remaining referee called the game when he realised he'd have to face the rest of us alone. Then he fled before we could contest his ruling. Since each team had scored a touchdown, the game was declared a draw.'

'I thought the one ref had negated my touchdown.'

'The surviving ref thought better of that, son,' Slick said. 'He reinstated it.'

Dunk grinned at that. His smile vanished when he looked back up at Pegleg. 'I'm sorry, coach,' he said. 'I did my best.'

'That, Mr. Hoffnung, is exactly what I'm afraid of.' Pegleg shook his head, then turned and left.

Dunk fell back into his bed. What a rude awakening this had been. He felt like crawling up onto the deck and throwing himself overboard. At least then he wouldn't be able to mess everything up again.

'Don't feel so bad, son,' Slick said. 'Pegleg's hard on everyone.' The halfling stared at the door. 'You should feel honoured actually. He's come in here every couple hours checking on you. Considering how stuck to that crystal ball of his he usually is, I'm impressed. I've never seen him leave his cabin before if we weren't docked.'

Dunk sat back up and shook his head. 'I guess that's something.' A question struck him finally. 'Why didn't we stay in Magritta?'

'Pegleg's not a stupid man. He did the math. With two losses, it's next to impossible to make the semi-finals.'

'Then where are we going?'

'Like most teams, we're off to the next of the Majors.'

Dunk nodded. He liked the thought of a fresh start somewhere else with another chance to prove himself. 'Which one's that?' he asked.

Slick flashed Dunk a smile that made him nervous. 'We're off to see the Dungeonbowl.'

'I thought there were three months between all the Majors.'

'Roughly,' Slick said. 'You can never tell exactly when the Chaos Cup will be played, for instance.'

'Where is the Dungeonbowl then?' asked Dunk as he tried getting to his feet. The world swam under his feet as he did, but he realised now that this was the ship, not his head. 'I mean, how long will it take us to get there? Three full months?'

Slick shook his head. 'The wizards of the Colleges of Magic host the tournament every year. Each of the ten colleges sponsors a team to represent it in the games. Originally, they set this up to resolve a horrible conflict among the colleges, but they liked the game so much that they decided to keep it going. They've been playing it for more than seventy-five years now.'

'The Colleges of Magic,' Dunk asked, his head suddenly pounding harder than ever. He sat down to wrestle with his stomach again. 'So we're going to Altdorf?' Dunk wasn't ready to go home, not yet, maybe not ever.

'Oh, no,' Slick said, waving off Dunk's ignorance. 'The wizards who run the colleges are too smart to host something as dangerous as the Dungeonbowl anywhere near their main campus. It's held in Barak-Varr, the dwarf seaport that sits right where the Blood River runs down from the Worlds Edge Mountains and into the Black Gulf.'

'Sounds like a lovely place,' Dunk said. His stomach settled down as he spoke.

'It's not so bad, son, so long as you like dwarfs. Of course, most dwarfs won't go near Barak-Varr, since it's so near the sea. They think the dwarfs who choose to live there are a bit off-balance, if you know what I mean. But then, they'd have to be to come up with the complexes in which they play the game, right?'

'Who's crazier, Slick?' Dunk asked as he got to his feet again. 'The people who create the game or those who play it?'

'WE'RE NOT GOING directly to Barak-Varr, Mr. Hoffnung,' Cavre said that night as Dunk took his dinner on the deck, sitting next to the blitzer. 'Right now, we're in the Southern Sea, heading southeast. Once we round Fools Point, we'll be in the Tilean Sea, which separates Estalia from Tilea. We'll follow that coast as closely as we dare, stopping in Remas for supplies. From there, it's on to Luccini and then through the Pirates' Current into the Black Gulf.'

'How long will all this take us?'

'A good few weeks. It's not as far as the trip from Bad Bay to Magritta, but we're not in as much of a hurry. With winter coming on, most of the Blood Bowl teams have gone into hibernation until spring. The Dungeonbowl is the only major tournament held in these dark months.'

'Who's sponsoring us in the tournament?' Dunk wondered if he'd get to meet some of the powerful wizards who ran the Colleges of Magic back in Altdorf. Those were the kinds of friends that might come in handy later.

'No one,' Cavre said. 'We're not playing.'

Dunk almost dropped his spoon. 'Then why are we going there?'

Cavre smiled. Dunk realised what a great player the assistant coach must have been. After nearly fifteen years of playing Blood Bowl, he was not only still alive, he even had all his own teeth.

'We're going to watch and to learn. We just hired a quarter of our team last week, as you know, and many of the others have only a year or two under their belts.'

Cavre clicked his tongue. 'It's a rebuilding year. Not so coincidentally, Mr. Hoffnung, we have a winter training camp set up on the north coast of the Black Gulf, in one of the lands of the Border Princes. We'll train there hard until the Dungeonbowl, and when that tournament is over, we'll head back toward the Empire and hope we're in the right place when the location of the Chaos Cup is announced.'

'You don't know where it is?' Dunk asked, surprised.

'No one does. It's kept a secret until a week or two before the event. That way, no one can disrupt it.'

'Does that work?' Dunk asked, rubbing the back of his head, which was still a bit tender.

'Not really,' Cavre said. 'Most of the time the fans do more damage than any invading army ever could.'

The two fell silent for a moment, and Dunk gazed up at the stars sparkling overhead. Cavre was right about the winter. Even this far south, he could feel it getting colder. He imagined Altdorf would be covered with snow already. The thought of his home town coated with a virginal layer of white made him homesick. He remembered running snowball fights with Dirk along the battlements of the family's keep, even though there wasn't much of a home left there to go back to.

'Have you seen Mr. K'Thragsh yet?' Cavre asked.

Dunk looked up to see the blitzer smiling at him softly. 'No. Is he all right?'

'Your "accident" shook him up a bit. He's lost a lot of team-mates over the past few years, and he thought you might be the next one. I think he's taken a real shine to you. He checked in on you more than anyone besides Mr. Fullbelly.'

Dunk snorted. 'I suppose it's better to have the ogre with you than against you. I have to say, though, I thought an ogre would be...'

'Less sensitive?'

'That's it.'

Cavre nodded. 'Mr. K'Thragsh is a special case. Years back, an Imperial army wiped out his entire village when he was just an infant. He was the only survivor.'

'That's horrible.'

'They *were* eating the people in the neighbouring village.'

'Ah. So what happened to M'Grash?'

The army's commander couldn't bear to kill an infant in cold blood. He picked up little Mr. K'Thragsh, who was probably already as big as Mr. Fullbelly, and brought him to the village. A woman who'd been widowed during an ogre attack took the baby ogre in and raised him as her own.'

'Amazing,' Dunk said. 'So, why did you ask about M'Grash?'

Cavre jerked his head toward the ship's stern. The ogre stood there, perched behind Percival Smythe, the catcher and sometimes pilot. When he caught Dunk's eye, he jumped for joy and nearly knocked Percy off the bridge. Dunk felt the ship sway with the ogre's movement.

'You'd better get over there before he capsizes the ship,' Cavre said.

Dunk put his empty bowl in the dishes bin as he walked down the deck to get the biggest hug he'd ever had in his life.

ONCE THE TEAM settled in at their winter camp, Pegleg drove them hard. 'I've never seen such a flabby and useless lot outside of Stirland!' he liked to roar at them. Slick tried to protest this slander against his people, but a wave of Pegleg's hook convinced him to let the issue lie.

Dunk took to the training as if his life depended on it. After his experience in the *Spike! Magazine* Tournament, he was sure that it did. If he didn't get better and smarter at this game, he knew it would be the death of him. Despite his initial discomfort about joining a Blood Bowl team, he wasn't ready to be murdered for it.

As the weeks wore on, Dunk found himself becoming not only a member of a team, but a family. The constant hours spent together forged the Hackers into a unit much stronger than the sum of its parts.

As with all families, though, there was some friction. Kur treated Dunk like an uppity child he felt compelled to humiliate at every turn. Dunk wasn't sure why the starting thrower disliked him so much, but he wasn't about to give in to the torture.

When, for what seemed like the fortieth time that day, Kur tripped Dunk as he raced past him while running a throwing route, Dunk leapt to his feet and belted Kur in the teeth. As soon as he did, he regretted it.

Instead of falling down, Kur just smiled at Dunk and pulled out one of his own front teeth. Then he made a fist around the tooth and pummelled Dunk with it.

Dunk's combat training had been with swords, not fists. He was faster than Kur, but he couldn't seem to get his arms up fast enough to block the taller man's hail of blows.

'Dumb kid,' Kur growled as he administered the beating like a malicious headmaster. 'If you want my job, you're going to have to *take* it from me.'

Under other circumstances, Dunk might have told Kur the truth, that he didn't really want his job, that he was content to wait on the bench and serve as a fill-in only when Kur couldn't manage it. Instead, he lashed out with his fist. His gauntlet cut the starting thrower across his forehead, splashing blood into his eyes.

Startled at how much damage he'd done, Dunk stopped, holding his fists before him to defend himself. He watched as Kur wiped the blood from his face, clearing his eyes with his fingers. Then the veteran of countless games snarled at Dunk.

'You cut my face,' he said. 'I'll cut your throat!'

Before Kur could close with Dunk to land another blow, a massive hand swept through and smacked him away. Dunk's head snapped up to see M'Grash standing between him and Kur now, growling at the veteran like a hungry lion.

'Stay away!' the ogre said to Kur, threatening him with a fist as big as Kur's head. 'Hurt Dunk, kill you.'

Kur got up slowly from where he'd been knocked to the turf. Everyone else on the team, including Pegleg had stopped to watch the fight. All eyes followed Kur, but no one spoke a word.

The veteran passer spat blood on to the ground. 'Your monster friend won't always be there for you.'

'Hold it right there, Mr. Ritternacht,' Pegleg said, cutting Kur off. 'You keep your rivalries on the field. If I hear different, then you've seen your last day on this team.'

Kur glared at Dunk, then bit his tongue and stomped off the field.

Dunk looked up at M'Grash and said, 'Thanks, big guy.'

The ogre patted him on the back. After weeks of this, Dunk was braced for it and managed to stay on his feet. 'Anything for friend,' M'Grash said. 'Anything.'

Ye Olde Trip to Araby was the kind of pub that Dunk thought he would have loved if he'd been born a dwarf. The bartender, a stubby creature, even for a dwarf, claimed that the place was the oldest known watering hole in all the dwarf kingdoms. It got its name from the fact that it was the last place dwarf warriors would stop for a drink before heading off to war against the soldiers of Araby in an effort to put an end to their jihad.

Unlike many of the other places Dunk had seen since entering the mostly subterranean city of Barak-Varr, the Trip was little more than a series of interconnected holes in walls. Most of the city featured the stunning, legendary architecture of the dwarfs, who were unparalleled in their skill with cutting and carving stone. The keepers of the Trip, however, had left the place pretty much the same over the centuries. Each chamber was little more than a natural cave with a levelled floor, a few torch-filled sconces on the walls, and scattered sets of low-slung tables and chairs. These were big enough for humans to sit at, but they were clearly meant for dwarfs instead.

Dunk had come here shortly after arriving in town because he'd heard that the Reavers often met here when they were in town. The Grey Wizards were sponsoring Dirk and Spinne's team in the Dungeonbowl, so Dunk figured he had a good chance of finding his brother here.

Shortly after waking up on the *Sea Chariot*, Dunk realised that he had never warned his brother about the murderous Skragger's threat. He promised himself he would do so at the first chance, so as soon as the Hackers arrived in Barak-Varr, he found his way to the Trip.

Dunk had never been in a city like this before, or in any dwarf settlement for that matter. There were dwarfs in Altdorf, of course, and Dunk had visited their pubs there to sample their legendary brews, but those places were only faint echoes of what he'd already seen here.

The docks of Barak-Varr had been lined with ships, many of which were fitted with paddles and mighty engines that drove them via steam. The city itself was carved into the faces of the cliffs that surrounded the Blood River as it spilled into the Black Gulf. From a distance, the cliffs looked like pock-marked cheese, but as the *Sea Chariot* grew closer, Dunk could see elaborate windows, doors, and balconies carved in and around the holes. High above, a flag of royal blue and a glittering gold axe and pick fluttered in the wind, declaring this place a home of dwarfs.

'It's the only major port the dwarfs have,' Slick had explained. 'They mostly live under mountains, and you don't get a lot of boat traffic there. They use those paddleboats to ferry goods up and down the Blood River to Everpeak, high in the Worlds Edge Mountains. That's how the people of Karaz-a-Karak get the supplies they need to survive. The rest of the world gets dwarf-made crafts and beers in exchange.'

'All the dwarfs I knew in Altdorf would spit if you mentioned the sea. Some of them wouldn't even cross the bridge over the River Reik. I'm surprised they have a port like this at all.'

'So are most of the dwarfs who don't live here. They think the dwarfs of Barak-Varr are mad. They call them "sea dwarfs", which is about as low as a dwarf can get. The ones who live here, though, they wear that title proud. They point out that there's money to be made trading goods here by the sea, and I've yet to meet a dwarf who didn't understand that kind of lure.'

A cheer from the largest of the pub's caverns went up again. This was where the Reavers were having their last dinner before the tournament started tomorrow, the bartender had said, but attendance was by invitation only. The pair of burly dwarfs flanking the doorway had kept Dunk at bay, so here he sat at the bar, nursing a delicious Gotrekugel's winter ale and waiting for Dirk to emerge. Dunk had sampled this beer in Altdorf, but it was miles better here. He wondered if it simply didn't travel well or if the Imperial dwarfs were secretly (and not nearly so masterfully) brewing it themselves.

'Hey, stranger,' a voice said from behind Dunk, 'buy a girl a drink?'

Dunk turned to see Spinne standing over him as he squatted on a short stool in front of the dwarf-sized bar. His heart melted like an icicle in a dragon's breath, and he smiled warmly at her.

Spinne reached out and caressed his cheek with her hand. 'It's good to see you again,' she said. 'After that match in Magritta, I was afraid I'd lost you.'

Dunk rubbed his head as he remembered that fall. He shuddered inwardly at the thoughts that sprang into his head.

'I never meant to hurt you,' she said. Then she caught herself. 'Well, not that badly.'

'Forget it,' Dunk said. 'Not remembering you were coming up behind me was a rookie mistake. It's my fault as much as yours.' He wasn't sure that was true, but he knew he wanted her to believe it. Then he added with a laugh, 'It won't happen again.'

'Well, well, well,' said a voice Dunk remembered far too well. He turned to see Lästiges emerge from a dark hole near the bar like some kind of a monstrous trap spider delighted to see not one but two victims come too close to her lair. 'It seems the rumours are true,' she said, innuendo dripping from her red-painted lips.

Spinne stepped back from Dunk immediately. 'There's nothing going on here,' she said, giving Dunk's cheek a playful slap. 'I'm just checking up on the health of a once and future victim.'

'That's not what my sources tell me,' Lästiges said, still gloating at her good fortune. 'I can see the headline now: "Black Widow Risks All for Rookie – and Loses Big!"'

'There's nothing wrong with what we have,' Dunk said defensively. He didn't see why Spinne would show this reporter any respect, much less fear.

'There's nothing wrong with nothing,' Spinne said, nodding in agreement. 'After all, it's common knowledge that the Reavers' contracts forbid the players from establishing relationships with members of other teams. It's a firing offence,' she said, looking right into Dunk's eyes.

Lästiges smirked at this. 'I have eyewitnesses that saw and then *heard* the two of you cavorting about during the *Spike! Magazine* tournament. I'm sure my editors would love to run a feature about this sort of thing. Sex really does sell, you know.' She looked Dunk up and down as if she could have eaten him alive, right there. 'Combine it with the violence of Blood Bowl and, oh, my!'

'I wasn't a Blood Bowl player that night,' Dunk said.

'What night?' Spinne said as she tried to surreptitiously grind her foot down on Dunk's toe. He rescued his foot and continued on.

'I didn't sign my contract until the next morning. Spinne didn't do anything wrong.'

The door to the Reavers' private room flew open. There was a roar of laughter and a tall figure stood silhouetted in the doorway.

'I hear I have family waiting out here for me,' Dirk said loudly. From his tone, Dunk could tell his brother had been drinking. A lot. 'Brother!'

Dunk rose from his stool and met Dirk halfway between the door and the bar. They embraced with a hug in which it seemed each was trying to squeeze the breath out of the other as they pounded each other on the back.

'It's good to see you again, Dunk,' Dirk said. 'Until I saw you go sailing over the top of that stadium, I don't think I realised how much I missed you.'

'Thanks,' Dunk said. 'I think.' Then he remembered what he'd come there for.

'Dirk,' he said, 'I have a warning for you from a black orc by the name of Skragger.'

'That old windbag,' Dirk said, noticing Lästiges and waving at her. 'What does he want?'

'He came and attacked me at the Hackers' camp on the opening day of the *Spike! Magazine* tournament. He said that if you broke his annual record for most touchdowns scored he'd kill you and everyone related to you.'

'Do you really think he could manage that second part? Maybe we'd be better off letting him try. Maybe he'd be the one to finally find our father again.'

Dunk frowned. 'I don't see how it would matter, if he kills us first.'

Dirk grimaced playfully at Dunk, one eye still on Lästiges. 'Don't let that old loincloth shake you, Dunk. He's harmless. I hear he does this kind of thing every year.'

'He's only killed three people so far,' Lästiges said.

Dunk glared at the reporter. '*Only* three.'

'This year.' She gazed at Dirk with her hungry eyes and drank him in. 'I'm sure a couple of young bruisers like you two could handle him.'

'He knocked me around pretty well,' Dunk said.

Dirk blushed for his brother and slapped Dunk on the back. 'I'm sure he caught you off guard.'

Dunk shrugged off Dirk's arm. 'Don't talk to me like that,' he said, letting his irritation show in his voice. 'You always do that. We're fine until I admit to a flaw, and then you're so superior.'

Dirk flashed a knowing smile at Lästiges, who giggled at it. 'I can't help what I am,' he said, grabbing Dunk's shoulders and shaking him playfully.

Dunk shoved him away. 'Don't,' he said coldly. 'I don't need any more favours from you. I know how you got Slick to do your dirty work for you. Trapping me to play this game just so you can parade yourself in front of me showing how successful you are.'

Dirk frowned. 'So it's like this again?' he said. 'That's gratitude for you. I thought maybe we were old enough to get past all that, but it's all the same, isn't it? I get myself set up in a new career, a new group of friends, and you can't stand it. You get jealous and just have to show everyone that the oldest Hoffnung is always the best.'

Dunk couldn't believe his ears, which grew redder and redder as Dirk spoke.

'You can just forget that,' Dirk said. 'This isn't the keep, and Lehrer isn't around to protect you. This is Blood Bowl. It's a killer's game, and you just don't have it in you to beat me at it.'

'He's a lover, not a fighter, I suppose,' Lästiges said, putting her hand on Spinne as she spoke, interrupting Dirk's rant. The younger brother stared at her, confused as to what she could mean. Then he saw the horrified look on Spinne's face, and the truth stabbed him in the heart.

'You didn't know?' the reporter giggled cattily. 'How tasty! Your older brother has been sleeping with your lady friend here.'

Spinne turned pale as the snow that Dunk used to play in with Dirk when they were kids. 'You thrice-damned bitch,' she breathed. Then she turned to Dirk, whose face was as red as a gargoyle's eyes. 'Please,' she said to him. 'I was going to tell you.'

Dunk stared at Spinne, trying to figure out just what was going on. He wasn't looking at his younger brother when he struck.

'You bloody bastard!' Dirk roared as his fist slammed into Dunk's face, knocking him back into the bar. 'How dare you!'

Dunk wanted to talk this over with his brother, who he loved deeply, despite the problems that had torn them and their family apart over the past few years. He wanted to sit down with him over a couple steins and figure out his history with Spinne and just what she'd been thinking about playing with their hearts. He wanted to do this peaceably and calmly, most of all.

Instead, his temper got the better of him. As Lehrer had called it, 'the red veil' dropped over his eyes, and the next thing he knew he was pounding at his brother's face with both fists, as hard as he possibly could.

Just before Dunk struck back, he heard Dirk whisper something like, 'I'm sorry.' But it was too late. When Dunk launched himself off the bar and smashed into his brother, the time for words, for apologies, was over.

Dirk raised his arms to fend off Dunk's fists. Frustrated by his inability to hurt his brother, Dunk lowered his shoulder and charged into him instead, sending him hurtling backward through the door by which he'd come. The two dwarf guards tried to stop them, but the one who managed to get a hand on Dirk only got pulled along, leaving the other to gape after them.

Dirk slammed his brother into the long dining table in the centre of the Reavers' private room. Half-empty steins of beer, stacks of dirty dishes, and bits of bones and other less sturdy foods went flying everywhere, splattering every person in the room.

The Reavers sitting at the table scattered as the brothers rolled across the table and through the remains of the meal. The veterans grabbed their beers as they backed away, leaving the rookies without a drink to enjoy during the brawl.

When the brothers finally came to a halt in the remnants of the roast boar, Dirk was somehow on top, and the Reavers let out a great cheer. This distracted Dirk, who glanced around at the others and flashed a sheepish grin.

Dunk flailed about until his hand fell upon a half-eaten haunch. He grabbed the bone by the end and swung it up hard against the side of Dirk's head, knocking him off not only himself but the table too. The crowd booed at this, but a few brave veterans applauded Dunk's resourcefulness.

Dunk leapt off the table to see Dirk scrambling away from him, heading for a shuttered window on the opposite side of the room from where they'd come in. As Dirk reached the window, he turned around just in time for the charging Dunk to hit him with a two-armed tackle.

The two brothers crashed through the window and fell atop a dining table in another underground chamber below. The dwarfs eating there had been in the middle of a toast to the Colleges of Magic for bringing the lucrative Dungeonbowl to their land once again when the two men landed on their table, shattering its legs and crushing it to the floor.

'You're mad!' Dirk said as the two crawled off the table in different directions, the wind momentarily taken from their sails. 'You could have killed us!'

'I don't have what it takes to kill,' Dunk wheezed bitterly as he staggered to his feet. 'Remember?'

'I didn't mean that,' Dirk puffed as he rose just as shakily. 'I was mad.' He gulped for air a moment before continuing. 'Spinne dumped me a few months back. She said she'd found someone else.'

'I didn't know!' Dunk said. 'I thought you were just team-mates.'

Dirk grabbed a stein from one of the stunned dwarfs and drained it as he stumbled toward an empty serving table sitting in front of a large window glazed with gold-tinted glass. 'Then stopped bedding my damned team-mates!' Dirk raged.

From the room above, the Reavers roared their approval. A couple of smaller voices said, 'Awww!'

Dirk smashed the stein on the smooth stone floor. 'Forget it,' he said. 'You can have the whore. I was through with her anyway.'

Dunk had been ready to call the fight done, but Dirk's comment about Spinne stuck like a knife in his ear. He growled with mind-numbing anger and charged at Dirk again. This time, his younger brother was ready.

Dirk grabbed the oncoming Dunk by the shoulders and rolled backward, allowing Dunk's momentum to send him flying toward the tinted window just beyond. Whilst Dunk was surprised at this manoeuvre, he managed to grab hold of Dirk through sheer determination, and refused to let go. As he smashed through the window and cascaded with the shattered glass into the open, sea air beyond, he hauled his brother with him.

A moment after they broke through the window, the two brothers looked around to see where they were.

In the distance, Dunk glimpsed the sun setting over the western side of the gulf, a red-orange orb that suddenly seemed like the entrance to some daemon-infested realm. He felt the wind rushing past his face as he and Dirk fell, and he saw the sunset-mirrored sea reaching up toward them like a sky toppling in the absolute wrong direction. He started to scream, and Dirk joined him in a horrified harmony that lasted until they blasted through the gulf's gleaming surface and into the frigid waters below.

Hitting the sea stunned Dunk for a moment, and the seawater threatened to race into his lungs, but he managed to hold his breath long enough to kick his way to the surface.

As Dunk broke back into the air, the first word from his lips was, 'Dirk!' He whipped his head about, searching for any sign of his brother, even a floating body, but there was nothing there. He panicked for three long seconds before his younger brother burst through the waves in front of him, gasping for air and coughing up the sea.

Dunk swam over to his brother with three painful strokes and grabbed him underneath his arms. He held him there until he was done coughing and could breathe again.

'You all right?' Dirk said when he could finally talk again.

'Yeah,' Dunk said, relieved. 'You?'

'Yeah.'

Dunk let his brother loose and the two of them started to swim toward the docks at the bottom of the cliff, only fifty yards away.

'Let's never do this again,' Dirk said as they headed toward a swarm of dock workers who had seen them cascade into the chilly gulf.

'Deal,' said Dunk.

THE NEXT DAY, Dunk sat in the stands for the first Dungeonbowl game of the tournament, alongside Pegleg and about half of his teammates. His nose was red and raw from all his sneezing, and every bit of him was sore. Falling into the Black Gulf from a dozen storeys up was better than being tossed over the edge of the *Spike! Magazine* Tournament's stadium, but not by much. And this time, he'd done it to himself.

'Mr. Hoffnung,' Pegleg said from where he sat behind Dunk. 'I understand your brother won't be able to start this game because of your fracas with him last night.'

Dunk hung his head in shame. 'Damn,' he said softly. Then he felt a hook rest gently on his shoulder.

'Well done, Mr. Hoffnung,' the Hackers coach said. 'I have a hundred crowns on the Champions of Death.'

Slick, who was sitting next to Dunk, smothered a cackle.

Dunk sighed and looked around at the large room in which they sat. They sat on hard, stone seats carved out of the rock in a stair-step fashion that allowed the people behind to see over the people in front of them. There was room for at least a thousand people in the room, maybe more, and the seats were rapidly filling up.

The crowd here seemed a bit more polite than the ones in Dunk's last Blood Bowl game. Perhaps that was because the dwarfs charged exorbitant amounts for the few tickets left over after team representatives got their seats. On the way into the observation room, one dwarf had offered Dunk five hundred crowns for his place. Another had made him a far more disturbing proposition involving a pair of young dwarf ladies and a stick of limp celery.

The far wall of the room was smooth and flat, and covered with several images depicting the interior of a well-lit dungeon somewhere in the depths of Barak-Varr. It was a moment before Dunk realised that the images were more than perfectly lucid paintings. When he saw a squad of six Reavers in their blue and white uniforms appear in an image to the left, he realised these were Cabalvision pictures of what was happening in the dungeon at that moment.

Dunk looked up behind him. At the top of the room, a score of dwarfs fiddled with a set of crystal balls through which they somehow shone bright lights. The light passed through the balls and a set of lenses which somehow focused the images on the large wall, allowing all of the spectators to watch and cheer for the players at once.

Six players dressed in the distinctive black uniforms of the Champions of Death appeared in an image on the right of the wall. These included a rotting mummy, a slavering vampire, a nasty wight, a hungry ghoul, a tottering zombie, and a rattling skeleton. As they appeared in the room, seemingly out of thin air, they grouped together into a horrifying huddle, their backs to the camra watching them.

Although Dunk had spent the past three months learning the fundamentals of Blood Bowl until they were second nature to him, he was mystified by what he saw. There was no field, no one had a ball, and the other images on the wall showed a series of rooms and passageways that had six identical chests scattered among them.

'What's going on here?' Dunk asked Slick.

'Do you really want to know?' Slick said. 'You're not going to play. You just have to sit back and enjoy.'

'My brother might end up out there soon,' Dunk said, not mentioning that he'd seen Spinne among the Reavers already in the dungeon.

'The way you two fought yesterday, I'd have thought you wouldn't care about his safety.'

Dunk just glared at the halfling.

Slick cleared his throat and put on his best instructor's voice.

'Seventy-five years ago, the head wizards of the Colleges of Magic decided to resolve a long-running dispute by sponsoring a Blood Bowl tournament. Each of the ten colleges backed a team. The supporters of the winning team won the argument. The wizards liked it so much, they made it a regular event. So, here we are.' Slick smiled broadly.

Dunk stared at him. 'That's it?'

'Ah, so you want the *whole* story? As you wish.' Slick cracked his knuckles before diving in again. He pointed at various images on the wall as he talked.

'Most Dungeonbowl games are just played in the Barak-Varr Bowl, an underground stadium complete with a regular field and stands. This year is a special occasion because we're playing under the classic Dungeonbowl rules, which haven't been used for decades.

'You see where the two teams are right now?' The halfling pointed at the images to the far right and left of the wall, where the representatives from both the Reavers and the Champions of Death milled about. 'Those are the two end zones. Each room has only one way in or out of it, so getting in can be a real battle. The real poser is that the players have to find the ball first.

'You see those chests scattered about the place?' Slick said, pointing them out as he went. 'There are six scattered throughout the dungeon. The ball is in one of them.'

Dunk rubbed his chin. 'What's in the other chests?' he said suspiciously.

Slick clapped Dunk on the shoulder proudly. 'Now you're thinking like a Dungeonbowl player! They're trapped, of course.'

'Trapped?'

Slick nodded. 'Nothing in them but explosives. They make a good, little boom when you lift the lid.'

Dunk shook his head in disbelief. 'So, five times out of six, the chest blows up in your face.'

'See, there's the fun of it!'

Dunk goggled at the halfling. 'If you're sitting here watching, maybe. They must go through dozens of players.'

'Not quite. The first team to score a touchdown wins the game. Also, the dwarfs know their explosives. Some of the players who open the wrong chests don't even have to be carried off the field.' Noticing Dunk's look of disbelief, Slick added, 'Son, it can't be any worse than having an ogre hit you, right?'

Dunk nodded along with that. Even the few times M'Grash had blocked him in practice had been enough for him to pause to rethink his recent career choice.

'How do they pass the ball with those low ceilings?' Dunk asked. As a thrower, he figured this was something he should know.

'They bounce it off the walls, believe it or not. Wait until you see it!'

Dunk looked back at Pegleg for help, but his coach just looked down at him. 'If the game bothers you so much, Mr. Hoffnung, perhaps you should thank Nuffle that we couldn't find a sponsor. The Colleges of Magic each select a team packed with members of certain races. The Grey Wizards favour humans, and they chose the Reikland Reavers this year, just as they usually do.'

Dunk turned back to watch the images moving on the wall. 'So unless we can prove we're better than the Reavers, we'll never get to play in the Dungeonbowl.'

'Or unless something happens to them,' said Slick.

Dunk shot him a dirty look.

'What?' the halfling said guiltlessly. 'It's a hard game. Things happen.'

'That's my brother's team,' Dunk said.

'Weren't you trying to kill him yesterday yourself?'

'Just to beat him *half* to death,' Dunk snapped, letting his irritation with the topic show.

'Ah,' Slick said knowingly, 'much better.'

Mercifully, a whistle blew at that moment, and the game began. 'That's the start of the game, folks,' said Bob's voice. 'The Reavers, led by catcher Spinne Schönheit, charge headlong into the dungeon. The Impaler leaps out in front of the Champions of Death, leaving "Rotting" Rick Bupkiss and Matt "Bones" Klimesh behind to protect the end zone.'

'This is going to be a real bloodletter of a game, Bob,' said Jim's voice, 'at least if the Champs get their way. None of them have blood of their own to spill!'

A flash of light on one of the images caught Dunk's eye, and he saw Spinne appear in the middle of a room.

'What happened there?' he asked Slick. 'With Spinne?'

'She stepped on the teleport pads in the room next to the Reavers' end zone. It's risky – some players who do it don't show up again for a few days – but it can really pay off.' The halfling pointed up at Spinne. 'See, she jumped three rooms ahead of where she was, and she ended up right near a chest.'

'And that's paying off?'

'Wait until she opens the chest to see.'

In the image in the centre of the wall, Spinne leaned over and grabbed the handle on the front of the chest. After taking a deep breath, she flung it wide.

A blast of noise and light knocked Spinne off her feet. For a moment, Dunk held his breath, his heart stopped too. But then Spinne staggered back up, holding her head. After a moment, she snarled and raced straight back toward the glowing circle on the floor that Dunk realised was the teleport pad.

Spinne blinked away, and Dunk snapped his head back to look at the room from which she'd originally come. She wasn't there.

'She disappeared!' Dunk choked.

'No, son,' Slick said, pointing off toward the right. 'There she is.'

Dunk followed Slick's finger to see Spinne appear in the middle of another room. The ghoul and wight playing for the Champions of Death were here, and they immediately charged toward Spinne.

'How?' Dunk asked. 'Ouch!' he said involuntarily as Spinne slammed the wight back into the ground. The ghoul, though, grabbed her and repaid the favour.

'Oh, that's going to leave a mark in the morning!' Bob's voice said.

'If she survives that long,' Jim's voice chipped in. 'Gilda "the Girly Ghoul" Fleshsplitter looks hungry. I hear their coach, the legendary necromancer Tomolandry the Undying, has been starving them for days!'

Spinne got to her knees and ploughed the grey-skinned ghoul back into the teleporter pad. The creature disappeared in a flash of light. With a quick look around to see that there were no chests in this room, Spinne raced off through the door to the east.

'The teleporter pads move people at random,' Slick said. 'They aren't linked in matched pairs. If you step on one, you could end up on any other, or nowhere at all.'

Dunk saw flashes at both ends of the wall. 'What's happening there?' he asked. He saw a new player appear in each end zone.

'That's how the players get into the dungeon,' Slick said. 'Each team's dugout has a teleporter pad too, but this one is matched to a spot in their end zone. The coaches can feed in new players one at a time, as fast as the teleporter will work.'

Dunk shook his head. 'Doesn't that make for a pretty crowded game?'

Slick smiled. 'It makes for mayhem, son. Beautiful mayhem.' The spectators roared as an undead player opened another chest that exploded in his face. Slick gestured all around him. 'You have to give the people what they want!' he shouted.

Suddenly a loud noise erupted from the images on the wall. The players in the dungeon all looked up for a moment. Several of them screamed in terror. There was a sickening rumbling noise. Then the wall went blank and bright, the white light from behind the crystal balls shining through nothing but clear glass.

'This is strange,' said Bob's voice. 'I haven't seen light this bright in three hundred years!'

The crowd buzzed in confusion for a moment. Then, almost as one, all of the dwarfs jumped up and raced toward the exits. This left the visitors, guests, and members of the other teams – those who had bothered to show up to watch this match – milling about and wondering what had happened.

'What happened?' Dunk asked. Slick just shrugged. It was then that Dunk noticed that one of the images was still there on the wall, although it was pitch black.

Before the halfling could open his mouth, Bob's voice rang out again. 'Jim, Nuri Nottmeeson, the Dungeonbowl grounds manager, has just handed me a note. Oh! By all of Chaos's craftiest gods, this is the darkest day in Dungeonbowl history!'

'Bob?' Jim's voice had lost its traditional swagger. 'Bob? What is it?'

'The dungeon the Reavers and Champions of Death were playing in has collapsed. I repeat, *the dungeon has collapsed!*'

THAT EVENING, DUNK tried to get into the Trip again, with Slick and M'Grash in tow, but the owner, a dour dwarf on the best of days, wouldn't hear of it. 'Have you not done enough damage around here?' he growled.

Dunk slunk away with his tail between his legs, his two friends behind. The dwarfs who passed them in the massive halls of Barak-Varr stared at the three of them: a halfling (small as a dwarf child), a human (taller than a dwarf, but barely as broad), and an ogre (bigger than the other two put together). With Dunk too depressed to think much, Slick took charge.

'Most of the pubs in this city are built for people only slightly larger than myself. They're large enough to accommodate a few humans, though not in big numbers. I only know of one other establishment in this complex that can seat an ogre at a table,' the halfling said as the trio wound through the labyrinthine passages cut expertly through the cliff face. 'This makes the choice much simpler.'

Slick guided the three friends through the Great Hall of Barak-Varr, a cavernous affair that made even M'Grash seem small by comparison. About halfway down the hall, on the right, they veered off towards a massive set of stone doors, in which was set a smaller set of dwarf-sized doors. A set of glowing dwarf runes blinked overhead in a pattern that seemed to call to Dunk, even though he could not read the Khazalid.

'It translates roughly as "House of Booze",' the halfling said. 'It's my kind of place.'

As the trio approached, the dwarf doorman called to someone inside. By the time they reached the pub's threshold, the stone doors were already rotating back silently on their massive stone hinges. The three then walked under the open archway, which stood at least twice as tall as even M'Grash.

As the giant doors closed behind them, the trio sauntered into the pub. It was a huge place with wide-open aisles running between tables with tops set at all different levels. The upper reaches of the room were filled with smoke rising from the long pipes on which many of the patrons puffed, but this was so high above that it almost seemed like a thick layer of clouds that might open up and rain down on the patrons below at any moment.

Slick led the others to a large table, the top of which stood far over his head. It was perfectly sized for M'Grash, who sat down comfortably at one of the chairs. Slick climbed up a ladder built into the side of one of the chairs, which cunningly had a tiered back. Slick sat on the highest of the tiers while a pair of dwarf waiters pushed him close enough that he could make use of the table.

Dunk had to climb into his own chair, although he was able to pull himself close to the table on his own. As he made himself comfortable, Slick ordered a round of drinks for them. They arrived only moments later, carried by dwarfs walking on multi-jointed steel stilts. Slick and Dunk received standard-sized steins of Delver's Doppelbock, a local specialty said to be brewed in the deepest of dwarf mines. M'Grash, on the other hand, was brought a barrel-sized stein of his favourite Killer Genuine Draft.

'Thank Nuffle that Dirk will be all right,' Slick said.

'And Spinne too,' Dunk said, raising his glass. It was a bittersweet kind of relief. Of the eight Reavers caught in the dungeon when it collapsed, four had been crushed to death in the disaster. Dirk, hurt though he was, had been the last Reaver to enter the dungeon.

'Have you visited them in the Halls of Mercy yet?' Slick asked.

Dunk shook his head. 'The doctors said they couldn't see anyone until tomorrow.'

'Isn't that convenient?' a voice called up from below. Dunk looked down to see Lästiges standing at the bottom of a chair next to his. She kept talking as she mounted the chair and climbed up to sit next the others, a pair of dwarfs ready to push her close to the tabletop. 'The loss of the great rookie phenom's main rival – his hated brother, who he nearly killed the night before – and the destruction of the team that handed the Hackers' their most recent defeat.'

Dunk glared at the reporter. 'This is a private party,' he said coldly.

'Excellent,' Lästiges smiled at a dwarf with orc's blood on his axe. 'I'm sure you have a lot to celebrate. Either way, I'm sure your employer won't mind if I cover it.'

'We're not here as a Blood Bowl team, miss,' Slick said. 'Just fans of the game.'

'Really?' Lästiges said in a mocking tone. 'Are you sure about that?'

'What's your game?' Dunk asked. He was tired, grumpy, and wanted to be left alone to have a drink with his friends.

'The question is, what's yours? Dungeonbowl is the answer tonight, it seems.'

Dunk opened his mouth to bark at the woman, but Slick silenced him with a wave of his hand. 'Wait,' he said, concern etched on his face. 'What are you saying?' he asked the reporter.

Lästiges smiled, her crimson-painted lips parting to reveal a set of perfectly even, sharp teeth. 'You haven't heard? Instead of dropping out of the tournament, the Grey Wizards have chosen another team to substitute for the Reavers.'

Dunk scowled at the reporter. 'Who?'

'Who else?' she smirked. 'What other human-centric team is right here in Barak-Varr and ready to play? Why the Bad Bay Hackers, of course!'

Slick let out a cheer, and M'Grash joined him, rocking the table with his enthusiasm. Dunk put his hands over his face and sighed.

'As I was saying,' Lästiges said once the cheers faded, 'how much more convenient can you get? This couldn't have worked out better for you if you'd planned it.'

'I didn't plan anything.'

'So it just happened? A kind of spur-of-the-moment sort of a thing? How opportunistic!'

'I had nothing to do with it!' Dunk shouted, standing half out of his seat. As he did, he realised the people at the neighbouring tables were looking at him. Then his eyes settled on two wizards in black robes with red sashes watching him from near the door. They were the same ones from that night in the Bad Water: the tall dwarf and the short elf.

'Ah,' Lästiges said approvingly. 'I see you've finally noticed my friends over there. They make a charming couple, don't they?'

'Are you working for them, miss?' Slick asked, a bit of an edge in his voice.

'I prefer to say I'm working *with* them. They're so clueless on their own. All they understand is *enforcement*, nothing about how to run an *investigation*.'

'And that's your specialty,' Dunk said.

Lästiges reached out and patted Dunk on the cheek. 'And everyone says that Dirk is the brains in the family.'

Dunk looked back over at the Game Wizards and waved at them with a mock smile. They ignored him and went back to muttering at each other over their glasses of dark red wine.

'They really are clueless,' he said. 'One of the biggest threats to the game is standing right behind them, and they haven't even noticed.'

Lästiges turned around to see who Dunk was talking about. She peered hard at the GWs and all around them. 'I think you're the clueless one, rookie,' she said. 'There's nothing there.'

'See that black orc standing at the bar behind your friends?'

Dunk jerked his head in that direction, and Lästiges, Slick, and even M'Grash stared after him.

Lästiges wrinkled her brow for a moment, then said, 'Skragger? You *can't* mean Skragger.'

'That's exactly who I mean,' Dunk said as he raised his stein in a toast to the monstrous orc. Skragger responded in kind with his own stein of Bloodweiser, then arched his eyebrows and jerked a long, sharp-nailed index finger across his throat with a wicked smile.

Dunk gave the black orc a thumbs-up sign and then turned back to Lästiges. 'He's afraid someone's going to break his record for most touchdowns in a season, remember,' he said. 'He says if Dirk tries it, he'll kill us both. He threatened Kur too. You were with me in The Trip when Dirk told me.'

Lästiges laughed. 'Kur doesn't have a chance.'

'You're missing the point,' Dunk said. 'He's trying to keep players from performing at their peak potential, and that can only hurt your friends and your employers at *Spike!*'

Lästiges wrinkled her snowy brow at that. 'How do you figure?'

'How many Cabalvision licenses do you think Wolf Sports could sell if someone was close to breaking Skragger's record. I mean, besides all the great, high-scoring games leading up to that. The few games before, during, and after the breaking of the record? Blood Bowl fans would be tripping over themselves to lay down their crowns.'

'That's an interesting angle,' Lästiges said, nodding her approval. 'Of course, it hasn't occurred to you that he might also have been behind the "accident" today. Or that having the GWs focus on him might take the heat off you for a bit.'

Dunk shook his head. 'I'm not worried about that. I'm innocent. I just want to keep people safe.'

Lästiges reached out and patted Dunk's cheek again. 'Well played,' she said. 'I'd love to think anyone is that altruistic, but, well, this is Blood Bowl we're talking about.'

Dunk smiled, 'Anything I can do to help a good friend like you.'

'Insincerity. Now, *that* I understand. You're serious about the threats though?'

'Slick was there.'

Lästiges grimaced at the halfling. 'I don't think I could cite someone with the name "Slick" as a reliable source.'

'Listen here, miss,' Slick began.

Lästiges cut him off and changed the subject, addressing Dunk again. 'I hear you were seen talking with Gunther the Gobbo in Magritta. That's interesting company you keep.'

'No more so than you.'

'Touché. What did he offer you?'

'Maybe I just wanted to place a bet.'

'That's against most team charters. It's in the fine print of your contract.' Lästiges hesitated. 'You *can* read, can't you?'

'Well enough to know you're not much of a writer.'

'Perhaps you read the exposé I did on the Gobbo last summer? No? That was before your time, I suppose.'

Dunk shrugged.

'I found evidence that the Gobbo is the head of a vast conspiracy of players that runs through nearly all of the top Blood Bowl teams. Together, they work his odds-making racket well enough for him to be able to pay off at least a score of players.'

'I didn't think anyone would care about cheating in Blood Bowl.'

'They do when it's their money on the line. People lay down bets on these teams assuming they're all doing their best to win.'

'And some of the players are professional chokers.'

'Not everyone is good enough to get paid for it.' Lästiges patted Dunk's hand as she said this, and he flashed back to that long fall over the edge of the stadium in Magritta.

'I suppose this conspiracy has a colourful name?'

'The Black Jerseys.'

'Cute. Did you come up with that?'

'I didn't have to. They use it themselves.'

'What's this have to do with the accident yesterday?'

Lästiges leaned forward, every bit serious now. Slick practically climbed on the table to get close enough to hear everything she said, and even M'Grash tilted an ear over her.

'Someone's been killing off Blood Bowl players like snotlings this year,' she said. 'Every time I turn around, I hear about somebody dying under mysterious circumstances. Take the Hackers, for instance.'

'I had nothing to do with those killings in the tryout camp.'

'So I hear, but that's not what I meant. Ever wonder why there were so many openings on the Hackers with such short notice before the first Major of the year?'

Dunk realised he had not, and the fact irritated him. As he finished his beer, the dwarf server was there with another for him in an instant.

When he picked it up, he felt a piece of paper wrapped around the grip. As he spoke with Lästiges, he tried to peel it off without her noticing.

Slick filled in the details for Dunk. 'The Hackers lost four players only a month beforehand, son. That's why I was out looking for recruits.'

'What happened to them?'

Slick shrugged. 'No one knows. They just never showed up for practice one day, and no one heard from them again.'

'Odds are they were murdered,' Lästiges said.

M'Grash's elbow slipped off the table, and the ogre bounced his chin off the tabletop, sending all of the other drinks leaping a foot into the air. Dunk was still working at the mysterious paper, so he kept control of his stein. Slick and Lästiges, on the other hand, ended up wearing what was left of their drinks.

'Sorry!' M'Grash rumbled with a sincerity Dunk was sure Lästiges couldn't understand. 'So sorry! Fell asleep!'

As the others – along with a handful of dwarf servers – fussed over the mess, Dunk tore the paper off his stein and unrolled it. On it was written a note. It read:

'My offer stands! Let's do business!'

It was signed 'The Gobbo.'

Dunk scanned the room, still in his chair while the others had dismounted to help the waiters get at the mess. There in the back of the room, directly opposite from the Game Wizards, sat Gunther the Gobbo, raising his stein and favouring Dunk with a greasy grin.

Dunk flipped the Gobbo an obscene gesture that drew gasps from everyone seated on that side of the pub. Then he slid down from his chair and said to Slick and M'Grash, 'Let's get back to our quarters. It seems we have a game tomorrow.'

THE NEXT AFTERNOON, Dunk stood in the visiting team's dugout, outside of a different dungeon, suited up and ready for the game. He'd tried sleeping last night, but wrestling with worrying about his brother and the things Lästiges had told him had ruined much of that. Still, he was ready to get in and play. Frustrated as he was, he felt like breaking something – or someone.

The game was to be a rematch of the game interrupted by the cave-in, with the Hackers taking the Reavers' place. The Champions of Death, being already dead, hadn't lost any players yesterday. A few of them had been flattened, but Coach Tomolandry had managed to patch them back together in time for the game.

Dunk looked around the room. The entire team was on edge. They'd had no time to prepare for this tournament, and Dungeon-bowl differed from traditional Blood Bowl so much that there were sure to be mistakes. Plus, there were the teleporter pads, which few of the players trusted.

Dunk sympathised with this. In his experience, magic was something to avoid. The people who worked it were either power-mad wizards who cut deals with unknowable forces or power-mad clerics who cut deals with inconstant gods. Being sponsored by one such group of wizards in a tournament overseen by the largest and most powerful organisation they had set his hair on end.

'Listen up!' Pegleg called from the front of the room, where he had stood on an empty bench in front of an open locker. 'We have five minutes to game time, and I have something to say.'

The room fell quiet, and all eyes stared at the coach, some glumly, some excitedly, but all intently.

'This game may be more than we bargained for when we came to Barak-Varr, but it's also the chance of a lifetime. If we do well here, we may end up with a long-term sponsorship from the Grey Wizards, and the Dungeonbowl could become a regular stop for us.'

No one cheered at this news.

'To sweeten the pot, the Grey Wizards put up another 50,000 crowns for us. We get half that just for showing up to play today, with 1,000 crowns going to each of you!'

The players whooped it up at the news. M'Grash picked up Dunk in a big hug that threatened to break his ribs.

'And we get the rest if we win the tournament!' The players cheered again, and a knowing smile spread across Pegleg's normally dour face. After giving the noise a moment to die down, the coach put out his hand and hook to signal for silence.

'I want these six players to line up in front of the teleportation pad: Mr. Ritternacht, Mr. Cavre, Miss Mardretti, Mr. K'Thragsh, Mr. Baldurson, and Mr. Otto Waltheim. You're our starters. When you're ready, say a prayer and step on the teleportation pad. With luck, you'll end up in our end zone.'

The six players hustled into position. As Kur strode by Dunk, he shouldered the rookie aside with a satisfied grin. Dunk picked himself up and told himself that three minutes before game time wasn't the right moment to practise his home lobotomy skills on the veteran thrower.

'The rest of you, line up in this order. As soon as the game starts, I'll send you on to the teleporter pad one at a time. Mr. Hoffnung, Mr. Andreas Waltheim, Mr. Klemmer, Mr. Reyes, Mr. Smythe, Mr. Engelhard, Mr. Karlmann, Mr. Hoffstetter, Mr. Albrecht, and Mr. Sherwood.'

The remainder of the team lined up behind Dunk as he stood right behind the starting six. He was thrilled that Pegleg had enough confidence in him to make him the seventh man. If he couldn't be in the starting six, this was literally the next best thing.

'There's no secret to this game,' Pegleg said over the heads of everyone but M'Grash. 'Find the ball and stick it in the end zone. What could be simpler?'

The players all laughed nervously.

'Oh,' Pegleg said, 'and try not to be too surprised if a chest blows up in your face.'

With that, the horn in the dugout sounded, announcing the start of the game. 'Get in there!' Pegleg shouted at the starters. 'And make us some gold!'

The starting six stormed onto the teleporter pad and disappeared in six quick flashes of light. Dunk rubbed his eyes and got ready to follow them. In two minutes, the game would begin, and he wanted to be in it as quick as he could.

These were two of the longest minutes of Dunk's life. He looked over to where Pegleg watched a Cabalvision feed of the match on a large crystal ball. He saw the starting Hackers flexing and stretching in the end zone.

'Mr. Hoffnung,' Pegleg said to him. 'You're my wild card. I want you jumping onto every teleporter pad you can find until you spot a chest. Then open it.'

'Then I take the ball and run.'

Pegleg laughed. 'If there is one. Your job is to eliminate as many chests as you can until you fall over.'

Dunk gulped at that, but he didn't have much time to think about it. The whistle went off, and the game was on.

'Wait,' Pegleg said, holding up his hook for a moment. Then he snapped it down. 'Go!'

Dunk stepped on the pad. For a moment, he was somewhere else, someplace horrible and twisted, both dark and light at the same time. He drew in a breath to scream, but before he could start the Hackers' end zone room appeared around him.

Dunk bit his tongue, then dashed off down the corridor leading out of the room. He could see M'Grash lumbering along in front of him. The ogre's job was to protect the Hackers' end zone, which Dunk thought he might be able to do just by sitting down in the hallway. As the rookie raced past, he clapped the ogre on the leg. This made him feel tiny, which – he realised then – must be how Slick always felt around him.

In the first room after the corridor, Dunk spotted the telltale glow of a teleporter pad. He raced over and stepped on it, closing his eyes as he did. He felt the hot wind of that other place on his skin for a moment, and when the cool dank air of the dungeon replaced it, he opened his eyes. He thought he'd heard screams while in between pads, but he couldn't be sure those hadn't been from somewhere in the dungeon instead.

Dunk found himself standing on a rickety rope bridge strung over a bottomless chasm. His hands lashed out to grab on to the guide ropes and steady himself before he cascaded over the edge and into oblivion. As he did, he looked up and saw the Impaler – a thick-muscled, pale-skinned man dressed in the Champs' black uniform – standing at the bridge's far end, the razor-sharp tips of his spiked gauntlet poised over one of the bridge's four main ropes.

'Velcome,' the vampire said in a Kislevite accent, his eyes glowing red with bloodlust as he bared his fangs in an evil smile. 'And goot-bye.' He brought his fist down, and the spikes slashed through one of the ropes Dunk held.

Dunk felt himself starting to fall, so he released the severed rope and started forward. He had to get to the end of the bridge before the vampire completed its lethal work.

The Impaler swung his other fist at the guide rope, and Dunk was forced to let that loose too or allow it to pull him into the abyss. He realised he would never make it to the end of the bridge before the vampire brought it down, and he glanced around desperately for some other means of escape.

Dunk's eyes fell on the teleporter pad behind him. If he could just reach it, he had a chance. He whipped about and raced back toward the pad. As he did, he heard the Impaler's steel-clad fist fall again and sever one of the bridge's two base ropes with a sickening chop.

Dunk dove for the glowing circle in the middle of the bridge, even as he felt the bridge's wooden planks start to give way beneath him. The toe of his boot found purchase in the gap between two boards, and he launched forward as hard as his legs would push him. Just as the planks spun away beneath him, he stretched out and slapped the pad with his open hand, and he was somewhere else.

Dunk felt himself falling, falling, falling, and when he arrived in another room elsewhere in the dungeon he hit the ground hard. Only his armour prevented him from cracking a rib or worse. He scrambled to his feet and smelled first rather than saw the Champs' mummy – the back of his jersey read Ramen-Tut – opening the chest on the other side of the room.

The scent of ancient must and disease made Dunk's eyes itch, and he flinched involuntarily as the creature flung open the chest. Dunk opened his eyes again when he realised there hadn't been a big boom, and he saw Ramen-Tut triumphantly pulling the ball from the open chest.

Dunk dug in his feet to charge at the mummy, but before he could, Kur raced past him, yelling, 'Get out of the way, punk! He's mine!'

Determined to not let Kur hog all the glory, Dunk chased after the man, straight at the mummy. Ramen-Tut turned, the ball in his spindly, gauze-wrapped arms, and hissed at the two oncoming Hackers. Green gases erupted from the mummy's faceguard, but if Kur wasn't going to back down then neither was Dunk.

The two Hackers slammed into Ramen-Tut at once. Dunk was surprised how light the creature was, but he supposed having all of your internal organs removed would do that to you. He and Kur knocked the mummy back into the chest and piled on him, trying to strip away the ball.

'Urrr!' the mummy groaned as the Hackers laid into him. Then the groan transformed into a desert-dry scream.

One moment Dunk was wrestling with a rotting mummy, trying to keep down his breakfast, and the next he found himself holding a loose bundle of bandages filled with nothing more than dust. Surprised, he inhaled a double lungful of the stuff and got it caked in his eyes.

Dunk stumbled back, hacking up whatever was left of Ramen-Tut from his chest while he wiped the ancient grit from his eyes. As he did, he nearly stepped on the football. Still coughing, he reached down and picked it up, then tucked it into his arms.

'Give me that ball, punk!' Kur snarled.

Dunk spun about to see Kur standing before him with his hands reaching out to him. 'Now!' The starting thrower said.

Dunk hesitated, and the impatient Kur lowered his shoulder and charged at him. More from reflex than anything else, Dunk dodged to the left, and Kur sailed straight past him.

'Nooo!' Kur shouted.

Dunk spun around to see that he was alone. The teleport pad pulsed softly where Kur had once been. The rookie couldn't help but grin as he turned to run from the room.

A moment later, Dunk dashed back into the room with three Champions of Death on his tail: a rattling skeleton and a pair of rotting zombies that smelled worse than a pile of dead skunks. The teleport pads had disoriented him, and he had no idea what direction he was supposed to even be headed in. He decided to take his chance with the teleporter pad again instead of trying to figure it out. They were supposed to toss people around the dungeon at random, so with luck he wouldn't end up wherever Kur had gone.

Dunk kept his eyes open this time as he flashed into the space between spots in his reality. In the spinning, swirling unreality, he thought he saw translucent stretching and moaning at him, and he felt insubstantial fingers tugging softly at the ball. Then the world spun out from under him, and he felt himself falling.

The ball still tucked under one arm, Dunk lashed out with his free hand. His fingers found purchase between two boards in a long series of them hanging strapped between two parallel ropes, nearly wrenching his arm from its socket.

Dunk's legs spun out wildly beneath him as he stared down into an all-too familiar abyss. He looked up and realised he was hanging from planks in the rope bridge the Impaler had cut from under him.

Gritting his teeth, Dunk pulled himself up with his aching arm and reached up high above him with the other, stretching for the teleporter pad glowing from the planks overhead. He slapped the ball into the light, and then he was gone again.

When Dunk snapped back into reality, an ear-splitting roar nearly stopped his heart. It was a moment before he realised someone was shouting his name. 'Dunkel, Dunkel, Dunkel!' it said. 'Dunkel has the ball!'

Dunk leapt to his feet and saw M'Grash standing in one of the room's two doorways, jumping up and down with glee like a schoolgirl spotting a pony. Dunk would have smiled at that were it not for the vampire in the skull-emblazoned armour and helmet darting at him.

'This time, I'll have the ball *and* your life!' The Impaler promised.

With no time to react, Dunk did the first thing that occurred to him after so many hours of practice. He threw the ball.

The ball sailed wide past the oncoming vampire, bounced off the far wall, and landed neatly in M'Grash's outstretched arms. The ogre stared at it for a second as if it was his brain that had suddenly slipped out of his head.

The vampire knocked Dunk flat, then turned and smacked his lips at M'Grash. 'Fantastic!' He said. 'I've just super-sized my next meal.'

The ogre looked up from the ball at the vampire and froze. Still on his back, Dunk shouted at him. 'M'Grash! Throw it back!'

The ogre stomped forward and shoved the Impaler aside. The vampire slammed into a nearby wall and crumpled into a heap. Then M'Grash scooped up Dunk in his free arm and kept moving.

When M'Grash stepped on the teleport pad, the room around them vanished, and the ogre nearly crushed Dunk in terror. After they reappeared in a well-lit hallway, M'Grash set Dunk down with a sheepish, 'Sorry,' and handed him the ball.

Staring ahead, Dunk spotted the Champs' end zone straight before them. Without a word, he charged straight for it, M'Grash hot on his tail. As the emerged into the end zone's room, though, a black armoured ghoul stabbed forth from a hidden corner and grabbed at M'Grash, its flesh-clotted teeth searching for a gap in the ogre's armour. It found it and bit deep.

Only steps from the end zone, Dunk turned around and drove his spiked elbow pad straight into the ghoul's helmet. It punched through with a satisfying pop and stabbed into the cavity where the cannibal's hunger-rotted brain rattled around.

Dunk wrenched his arm free, and the creature fell limp. M'Grash tore the ghoul off his bicep, taking a bit of his muscle with it. 'Thanks, Dunkel,' he said. 'Best friend! Now score!'

M'Grash scooped Dunk up again and carried him into the end zone where he set the rookie down, the ball still cradled in his arms. From somewhere, Dunk heard a whistle blew, and he knew that in the observation theatre the crowd was going wild. He thrust the ball over his head – checking first for angry foes looking to get in a last cheap shot – and grinned.

'ROOKIE!' KUR SHOUTED as he hurled his helmet at Dunk once they were all back in the Hackers' dugout. 'You're dead!'

M'Grash caught the helmet before it could hit Dunk, then glared at Kur as he crushed it in his bare hand. 'Leave Dunkel alone!' the ogre said.

'That's enough, Mr. Ritternacht,' Pegleg said, his voice filled with more menace than M'Grash could manage with his worst hangover. 'Thanks to Mr. Hoffnung's efforts, we have another mark in our win column.'

'That was *my* score!' Kur said, stabbing his finger at Dunk. 'If you ever take my ball from me again–'

M'Grash stepped between the two men and glowered down at the starting thrower.

'You'll what?' Slick asked in his most innocent voice, which wasn't very.

Kur ignored the halfling and arched his neck around M'Grash's bulk to scowl at Dunk. 'I'll teach you to respect your betters, punk. Your friends won't be able to protect you.'

'Mr. Ritternacht!' Pegleg said. 'Come into the coach's office with me!'

'But coach!'

'Now!'

169

Kur curled his lip, then spat at M'Grash as he turned and followed Pegleg out of the room.

Slick walked along an empty bench to slap Dunk on the back. 'It's all right, son,' he said. 'Kur's just jealous.'

Dunk hung his head. Moments before, he had been flying high, thrilled at the Hackers' win, but Kur had dragged him back to earth and promised to bury him beneath it. 'It's fine,' he said. 'Let's just go.'

Dunk opened the door to the Reavers' room in the Halls of Mercy, the place where the sick and injured were cared for in Barak-Varr. The healers in charge of the place always opened an extra wing during the Dungeonbowl tournament. The wing had many large private rooms in it so that team members could convalesce with each other while not having to share space with players from other teams.

Dirk and Spinne were alone in the room, each in a bed on opposite sides of the room. Spinne's bed lay near a beautifully carved, wide and open window in the room that looked out over the gulf far below, and the afternoon light spilled in on her, bathing her in its golden glow. When Dunk entered, she turned to see who it was and smiled.

Dirk's bed was tucked back nearer the door, out of the light. He was sleeping when Dunk entered, but as quiet as Dunk strove to be, Dirk awoke as his brother stepped into the room.

'How are you?' Dunk asked, reaching out to put his hand on Dirk's unbandaged shoulder.

Dirk gave Dunk a weak smile. 'I've been better,' he said. 'First some guy knocks me through a window the night before a big game, and then – in the middle of the game – the whole damn mountain drops on my head.'

'Sounds like a rough week.'

'Just part of a rough life.'

'You're a Blood Bowl player,' Dunk said. 'You thought it would be easy?'

Dirk just smiled. Then he looked over at Spinne, who watched them from where she reclined in the sun. 'I think she got the worst of it. They already let out Schembekler and Karr.'

'I'm all right,' Spinne said wanly. She smiled at Dunk as he came over to stand next to her. She reached out and took his hand and held it in her lap.

'I've been thinking,' Dirk called over from his bed. 'You can have her.'

Spinne gasped in horror.

'I mean, look at her,' Dirk continued. 'Talk about damaged goods.'

Spinne tore a pillow from her bed and hurled it at Dirk. It bounced off his upraised arms.

'Hey,' he said, 'I'm an injured man.'

'You'll get a permanent disability if you keep talking like that.'

'Look,' Dunk said. 'Spinne and I, we had a lot of fun, but you're my brother. We can't let a woman come between us.' He carefully avoided looking at Spinne as he spoke, but he braced for a punch at the same time. It never came.

'What?' Spinne said. 'You've let everything else come between you over the years. Why not…?'

'Why not what?' Dunk asked.

'Fine!' Spinne said angrily. 'Have it the way you like. Or not, as the case may be. We can't be together anyhow. You're a player.'

'I was before.'

'You hadn't signed your contract yet.'

'Ah.' Dunk's heart sank. He was torn between what he felt developing between himself and Spinne and his loyalty to his brother. 'Well, I suppose I didn't speak to Dirk for three years. I could go a little longer.'

'Hey!' Dirk said. He reached out for a chamber pot and tossed it over at Dunk. It missed the rookie and skittered under the bed.

'Ow!' someone said.

'I didn't even hit you!' Dirk complained.

'That wasn't me,' Dunk said, his wide, round eyes locked with Spinne's . She shrugged at him, confused, and he dropped to the floor as if Pegleg had screamed for a hundred push-ups.

Staring under the bed, Dunk found himself eye to eye with Schlechter Zauberer. The wizard squeaked in terror and tried to stab the prone rookie with a thin knife that looked to Dunk like an oversized letter opener.

Dunk deflected the feeble attack and grabbed the wizard by the wrist and squeezed until he dropped the knife. He then hauled the pathetic creature bodily out from under the bed, with Zauberer whimpering the entire time.

'I didn't hurt anyone,' the wizard said.

When Spinne saw Zauberer, a short scream escaped her before she could stifle it. Dirk just stared at the thin man in the oversized robes.

'Who is that?' he asked.

Dunk hauled his prisoner to his feet. 'His name is Zauberer, and he's a wizard who trucks with daemons.'

'You *know* him?' Spinne asked, edging away toward the far side of her bed.

'I caught him rummaging through my coach's tent during a game in Magritta. He had a gargoyle with him then.'

Dirk got half out of his bed to peer underneath his mattress. He popped back up immediately and shook his head. 'Nothing there, at least.'

Dunk shook Zauberer by the collar. 'What were you doing under there?'

'Spying on us, I'll bet,' said Spinne. 'Which team are you working for? Did the Chaos All-Stars send you? Or the Dwarf Giants?'

'No!' the wizard protested, his feet barely touching the ground. 'It was nothing like that.'

'So you're just some kind of twisted fan then, hoping to get a good look at Spinne's rack?'

'Hey!' the catcher said.

'No! Really!' Zauberer said. 'I didn't mean to be here this long. I snuck in, and then the woman here woke up, and I was trapped. I thought I'd wait for them to fall asleep before I left.'

'And then I came in, and we found you?' Dunk asked, letting the wizard's heels touch the ground again.

Zauberer nodded as he shrugged his robes back into place. 'And now I'll be going,' he said evenly.

Dunk tightened his grip on the wizard's collar. 'What were you doing here?'

Zauberer pressed his lips together and refused to talk.

'Just throw him out the window,' Dirk said. 'Problem solved.'

Dunk goggled at his brother. 'I'm not going to kill him in cold blood.'

'It's not cold blood. You found him here. He surprised you. He tried to escape.'

Zauberer pulled against Dunk's grasp, but the rookie just hauled the wizard in. 'He's not going anywhere, and he's not much of a threat to us.'

Dirk nodded. 'He is a bit of a scarecrow.'

'Didn't he try to stab you?' Spinne said. 'I thought I heard a knife hit the floor.' She glared at the wizard, 'Did you try to stab him?'

Dunk wasn't sure she wasn't laughing at the man.

Zauberer hung his head. 'Yes, I did,' he said. 'I deserve death.'

Dunk stared at the wizard as if he'd just announced that he wanted to show them his mutant third arm. 'Are you mad?' he asked.

Zauberer shuddered. 'You don't understand. I'm not in the kind of position where I'm allowed to fail. I'd rather die. The alternative is worse.'

Dunk almost relaxed his grip, but he tightened it again when he felt the wizard try to pull away. 'You're out of your mind.'

'Give him what he wants,' Dirk said, sitting up in his bed. 'He's happy, we're happy. What's the harm?'

'He'd be *dead*.'

Dirk stood up and hobbled over to the wizard and his brother. He stretched to his full height when he reached Zauberer, so he could look down at the pathetic man. He glared into the sneak's eyes for a moment then said. 'He's lying.'

'He doesn't want to die?'

Dirk shook his head. 'This guy loves life too much. I can smell the stench of Chaos on him. He's after power, power, and more power. He can't get that if he's dead.' He peered into Zauberer's eyes. 'Let him go.'

'No,' Dunk grimaced. 'He's slippery. Let's call the Game Wizards and turn him over to them.'

'No need,' a voice said from the doorway. 'We're here.'

Dunk looked over his brother's shoulder to see the tall dwarf and the short elf standing next to each other in the doorway like some kind of strange set of salt and pepper shakers. 'Have you been following me?' he asked.

Dunk was so distracted he let go of Zauberer's collar. The wizard turned and bolted toward the window.

'No!' Dunk shouted, dashing after the thin, wizened man, but he was too late.

Zauberer scrambled over Spinne's bed (and her protests) and leapt straight out the window, kicking off from the sill to force himself further away from the cliff wall.

'Damn!' Dunk said as he crawled over Spinne too. She drew her legs out of the way for him, and he peered down toward the gulf far below.

The wizard had vanished.

'Where'd he go?' Dunk asked aloud. As the words left his lips, a gargoyle zoomed past him, nearly cutting him with the tips of its wings.

Zauberer hung from the creature's hands. As he passed by, he cackled, 'One more sacrifice for the Blood God!'

Dunk ducked back into the room, stunned. He saw the two Game Wizards standing stoically in the door. 'What are you waiting for?' he asked. 'Go after him?

The dwarf turned to the elf and said, 'Do you have a gargoyle waiting outside that window for you, Whyte?'

The elf kept looking straight at Dunk as he shook his head. 'No, I can't say I do, Blaque.'

'Shame that,' the dwarf said, looking back at Dunk. 'Can't help you there.'

Dunk just goggled at the pair in amazement.

'And to answer your earlier question,' Blaque said, 'Yes, we were following you.'

'Why?' Dunk asked.

'I like that,' Blaque nodded as he stroked his short, ebony beard. 'Straight to the point.'

'Don't care for it myself,' Whyte said flatly.

'Are you going to answer his question now or wait for another murderous daemon-conjurer to leap from hiding first?' asked Dirk.

'We've had our eye on Dunk here for a while,' the dwarf said. 'And you're not as funny as you think.'

'What's he done?' asked Spinne, who was now edging away from the window to the nearer side of her bed.

'There's what we think he's done and what we know he's done, right?'

Whyte answered the question. 'There have been a string of murders throughout the Blood Bowl teams this season, far more than usual. They point to a single, bloodthirsty individual methodically killing off any and all who stand in his way.'

'And you think that's Dunk?' Spinne asked, her eyes wide.

'Correct,' said Blaque.

Dirk laughed out loud. 'You're nuts. Dunk, a crazed killer?'

The dwarf fixed his dark eyes on Dirk. 'Didn't he knock you through a window to fall a hundred feet into the gulf?'

Dirk grinned. 'That was more of a mutual thing.'

'There's the matter of the prospects killed in the Hackers' tryout camp,' said Blaque.

'And the Broussard brothers,' added Whyte.

'I couldn't have done that!' Dunk said. 'Lots of people saw me in the Bad Water that night. Gods, *you two were there!*'

'Did I say he was working alone?' asked Blaque.

'I didn't hear you say that,' said Whyte.

'Good,' said the dwarf. 'I'd hate to give the wrong impression. Then there was the collapse of the dungeon yesterday.'

'I was in the theatre!'

'Am I going to have to repeat myself?' Blaque asked.

'I hope not,' Whyte said. 'It's tedious.'

'So I won't,' Blaque said. 'But we're really hear to talk about the killing earlier today.'

'Which one?'

Blaque raised an eyebrow at this but continued on. 'You may remember Ramen-Tut.'

Dunk narrowed his eyes. 'He fell apart in my arms. And it was in the middle of a game.'

'You killed Ramen-Tut?' Dirk said in proud amazement. 'Good job!' When he noticed the GWs glaring at him, he added in a whisper, 'I always hated that guy.'

'We have Cabalvision images of you and Kur Ritternacht attacking Ramen-Tut,' the dwarf said.

'Tackling.'

'Most tackles don't cause their victims to crumble irreversibly to dust.'

Dunk shrugged his shoulders. 'My first time tackling a mummy.'

'During the attack, someone administered a magical charm that caused the victim's dissolution. It had to be either you or Kur.'

'So it was Kur.' Dunk folded his arms across his chest. 'Wait,' he said with a smile, 'You don't know who it was, do you? You can't prove anything?'

'True enough,' Blaque said. 'That's why the Hackers have been banned from the tournament.'

'You can't do that!' Dunk said, stunned. 'Can they do that?' he asked Dirk and Spinne.

'They're not technically in charge of any league,' Spinne said. 'There isn't any league. Each team is in charge of itself.'

'But Wolf Sports broadcasts the tournament,' said Blaque. 'Do you think they know who the vice president of Wolf Sports is?' he asked Whyte.

'I can't say they do,' answered the elf.

'It's Shawbrad-Tut,' Blaque said. 'Father to the deceased.'

Dunk's heart sunk.

'Pack your bags, Dunk,' the dwarf said. 'You're going home; if you survive the trip back with all those angry team-mates, that is.'

'Don't forget Pegleg,' said Whyte.

'True,' Blaque nodded. 'That's one vicious hook.' He shook hands with Dunk, as did the elf.

'If you make it to the Chaos Cup, we'll see you there,' Blaque said. With that, the two Game Wizards left.

Dunk, Dirk, and Spinne stared at the empty doorway for a moment.

Dirk put his arm around his brother. 'Don't worry,' he said. 'It can't get much worse, right?'

Dunk coughed. 'Did I mention a threat on our lives by a black orc named Skragger?'

THE TRIP BACK to Bad Bay was a long one for Dunk. Pegleg had been furious at what the Game Wizards had done, and he let them know about it. He told Dunk that he didn't blame him in the slightest, but the rookie found it hard to believe that in his heart. Some of the other players, especially Kur, lay all the fault with Dunk, and they expressed their opinion at every opportunity.

Dunk took to sleeping on deck as the *Sea Chariot* made its way along the Old World's long, convoluted coast. M'Grash stayed out there with him every night, and Slick spent many a night up there too, although he enjoyed his comforts too much to make a commitment to it.

As the *Sea Chariot* went north, the weather grew colder and colder. Eventually, about the time the travellers spotted snow on the shore for the first time, Dunk gave in and went back to sleeping below deck. It was just too cold out in the open air.

'Pegleg had planned to return to the winter training camp for a while after the Dungeonbowl tournament,' Slick told Dunk one night, 'but he was so angry at Wolf Sports he decided to head home right away. He claims it will toughen up the players to get them used to the cold. He's even talking about scheduling some games with a Norse team or two.'

Kur tried to start a fight with Dunk more than once, but the ship wasn't big enough for the thrower to avoid M'Grash at the same time.

For a while, Dunk worried that Kur might try to throw him overboard in the middle of the night, but Kur never got up the courage to brave M'Grash's wrath.

'Dunkel hurt, you die,' the ogre told Kur one evening when the thrower had been picking on Dunk.

'I promise not to harm a hair on his head,' Kur said mockingly.

'None of Dunkel's hairs! He hurt, you die.'

'What if someone else hurts him?' Kur said. 'You can't hold me responsible then.'

'Dunkel hurt,' M'Grash said as clearly as he could, 'You die.'

Kur glared at the ogre's massive skull and said just as clearly, 'Understood.'

THE HACKERS SETTLED back into Bad Bay well, but for Dunk it was a bit of an adjustment. Bad Bay was a small farm town on the edge of the River Reik's delta, right where it flowed into the Sea of Claws, in a part of the world north of the Empire, known as the Wasteland. Its biggest export was beef, which shipped out of the place's small port almost daily, bound for places like Marienburg, L'anguille, and even Altdorf.

This was, in fact, where the Hackers' name came from: the method by which the cattle were traditionally slaughtered in the warehouses next to the port. The water in the bay often ran red with blood, which might also have been how the bay got its name, although Dunk suspected a darker and nastier truth beneath that tale.

There were few places to drink in Bad Bay, and even fewer places to eat. While his salary had made Dunk rich, he had little or nothing on which to spend his money. On off days, he sometimes wandered down to the docks, hoping to find something exciting to buy or even news of Altdorf or other, further lands.

The Hackers practiced five days a week. They played a game once a week. Sometimes, if Pegleg couldn't find an opponent, they just scrimmaged each other, but normally there was a proper team on the schedule. Marienburg had a pair of teams there. The legendary Marauders (once from Middenheim) had settled there a few years back, and just five years ago the Wasteland Wasters had finally mustered enough financial backing to go pro.

Kur had a great season, which meant a lot of time on the bench for Dunk. Once the outcome of the game was determined, Pegleg often substituted Dunk as the team's thrower just to give the rookie some time on the field against real opponents. For a while, the coach had even experimented with a two-thrower line-up, but the fact that Kur and Dunk would never give each other the ball hampered its effectiveness.

Other times, Pegleg put Dunk in as a catcher. 'There is no better training for a thrower, Mr. Hoffnung, than to see how hard it is to catch the ball.'

This meant that Kur had to throw the ball to Dunk, but he almost never did. Kur would rather throw the ball straight out of the opponent's end zone than put it in Dunk's hands.

However, towards the end of a close game against the Wasters, Dunk found himself alone in the end zone. He shouted and yelled for Kur to throw him the ball. By now, the Wasters had figured out that Kur didn't want to do this, so they didn't bother to cover Dunk at all.

'Throw Mr. Hoffnung, the damn ball!' Pegleg roared from the team dugout.

With time ticking down in the final half of the game, Kur had no choice. No one else was open, and running the better part of the field was not an option for him. He hated getting hurt even more than he hated Dunk. So he reared back and hurled the ball at Dunk as hard as he could.

As soon as Dunk saw the pass, he knew it was going to be long. He back-pedalled to the deepest corner of the end zone and leapt straight up into the air for it, but the ball still sailed over his head and landed in the stands. For a moment, he thought about chasing it, but one good look at the Marienburg fans convinced him to call the ball a loss. The fans eventually coughed it up, but it was too late. The clock ran mercilessly out, and the Hackers lost the game.

As the Hackers returned to their dugout, Kur charged Dunk. As he did, he took off his helmet and started beating Dunk with it. 'You missed that throw on purpose!' he raged at the rookie. 'You just cost us that game!'

Although M'Grash had kept Kur from actively hurting him, Kur had made Dunk's life miserable for the past couple months. He took every chance to cause trouble for the rookie. Dunk had had enough. When Kur opened his mouth to berate him again, he reached out and popped the man across the chin.

Kur collapsed like a skeleton turned into a pile of bones. He was out cold before he hit the ground.

'Pick him up,' Pegleg said, 'Him and his stinking glass jaw.'

The Waltheim brothers each got under one of Kur's arms and hauled him off to visit the arena's apothecary.

'You, Mr. Hoffnung,' Pegleg said. 'He had it coming for sure, but this is over. I want the two of you to work this out tonight, or I may have to start talking with the other teams about a trade, and who knows which one of you they'll want.'

* * *

WHILE IN BAD BAY, Kur stayed at the best inn within fifty miles, the Hacker Hotel. That night, Dunk walked over there from his decidedly less posh place at the FIB Tavern – which took its name from an obscene variety of Imperial Bastards – to make peace. He suspected he would only get into another fight, particularly because he'd made M'Grash stay back at the tavern, but he had to try. He was embarrassed that he'd lost his temper at a team-mate and actually hurt him, even if that team-mate was Kur. This was something he had to do.

When Dunk reached Kur's private room on the hotel's third floor, he knocked on the door. He knew Kur had to be there. From what Slick had told him, Dunk had broken Kur's jaw, and the medicines the apothecary had given him would ensure he wouldn't be too mobile tonight.

Dunk waited for a moment, and when no one came to the door, he knocked again. There was still no answer.

Dunk listened at the door for a moment and heard voices inside. Perhaps Kur was watching another game on Cabalvision, or maybe some of the other Hackers had come to play him a visit. Either way, Dunk wasn't ready to turn around and go home now. He was afraid he'd lose his resolve if he didn't do this now.

Dunk pushed on the door, and it swung open. In a corner of his mind, he saw that the lock had been shattered, but the sound of someone choking in the other room made him dash right by without inspecting it.

Kur's place featured three rooms: a dining room, a sitting room (complete with a fireplace big enough to stand up in), and a bedchamber. The entrance let into the sitting room, but a quick glance around told Dunk no one was there. The sounds he heard came from the bedroom.

Dunk crept toward the bedroom door and flung it open. There in front of the bed stood two figures. The first was Kur, whose face was both bruised and blue. Next to the Hackers' thrower, his meaty hands wrapped around Kur's throat, stood Skragger.

The black orc turned to see who was interrupting his murdering. When he saw Dunk, he bared his tusk-like teeth and let Kur drop to the floor. The injured man lay there on the ground, gasping for breath.

'Want some of this?' Skragger asked.

Dunk drew his sword. He'd bought himself a fine blade in Marienburg, perhaps the best he'd ever owned, but it had yet to taste blood.

'Put that pigsticker away,' Skragger growled. 'Just talking with yer friend. Sez you didn't give him my message.'

'He's a liar,' Dunk said, still keeping the tip of his blade between himself and the retired record-holder.

'Bad one too.' Skragger looked down at Kur, who was crawling onto his bed, still coughing and hoping for more air. 'Think I made my point.'

With that, Skragger walked straight toward Dunk. 'Leaving now,' he said. 'Move and live.'

Dunk stepped back into the sitting room and gave the black orc a clear path to the exit. Once Skragger was gone, Dunk sheathed his blade and went to check on Kur.

The thrower sat in a pool of vomit on the edge of the bed, still coughing. When Dunk walked in, Kur stood up and charged the rookie. 'You did this!' he said, his voice as hoarse as a stage whisper.

Dunk held up his hands to calm the veteran, but Kur kept straight at him barely able to walk. Dunk caught the man in his arms and carried him bodily back to his bed.

'I had nothing to do with this,' the rookie said as he sat Kur back down, holding his shoulders so the man couldn't leap up and attack him again. 'Pegleg warned you about Skragger. You wouldn't listen.'

Kur sneered at Dunk through his busted lips and broken jaw. 'You little codpiece. You waltz in here and think you can just take my job.' Kur shook his head so softly Dunk wasn't sure the man wasn't just shuddering. 'No one takes my place, in anything, ever. You know why?'

Dunk shook his head. He saw Kur fumbling around with something around his belt buckle, and he feared the man might need to vomit again.

'Because I'm willing to do anything to make sure it never happens.'

With those words, Kur drove the secret punch dagger he'd drawn from his belt buckle straight into the spot above Dunk's heart.

The blade turned on something hard and unyielding. As it did, its honed edge sliced through Dunk's shirt, exposing the breastplate hidden beneath.

'You must not think much of me,' Dunk said as his hand snapped out and knocked the punch dagger away. 'You think I'm dumb enough to come see you alone without some kind of protection. I know you a little too well for that.'

Kur reached up with both of his hands and wrapped them around Dunk's neck. Dunk ignored the feeble attempt to strangle him and drove his fist right into Kur's jaw again. It gave a satisfying pop, and Kur flung himself backward, clutching at his face.

Dunk stared down at the man, struggling to master the rage in his heart. He considered killing Kur – he could honestly say it was in self-defence – but the impulse faded quickly. Instead, he drew his sword and kicked the man in the ribs.

Kur whipped his head around to snap something at Dunk, but he stopped when he came nose to tip with the rookie's blade. He started to say something again, but a jab forward with the sword stopped him.

'Shut up,' Dunk said coldly. 'I've been taking your shit for months now, but that just ended when you tried to kill me. You listen to me now.'

Dunk waited for those words to sink in. When Kur nodded slowly, the rookie continued on.

'I've been letting M'Grash keep you off my back, but that's done too. I don't need him around for that. I'm trained in a half-dozen ways to kill a man, and I'd be happy to try them all out on you.'

Dunk placed the tip of his blade over Kur's heart and leaned forward. 'I want you to think back to earlier today, if you can manage it. I took you down with a single blow. I can do it again any time I like.

'I'm faster than you, stronger than you, and better looking than you. I'm better than you in every way. The only reason you still have your job is that I haven't tried to take it.'

Dunk paused here for a moment and glared into Kur's eyes. 'But I want to make one thing absolutely clear. You shouldn't be afraid of M'Grash. You shouldn't be afraid of Pegleg. You shouldn't even be afraid of Skragger.

'No, you dumb son of a bitch,' Dunk whispered. As he spoke, he sheathed his blade with one smooth move, his eyes never leaving Kur's rattled orbs. Then he leaned forward and pushed Kur back flat on the bed with a single index finger.

Dunk turned to leave then. As he reached the door, he looked back and spat at Kur. 'You should be afraid of *me*.'

A FEW WEEKS later, Pegleg stormed into the morning chalk talk and made an announcement. 'I just got word that the Chaos Cup is being held in Mousillon in one week. If we get the *Sea Chariot* underway today, we can just make it.'

The players all stared at their coach with blank faced.

'Well?' Pegleg said. 'What are you all waiting for? *Move out!*'

THAT AFTERNOON, AS the tide pulled out, so did the *Sea Chariot*. Dunk and Slick stood at the rail with M'Grash sitting beside them. Most of the other players avoided Dunk these days. After his incident with Kur, Dunk started keeping to himself more and more. He worried that the team captain would try to kill him during a weak moment, so he promised himself not to have any. With the exception of Slick and M'Grash, he didn't know he could trust any of them to not take Kur's side over his. The only exceptions were Cavre and Pegleg, but keeping the Hackers going gave them enough troubles of their own.

'Ever been to Mousillon?' Slick asked.

M'Grash and Dunk looked at each other, then both shook their heads.

'It's an evil place, son, if ever there was one. Some call it "the City of the Damned" and once we get there you'll see why.'

'Full of daemons?' M'Grash asked, a bit of a tremor in his voice. The ogre wasn't afraid of much, but magic, especially dark magic, always set him on edge.

'Nothing so spectacular, I'm afraid, but sometimes more sinister,' Slick said. 'Something went wrong with the city a few generations back. It used to be a wonderful place, nestled there next to the River Grismerie. Then it got hit with something like a dozen earthquakes in the space of a month. It never really did recover.'

'That's it?' Dunk said. 'That doesn't sound so bad.'

'Wait until we get there. When a place like that doesn't come back, there's always a reason.'

THE SEA CHARIOT swung through the Middle Sea and sailed north into the Great Western Ocean. Then it made its way into the Bay of Hope and up the River Grismerie until he reached the quay at Mousillon.

Even from the river, Dunk could tell that this was a city with troubles. Not one of the houses or buildings he saw bore a lick of paint. Most of the once-proud roofs were either caving in or had already fallen. A number of towers that once stabbed proudly into the sky now reached up like broken fingers.

In the city, the people were just as dour and colourless as their homes. Many of them wore little more than rags, and even the best-dressed people wore clothes that even M'Grash would have turned up his nose at. Voluminous hoods and cloaks seemed to be the style here. Everyone wore them: men, women, and even children.

Dunk thought this was odd, especially when he saw a mother carrying an infant swaddled in such a garment. As the child began to cry, though, a prehensile tongue at least a foot long slipped out of its hood and snagged a hapless deerfly from the air. It stopped crying then.

'The taint of Chaos is strong here,' Slick said, sticking close to Dunk. Any one of these people could bear mutations from exposure to its unwholesome essence.'

'Any?' M'Grash said, looking at all the hoods around them. 'All!'

'Dirk said he'd be here at Ye Olde Salutation,' said Dunk. 'Any idea where that is?'

Slick pointed to a sign hanging over the door of a run-down inn down a broken street off to the left. It showed a hand making an obscene gesture. 'They may have changed the sign since the earthquakes,' he said. 'I was here before that once, and it was a much friendlier place.

Dunk led the way to the inn, weaving his way through people in hoods of all sizes. Only a few were not wearing the dark garments, but since they were such large people walking around with such beautiful members of their race, Dunk could only guess they were other Blood Bowl players and even cheerleaders.

Inside, the Sal, as Dunk later learned the locals called it, was just as depressing as it looked from the outside. The tables were all warped and crooked, and the stools were just as low and mean and often sported fresh splinters. Black candles illuminated the common room, but just barely. It was the sort of place in which a local could doff his hood and still stay hidden from prying eyes.

After ordering a round of drinks – a local brew called Mutant High Life – from a three-eyed bartender, Dunk asked if he'd seen anyone that looked like Dirk and Spinne. The man pointed him toward the back of the dim and smoky room. As Dunk turned to leave, he noticed the man's thumb was split in two like a devil's fork.

'Have a seat,' Dirk said as Dunk, Slick, and M'Grash walked up and set down their drinks. They all shook hands with him and Spinne, who gave Dunk a hug, friendly, but nothing more. 'Sadly, we're not alone here.'

'Who's the problem?' Dunk said, peering into the surrounding gloom.

'At first, I thought it was Skragger. I think he's been following me around town ever since we arrived. He really has me spooked.' It struck Dunk that for his brother to even admit he was 'spooked' meant he was probably truly terrified.

'Who is it then?'

'I knew you'd show up here eventually,' said Lästiges as she emerged from a nearby booth. 'These two always attract the most interesting sort of garbage, kind of like flies but in reverse.'

'We have to stop meeting like this,' Dunk said.

'Or you'll kill me, just like anyone else who gets in your way?'

Dunk narrowed his eyes at the reporter. 'That means what?'

'I know how the Hoffnungs work. You never let anything or anyone get in the way of what you want. And now I have proof.'

Dunk shook his head. 'You can't. I didn't do it.'

'That doesn't mean she doesn't have proof, son,' said Slick. 'Evidence isn't always honest.'

Lästiges smirked at that. 'I have incontrovertible proof that Dunk here killed most of the other prospects from his recruiting class and that he brought down the roof on the Reavers and even killed Ramen-Tut.'

Dunk waved her off. 'No proof of a plot to kill the Emperor?'

'Give me time.'

'Look,' Dirk said as he stood up to talk with Lästiges, 'this is my brother. I've known him all my life, and he's just not capable of these things.'

Lästiges eyes flashed hot and then icy cold. 'The facts don't lie.'

'But people lie about them all the time,' Dirk said. He looked around the pub. 'Can we all go someplace a bit nicer to talk about it?'

'Is there such a place in town?'

'I have a few ideas.'

'I'm not going anywhere,' Dunk said. 'I don't have anything to prove.'

Dirk rolled his eyes. 'I just think it might help if the lovely young Lästiges got to hear our side of the story.'

'Certainly,' the reporter said, eyeing Dirk. 'It should make for a good laugh.'

'That's just the lack of bias I've come to expect from the media,' Dirk said as he took Lästiges by the arm and led her from the pub.

Slick raised his eyebrows at Dunk as the two left, but Dunk ignored him. He was about to say something to Spinne – he didn't know what – when another repulsive figure shambled out of the gloom.

'I thought she'd never leave,' Gunther the Gobbo said as he oozed onto the stool that Dirk had vacated.

'What is he doing here?' Spinne asked.

'So, kid,' the corpulent Gobbo wheezed at Dunk through his greasy mouth, 'It looks like you're turning into a real up and comer. Killing Ramen-Tut? That was brilliant!'

'That was Kur,' Slick said.

The Gobbo waived the halfling off. 'Whatever. It was a good move, and it shows our little prodigy's ability to be in the right place at the right time.' At this point Gunther's smile grew impossibly wide as he focused his watery eyes on the rookie, and Dunk wondered if maybe Mousillon was the creature's hometown. 'And that's just the kind of service I'm interested in renting from you.'

Spinne threw the contents of her stein at the Gobbo, drenching him. He smiled at her as he strove to lick as much of the beer from his face as he could with his unusually long tong. 'Don't you worry, sweetie,' he said to her, still smiling. 'I'll get around to making you an offer next.'

Spinne's arm lashed out and grabbed the Gobbo around the collar of his hooded cloak. He gurgled as she stood and wrenched him out of his seat. 'Stay away from him,' she said. 'He's not your kind of player, and he never will be.' Then she shoved him so that he fell and skidded off into the gloom again.

Dunk heard the Gobbo scrabbling away, but as the creature left he called out. 'I'll get back to you later, kid, when you have a better selection of company. We'll do lunch!'

Spinne tossed her stein in the direction of the voice. Dunk heard a satisfying cry of pain come from where the stein went. He hoped it was Gunther's voice and not someone else's.

'Thanks,' Dunk said to Spinne in a tone that was anything but grateful. 'I'll be sure to run all of my acquaintances past you for approval.'

'He's scum,' Spinne said. 'You don't want to have anything to do with him.'

'What gives you that right?' Dunk asked. 'Sleeping with me to get under my brother's skin?'

Spinne gasped in anger. Looking down at her hands, she realised she'd already thrown both her beer and her stein, so she just steamed at Dunk instead. It was the kind of look that could peel paint from walls, had there been any left in this town.

'No,' said Dunk, who was feeling meaner all the time. Was it the beer talking already or just the air in this damned town? 'Maybe it's the way you hide behind your contract so you can't repeat your mistake.'

Spinne grabbed Slick's stein and threw the beer in it at Dunk. The rookie dodged out of the way, and before Spinne could follow the beer with the stein, Slick snatched it from her hand.

'Think what you like,' Spinne said. Dunk thought he saw tears welling up in the woman's eyes, but it could just have been from the odd conglomeration of smells in the pub. 'I'll leave you alone from now on.'

With that, Spinne spun on her heel and disappeared into the darkness.

Dunk looked into his beer for a moment, then handed it to Slick and took after the Reavers catcher. 'Spinne!' he said. 'Wait!'

'Thanks, son,' Slick said as Dunk left. 'I like a client who knows how to take care of his agent.'

Outside the Sal, Dunk spotted Spinne marching away up the street. He started after her, calling for her to stop, but she only moved faster. He caught up with her as she raced through a door beneath a sign that read 'The Mousillon Tentacles Hotel'.

'Hold it!' said Dunk as he followed Spinne into the dimly lit lobby. The place was made of crumbling bricks that seemed to be covered with a glowing green mould. 'Please! I want to apologise.'

'For what?' Spinne asked.

Dunk paused a moment, hoping that Spinne would help him out here. He knew he'd behaved badly, but now that she was angry with him, bringing her down was sure to be tricky.

Spinne just glared at him with her blazing blue-grey eyes, daring him to say the wrong thing.

'For being a complete ass,' Dunk said. 'I thought maybe there could be something between us, and well...'

'You decided to make sure that could never be.'

'No,' Dunk said, confused. 'Wait. I thought we were already at that point.'

Spinne frowned at him. 'Only as long as we're both players who play by the rules.'

Dunk smiled nervously. 'What Blood Bowl player ever paid attention to the rules?'

'Exactly!' Spinne said, throwing her hands up in frustration. She spun on her heel again and headed up to her room.

'So, wait!' Dunk said as he chased Spinne up the stairs. 'Are you saying there's a chance for us?'

Spinne stopped in front of a battered door, a tarnished key in her hand. 'Anything can happen, Dunk. It's like Blood Bowl. Sometimes, success is a matter of how much you want it.'

She stuck the key in the lock. 'So,' she said seriously, 'how much do you want it?'

Awash in a mixture of relief and uncertainty, Dunk said the only thing that popped into his head. 'More than anything.'

'That,' Spinne said with a smile as she turned the key and shoved open the door, 'is the first step.'

As the door swung open, Dunk's jaw dropped. Spinne looked at him, confused at his reaction, then turned to see what had stunned him so. As she did, she let out a little scream.

Dirk and Lästiges lay on the bed in the room's far corner, entangled in each other's arms.

AT BREAKFAST THE next morning, Dirk said, 'My roommate was in my room. I knew Spinne's place was empty.' He grinned at Dunk. 'I didn't think you'd drive her out of the pub that quick.'

'Shows how well you know her, I suppose.' Dunk sighed over his meal. Despite ending up alone in his own bed, he'd not slept much that night.

'Look,' Dirk said, 'Spinne and I have had a fling or two before – mostly drunken celebrating after a big win – but there's nothing there. We're team-mates.'

'Thanks,' Dunk said. He wanted to sound depressed and sarcastic, but he was having a hard time pulling it off. Dirk's words sparked just a bit of hope in his heart again. After Spinne had kicked everyone out of her place last night, he had thought his chances with her had been ruined. Now he wasn't so sure. Just how bad do you want it? he thought.

'Think Lästiges is going to get over it?' Dunk asked. After being kicked out of Spinne's room, the reporter had slapped Dirk in the face. 'I think she's under the impression you were just using her to get her off my back.'

'What makes you think that?' Dirk said with a not-so-innocent smile.

'I think it was the part where she slapped you and said, 'You were just *using* me!' But I might have read that wrong.'

'I prefer to think of it as a happy coincidence.' Dirk said, grinning devilishly. 'Sleeping with a beautiful woman will help my brother? Just call me an altruist.'

THE HACKERS PLAYED three games over the course of the next week and won two. The loss had been a heartbreaker against the Oldheim Ogres. The creatures had physically outmatched the Hackers, but Kur and Cavre had kept their team in the game until the very end, when Percival Smythe had been crushed in a pile-up after catching a pass near the end zone.

Pegleg had forgone a funeral after seeing Percy's body. 'He went how he would have wanted to,' the coach said, wiping away a single tear with his shining hook. 'Besides,' he pointed down at the ground where the pile of ogres had pressed Percy straight through the turf, 'he's already buried.'

Despite the loss, the Hackers made it into the semi-finals against the heavily favoured Chaos All-Stars. The morning of the game Slick said to Dunk, 'The Gobbo gives them a three-point spread, which is more than I suspected. Are you sure you didn't take him up on his offer?'

'You just want your cut,' Dunk said with a smile.

Slick stuck out his open hand, ready for a bag full of gold to fall into it. 'You're a great player, son, but this *is* business.'

'I know,' Dunk said, 'but I don't do business that way.'

'Bah!' Slick said, but Dunk saw the halfling smiling as he walked away.

* * *

As THE GOBBO predicted, the All-Stars pounded the Hackers hard. The All-Stars' captain, Schlitz 'Malty' Likker, a mutant minotaur with six horns on his head, kept M'Grash on his heels the whole first half. Kur threw two interceptions, and a cheap shot from Baron Redd the Damned put Cavre down for the rest of the game with a case of skin rot.

At half-time, the Hackers assembled in their dugout, ready for one of Pegleg's traditional 'you bunch of losers' rants. Instead, their coach told them to turn their attention to the field. 'Orcidas has something going on, and since they're hosting this party, all us guests have to play along.'

'What's happening, coach?' Guillermo Reyes asked, the pockmarks from one of the All-Stars' tentacles still pink and puckered across his face.

'They're milking every last bit they can get out of one of their top endorsement contracts by 'honouring' him with a ceremony during half-time,' Pegleg snarled.

'Who is it?' Kai Albrecht asked, still scratching the rash he'd broken into after getting coated with the green goo that passed for one All-Star beastman's blood.

'Skragger, of course.'

Dunk hadn't been interested before, but the name of the black orc snapped him back to attention. He craned his neck over the lip of the dugout to see the temporary stand a herd of goblins and snotlings had dragged into the centre of the field. 'Anyone notice that the Chaos Cup symbol in the middle of the field looks a lot like a pentacle?' he asked.

'It *is* a pentacle, Mr. Hoffnung,' Pegleg said. 'Strange things happen at the Chaos Cup all the time, and the teams finally insisted on some kind of protection. If you see a daemon, get your tail inside that pentacle's circle, and you'll be safe.'

Dunk eyed the circle carefully. 'Are you sure about that, coach?'

'No,' Pegleg said. 'Ain't magic grand?'

'And now, here to accept the Orcidas Golden Spikes for the third year in a row,' Bob's voice said, 'the greatest black orc player of them all. The Prince of Pain. The Captain of Calamity. The Duke of Dirty Play. Ladies, gentlemen, and creatures of all kinds: Skragger!'

The crowd roared with approval as the black orc stepped up to the front of the makeshift stand that somehow looked much sturdier than anything else in the stadium. Skragger, dressed in a vibrant black Orcidas sweat suit trimmed with blood-red piping, waved at the fans, and they roared back louder.

'He's something, huh?' marvelled Milo Hoffstetter.

'A couple decades of top play and high casualty counts, and you might be there too,' Pegleg said. 'But concentrate on surviving today first.'

Despite his misgivings, Dunk found the event fascinating. This psychopathic orc – a redundant term, Dunk suspected – was the hero of all these fans. And how had he gotten there? Images of Skragger strangling Kur flashed through Dunk's mind. He glanced at Kur and saw the man had turned white as Skragger took the field.

Dunk turned back to the ceremony, where he saw a man in dark robes walking up the steps of the stand in the centre of the pentacle with a pair of golden spikes in his hands. The rookie rubbed his eyes and then looked again, but the image was still the same. 'That's Zauberer out there!' Dunk shouted.

Before anyone could respond, Dunk sprinted out toward the stand. He didn't know what was happening here, but if Zauberer was involved he couldn't let it happen. 'Zauberer!' he shouted at the top of his lungs. 'Stop!'

'Well, Bob,' Jim's voice said, 'it looks like one of the Hackers has decided to join the ceremony.'

'That's number seven, Dunk Hoffnung,' Bob said, 'and he looks excited. Perhaps Coach Pegleg chose him for the traditional human sacrifice.'

'I thought Orcidas gave up on those after last year's summoning of the great daemon Nurgle nearly started another Red Plague.'

'It looks like tradition may have trumped safety concerns once again, Bob. This is the Chaos Cup we're talking about!'

The crowd fell silent with anticipation as Dunk charged the stage. He leapt onto the raised platform and tackled Zauberer just as he was about to present the golden spikes to Skragger.

'Wow, Bob! Hoffnung just waltzed right in there and took that man down. I wish he'd tackle like that during the games!'

'I know what you mean, Jim. I wonder where the defence is at a time like this. Doesn't a player like Skragger rate any bodyguards?'

'Just look at him,' Jim's voice laughed. 'Does he look like he needs them?'

'I don't know what you're up to, wizard,' Dunk snarled at the terrified Zauberer, 'but it ends here!'

The wizard struggled to stab Dunk with the spikes, but the rookie smashed Zauberer in the face first. He was about to follow up with a knockout blow, when someone pulled him bodily off the wizards.

'Gots a death wish, punk?' Skragger growled into Dunk's ear. The crowd screeched with approval.

'Wait!' Dunk shouted. 'This man is an evil wizard! He was going to kill you!'

Skragger just shook his head as he threw Dunk back over the edge of the stage. 'Look around, punk. Game's fulla evil wizards.'

Dunk scrambled to his feet to see Zauberer standing behind Skragger, who was still sneering down at Dunk, the two golden spikes raised high in his fists, poised to stab into the black orc's back.

'No!' Dunk shouted, although he knew it was too late.

Just as Zauberer struck, Schlitz the six-horned minotaur, who'd been up on the stage to help present the award, dove between the wizard and the black orc. When Zauberer brought down the spikes, they drove straight into Schlitz's chest.

Schlitz screeched in horror as the spike plunged into his flesh.

'What?' Skragger said as he turned to see what had happened. 'You bloody bull!' he shouted at Schlitz. 'No one steals my trophies!'

Dunk stood up and craned his neck around Skragger to see what was happening to Schlitz. As he did, he noticed Zauberer skulking away, but he was more concerned about the minotaur than the wizard at the moment.

Sparks of some nameless crimson energy arced between the spikes in Schlitz's chest and quickly grew to cover the creature's entire body. Then a vermilion bolt cracked down from the overcast sky, bathing the clouds and the stadium beneath in a hellish light. The bolt shot straight down through the minotaur and the stage, then flooded through the pentacle, illuminating its every line and edge. There were many gaps in the outer circle.

Dunk reflexively covered his eyes against the flash, and when he drew his hands away he saw Schlitz still standing on the stage, bent down on one knee. The creature's fur and skin glowed an angry orange and red, reminding Dunk of the colour of flowing lava. When the minotaur looked up, Dunk could see that his eyes were a blazing scarlet from rim to rim.

'Who beckons the servant of the Blood God?' Schlitz roared in a voice that carried further than Jim or Bob's. 'Who shall be the first penitent to slake his thirst?'

'Bob,' Jim's voice said. 'I think we're in for a real show here tonight.'

Skragger lowered his shoulder and stomped up to the minotaur, trying to knock him flying from the stage. Schlitz, or whatever daemon rode his flesh, swatted the black orc away like a gnat

Dunk ducked as Skragger went sailing over his head to bounce off the turf behind him. Under most circumstances, this would have brought a smile to the rookie's face. At the moment, though, Skragger's fate was the furthest thing from his mind.

'You!' the blood-eyed minotaur roared as it stabbed a broken-nailed finger at Dunk, red energy still arcing among its six horns. 'You're next!'

Dunk stared up at the minotaur for a moment, then turned and ran.

Schlitz charged after the rookie thrower as he raced down the field.

'It looks like Hoffnung's decided to challenge Khorne's impromptu proxy here to a foot race,' Bob's voice said. 'Jim, do you think he has a chance?'

'Does a zombie smell like roses? Minotaurs are renowned for their hoof speed. I'd say it's only a matter of seconds before the stampeding Schlitz puts an end to a very promising rookie season.'

Dunk knew the announcers were right. He had no hope of out running the minotaur in a fair race. Fortunately, 'fair' didn't enter into his plans.

As Dunk sprinted along the field toward the Hackers' end zone, he heard Schlitz thundering after him, the minotaur's hooves thumping along faster than the rookie's heart. Dunk put everything he had into making the minotaur sweat. The longer the race lasted, the more careless the creature would be.

When Dunk felt the minotaur's hot breath blasting down on his neck and could hear the energy arcing between his horns crackling in his ears, he threw himself to the turf and curled up into a tight ball.

Schlitz's shins ploughed into Dunk's back and knocked the rookie spinning. At the same time, the kneecapped minotaur went sailing over Dunk's armoured form, his momentum sending him soaring into the air.

Schlitz landed headfirst in the Hackers' end zone, his six vicious horns stabbing through and embedding themselves in the turf there. His momentum brought his hooves flying up over his head until they landed hard on the turf in front of him. As this happened, there was a loud and sickening snap.

Bruised but still whole, Dunk scrambled over to where the minotaur lay, his head pointing in one direction and his body in another. Crimson energy arced around Schlitz's body as the orange and red fire under his fur began to flicker and fade. His unholy screech of protest rang throughout all of Mousillon's damned streets and alleys.

Unsure what to do, Dunk reached out and pulled the golden spikes from the minotaur's chest. The unnatural lights blinked out immediately, and the screech dampened to a feeble cry.

Having fallen silent during the possessed minotaur's death scream, the crowd now stared blankly and quietly down at the field to where the minotaur lay.

Still on his knees, Dunk crawled around to where Schlitz's eyes still stared back at his own team's end zone, all the way at the other end of the field. 'Thanks, kid,' the minotaur whispered as the life went out of his soft, brown eyes.

Dunk reached out and closed those eyes, then stood over the minotaur, the golden spikes still in his hands.

'Gimme those, punk!' Skragger said as he came trotting down the field.

Angry, Dunk waited until the black orc was close enough and then flung the spikes at his face. Skragger splayed out his hands and caught them each neatly. Stomping to a halt, he brought the spikes up in front of himself and pointed them at Dunk.

'No one takes my trophies!' With that, he thrust his fists high into the air, the tips of the spikes facing toward the sky, and the crowd erupted.

When the noise came down a bit, Skragger lowered his arms and pointed the tips of the spikes at Dunk's chest. 'Next time I see ya, yer dead!' he snarled.

Unable to hear the black orc's words, the crowd seemed to understand the intent. The people in the stands roared again, and Skragger trotted back to the stage, the spikes held high, basking in the adulation.

As Dunk watched the black orc enjoy his moment, he felt something on his shoulder. He turned to see a snake-headed creature with a trio of tongues standing behind him, dressed in a black-and-white striped shirt. The referee retracted its tentacle as soon as it realised it had Dunk's attention.

'Sssorry, sssir,' the ref said, 'but you're going to have to leave the game. The rulesss againsssst killing other playersss during half-time are quite clear.'

Dunk stared at the snakeman, uncomprehending. 'I may have just saved the life of every person in this stadium,' he said, 'and you're worried about the game.'

The snakeman's headed weaved and bobbed nervously as he spoke. 'You may – I'll ssstresss 'may' – have sssaved livesss today, but you alssso killed the captain of the Chaosss All-Ssstarsss. Our sssponsorsss frown on that.'

Dunk glanced back over his shoulder to where the referee was looking. Blaque and Whyte were standing next to a furious Pegleg in the dugout.

'If you leave right now,' the referee said, 'we will let your team continue the game.'

Dunk didn't look back at the snakeman. He just nodded as he began the long walk back toward the Hackers on the sidelines.

'What in Nuffle's name were you doing out there, Mr. Hoffnung?' Pegleg demanded as Dunk stepped down into the dugout. Blaque and Whyte stood silently in a far corner, watching everything.

'Saving us all,' Dunk said, staring dejectedly at the wall before him. The other players didn't say a word.

Pegleg grabbed one of Dunk's spiked shoulder pads with his hook and pulled the rookie about to face him. 'That's not what you're here for, Mr. Hoffnung. That's *not* what I'm paying you for. If you even think about doing something like this again, you will be terminated, and I'm not just talking about your contract.'

Dunk brought his eyes up to look into Pegleg's. 'You can't fire me, coach,' he said flatly. 'I quit.'

THE CHAOS ALL-STARS, energised by the death of their captain – all the surviving players wanted to compete for his spot – thrashed the Hackers in the second half of the game. Dunk was back in his hotel room when Slick brought him the news.

'It's too bad, son,' the halfling said. 'You did the right thing.'

'That's behind me now,' Dunk said, grimacing as he spoke. 'I don't want to have anything to do with that game now.'

'Wait,' Slick said, concern etched on his brow. 'You're not serious about quitting, are you? That was in the heat of the moment. I'm sure Pegleg will let it slide.'

Dunk shook his head. 'That's not going to happen,' he said. 'I'm sick of this game. I'm sick of the death. I'm sick of the threats. I'm sick of the media trying to pin everything on me.' He sat down on the edge of his bed and buried his head in his hands. 'I've had it. No more.'

'Son,' Slick said, his hands spread wide and open, 'that's part of the game, all of it. I thought you knew that going into it.'

Dunk threw himself back on the bed. 'I knew it, yeah, but I had no idea. It's one thing to want gold and glory. It's another to get it.'

Slick climbed up into the chair next to the bed. 'It's all over then, is it?' he said. 'The gold and glory? You've had enough of it?'

Dunk put his hands over his face. He didn't want to hear what Slick was saying to him. He didn't want to think about it at all. The only thing he wanted was to be out of Blood Bowl for good.

'What then?' the halfling said. 'Back to chasing dragons? We know how well that went.'

Dunk didn't say a word.

'You have perhaps a bit too much of the hero in you, son. You certainly proved that today. But where else can you feed that part of yourself?'

'And where else can I get paid so well for it, right?' Dunk said.

'True enough,' Slick said, 'although that wasn't my point.'

Dunk sat up and glared at the halfling. 'Face it, Slick, if it wasn't for my "potential" as a Blood Bowl player, you wouldn't have crossed the street to spit at me.'

Slick stood up on the chair and glared back down at Dunk. 'Think that if you will, but I didn't have to open that door for you that night in Dörfchen, did I? I didn't have to hand you that spear. That we've since made each other wealthy, well, I'd be lying if I said it wasn't important to me.

'You've never been poor, son. You may have left Altdorf and your family behind, but you never had to scrabble around in the gutter for scraps. You never had to wear rags for clothes. You're so well off now, you don't know how good you have it.'

Slick swung his arms around the place to show Dunk what he meant. As he looked around the grungy, leaky, draughty place, he grimaced and leapt down from the chair. As he headed for the door, he looked back and said, 'There are worse places to be in Mousillon, you know. Playing Blood Bowl – having that kind of gold and glory – lets you make the best of a bad deal. Consider that before you throw it all away.'

THE NEXT MORNING, Dunk climbed aboard the *Sea Chariot* with the rest of the team. He didn't say a word to anyone, and he studiously avoided Pegleg's gaze. But as he walked past the coach, Pegleg simply said, 'Welcome aboard, Mr. Hoffnung.'

The trip back to Bad Bay gave Dunk a lot of time to think. He spent his time above decks, day and night, gazing out into the sky like some mad prophet looking for meaning in the clouds and stars. No one bothered him. Slick brought him his meals, and the halfling and ogre sat with Dunk as they ate, but they seemed content to share each other's company without spoiling the moments with talk.

When the Hackers got to Bad Bay, Dunk was among the last to disembark. He watched the families and friends of the other players greet them at the dock, thrilled to find their loved ones had survived yet another tournament. There would be many a celebration in the tiny town that balmy spring night.

When Dunk finally did leave the ship, he saw Cavre limping up to him on a set of crutches, holding something in his hand. A beautiful woman and a gaggle of children stood at the end of the dock where they'd greeted the man, and they waited for him to return with wide and eager eyes.

'What is it?' Dunk asked as respectfully as he could. For all the problems Dunk had been having with the team, Cavre had always treated him with patience and respect.

'Congratulations, Mr. Hoffnung,' Cavre said, handing him a sheaf of bound papers that featured a colour image on the front. 'You just made your first cover of *Spike! Magazine*.'

Stunned, Dunk flipped the magazine over to look at the cover. There was a picture of him standing over Schlitz's body, the bloodied golden spikes still dripping in his hands. The headline read: 'The Hackers' Hoffnung: The Greatest Killer Ever?'

Dunk narrowed his eyes at Cavre. 'Is this good or bad?' he asked. 'In some circles, this would be a compliment.'

'Look at the by-line on the article,' Slick said, pointing at the cover again. It read: 'Story by Lästiges Weibchen.'

M'Grash put his hand on Dunk's shoulder and said, 'Not good.'

DUNK THANKED CAVRE, who went home with his overjoyed family, and strode over to the Hacker Hotel. There, in the Hacker-decorated common room, he sat and read the article. He ignored the number of people staring at him as he did.

'Good on ya,' the bartender said as he brought Dunk and his friends a round of Hackers Stout, a dark and heady brew that was drinking more like bread than water.

Dunk looked up from the magazine, startled. The bartender – a sandy-haired young man named Henrik, with a Hacker logo tattooed on his forearm – smiled at him. 'It's great to see one of ours hit the big time,' he grinned. 'These are on the house.'

'Thanks,' Dunk said, a bit confused. He sipped the beer as he continued to read.

Lästiges had assembled a cadre of 'anonymous sources' who swore to Nuffle that Dunk had been behind a large number of the off-field casualties surrounding the tournaments over the past year. This included the murders of the prospects in the Hackers' training camp before the *Spike! Magazine* tournament, the killing of the Broussard brothers, the collapse of the dungeon in the Reavers-Champions of Death game, and the dissolution of Ramen-Tut, capped off by the slaying of Schlitz 'Malty' Likker in the Chaos Cup semi-finals.

Dunk had to admit that a disturbing number of people had died around him this year, and Lästiges had done a solid job of either lining up liars or fabricating accusations about him. If he hadn't known better, he might have thought he was guilty too. She even tied him to

some other killings he hadn't even known had happened. He wondered for a moment if someone was wandering around disguised as
him and killing people.

As Dunk kept reading, he became more and more angry. True, he
had killed Schlitz, but it was more like the poor, possessed minotaur had killed himself while trying to turn Dunk into paste. He
had done nothing to be ashamed of, at least as far as these killings
went.

'This is awful,' Dunk said. 'Lästiges is on a crusade for my head
here, and if the Game Wizards believe this stuff, she might actually
get it.'

'Will they?' M'Grash asked, his boulder of a face filled with concern.

Slick shrugged as Dunk handed him the magazine to read. 'It's possible. First, they've been following you and her around for much of
the time she's been "investigating" you. Second, *Spike! Magazine* is the
most important magazine in the sport. If the GWs don't make an
example out of Dunk, lots of other players might figure they can get
away with this kind of stuff. The whole sport could dissolve in a rash
of off-field murders.'

Dunk shrugged nonchalantly. 'What can they do to me? Suspend
me for a few games? Kick me off the team?'

'Publicly execute you?' said Slick. It wasn't really a question. 'You
need to go back and read your contract more thoroughly.'

Dunk sat up straight. 'You said it was a 'standard contract'!' Dunk
protested.

'That sort of stuff *is* standard!' Slick said.

'Gah!' Dunk slouched back in his chair and put his hands over his
face. 'How did I get wound up in all this?'

While Dunk sulked, Slick read the article, and M'Grash drank his
bucket of beer. When the ogre set it down, his hands shook so badly
that he nearly knocked it off the table.

'You okay?' Dunk asked. 'This article has really thrown you.' He
leaned forward and put his hand on the ogre's massive arm. 'Don't
you worry about it, M'Grash.'

'And why should he, Mr. Hoffnung?' Pegleg said as he walked into
the hotel's common room. 'You can't buy this kind of publicity!' He
grinned from ear to ear.

Dunk goggled at his coach for a moment. 'What?'

'This is the best thing that's happened to us since we founded the
team,' Pegleg said as he pulled up a chair and sat down. Dunk had
never seen him so excited. 'We're going to have teams lining up to
play us after this, and the venues will have to offer us a better cut of
the gate to make it worth our while.'

'So, this is good?'

Pegleg put his hand on Dunk's shoulder. 'No, Mr. Hoffnung, it's phenomenal.' Then he leaned in conspiratorially and said, 'So, when do you think you might kill again?'

Dunk froze. He couldn't believe the coach's words.

'You see, the trick is to not do it too often. You need to leave the public wanting more.' Pegleg waved the magazine at Dunk. 'You have to avoid over saturation while still keeping yourself and the team in the public eye. It's a fine line to walk.'

'Coach.'

'Also, if you are open to suggestions, there are some people in the game that might be better dead than others, if you know what I mean. I can provide you with a list and reasons for each if you like.'

'Coach.'

'Or just let your murderous appetites lead you where they may. They've done well by you so far. Perhaps it's best to not mess with a savant's instincts, eh?'

'Coach!' Dunk glared at the startled Pegleg until he was sure the man would be silent. 'I didn't do it. None of it!'

'Come now, Mr. Hoffnung. I saw you kill Schlitz myself, as did thousands of others. Masterfully done, by the way.'

'That was self-defence! I didn't touch any of the others.'

A light went on under Pegleg's yellow tricorn, and he favoured Dunk with a knowing smile. 'I see. If that's the way you like it, Mr. Hoffnung, than so be it. I'm just as pleased either way.'

With that, Pegleg stood and left with a tip of his hat and a sly wink at Dunk.

'Dunkel,' M'Grash said. The rookie looked up at the ogre, who seemed to be near to tears.

'Yes?' Dunk said, putting his hand on M'Grash's monstrous mitt.

'We talk?' The ogre looked as if he might burst if he didn't get to say his piece soon.

'Go ahead,' Dunk said. 'You can tell us anything.'

M'Grash looked sidelong at Slick. 'Talk alone?'

Slick gave the ogre a good-natured smile. 'I can tell when I'm not wanted, big guy. I'll leave the two of you to your chat.'

As Slick rose from the table, he walked behind the ogre and mouthed at Slick, 'Tell me later.'

Dunk stifled a laugh and waved the halfling off. 'Do you want to go somewhere more private?' he asked M'Grash.

The ogre nodded, so Dunk led him from the common room and up into his own quarters. M'Grash had to bend down to get through the door, but once inside he was comfortable enough.

'So,' Dunk asked, a little amused by the sight of the ogre sitting on the floor of his parlour, as none of the chairs were close to large enough. Even the couch would have been crushed under M'Grash's bulk. 'What do you have to say?'

The ogre's faced reddened and screwed up horribly. Dunk braced for an ear-splitting wail, but it never came. Instead, M'Grash whimpered and pointed a trembling finger at the copy of *Spike! Magazine* still in Dunk's hand.

'Me,' the ogre rasped. 'My fault.'

Dunk shook his head. 'Don't be silly, M'Grash,' he said. 'If it's anyone's fault, it's Lästiges for writing such lies.'

'No,' M'Grash said, his voice louder now. He pointed at his chest sombrely. 'Killed them. Me.'

Dunk cocked his head at his monstrous friend as what M'Grash was trying to tell him finally dawned on him. 'You,' he said, collapsing on the couch as he tried to absorb this.

'You killed the other prospects in the camp?'

M'Grash shook his head slowly as he wiped his wet eyes dry. 'Broussards.'

'Luc and Jacques killed all those people?'

M'Grash nodded.

'And then they planted that knife in my tent to make it look like I did it.'

'Uh-huh. Wanted you off team.'

Dunk blew out a long sigh. 'It worked. If they hadn't been killed, I never...' He shot M'Grash a hard look. 'You killed them, didn't you?'

The ogre nodded. 'Wanted Dunk with Hackers.'

Dunk reached out and clapped M'Grash on his massive shoulder. 'You got that, all right.' He wasn't sure how he felt about M'Grash killing the Broussards, but he was sure they'd have been happy to do the same or worse to him. 'Thanks, big guy.'

'Ceiling?' M'Grash said. 'Me.'

Dunk's eyes went wide as he thought of Dirk and Spinne nearly being killed. 'No one actually died there,' he said slowly. 'The Champions of Death got the worst of it, and they just needed to be unburied.' Several of the Reavers had been crushed to death of course, but Dunk was far from certain how capable the big ogre was of comprehending his actions; best not to burden him with distractions like the truth.

Dunk narrowed his eyes at M'Grash. 'You didn't have anything to do with Ramen-Tut, did you?'

'No. Was Kur. Magic knife.' The ogre pointed at his waist.

'Ah. The belt-buckle blade.' Inside, Dunk breathed a sigh of relief. Kur had almost slain him with that same knife.

'Why did you bring down the ceiling?' Dunk asked.

'Coach wanted Dungeonbowl game.'

'So you eliminated the team playing in the one spot that could be open to us.' Dunk marvelled at the ogre for a minute. 'You're not so dumb as people think.'

M'Grash grinned widely, showing all his teeth. 'Thanks!'

'What about Schlitz?'

M'Grash shook his head. 'Saw wizard talk to Gobbo before game.'

'So Gunther was behind it?' Dunk thought about this for a moment. 'He must have wanted our team to lose. If he's working with Zauberer, he probably knew I'd chase out there after the wizard and either get myself killed or kicked out of the game.'

M'Grash nodded along, although Dunk suspected the ogre didn't really understand. Still, he'd underestimated the ogre before, and he was wary of doing so again.

'Anything else?' Dunk asked.

M'Grash nodded. 'Before you came. Killed Hackers.'

Dunk forced himself to breathe slowly. 'That's why the Hackers were looking for so many new players. Why did you kill them, M'Grash?'

The ogre frowned. 'Mean people. Kill mean people.'

Dunk smiled faintly. 'Remind me to never be mean to you.'

M'Grash gathered Dunk in a hug so tight and long that for a moment he feared he was to be the ogre's next victim.

'Dunkel friend!' M'Grash said as he set the gasping rookie down.

'Yes,' Dunk wheezed as he looked up at the gentle killer. 'The question now, though, is what do we do about all this?'

Before M'Grash could respond, there was a knock at the door. 'Who is it?' Dunk called.

'Blaque and Whyte,' the dwarf Game Wizard's gruff voice said. 'We'd like to have a few words with you.'

Dunk slipped around M'Grash and opened the door a few inches. He kept the side of his foot braced against the inside of it. The odd-sized elf and dwarf stood there in the hallway in their black robes, the words 'Wolf Sports' embroidered across their chests.

'What's this about?' Dunk asked.

'Aren't you going to invite us in?' Blaque said.

'I just got back from the Chaos Cup,' Dunk said. 'The place is a mess.'

'Have you read the latest issue of *Spike! Magazine* yet?'

Dunk grimaced. 'I'm just getting to it now.'

'I like that cover. It's a good image of you. Don't you like that cover, Whyte?'

'Fantastic,' the elf said. 'Almost like being there.'

Dunk closed his eyes for a moment. When he reopened them, the two GWs were still there. 'I'm beat,' he told them. 'I appreciate you checking in on me, but I'm going to bed.'

'I'm afraid we can't let you do that quite yet,' Blaque said.

Dunk looked down and saw that the dwarf had wedged his foot in the gap in the door.

'Hold on for a moment,' Dunk said as he held up a finger toward the GWs.

Dunk turned toward M'Grash, who'd been watching him with a confused look on his face. He beckoned the ogre over, then pointed at the door and whispered in M'Grash's ear, 'Don't kill them. Just slow them down.'

The ogre grinned down at Dunk as he put his hand against the door.

'My apologies,' Dunk said, poking his nose back through the gap in the door, 'but I have to go.'

'Look here,' Blaque began. Dunk noticed the two wizards now had wands in their hands.

'Wish I could help,' Dunk said. 'While I'm gone, my friend here will take care of you.'

With that, Dunk turned and headed for the window.

As DUNK URGED Pferd to gallop faster on the road that headed south, toward Marienburg, he heard an explosion from the direction of the Hackers Hotel. He looked back toward his still-open window and saw a shower of sparks erupt from it, followed quickly by a medium-sized form in a black robe that went sailing into the bay.

Dunk hoped M'Grash would get through the incident without being turned into a toad. Before the wizard in the water could spot him, he dug in his heels, urging Pferd to move faster than ever.

Once Dunk had left Bad Bay far behind, he began to think what he might do next. Going back to the Hackers was out of the question for now. There were a couple months left until the next of the Majors: the legendary Blood Bowl itself. The team would be all right without him until he figured out what to do about the GWs and his growing reputation as a player-killer.

As he headed south through the Wasteland, alongside the River Reik, his thoughts returned to his childhood and to the one person he always knew he could trust.

The city of Altdorf lay somewhere down the road ahead of him. Lehrer lived in Altdorf. So Altdorf it was.

THE FAMILY KEEP still stood there in the heart of Altdorf's wealthiest district. It was part of a collection of such places piled up on top of each other, each of them built to be more impressive than the last. As the birds darted in and out of the ivy-covered walls, Dunk's thoughts turned to better days.

Dunk had spent his entire childhood in the keep, never venturing any further than the limits of Altdorf itself, with the occasional jaunt a few leagues up or down the Reik. At the time, he'd never known he could ever want anything more. In many ways, Altdorf was the centre of civilisation, and the rest of the world just seemed like the wolves scratching at the door.

Dunk waited outside the keep until dark, which came late in these last days of spring. He saw his target slip out of the place at dusk, dressed in the same grey cloak Dunk still remembered.

Lehrer moved like a panther prowling through the city's undergrowth, constantly on the lookout for other predators. He sauntered past Dunk, keeping to the shadows, and moved silently down the street. Dunk waited for him to pass, then followed him as he ducked into a dark alley.

When Dunk entered the alley, he found it bare but for a few scraps of litter blowing in the breeze shunted down the narrow passage. He drew his sword as he stepped into the darkness and said quietly, 'I only want to talk.'

Dunk parried the blade that cut at him from the darkest part of the shadows. He knew Lehrer would be there, just as he knew he'd be dead if he hadn't been prepared for the blow. His old teacher didn't care to ask questions of people outside of the keep's walls.

'It's been a long time, kid,' Lehrer said as he moved into the half-light of a nearby streetlamp pouring into one corner of the alley. 'I hear you been keeping busy.'

The shorter Lehrer drew back his hood and glared at Dunk, who recognised that look from his long hours in the man's training; slightly impressed, but never enough to really show it. The slight man's silver hair matched the grey of his eyes now and blended in well with his cloak and the drab colours of Altdorf by night.

'Not as busy as some might say,' Dunk answered, sheathing his blade.

'Warmed my heart to see you and your brother in the same line of work,' Lehrer said. He kept his sword out, although he lowered its tip to the ground.

'I doubt my parents would have said the same.'

'Greta would appreciate the gold you're making,' Lehrer said with an ironic smile. 'Lügner would care more about the kills.'

Dunk snorted softly. 'Have you heard from them?' he asked, struggling to keep any taint of hope from his voice.

'Not a peep,' Lehrer said. 'The Guterfeinds are still looking for them, but they've not had a lick of luck yet.' He hesitated for a moment before continuing on. 'They're looking for you too.'

Dunk nodded. 'I,' he started, 'I thought I could make a name for myself as a hero. You know, slaying dragons and all that.'

'Gold and glory.'

'Right.'

'You've been listening to too many stories,' Lehrer said.

Dunk shook his head. 'So it seems. I just wanted to be able to come back here and save everyone, to make things right.'

'It's going to take more than fame and fortune to do that, kid.' When Dunk's face fell, the old teacher added. 'At least it would give you more choices about how to do it.'

'Maybe.' Dunk began to wonder if this was all a mistake.

'Dirk had the right idea,' Lehrer said. 'Leave here and get himself set up in a whole new life. He never looked back.'

'Ironic he got traded to the Reavers then and ended up back here.'

Lehrer laughed. It was a low sound bereft of humour. 'That's fate for you.'

Dunk waited for Lehrer to say something more. When that didn't happen, he realised his old teacher was waiting for him.

'I'm in some serious trouble,' Dunk said.

'So I read.'

'What can I do about it?'

Lehrer stuck out his chin. 'I take it fighting's not an option.'

Dunk shook his head. 'It involves wizards. There's only two of them right now, but there could be more at any moment.'

'Did you do it?'

Dunk's breath caught in his throat. 'What's that?'

'Did you kill all those people?'

Dunk frowned. 'Does it matter?'

'Not to me,' the old man said, shifting his weight.

'I need to make this go away,' Dunk said. 'Otherwise, I won't be able to settle in a major city for the rest of my life.'

'If the Game Wizards put a bounty on your head, you can expect more hassles than that.'

'So what do I do?'

'Well,' Lehrer said, 'if there's anything my time with the Guterfeinds has taught me, it's that no job is complete until you pin the blame on someone else.'

Dunk grunted. 'After so many years with our family, how can you work for those people?'

Lehrer eyes Dunk carefully. 'They're not all bad. Your family wasn't all good either.'

'We had nothing to be ashamed of.' Dunk surprised himself with how angry he sounded.

Lehrer shook his head. 'You still see your family through the eyes of a child. It's time to grow up, kid.' With that, he turned and slinked back into the shadows. 'Good luck.'

Dunk thought about following the old man, but if Lehrer wanted to leave he wasn't sure how he could stop him.

'Just know one thing,' Lehrer's voice called back through the darkness from somewhere further down the alley. 'It wasn't your fault, kid. Not all of it.'

THAT NIGHT IN the Skinned Cat, Dunk just wanted to be left alone with his thoughts. This was the kind of place where hard people drank hard drinks and gave each other plenty of space, which suited Dunk just fine. In his younger days, he'd heard many a tale about the place, most of which seemed too fantastic to believe. The only thing that he'd been sure of was that he never wanted to set foot in the place, yet here he was.

As Dunk finished off what he'd promised himself was his last stein of the horribly potent dwarf draught Bugman's XXXXXX, the only thing he was closer to was leaving his dinner in the gutter outside the pub. He'd turned Lehrer's advice over and over in his mind, but he couldn't figure out a way to make it work.

'Pin the blame on someone else.' It sounded like a fine notion, but Dunk couldn't think of where to begin. The only obvious people to shift the blame to were either his friend (M'Grash) or dead (the Broussards).

There was Kur, of course. Not only had he let Dunk share the blame for Ramen-Tut's death but he'd tried to kill the rookie too. Dunk didn't think he'd shed a tear for the veteran thrower if he were to take the fall for all those murders. Still, it wouldn't be simple to make that happen.

The easy way to handle it would be to give up M'Grash. The ogre had been responsible for enough of the mayhem that it wouldn't be hard to make the rest stick to him. Dunk didn't want to try that quite yet though. The ogre had been a friend to him when he needed one and had saved him from Kur more than once. He even owed his spot with the Hackers to M'Grash.

Dunk wished he could leave the blame with the Broussards. How he'd explain their own deaths and all those who came after though, he didn't know. Sure, the dead sometimes walked, and even played Blood Bowl, as he'd seen with the Champions of Death, but this would be a long stretch.

Dunk had given up and was motioning for the bartender to bring him another pint of the Bugman's when the last person he'd expected to see slipped into the other side of his booth.

Gunther the Gobbo smiled across the dagger-scarred table at Dunk. 'I've been looking for you everywhere, kid,' he said. 'I never thought I'd find you in a dive like this.'

Dunk fought an urge to shove the table into the Gobbo's greasy, overfilled gut and crush him with it. 'How did you find me at all?'

The Gobbo grinned as wide as an alligator. 'I read, kid, and I know a little bit about you.' He leaned over the table and nearly drooled on the wood. 'Don't be so surprised. The kind of business I'm in, it's my job to know as much as I can about hot new talent like you.' He winked at the bartender. 'And to know as many different kinds of people as I can. You never know where the next star player's going to crop up.'

'What do you want?' Dunk said, glancing around the place nervously. He didn't see any sign of Blaque and Whyte, but he was ready to flee at the first sign of them.

The Gobbo slapped his clammy, wart-covered hand on the table, and Dunk nearly leapt from his skin. The bookie laughed. 'A little jumpy there, aren't you, kid? No need for that. I'm here to help you.'

'Like you did at the Chaos Cup?' Dunk said.

The Gobbo chuckled at that. 'You're not going to hold that one against me, are you? How was I to know you'd chase out there after Zauberer? That little madman told me he'd be wearing a disguise.'

'Then what was he doing out there?' Dunk asked suspiciously.

'He was going to kill Skragger, of course,' the Gobbo said. 'I thought you were smarter than that kid.'

'But why?' Dunk hated even talking with the Gobbo, but his curiosity had to be satisfied. This just didn't seem to add up.

The Gobbo folded his hands in front of him on the table. A pint of Bugman's appeared in front of Dunk, while the barmaid slid a massive stein of Bloodweiser in front of the bookie.

'Ever heard of a dead pool, kid?' The way the Gobbo leered at Dunk, he was sure it was something horrible, but he had to shake his head.

'It's a kind of bet based on a list of famous names, a pool in which the gamblers wager on which of the names will die next. With the right crowd, you can end up with a lot of money on the line.'

'And Skragger's name was on that list?'

The Gobbo nodded. 'This is a list for Blood Bowl players only, and he's been on it forever. I put a ton of money on the guy back when he was a rookie, and I've just been letting it ride ever since. Can you imagine how he managed to survive all those years?

'Do you know how many Blood Bowl players make it to retirement? About one in ten. It's even harder for the better players. They set themselves up as targets, and everyone wants to take them down. Skragger was the biggest target there was.'

The Gobbo stopped for a moment to throw back the entire stein of Bloodweiser in one gulp. 'Another Blood for me!' he shouted at the bartender, who pointed at the barmaid already coming their way with a refill.

'By his last year, Skragger was at the top of most dead pools. A lot of people lost money on him. They pulled theirs out when he made it to the end of the season, but not me. I just let it ride. In fact, I doubled what I had down.

'Most people just thought it was a long-term investment. After all, he's got to die sometime, right? Probably in a violent way, knowing him.'

'And now you stand to gain a lot if he dies.'

The Gobbo shook his head. 'Not anymore. Now that everyone knows someone's gunning for the guy, they all leaped on his name too. If he dies this year, the take will be split so many ways I'll lose my shirt.'

'Sorry to have ruined your year,' Dunk said deadpan.

The Gobbo cocked his head at the rookie. 'Don't worry about it, kid. There are more bets where that one came from. In fact, that's where you come in.'

'Here it comes.'

The Gobbo grinned wide enough for Dunk to wonder if the bookie ever cleaned his teeth. 'I need someone like you to work for me.'

'I don't know if I'll ever play Blood Bowl again.'

'You leave that to me. With enough gold to grease the way, anything can happen.'

Dunk goggled at the man. 'You could buy off the GWs?'

The Gobbo winced. 'Maybe, maybe not. Everyone has his price. Besides, there are lots of ways for a resourceful fellow to get what he wants.'

'Does this have anything to do with the Black Jerseys?'

'Shhh!' The Gobbo put a fat finger in front of his mouth, then leaned forward again and said, 'Let's just say I think you'd look good with a black shirt under your Hacker green.'

'What's in it for me?' Dunk asked.

'Besides getting the GWs off your tail?' The Gobbo stared at Dunk incredulously. It didn't suit him. There was so little about him that was credible in the first place.

Dunk shook his head. 'How do I know you're not just setting it up so you can turn me in? Is there a bounty on me already?'

'Five hundred stinking crowns,' the Gobbo said with a snigger. 'You don't have to worry about me, kid. Adding another name to my little metateam's roster is worth far more than that.'

'Metateam?'

'Zauberer came up with it. You know how wizards are with words. Or maybe you don't. Anyhow, it's a team made up of parts of other teams that covers them all like a blanket.'

'Which is you make sure the games come out the way you need them to in order to give you the most profit.'

The Gobbo nodded. 'You're not as slow as you look, kid.' He leaned forward again, whispering this time. His breath smelled of verdigris.

'Let's quit dickering around here, kid, and get down to business. The Black Jerseys make a lot of money for me and from me. If you don't end up working for us, then you'll be against us.'

Dunk held up a hand. 'Are you saying there are Black Jerseys already on the Hackers?'

The Gobbo gave Dunk a sardonic grin. 'What do you think, kid?'

'Then what do you need me for?'

'Insurance, kid. I always like to have a backup plan or three. After all, that guy gets hurt, then where am I with the Hackers?'

Dunk sat back. 'I don't know. I'm thinking of washing my hands of all this and leaving the game behind. There's always Albion, or the New World.'

The Gobbo shook his head. 'Don't do that, kid. You got one hell of a career here. You'd be throwing it away.'

'It looks to me like it's already gone.'

'I can fix that. Let me outline a deal for you.'

Dunk nodded to show he was listening.

'Smart money – okay, *my* money – is on your Hackers making it into the Blood Bowl finals this year.'

'Are you serious?'

'As a Chaos cultist. The trick is that the Hackers will then lose the game. I need you in there to help make sure that happens.'

'But I can't play in the game. If I show up in the stadium, the GWs will grab me for sure.'

'If you manage to pull it off, I'll make that problem disappear. Plus, you'll be on my salary from there on out. That game alone could make you fifty thousand crowns.'

The number nearly took Dunk's breath away, but he focused on the GW problem instead. 'That money won't do me any good if I can't spend it.'

'I have the perfect patsy for you. I'll even provide the evidence for Blaque and Whyte to nail him to the stadium wall.'

'Who is it?' Dunk asked.

'Zauberer, of course.'

Dunk smiled despite himself. Then he heard his voice say, 'All right, I'll do it.'

DUNK SPENT THE next month holed up in a number of different inns. He kept changing his address every few days, just in case someone recognised him. Luckily, in a city the size of Altdorf there were plenty of places to stay and thousands of other transients for him to hide among.

While he waited for the Blood Bowl to roll along, Dunk did his best to stay in training. Although he couldn't get in any practice time without raising suspicions, he spent much of his days working out in whatever room he was staying in at the time. He wanted to be ready for the big game when it came along, and the grunts and growls he made tended to convince the others staying in the inn that it wasn't worth bothering the lunatic down the hall.

Every now and then, Dunk wandered down to the Altdorf Oldbowl, the home stadium of the Reikland Reavers. Eventually, he saw what he wanted: a home game coming up the next week.

THE CEILING OF the halfling inn known as Slag End was so low that Dunk had to enter on his knees. In a city as cosmopolitan as Altdorf, there were many places like this, but Slag End was the closest to the Oldbowl. Dunk suspected he'd find who he was looking for there, the night before the Reavers' home game.

Slick sat in a dark corner in the main parlour, smoking a pipe that was nearly as long as he was and sipping at a mug of Teinekin Beer. When he saw Dunk walking over to him on his knees, the halfling let the pipe drop from his mouth and said, 'Esmerelda's sacred pots, son. Is that you?'

Without waiting for a reply, Slick leapt to his feet and charged into Dunk's outstretched arms. The two embraced for a moment, then Slick pulled back to look at Dunk. 'How have you been? *Where* have you been? You look good – great even! Sit, sit, and tell me every-thing!'

Dunk squeezed himself into the corner next to Slick's chair, refusing a seat himself, as they were all too small to hold him. 'My apologies, son. It's the reason I come here, most big folk won't, but it makes it hard to entertain such guests. Come, let's go someplace else.'

Dunk refused. 'This is fine, Slick. I need to talk, and I can't stay long.' With that, he told Slick everything that M'Grash had told him and what he'd been doing since, including the offer that Gunther the Gobbo had made to him and the fact that he'd accepted it. Throughout it all, Slick sat and puffed on his pipe, blowing the occasional ring but mostly just listening and taking it all in. Later, Dunk would realise that this was the longest he'd ever seen the halfling stay quiet when there was a conversation to be had, but that fact made it clear that Slick was giving his words his full attention.

'I knew it,' Slick said when Dunk was done. 'That ogre always worried me. He's a good one to have on your side, to be sure, but he's trouble too. Ogres don't have any sense of morals, no way to tell right and wrong. M'Grash's childhood may have "humanised" him a bit, but he's still an ogre beneath it all.'

The halfling looked over at Dunk. 'You did the right thing by coming here, though. Those GWs were ready to hang you from gates of the nearest stadium. They need to make an example out of someone, and you're at the top of their list.'

It was here that Slick became grave. 'You should consider handing them M'Grash,' he said. 'It's the simplest way out of this. Everything else involves too much risk.'

'I can't do that,' Dunk said. 'That ogre did everything out of loyalty to me and the team. The only people he killed were the Broussards, and that couldn't have happened to a better pair of bastards.'

'Son, this isn't about loyalty. It's about two of the most important things in life: money and breathing. Blood Bowl has made us both wealthy, but you can't enjoy money without breathing, and you can reverse that, and it's just as true!'

Dunk shook his head. 'I won't allow it. Loyalty, friendship, has to count for something. I won't sell out M'Grash to save my own skin. Money's not that important to me.'

Slick gasped at this. 'Spoken like someone heady with the possibilities of youth!' He waved his hands at himself. 'Look at me. I'm not a young halfling anymore. I don't have much in the way of talents, and my only skills centre around smoking, drinking, and the gentle art of conversation, particularly in convincing coaches to hire players for a bit more than they're really worth.'

'Is that more important than a friend's life?' Dunk asked. He wasn't really sure he wanted to hear Slick's answer.

'You should ask M'Grash that. He seems happy to let you take the blame for what he did.'

'And if he came forward? The GWs would still pin all the other killings on me. Then we'd both be in for it.'

'You might be able to pin it all on him.'

'Or not. I'd rather try that with someone else. That way if I blow it, at least I'm not hurting a friend too.'

Slick shook his head as he stood up and approached Dunk. In the cramped quarters, the move made Dunk more than a little claustrophobic.

'He's your friend, not mine. As your agent, I feel compelled to inform the GWs about all of this and establish your innocence. For your career, it's the right thing to do.'

'Keeping me and M'Grash away from the GWs is good for the Hackers over the long term. That's good for my contract too. It makes it a good investment for you.'

'I don't know, son,' Slick said. 'It sounds like a good theory, but I'm more worried about the short-term. If the GWs catch up with you, what's going to happen to *you*?'

Dunk smiled softly. It wasn't the money that Slick was worried about after all.

'Well.' Dunk sensed that Slick wanted to do the right thing but needed a good excuse for it. 'What if M'Grash was your client too?'

Slick furrowed his brow for a moment, then sat down. 'That's a mighty good question, son, but it's moot, isn't it? Why would he make me his agent?'

'He doesn't have one now, and I'll bet Pegleg screwed him on his contract,' Dunk said, warming to the idea. 'Just think of the gains you could make for M'Grash, and your percentage.'

'Of course,' Slick said, instantly warming to the idea. 'Do you think you could get him to do that?'

'Hey, he's my friend, right?' said Dunk. 'Besides, I'd say he owes me a favour or two.'

A FEW WEEKS later, Blood Bowl fever hit Altdorf hard. Throughout his years of living here, this was the season that Dunk had hated most. Hundreds of thousands of 'people' of all races descended on the city, swelling it nearly to bursting and straining its normally bountiful resources to the limit.

Most years, Dunk would simply hole up in the family keep and avoid the craziness around the big event as much as he could. After all, even walking across town could turn from a simple jaunt into an epic quest. It just wasn't worth going outside.

In those days, the roar of the crowd and the chants of the fans roaming through the streets terrified the young Dunk and annoyed his teenage self. For weeks after, he'd hear, 'Here we go, here we go, here we go,' echoing in his dreams.

This year was entirely different.

Dunk couldn't wait for the Blood Bowl tournament to begin. It would be three weeks of open games arranged by the team coaches, followed by a semi-final round and then a final round for the big prize: the Blood Bowl trophy and the lion's share of the half-million-crown purse. It was also Dunk's chance to redeem himself if everything went to plan. It was an insane, risky plan, of course, but it was all he had, so he clung to it like a rabid fan to a stray football.

At Slick's advice, Dunk had shaved his head bald and painted it so it looked like a Hacker's helmet. 'You're hiding in plain sight,' the halfling said. 'Who would think the fugitive thrower from the Bad Bay Hackers would walk around dressed up as one of its biggest fans?'

Dunk had to admit that he looked very little like himself. People did stare at him as he walked down the street, but it seemed they were looking at the decorations on his head rather than him. He even went out and bought himself a replica jersey that had his number, ten, on it and his name emblazoned across the back.

In the pubs, Blood Bowl fans hailed Dunk and slapped him on the back. 'Go, Deadly!' they shouted at him, thinking he was emulating the 'Deadly' Dunk Hoffnung mythologized in the pages of *Spike! Magazine*.

Lästiges had followed up her 'exposé' of Dunk's killing spree with another feature article detailing Dunk's short career and his links to Dirk, Spinne, Slick, and anyone else Dunk had ever met. According to the report, Dunk had killed half a dozen Game Wizards while making his escape and then dared the world to find him.

Accordingly, although they had to know the story wasn't true, the GWs had raised the bounty on Dunk's head to five thousand crowns. That was more than most people in Altdorf made in their entire lives, and it was enough to grab the attention of more than a few bounty hunters. Fortunately, no one was able to penetrate Dunk's disguise.

Rumours placed Dunk all over the place. Some said he'd escaped to the New World. Others claimed he'd struck a deal with the gods of Chaos and would be the new starter taking the place of Schlitz for the Chaos All-Stars. One local rag even claimed that Dunk was an illegitimate grandson of the Emperor himself and had been secreted away in the Imperial Palace.

While all this insanity swirled around him, Dunk got Slick to find a ticket for him to the Hackers' games. 'Where else would someone dressed like me be on game day?' he asked.

'I don't know, son,' Slick said. 'The Game Wizards will be there in force. Do you think they'll be as easy to fool as everyone else?'

'I'll be standing in a crowd of over a hundred thousand raving fans, dressed like this. If they can pick me out of that, they deserve to catch me. As part of my contract I get seats to all games in which we play. Get me one of those.'

'You're not still playing for the Hackers, son.'

'Has Pegleg torn up my contract?'

'No,' Slick smiled, 'he hasn't. He'd have to spend a fortune to fire you. Besides which, he's milking the publicity of you being a Hacker for all it's worth.'

'How'd you negotiate a severance clause like that?'

'It was easy, son. Pegleg figured you'd be dead long before he thought about firing you. Most bad Blood Bowl players end their career on the field. It's rare that they live long enough to refuse to play.'

IN THEIR FIRST game, the Hackers were set to take on the Moot Mighties, a halfling team from Mootland. 'The "halfling reserve" as some like to put it,' Slick said as he gave Dunk his ticket.

'Does a halfling team stand a chance against the Hackers?' Dunk asked. 'I don't mean to offend, but it sounds like a mismatch.'

Slick shook his head. 'You really need to start following the sport more.' He drew a deep breath, then spoke. 'In most circumstances, you'd be right. Most of the halfling Blood Bowl teams only ever play each other in their own stadium, known as the Batter Bowl, named after former Mootland League Commissioner Balbo "Beery" Batterman, of course.'

'That's fine, but the Hackers will murder them. Literally. M'Grash could probably take on the lot of them alone.'

Slick winced. 'It's been done before. The Mighties got tired of all the grief they got for being so small. The legendary ogre player Morg'th N'hthrog boasted he could take them all on at once, and they dared him to prove it.'

'What happened?'

Slick pursed his lips. 'Let's just say the next season was a rebuilding year for the Mighties.'

'And they won't meet the same fate against the Hackers? It sounds like M'Grash could trash everyone on the field and then use the scrubs to pick his teeth.'

'On any given day, any team can beat any other team.'

'That sounds like something the Gobbo would say. I smell the Black Jerseys at work here. Why give the Hackers such a creampuff of a team to play though? Who's going to bet on the Mighties?'

'All they have to do is beat the spread.'

'What's the spread?'

'Six touchdowns.'

Dunk frowned. 'That's all?'

'The Gobbo's giving even odds the Mighties won't survive the game long enough for the Hackers to score seven times.'

Dunk nodded. 'The Black Jerseys could make sure the Hackers lose somehow, and the Gobbo would rake in a dragon's hoard.'

'But you said the Hackers have to lose in the finals for the Gobbo to make his big score. So the Hackers play the Mighties and get an easy win and rack up a bunch of points. I heard the Mighties coach actually challenged the Hackers. I'll bet the Gobbo set that up.'

'I'm surprised the players don't refuse to take the field. They'll get creamed.'

'Maybe,' Slick said. 'The Moot Mighties, though, aren't just any halfling squad. They have a treeman on their team by the name of, well, his real name is unpronounceable. The Mighties call him Thick-trunk Strongbranch.'

Dunk goggled at his agent. 'A treeman player? What position does he play?'

Slick grinned. 'Thrower, of course.'

Dunk shook his head. 'This, I have to see.'

COME GAME TIME, Dunk sat in the stands, surrounded by thousands of newly minted Hackers fans. Scores of them wore replicas of his jersey, and a few even had their heads painted like him. They seemed uniformly drunk and rowdy, but Dunk found their unbridled enthusiasm contagious. He was soon cheering along with the rest of the fans, screaming and chanting until he was sure he'd never be able to talk again.

When the Hackers took the field, they charged out there like champions. Dunk wasn't sure what Pegleg had said to the players in the locker room ahead of time, but they came out ready to play. He watched them down there with a pang of regret. He surprised himself by how much he wanted to be out there playing alongside them.

A quick head count told Dunk that the Hackers had yet to replace him. They only had fifteen players on the field. In some strange way, that gave him hope that everything would somehow all work out for the best.

When the Mighties rolled out onto the field, the crowd erupted into laughter, all except for a sizeable halfling cheering section in along the eastern end of the field. The little fans rooted at the top of their lungs for their homeland heroes and were just as rowdy as any of the other spectators. Dunk noticed there were more beer vendors walking the aisles in the halfling section, selling Bloodweiser draughts in commemorative steins to all the thirsty fans there, who seemed able to drink twice their weight in cheap, watery beer.

The halflings went mad as the treeman strode onto the field. Thick-trunk Strongbranch towered over the field, dwarfing even M'Grash. He waved his leafy boughs at the crowd, greeting the fans of Mighties and taunting the Hacker Backers, as a blood-streaked banner a crew of battle-scarred rowdies standing well behind Dunk proclaimed the Bad Bay fans.

The Hacker Backers started to chant right away. 'The tree! The tree! The tree is on fire! We don't need no water! Let the bugger burn! Burn, bugger, burn!'

Strongbranch just smiled at them all as he sauntered out to the Mighties' end of the field.

The coin toss went to the Mighties, but that was the only thing that did. They elected to receive the ball. Gigia Mardretti kicked it deep into the Mighties territory, and one of the halflings pitched it to the treeman.

M'Grash was the first Hacker down the field. He lowered his shoulder and slammed into Strongbranch with all his incredible might.

The treeman struggled to stay upright, but it was a futile effort. The towering oak of a player toppled over backward, slowly at first and then accelerating to bone-crushing speed.

'Tiiiiiim-beeeerrrrr!' the Hacker Backers sang in unison as the treeman was laid low.

Strongbranch dropped the ball as he fell, and Kur was there to scoop it up. An instant later, he was in the end zone, celebrating the Hackers' first touchdown.

Two of the Mighties had been standing in the wrong place when Strongbranch fell. A well-experienced crew of halfling litter bearers raced on to the field and carried them off. Two more players bravely took their place to the hooting of the Mighties' fans.

'Wow, Jim,' Bob's voice said as the teams set up for the Hackers to kick the ball again. 'That was a quick score. Isn't that some kind of record?'

'You'd think so, wouldn't you, Bob? The fastest score ever though was made in literally no time at all, since the clock doesn't start until someone touches the ball.'

'I think I remember that. Wasn't that Old Goldenhooves?'

'You got it, Bob! The centaur player was so fast that he reached the Elfheim Eagles' end zone before the kick-off hit the ground and caught it in the end zone!'

Dunk looked up towards the top of the stadium above the north end zone. There he saw a live Cabalvision broadcast of the game displayed on a massive white wall. The images of Jim and Bob chatting with each other flashed up for a moment, along with a grainy replay of that long-ago centaur score.

'The Mighties have only taken two casualties so far, Jim, so you owe me a crown!'

'Those little guys are tougher than they look, Bob. Let's go to our new sideline correspondent, the lovely Lästiges Weibchen, to get a report on how they're doing.'

Dunk stared in disbelief as Lästiges's face splashed onto the wall, her head alone taller than M'Grash.

'Thanks, Jim!' Lästiges said with a winning smile. 'It's not looking too good for Perry and Mippin down here. The Mighties' team apothecary tells me they won't be back on the field today. More stunning, they might even miss dinner tonight!'

The rising noise of the crowd drew Dunk's eyes away from the monstrous image to watch the next kick-off. As he scanned the sidelines he spotted Lästiges down there near the Mighties' bench, a fist-sized golden ball floating near her head, watching her and broadcasting the image via Cabalvision to the Wolf Sports team.

One of the halflings near Strongbranch caught the ball again. This time, instead of tossing the treeman the ball, the stubby player dashed into Strongbranch's arms.

'Throw him! Throw him! Throw him!' the crowd chanted as the treeman raised the halfling over his head. Dunk couldn't believe what he was seeing, but neither could he look away. Strongbranch reared back an arm, the one with the ball-carrying halfling in it, then hurled it down the field over the heads of everyone, including M'Grash who leaped up to try to knock the little guy down.

The halfling, who had rolled himself up into a well-armoured ball, went sailing down the field and hit the turf just shy of the end zone. From there, he bounced once and spun out flat, just on the other side of the goal line. The little guy stood up and stabbed a fat-fingered hand into the air. The ball was in it.

The crowd went nuts. Even the Hacker Backers cheered. Dunk found himself screaming his heart out for the little guy.

It was the last time the Mighties would score. Now wise to the treeman's strategy, the Hackers put two receivers back in their own end zone. They camped there until Strongbranch decided to try his halfling-hurling trick again.

When the halfling zoomed toward the end zone, Cavre stepped up and caught the flyer before he could land. Then he tucked the hapless halfling and the ball he was carrying under his arm and raced him all the way back down the field to the other end zone, scoring a touchdown for the Hackers instead.

Cavre was so excited by the strategy's success, he spiked the halfling along with the ball. The halfling litter bearers were already waiting in the end zone for this and toted the little guy off in seconds.

The rest of the game was a rout. The Hackers pounded the Mighties into the dirt, sometimes literally. After only six scores, the Mighties no longer had enough players left to field a whole team and had to concede the game.

The crowd rushed the field as the referees announced victory for the Hackers, and Dunk went down with them. He was careful to avoid the Hackers, though, for fear that his disguise wouldn't be enough to fool any of them. He knew that some of them, Kur in particular, wouldn't hesitate to turn him in for the bounty on his head.

As Dunk watched, a battalion of Hacker Backers upended Strong-branch, who toppled into the crowd to another rousing round of 'Tiiiiiim-beeeerrrrr!' It was then that he felt a hook snag his shoulder. He turned to see Pegleg staring at him.

'That's quite a getup you have there, sir!' the coach shouted over the noise of the crowd to Dunk, his sea-grey eyes piercing right through the rookie. 'We hope to one day see our friend, Mr. Hoffnung, back among us!'

'I don't think it will be too much longer!' Dunk shouted back.

'Let's hope not!' Pegleg shouted. 'This team needs him more than he might know!'

'Tell us, coach!' Lästiges's voice shouted at Pegleg over Dunk's shoulder. 'How does it feel to be one step closer to the Blood Bowl?'

Pegleg shot a knowing glare at Dunk for a moment before devoting his attention to the reporter. 'Like coming home!' he shouted as Dunk slipped back into the crowd, not once looking back. 'Like coming home!'

THE HACKERS PLAYED two more games in the playoffs. In the first, they faced off against the Underworld Creepers, a team made up of skaven and goblins who normally scrimmaged in the sewers of the largest cities in the Empire. The final score was 7 to 2, in favour of the Hackers. It wasn't much of a game after a pivotal moment in the first half.

As Dunk watched the game, he saw that one of the Creepers was smoking – and not tobacco. Smoke and sparks poured out of a black, round shell the lanky, green goblin had tucked under its arm as it raced down the field.

'Look, Jim,' said Bob's voice. 'Number fifty-eight, Gakdup Goremaker, seems to have a bomb!'

'He sure does, Bob! And look at him go! He's trying to get rid of that deep in Hacker territory.'

'For the folks at home, Jim, can you tell us if this sort of thing is legal?'

Jim's voice laughed. 'As in "within the proper rules of the game"? Of course not. But I can't remember a game featuring goblins that didn't feature some kind of cockamamie scheme. Do you remember the Pogo Stick of Doom?'

'Remember it? I think I'm still cleaning the turf out of my teeth after the last jump of the pogo stick's inventor Pogo Doomspider. Attaching a rocket to it in a game versus the Dwarf Warhammerers just wasn't too wise!'

Goremaker scrambled down the field, carrying his deadly cargo straight to Kur and tossing it into the surprised thrower's arms. Kur was no fool though. Even from Dunk's spot in the stands, he could see the thrower recognise the bomb for what it was instantly. He brought back his arm and fired it into the Creepers' dugout.

Dunk had been prepared for a loud blast, but the ear-splitting boom that followed almost deafened everyone in the Emperor's Bowl. From the large number of skaven and goblins that vacated the dugout as the bomb came in, Dunk could only guess that the Creepers had had a whole stockpile of explosives stored away there.

Despite the blast, play on the field didn't pause until M'Grash brought the ball into the end zone a full minute later. He'd have been there quicker if he hadn't stopped to kick every deafened goblin out of his way.

As the Hackers were setting up for the next kick-off, Wolf Sports cut down to Lästiges again. 'The Underworld Creepers suffered a staggering ten casualties from that self-inflicted explosion,' she told the camra. 'Despite this and the restriction keeping the total number of players on a team to sixteen, the Creepers still have eleven eligible players ready to take the field.'

'That's goblin maths for you, Lästiges!' Jim's voice said.

'What happened with the referee this time?' Bob's voice said. 'Where was the penalty call?'

'The Creepers are old hands at this sort of mayhem, Bob,' Lästiges said. 'Apparently one of their cheerleaders slipped a small bomb down the referee's pants before Goremaker made his ill-fated dash for glory. I'm being told that he will not return to the game, leaving only one referee to cover the entire match.'

'No other referees are willing to step up?' asked Jim's voice.

'As you know, the high casualty rate among referees has crippled recruiting efforts. Besides this, most referees consider it horrible luck to take over in a game during which another zebra has already been slaughtered.'

THE NEXT GAME, the Hackers took on the fabled Elfheim Eagles, a team composed entirely of high elves, the most sophisticated, long-lived, and flat-out haughty people on the planet. Dunk wondered how the Gobbo would have allowed such a match-up. The honour of the high elves was legendary, and Dunk doubted there could be a Black Jersey among their number.

The captain and coach of the Eagles, Legless Warwren, spent much of the game raging at the referees, who'd clearly been bought. Dunk couldn't be sure whether the money had come from the Hackers' coffers or those of the Gobbos, but when he saw Kur kneecap an Eagles blitzer right in front of the end zone, and in full view of the orc ref standing there, he knew what had happened.

As honourable as they were, the Eagles refused to lower themselves to the Hackers' level and cheat, whether blatantly or not. They managed to complete the game, which was more than could be said for the Moot Mighties or the Underworld Creepers, but the outcome was never really in doubt.

ONCE THE PLAYOFFS were over and the tallies were in, the Hackers were the top-rated seed of the four teams to move on to the semi-finals, the others being the Reavers (of course); Da Deff Skwadd, a team of orcs hailing from the Badlands far to the Empire's south; the Dwarf Giants, a team of dwarfs from Karaz-a-Karak in the Worlds Edge Mountains.

As Da Deff Skwadd had barely squeaked into the semi-finals, their seeding pitted them against the Hackers, while the Reavers faced off against the Giants. Dunk hadn't heard much about the orcs, other than that they had a troll on their team and were all terrible at spelling. In the end, Dunk thought, it probably didn't matter much. If the Gobbo couldn't figure out a way to pay off a bunch of orcs to throw a game, he wasn't really trying.

Dunk almost hoped the Hackers would lose to Da Deff Skwadd. Then he wouldn't have to go through with his plans for the final game. Of course, he'd then be on the run with a huge bounty on his head for whatever might be left of his miserable life.

When the game came around, Dunk sat in the same spot as always. The other fans around him were just as rabid as he was about the game at this point, and they suited him fine. When the Hackers took the field at the start of the game, the Hacker Backers almost knocked each other out by cheering too hard. They were so worked up they all spent the entire game standing on their seats, screaming for more touchdowns and orc blood – not necessarily in that order.

It wasn't too far into the game when Dunk felt something tugging at his leg. He looked down to see Slick standing there in front of his seat, desperately beckoning him to sit.

Dunk slipped to his seat immediately. He knew that something horrible must be wrong if Slick had risked coming into this section of the stands. 'What is it?' he asked.

'Blaque and Whyte are here, son,' the halfling said.

'I figured they would be,' Dunk said. 'But how are they going to find me up here?'

'They were down in the dugout at the start of the game, questioning people. Kur wanted to give you up so badly I thought he'd start making up stuff in the hopes it would be true. The GWs were too sharp for him though and ignored him right away. Then I heard them say they'd start scouring the stands today. Blaque mentioned the Hacker Backers, and I knew I had to warn you.'

Dunk closed his eyes in frustration and then opened them. 'Did it ever occur to you,' he asked the halfling, 'that they might have known you were listening?'

Slick gasped. 'They said that so I would hear them? And then…' The halfling's face threatened to turn Hacker green. 'Oh, dear.'

Dunk popped up from his seat to peer around the stadium like a prairie dog in a sea of drunk, violent, and over-decorated people. As he craned his neck around, he saw the tall dwarf Blaque stomping down the aisle to his left. He glanced the other way and saw the short elf Whyte prancing down the aisle to his right. The two were matching time perfectly, and they would converge on his seat in mere seconds.

Dunk dunked back down and hissed at Slick. 'Let's scatter! They can't follow us both at once.'

'They only want you, son,' Slick said as he slapped a thick hand over his face, miserable with grief. 'I'm worthless.'

'If I do manage to get away, and I'm going to go for it right now, they'll go after you next. Now that you've shown that you're in contact with me, you're not safe either.'

A look of horror dawned on Slick's shamed face as the truth of Dunk's words hit him.

'Someone your size shouldn't have too much trouble hiding here for a few minutes. They're going to chase me out of here. When that happens, that's your chance.'

'What *are* you going to do, son?' Slick said, putting his hand on Dunk's arm.

'I'm making this up as I go,' Dunk confessed.

Blaque appeared at the end of the aisle, over Slick's shoulder. Dunk looked back and saw Whyte completing the pincer move from the other side. With the vast sea of people crowded around them, there was nowhere for the rookie to run.

Dunk jumped up and smacked the man next to him, a barely standing brute who'd tottered his way through every game so far, loyally screaming his lungs out for the Hackers. The man glared back at Dunk, who suddenly realised the man hadn't just had the Hackers' logo painted on the side of his shaved head. It was tattooed.

'What do *you* want?' the man screamed in Dunk's face, spittle flying as he spoke.

Dunk raised one knee and shouted. 'Give me a boost, pal! I'm going over!'

The drunk fan smiled and laced his fingers together in front of him. 'About time someone round here finally showed some bloody team spirit!' He shouted with a grin.

Dunk put his boot in the man's hands and then jumped up. As he did, the man pulled upward, shoving Dunk high into the air. 'Body pass!' The drunk shouted as his hands came over his head.

The people all around turned their heads in time for them to toss up their hands and catch Dunk. The rookie breathed a sigh of relief as he felt a dozen hands cradle him for a moment. He'd seen crowds that were just too drunk or mean to care drop people instead of grabbing them, and the last thing he needed was to land headfirst on the stone steps right in front of Blaque and Whyte.

The crowd beneath him started to pass him up toward the top of the stadium, just as they had during Dunk's first game. Visions of hurtling over the top of the Emperor Stadium flashed through his head as he spotted the GWs turn tail and head back toward their aisles. If they couldn't catch him now, they'd just follow him until it was safe.

Dunk reached down and grabbed one of the fans holding him. It was a tall burly man with a blood-red mohawk and a set of piercings that followed cheekbones sharp enough to cut diamonds.

'Leggo, deader!' the man shouted. 'You're going over!'

'No!' Dunk insisted. 'I got up here for one reason only. I want to kiss a Hackette before I die!'

The Hackettes were the Hackers' squad of professional cheerleaders. They were uniformly gorgeous in the kind of way that Dunk couldn't really fathom but from a distance. He'd never even stood close to them, for two reasons. First, they only showed up at real games, and Dunk was either in the dugout, on the field, or nursing a possible concussion at those times. Second, Pegleg absolutely forbade even a conversation with these ebullient young beauties for fear it would distract the players from the task at hand; winning the game.

The fans all around Dunk roared with approval at his choice of how to end his life. They all suspected that the security guards that protected the ladies would tear Dunk into tiny bits. The burly guards, often washouts from one Blood Bowl team or another, or a former player who'd taken one too many blows to the head, were rumoured to be testy because they supposedly had to be castrated to take the job, although Dunk had no proof that this was true. He hoped that whatever the reason, the guards would be in a less-than-murderous mood when he landed before them.

Being passed down toward the field went faster than being pushed toward the top. As Dunk slid along the raised hands of the people in front of him, he looked back to see Blaque and Whyte turn around and then race down after him. As they got closer to the bottom rows, they had to fight their way through the rowdiest of the spectators, people who had left their seats to stand at the bottom of the aisle and were strong and tough enough to maintain their positions against all rivals.

Dunk grinned, but as he reached the restraining wall that supposedly kept the fans from the field, he braced himself. The last of the fans, the ones who were standing in the front row, right in front of the lovely Hackettes, gave him the kind of heave-ho that only comes with lots of practice and tossed him straight over the heads of the guards.

Two of the ladies linked their arms together and caught Dunk as he hurtled into their midst. He smiled at them as they set him down gently. They returned the favour with dazzling grins.

'My undying thanks,' Dunk managed to say.

'It happens all the time,' one of the women said, a stunning blonde with bright blue eyes. 'Someone isn't paying attention and his friends decide to send him for a ride.'

'We used to beat the guys senseless,' a ravishing brunette with an amazing tan said. 'Then one of them managed to tell us it wasn't his fault.'

A mind-blowing redhead stepped up and said, 'Since then, we've been a bit gentler with the guys. After all, who can blame them for wanting to get a closer look?'

The rest of the women giggled. Dunk wondered if the stadium had suddenly gotten a lot warmer or if it was just him.

'Of course, we're not really the ones you should be worried about,' the blonde said. 'It's them.'

Dunk turned to see a pair of guards charging toward him. They looked like they'd been castrated that morning and were looking to take out their aggravations on someone.

'Hey, ladies,' Dunk said, pointing up towards Blaque and Whyte, who had just managed to finally fight their way through the fans on the other side of the restraining wall. 'You see those two guys with the Wolf Sports robes? Network executives.'

The cheerleaders squealed with delight and charged toward the two Game Wizards, sweeping the guards back with them. The two men were charged with protecting the women, so they went along with them rather than chasing down Dunk.

The rookie smiled to himself as he raced toward the tunnel that led to the team locker rooms. In less than a minute, he lost himself in the maze of passageways that riddled the underside of the stadium and left Blaque and Whyte and the rigged semi-final game far behind.

Dunk watched the rest of the game in a sports pub he picked out at random, a place known as the Spiked Ball, and then stuck around for the second game too. The Reavers handed the Giants their heads – sometimes literally. This means the Hackers would end up playing the Reavers in the finals, just as Dunk had hoped.

Dunk wanted to meet with Slick somewhere, but he didn't dare go to Slag End or to Slick's hotel. The GWs would follow the halfling around if they could find him, and Dunk just couldn't take that risk. He thought about going to the Skinned Cat to see some familiar faces, but he feared the Gobbo might show up there. He didn't want to see Gunther until the final match.

Dunk had a week until the next game, and he spent most of that time working out and moving around a lot. Since the GWs had seen him in his fan costume, he had to change his look again. He washed his head clean and got rid of his replica jersey. Soon he hoped to be wearing the real thing again.

In Beggars Square, Dunk picked up a new outfit: the simple brown robes of a monk and a fist-sized football carved from wood and spiked with blackened nails, Nuffle's holy symbol, hanging from a rough length of jute around his neck. Dunk pulled the hood low over his head as many of the penitents did during these wild days in Alt-dorf to serve as an example of restraint. They stood out like bears in a beehive, but everyone in town considered them sacrosanct and left them alone. No one ever bothered one of Nuffle's own, especially during the Blood Bowl tournament, for fear of jinxing both themselves and their favourite teams. As long as Dunk didn't run into some other monks who tried to drag him along to services in one of the churches that spotted the town, he would be just fine.

THE NIGHT BEFORE the big game, Dunk set his plan into motion. To guarantee a loss for the Hackers, he'd have to play for them, and that meant getting back on the team. It wasn't going to be easy to arrange, but Dunk didn't see how he had a choice.

Still dressed as one of Nuffle's monks, Dunk strolled into the Jaeger Inn, one of the handful of first-class hotels located near Emperor Stadium. The teams who played in the Blood Bowl tournament stayed in these places, so much so it was almost impossible for anyone else in the area to take a room here.

Dunk walked straight to the Jaeger's private dining hall and let himself in. The doors were guarded, but when he pulled back his hood for an instant to reveal his face, the sentries were so stunned they let him in. He was still a part of the Hackers after all.

Inside the dining hall, Pegleg was just finishing a toast when Dunk walked in and stood at the foot of the table. Every eye in the room turned to look at the man in the monk's robes, unable to see who he really was under his hood. The murmur of voices in the room fell silent.

It was Pegleg, standing at the head of the table, who broke the silence. 'To what do we owe this honour, good brother?' he asked. 'Are you here to tell us that Nuffle himself has blessed our efforts and that we can expect him in our dugout tomorrow afternoon?'

The rest of the Hackers laughed nervously at this. Then all fell silent again.

Dunk reached up and drew back his hood, exposing his face and head. The collective gasp almost sucked every bit of air from the room.

'Mr. Hoffnung,' Pegleg said, 'welcome back.'

No one else said a word. Down at the far end of the table, next to Pegleg, Slick gave Dunk a hearty smile and wave.

'It's good to be back,' Dunk said.

'It's a pity you can't stay long,' Kur said as he stood up from his spot halfway down the table. 'We have no place for murderers here.'

The rest of the team burst into peals of nervous laughter at this. When they were finished, Dunk spoke.

'I heard you might need another thrower for the final game.'

Kur sneered at the rookie. 'We've gotten this far without you, punk. We don't need anyone's help, especially not yours.'

Dunk smiled knowingly. 'That's not what the papers are saying, especially after those three interceptions you threw against the Da Deff Skwadd. Those orcs picked you off more often than they picked their noses.'

'That was all part of my plan,' Kur said, although Dunk was sure no one in the room, Kur included, believed it. 'I just put the ball deep into their territory so we could take it from them there. Those moronic orcs never stood a chance. I could have taken on the whole lot myself.'

Dunk had seen Kur say the same thing on Cabalvision in an on-field interview with Lästiges after the game. 'I think the orcs would love to see you try that,' he said.

Kur stepped away from the table. 'Isn't there a fat bounty on your head?'

'Better that than to have a bountiful, fat head like yours.'

Kur strode toward Dunk and stood in the rookie's face. Their eyes met and locked. They were still the same height, but Dunk had filled out over the course of the last year and was just as broad across the chest as the veteran. The week's worth of stubble on his head made him look harder than his shaggy locks ever had. He was more than ready to stand toe to toe with Kur.

'I'm claiming you for your bounty,' Kur said. Dunk thought he detected a hint of desperation behind the veterans' bravado, and he smiled.

'Sorry, *old* man,' Dunk said. 'You have to catch me first.'

Kur's hands snaked out and caught Dunk by the collar of his robe and held him fast. 'That's easily enough – ow!'

Dunk smashed his forehead into Kur's sharp nose, smashing it flat. Despite the shock and pain, Kur refused to let go of Dunk's robes, even as the blood poured from his face.

Dunk threw up his arm and bent over, letting his robes slip right over his head. Kur, who'd been trying to hold Dunk in place, staggered backwards and fell into the end of the table, striking the back of his head on its edge.

Kur grabbed the back of his head and brought his hand around to his face. It was coated with blood. On his knee now, he glared up at Dunk and snarled. 'I'll skin your skull!'

All eyes in the room went to Dunk, who stood framed in the doorway, wearing a Deff Skwadd jersey. 'Give it a try,' he said with a cocky smile. Then he turned and fled.

Dunk raced down the hall and out the front door of the Jaeger Inn. As he ran down the brightly lit boulevard, dodging back and forth through the people milling about the crowded streets, he could hear Kur stomping after him.

Dunk charged around the next corner and then another, each time far enough head of Kur that the rookie could still be seen but not caught. As Kur got closer, Dunk ducked through a rough door, over which hung a sign that depicted an elf's decapitated head.

A pair of hands grabbed at Dunk as he raced through the dimly lit place, but he spun away from them, just as he'd been trained to shake a tackle. Dunk smiled at that, knowing that Pegleg would have been proud.

Dunk raced down a corridor and stopped dead in front of a pair of double doors that barely hung on their hinges. In the room beyond, he could hear plates and steins clanging, accompanied by rough words and off-key songs. For a moment, he worried that he'd lost Kur at the door, that he'd not been able to shake the bouncer as Dunk had. Then he saw the starting thrower appear at the end of the hallway.

'Nowhere to run?' Kur said, venom dripping from his voice. Dunk saw that the man had the punch-dagger from his belt in his fist. Fresh blood dripped from its blade.

Dunk stepped back until he had both hands on the doors behind him. He pressed back against them and felt them give.

'You're as dumb as you are weak,' Kur said as he stalked down the hallway. 'First, you take the fall for all those killings, including some that I committed. Then, you show up at our dinner to ask for your job back when there's a 20,000-crown bounty on your head.'

'I didn't realised they'd upped it,' Dunk said.

'They made an even better change too,' Kur said as he came within striking distance and brought his blade high. This was it, Dunk knew as he leaned back into the doors behind him and braced for the attack.

'Now,' Kur said, 'it's "dead or alive".'

Kur roared as he charged at Dunk and drove his bloodied blade home. Dunk grabbed Kur's arms as he stepped back into the room beyond. Then he spun and used Kur's momentum to throw the man behind him with all his might.

Kur sailed through the air for a moment before he came crashing down into a battered dining table. He landed in the remnants of a platter of roasted boar and skidded along the length of the table until he came to rest near the head.

Kur looked up to see more than a dozen gruesome, green-skinned creatures with rough, tusk-filled mouths gaping wide at him as they glared down through wide, yellow eyes. The room had fallen silent, except for one slurred voice in a corner somewhere rasping out the last refrain of a drinking song.

'Kur Ritternacht, starting thrower for the Bad Bay Hackers,' Dunk announced brightly to the orcs assembled around the room, who stared first at Kur, who was still lying on their banquet table, and then him. Dunk pointed to the red Deff Skwadd jersey he wore. Then, before he backed out of the room and closed the doors behind him, he called out, 'Consider him a gift from a fan!'

The screams and pleas for pity that emanated from Da Deff Skwadd's year-end dinner followed Dunk all the way out to the street. He tried to stop himself from smiling but failed utterly.

THE NEXT MORNING, Slick and Dunk reported for the game at the Hackers' locker room as if nothing had happened. Dunk wore another set of monk's robes to the stadium, and Slick used his personal pass to walk him straight past the tight security.

Once inside the locker room, Dunk held back near the exit and Slick walked straight up to Pegleg. The coach didn't wait for the halfling to speak before laying into him. He snagged Slick's shoulder with his hand and said, 'What kind of stunt was that your boy pulled last night, Mr. Fullbelly? It's less than an hour before the biggest game in this team's history, and I don't have a single thrower to show for it!'

Pegleg held up his hook, which had a deflated football impaled on the end of it. 'I even thought of playing the position myself,' he said, 'but I'm just not equipped for it!'

'Calm yourself, Pegleg,' Slick said smoothly. 'Don't fear. I have the solution for you right here.'

The halfling motioned to Dunk, who drew back his hood again and strode up to Pegleg. 'Ready and reporting for duty, coach,' he said.

'Dunkel!' M'Grash cheered. Everyone else in the room simply gaped at the rookie as if he were some sort of ghost.

Pegleg frowned and narrowed his eyes at the thrower. 'You had this in mind all along, didn't you, Mr. Hoffnung?'

Dunk started to nod proudly, but Pegleg cut him short, brandishing his football-blunted hook at him. 'I should gut you right here!' he shouted.

M'Grash stepped forward and covered Pegleg's hook and ball with a monstrous hand. 'Don't!' he growled. Then he grinned broadly at Dunk. 'My friend!'

Dunk winked at the ogre then stared coldly back at his coach. 'If you'd rather I leave,' he started.

At that moment, the door to the locker room slammed open, and Blaque and Whyte stormed in, their wands out and crackling. 'Hold it right there!' Blaque shouted at Dunk.

'It's the Game Wizards,' Slick said in a not terribly convincing tone. 'Thank Nuffle you're here!'

The halfling walked over to Dunk and took him by the hand. 'Come with me, son,' he said as he led Dunk over to stand in front of the two GWs, who stood there panting for breath.

'You've led us on a merry chase,' Blaque said to Dunk between deep breaths. 'But it ends here.'

'That it does, my friends,' Slick said as he presented Dunk to the pair. 'I'm pleased to finally hand over this dangerous threat to you.'

Blaque shot Slick a curious look. 'The Game Wizards thank you,' he said slowly. 'Now, what's your game?'

'No game,' Slick said. 'I just want to make sure that you know that it was Slick Fullbelly who placed Dunk Hoffnung in your hands, right in front of all these wonderful witnesses.'

'You sawed-off bastard,' Dunk growled. 'I thought I could count on you!'

'You can mull that over all you like, son,' Slick said with a self-satisfied grin, 'while I count every crown in that bounty.'

Blaque looked to Whyte. The elf just shrugged at him and put his hand on Dunk's shoulder.

'Now wait just a minute,' Pegleg said, his voice coated with menace. 'Where do you two think you're going with my thrower?'

'We're taking him back to headquarters for now. We'll schedule a disciplinary hearing after that,' Blaque said. 'You'll be invited to testify on his behalf.'

'Once you get him to wherever you're taking him,' Pegleg said, 'he'll only be good for playing for the Champions of Death, I'm sure. I need him now!'

Whyte stopped binding Dunk's hands behind his back with a length of thin rope.

'What happened to Kur?' Blaque said, glancing around the locker room for the veteran.

Pegleg glared at Dunk for an instant before answering. 'He took a wrong turn somewhere last night and fell into the wrong hands. He won't be playing for some time, maybe months, and I need a thrower today!'

'Let me play,' Dunk said to the GWs. 'Let me play one last time before you take me away.'

Unsure about all this, Blaque turned to Whyte. 'Now that we finally have our hands on this fugitive, does it make sense at all to let him go?'

The elf shook his head slowly. 'I just can't see it.'

'I'll turn myself back over to you right after the game,' Dunk said. 'You have my word on it.'

Blaque burst into laughter at that. Whyte just stood there stoically until his partner finished.

'You want us to take the word of a Blood Bowl player?' Blaque finally said. 'You *are* a rookie.'

'A rookie who's been bringing in some top ratings!' a voice thundered from the locker room's entrance. All heads turned to see an angular man in the bright blue robes of a Wolf Sports wizard stroll in through the doorway, his close-cropped white hair swept back in a tight widow's peak. The smug look on his face told people he thought he owned the place. The phalanx of weapon-bristling bodyguards who surrounded him only emphasised the attitude.

'Ruprect Murdark!' Slick blurted as everyone else in the locker room gasped. 'My, what a coincidence that the owner of the Wolf Sports network would grace us with a visit right now.'

The wizard favoured Slick with an arrogant wink. 'A true mystery that,' he said, 'but that will have to wait for later! Right now, I'm more concerned with that young man's fate!'

Blaque and Whyte lined up on either side of Dirk and grabbed him by his elbows. 'We were just bringing him in, Mr. Murdark,' Blaque said eagerly.

'You're not taking him anywhere!' the wizard pronounced. His spotless and stylish robes swirled about him as he spoke. 'Think of the ratings!'

'I'm sorry, sir,' Blaque said. 'I don't believe I understand your meaning.'

'I said, "think of the ratings". Dunk Hoffnung, player on the run, returns to the game for one last match, in the Blood Bowl itself!' Murdark held up his fingers in a wide circle, as if framing a crystal ball.

'The ratings will go through the roof! I only wish I had more time to publicise it! This is high drama! Blood Bowl at its best!'

'But sir…' Dunk felt the Game Wizards' grips tighten on him as if he might be torn from their grasp at any moment.

'No buts,' Murdark said. 'That man plays today! Let him go, or I'll fire you both on the spot!' Sparks of energy crackled between the wizard's fingers as he spoke, the electric arcs dancing wildly in his eyes. 'And that will be the least of your troubles!'

Blaque turned as pale as Whyte. The dwarf gaped at Murdark for a moment, then glanced over at the elf, his eyes pleading for some kind of advice. Whyte had none to give.

The dwarf grimaced as he looked up at Dunk and said, 'All right. One last game.'

'Don't get your robes in a bunch!' Murdark said with a smug smile. 'You can arrest him again right after the game! No better way to cap a Blood Bowl tournament than a public execution!'

Dunk shot a frightened look at Slick. The halfling shrugged at him with a nervous smile. 'That's entertainment,' he said.

'BLOOD BOWL FANS of all ages,' Bob's voice said, ringing out over Emperor Stadium, 'welcome to the ninety-eighth Blood Bowl!'

The roar shook the stadium to its roots and gave Dunk reason to wonder if a sufficiently loud noise could actually stop a beating heart. Standing in the dugout, he stared out at the stands before him and held his breath. This was the sort of adulation and attention reserved only for kings and emperors, and only rarely then. Dragon slayers never rated this.

To start the game, Jim and Bob announced the names of each of the players on both teams as they trotted out to the centre of the freshly re-laid Astrogranite field, waving at the crowd and absorbing the raw power of all that intense, nearly tangible emotion focused on them. The announcers got through all of the names on both of the team lists, and Dunk found himself standing his the Hackers' dugout alone. For a moment, he feared that Blaque and Whyte had changed their minds and would snatch up him there on the spot. Then he heard Bob's voice again.

'Last, but certainly not least, we have the Hacker's starting thrower: Kuuuuurrr–'

'Hold it, Bob,' Jim's voice said. 'We have a last-minute substitution here. It's – Nuffle's spiked balls! In as the Hacker's starting thrower: Dunkel Hoffnung!'

The crowd went insane. Dunk kept his head down and trotted out to the middle of the field where the rest of his team was waiting for him. As he did, he saw Dirk and Spinne standing with the Reavers on the other side of the referee holding the game coin in the middle of the field. They stared at him with open mouths.

'Talk about the comeback of the year!' Bob's voice said.

Dunk raised his hand to acknowledge the crowd's exultant roar of approval. As he did, he knew that he'd play this game until the day he died. There was simply no better place for him to be.

The Hackers won the coin toss, and Cavre informed the ref that the team would receive the ball. When the two teams met to shake hands before heading to their own ends of the field, Dirk and Spinne grabbed Dunk.

'What are you doing here?' Dirk demanded. 'The GWs will haul you in for sure.'

'They already have,' Dunk said. 'I'm just here to do a job.'

'What could that possibly be?' Spinne asked.

Dunk discovered that he enjoyed the note of concern in her voice. 'If I help the Hackers lose the game, the Gobbo will pin all the killings on Zauberer instead. I'll be a free man.'

Dirk and Spinne glanced at each other, looks of horror painted on their faces.

'Can I count on your help?' Dunk asked.

Dirk grimaced. 'Normally, sure, but…'

'What is it?'

Spinne spoke up. 'Skragger has promised to kill you, Dirk, and everyone else in your family if the Reavers win, especially if Dirk scores three more touchdowns and breaks Skragger's record.'

Dunk grabbed Dirk by his shoulder pad. 'He knows where the rest of our family is?'

'He claims to,' Dirk said. 'I'm not willing to risk it.'

The whistle blew to start the game. 'What's the worse fate?' Dunk asked. 'Death or prison?'

Dirk frowned before he answered. 'You brought it on yourself, Dunk.'

Dirk turned and trotted down to the Reavers' end of the field. Spinne looked after him in shock for a moment, then turned and gave Dunk a quick kiss. 'I'll talk to him,' she said. 'Wish me luck.'

Dunk nodded at her as she took off running. 'I hope you kick our asses.'

'Did you see that, Bob?' Jim's voice said.

'I sure did, Jim! It looks like the rivalry between two of the players down there might be more than just friendly! Let's see that again!'

Dunk looked up at the massive image displayed on the wall over the end zone and saw Spinne kiss him. The crowed hooted like mad as Dunk strapped on his helmet to hide how much he was blushing.

Moments later, the kick-off sailed down the field toward the Hackers. Cavre fielded the ball and then pitched it over to Dunk.

Dunk fell in step behind M'Grash, who bowled over a pair of Reavers trying to get past him. Then Dunk stepped back and hurled the ball downfield.

The throw sailed wide over the head of Gigia Mardretti and landed in Spinne's outstretched hands instead.

'Wow!' Bob's voice said. 'It looks like Hoffnung has just given his girlfriend an early birthday present! You don't see turnovers that clean every day!'

Before Jim's voice could respond, Gigia charged into Spinne and knocked her flat. The ball rolled from her grasp, and the Hackers' catcher scooped it up. Another Reaver hit her before she could go another step and the ball game rolled on.

Within minutes the Hackers had scored their first touchdown as Andreas Waltheim ran the ball into the end zone. Dirk should have been able to bring him down, but he seemed to have tripped when trying to tackle the Hacker blitzer.

After the next kick-off, Dirk got the ball and hurled it down the field straight toward Dunk. He caught the ball and ran towards M'Grash again. This time, he flipped the ball to the ogre and shouted, 'Cavre's open. Throw it!'

To Dunk's knowledge, the ogre had never thrown the ball before in his life. Dunk was sure that M'Grash had plenty of strength for the job, but that wasn't all there was to throwing the football. He watched as the ogre slung back his arm and then fired it down the field toward the distant Cavre.

A Reaver blitzer dashed over and got in front of the ball. It hit him like a warhammer and knocked him flat, but he kept a hold of it, perhaps because of how it had dented his armour. A nearby Reaver lineman gathered the ball up from his fallen friend and raced it back toward the end zone.

Dunk saw M'Grash heading for the lineman and waved the ogre off. 'I got him!' he shouted as he ran toward the ball carrier. The lineman hung out a stiff arm which Dunk promptly collided with and moments later the Reavers' had their own first touchdown.

BY HALF-TIME, THE Reavers had a 3 to 2 lead over the Hackers. As Dunk and the rest of the players filed into their locker room, Pegleg grabbed the thrower with his hook and pulled him aside.

Out of earshot of the rest of the team, alone in the tunnel, Pegleg shoved his hook into Dunk's face and said, 'What in Nuffle's sacred rules are you doing out there?'

Dunk decided to play dumb. 'I don't know, coach. I guess I'm still a bit slow from so many weeks off. It's coming back to me though. I'll make it up in the second half.'

'That's not what I'm talking about, and you know it, Mr. Hoffnung,' Pegleg hissed. 'You're moving around just fine out there. Too well, in fact, for how rotten you're playing. Answer me this,' he said. 'Are you trying to lose this game?'

Dunk hesitated. He wanted to come clean about what he was doing. Maybe the coach could even help him out. He knew that Pegleg wanted to win the game, but perhaps he could see that a loss would be in the Hackers' long-term interests. After all, it would ensure that both Dunk and M'Grash would be able to keep playing for the team. Otherwise, the Hackers would be gutted.

Dunk looked Pegleg straight in the eye and said, 'Yes.'

Pegleg backhanded Dunk with the blunt side of his hook, knocking the thrower to the ground. 'Are you out of your damned mind?' he raged at the rookie.

'But coach!' Dunk said, cowering before the man's wrath. 'Let me explain.'

'There is *nothing* to explain!' Pegleg roared. 'You have betrayed the trust of *every* member of this team.'

'But–' Dunk ducked under another swipe from the coach's hook, this time with the sharpened end.

'But nothing! I can only assume, Mr. Hoffnung, that someone got to you somehow. This is *not* the man I've watched develop into one of the most promising Blood Bowl players I've ever seen. This is *not* the man who's gone from a dilettante to a dedicated leader.'

Pegleg leaned over Dunk and shook his hook at him. 'I don't know what they promised you, Mr. Hoffnung. Money, women. Maybe they threatened your life. *None* of that matters now because you're life ends *here!*'

Before Pegleg could slash Dunk's neck open with his hook, Dunk lashed out and knocked the coach's legs from under him.

'This is about my life, M'Grash's life, and the fate of this team,' Dunk grunted as he leapt on top of the coach and pinned him to the ground. 'If we lose this game, Gunther the Gobbo will provide us with a patsy to pin all those murders on.'

'If you really killed all those people, Mr. Hoffnung, then good riddance to you!' Pegleg snarled as he struggled to pry his hook free from Dunk's grasp.

'I didn't do it,' Dunk said. 'It was M'Grash!'

Pegleg stopped wrestling against Dunk for a moment. The look in his eyes was tired but still defiant. 'So,' he said, 'you're telling me that Mr. Gobbo will provide you and M'Grash, two of my best players, with a clean slate should you lose the game for him?'

Dunk nodded. 'It's all part of Black Jerseys conspiracy of his. He sets the odds the way he likes and then forces the game to go the way that earns him the most money.'

'Of course he does, Mr. Hoffnung.'

Dunk nearly let go of the coach, but he remembered the man's vicious hook just in time to keep from being gutted. 'You know about this?'

'I read, Mr. Hoffnung, and I've been coaching this team for a long time.' Pegleg squinted up at Dunk. 'You know what the most stunning thing about this year has been?'

'Getting to play in the Blood Bowl.'

'Certainly, but more than that. It's that I know this isn't our year. We didn't get here on our own. Someone arranged for it.'

'The Gobbo,' Dunk said, exasperated that Pegleg wasn't getting it.

'No, Mr. Hoffnung,' Pegleg said softly. 'It was me.'

This time Dunk did let go of the coach. He leapt backward before Pegleg could renew his attack, but the coach's hook didn't twitch as he scrambled up against the wall.

'I am part of the Black Jerseys, Mr. Hoffnung,' Pegleg said as he sat up and placed his back against the tunnel 's opposite wall. 'I persuaded Mr. Gobbo to make us the champions this year. I promised him half of our purses all the way through the tournament in exchange for his help.'

'You… you were behind it?' Dunk couldn't even believe the words as they left his lips.

Pegleg nodded slowly. 'And now you tell me that I've been double-crossed.' He doffed his yellow tricorn. The wig attached to it came off too, and he sat there with his grey stubble showing.

'I knew it would happen eventually,' Pegleg said. 'I just didn't know when. I'd hoped…' He fell silent for a moment, and Dunk wondered if he was about to cry.

'I'd hoped it would be next season, sometime, *anytime*, after this game.' Pegleg crumpled up the hat and wig in his hands. 'Just once,' he said, staring dully into Dunk's eyes. 'Just once, I wanted to be a *champion*.'

Dunk reached out and put his hand on Pegleg's knee. 'Coach,' he said, 'I think there's still a chance that could happen.'

As Dunk charged back out through the tunnel after the rest of the
team for the game's second half, Slick reached up and caught his arm.
'Hold on a moment, son,' he said. 'I have someone who wants to have
a chat with you.'

Fearing it was the Gobbo, Dunk tried to pull away. 'Not now, Slick,'
he said, 'I have a game to play.'

Slick grabbed on with both hands, though, and insisted. 'Trust me,
son,' he said. 'I set up a quick interview with you on live Cabalvision.
Think what it'll do for your career!'

'Look,' Dunk stopped and said, 'you should get out of here, distance
yourself from me.'

Slick narrowed his eyes at Dunk. 'Now why would I do something
like that, son?'

Dunk grimaced and checked to make sure no one else was listening. The tunnel was empty again. 'I'm going to double-cross the
Gobbo. From here on out, I'm playing to win.'

Slick grinned. 'You don't know how pleased I am to hear that.' Then he
grew concerned again. 'But what about the GWs? The only reason I
turned you in there was I figured you'd go free at the end of the game. If
that was so, then why let all that lovely reward money go to waste.'

Slick reached down and tousled the halfling's curly hair. 'I figured,'
he said. Then he sighed. 'I'm not sure what I'm going to do about

them. Right now, I'm just going to play the best game I can and let the dragon's scales fall where they may.'

Slick grinned. 'In that case, you really should do this interview.'

Dunk let out a good-natured groan and let his agent lead him by the hand out of the tunnel. When he emerged into the sunlight, the crowd roared its approval. Before he could turn to acknowledge it, he found Lästiges stepping right into his face.

'Thanks, Jim!' the reporter said to someone Dunk couldn't see as she turned to him. He noticed a small golden ball hovering next to them, a small, eye-sized hole pointing first and her and then him, flickering back and forth between the two.

'I'm down here on the field with Dunk Hoffnung, the rookie sensation slash mass murderer, whose story seems to have taken Blood Bowl fans everywhere by storm.' Dunk heard Lästiges voice booming above him like that of some sharp-tongued goddess. The crowd cheered in response to her words.

'Tell me, Dunk,' Lästiges said as the eye in the golden ball pointed toward the thrower, 'how does it feel to be playing in what we're told will be your last game with the Hackers?'

Dunk grinned. 'Don't tell me they're talking about trading me already.' His voice boomed alongside Lästiges's – or so it seemed. He was sure he couldn't really sound so confident as that voice did.

Lästiges smiled like a crocodile at Dunk's response. 'I'm referring to the bounty placed on your head, which the Game Wizards tell me was claimed by your former agent. Tell me how it must have felt to be betrayed like that.'

Dunk just smiled again. 'My *current* agent, you mean,' he said, gesturing down to Slick standing beside him. The floating camra pointed down at the halfling, who watched himself waving at the crowd, his face almost fifty feet high. 'Anyone who can get that kind of money out of Wolf Sports is a keeper! My only question is whether I get the standard ten percent!'

Lästiges smiled wider, and this time it almost seemed real. 'Rumour has it you tricked Da Deff Skwadd into nearly beating to death Kur Ritternacht last night, opening the way to your start in today's game. Can you comment on that?'

Dunk opened his mouth but then slammed it shut again when he saw someone hobbling up behind Lästiges on a new set of crutches. 'Here comes Kur right now,' he said, pointing at the veteran thrower who was stamping his way along the sidelines toward Dunk. 'Why don't you ask him yourself? I've got a championship to win!'

With that, Dunk trotted on to the field, leaving Lästiges and Kur behind. As he went, he heard Slick say, 'That's an amazing rig you have there, miss. Do you mind if I have a look at it?'

The second half of the game was much different than the first. Before the two teams lined up for the kick-off, Dunk met Dirk and Spinne in the centre of the field again.

'New game plan,' Dunk announced with a grin. 'We're going to whoop your ass.'

Spinne was stunned. 'You're not worried about the Game Wizards?'

'It's a trick,' Dirk said, measuring his brother's reaction.

Dunk shook his head. 'I'm not worried about any of that anymore. Just look around you. See where we are.' He flung his arms wide as if he could throw then around the entire stadium. 'This is the Blood Bowl. *The Blood Bowl.* We may never have a chance to play in a game like this again. I don't know about you, but I'm not going to waste it on someone like Skragger or Gunther the Gobbo.'

Dirk frowned. 'Nothing's changed. You just want us to try to beat you.'

'No,' Spinne said, intrigued. 'I think he's serious.'

'You can *try* to beat us,' Dunk said, 'but you're going to have to play your best to do it.'

'If you want to win so badly, why tell us?' Spinne asked.

Dunk smiled at her and then chucked his brother on the side of his helmet. 'I'd love to win, but I came here to *play!*'

The whistle blew, and Dunk trotted into his position at the far end of the field, so excited to finally play for real that he practically bounced along the Astrogranite. When the ball came sailing through the air, he made a running dive and came up with it. Directing Kai, Henrik, Lars, and Karsten to form a line for him, he made some good yardage forward while Cavre and Simon blasted downfield to get open for a pass.

Meanwhile, Dunk motioned for M'Grash to get in front of him and charge forward. Dunk pumped his arm downfield, faking a pass to Carve, then blasted right through the hole the ogre had opened for him. He was halfway to the end zone before any of the Reavers came close to touching him, and he raced straight past them.

Only Dirk stood between Dunk and the goal line now. As Dunk sprinted closer to where his brother waited for him, he could see that the younger Hoffnung still hadn't made up his mind about whether or not Dunk was really here to play, and he smiled to himself.

Dirk had the angle on Dunk and came at him just shy of the end zone. Rather than trying to juke around his brother, Dunk lowered his shoulder and drove into him as hard as he could, his legs pumping like a stallion at full gallop.

Dunk smashed into Dirk's chest and knocked his brother back into the end zone. He followed after him, holding the ball into the air as he crossed the goal line, soaking up the crowd's rabid cheers.

As he passed by Dirk, Dunk spiked the ball right into his brother's helmet. It bounced high off Dirk's head and landed in the stands. The fans there went wild, screaming, 'Dunk! Dunk! Dunk!'

Dirk stood up and beckoned for his older brother to come over to him. When Dunk complied, the two butted their helmets against each other like rutting rams.

'All right,' Dirk said. 'You wanna play? Let's go!'

With the score now tied, it was a real game once again. The Hackers and Reavers faced off against each other like two punch-drunk boxers, throwing everything they had into every punch, hoping for a knockout blow.

The Reavers scored next. Dirk connected with Spinne for a long bomb that put her in the end zone. Dunk raced up behind Spinne, hoping to intercept the ball, but it was just out of his reach. He then tried to tackle her, but she put on a burst of speed and left him in her dust.

As Spinne danced around the end zone, celebrating her victory, Dunk had the chance to take a cheap shot at her and knock her into the stands. Instead, he crept up behind her, tapped her on the shoulder, and said, 'Boo!'

Spinne nearly jumped out of her armour, and Dunk dashed away before she could take her revenge. The crowd exploded into laughter and shouted for more.

When the next kick-off came to the Hackers, M'Grash somehow ended up with the ball and managed not to drop it. Confused, the ogre glanced around for some sort of direction. He was used to hitting people carrying the ball, not handling it himself.

'Go, go, go!' Dunk shouted. 'I'm right behind you!'

With a wild, ear-shattering howl, M'Grash launched himself straight down the field like a mad bull, only much more dangerous and bigger. Reaver after Reaver stepped up to take him on, only to find themselves face down in the Astrogranite. Eventually they brought him down, only yards from the end zone, but it took six of them to do it, one on each limb another on his head, and the last, Dirk, stripping the ball.

Dirk landed hard and rolled away from M'Grash before the ogre toppled over onto him but held on to the ball and scrambled to his feet. Looking downfield, he didn't have anyone open. Most of his team was still prying themselves loose from M'Grash. So he tucked the ball under his arm and sprinted ahead.

Dunk knew that he had to stop his brother or it would be another Reaver touchdown for sure. He looked up at the clock and saw that time was running out. If the Reavers scored again here, the game would be over. There would be no catching them.

Dunk charged straight at Dirk, who corrected his course to avoid his brother's path, angling toward the far sideline. Dunk changed his route as well, putting the two of them on a collision course well shy of the end zone.

When the two brothers reached each other, Dirk juked left, then right, in a vain attempt to throw off Dunk's tackle. Dunk, though, remembered his training. He kept his eyes on Dirk's waist, not his shoulders or feet, and he threw his arms wide to wrap them around his brother and bring him down.

Dunk hit Dirk hard enough to dent both armours. Dirk grunted and started to topple, but as he did he managed to get rid of the ball.

Dunk crushed Dirk to the ground. He smiled as he heard the air whoosh from his brother's lungs. He'd done his job well. He was a good Blood Bowl player, maybe even a great one, and he knew it.

The crowd erupted into a mind-numbing cheer, and Dunk wondered what had happened. He rolled off of Dirk and looked back toward the end zone to see Spinne standing there alone, holding the ball triumphantly over her head.

Dunk looked up at the Cabalvision images playing on the wall high over the end zone. On the replay, he saw Dirk's pass wobble along like a wounded duck until Spinne plucked it from the air and carried it the last few steps into the end zone.

The Reavers now had a two-touchdown lead. The game was over. The Hackers had lost.

'Sorry, Dunk,' Dirk said as he stood up and offered his brother a hand. 'The best team won.'

'Hey,' Dunk said wistfully, 'it's not all bad. We actually got to *play*. And at least now I can get the Gobbo to hand over Zauberer to take the blame for those killings.'

Spinne charged over and grabbed Dirk in a victorious embrace. 'We did it!' she screamed. 'Reavers win!' The crowd echoed her over and over as the rest of the Reavers rushed over to them and grabbed them up as they exulted over their triumph.

A large hand fell on Dunk's shoulder as he took off his helmet. 'Tried Dunk,' the ogre said as Dunk turned toward him. A tear as large as an apple fell from the creature's eye.

'It's all right, big guy,' Dunk said, patting M'Grash's arm. 'We did the best we could.' He blew out a big sigh. 'I guess there's always next year.'

As Dunk spoke, he looked over to the sidelines to see Blaque and Whyte waiting for him there. He flipped them a quick salute. 'Or, maybe not.'

Dunk started to make the long walk back to the Hackers dugout when someone grabbed his arm and whipped him around. It was

Spinne. She wrapped her arms around him and planted the most incredible kiss Dunk had ever experienced square on his lips.

After a stunned moment, Dunk brought his arms up around Spinne and returned the kiss, his passion matching her own. The crowd bellowed its approval.

'Hi,' Dunk said as they broke their embrace. 'I think they like it.'

'Nothing like a little sex to spice up the violence,' Spinne said. Then, with a wink, she was gone, back to celebrate the Reavers' victory with her team.

'Wait!' Dunk said. 'Sex?' But she was too far away already to hear.

While Dunk stared after Spinne, Dirk came up and chucked him on the shoulder. 'Good game,' Dirk said. He stuck out his hand, and Dunk took it and pulled his brother into a back-thumping hug.

'By my count,' Dunk said, 'that last pass of yours broke Skragger's record.'

Dirk smirked. 'You know,' he said, slinging an arm around Dunk, 'I think you're right.'

'So,' Dunk said, 'what are we going to do about him?'

'Skragger?' Dirk said with a swagger. 'Against the Brothers Hoffnung? He doesn't stand a chance.'

DUNK STOOD ON the sidelines and looked up at the stage a horde of halflings had hauled into the centre of the field for the presentation of the Blood Bowl cup to the Reavers. The cup itself, a travelling trophy that stayed with the winning team for only a year at a time, was a mithril and gold cup covered with skulls and spikes. Dunk could have sworn that he saw the eye sockets of one of the skulls glowing with red malevolence, but he was too far away to be sure.

'Good work, kid,' a voice behind Dunk said. He turned to see Gunther the Gobbo standing there, a greasy, gap-toothed grin on his face, a furry bit of rat-on-a-stick still caught between his incisors. 'You just made me a fortune.'

'I'm sure,' Dunk said with a frown. He'd gotten what he thought he'd wanted, but it left him feeling hollow inside.

'No, kid, really,' the Gobbo said in a low voice. 'Didn't you ever wonder why the Reavers were trying to lose so hard?' His eyes gleamed with daemonic delight.

'Skragger threatened my brother,' Dunk said.

'Sure, sure,' the Gobbo said, grinning. 'Skragger's been a Black Jersey from way back.'

Dunk blinked at that. 'You mean you wanted the Reavers to lose?'

The Gobbo's grin grew so wide that Dunk expected the top of his head to flip backward.

'You played both sides here, didn't you?' Dunk said gaping at the grimy, flabby creature. 'You betrayed the Black Jerseys to line your own pockets.'

'Think whatever you want to, kid,' the Gobbo said. 'I'll just say one thing: nothing pays like treachery.' He patted Dunk on the arm and turned to leave. Before he did, he said one last thing.

'By the way, as far as the GWs go, you're on your own. Pleasure doing business with you, kid.'

Dunk's heart sank as he watched the bookie stroll down the field to chat with Skragger, who stood fuming in one of the end zones.

In the centre of the field, the Reavers accepted the Blood Bowl cup. Dirk raised it high above his head, and the crowd erupted with nearly insane applause.

To Dunk, it seemed like a Cabalvision broadcast from someplace far, far away. He felt a tiny hand reach up and grab one of his. He looked down and saw Slick smiling up at him. The halfling's happiness tore at Dunk's misery, and he felt the corners of his own mouth tugging upward.

'Give me some good news, Slick,' Dunk said. 'I could use some right now.'

'Well, since you asked so nicely, son, I'd be happy to.' The halfling rubbed his chin as he spoke, a sure sign he'd been up to something. 'While you were playing your heart out, I had a long conversation with Lästiges.'

'Selling the rights to my execution?'

'Of course not,' Slick said in mock horror. 'For those, I'd hold an auction with the Cabalvision networks. Something like that's too big for a sidelines deal.

'However, I did strike a deal with her. She gets the exclusive rights to your story, for this past season, that is. In exchange, she does me a small but vital favour that will help us all.'

Dunk squinted at the halfling. 'I have no idea what you're talking about, Slick, but I'm glad you're on my side.' He smiled as Slick trotted off to talk with Blaque and Whyte, who were standing at the entrance to the tunnel that led to the Hackers' locker room.

It was then that Dunk felt the tip of a knife prick his side. 'You little bastard,' a voice said in Dunk's ear. 'You ruined everything.'

Dunk's breath caught in his throat, and he said softly, 'Hi, Kur.'

The Hackers' injured thrower pulled the tip of his knife slowly from Dunk's kidney toward his spine. The rookie felt his blood well up under the blade's razor-sharp caress.

'Make a move, and I'll kill you where you stand,' Kur said.

'Had a rough day?' Dunk said with false concern.

'I'm with a group called the Black Jerseys,' Kur said. 'We run things around here. No one wins a Blood Bowl without our say so. And you've messed that up.'

'My deepest apologies,' Dunk said. As he finished, he felt the knife jab into his skin, just a little, enough to make him want to jump. Instead he gritted his teeth.

'Don't you dare mock me,' Kur said. 'You think you're so damned clever. Well, this is the end of the road, smart guy. The Hackers were supposed to win today. I was supposed to lead us to victory. And you bollocksed it all up.'

'So now you'll kill me with that little knife of yours, just like Ramen-Tut?'

'Just like I've killed dozens of players. Scores, maybe, you high-bred moron. You're just another notch on the crest of my helmet. I don't spend my nights out drinking with 'friends' like that post of an ogre of yours. I'm out there carving out my future, my legacy, in blood.'

'The best part of it,' Kur said in Dunk's ear, 'the very best part, is that I know you had nothing to do with all those murders.' He started to snigger. 'Did you, "killer"?'

It was then that Dunk realised that the entire stadium had gone dead quiet. He looked out at the Reavers and saw Dirk and Spinne staring back at him, their jaws gone slack. Everyone else on the stage was gaping at something above the end zone.

Dunk glanced in that direction and breathed a smile. 'Care to repeat that for me again?' he said to Kur. 'I don't think the people in the cheap seats quite heard you.'

Dunk felt Kur turn his head to see what the rookie meant. Dunk knew that the sight of the two of them displayed on the jumbo wall looming over the end zone would stun the injured thrower for a moment. That was when he made his move.

Dunk took a half step away from Kur and then spun back, slamming a spiked elbow pad into the man's face. The unarmoured Kur never had a chance. The spike took him right between the eyes and plunged straight into his brain. He was dead before Dunk could shake his wide-eyed corpse off his arm.

The crowd went nuts.

Dunk looked up and saw a floating golden ball looking straight at him. He smiled at it as Lästiges stepped up toward him.

'That's quite a revelation, Dunk,' the reporter said to him, a broad smile on her crimson-painted lips. 'I suppose this puts the facts about your case in a new light.'

Dunk glanced behind him and saw Blaque and Whyte hauling Kur's body away.

'I hope so, Lästiges,' Dunk said breathing a massive sigh of relief. 'I just want to say thanks to everyone, to my coach Pegleg, to my agent Slick, to the rest of the Hackers, and to all the fans for all their support. It's been a hell of a year.'

'Is this a retirement speech?' Lästiges asked, mock concern marring her smooth brow.

Dunk shook his head. 'Pretty much the opposite, actually. Dunk Hoffnung is here to stay!' he roared up at the crowd, and the crowed roared back. '*I love this game!*'

LATER, IN THE Hackers' locker room, after everyone else had left, Dunk gave Slick a massive hug that threatened to squish the halfling. 'You,' he said, 'are the best agent ever!'

Slick gave a little bow after he extricated himself from Dunk's grasp. 'What have I been telling you since we met?'

'All those interviews kept us here forever,' Dunk said as he slammed his locker shut. 'We need to hustle if we're going to make the team dinner.'

'You don't think they'll all want to hang you for losing the game?' Slick asked.

'We played the best we could,' Dunk said. 'We shouldn't have even been in that game. We wouldn't have been without the Black Jerseys rigging it. The Reavers were the better team.'

'And there's always next year,' Slick added.

'There's always next year,' Dunk agreed, smiling in spite of himself. 'I tell you, losing never felt so good.'

'It palls pretty quickly, kid. Take it from me.'

Dunk and Slick turned to see the Gobbo slither in from the tunnel to the Hackers' dugout. The creature wore a murderous frown.

'You cost me today, kid,' the Gobbo said, waving a fat finger at Dunk.

'I thought you got what you wanted,' Dunk said evenly. 'The Hackers lost.'

'Sure,' the Gobbo said, throwing his hands in the air. 'Today was a good day for me, but with Kur blabbing on Cabalvision about the Black Jerseys, I'm ruined! I'll never be able to use them again!'

'You double-crossed me,' Dunk said. 'Suck it up.'

'Come on, kid,' the Gobbo said, 'you don't think I was serious about that, do you? A little joke among friends.'

'Not funny.'

'Well, if we're not friends anymore, I suppose it's only fair that I tell the GWs all about your ogre friend's killings. Or I could tell the Colleges of Magic about how he destroyed their dungeon. Wizards don't appreciate things like that the way you and I do.' The stunted creature stood staring defiantly at Dunk and Slick, confident he'd played the last, winning card.

Dunk stalked toward the Gobbo and thrust a thick finger into the creature's soft chest. 'You breathe a word about M'Grash to anyone, try to destroy me or any of my friends, including my brother and I'll crucify you.'

The Gobbo sneered up at the Blood Bowl player. 'How do you think you're going to do that?'

'There are still a lot of Black Jerseys out there,' Dunk said as he leaned over to growl into the Gobbo's pitted face. 'If they learn you rigged the Blood Bowl to cut them out of the winnings, there won't be a place in the Old World you can hide.'

'You wouldn't,' the Gobbo started, then caught himself mid-sentence. He snorted angrily as he glared into Dunk's unforgiving eyes. 'Yes. Yes, you would.'

'Get out of here,' Dunk said. 'If I so much as smell you again, I'll beat you into a puddle.'

The Gobbo gasped, offended by the threat, but he turned and skulked off towards the tunnel again. As he reached the exit, he looked back and said, 'You owe me, kid. You owe me big. And Gunther the Gobbo always collects his debts!'

'DID YOU SEE the look on his face?' Dirk asked. 'Just before you killed him? When he looked up at the Cabalvision and saw what everyone else in the stadium was watching. Priceless!'

Dunk shook his head and smiled sidelong at Spinne, who sat there at a private table in the Skinned Cat with them and Slick as they held their own celebration of the day's events. 'I'll have to look for it on the commemorative recording,' he said wistfully.

'Be sure you get it on Daemonic Visual Display,' Dirk said. 'I picked up a player this year, and the DVDs are just amazing.'

Spinne put her arm around Dunk and gave him a hug. 'You did great today,' she said. 'I was impressed.'

'Look who's talking,' Dunk said. 'That catch you made to finish off the game? Incredible. I'll watch that part of the recording over and over.'

'You should watch how I got rid of the ball,' Dirk said, waving a half-eaten turkey leg at his brother. 'You might finally learn something about how the game is played.'

'Next year, Dirk,' Dunk said between hearty swallows of his Killer Genuine Draft. 'Next year. Assuming the Hackers are willing to take me back.'

'And why wouldn't they?' Slick asked, his concern exaggerated by the vast quantities of Teinekin Beer he'd already consumed. 'We have a contract, for one.'

'In case you hadn't noticed,' Dunk said, 'I missed about a quarter of the season. On top of that, Coach nearly killed me during half-time for trying to throw the game.'

'Tish-tosh,' Slick said. 'Pegleg saw how you played your heart out in the second half. That quick score you made when you got back onto the field had the entire team cheering for you, even the scrubs.'

'Really?' Dunk said, slightly amazed. He raised his stein for a quick toast. 'I guess there's hope.'

'Besides which, aside from any meetings in the Majors, of course, I think I can help Pegleg arrange for a few grudge matches between Hackers and Reavers next year,' Slick said. 'But they'll only really work if you two Hoffnungs are on the teams. We'll negotiate the Cabalvision rights separately and rake in a fortune. Who wouldn't want to see it?'

The laughter from the four friends ended abruptly as the door to their private room smashed inward off its hinges. They spun about in their chairs to see Skragger framed there in the doorway, crushing the throat of the hapless serving girl who'd tried to stop him. He dropped the girl's lifeless body to the floor and stepped into the room.

'Blew deal,' the black orc growled as he pointed a crooked finger at Dirk. 'Broke record. Gotta pay.'

Dunk, Dirk, and Spinne leapt up from the table while Slick scooted under it. Dunk glanced around the room and saw that it was a dead end but for a single window that looked down over a forty-foot drop. He wasn't quite ready to try that, yet.

Dunk flipped over the table, placing it between Skragger and the rest. Slick squeaked like a mouse as he found himself exposed. He scrambled around to one edge of the overturned table to get a better view.

'There are three of us,' Dirk said nervously. 'We can take him, right?'

Skragger strode forward and kicked the table into splinters with a single blow. Slick skittered back against a wall and then made a dive for the now-open door.

'Maybe not,' Spinne said, 'but we'll go down fighting.' As she spoke, she stepped up and levelled a bone-crushing roundhouse kick to Skragger's chest.

Skragger took two steps back from the force of the blow and smiled, showing all his tusks and broken, rotten, vicious teeth. Spinne grabbed her broken toes and hopped around, yelling, 'Ow! Ow! Ow!'

Dunk stepped up, ready to take on the black orc, but his brother breezed by him and slammed into Skragger like a blitzer taking down a thrower who'd held on to the ball too long. Skragger grunted as Dirk's pumping legs drove him backward into the wall next to the door.

Once they'd come to a stop, Skragger balled his fists together and brought them down on Dirk's back like a warhammer on an anvil. Dirk collapsed at Skragger's feet, and the black orc kicked him aside with a steel-booted toe to the ribs.

Dunk glanced back at the window and gauged his chances. A fall from the window would likely mean a broken leg at least, probably worse. At the moment, though, it seemed like staying in the room with Skragger would be certain death. Though if he jumped, he'd be abandoning Dirk and Spinne to the black orc's non-existent mercies. Looking at his brother and then at Spinne as she hobbled over next to him, he realised he couldn't do it.

'Your turn,' Spinne said to him.

'Can I pass on that?' Dunk said as he watched Skragger crack his neck and knuckles to prepare for his next challenger.

'It's you or me,' Spinne said, looking at her damaged foot.

'Since you put it that way,' Dunk said. He leaned over and gave Spinne a tender kiss on her soft, sweet lips. 'Wish me luck.'

'Awwww,' Skragger said. 'Saying goodbye? Don't. All be in hell tonight!'

Dunk strode up to Skragger and feinted left. The black orc went for it, and Dunk pulled back and levelled his best right hook into the creature's jaw, putting everything he had into it.

Dunk felt a tusk break against his fist, but before Skragger could spit it out, he hit him again, this time a hammering blow to the belly. The black orc bent over double, and Dunk smashed his right into him once again.

Dunk pounded at Skragger mercilessly, keeping the black orc on defence the entire time. As he rained blow after blow into the murderous veteran, Spinne cheered him on. Her voice put new energy into his arms, and he brutalised the orc until the skin peeled from his bloodied knuckles and he felt like he might never be able to raise his arms again.

Dunk staggered backwards, exhausted, straight into Spinne's arms. She propped him up as best she could with her injured foot.

'How'm I doing?' Dunk panted.

'Looked good from here,' Spinne said. Then she gasped as the blood-covered Skragger stretched himself back up to his full height and favoured her with an evil smile.

'Finished?' Skragger asked Dunk. It was all Dunk could do to just goggle at the creature. The black orc growled as he stepped forward. 'Will be, soon.'

Spinne let Dunk slide to the ground, then stepped between him and the black orc. 'Come get some,' she said to him.

Skragger growled and lashed out at the catcher. She ducked beneath his blow and then came up and popped him in the throat. He stumbled back, coughing hard and clutching at his throat.

Spinne stepped in for the kill, and the black orc's clawed hand reached out and snagged her around the neck. Keeping her at arm's length, he pulled her up off her feet and began to squeeze the life from her. She tried desperately to pull his fingers from her throat as her legs kicked feebly beneath her, but it was like trying to pull apart an iron band.

Dunk knew he had to do something or Spinne would be dead in seconds. He glanced over at Dirk and saw that his brother was rousing but would be far too late. Throwing caution to the wind, he vaulted up onto his haunches and charged straight at Skragger's legs.

Dunk hit the black orc right in the knees and heard one of the joints crack. Skragger howled in pain and hurled Spinne against the far wall, where she narrowly avoided spilling out through the high window.

The black orc's leg gave way, and he slammed down atop Dunk, crushing the air from him. With another howl no less bloodthirsty than the last, Skragger pulled Dunk from under him and wrapped both hands around the rookies' throat.

'Dead!' the orc snarled. 'Now!'

The world around Dunk seemed to pull away from him as if he was looking at it down a long, dark tunnel. He knew that in a moment the light at its end would flicker and go out forever.

'Put that man down!' a voice demanded from the doorway.

Dunk felt the grip on his throat slacken, and the world became bright again. He gulped for air as he turned to see who had come to his rescue.

There, framed in the doorway, stood Slick, backed up by Pegleg and Cavre. Dunk could see the rest of his team-mates peering over their coach's shoulder as he levelled his legendary hook at the black orc.

'You have two choices, Mr. Skragger,' Pegleg snarled as he stepped into the room, the rest of the Hackers following him into the cramped space. 'You can try to take us all on, in which case I'll gut you with my hook while the others hold you down.'

'Or?' Skragger said as he let Dunk slip to the ground and stood to face the wrath of a full Blood Bowl team.

'You can take the easy way out,' Pegleg said, nodding at the window.

Skragger nodded as he considered the scowling faces of the players facing him. Then he noticed Dunk tapping him on the leg.

'Take them on,' Dunk croaked as he glared into the black orc's shaking eyes. 'I want to see you get torn apart.'

'Not today,' Skragger sneered. He turned and sprinted three long steps toward the window. He dove through it as if he was stretching out to reach his last end zone and then disappeared over the edge. He didn't scream, but a moment after he left the room there was a sickening splat.

Cavre came over to help Dunk to his feet while Pegleg did the same for Spinne. Slick directed Karsten and Henrik in getting Dirk steady again. M'Grash watched the whole thing from the doorway, too large to join the others in the smallish room.

'I thought we might have lost you there, Dunk,' Cavre said. 'When Slick told us Skragger was trying to kill you, I thought we'd never get here in time.'

'Yes,' Pegleg said, a hint of admiration colouring his voice. 'You did well in keeping the orc busy until we could get here. Many would have given up before then.'

'I… I didn't know you were coming at all,' Dunk said.

'Come now, son,' Slick said, 'you didn't think I'd just run off to let you die.'

'The thought crossed *my* mind,' Spinne said, now sitting on a chair that Gigia had shoved under her.

'You were the last people I expected to see come through that door,' Dirk said, stretching his back as Guillermo checked him for a concussion.

'And why would that be, Mr. Hoffnung?' Pegleg said. 'You're a Hacker, and the Hackers back their own.'

'Really?' Dunk said to the coach. 'I wasn't sure you'd want me any more.'

Pegleg smiled warmly. 'We can always use someone with your talents and love of the game. Besides which, we only have just over two months before the start of the *Spike! Magazine* tournament.'

Dunk shook his head as he came over to put his arm around Spinne. He smiled at Slick and Dirk and then up at Pegleg as he said, 'It never ends, does it?'

'It never does, Dunk.' Pegleg flashed the rookie a broad, gold-toothed grin under his yellow tricorn hat. 'And that's the best part.'

DEAD BALL

1

THE LAST THING that went through Henrik Karlmann's head was the spike on the front of the football.

Dunkel 'Dunk' Hoffnung, star thrower for the Bad Bay Hackers, stood close enough to Henrik to catch the lineman when he fell. The ball juddered from Henrik's forehead on its long, sharp tip. His dead eyes were crossed, still trying to focus on the thing that had killed him, his arms caught halfway up to where they would have been needed to save his life.

'And Karlmann's down!' Bob Bifford's voice echoed through the stadium via the Preternatural Announcement system, magically audible over the near-deafening roar of the crowd. 'Ooh, Jim, that's going to leave a mark!'

'More like a marker, Bob – over his grave!'

'That's already three in the kill column for the Chaos All-Stars today, Jim. Do you think they could break their team record?'

'To do that, they'd have to top their TPK from the Chaos Cup play-offs against the Stunted Stoutfellows. The Hackers are a bit tougher than halflings at least.'

'I always thought it should be TOK for Total Opponent Kill, Jim.'

'Well, Harry "The Hammer" Kehry coined the phrase back in 2482, and he never could spell. When he said 'Total 'Ponent Kill', would you argue with him?'

'Not unless I wanted to end up like poor Karlmann there. Let's hope the Hackers have a generous funeral insurance plan. It looks like they're going to get a lot of use out of it.'

Dunk's silvery eyes took one look up at Chthton – the octopus-armed beast that had thrown the bullet-like ball at his friend – and snarled. In one swift move, he snatched the ball from his fallen friend's forehead and tucked it under his arm, taking care not to stab himself on its bloodied spikes. With the slavering, tentacled beast in the all-black helmet and jersey bearing down on him, Dunk had no time to get rid of the ball by passing it downfield. First, he had to scramble clear.

Dunk jinked to the left then broke right, but the Chaos-tainted Chthton spread his tentacles wide. One of them wrapped around Dunk's arm as he tried to dash past, its wet, puckered cups adhering to Dunk's shoulder pad and holding fast.

Dunk heard the fluid from Chthton's tentacle flowing down his armour, sizzling as it went. Where it dripped off the shoulder pad onto his bare bicep, it burned like a red-hot brand. The second-year thrower howled in pain and pulled on the hard-stuck tentacle like an ox hauling a plough.

Chthton snorted something green and wet as he pulled back against Dunk, and the young Hacker felt his forward progress grind to a halt. He looked back at the warped creature and growled in pain, anger, and frustration. If he didn't break free of Chthton soon – if the creature managed to tackle him – this game might be his last.

A thin hand shot out and hacked down at the tentacle, cutting it in half. As Chthton fell backward, blood spurting from the maimed stump of its arm, Dunk stared at his saviour.

Gigia Mardretti stood nearly as tall as Dunk's six feet. Long, black hair cascaded from beneath her golden helmet, on the side of which a green, block H was emblazoned, overlaid with three crossed swords that followed the lines of the letter. Blood ran down her arm where it had sliced through the overstretched tentacle. She bore a satisfied little grin on her ruby-painted lips.

The blade embedded in the edge of Gigia's gloves was illegal in Blood Bowl. In this sport, the players – and their armour, and maybe the ball – were supposed to be the weapons. Using anything else in the course of a match broke the rules.

Not that anyone paid much attention to the rules, including the referees. Perhaps especially the refs, who seemed to have taken their dangerous jobs just so they could solicit large bribes. Some sold themselves to both sides, their loyalties swapping back and forth faster than they could pocket their money.

'Thanks!' Dunk said as he spun to face back toward the All-Stars' end of the field. Henrik had fallen deep in the Hacker's territory, and now Dunk stared down eighty yards of Chaos-infested Astrogranite standing between him and the goal line.

A pair of All-Star blitzers came stampeding down the field toward Dunk as he cut right, looking for some daylight. None of his team-mates were open downfield, so he sprinted to the right, hoping to find some blockers or at least keep out of the blitzers' grasp until he could get rid of the ball.

'Would you look at that human run?' Bob's voice thundered over the PA. 'He looks like a halfling being told mealtime's almost over!'

'You'd run for your life too if the All-Stars had the kind of grudge against you that they have for poor Hoffnung,' said Jim. 'Don't you remember what happened when they met in the Chaos Cup finals last year?'

'How could I ever forget? It's not often you see someone kill the opposing team's captain in the middle of halftime. Not to say that players don't try it all the time, but to succeed, that's something else.'

'Especially against a mutant minotaur like Schlitz 'Malty' Likker. That bull had a six-pack of horns that could open most players up like a keg of ale. What was Hoffnung's defence again?'

Dunk tried to shut out the blather coming over the PA. None of that mattered now. The Hackers had lost that game, and it had been over six months ago. In the world of Blood Bowl, that was a dozen life-times past – maybe more if you added in how many players the Hackers had lost just today.

Lars Englehard stepped up between Dunk and the two All-Stars on his tail. The lineman lowered his shoulders and took out both of them at once. It wasn't until Dunk heard Lars start to scream that he wondered if the All-Stars weren't really after the ball anyway.

'I think Hoffnung said that Malty was "possessed by a daemon,"' Bob said with a laugh. Jim joined in.

'I think half the All-Stars on the field today might meet that criteria. And what about Nurgle's Rotters?'

'Too true, Jim. If we start removing players for any kind of posses-sion, we won't have many teams left!'

As Dunk stiff-armed a goat-headed blitzer wearing a carved-up All-Stars' helmet, he thought perhaps that wouldn't be such a bad idea. The game was lethal enough without adding daemons from hellish realms of Chaos into the mix.

The goat-man's horns sprang forward and clamped around Dunk's forearm like the jaws of a tiger. His vambrace there protected his flesh from being torn away, but when he tried to pull his arm free he dis-covered he was caught. The goat-headed creature bleated in low, guttural glee as it raked at Dunk's face with its arms, which ended in cloven hooves.

Dunk swung his free arm around and stabbed the spiked ball up under the goat-man's chin with desperate strength. The horns fell slack as the All-Star went silent and slid off Dunk's hand.

'Now that's a turnabout for you,' Bob said. 'Hoffnung gets free, and the Hackers chalk up their first kill for the day.'

'That ball's getting a lot of action out there today, Bob. I'm glad to see they brought "Ol' Spikey" back for the *Spike! Magazine* playoffs. Believe it or not, some people complain that a ball like that makes the games too deadly.'

Bob scoffed at Jim. 'That's like saying you can have too much Bloodweiser after the game. Wait, I didn't think we were talking about what happened to you last night. I don't think I've ever seen an ogre that tipsy.'

'That's not fair,' Jim said. 'Vampires like you can't get drunk.'

'Right,' Bob said sadly. 'Now *that's* unfair.'

'Such is unlife.'

Free from the goat-man, Dunk scrambled back to his left, saw two more All-Stars blocking that way, and dropped back to his right again. Then he saw what he wanted: an open Hacker downfield.

Percival Smythe stood near the end zone in his green and gold uniform, sweeping his arms up and down in the universal signal for 'I'm wide open!'

Dunk cocked back his arm and hurled the ball down the length of the field. It flew in a perfect spiral, the spikes spinning around its sides like a set of lethal wheels. Dunk wondered, not for the first time, how anyone could catch a pass like that without getting killed, but thankfully that was Percy's problem, not his.

'Oh, that's a beautiful pass!' Bob's voice said. 'And not an All-Star within 10 yards of Smythe!'

'Yeah,' Jim said, 'but do you see Mackey?'

Dunk glared down the field and wondered what the announcers were talking about. Mackey Maus was the All-Stars' new team captain, the one who'd taken over after Likker's death, but he wasn't anywhere near Percy. No one was.

The crowd, scores of thousands strong, roared as the ball sailed into Percy's grasp. The noise drowned out anything else, so he didn't hear the footfalls of the player who came up behind him and slammed him into the Astrogranite.

'Hackers score!' Bob's voice said, his magically enhanced voice ringing out over din.

Dunk would have cheered, but he found that he couldn't breathe. The player on top of him had driven the air from his lungs. He tried to push himself up on his arms, and something hit him hard in the back of the head. If not for his helmet, the blow would have caved in his skull. As it was, he felt the metal protecting his cranium dent in and dig into his scalp. Stars danced before his eyes.

'Enjoy those cheers,' Dunk's attacker shouted, 'until I tear off your ears!'

A long, sharp talon reached under Dunk's neck and slashed at his throat. He felt something give and then wetness. Adrenaline coursed through Dunk's veins, despite the fact he thought it was too late. He had to be dead already, but his body just didn't know it.

In one desperate move, Dunk wrenched his body around. As he did, his helmet came off, and he realised that it was its leather strap he'd felt giving way. The cut on his neck burned, but the hope that it was only superficial surged in his heart.

The creature atop Dunk managed to maintain its position, even while the young thrower squirmed beneath him. It glared down at him from behind a greasy-furred, rat-like snout poking out through the open face of its jet-black helmet. Its ebony eyes glittered with madness as glowing, green spittle dripped from its long, narrow muzzle filled with short, sharp teeth. Dunk recognised the spitting-mad beastman instantly: Mackey, the Chaos-mutated skaven who'd been taking cheap shots at him all day.

Throughout it all, Dunk had tried to tell himself it was nothing personal. Death and dismemberment was all part of the game. Maybe it wasn't legal by the rules, but people expected it. The fans, the coaches, the players, they all expected it.

Even the referees expected it. They didn't haul the killers off and throw them in jail. They just hit them with a penalty.

But when a blood-parched, mutant skaven sat on top of Dunk and drooled something green and viscous on to his face, where it stung and burned like fire, he had his doubts.

'Don't let them get to you, son.' Dunk's agent, a rotund halfling by the name of Slick Fullbelly, had said the same thing to him over and over. 'It's their job to try to put you down, just as it's yours to do the same to them. The trick is to do unto others *before* they do unto you. It's nothing personal, for you or them. Remember that.'

'This one's for Schlitzy,' Mackey said as he raked down with his long, filth-caked claws. 'Say hi to him for me in hell!'

Faster than he could think, Dunk's hands snapped up and caught Mackey by the wrists. He held the skaven's arms out away from him, the tips of his talons only inches from Dunk's face.

The crowd booed, hissing at the All-Star. It was one thing to kill someone while the ball was in play. Watching mayhem like that happen was a good part of why most of the fans showed up to the games.

The chance to be spattered with warm blood proved too much for them to pass up.

After a score, though, it was time for the gridiron warriors to return to their respective corners, to lick their wounds until it was time to face each other again. To violate that understanding was more than just breaking the rules. Players chewed up the rulebook and spat it out during every game.

To try to kill someone during one of these few down moments, though, was known as a dead ball foul. Few fans would tolerate this worst kind of cheating. Not even the best-bribed referees could afford to ignore so flagrant a foul.

So the crowd cheered when Dunk sat up hard and bashed his fore-head into Mackey's sneering mouth. He felt teeth snap and flesh shred in the skaven's mouth, and when he drew back, blood, mucous, and the creature's glowing saliva coated his own forehead.

Dunk tried to shove Mackey off, but the skaven snapped down at him instead, trying to savage him with its broken front teeth. To keep himself from the creature's reach, Dunk fell back again. When his head hit the Astrogranite, though, he knew he had nowhere else left to go.

Panicked, Dunk pressed up against Mackey again, trying to throw him off, but the skaven, mad with pain, refused to relent for a moment. He used his weight to press down against Dunk's arms, low-ering his snapping, bloodied snout inch by inch toward Dunk's exposed neck.

Dunk tried to swing his legs up and throw the skaven over his head, but Mackey's legs clamped around his waist like iron bands. Those jaws of his kept getting lower and lower.

Mackey had Dunk's arms pressed hard against his chest now. The Hacker thrower tried to butt the skaven with his head again, but he couldn't get the momentum to do more than annoy the insane beast.

Mackey chortled at this, coughing and snorting up blood and mucous that dripped through his shattered teeth. He shoved his snout down at Dunk's neck, but the thrower managed to deflect the skaven's nose with his chin. Quick as a snake, Mackey forced his sop-ping-wet snout past Dunk's cheek and began to pry the Hacker's chin up with the end of his pointed nose.

'Stop it!' Dunk said, unable to think of anything else to do. Where were the referees when you needed them? Probably they didn't want to get involved in the middle of a mortal combat like this. It was one thing to give out a penalty to someone who committed a foul. It was something else entirely to risk your life trying to get between two trained and armoured Blood Bowl players.

Mackey responded by snuffling its nostrils against the underside of Dunk's jawline.

'Hey!' Dunk shouted. 'Not on a first date!'

'Your blood.' Mackey growled softly into Dunk's ear. 'It smells delicious.'

At times like this, Dunk sometimes wished he was a praying man. He'd seen enough of the fickleness of the gods to know that using your last breath calling on them was a waste. Still, nothing else more useful came to mind either.

Dunk tried to think of something pithy, some last words that would sting his killer or at least give the world a reason to remember him. The jagged touch of the creature's teeth pressing down over his jugular vein, though, forced everything but blind panic from his head.

Dunk gritted his teeth and closed his eyes. As he did, he found images of Spinne Schönheit whirling through his mind. The beautiful catcher for the Reikland Reavers had only been dating him for a few months, but he already knew that he loved her with all his heart, that he wanted to marry her, to have kids, to grow old. Now none of that would happen – growing old, most of all.

Dunk felt Mackey spread his teeth, readying himself for the bite that would end Dunk's life. He felt the skaven's acidic drool burn its way around his throat as if preparing the way for the mortal wound.

His eyes still closed, Dunk felt Mackey's face draw back, and he stiffened for the final blow. Instead, he heard a sickening snap and felt Mackey's grip on him fall slack.

Dunk peeled one eye open and then the other to find a massive creature towering over him. He stood over eight feet tall and massed at least four hundred pounds, twice the size of Dunk. Polished tusks jutted from his lower jaw, and a golden ring the size of a bracelet hung like a doorknocker from the septum of his broken nose.

The ogre peered down at Dunk, Mackey's head in one hand and his body in the other, hot blood pouring from them both.

The crowd went nuts. The cheers were so loud Dunk wondered if his ears might bleed.

'Dunkel okay?' the ogre said, concern furrowing his massive brow as he let the separate parts of what had once been Mackey drop to the Astrogranite.

'I am now, big guy,' Dunk said as he took the ogre's hand and let the creature haul him to his feet. 'Thanks, M'Grash.'

As Dunk wiped Mackey's blood, snot, and spit from himself, a tall, thin orc in a black-and-white striped shirt ran up and threw something at M'Grash: a sack of sand wrapped in a long, yellow ribbon of cloth. It fluttered to the ground after bouncing off the ogre's chest.

'I don't believe it!' Bob's voice said over the PA. 'They're going to call a penalty on K'Thragsh!'

The crowd's cheers turned to boos. Dunk started to shout something at the referee, but the official just waved him off. Then the orc stood to face the announcer's box and crossed his arms in an X over his head. Then he pointed to M'Grash.

'Holy Nuffle's battered balls!' Bob said. 'It's a dead ball foul on M'Grash!'

'What's the penalty going to be?' asked Jim.

The ref pulled back his hand and then stabbed his finger to point out over the top rows of the stadium.

'He's kicking M'Grash K'Thragsh out of the game!'

'Oh, the crowd doesn't like this, Jim.'

Dunk put his hand on M'Grash's arm and felt the ogre flex his muscles. They were like steel.

The ref started to back-pedal as he watched M'Grash glare at him with his saucer-sized eyes. He put up his hands and flinched when the ogre snorted. The crowd went wild.

'Give! Him! To! Us!' the fans chanted. 'Give! Him! To! Us!'

The ref turned and sprinted away down the field.

'M'Grash,' Dunk said, trying to hold on to the ogre's arm. 'Don't do–'

Before he could finish, though, M'Grash tore free and lumbered after the fleeing ref with a stride twice as long as his prey's.

Dunk threw up his hands and decided to watch and enjoy the chase. 'They've already kicked him out of the game,' he said. 'What else can they do to him?'

'CAN YOU GET that through that thick excuse for a head you keep stitched on top of your shoulders?'

Dunk had rarely seen Captain Pegleg Haken, the head coach of the Hackers, so mad. The ex-pirate had the hook that stabbed from his left sleeve linked through M'Grash's nose ring and had pulled the ogre's face down to his so he could scream right into it.

'Sorry, coach,' M'Grash said, whimpering like a kicked puppy.

Dunk knew the ogre could kill Pegleg in an instant, just as he'd torn Mackey apart out on the field, but he also knew he wouldn't. To M'Grash, Pegleg stood at the right hand of Nuffle, the sacred god of Blood Bowl that most of the game's players and many of its fans worshipped. From the way most of the other players in the locker room pressed against the walls, trying to stay as far away from Pegleg's wrath as possible, Dunk guessed that M'Grash wasn't the only one who felt that way.

'Sorry isn't going to cut it!' Pegleg said. He gave the ogre's nose ring a last tweak and let it go from his hook. Then he turned to glare at the rest of the players. Sweat ran down his reddened face, and his eyes blazed with fury.

'What in Nuffle's name is wrong with the lot of you?' Pegleg asked. 'It's only halftime, and we've lost five players!' He shot a murderous look at the ogre. 'Besides M'Grash, we'll need funerals after the game for four of them!'

'Coach,' Dunk said, interrupting Pegleg's rant. He instantly regretted it. The temperature in the room seemed to drop from hot and bothered to ice-cold mean in the space of a second. No one moved, apparently frozen in place. Pegleg might have stopped shouting, but Dunk couldn't hear anyone else breathing, not even himself.

He glanced over at his agent, Slick Fullbelly, who stood hiding in the room's far corner. At only three feet tall, the rotund halfling seemed to be trying to hide under his unruly mop of curly dark hair. None of the other players' agents dared to come into the locker room for fear of incurring Pegleg's wrath. The coach considered most agents vermin and would as soon stab one as talk to him, but he tolerated Slick, who always walked around like he owned the place.

Pegleg turned to stare at Dunk; his eyes wide and amazed as if the young thrower had just had a second head sprout from his nose. 'Yes, Mr. Hoffnung?' he said with a formal smile that showed a gold tooth in the centre of his rotted teeth.

A shiver ran down Dunk's spine. Ever since the Blood Bowl finals last season, Pegleg had called him by his first name as a sign of the respect he'd worked so hard to earn.

Slick stared at Dunk in horror and mouthed a single word to him: 'Run.'

Dunk ignored the halfling's advice, even though a part of him wanted nothing more than to run screaming into the relative safety of the playing field. Instead, he met Pegleg's steely glare and spoke, taking care to not let his voice crack.

'Coach, they're killing us out there, literally. Maybe we should–' Dunk stopped here to swallow. 'Maybe we should call it a day.'

When Dunk stopped talking, the room fell silent. No one else breathed a word. For a moment, Dunk wondered if some horrible magic had frozen them all in place, including him. He thought of trying to test it, but he couldn't manage to convince his body of the promise the idea held.

Pegleg reached up with his hook and inserted it into his ear, where he screwed it around two or three times before taking it back out. 'Would you care to clarify that? I don't think I could have heard you properly.'

Dunk looked down at Pegleg's hook and saw blood smeared on it.

'Maybe.' He took a deep breath. 'Maybe we should forfeit.' He held up his hands as he heard everyone in the room gasp – everyone but Pegleg, who stood watching him like a statue.

'Coach, we've lost five players. That brings us down to eleven. If we lose another, we won't have enough left to field a team.'

'What, Mr. Hoffnung, is your point?' Pegleg reached up and wiped the stone-sharpened tip of his hook clean on his tricorn hat as he spoke. The blood left a dark red streak along the bright yellow crown.

'If we lose another player, we'll have to forfeit anyway, right? Since we've already lost five players in one half, I don't doubt–' Dunk cut himself short as he realised some of the other players, the ones not too terrified of Pegleg, were laughing. 'What?' he asked, flushing with anger. 'We're going to lose this match. Let's call it quits before another of us has to die.'

The rest of the players started to snigger, and soon the locker room shook with laughter. Pegleg had to sit down to hold his belly with his hook and wipe the tears from his face with his good hand.

'What?' Dunk asked. 'Are you all so jaded you don't care if one more of us dies before we lose the game?'

Rhett Cavre, a hard-muscled, dark-skinned man standing next to Pegleg, spoke. 'Dunk, you don't need eleven players to keep playing.' Cavre had been on the team longer than anyone and had become a legend on the Blood Bowl pitch. He also worked as the team's assistant coach and, when travelling by sea, Captain Haken's first mate. Dunk knew Cavre took the game as seriously as anyone, but he couldn't believe his own ears.

'You don't? But if we don't have at least eleven, they won't let us on the field, right? Remember that game in Kislev? We could barely get six of us on the field, and they made us forfeit the game.'

'That's because the rest of us were too hung over to move,' Percy said from a far corner of the room. Maybe the catcher was still riding high from his touchdown reception. Most days he'd have been too cautious to say something like that in Pegleg's presence.

'Damn that Bloodweiser they serve there,' Slick said, turning toward Pegleg to keep him from turning and plunging his hook into Percy's chest. 'They call it by the same name, but it's not. They've been brewing that stuff in the same cauldrons for a thousand years, and it's strong enough to bring an ogre to his knees.'

M'Grash let loose a whimper at the thought of the hangover he'd endured that day. It had taken three men to pull his head out of the bog.

'Blüdvar, the Kislevites call it. Translates into "Blood War", I think.' Slick's voice trailed off as he noticed Pegleg looming over him like the shadow of death, his eyes trying to burn holes down through the halfling's head, straight to his furry, unshod toes.

'Anyway, son,' Slick said, scurrying toward Dunk to get out of range of Pegleg's hook, 'you only need eleven players to *start* the game.'

Dunk stared at the halfling for a moment, and then glanced over at Pegleg. The captain wore a grim look on his face that Dunk could not read.

'But, coach,' Dunk said, 'how many people are we willing to lose before we – well, before we give up?'

Pegleg hobbled over on his good leg and the wooden stump that sprouted from the bottom of his right knee. Standing as tall as Dunk, he stared deep into the young thrower's eyes. His were the blue of the open sea, filled with the wisdom of his years but deep and hidden all the same. Although his voice was rough and low, it carried throughout the room as if he spoke over the stadium's PA system.

'This is the nature of the game, Dunk. Some teams play to score points. Others play to kill.'

'What about us?'

'We play to win.'

Dunk swallowed hard, and then nodded, never taking his eyes from Pegleg's.

A tiny snotling, a goblin-like creature only half the size of Slick, poked his head into the locker room and said, 'One minute until the second half.' His high-pitched voice sounded like that of a child with a bad cold, but no one laughed.

The snotling peered around the room at the Hackers' sombre faces. 'You always have such rousing halftime speeches?' he said.

Pegleg snatched off his hat and hurled it at the little, green-skinned creature. It sailed toward him, spinning like a disc, and smacked into him with a non-hat-like *thunk*. The snotling let out a little 'Eep!' and dropped to the ground unconscious.

'I've hit my limit today for stupid questions,' the coach roared as he spun around to glare at each of his players in turn. 'The next person to ask one will think the snotling got off easy. Now let's get out there and win this damned game!'

Dunk charged past the coach and led the way out on to the field.

IN THE MIDDLE of the second half, Dunk threw another touchdown pass to Otto Waltheim, one of the Hackers' best catchers. The score put the Hackers ahead of the All-Stars, three to nothing, but after the catch an All-Star with an octopus for a head knocked Otto into the stands.

Dunk and the other Hackers could do no more than watch as the fans grabbed Otto and passed him up to the top edge of the stadium and pitched him over. The same thing had happened to Dunk in last year's *Spike! Magazine* tournament, and he'd survived only by the sheer luck of tearing through a series of awnings before landing on a food vendor's cart. By the way the crowd roared again soon after they tossed poor Otto over the edge, Dunk guessed his team-mate hadn't been so fortunate.

As Dunk and the remaining Hackers lined up to kick the ball, he allowed himself a quick headcount. Only ten Hackers were left. There were three catchers: Gigia Mardretti, Percival Smythe, and Simon Sherwood; three blitzers: Andreas Waltheim, Milo Hoffstetter, and Rhett Cavre; and three linemen: Kai Albrecht, Karsten Klemmer, and Guillermo Reyes. Dunk, the only thrower left, made ten. M'Grash was the only player left on the sideline, and he'd been banned from the game.

Milo kicked the ball, and the rest of the team raced down the field to take it away from the All-Stars. As Dunk sprinted along next to Guillermo, he smelled something dark and pungent that made him want to cough. Downfield, he spied a plume of smoke coming from the area where the ball had landed.

'What are those Chaos cultists burning down there?' Dunk asked Guillermo, but the big, bearded Estalian just shrugged his shoulders.

'Smells like oil,' Guillermo said. Then a loud buzzing noise, like the sound of a hive of angry, giant bees, came from the same direction. 'Sounds like mayhem.'

With all the players still between him and the ball, Dunk couldn't see what was going on. Kick-offs often ended up in pile-ups of players that sometimes had to be pried apart before the game could continue.

Then the screaming started, and the crowd went wild.

'Did you see that, Bob?' Jim's voice rang out over the loudspeakers. 'I think I saw an arm come flying out of that scrum down there.'

'It could have been a leg – or a tentacle. It's hard to tell from here. Let's take a look at the Jumboball image at the end of the field, brought to us by Wolf Sports, the top name in Cabalvision broadcasting. And I'm not just saying that because they sign our cheques!'

'No, the network's Censer Wizards make sure of that. Nothing like the threat of being roasted over a crucible filled with red-hot coals to motivate an on-air personality, eh?'

Dunk shaded his eyes to glance up at the twenty-foot-tall crystal ball mounted over the rim of the stadium's west end. It hadn't been there last year, but he'd heard that Wolf Sports had installed it to show the fans in the stadium what they were missing at home.

The Jumboball didn't produce any sound, but the screams still threatened to pierce Dunk's ears as he and Guillermo stampeded toward the pile. In the Jumboball, Dunk saw a close-up image of the stack of players piled over the ball. The players in the pile would normally all be jabbing and stabbing at each other, trying to inflict an injury that a referee wouldn't be able to see. Now, though, smoke and a reddish mist that could only be blood obscured most of the view. On the edges of the pile, Dunk saw the Hacker players trying to break free while the All-Stars pulled them back into the pink smoke.

The buzzing from inside the pile grew to a roar as Dunk charged into the fray. Then a dwarf in Chaos All-Stars armour burst from the smoke, madness pirouetting in his wide, ice-blue eyes. These were the only things that showed clearly under the splattered blood and gore that coated the front of the dwarf's armour and his face and bushy beard in a thick layer of red.

Something horrible growled in the dwarf's hands, the like of which Dunk had never seen before. It stretched from the Chaos-tainted creature's hands the length of a sword, but its handle roared like a dragon and belched black smoke into the air. The edge of the sword's blade bore three-inch long serrations shaped like a manticore's teeth, and they carried bits of bone and gristle caught between them.

The dwarf cranked something on the weapon's handle, and the serrations began to move. They started slow but soon spun around the edge of the blade so fast they became a blur of crimson and steel.

'Nuffle's holy gridiron!' Bob's voice said over the PA. 'It's Gimlet the Lost, and he's got a chainsaw!'

Somewhere, Dunk heard a whistle as a referee called the play dead, but he knew it wouldn't matter. From the look in Gimlet's eyes, he wasn't going to let anything stop him until he ran out of fuel, and the chainsaw – if that's what that thing was – seemed fully loaded.

Dunk gave Guillermo a shove and pointed for the lineman to circle to Gimlet's right. Without looking to see if Guillermo complied, Dunk veered left, hoping to catch Gimlet in a pincer move. He hoped this might confuse the blood-drenched dwarf, but if it didn't at least it would mean he could only attack one of them at a time.

Gimlet swung his chainsaw in a wide circle, trying to gore both of the Hackers as they came at him. The blade missed Dunk, but it caught Guillermo on the side of the helmet and sent him sprawling. Gimlet followed up on the attack, raising the chainsaw over his head as he stomped after the downed lineman.

With Gimlet's back to him, Dunk charged at the All-Star and tried to tackle him. He wrapped his arms around the dwarf, but he could not bring him down. It was like trying to tackle a rock. His grasp kept the dwarf's arms trapped close to his body, but Gimlet kept marching forward, step-by-step, dragging Dunk along behind him like an overlong cloak, until he stood over Guillermo's body.

Dunk peered over Gimlet's shoulder to see that the dwarf's first blow had cracked open the lineman's helmet and spilled out the contents like a rotten egg. Gimlet cackled with mad glee and began to bring his hands up, angling his wrists so that the chainsaw pointed back over his shoulder, straight toward Dunk's own helmet.

As the chainsaw's buzzing blade came lower and lower, the sound almost drowning out the shouts from the crowd, Dunk squeezed

Gimlet harder and harder, trying to force the dwarf's hands back down. All he managed to do was slow the blade's inexorable progress. He had to try something else, fast.

Dunk wrapped his leg around to plant his foot in front of Gimlet's legs. The dwarf snorted, perhaps thinking Dunk only meant to try to squeeze him with his legs as well. Gimlet leaned forward harder, pushing the chainsaw back behind him as he did so. The whizzing blade met, screeching and sparking against Dunk's helmet.

Dunk let go with his arms, keeping his foot steady where it was. Freed from the Hacker's arms, Gimlet brought his blade back down in front of him and let out a wild laugh. As he tried to step forward, though, his feet met Dunk's booted foot, and he tripped.

Gimlet landed on his chainsaw face first. The blade screeched right through his exposed face and then his breastplate, digging its way through his hot, gurgling corpse.

The machine was still running when the referee came over and shut it off. The scene played over and over again in glorious crimson colour on the Jumboball high above them.

'Did you see that move, Jim? And the way that chainsaw parted Gimlet's armour? Amazing!'

'It sure is, Bob! It looks like Dunk Hoffnung, one of last year's most promising rookies, is taking charge of this game.'

'It's about – wait! What's this?'

Dunk looked up to see what the announcers were chatting about, and he saw a yellow penalty flag flutter over the Astrogranite and land at a bloodied player's feet. Then he looked down at the artificial turf before him. The flag sat right there.

'They've called a penalty against Hoffnung! Can you believe it?'

'Well, Jim, it's clear whose gold is lining the ref's pockets today. What's the call?'

'Illegal use of a weapon! The ref is accusing Hoffnung of using that chainsaw to kill Gimlet!'

'You can't do this!' Dunk screamed into the ref's face. He pointed down at Gimlet. 'It's his chainsaw. He killed all those people!'

The tall, thin elf sneered back at the Hacker. 'So you say. You see it your way, and I'll see it mine. But only mine counts.'

Rage threatened to explode Dunk's head from the inside. A red veil dropped down over his eyes, and the next thing he knew he found himself chasing the ref back up the field.

The crowd loved it.

Dunk never caught up with the referee. The dark elf ran with the grace of a gazelle – which probably explained how he'd survived so long as a referee – and Dunk's armour and injuries slowed him down. He kept pace with the ref until they reached the Hackers' end zone, on the opposite end of the field from all the carnage, but as he crossed the goal line his rage lost its battle with his legs, which refused to run any more.

Dunk bent over and grabbed his thighs as he tried to suck more air into his lungs. As he did so, the crowd booed. The fans had tasted plenty of blood today, but it had only made them hungry for more. To Dunk, it seemed they wanted the referee dead as much as he did.

'The crowd is not happy about this!' Jim said.

'No, Jim, they're not. I haven't seen a referee show such a blatant disregard for the rules and for any sense of fair play since the Athelorn Avengers played the Dwarf Giants.'

'Bob, that was only last week!'

Dunk raised his head and stared up at the Jumboball. Images of Gimlet's death flashed through it. Then he saw the referee racing away from him, thumbing his nose first at Dunk and then the crowd.

The sequence played through again, although more wobbly this time, and Dunk – enough air in his lungs at last – stood up to glare at the ref. He considered chasing after the corrupt dark elf again, but the way his vision had been shaking he didn't think he was up for it. As he stared at the ref, though, he realised there was nothing wrong with his vision.

'I think the fans have a plan for revenge here, Bob,' Jim's voice said.

'Sure,' Bob said, 'but do you think they've really thought this through?'

'They wouldn't be Blood Bowl fans if they had. Look at that Jumboball shake! The fans up there in the cheap seats are going to get more than nosebleeds if they keep that up!'

Dunk peered up at the far end zone and saw the Jumboball juddering like – well, like the spiked football had in Henrik's head. A sense of dread filled him, but before he could give it voice, the wooden stand that held the boulder-sized crystal gave way with a crack he could hear clear across the stadium.

The ball hung there in the air for a moment before spilling forward onto the people standing in the seats beneath it.

The crowd howled in pain and fear as the ball began to roll down the inside of the stadium's bowl, crushing both the slower fans and the stands from which they sought to scramble. It picked up speed as it went, and it reached the Astrogranite in mere, bloody seconds, busting through the low restraining wall meant to keep the fans from making easy grabs at unwary players.

When the Jumboball entered the All-Stars' end zone, the players still stuck in the remnants of the pile-up around the ball realised something was wrong. Dunk saw Gigia stand up and try to pull a wounded Milo out of the massive thing's rolling path, but he was too injured to do more than slow her down. Andreas tried to pitch in to help, but he only doomed himself as well. The red-stained crystal smashed all three Hackers beneath its rolling bulk.

A number of the All-Stars went down too, as the Jumboball didn't take sides in this, the first game it had ever entered. It just kept rolling along, oblivious to the destruction it left in its wake.

Dunk peered past the ball, forgetting the treacherous referee in the face of this new threat. He saw Cavre and Simon racing away from the ball, running north, toward the Hackers' dugout. With any luck, they would be safe.

In the centre of the field, Karsten and Guillermo sprinted toward Dunk at top speed. If they were hoping to outrun the monstrous crystal ball, it seemed they were doomed to lose. The two linemen realised this and turned right, heading toward the All-Stars' dugout.

Dunk breathed a sigh of relief and started for the Hackers' dugout himself. First he headed north, planning to hug the edge of the field to keep as far from the Jumboball's path as he could.

To Dunk's amazement, the Jumboball veered off to the left, forging a new path that would intercept Karsten and Guillermo long before they made it to the relative safety of the All-Stars' dugout. Dunk was sure that any Hackers who literally landed in their foes' laps were in for a savage beating, but at least they'd survive that. Probably.

Dunk shouted a warning to Karsten and Guillermo, but the roar of the crowd at the Jumboball's abrupt change of course drowned out any hope of his friends hearing him. Despite this, the two Hackers glanced back to see where the Jumboball was and found it hot on their tail. Guillermo shoved Karsten to the left and took off to the right himself, splitting them so that the Jumboball would pass between them and roll right into the All-Stars' dugout.

This dugout, like the Hackers', featured a set of steps that led down into the ground. Tall players standing on the broad floor could look out over the field at about eye level. Others could achieve the same effect by climbing a few steps.

A concrete roof angled back to protect the occupants of the dugout from the fans in the stands behind it. Riots seemed to break out in just about every game, and when they did the players could dive right into their dugouts to avoid thrown beer steins, rotten tomatoes, and even rusty knives.

Dunk wondered if the roof would be enough to stop the Jumboball. Or would the massive sphere crush the structure and everyone in it? As much as he hated to see people die, a part of him felt that if any team deserved such carnage it was the Chaos All-Stars.

The Jumboball ground to a halt before it reached the dugout. It hesitated there for a moment and then veered left.

'Wow! Have you ever seen anything like that, Bob? Talk about playing on an unlevel field.'

'Uh, no. Never! It seems like that rogue Jumboball has a mind of its own.'

Dunk wondered for a moment if he was seeing things. Then he spotted a familiar face in the All-Stars' dugout: Schlechter Zauberer.

Dunk had last seen the middle-aged wizard at last year's Chaos Bowl, in the middle of the same game at which he'd killed the bull-headed Likker. He wore the same midnight-blue robes with bluish-white piping that highlighted their edges, and the same polished silver skullcap that glinted in the midday sun. He waved a wand that resembled the blackened thighbone of some large bird, and the Jumboball followed his gestures.

Although Dunk had almost made it to the safety of the Hackers' dugout, he saw only one course of action. He sprinted across the gridiron to rip Zauberer's wispy white beard off his receding chin.

'Dunk!' Pegleg called after him. 'Get back here, damn your meaty legs!'

The thrower ignored his coach's pleas, pretending he couldn't hear them over the crowd. It wasn't hard to do.

As Dunk neared the All-Stars' dugout, a pair of benchwarmers leapt from the dugout and charged at him. The first, a twisted lizardman bearing two massive tails, threw back its head and hissed a challenge at Dunk. A pair of eyeballs twisted on the end of its long, sinuous tongue as it slipped in and out of its toothy maw.

The second creature worried Dunk more. The stone-skinned troll stood twice as tall as the Hacker and bore spike-knuckled fists, each as large as Dunk's head. It bellowed at the thrower as it lumbered toward him, smashing holes in the Astrogranite for emphasis.

The crowd cheered. Dunk glanced to his left to see Karsten's flattened remains come slipping off the backside of the Jumboball, which had just run him over. The ball came to a halt, then backed up, running over Karsten again and heading straight for Dunk.

Dunk looked back toward the All-Stars' dugout and saw that the lizardman and troll were coming at him like a pair of runaway battlewagons. He turned and ran in the other direction. Zauberer would have to wait.

For a moment, Dunk thought he had a chance. Despite the troll's long strides, he could outrun him in a fair race. The lizardman, though, wasn't going to give Dunk a chance. The lizardman couldn't run any faster than Dunk, but he was fresh off the bench. Dunk's legs felt like he wore lead anklets that became heavier with every step.

And then there was the Jumboball.

'This is amazing, Bob,' Jim's voice said. 'Hoffnung seemed to be hunting for an epic death with his charge into the All-Stars' dugout, but at the last moment he lost his nerve.'

'It's one thing to die,' said Bob. 'As a vampire, I know all about it. It's something else to be torn to pieces and eaten. Chaos trolls like Krader there have been known to do that.'

'That's if Sseth Skinshucker doesn't get a hold of Dunk first. As we know from last year's Blood Bowl qualifying rounds, Sseth doesn't like to share.'

'I've never seen anyone swallow a halfling whole like that before. I understand it took him the better part of the week to digest poor Puddin Fatfellow.'

'True, although I hear the Greenfield Grasshuggers took longer than that to select a new captain!'

These words spurred Dunk on toward the All-Stars' end zone. As he leaped over the pile of dead bodies near where Gimlet fell, he heard a low rumbling noise under the maddening roar of the crowd. He glanced over his shoulder and saw the Jumboball bounce along over the corpses only a dozen feet behind him. Sseth and Krader had veered off to the south to give it room to pass, but they still kept pace.

'Ooh! It looks like the jaunty Jumboball is going to win that footrace instead, Jim.'

'It could be – but wait! We have a new entrant into the fray!'

Dunk snapped his head around to see what Bob could mean. As he did, he saw M'Grash come stampeding in from the Hackers' dugout and hurl himself into the Jumboball's spinning side.

Despite the ogre's size, the Jumboball stood more than twice his height. This didn't faze him for a moment. He lowered his shoulder and smashed his spiked spaulder flat into the massive crystal. A loud crack rolled through the stadium like instant thunder, and the ball's path skewed south.

Sseth leapt out of the way on his powerful haunches. To Dunk it looked like the lizardman's tail propelled him out of the way. The troll, however, wasn't so fortunate. Krader roared in protest before the Jumboball rolled over him, crushing him behind it as it smashed into the south stands.

Dunk skidded to a halt then ran back around to where M'Grash stood, holding his bruised shoulder. 'What did you think you were doing?' the thrower shouted. 'You could have been killed!'

To Dunk's surprise, the ogre blushed. 'Me sorry, Dunkel,' he said, lowering his eyes. 'Didn't want Dunkel to die.'

Dunk's heart fell. M'Grash had the brains – and the moral frame-work, sadly – of a two-year-old. He hadn't considered the risk to his own skin. He'd only known he had to save his friend's life.

Dunk clapped M'Grash on the arm. 'It's all right, M'Grash. Actually, it's better than that.' He leaned over to peer up into the ogre's weepy eyes. 'Thanks.'

'Mean it?' M'Grash said as he wiped his eyes, a half-proud smile spreading across his face.

The thrower nodded. 'Damn right. If not for you, I'd be– '

Dunk had to stop talking when Sseth's tail knocked him clear past the ogre to land face first atop the pile of chainsaw-savaged cadavers.

'Wow!' said Bob. 'You don't see cheap shots like that every – wait! Yes, I guess you do!'

'Too true, Bob,' said Jim, 'but that was a classic of the genre. The Cabalvision networks will be playing that one on the highlight feeds all week long.'

Dunk pushed himself to his knees, his battered back painfully protesting. He looked down and saw a body in a green and gold uni-form beneath him. He had to squint, but it looked like Kai. Just three feet to his left, he spotted Percy's severed head staring out at him through his intact helmet.

To Dunk, this had long since stopped being a game.

He stood up and cheered as he saw M'Grash grab Sseth by his long, green-scaled tail. The ogre leaned back and started to spin around, swinging the lizardman around by his extra appendage. After a half-dozen rotations, M'Grash let go and hurled Sseth right over the Jumboball and into the south stands.

'So, Jim, what do you think the chances are of Skinshucker making it out of there alive?'

'If the Gobbo was here, he'd lay six to one odds, Bob. Ooh! It looks like the fans might be putting Skinshucker's last name to the test. That's gotta hurt! I haven't seen that many scales ripped off someone since my wife's last trip to the spa!'

Before Dunk could run over to M'Grash to congratulate him, a sound like the bellow of a wounded dragon came from behind the Jumboball. The gigantic crystal dislodged from where it had come to rest against the crushed restraining wall separating the field from the stands. As it rolled to the right, Krader appeared from behind it, pushing himself up from where he'd fallen.

As Dunk watched, the troll's battered skin and broken bones reknit themselves together. The crowd gasped, then cheered with delight.

'With their regenerating powers, Bob, it's hard to keep a good troll down.'

'Or a bad one for that matter, Jim!'

Dunk looked down at his feet and spotted the end of the chainsaw sticking out through Gimlet's armoured corpse. It would certainly make a better weapon than the thrower's bare fists.

Dunk flipped Gimlet over and dragged the chainsaw out of his corpse. He'd never seen anything like this before, some strange amalgam of sorcery and alchemy, he guessed. Still, if a creature like Gimlet could run it, then perhaps Dunk could too.

He fumbled with the contraption for a moment until his hands found the proper grip on it. How had Gimlet turned the thing on? Dunk had been too far down the field to see the chainsaw start up.

'It looks like Hoffnung has decided turnabout is fair play, Bob.'

'Too bad no one engraved a set of instructions on the side of that thing!'

Dunk cursed and glared up at the announcers' box, high above the stadium's north flank. It was bad enough he couldn't figure out the damned thing without disembodied voices mocking him in front of thousands of people.

Then an odd thought struck Dunk. He turned the chainsaw over on its side. There, just under the left handle, someone had scratched a set of instructions: 'Grab left handle. Pull chain with right.'

Dunk looked at the serrated chain running along the outside of the blade. He couldn't imagine anyone would want to grab that to get the thing going. Not even a Chaos worshipper like Gimlet could be that willing to risk his fingers every time.

'Try the T-grip,' Guillermo said.

Dunk almost leapt from his armour at the sound of the Hacker's voice behind him. He swung the chainsaw around to smack the man but managed to recognise him in time. 'Where in the Chaos Wastes did you come from?' he said.

Guillermo tossed a thumb back at the stands. 'Been hiding in the crowd.'

Dunk scowled as he looked for this 'T-grip' Guillermo had mentioned. 'They didn't pass you up over the edge?'

'Too busy watching the show.'

Guillermo tapped a fist-long wooden dowel dangling from the right side of the chainsaw's handle. Like most of the rest of the machine, it was stained with fresh blood. Dunk reached down and grabbed it with his right hand. Bracing the chainsaw in his left hand, he hauled back on the T-grip with all his might, and the smoke-belching beast roared to life.

Dunk nodded his thanks to Guillermo over the machine's deafening roar and turned to see Krader and M'Grash pummelling each other to death. The ogre seemed to be getting the worse of it, which was no surprise. The troll had a couple of feet of height on him and countless pounds. Worse yet, Dunk could see every wound M'Grash inflicted on the troll was already healing. The same couldn't be said for the half-dozen gashes Dunk spotted in the ogre's hide.

'Let's finish this!' Dunk said, charging forward with the chainsaw buzzing in his hands.

As he approached the massive combatants, though, he saw the Jumboball start to move again.

'Gee, Jim,' Bob's voice said, 'that hardly seems fair.'

THE CROWD ROARED at Bob's joke as Dunk turned to face the twenty-foot-tall crystal ball rolling toward him. Then he did the only thing he could think of, and charged straight at it.

Dunk knew that if he tried to run the ball would outpace him before he could reach safety. It would have done so before if M'Grash hadn't stopped it, and the ogre was too busy to lend a hand right now. So he ran straight at the thing, hoping it wouldn't build up too much speed before he reached it.

As Dunk neared the Jumboball, he dived to the right. He misjudged the ball's size, though, and it clipped his shoulder as it rolled by him, sending him sprawling to the ground.

Dunk wrestled with the chainsaw as he fell, refusing to share Gimlet's horrible fate. He landed on his back, holding the machine over him in his outstretched arms, its vicious teeth whirring only inches from his face.

'I think Hoffnung's taken too many blows to the head today, Bob,' Jim said.

'Lots of people have underestimated the Hoffnung brothers before. Remember how Dunk's younger brother Dirk pulled out that win in last year's Blood Bowl final?'

'Are you kidding? That was the best Blood Bowl I've seen since the glory days of Griff Oberwald. Somewhere in a dark corner of hell, Reavers' founder D. D. Griswell is still smiling about it!'

Dunk scrambled to his feet and saw that the Jumboball hadn't got far. It had stopped rolling away and stood hesitating only a few feet away from the Hackers' thrower. As it started toward Dunk again, he launched himself forward and stabbed the chainsaw's roaring blade into it.

Where the blade met the crystal, it chipped off large chunks of it, and the ball slowed to a stop once again. Sensing the advantage, Dunk jammed the chainsaw forward, taking larger and larger pieces out of the thing. A moment later, though, the sphere pressed forward harder, and Dunk had to dodge out of the way once again.

Dunk spun around as the ball passed him. He spotted a pair of large cracks running through the thing. The first came from when M'Grash had smashed into it, and the second sprung from the deep gouges he'd managed to carve into it. These same divots didn't keep the Jumboball from still rolling along the Astrogranite in fine form though.

Beyond the glassy sphere, now smeared with layers of blood, Dunk saw Krader beating M'Grash into the Astrogranite. The ogre had fought valiantly, but he looked like he might fall over exhausted at any moment. Dunk had to do something to help him now, or he might never get another chance.

Dunk ran around to the other side of the sphere. It wobbled there for a moment as if unsure which way to go. Dunk jabbed at it with the chainsaw again, and huge hunks of crystal spun away from it. The ball leaned toward him once again.

Dunk ran straight for the battle between the ogre and the troll. Krader had knocked M'Grash to his knees, and he was about to finish the bleeding, battered ogre off. He had his back to Dunk and didn't hear the chainsaw over the crowd until it was too late.

Dunk shoved the tip of the chainsaw straight into the troll's back and fought to hold it steady as it bucked against the creature's rocky hide. At first, he thought the creature didn't feel the whirring teeth biting into its skin, but then Dunk realised that M'Grash had wrapped his fists around Krader's arms and was holding him down.

Krader pulled back his head and screamed. Dunk's ears rang so hard he thought he might never hear again. At the moment, though, that was the least of his problems.

In his pain-fuelled rage, Krader backhanded Dunk, who went sailing off to the west. As he wondered whether his jaw might be broken, the thrower looked up to see the Jumboball roll right into Krader and knock him flat.

The crowd went nuts.

'Now that's the kind of turnaround I like to see in a Blood Bowl game, Bob. This is fantastic! I wonder how we can top this next week?'

'Careful what you wish for, Jim. I wouldn't be surprised to see the rogue Jumboball become a regular event!'

The Jumboball tried to slow down before it smashed into Krader, but it failed. The troll reached up to stop it too, but he only ended up being able to put up his arms to keep it from crushing his upper body, even as it pulverised his legs.

M'Grash summoned up some hidden reserve of energy and sprang at the Jumboball. At first, Dunk thought the ogre might try to attack it with his bare hands, but he soon realised that M'Grash just wanted to hold the thing in place.

'Hit it, Dunk!' Guillermo shouted from behind.

The thrower didn't need another prompt. He launched himself forward and slammed the chainsaw into the Jumboball, searching for a weak spot, digging at the cracks that had already formed. Under his assault, those cracks widened into seams and then to gaps.

'So, Bob, how much do you think one of those babies costs?'

'I don't know, Jim, but I'm glad it's not coming out of *my* pay cheque.'

'No!' Krader shouted. 'Stop! Please!'

For a moment, Dunk considered showing the troll mercy, but before he could even haul back on the chainsaw, Krader lashed out with his arms and knocked M'Grash's feet from under him. The ogre went down like a brick wall in an earthquake.

'I'll kill you!' Krader said. 'I'll kill you all!'

He reached for Dunk then, but the thrower ignored him. The Jumboball, he saw, was rolling towards him once again.

Dunk took three steps back and looked up at the monstrous sphere. His arms felt like wet logs, and his fingers wanted nothing more than to let the sputtering machine in his hands fall from their numbed grip.

The chainsaw coughed twice and then went dead.

Dunk grabbed at the T-grip and pulled. Something in the machine whirred around, but the chainsaw failed to leap to life.

As the ball rolled closer, Dunk tried the T-grip again and again.

'Run!' Guillermo shouted.

Dunk didn't bother to glance back at the lineman. This had to work. It *had* to. He pulled the T-grip again, and the machine choked and rumbled again, then let loose a hungry roar.

The Jumboball loomed over Dunk now, the midday Estalian sun gleaming off its gore-spattered surface. The thrower hefted the smoking, coughing chainsaw behind him and then pitched it right into the sphere's path.

The sphere rolled over the still-whirring chainsaw, its teeth scoring huge gashes in its underside. As the crystal fragmented along the bottom, Krader came crawling around from its far side, his legs starting to heal even as he dragged himself along by his boulder-like hands and powerful arms.

'I'm going to pick my teeth with your bones!' the troll snarled, blood spluttering from between its broken teeth. 'I'm going to use your hide to wipe my–'

The chainsaw's fuel tank exploded under the Jumboball, which smothered the blast. The resultant shock sent thousands of cracks through the sphere and shattered the already cracked crystal into billions of shards. For a moment, the shards hung there in the air, nothing holding them together any longer but memories. Then they cascaded downward like water from a burst skin, driving themselves into the hapless troll below. The tremendous weight of the countless razor-sharp shards shredded Krader's flesh into a bloody stew.

Dunk lurched backward to avoid the falling remnants of the Jumboball. The crowd's cheers hit him with the force of a wave. He fell to his knees and wondered what might happen next.

'Well, Bob, that's one way to kill a troll I've never seen before!'

'True enough, Jim. I prefer to barbecue them myself, but to each his own!'

'I CAN'T BELIEVE that after all that we had to forfeit the game?' Back in the locker room, Dunk shook his head, his short-cropped black hair still dripping with sweat, as the apothecary the team had hired stitched up his wounds. The white-haired woman didn't believe in painkillers, but her needle was so sharp that Dunk barely felt it. He'd waited for the old Estalian mystic to help out some of the others first. He'd wanted her to take care of M'Grash too, but the ogre had threatened to smash her skull between his thumb and forefinger if she didn't minister to Dunk first.

'We only have five players left alive, son,' Slick said, his voice filled with a rare reverence. 'And you and M'Grash were kicked out of the game. Even Pegleg won't fight odds like those.'

'Weren't you the one telling me I should give up when we had eleven players left, Dunk?' said the coach, who stood nearby, watching over the apothecary's handiwork. 'Now there's only M'Grash, Cavre, Sherwood, Reyes, and you.'

Dunk let his head hang down. He focused on the stab and pull, stab and pull, of the old woman's needle and thread. It kept his mind off the grief.

'It is okay to mourn our lost, Mr. Hoffnung,' Cavre said from his spot on a bench across the room. Dunk raised his head to meet the man's gentle stare. 'Tonight, we number eleven less than this morning. This is much for even the hardest minds to comprehend.'

'It's like we've been through a war, innit?' said Simon in his clipped, Albion accent. His eyes bore a haunted look, rounded with deep, dark circles that reminded Dunk of the black paint many players wore under their eyes to cut down on glare during a game. Simon had washed off his black grease long ago, but the darkness remained.

'Ah, the shame,' Guillermo said, 'it is tremendous. Here, in my homeland, in front of my family and friends, to be humbled so.' He fell silent for a moment. 'I cannot wait until we leave.'

'Aren't we going to stick around for the rest of the tournament?' Dunk asked. 'The finals are next week. The Reavers still have a shot.'

'We don't really care about your brother and your girlfriend, now, do we?' Simon said. 'We have enough problems of our own.'

Slick stepped in front of Simon. 'There's no need to get personal about it,' he said sharply. 'If it wasn't for my boy there, we'd be down to the three players who managed to hide the best.'

Simon unfolded himself to his full height and glared down at the tiny Slick. 'I don't care for how you choose to talk to me.'

'Sure,' said Slick, 'now you can play the tough guy, when you're facing down someone less than half your size.'

Simon raised his foot high enough to stomp on Slick's head. A large man, Simon stood taller than Dunk, and far more than twice the halfling's height. He looked like he could squish the little agent like a cockroach. 'You watch your little tongue–' the catcher started.

He stopped when the even larger M'Grash grabbed him by the scruff of the neck and hauled him into the air like a helpless kitten. Simon's feet pedalled in the open air beneath them as he strove to pry the blitzer's massive hand from around his neck. M'Grash held the full-grown man out at a safe arm's length and shook his head at him.

'Put me down,' Simon snarled, his dark eyes blazing at the ogre as his face flushed to the colour of a watermelon's flesh. 'Put me down, or I'll – urk!'

The catcher's tirade came to an abrupt end as M'Grash squeezed off the last bits of air flowing through Simon's throat.

'Stand down!'

All heads snapped around to stare goggle-eyed at Pegleg, who stood atop one of the benches in front of the lockers, glaring down at the others. 'What in Nuffle's nine nastiest names do you lot think you're doing?' he said. 'It's not enough that we lost eleven players to the Chaos All-Stars today, is it? You have to go finish the job for them?'

The others hung their heads in shame. M'Grash let loose his grip on Simon, and the catcher came crashing to the floor. He missed crushing Slick by scant inches.

'I'm all right,' Simon said after a long, silent moment.

'For now,' Pegleg said. 'If I catch any of you fighting with each other again, I'll kick you off the team.'

The players looked at each other for a moment, none of them willing to risk their coach's wrath. Or so Dunk thought.

'You're joking,' Simon said as he stood up and brushed himself off. He looked around at the others. 'With only five of us left, you can't afford to lose any of us.' He smiled, and the sight of it felt like a knife in Dunk's belly. 'I'm the only catcher you've got.'

Pegleg leapt down from the bench and landed right in front of Simon. As he did, his hands moved quicker than Dunk could see. Pegleg's hook caught Simon around the back of his neck, and a short, gleaming knife appeared in the coach's other hand, pressed against Simon's throat. A line of blood appeared along its edge, right where it met the catcher's flesh.

'Coach!' Dunk started toward the ex-pirate, but Cavre's firm hand on his shoulder held him in his place.

The thrower couldn't let Pegleg murder Simon. No matter how much of a bastard he might be, the Albionman was a team-mate, and that had to mean something.

Pegleg ignored Dunk as he hissed into Simon's ear. 'I already have to replace eleven players after today, Mr. Sherwood. What's one more body dumped in the deep?'

Simon's flesh turned a ghostly pale. 'You – you misunder– my apologies, Captain Haken. I was out of line.'

'That you were, Mr. Sherwood.' Pegleg removed his hook from the back of Simon's neck and pushed him away. The catcher fell back into M'Grash's arms, blood trickling from the shallow cut on his throat.

The coach glared down at Simon and then around at each of the others in the room, like a wild tiger who'd awakened to find himself in a cage full of fresh, poisoned meat. 'If you – any of you – cross that line again, the consequences will be swift and horrible.'

With that, Pegleg turned, his long green coat flaring out behind him, and fled the locker room.

'Well,' Simon said, 'that was a bit much, wasn't it?'

'Shut up,' Slick said, shaking his head at the catcher in disgust. 'You're lucky he didn't cut you right there.'

'From the team?'

'From life.'

Simon started toward the halfling, but Cavre stepped between them and put a hand on the catcher's chest. 'There's been enough blood shed here today, Mr. Sherwood.'

Simon opened his mouth to speak, then reconsidered and closed it. He nodded at the team captain's cool-headed wisdom and took a step back.

'So,' Dunk said, trying to fill the awkward silence. 'What happens now?'

Cavre answered, thankful for the change in subject. 'I suspect it's back to Bad Bay for us,' he said. 'We might stay here a bit to see if we can round up some new recruits, but the other teams snapped up most of the top prospects before the tournament began.'

Dunk nodded, remembering how he'd joined the team that way just over a year ago. He hadn't made the first cut then, although Simon and Guillermo had. That thought shocked Dunk. Of the Hackers still left standing at the end of today's game, only M'Grash and Cavre had been a part of the team for more than a year.

Pegleg had only offered Dunk a job after someone murdered the 'top prospects'. Dunk hadn't known then that he owed his job to M'Grash's amoral efforts to get him placed on the team. When he'd found out, he'd nearly choked.

Thankfully, Dunk had been able to clear all that up during the last Blood Bowl tournament, casting the blame on Kur Ritternacht, then the Hackers' starting thrower and Dunk's chief rival. Kur had killed enough others and had tried to destroy Dunk enough times that Dunk felt no guilt for that. Sadly, it seemed to be just another part of the game.

'Maybe we should go to Albion instead,' Simon said.

Everyone turned to gawk at the catcher. 'This isn't a chance for a quick vacation,' Slick said. 'We have to rebuild fast for any chance to play in the Dungeon Bowl tournament.'

'Will the Grey Wizards sponsor us again?' Dunk asked. 'After all, the only reason we got in last year was that cave-in that almost destroyed the Reikland Reavers.'

M'Grash had been behind that too, Dunk recalled. Fortunately, his brother Dirk and lover Spinne hadn't been killed. Otherwise, he might never have been able to forgive the ogre.

Dunk glanced over at the massive, morose creature. He'd never seen M'Grash so quiet, so depressed. The ogre's simple nature meant he probably felt the loss of their team-mates sharper than anyone else, Dunk guessed.

Cavre frowned. 'They've said as much, but this may change things. Wizards love their plans. They set schemes in motion that take years to bear fruit. They do their best to eliminate uncertainties.'

'And a team with just five players left, she qualifies as 'uncertain'?' Guillermo said.

Carve shrugged. 'It's hard enough to fathom the mind of a single wizard. I won't hazard a guess at the thoughts of an entire college.'

'I wasn't talking about taking a holiday,' Simon said. 'Albion is a cold, dreary place. If I never went back, that would sit fine with me. I'm talking about going after the Far Albion Cup.'

Dunk's face went blank. He'd never heard of this cup before, but then he'd avoided anything to do with Blood Bowl until that incident with the 'chimera that wasn't anything at all like a dragon' last year, after which Slick had convinced him to forget about dragon slaying and give the game a try.

Dunk's agent saw his confusion written on his face. 'It's the Albion-ish equivalent of the Blood Bowl tournament, son,' Slick said. 'If you can call what they play over there by the same name.'

'It's not 'proper' Blood Bowl, for dead sure,' Simon said. 'But the teams play hard. I was a star player for the Notting Knights before I joined the Hackers.'

'Happens all the time,' Slick said to Dunk. 'Far Albion League play-ers get full of themselves playing in their little league and decide to try their fate in the real league. Most of them get sent back home in a pine box.'

'We have some cracking players,' Simon said. 'But the Old World league pays far better. It drains away all the real talent.'

'So how'd you get in?' Slick asked.

Simon ignored the halfling. 'I wasn't talking about the Far Albion League though. I meant the Far Albion Cup, the league trophy. The actual cup from which the gods of Albion drank the blood of their slaughtered forebears. The great god Feefa himself handed it down from the Highlands to the founders of the Far Albion League.'

'The legends say that those who control the cup cannot lose,' Cavre said softly. Dunk couldn't remember ever seeing the unflappable man so impressed.

'Must have made for some dull tournaments,' Dunk said. 'Right? Once a team won the trophy once, who could beat them?'

'It's a travelling trophy,' Simon said. 'The winners have to give it up before the start of the tournament every year.'

'If we had the cup, Mr. Sherwood,' Cavre said, his eyes wide and dis-tant, 'we'd never have to suffer through a game like this again.'

'Do we even know where this thing is?' Dunk said. 'This all sounds a bit too easy: Steal the cup and never lose again? What are we wait-ing for?'

'You confuse 'straightforward' with 'easy,' Mr. Hoffnung.' Cavre nod-ded at Simon to continue.

The catcher cleared his throat. 'Sadly the Far Albion Cup was lost.'

'What happened to it?'

'It was stolen – over 500 years ago.'

'And where do you think you're going to find that?' Slick snorted. 'Everyone but Nuffle himself has been hunting for that old trophy for centuries. They all failed. What makes you think you'll be any differ-ent?'

'When I was with the Knights, our team wizard was Olson Merlin.'

An unsettling silence fell over the room. Slick, Cavre, and Guillermo stood with their mouths gaping wide. Even M'Grash stopped picking his nose for a moment, withdrawing a chipped, mucous-coated nail from a nostril large enough to engulf Slick's head.

'Who?' Dunk said.

'The immortal wizard of Albion,' Simon said, smiling. 'It's said he's cursed to wander this earth forever – or until he finds the cup and drinks his own blood from its gold-lined bowl.'

'Now that's what I call an incentive clause,' Slick said.

MOST NIGHTS DURING the *Spike! Magazine* Tournament, Blood Bowl fans in Magritta packed the wharf-side tavern known as Bad Water to the rafters. When Dunk and Slick entered the place, though, just after the game after theirs had started, the place was half empty. The bartender, a sun-worn dwarf with a long, damp beard, waved the pair over from behind a thick, wooden bar that bore the scars of countless fights.

'Well met, Sparky,' Slick said to the bartender. 'Get us a round of Killer Genuine Drafts, would you?'

'Got a special on Poor's Silver Bullets,' Sparky said. He narrowed his eyes at his two new customers. Thanks to a narrow shelf that ran the length of the bar's interior, about three feet off the ground, his eyes met Dunk's at the same height. 'Neither of you werewolves, are you?'

'No!' Dunk said, startled at the implications. His head snapped about so he could glance at the other patrons, and he wondered how many of them might transform into a wolf as night fell.

Slick smirked. 'You get a lot of that sort around here, do you?'

'Just enough that it pays to ask.' Sparky used the end of his beard to wipe up some of the spilled beer on the bar in front him.

'What happens?' Dunk asked.

Sparky cursed as his tangled beard caught on something white and jagged sticking out of the bar. He reached under the bar and brought

303

out a long pair of rusty pliers. 'Ever seen a man try to tear through his belly and rip out his own stomach?'

Dunk shook his head as Sparky yanked at the white thing with his pliers. After a moment of wiggling back and forth, it popped free. Sparky smiled and held the thing up to the light: a long, jagged tooth over two inches long. Blood coated the part of it that had been shoved into the bar.

'I thought Kurtz left something behind.' Sparky wiped the thing clean with his beard, and then stuffed it into a pocket on his shirt.

'Kurtz?' Slick asked. 'The starting blitzer for the Orland Raiders?'

Sparky nodded. 'He's a big fan of your Hackers, he is. Had a hundred gold on you in the game. When Dunkel got kicked out of the game, he had a fit. Threatened to kill every All-Stars fan in the bar.'

Dunk smiled. 'Too bad he lost then.'

Sparky stuck the end of his beard into his mouth and started sucking on it. 'Oh, he didn't lose,' he said around the blood- and beer-soaked hair. 'You should have seen the other guys. Took our cleaning crew three buckets of clean water to mop it all up.'

Slick looked at Dunk, then said, 'We'll take a couple of Killers, Sparky.'

The dwarf shrugged and went to pull a pair of pints for them. 'Suit yourselves.'

A crystal ball hung in one corner of the ceiling over the bar. Bob and Jim's voices blared out of it, but Dunk ignored them, concentrating on the images instead. Slick remained quiet while waiting for the beers to arrive, for which Dunk gave thanks.

'Dirk and Spinne look good,' Slick said as Sparky slid a pair of commemorative steins in front of Dunk. The thrower tossed Sparky a coin for the drinks, which the dwarf tucked somewhere into his snarled mess of a beard.

'They always do.' Dunk didn't feel much like talking, but he knew that Slick could never stay silent for long. 'Who are they playing again?'

'The Evil Gitz,' Slick said. 'A goblin team from the Badlands.'

'They don't look like much.'

Slick smiled and sipped his beer. 'They're not.'

'How'd they make it to the playoffs then?'

'Same as always. They play dirtier than anyone else around. This time around, I hear they managed to find mostly halfling teams to play.'

'Ah,' Dirk nodded. 'So that's what happened to the Tinytown Titans. I saw the funeral procession last Tuesday: sixteen little coffins headed for the cemetery.'

'It's getting awful crowded up there, son,' Slick said. 'The game's more violent than ever, these days.'

'I wouldn't know. I've only been at it for a year. Fatal is still fatal, as far as I can see.'

Slick pursed his lips for a moment before taking another belt of his beer. 'Ever think about giving it all up?'

Dunk stared at Slick as if he'd just sworn off food. He peered around the top and sides of the halfling's head and said, 'Did you get hit by a flying body part during the game? You practically begged me to give Blood Bowl a crack, and now you want me to walk away?'

Slick stuck up a short, thin finger. 'I never said that, son. I only inquired as to your own feelings on the matter. After all, you've seen a lot of death in your short time in the league. I just want to know where you stand.'

'Why?' Dunk said, leaning closer to Slick. 'You worried I'm going to quit and leave my salary behind – along with your cut?'

Slick scowled and pressed a hand to his chest. 'That hurts, son. That really hurts. You think just because I'm half your size my heart doesn't beat as fast? Do you think I don't care?'

'I think you're an agent, Slogo. You didn't get the name 'Slick' for your way with the lady halflings.'

Dunk took a long pull from his beer too. When he finished he saw Slick staring at him aghast. 'Hey,' Dunk said in awe, 'you're serious.' He leaned forward to apologise, but Slick pulled back.

'No,' Slick said, putting his hands in front of him. 'I deserve it I suppose. I've put a lot of effort into farming that image, so I shouldn't be surprised when even my closest friends buy into it too.'

'What are we buying here?' a high-pitched crackle of a voice said off to Dunk's left. It could only belong to one person, and the thought made the thrower groan out loud.

Slick and Dunk turned as one to see a pale, greasy creature with wide, bloodshot, baggy eyes and a large, wart-coated nose over a wide, repulsive smile that showed a mouth of blackened and broken teeth. His oily hair hung in long, dirty locks over his face and broad, bald pate, except where he'd drawn it back into a greasy ponytail that looked like a fire hunting for a match.

'Gunther the Gobbo,' Dunk said, ignoring the hand Gunther stretched out in greeting. 'You're looking well.'

'Thanks, lad!' the Gobbo said. 'I'm glad someone's finally noticed how I'm trying to better myself.'

Dunk grasped the edge of the bar to keep himself steady, as the odour of Gunther's breath threatened to knock him over. The thrower picked up his stein and did his best to breathe through his beer until the vertigo passed.

'We were having a private conversation,' Slick said, glaring at Gunther with open disdain. 'No one around here is interested in doing any kind of business with you.'

'So you say, so you say.' Gunther grinned, and Dunk feared that several of the Gobbo's teeth might decide it was better to dive from his polluted mouth than remain there a moment longer. 'But you're involved in Blood Bowl, and Blood Bowl is my business. Sooner or later, everyone thinks they have a sure thing in a game, and that's when they come to place their bets with me.'

'There's no such thing as a sure thing,' Dunk said. 'Didn't the Black Jerseys teach you that?'

Gunther's smile fell into his face. 'Kid, you're not suggesting I had anything to do with that horrible group of game-fixing players, are you?' He spoke louder than ever, his voice warbling with nervous energy.

'No,' Slick said, trying to wedge himself in between Gunther and Dunk. 'He's not *suggesting* anything.'

Gunther stared into Dunk's eyes as the thrower remembered how the notorious bookie had tried to draft him into that 'meta-team' of Blood Bowl players who worked with him to force the maximum profit from the multitude of fans who wagered on the big games. He'd managed to avoid that until the Game Wizards from the Wolf Sports Cabalvision force had put an end to the Black Jerseys' reign.

The Gobbo let his eyes fall to the ground. 'All right then,' he said, his voice tinged with regret. 'I thought businessmen like ourselves could let the past stay in the past.'

Slick gasped. 'You're starting them back up again, aren't you? I'm surprised any respectable player would come within ten feet of you of his own accord. What will you call your group of crooks this time? The Black Benchwarmers?'

Gunther scoffed, bringing up a hunk of dark phlegm that landed on the bar. Sparky reached over and wiped it up with the end of his beard. 'Poor's Light for you, Mr. Gobbo?' the dwarf said.

'Make mine a Bloodweiser,' Gunther said. 'Got to support the sponsors of my pre-game show on the Extraordinary Spellcasters Prognosticated News Network, after all.'

'I thought you were with Wolf Sports,' Dunk said. 'Get fired?'

Gunther's greasy smile returned. 'Let's just say I saw a better future with ESPNN.'

'So you've reformed entirely,' Slick said, shaking his head.

Gunther sniggered. 'You and your lad here have nothing to fear from me,' he said. 'I've given up buying players.' He leaned in and whispered, 'It's far more economical to purchase referees instead.'

Dunk nearly spit out his beer. 'Wait,' he said. 'What happened in the game today. You didn't–'

'*I* didn't do anything,' Gunther said, wearing his mock innocence like a halfling's dress. It didn't do anything to really cover him and looked horribly inappropriate. 'Those were some really awful calls though.' He patted Dunk on the shoulder with a slimy paw.

Dunk shrugged off the hand. He wanted nothing more than to tear off the Gobbo's head and hurl it across the room. He clenched his fists instead and spat out, 'We lost eleven good players today.'

Gunther shook his head, unaware of Dunk's designs on it. 'That's why it's called *Blood* Bowl, right? At least your finest players made it through. It's survival of the fittest at its best!'

'I ought to kill you right here,' Dunk said.

'Hey, kid, don't take it personally. It's just business after all.' Despite his jovial manner, Gunther started to back away. Then he stepped forward again and whispered, 'Be sure to tell Pegleg that, for the right price, things could start to go the Hackers' way again.'

Dunk gritted his teeth and brought up his hands to lunge at Gunther, but before he could Slick leapt from the top of his barstool and thrust his fingers into the bookie's watery eyes.

Stunned, Dunk froze where he stood and watched as Gunther screamed out in pain. Slick landed on the bookie's chest and started to hammer at him with his little fists, giving everything he had in his murderous rage.

Sadly, it wasn't much. The blows bounced off the Gobbo's corpulent head and shoulders like rain on a helmet.

'Get off!' Gunther squeaked, shoving Slick away from him and catapulting the halfling over the bar.

Dunk thrust himself up and backward and reached out with both hands, catching Slick between them. He hauled his little friend back in and cradled him in his arms like a child, protecting him as he crashed down behind the bar.

Everyone in the bar had turned to watch the fight. As Dunk and Slick disappeared behind the bar, the onlookers all gasped and fell silent. When Dunk sprang back to his feet, holding Slick up in his hands like a prized trophy, the rest of the patrons cheered at the top of their lungs – all but Gunther, who skulked out of the bar as fast as his podgy legs would carry him.

As Dunk set Slick down on the bar, the halfling scooped up his stein and sent it flying after the bookie. It shattered on the doorframe just as Gunther raced through it.

Once Gunther left, Slick turned around and dusted himself off. As he did, he looked down at Dunk and said, 'Do you still think the league's no more dangerous than normal, son?'

Dunk shrugged. 'How could it get much worse?'

A GENTLE RAIN fell on Magritta the next day as Dunk, Slick, Cavre, M'Grash, Simon, Guillermo, and Pegleg stood by the graves of their fallen friends. Thunder rolled in the distance, but Dunk never saw any lightning to go with it. Three other groups of players huddled together at other points in the cemetery, each of them mourning their own losses.

One of them, a group from the Oldheim Ogres, sang a dirge that reminded Dunk of nothing more than whale songs. Slow and mysterious, it moved him, although he could not understand a word of it.

M'Grash, on the other hand, wept like a battered child. Some claimed that being raised by human parents had stripped the ogre of the savagery that was his birthright. The way the Oldheimers wailed for their lost compatriot, though, Dunk wondered if all ogres were like his friend under their ferocious facades.

A band of Norscans from the Thorvald Thunderers cheered off to the west. From the slurring of their songs, Dunk guessed they'd been there since daybreak, toasting their friend's toasted remains atop a burnt-out pyre that had stayed lit throughout the night.

Off in the distance, Dunk spotted a trio of lovely, pale women dressed in black corsets. They didn't seem to be part of any entourage of mourners, instead watching each of the ceremonies intently. The thrower nudged Slick and nodded at the blanched beauties.

'Them?' Cavre said softly. 'They're recruiters for the Deathmasques, an all-undead team. That blonde one in the middle is their coach, Rann Ice.'

Slick scowled. 'It used to be those bloodsuckers would at least wait until nightfall before coming around, looking for fresh kills. Damn Sun Protection Fetishes. SPFs like those have ruined the traditional night games.'

'I thought this was hallowed ground,' Simon said. 'Don't their sort have to stay far away from here?'

Everyone looked to Pegleg. The coach hadn't said a word since they'd entered the cemetery. He'd taken off his yellow tricorn then and let the rain mat down his normally curly locks, but not a word had crossed his lips. He'd just walked from one grave to another, spending a few minutes staring down at each as if he could engrave some additional words on the gravestones with invisible beams from his eyes.

After a moment, Pegleg detected the silence, and his head snapped up. 'What, me hearties? What is it?'

Without a word, Cavre pointed at the three vampires standing to the east. Pegleg's face flushed as he spotted them, but it faded just as quickly. 'What? Do I look like a priest?'

'Isn't this hallowed ground?' Simon asked.

Pegleg sucked in his lips for a moment, then shook his head. 'No. These poor souls didn't rate such treatment.' He stabbed his hook toward a hill to the north, a grassy patch of land that looked down over the city below and the sheltered bay beyond.

'Don't you – doesn't the team have enough money to pay for it?' Guillermo asked.

Slick slapped him on the back of the leg, and the Estalian realised he'd made a terrible gaffe. He started to apologise to Pegleg, but the coach raised a hand to cut him off.

'Only the greatest players are buried on the Hill of Fame, which is hallowed by priests of a dozen denominations. You can't buy your way into it. You have to earn it.' Pegleg glared down at the eleven gravesites before them. 'None of these fine people were granted that honour.'

'So now these teams of undead can recruit our friends at will?' Dunk said with a visible shudder.

Cavre spoke up. 'They only want the best players, Mr. Hoffnung. Players who cannot survive a match don't meet their needs.'

Dunk cocked his head, confused. 'If they're not recruiting, then why are they here?'

A white smile cracked Cavre's dark-skinned face. 'They are recruiting, Mr. Hoffnung. They're looking for the better players – those who survived: us.'

A silent terror fell over the Hackers. Dunk wondered how powerful the vampires were and if he and his friends could manage to leave the cemetery alive. Before he could say anything though, a mighty roar erupted from the west, and he looked over to see the Norscans come stampeding across the cemetery toward them.

A moment later, the Norscans veered around the Hackers and headed straight for the three pale ladies. Just as the Thunderers reached the vampiresses, though, they faded to mist and disappeared. For a moment, Dunk thought the Norscans might turn on each other for lack of a clear foe, but then another cheer went up as the man who carried the keg of ale finally caught up with the others.

The Hackers turned to each other and smiled. Although they'd lost nearly a dozen of their number, they somehow managed to find room in their hearts for a hint of laughter. Dunk felt a good deal better because of it.

'On that note,' Pegleg said, drawing attention from the Thunderers and back to himself again, 'I have some good news and some bad news.'

The Hackers each composed themselves and readied themselves for their coach's revelations. He cleared his throat hard before he began, covering his mouth with his hook.

'The Grey Wizards have pulled their sponsorship of us.' Pegleg waited a moment for that to sink in. 'We are no longer invited to play in the Dungeonbowl Tournament. Instead, they will return to using the Reikland Reavers as their representatives.'

Dunk frowned. In one way, not having to play in the Dungeonbowl was a relief. So soon after losing eleven players, he found the arena held few thrills for him. He didn't know when he'd be ready to return, but not so soon he'd hoped. It seemed his wishes had come true.

On the other hand, he didn't want the Reavers to take the Hackers' place. That meant Dirk and Spinne would be at risk again. They survived their game last night – won it, even. Even though he'd seen them risk death week after week for the past year, he worried about them now in a way he hadn't considered before.

'Is it back to Bad Bay for us then?' asked Slick.

Dunk grimaced. Even though they wouldn't play in the Dungeonbowl, it didn't mean they wouldn't have a full slate of games before them. As soon as Pegleg managed to line up enough recruits to fill the team out again, they'd be at it, playing in local or regional games until the Chaos Cup came around. That was six months off though. At least the Hackers would have a chance to practice with their new teammates and ease back into the game with a few patsy matches before facing their next tournament.

Pegleg shook his head and allowed a shadow of a smile to spread across his face. 'That's the good news, Mr. Fullbelly. Instead of crawling back home to lick our wounds, we're going to take the kind of bold, decisive move that defines champions, both in the game of Blood Bowl as well as life.'

The bottom of Dunk's stomach fell out. Even as Pegleg spoke, the thrower knew what his coach was going to say. As much as he dreaded it, he couldn't turn away.

'We're going to Albion, my Hacker dogs!' A mad light of greed danced in Pegleg's eyes. 'There, we'll find the Far Albion Cup and bring it back to dominate the Blood Bowl League – or die trying!'

'SO YOU'RE DEAD for sure,' Dirk said, raising his voice to be heard over the noise in the Bad Water. The other patrons cheered as Khorne's Killers scored another touchdown against the Chaos All-Stars. The Killers' team captain, Baron Von Blitzkrieg, celebrated by ripping the second, vestigial head off one of the All-Stars' linemen and spiking it in the end zone.

Dunk scowled at his brother. Although Dirk had been playing Blood Bowl for a few more years than he – under the assumed last name Heldmann – Dunk was still the elder. It galled him that his little brother – who stood an inch taller than him – liked lording this difference over him so much. But that was the point, Dunk supposed.

'We're going to Albion,' Dunk said. 'We'll wander around there for a while looking for a trophy that no one's seen for over five hundred years. We'll come back in time for the Chaos Cup.'

'You'd better,' said Spinne. Sitting next to Dunk, her arms wrapped around him, she gave a squeeze tight enough to make sure he knew better than to argue with her.

Dunk smiled as he looked deep into Spinne's grey-blue eyes. He pulled an arm free from her grasp and used it to brush a few stray strands of her strawberry blonde hair from her eyes. Most of it still hung in a long braid that hung behind her, but it had been a long day.

After Pegleg announced the Hackers' plans, Dunk had gone looking for his lover. He'd tried the Reavers' camp first but had been told she'd left for a run. He'd caught up with her on a beach on the western shores of the bay, and they'd spent the rest of the day frolicking in the surf and sun.

Dunk had told Spinne right away that he'd be leaving the next morning, and she'd only nodded silently. They'd never said another word about it – until they met Dunk's brother Dirk on his way for a drink at the Bad Water. He'd insisted they join him and fill him in. Dunk hadn't seen a good way around it, despite the fact he knew it would break the spell of denial Spinne and he had spun around themselves.

'It sounds like madness to me,' Dirk said. 'Making an open-sea voyage in Captain Haken's rickety old boat, across the Sea of Claws, so you can wander around that hapless excuse for an island nation. And what if you do find the Far Albion Cup? How are you going to get it out of the country if everybody there wants it just as bad as you do?'

'One step at a time,' Dunk said. 'It can't be any more dangerous than playing a match of Blood Bowl.'

Dirk shook his head. 'I'll take my chances on the gridiron any day. Those Albionmen are just weird. They talk funny, they have strange, stuffy manners, and they dress like fops. They're all 'cheerio' and 'pip, pip,' and all the while they're looking to stab you in the back with a polished blade. I'd rather take a tour of the Troll Country. At least there you know when someone's trying to kill you.'

Dunk stared at his brother. 'What do you know about Albion culture? Just what you've seen on Cabalvision?'

Spinne snorted, then looked at Dunk, surprised. 'You don't know?' She goggled at Dirk, and then grinned. 'You never told him!'

Dirk blushed. 'There's never been, well…. I just haven't been able to….' He scowled. 'It never came up!'

'What?' Dunk said staring back and forth between his brother and his woman. Then it dawned on him, and he gaped at Dirk. 'You played in the Far Albion League!'

'No,' Dirk said, raising a finger. Then he dropped it. 'Well, yes, but not even for a full season.'

Spinne held Dunk's arm, enjoying Dirk's discomfort. 'Your brother tried out for the Reavers, but he didn't know much more about Blood Bowl than you did when you started.'

'Hey,' said Dirk, 'at least I was a fan. I knew how to play the damned game.'

'Not very well, it seems,' said Dunk.

'I – it's not as easy as it looks. *You* should know.'

Before Dunk could respond, Spinne cut in. 'After your brother got cut from the Reavers' tryouts, he jumped the first ship to Albion to try his luck there instead.'

Dirk threw up both his hands. 'It's my story, damn it. Let me tell it.'

Spinne nodded and gestured gracefully for Dirk to continue. 'Please. I'm sure it will be inspirational,' she said with a giggle.

Dirk ignored Spinne and focused his attention on Dunk. 'You know how our family never wanted me to play Blood Bowl.'

'Either of us.'

'But I was determined. Hells, there I was – fresh sprung from the life of an aristocrat – and I wasn't about to live like a peasant. But the only skills I had came from our tutor, Lehrer. Sadly, the things a noble child learns are meant to help him keep his wealth. They don't do a damn thing to help you get rich in the first place.

'Working a regular job is no way to get ahead in this world. Sure, I could have tried my hand as a guard or a mercenary, but the people who hire you are the ones with all the money. They keep you around to protect it, not share it.

'So, I figured I had two options. I could either become a Blood Bowl player or a dragon slayer. And what kind of idiot wants to go up against dragons?'

Dunk's face reddened at this as he remembered his own ill-fated stab at that career path. He'd thought it more honourable than playing Blood Bowl, despite the inherent dangers in challenging monsters the size of small castles. Slick had talked him out of that.

Sometimes Dunk wondered if he'd made the right choice. As a Blood Bowl player, he had plenty of money and more fame than he cared for, but he knew his parents would be as disappointed with him as they had been with Dirk. Still, being a live football player beat being a dead dragon slayer any day.

'When the Reavers turned me down, I thought I might head for the Grey Mountains and try my hand at hunting dragons instead. I'd heard one had been haunting the area around Dörfchen for years.'

'That's just a rumour,' Dunk said, clearing his throat. 'Trust me.'

Dirk looked at Spinne and shrugged before continuing.

'Anyway, one of the other hopefuls who got cut was an Albionman by the name of Nigel Priestly. 'It's a bad spot of luck,' he told me, 'but at least I can always fall back on the Far Albion League for another season.'

'I hadn't heard much about this before, but Nigel filled me in on it. He told me it was much easier to make a team there and that the Old World leagues sometimes used the FA League as a farm system, recruiting the best players to join them in the big time.

'It sounded better than dragons to me, so Nigel and I worked our way across the Sea of Claws on a vessel of fortune.'

'I heard you went drinking in the wrong pub and ran into a pirate ship's press gang,' Spinne said.

Dirk grinned. 'All part of the master plan. It was hard work, but since Nigel and I didn't have a gold piece between us it made good sense. Best of all, they grabbed us before we settled up with the bartender that night, so we got a free night's drinks out of it too.' He tapped his temple with a forefinger. 'Clever.'

Dunk shook his head. 'Only you could say that about that plan with a straight face.'

'You're just jealous. When we made it to Albion, it was just as Nigel had said, only much, much worse. The Albionmen are a weak-spirited sort, living on the scraps of dignity left over from some former empire they claim to have once been a large part of – the Far Albion Royal Consortium Empire. I'd never heard of it before, but they made sure to tell me all about it every chance they had.

'It's all long gone now, of course. As Nigel put it, they "live on in the fading echoes of their former glory." I don't know about that. All I can say for sure is that their taverns close too damn early for anyone to make a proper night of it and that their football teams suck.'

'It's probably because we take all of their top talent, right?' Dunk said.

'That and a true lack of a killer instinct. How many Albionmen do you see in the Blood Bowl League?'

'There's Simon Sherwood,' Dunk said.

'He's a catcher. Catchers don't count. I'm talking about *real* – ow!'

Dirk lurched to the side, rubbing the ribs into which Spinne had jabbed her elbow.

'Thrower,' Dunk said to his brother, 'meet your star catcher.'

Dirk flushed, but his face didn't turn as red as Spinne's.

'What's that supposed to mean?' she demanded. 'Catchers are just as tough as any other players.'

'Catchers are tall, lean people with the legs of a horse and the hands of a spider. They can't tackle to save their lives, and they fold like cheap chairs when you smash into them.'

Spinne raised her fist to punch Dirk again, but another hand snapped out to hold it back. The catcher snarled and pulled her arm around, dragging her attacker after it.

A gorgeous woman in an attractively cut version of a nobleman's clothes rolled over Spinne's shoulder and landed in Dirk's lap. She pulled her long auburn hair out of her deep, dark eyes and glared up at Spinne. 'Careful there, player!' she said through her ruby-painted lips. 'I was just trying to defend my man.'

'Lästiges Weibchen!' Spinne said. 'You're lucky I didn't throw you over the bar.'

Dunk nodded. 'It's pretty nasty back there. Take it from me. I hear they used to let the rats lick it clean, but they kept vomiting everything back up.'

Dirk started to say something, then thought better of it and planted a big kiss on Lästiges's full, pouty lips. Dunk and Spinne watched them for a long, uncomfortable moment. Then they picked up their beers and each took a long pull. Then Spinne let loose a loud, long belch.

Dirk and Lästiges broke their embrace and stared over at Spinne. She smiled at them with closed lips, then said, 'Excuse me.'

'Good to see you again, Lästiges,' Dirk said before the others could respond. 'I thought you'd be busy covering the game for Wolf Sports.'

Lästiges extricated herself from Dirk's arms and took an open chair between him and Dunk, across the table from Spinne. 'Normally, I would be, but I don't care much for those all-Chaos games. They're just too…'

'Chaotic?' Spinne said.

'Messy. Some of those mutant parts just aren't attached as well as they should be. I suppose that's what you should expect, they being so unnatural and all, but it's no fun working as a sidelines correspondent when you're getting splashed with hot ichor during every change of possession.'

'So you pulled some strings to get a night off to be with me?' Dirk said with a hungry grin.

'Don't I wish, darling.' Lästiges caressed Dirk's square chin with her well-manicured, crimson-tipped fingers. 'If I had that kind of pull with the network, I'd never work a Chaos game again. No,' she said looking at Dunk and then Spinne. 'I've been given a new assignment for which I must ship out in the morning.'

'That's just too bad,' Spinne said without a dash of sincerity. 'What are you on to next? Writing an exposé on the mating rituals of trolls? A hard-hitting investigation of what's rotten in Kislev? Or perhaps you're off to stir the ashes of Middenheim?'

Lästiges's Cabalvision reporter's smile dazzled Dunk with its falsity. 'I thought of following around a trollslayer until he finally found his doom, but then I thought "that's been done to, well, death." I could have charted the meteoric rise of great female catchers in the league, but then I realised there weren't any.'

Dunk put a hand on Spinne's arm to keep her in her seat. The reporter continued quickly before the catcher could throw off the restraint.

'Then my boss, Ruprect Murdark, he heard that one of the Blood Bowl league's premier teams was going to leave town with its collective tail between its legs and run off to the Far Albion League.'

Dunk took his hand from Spinne's arm, but before he could get up to protest he felt her hand pull him back into his seat.

'He thought that would make a great story,' Lästiges said. 'Since he owns the network, I could hardly disagree with him. Right then. In public.'

'You're probably right,' Dirk said. 'I can't imagine who would care about something like that. A bunch of major leaguers going to romp around in the minors? Who'd–'

Dirk stopped cold then stared at Dunk. 'Oh.'

'Welcome aboard,' Dunk said to Lästiges.

'Literally,' the reporter said, the same patently false smile on her perfect face. 'I've booked passage aboard the *Sea Chariot*.'

'On the Hackers' own ship?' Spinne said. 'Pegleg would never rent space out to outsiders.'

'He let Slick and I join him on the way to Magritta last year,' Dunk pointed out.

'You were a prospect. She,' Spinne pointed a long finger at Lästiges, 'she is a reporter.'

Lästiges let her smile drop. 'Look, dear,' she said. 'I'm not thrilled about this either, but Mr. Murdark is dead set on it. Reality shows are all the rage on Cabalvision these days, second only to Blood Bowl itself. A reality show about a Blood Bowl team? It's sure to be a smash hit!'

'Then why don't you want to go along?' Dunk asked. 'I mean, you're as aggressive a ladder-climber as I've ever seen. Don't you want to host a hit show?'

Lästiges reached over and grabbed Dirk's hand. 'Normally, yes, but your brother here has, well…'

Dunk couldn't believe the woman actually blushed. He'd thought nothing could embarrass the shameless story-hound.

'Altered my priorities,' Lästiges finished. 'I pushed for being assigned to follow the Reavers, but Mr. Murdark said he needed his top reporter on this job.'

'What happened to Cob Rostas?' Spinne asked. 'Or Mad Johnny? Or–'

'He chose me,' Lästiges said. 'I'll be leaving with the Hackers tomorrow morning.'

'Dirk was just telling us about his time in Albion,' Spinne said.

'Really, darling?' Lästiges turned to the startled Dirk. 'Don't let me interrupt.'

'Um, there's nothing much to tell, really,' he said. 'I spent a few months there playing for the Blighty Blighters before the Reavers figured out what a mistake they'd made and offered me a contract. I slipped out of the country like a thief in the night and never looked back.'

'Did you ever play for the Far Albion Cup?' Dunk asked.

Dirk nodded. 'Once. Turns out the 'cup' is just this battered tin replica of the real thing. It's been passed around from team to team so many times, you almost can't recognise it as a cup any more. Kind of disappointing, you ask me.'

'Sounds like you didn't care much for Albion, my sweet,' said Lästiges as she cuddled up next to him.

'It's nothing like home,' Dirk said. 'Most of the people there are so damned proper you'd think they hadn't figured out sex and violence yet. They pour a damn fine pint, but most of the time when I was over there I was just, well, bored.'

Spinne frowned as she put her hand on Dunk's. 'Let's hope your trip is just as uneventful.'

'Nuffle's 'nads!' Lästiges said. 'I hope not. I need the ratings!'

'So,' DUNK SAID, wrapping his arms around Spinne as they lay naked next to each other in the wide, feather-stuffed bed. 'What's next?'

'I was thinking about ringing for some room service,' Spinne said, a contented smile on her face. 'That always gives me an appetite. I hear they make a great paella here.'

'They should, for how expensive it is.'

Spinne gave Dunk a gentle poke in the ribs. 'You have regrets? Or are the Hackers not paying you enough?'

Dunk grinned. 'As a Blood Bowl player, I make more money than I've ever seen before in my life. I remember having less gold, though, and prices like that still shock me a bit.'

She spun over and lay on his chest. 'So, it's regrets then?'

'Not one.' Dunk's lips met hers in another passionate kiss. 'I just wondered what might happen next between us.'

The afterglow faded from Spinne's beautiful face. 'What do you mean?' she asked.

She sat up and moved to the edge of the bed. 'This is just one last fling, right?' She started to put her clothes back on. 'I've been down this road before. You're leaving town. You want to see other people.'

'Wait,' Dunk said, getting out of the bed and reaching for her. 'That's not it.'

'Ah,' Spinne said, turning her shoulder to him. 'It's the old "it's not you, it's me" speech then.'

'No,' Dunk said. 'I want to be with you, I just–'

'What?' She spun to face him, her flashing eyes the colour of a stormy sea.

'Do you want to be with me?'

A tiny gasp worked its way past Spinne's soft, sweet lips. She stared at Dunk for a moment, and he saw tears welling up in her eyes. She looked like she might attack him right there. He braced himself for anything.

Still, he didn't expect the kiss. She wrapped her arms around him and kissed him so hard he fell backward onto the bed once again.

When they broke their embrace, Dunk looked up into Spinne's eyes once more. They were bright and happy.

'Is that a yes?' he asked.

She kissed him again, and they needed no more words.

LATE THAT NIGHT, as Spinne slept in his arms, Dunk lay awake and thought of the future. He'd never loved anyone as much as he loved this woman. In his younger days, he'd dallied with a few damsels, but most of them had been after his family's money. When that had disappeared, so had they – all except for Lady Helgreta Brecher, to whom he'd been betrothed.

While Dunk had liked Helgreta well enough, the thought of marrying her had given him many restless nights. He'd not been a good fiancé to her, but she'd stuck by him, even through his family's fall from grace. Her parents had demanded that she abandon her commitment to him, but she'd refused. It had been Dunk who'd had to dissolve their agreement.

Marrying Helgreta would have restored Dunk to some semblance of nobility in Altdorf, but at the cost of his self-respect. He'd only discovered after the fall of his family that he had any, and he wasn't about to sacrifice it so cavalierly again – even for a shot at getting his old life back.

Dunk had never wanted to play Blood Bowl. He'd shared his father's contempt for the game, and he'd joined in the family's scorning of Dirk when he left home to play. Still, so many good things had come to him since he'd let Slick talk him into trying out for the Reavers: wealth, fame, and now even love. He had a hard time imagining why he'd fought it for so long.

Then Dunk remembered the fallen on the gridiron. He'd lost many team-mates – friends, even – in the past year. Were all the gains in his life worth having to watch good men and women die?

As Dunk's eyes wandered about the room, his gaze drifted past the window, and he saw something there that made him leap from the bed. His movement thrust Spinne away from him, and he heard her sleeping form crash to the floor as he reached the window and threw open the sash.

'Ow!' Spinne said as she awoke. 'What in the Chaos Wastes?'

Dunk shoved his head out the window and glared all around. They were on the building's third floor. He couldn't have seen what he saw.

'What is it?' Spinne said, her voice filled with concern as she crept up behind him.

From down on the street below, a shout went up. Dunk looked down and saw a small group of Blood Bowl fans staring up at him and pointing and laughing. He waved down at them as he wondered how they could recognise him from this distance and in the dimness of a half moon.

Then he looked down at himself and saw that he was naked.

Dunk slammed the window shut and turned to find himself nose to nose with Spinne.

'Trying to give your fans a free show?' she asked.

Dunk blushed, first with embarrassment, then with frustration. 'I just – I thought – I saw something outside.'

Spinne peered around him at the half moon framed in the window, the silvery light spilling over her toned body and smooth skin. Then she reached up and put her arms around his neck. 'You had a bad dream,' she said.

'No.' Dunk shook his head. 'I saw it. It…'

Spinne stared up into his eyes. 'What?' she said. 'What was it? What could upset you so much you'd knock me clear out of bed?'

'Sorry about that,' Dunk said, caressing her thighs. 'Are you all right?'

'Are you?' she asked.

He hung his head sheepishly. 'It…' He drew a deep breath. 'I thought I saw Skragger.'

Saying the name somehow made it all seem even more real. As a star Blood Bowl player for the Orland Raiders, Skragger had held the record for most touchdowns in a year. When Dunk's brother Dirk had closed in on the record, Skragger had threatened to kill them both. He almost had.

Spinne's eyes grew wide. 'He's dead. We all saw him jump out of that window in Altdorf. We saw his body after he landed.'

'I know,' Dunk said, 'but…'

Spinne took Dunk's arm. 'Come back to bed. It's the middle of the night, and you're anxious about your trip.'

He let her pull him back into the bed. 'Are you hurt?' he asked as she pulled the sheets over them and settled down next to him.

Spinne winced a little as she curled into his arms. 'If I didn't love you so much…'

Dunk froze for a moment before his face broke into a wide, toothy grin. 'What did you just say?'

'Shh,' Spinne said, laying a finger across his lips before resting her head on his chest. 'Don't make a big deal out of it.'

Dunk gazed down at her face as she closed her eyes and melted into him. He'd never seen anything so beautiful. 'I love you too,' he said.

Spinne smiled.

DUNK VOMITED OVER the side of the *Sea Chariot* as the sea churned beneath the Hackers' ship. He watched as the remains of his breakfast splashed into the briny waters and swirled about. A school of sharks following in the ship's wake attacked it as if it was alive, devouring it in seconds.

'Dunk gonna die?' M'Grash said from behind, patting the thrower on the back.

Dunk peered back over his shoulder to see the honest concern etched on the ogre's massive face. The creature had lost most of his own meal half an hour earlier, and he looked a bit less green now than he had before. Dunk suspected that incident had attracted the sharks in the first place.

'I'm not that lucky,' Dunk said, reaching back to pat the back of M'Grash's kettle-sized hand.

'That's what you get for blowing off Nuffle's services before every game,' Simon said with self-righteous dignity. The fact that he looked happy and healthy only made it worse.

'How are you not dying along with the rest of us landlubbers?' Dunk asked, thinking he might have to force some sort of misery on Simon just to even the score.

The Albionman patted his belly. 'Iron stomach,' he said. 'Runs in the family. I come from a long line of seamen.'

'Don't we all,' Slick cracked. He bore a steaming bowl of something in his hands.

'What's that supposed to mean?' Simon asked, his happy façade cracked.

'Never mind,' Slick said as he handed the bowl to Dunk.

The thrower tried to shove it away. 'I don't care if that's food from the fields of the gods,' he said. 'I'm not putting it in my belly just so it can launch itself straight out again.'

'Nonsense, son,' said Slick, pressing the bowl into Dunk's hands. 'Pegleg made this himself. A weak broth to help settle your stomach. It's a long way to Albion still, and you have to keep your strength up.'

Dunk accepted the bowl but couldn't bring himself to try the broth. It was so thin he could see through it to the bottom of the bowl, but it still seemed like too much. He bent over it and gave it a good, long sniff. Then he shoved the bowl back at Slick and went back to his spot on the railing.

The halfling shrugged. 'Suit yourself.' He took up the spoon and tasted the broth himself. 'Ah, now that's good stuff.'

Dunk tried to retch, but his stomach refused to produce anything from its emptiness. After a moment, he turned back and slumped down on the deck, his back to the railing. As he did, Guillermo dashed up next to him and blew his own breakfast into the rolling waters.

When Dunk could look up again, he saw Cavre waving at him from the bridge. The dark-skinned man looked at home there behind the wheel, as comfortable on a ship as he was on the gridiron.

'Only another day from here, Mr. Hoffnung,' he called.

Dunk groaned at the thought of the torture ahead of him. He'd felt fine for the first part of the trip, but they'd reached the open sea sometime last night. Between that and a squall that had stirred up the rough seas, his stomach seemed determined to crawl up his oesophagus and leap straight out from his mouth. If he could have, he would have let it.

'How's Pegleg?' Dunk asked.

Slick drained the last of the broth from the bowl and put it down on the rocking deck. 'Fine,' the halfling said. 'Good thing too, as he absolutely refuses to leave his cabin still.'

'Does he ever?' asked Simon.

'Not while we're at sea. You know how he is about studying game tapes.'

'Can't he get those on Daemonic Visual Display yet?' Dunk asked. 'Dirk was right. Those DVDs are amazing.'

Slick shook his head. 'These all come from Albion, and they don't use the same broadcast standards as we do in the Old World. Pegleg had to buy an Albion-made crystal ball just so he could watch the tapes.'

'Really?' said Simon, perking up even more than usual. 'I'll have to ask if he gets any Soaring Circus broadcasts on that cryssy. I haven't seen that show since I left home.'

'Does anyone else wonder why we haven't seen any other ships out here?' Dunk said as Guillermo slipped down next to him, wiping his mouth clean. 'Maybe it's because everyone smarter than us turned back. Here we are with an ex-pirate captain – who's afraid of water – and a crew of six others, three of whom are too sick to stand.'

'Don't you worry about it, son,' Slick said, patting the thrower on the shoulder. 'Cavre is an excellent sailor. Why, he could take this ship all the way around Albion and back home by himself.'

'Can't he save himself the trouble and start back now?'

'You'd miss fair Albion entirely?' Simon asked, staring out to the northwest. 'What a pity that would be.'

Dirk turned and saw nothing but rolling seas stretching to the horizon. He had to sit down again. 'The way you talk about the place, I thought you didn't miss it.'

Simon seemed to ponder this for a moment. 'I often like to say that Albion is a fine place to be *from*.' He smirked a little at this. 'Still, it's where I was born, and I still have many friends and family there. It's a land unlike any other, an island unto itself in more ways than mere geography. I shall enjoy my time there again, and I shall miss it when I leave.'

'And will you leave it again?' Guillermo asked. 'If this home of yours is so fantastic, I would think you would stay instead.'

Simon bowed his head before he spoke. 'Leave it I shall, I'm afraid, for leave it I must. Its pull increases as I draw near, I confess, but there are other matters drawing me away as well.'

With that, the Albionman turned and strode back across the deck toward the bridge where Cavre stood waving at him to lend a hand.

'Seems the nearer he gets, the more his mouth runs on about it,' Dunk said.

'Perhaps,' Slick said, 'he protests too much.'

'Now THIS IS more like it,' Dunk said as he hefted a massive glass of beer to join in a toast to the Hackers' arrival in Albion. He'd not had anything to eat in two days. Even when they'd finally made it to the shores of this distant land, his stomach had been too busy swirling around inside of him for him to attempt to put food in it.

The Albion beer, though, looked too good to pass up. He'd ordered a round of ale upon walking through the door of the nameless, white-washed pub. It had taken the bartender half of forever to supply it,

with Simon blathering all the while about how the pints here were
hand-pulled in the old way – none of those magical taps so popular
on the Continent, as he'd now taken to calling the Old World.

But the beer was here now, and a table full of food that Simon had
ordered for the team was on its way. Dunk raised his glass and joined
the others in saying, 'Cheers!'

When Dunk knocked back the beer, he almost choked. Although it
looked just a bit darker than the Killer Genuine Draft he favoured
back home, this stuff had far more flavour. So instead of the refreshing cold drink he expected, he got a mouthful of warm sludge.

Dunk glanced around. Slick, sitting on a high stool that brought
him up to the height of the others – who sat on leather-upholstered
benches around the low table that squatted between them – smacked
his lips as he put lowered his drink and cradled it in his hands like a
long-lost child perched safely on his lap. Simon put his pint down
after draining half of it, a wide and satisfied smile on his face. Pegleg
drained his entire glass and then smashed it on the floor.

Cavre put down his pint with great care, the liquid in the glass
barely touched. M'Grash had popped back his first and second pints
while waiting for the others to finish their toast. Now he nursed his
third. Guillermo drained about half his pint, and then stopped dead,
his eyes bulging. He turned and spat everything in his mouth onto
the floor, gagging and coughing as if nearly drowned.

The others stared at him for a moment, none of them moving. Pegleg nodded at M'Grash and said, 'Give Mr. Reyes a hand, Mr.
K'Thragsh, would you?'

The ogre nodded, then reached out and slapped Guillermo on the
back with a meaty mitt. The blow knocked the Estalian from his feet
and into a nearby table, where Guillermo made a poor first impression on a group of local dockworkers by smashing their table to
pieces and spilling all their drinks in the process.

The angry dockworkers dragged Guillermo to his feet. One of them,
a surly dwarf with a blue-tinged beard and a series of piercings along
his right cheekbone, smashed the top of his glass off on the back of
his chair and jabbed it at the Estalian's face. An instant later, the same
dockworker smashed into the far wall of the pub and slid down to the
floor in a broken heap.

Dunk clapped M'Grash on the arm for taking out the primary
threat so quickly. Then the other dockworkers – none of whom
looked any more reasonable than the first – turned on the Hackers
and snarled at them like a pack of hungry wolves.

'Now, gentlemen,' Slick said, spreading his arms open wide as he
stood upon his stool. 'It was a simple accident followed by a misun-
derstanding. Can we buy you a round and call it even?'

One of the dockworkers – a balding, pot-bellied man burned a deep brown from constant exposure to the sun – stepped forward, a pair of short, sharp knives filling his hands. 'Ye killed the Runt,' he snarled. 'Ye won't be leaving the pub alive.'

Dunk nodded at the man, and then turned to M'Grash. 'Take care of them, would you, big guy?'

The dockworkers each took a step back as M'Grash stared out at them. Then the ogre looked down at Dunk, confused. 'Hurt them?' he said. 'Dunkel said hurting wrong.'

Dunk goggled at the ogre. In the previous season, Dunk had discovered that M'Grash had murdered people to help out his friends – Dunk included. The thrower had put a stop to that and had sat M'Grash down to explain to him in no uncertain terms that killing was wrong.

'Remember what I said about self-defence,' Dunk said. 'These people want to hurt us. Isn't protecting your friends why you knocked the Runt clear across the pub?'

'That wrong?'

Dunk grimaced at how eager the ogre was to please him. He'd worked hard to try to impart some sense of morality to the creature. He should have expected something like this to happen.

'No, M'Grash,' he said, patting the ogre on his elbow. 'There are exceptions to every–'

A pint of ale sailed through the air and smashed into the side of Dunk's head, coating him in beer and broken glass. He fell to the ground, dazed. A mighty roar from next to him nearly ruptured his eardrums. Still, he heard a stampede of footfalls rushing away from him and then the screams of souls in mortal fear of losing their lives. Many things smashed, and a chair flew over his head and crashed into the wall behind him before he could raise his head again.

'You'll be all right, son,' Slick said, standing at Dunk's side. 'M'Grash could take down the whole lot of them by himself.' A series of pounding noises punctuated the agent's words. 'Ouch. That has to hurt.'

When Dunk managed to stagger to his feet, he looked up to see the Hackers standing in the centre of a ruined room. Every set of tables and chairs lay in chunks on the floor; unconscious patrons sprawled across them, sleeping as if the bits of smashed furniture were more comfortable than any bed. In the opposite wall, three men hung slack from their necks with their heads shoved straight through the battered plaster.

'Any of the rest of you scurvy dogs care to try your luck?' Pegleg snarled, brandishing a bloodied hook before him.

The other patrons of the bar, who'd all stopped whatever they were doing to watch the fight, turned back to their drinks and restarted their conversations. All but one man, that was.

The man stepped up from a distant corner of the pub. He wore a royal blue cloak with a set of ram's horns embroidered in gold thread on his cowl. Underneath the cloak, he stood tall and broad, unbent by his years, at which Dunk could only guess from the wrinkles on his hands and the tip of his reddish-grey beard that jutted from the darkness under his hood.

The man strode forward with an athlete's grace. The others in the bar parted for him as he approached and closed behind him again as he passed. He walked straight for Dunk and Slick, ignoring the others. The other Hackers, sensing a threat, closed in around the stranger. M'Grash reached out to grab the man and hurl him out of the pub, but a gesture from Pegleg froze the ogre in his tracks.

When the man stopped in front of Dunk, the thrower could see his eyes glittering under the cowl. Blue and piercing, they seemed as if they could peer straight into Dunk's soul. The thrower felt a strong urge to ask the man what he saw there. Before he could, though, the man spoke, his words flavoured by a thick brogue.

'Faith, it's been a long time since We've seen a man who tried to face a foe with words 'stead of a fist.'

The man's lilting accent tickled Dunk's ear and threatened to make him smile. Instead, he stuck out his hand in greeting. 'The pleasure's mine.'

The man hesitated for a moment, then grasped Dunk's hand and shook it. He had a strong, rough-handed grip.

'You're with the Bad Bay Hackers,' the man said. 'Your name is Dunk Hoffnung. We've been expecting you.'

Dunk wondered if this man was some kind of mind reader. Then he realised that he was probably just a Blood Bowl fan who'd seen him on Cabalvision. Lästiges had made sure that their departure from the Old World was seen far and wide. It must have reached Albion as well.

'You don't speak like an Albionman,' Dunk asked. 'Can I ask your name?'

'Surely,' the man said, pulling back his cowl and revealing a wizened face under a full head of the same reddish-grey hair as his neatly trimmed beard. His eyes were the same grey as the overcast Albion sky, but they burned with knowledge and deep intent. The other thing Dunk noticed were the man's ears, the tops of which came to a sharp and elegant point.

'You're an elf,' Dunk said. As he did, he regretted his words, which sounded as profound as announcing that he was still actually breathing.

'Our name is Olsen Merlin,' the elf said. 'And we think we could be a great deal of help to each other, you and us.' He turned to look at the other Hackers staring down at him. 'And the rest of your friends, as well.'

Simon stepped forward and shook Olsen's hand. 'Mr. Merlin,' he said with a wide grin. 'I had the pleasure of playing on the Notting Knights a few years back. You were our team wizard.'

Olsen's face fell. 'Ah, sure 'twas, laddie, but we've put all that behind us now. There's nothing left in the game for us any more.'

'Why's that, sir?' Cavre asked. Dunk had never seen the man treat anyone with such reverence before, and the star blitzer was renowned for his respectful ways.

'Perhaps you've decided that the game that once sustained you has nothing left to offer you?' Pegleg asked. Olsen just shook his head.

'Or maybe you long to return to your homeland once more and leave Far Albion behind?' said Guillermo.

'Nay,' said Olsen. 'We bid good riddance to Hibernia when we left it centuries ago. Too damn many of the wee folk wandering around the place for our taste.' He eyed Slick carefully. 'You're a bit large for a fairy, aren't ye?'

'I'll have you know I'm a halfling born and proud of it,' Slick said, mustering every bit of indignity he could find. 'There's nothing the least bit "fairy" about me.'

Olsen reached down and patted Slick on the shoulder. 'No need to be so *dramatic* about it our wee friend.'

Dunk thought he saw steam escaping from his agent's beet-red ears.

'Did you decide to retire to a life of rest and riches?' Dunk asked, hoping both to distract the wizard and to get Slick's refocused on something that mattered much to him: gold.

Olsen shook his head. 'Nay. A team wizard can make a pretty penny, to be sure, but ye rarely have a steady contract, no damn benefits, and ye constantly have to worry about the other team trying to either bribe ye or assassinate ye. It's not a life fit for any self-respecting elf.'

'Friend?' M'Grash said, reaching out a monstrous hand to the downtrodden wizard.

The Hackers all froze. As Dunk knew, when M'Grash made a friend, the two were bonded for life. The ogre's brain held no room for two opinions about a soul. It branded each person it met with a label, and that stuck for pretty much ever.

'That's kind of ye, laddie,' Olsen said, patting the back of M'Grash's hand like that of a small child, despite the fact it was three times as wide as his own. 'But we've never been much of a friend to anyone, we fear.'

M'Grash's face fell so hard Dunk thought he might hear it bounce along the floor.

'Ah, cheer up, me grand ogre,' Olsen said, his eyes sparkling as he chucked M'Grash under the chin. 'We dinnae mean anything against your gentle soul. We're just too tired and crusty to think much on such things anymore.'

'So, why don't you just bugger off then?' asked Slick, who stood tall on his stool, glaring into the wizard's eyes.

'No!' the rest of the Hackers shouted in unison. According to Simon, Olsen alone had any hope of helping them find the Far Albion Cup, and they weren't about to let Slick run him off.

Cavre pulled out a chair for wizard, and Guillermo helped him into it. Pegleg cleared off the space on the table before Olsen with his hook, shoving the glasses there to shatter on the floor. Simon grabbed an unattended pint from the bar and placed it in front of the wizard, over the bartender's half-hearted protests.

Dunk placed himself between Slick and Olsen, hoping that the halfling wouldn't be willing to go through his meal ticket – Dunk – just to get at the wizard. M'Grash just sat down on a low bench against the wall, looked down at the bewildered elf, and flashed a toothy, too-innocent smile.

'Now that's what we call service, lads,' Olsen said. 'Good on ye.'

Then the wizard turned serious. 'Of course, we don't expect that you're being so kind for nothing. we may be old, lads, but we ain't that kind of fool.'

He leaned over the table as the others took their seats around him, each of them focusing every bit of their attention on his face. When he opened his lips to speak, they hung on his every word – even Slick.

'Aye,' Olsen said. 'You're here to learn all about the original Far Albion Cup, are ye not?'

The Hackers all nodded with excitement they could not contain. The wizard took a long pull on his pint, and then put it back down without bothering to wipe the foam from his moustache. He cleared his throat and then leaned forward again.

'Lend us your ears, lads. We've got a tale to spin.'

'A LONG TIME ago,' Olsen said, 'before any of ye were born, we played Blood Bowl like we meant it.'

Dunk glanced around and saw that every eye in the place was on Olsen, including those of the bartender and the other patrons. He got to his feet, his chair scraping out behind him loudly in the silence, and stared out at the others in the room. They all turned back to their own companions, and the bartender set to sweeping up the mess from the brawl once again.

'You were a Blood Bowl player?' Simon said. 'I thought you were just a wizard. I mean, not *just* a wizard – a wizard's a very fine thing to be, of course – but I never imagined that you played the game as well.'

'Ayé,' Olsen said, giving Simon a hairy eye. 'As an elf, we've led a long, long life, and we've done many a thing, some great and some not so much so. But we did play Blood Bowl, we did.

'Our team was called the Eiremen.'

'Ire Men?' Guillermo asked. 'I, R, E?'

'No, lad. E, I, R, E. Eire. As in another name for our fair homeland, Hibernia.'

'This is good,' Guillermo said blushing. 'I thought you might all be angry all the... Um, never mind.'

'Never will, laddie.' Olsen clapped his hands together. 'So, where were we?'

'Just about to tell my audience everything!' a feminine voice said as its owner burst into the pub.

Lästiges stormed through the room, straight up to the Hackers' table. A small golden ball hovered in the air just in front of her. As she reached the table, it turned around, and Dunk spied a small, eye-sized hole in the thing, staring out at him and the rest of the Hackers.

'Ah, Miss Weibchen,' Pegleg said as he got to his feet and doffed his yellow, tricorn hat. 'A pleasure, I'm sure. I didn't think you'd catch up with us this quickly.'

'Captain Haken, Wolf Sports paid you good gold to reserve a berth for me on your ship, the *Sea Chariot*. Why did you set sail from Magritta without me?'

Dunk could see that Lästiges was furious with Pegleg but unwilling to admit it to anyone. A sparkle of light flashed on the golden camra ball with its floating daemon inside, recording everything it could see and hear through the ball's open end. Dunk wondered if Lästiges could shut the thing off or would have to live with it recording everything she did until she returned home. Then he asked himself which of either Wolf Sports or his brother Dirk must have been behind such a thing. Maybe both.

Pegleg cleared his throat and shot an apologetic look at Olsen, like a parent embarrassed by an obnoxious child. He stood to address Lästiges, doing his best to ignore the floating globe that zipped around her head, trying to find a good angle from which to film them both.

'My dear,' the pirate said, flashing her his best smile, which proved to be far more creepy than comforting. 'We would have waited for you, but we were on a tight schedule. If we were to meet our new friend here, I knew we'd have to be gone at high tide or we'd be lost for sure.'

Lästiges showed Pegleg a pouty frown. 'Because of you, captain, I have no images of you and your players aboard the Sea Chariot. That was supposed to be the starting scene of my report. What will I do without it?'

Pegleg patted Lästiges on the shoulder and said, 'Do not worry yourself with such trivial matters. When we return, you can record our trip then. Just use those images for our venturing forth as well. No one will be able to tell the difference.'

'Huh,' Lästiges said, narrowing her eyes at Pegleg. 'I suppose that *might* work.'

Before the reporter could press Pegleg again, Cavre stood up and said, 'May I ask how you got here so quickly after us, Miss Weibchen?

I thought that you would have been delayed at least until the next high tide, putting you half a day behind us.'

A smile snaked across Lästiges's face. 'I've been here waiting for you for days. My employers at Wolf Sports have deep pockets,' she said. 'Very deep pockets. They paid to have me flown out here immediately once I'd realised you'd left without me.'

She looked around at the wreck of the room, including the sunlight shining in through the three holes in the far wall, from which the hapless patrons had finally been extracted while the Hackers spoke with Olsen. 'All I needed was to find you once you showed up. You and your team-mates didn't make that too difficult.'

'Well,' Pegleg said, pulling over an empty chair with his hook, 'now that you're here, why don't you make yourself comfortable?'

'We're not 'comfortable' with that,' Olsen said.

'And you are?' Lästiges wrinkled her nose at the wizard.

'Merlin,' he said, pointedly not extending his hand in greeting. 'Olsen Merlin.'

'Whatever.' Lästiges rolled her eyes at the wizard. 'Wolf Sports didn't send me here to follow some old coot of an elf who wants to cadge free drinks out of the tourists with stories born of his dementia.'

All of the Hackers winced at this, including Dunk, who half-feared – well, hoped maybe – that the reporter might disappear in a flash of smoke to be replaced by a warty frog. They all gaped in horror at Lästiges and then looked to Olsen to see if they might have to flee from his reaction to avoid any collateral damage.

The wizard stared coldly at Lästiges for a moment, and Dunk thought he saw his hands twitch beneath his cloak. The thrower prepared to grab Slick and throw them both behind M'Grash for safety.

Then Olsen drew forth a long, gnarled finger and pointed it directly at the reporter's nose. He opened his mouth to speak, and out came a deep, hearty chortle. 'You, you, you,' he said to Lästiges, punctuating every word with a stab of his finger as a smile curled on his lips. 'You have spunk. We like you.'

Tentatively, the Hackers joined in with Olsen, offering up half-hearted chuckles of relief – perhaps masking a bit of disappointment.

Dunk leaned over and whispered in Lästiges's ear. 'This wizard is going to help us find the Far Albion Cup. He's ancient and powerful. Don't make him mad.'

Lästiges's dark eyes twinkled as she glanced at Dunk. She turned to whisper in his ear. 'I think he's been mad since long before he met me.'

'And we've been able to hear people whispering about us since before any of you were born.'

Dunk and Lästiges, shame flushing their faces, looked up to see Olsen and the rest of the Hackers staring straight at them. Dunk cleared his throat.

'I was just trying to impress upon our friendly reporter here the reverence with which one should treat a person as important as yourself,' Dunk said.

'My deepest apologies,' Lästiges said. 'After spending years interviewing people who think they're something special, it's a pleasure to finally meet someone who really is.'

Olsen raised a hand to cut them off. 'Don't think we don't appreciate the obsequious utterances, lass, but we tire easily of such things. Besides which, we believe we have more pressing matters than massaging an old elf's battered ego.'

The wizard glanced up at the golden ball hovering over Lästiges's head. 'Is that camra on?' he asked, running a spit-slicked hand through his hair. 'We'd prefer to not have to repeat ourselves later.'

Lästiges's ruby-red lips spread in a hungry smile. 'I'm ready anytime you are – sir.'

Olsen grinned and then gestured for everyone to sit down and gather close. 'All right, then. Let us tell you the story of the Far Albion Cup.'

Lästiges, Slick, and all of the Hackers huddled tight around the wizard, each of them giving Olsen their undivided attention. Even M'Grash, who often had a hard time focusing on anything more complex than a meal, hung on the wizard's every word.

'Over five centuries past, the people of Albion caught Blood Bowl fever. We'd only just heard rumours of this most amazing of sports back then, and when Farley 'the Foot' McGintis returned from a tour of the Old World, he triggered off a national rage over the game.

'Farley had played in the NAF – the old Nuffle Amorical Football league – for a while, for the Champions of Death. He'd had a good run there until an opposing team's wizard resurrected the poor sod right in the middle of a kick-off return. They tore the poor lad to pieces.

'Of course, that's not always the end for the undead players of the Champions of Death. Farley wanted to play so badly he offered to kill himself again right there on the spot. Coach Tomolandry, the greatest necromancer to ever field a team, wanted to help Farley out, but they never were able to find all of Farley's parts to put him back together again. Seems that some vital pieces got thrown into the stands and disappeared. Rumour has it some bits appeared in a nearby rat-on-a-stick stand sometime in the second half.

'In any case, old Farley's career as a player was over. He packed up his things and caught the next boat back home to Albion. On the way, though, he realised that just because he couldn't play any more didn't mean he had to give up the game entirely. Those who can't do, coach.'

Pegleg harrumphed at this, but when everyone else at the table shot him a steely glare, he sealed his mouth once more.

'Within a week of his return, Farley had assembled enough players for four full teams. After that, it was just a matter of finding sponsors and venues. For that, he lined up Bo Berobsson, who had formerly been in charge of Big-Ass Ales – or B'Ass, as it came to be known. Bo got all the finances arranged while Farley taught the players and the coaches how to play the game.

'Now, Farley knew the rules as well as anyone else, but he didn't exactly teach us the right ones. Instead, he told us that football was a game in which you weren't allowed to use your hands. Also, when he figured out that kicking around a properly oblong pigskin didn't work all that well, he introduced a round ball with black and white panels into the game instead. Rather than carrying it into the end zone, you had to kick it through a big, white frame he called a goal.'

'Wait,' Lästiges said. 'You're telling me that this Farley changed the game all around? But why? Just to be different?'

Olsen tapped his nose twice, then pointed at the woman. 'Aye, that's what many thought at first when we figured out just what Farley had done, but it was too late then. We'd already played a dozen seasons of Albion Blood Bowl, and the people here loved it. There was no way for us to go back.

'Sure, some of the purists were appalled at Farley's lies, but as the 'father of the game' here in Albion, they couldn't touch him. They tried to change the rules to the proper set, the ones decreed by Nuffle so long ago, but they didn't take. We just played our variety of football here, and the Old Worlders played their way over there.'

'But why?' Lästiges said. 'Why did Farley do it?'

Olsen shook his head with a sad grimace. 'Ah, well, the injuries that poor Farley sustained in his playing days, they altered the man's makeup in some serious ways. If you'd seen him, you'd have no questions as to why he'd do something like that.

'Perhaps the old lad thought he might be able to play again himself someday, although he never did. Maybe he thought no one would listen to him as a coach of the proper game. It's hard to say. Still, he did what he did.'

Lästiges leaned forward, pressing the question. The golden ball closed in tight over her shoulder, as focused on the wizard's face as any of the other listeners.

'Why?' she asked.

Olsen let loose the sigh of a person who'd seen more than his share of tragedies in his centuries-long life. 'There's the rub of it, lassie. Not to put too fine a point on it, but poor Farley lost both his arms in his last game. He couldn't pick up the ball himself, so he made sure that no one else could either.'

Not waiting for a reaction from his listeners, Olsen pressed on with his tale. 'Of course, when Berobsson found out about Farley's deceit, you could have steamed a fish on the man's forehead. He decided he'd find out for himself just what the real game was like. This time, he refused to take anyone else's word for it. So he founded a team he dubbed the Albion Wanderers, and he took them off to tour the Old World and play against some of the NAF teams.

'Needless to say – but I'll say it anyway for your delightful camra there – the Wanderers were nearly eaten alive in their inaugural season. Literally. They lost three players to the Gouged Eye, and those damned orcs spit-roasted them right there on the sidelines, with Berobsson and the rest of the Wanderers powerless to stop them.'

Many of the players gasped in horror. Pegleg nodded knowingly. Dunk noticed that M'Grash licked his chops instead.

'When Berobsson came back, he pilloried Farley in every public venue he could find. He forced the man to buy his shares of Albion League Football, and he used the proceeds to found the Far Albion League, a proper, Nuffle-would-be-proud group of football teams dedicated to bringing real football to the Isle of Albion.

'Despite Farley's best efforts, Berobsson's work led an exodus of fans and players away from his weaker variety of football to the real thing. Still, we have a strong contingent of Albionmen who, to this day, claim that ALF football is the real thing. They've gone so far as to even come up with their own god – a rough sort of chap by the name of Sawker.'

'Sucker?' Slick wondered aloud. When he realised others had heard him, he slapped his hand over his mouth and blushed.

Olsen clapped the halfling on the back with a smile, nearly knocking Slick off his high stool. 'Some say so, wee one, but Sawker's adherents take him dead seriously. We have a bit of a feud that goes on here between those who revere him and the right-minded souls who appeal to Nuffle instead.

'Fans of Sawker have felt the pinch hard in this past while. For decades now, we've had to worry about these hooligans rampaging through the streets after an ALF game, kicking over everything they can find. They refuse to use their hands, of course, which means the believers of Nuffle can usually take them in a straight fight, but against helpless, inanimate objects Sawker's devout do a great deal of pointless damage.'

'Can anything be done to stop them?' Lästiges asked in her best investigative reporter's voice. Dunk saw the corners of her mouth turn up in a measure of perverse pride.

'Aye, lass,' Olsen nodded. 'That's where the Far Albion Cup comes in. Thanks for your kind prompting to keep an old elf's mind on track.'

Dunk couldn't tell if Olsen meant to be sincere or not, but the elf pressed on before he could guess.

'When Farley started the ALF, he produced a cup to use as the league trophy. It was an amazing thing, made of a reddish metal rarer than gold and set with a fortune in emeralds and diamonds. Legend has it that Farley stole the cup from Tomolandry the Undying, but we've not been able to confirm that. Farley's long dead now, and no one else seems to know for sure.

'When Berobsson started the FAL, he took the cup from Farley and made it the league championship trophy. It lasted in that position for six years before it disappeared.'

'It was stolen?' Pegleg said, scratching his hook across the table, scarring its already abused surface.

'It didn't take itself out of the Notting Knights trophy case, now did it?' The wizard's irritation shone through, but Dunk couldn't tell if it was from frustration with the disappearance or with the question itself.

'Our apologies, lad,' the wizard said. Dunk had never heard anyone call Pegleg anything other than captain, coach, or sir. 'We've been searching for the damned thing for the past 500 years, and we don't seem any closer now than we were then. It's the most stubborn mystery we've ever encountered, and no one seems to have any notion how to resolve it.'

'So what's the big deal?' Slick asked.

All heads swivelled toward the halfling. Dunk couldn't believe his ears. It wasn't like his agent to not care about something as valuable as the Far Albion Cup.

Slick checked his nails for a moment before pretending to realise everyone was waiting for him to continue. He favoured Olsen with a condescending smile.

'I mean, a wizard like you would hardly spend his whole life searching for such a thing if we were only concerned about the jewels in it, right? You can get diamonds anywhere. All it takes is money, and if you're involved in Blood Bowl, you're probably swimming in that. You're after something you can't buy, aren't you?'

Dunk watched the wizard seethe, his mouth drawn into a tight, straight line, and his eyes narrowed almost to a single point. The thrower thought the wizard might summon up the ability to spit fire and fry Slick to a cinder right there atop his stool. He braced himself to move, although whether toward Slick or away he wasn't sure.

'You're a cunning wee one, you are, laddie,' Olsen said in a flat, reserved tone. He nodded as he continued. 'The Far Albion Cup isn't just a fancy beer stein. It has devilish powers that no one has ever been able to duplicate. Blood has been spilled over it. Bodies been buried for it. And now it's up to us lot to find it, before it's too late.'

'Too late for what?' Dunk asked.

The wizard swivelled in his chair to stare deep into Dunk's eyes. When he spoke, his voice rasped like the scraping of a stone lid being removed from a long-buried grave.

'Too late to save the world.'

'You've LOST THE stitches on your balls,' Slick said. 'If you're looking to save the world, I hope you've hunted for better help. We're not heroes. We're football players.'

'You're not,' said Guillermo to the halfling.

'Good point,' Slick said, nodding forcefully. 'And neither is Pegleg or the lovely Lästiges over there. You've got five players, a halfling, a twice-maimed ex-pirate, and a hack of a lady reporter hurtling straight from up-and-coming to washed-up has-been – sorry, never-was – and you expect us to save the world?'

'All right,' Olsen said, ignoring Lästiges's protest at Slick's evaluation of her career arc. 'Fine. Point granted. Recovering the Far Albion Cup may not save the world, but it will put a stop to the plotting of a fiendish coven of cultists who plan to use it to cast all of Albion into their master's hellish realm!'

The wizard climbed to his feet as he spoke, and he kept going. By the time he finished, stabbing his finger into the air as he did, he'd clambered atop the table in the middle of the group. The table shook beneath him as he gazed down at the others, realising how far he'd let his fervour carry him.

'*All* of Albion, Mr. Merlin?' Pegleg asked, giving the wizard the respect that Slick had neglected to supply.

The wizard bowed his head, and his shoulders slumped. 'Well, maybe not *all* of it. But a damned good chunk, mate!'

'Which chunk?' Slick said, squinting into Olsen's eyes.

'Uh, well…' The wizard lowered his eyes.

'Aren't you really doing this for your own reasons?' Slick asked. 'Legend has it that you can only die by drinking your own blood from the cup. Perhaps you tire of this life and want to use us to help you out the door?'

M'Grash stood up and cracked his knuckles at this, his head scraping against the ceiling of the pub, which hadn't often hosted an ogre before. 'Help now,' M'Grash said with a smile.

'Aye, lad,' Olsen said, reaching over to pat the ogre on the shoulder. 'We appreciate the offer, but we're afraid it would do us no good. You could pummel us into a pink paste–'

'I could!' M'Grash tried to jump for joy but smashed a dent in the ceiling's plaster instead.

Olsen put up his hands. 'Not that we're asking you to. Faith! We wish it would work. We've been killed many a time, to be sure, but the next morning we always wake up without a scratch on us.'

'So you can't be killed, then?' Lästiges said. 'Permanently, I mean.'

Olsen shook his head, a grim smile on his face.

'Does it hurt?' Dunk asked softly, without meaning to. Every face turned toward him, but he ignored all but Olsen's. 'Dying. Death. Does it hurt?'

Olsen nodded sagely. 'Aye, lad. Dying's never any fun. Being dead's not so bad, especially for one so ancient as us. It's getting to that point that's the trouble.'

'And that's where the Hackers come in,' Lästiges said, a smug grin parting her lips.

Before anyone could respond, Pegleg held up his hook for silence. Then he turned and spoke to the wizard.

'The question, it seems to me, Mr. Merlin, isn't why you want the Far Albion Cup. It's why should we bother to help you?'

Olsen smiled as he reached out and shook the ex-pirate's hook. 'Exactly right, lad. Got it one, you did. There's nothing we appreciate more than a mercenary point of view. You know where you stand with such people at every moment. It's not about saving the world or even lending a helping hand to a poor elf in need. It's all about the gold.'

'That's not quite–' Cavre started, but Pegleg cut him off.

'So?' the pirate said, a steely glint in his eyes.

The wizard glanced around, making sure everyone at the table was ready for what he had to say. 'If you lot agree to help, and if we – meaning all of us – manage to recover the Far Albion Cup, then we –

meaning ourself – will agree to remand the cup entirely into your keeping once we have employed it in the way we desire most.'

A confused M'Grash looked at Dunk. 'What?'

'If we help him out, we get to keep the cup.'

'Ah,' the ogre nodded with a pleased expression. 'Good.'

'Mr. Merlin,' Pegleg said, doffing his yellow tricorn hat, 'I think we have a deal.'

'WHERE IS IT that we are again, please?' Guillermo asked.

Dunk was grateful that the Estalian had asked the question that he was sure had been burning in most of their minds for the past day. After leaving the pub, they'd gone with Olsen to hire enough horses to carry them all – except for M'Grash. None of the mounts Dunk had yet seen in Albion could have ever hoped to carry the ogre.

Walking seemed to suit M'Grash just fine though. He hadn't complained a whit since leaving town, just strolling along beside his friends' mounts, matching their walking speed with his long, smooth strides. It struck Dunk that M'Grash must have felt cramped for most of his life. Having been raised by humans gave the ogre the necessary civilization that allowed him to play on a human Blood Bowl team like the Hackers, but it also meant that the ogre had never been able to use his body to its fullest – except on the gridiron.

Walking next to Dunk most of the time must have felt to M'Grash like stumbling along with a slow child at his side. Now, able to stretch out and move at something closer to his own pace, the ogre wore a wide and toothy grin on his face.

'This is the Sure Wood,' Olsen said, gesturing at the tall, leafy trees all around them. As the Hackers had followed the wizard down the iffy and fading trail that led into the forsaken place, the branches had grown higher and thicker together until they almost blotted out the midday sun.

'Sherwood?' Slick said, looking over at Simon.

The Albionman shook his head and spelled out the place's name. 'My family does hail from the far side of the wood though. Our name is probably a corruption of the original.'

'A corruption of a corrupted place,' Guillermo said with a shiver.

'Does this make your family doubly damned,' Lästiges asked, her camra swivelling to aim at Simon, 'or do the two effects cancel each other out?'

'Doubly damned is nothing,' Olsen said. 'These woods are thrice-damned at the least.'

'You paint such a pretty picture,' Slick said to the wizard. The halfling bounced along astride a stalwart, russet-coloured pony that was the fattest such creature Dunk had ever seen. It wheezed as it rolled along, and the thrower feared it might fall over at any moment.

'This was once a clean, well-lit place, as such things go,' the wizard said. 'Upon a time, a clan of bright-leafed treemen called these woods home, and it was them from which the place took its name.'

'Were they 'friends sure and true'?' Dunk asked.

'Nay,' Olsen said. 'They were righteous bastards, always going on like they knew everything there was to know. They were never wrong – could never be wrong – and they let you know it.'

'Awful *sure* of themselves, weren't they?' Slick said, unable to suppress a snicker.

'Exactly. But that was the source of their downfall. When they finally encountered something for which they had no good explanation, they fell to pieces.'

'Literally?' Cavre said.

'Nay right away. The thing they were surest about was the fact they were immortal. When they started dying off, they couldn't figure out why. At first, they just chalked the first few deaths off to accidents. But they kept dying, one by one.

'When there were only a few left, they called us in to figure out what was happening to them. You'd never seen such a sorry lot in your lives. They'd pulled out most of their own leaves in worry, and those they had left had turned a bright red from the shame they felt straight down to their roots.'

'Did you ever figure out what happened to these legendary creatures?' Lästiges asked.

The wizard nodded. 'Root rot. It ate away at their nether regions until they were too fragile to stay upright any longer. Then, well, tim-beeerrr!'

'And that killed them?' Dunk asked. He looked up at the woods around them, which seemed to be growing darker and closer by the minute.

'Nay, lad.' Olsen peered out at the trail, which looked to be disappearing as they followed it. 'That just brought them down to where the cultists could get at them with their axes. They could have just waited for the rot to take them entirely, but that might have taken years, of course.

'Root rot's a horrible thing for a treeman, but when it gets to their knotty excuse for a brain, it's even more terrible. We found one once that the cultists had somehow missed. He'd been lying there in a gully for months, trapped and waiting for the rot that immobilised him to finally force his grip from life.

'The thing's voice was long gone, whittled down to a rasp from weeks of screaming for help that never came. We only stumbled upon him after following a trail of rot spoor that he had left behind as he wound his way into the gully. At first, we didn't even recognise him as a treeman, stretched across the old streambed like a fallen log. We were walking across him, using him like a bridge when he awoke.

'The nasty creature spun as we crossed over on him, sending us spiralling into the stream. He tried to tear us apart with what few limbs he had left but we'd fallen out of his reach. Soon enough, we figured out what had happened to him. He whispered a plea for us to finish him off. Those were his last words, lads. His last words.'

'So the cultists just took advantage of this rot to kill all the treemen?' Lästiges asked. 'How awful.'

'That's not the half of it, lass,' Olsen said. 'The cultists weren't just opportunists. Nay, they were *instigators*.'

'How do you mean?'

'They caused that root rot in the first place. It was all part of their master plan to make the Sure Wood theirs.'

'Or ours!' a voice shouted from somewhere in the darkness.

Guillermo let out a startled yip. Lästiges caught herself starting to scream. Dunk didn't even have time for that before he saw several piles on the leaf-strewn floor of the woods around them rise up and point swords and arrows in their direction.

At first, Dunk feared that a group of young treemen – Treelings? Saplings? – had ambushed them, ready to tear them to pieces in moments. Then he realised that such creatures wouldn't bother with weapons, instead using their own whip-like branches to flay the intruders to death.

These were men covered with sticks and leaves. They must have heard the Hackers troupe coming from a mile off and decided to set a trap for them. By burying themselves in the thick layer of rotting detritus on the forest's floor, they'd kept hidden until the Hackers were right on top of them.

Dunk cursed himself for not paying better attention to everything happening around him. Lehrer, his old teacher, would have smacked him on the back of the head for such a mistake, pointing out that it could cost him his life. Now it was time to find out if the old man had been right.

'Stand and deliver!' a leaf-swaddled man standing in front of Olsen's mount said. 'Make a false move, and we will knock your mounts from beneath you.'

'What scurvy fools–?' Pegleg started. Olsen cut him off with a curt wave of his long, thin fingers.

'Faith, we don't know how we get ourselves into these things, but,' he sighed, 'we know how to get us out.' The wizard pointed at the one who'd spoken, assuming him to be the leader of the group they faced. 'You. What god would you like to pray to before we strike you dead?'

The man stood silent for a moment, then threw back his head and laughed. He stood tall enough to look Olsen's horse in the face, and the sword he bore danced lightly in his hand as he spoke. 'You are a man of great bravado,' he said with a wide grin. 'I like that.' He gestured wide with his sword. 'Sadly, it will do you no good. Do I need to point out that we have you surrounded and outnumbered?'

Dunk noticed Cavre's head nodding as he finished tallying up the opposition. 'They have nineteen men on their side,' he said. 'We are but nine.'

A flash like a bolt of lightning filled the air, followed by painful crack of thunder. The blackened outline of the outlaw who'd been standing in Olsen's path stood there for a moment before crumbling into a steaming pile of ash.

'Right,' the wizard said. 'Now it's only two to one. Do those seem like fair odds, lads?'

'Robin!' a tubby man carrying a worn quarterstaff cried, shrugging off his mantle of leaves to reveal his shaven head. He gaped at the low pile of the robber's remains and shook, although with rage or fear Dunk could not tell.

'You killed him!' said a large man who stood nearly as tall as M'Grash. He stretched back his bowstring and pointed an arrow the size of a branch at Olsen's heart.

'And we'll do the same to the lot of you unless you let us pass,' Olsen growled. 'None dare threaten our life without tasting death themselves.'

'I thought you'd been killed a dozen times over,' Slick whispered from atop his pony. The halfling had his hands up in the air and bore a fake grin on his face as he watched the outlaws gape at the wizard's power.

'We never went down without a fight.' Olsen's hands crackled with power.

'Great,' Slick said. 'Let's follow the lead of the immortal who rises again the next day every time he's slain. He'll have a real incentive to get the rest of us out of here alive.'

'Hold it!' Dunk said, climbing down from his horse and stepping between the tall robber and Olsen. 'We don't have to do this. If we fight here, now, people are bound to die on both sides.'

'We think that's the point,' Olsen snarled.

'Perhaps we can see now why he had trouble finding others to help him in his quest,' Lästiges said into her camra. 'Did word of the wizard's ways scare off potential aid, or did all of his other protectors get killed on the job due to his abrasive manner?'

'Look,' Dunk said, desperation cracking his voice. He stretched his hand toward the tall man and asked, 'What's your name?'

'Wee Johnson,' the archer said, switching his aim from the wizard to the thrower. 'What of it?'

'Oh,' Slick said, slapping a hand over his face. 'You, son, need to find some better friends. Anyone who'd give someone a nickname like that?'

Wee Johnson adjusted his aim again and loosed his arrow. It zipped past Dunk's shoulder like a hurled log. The thrower turned just in time to see Slick get knocked back off his pony with a strangled cry.

Dunk leaped forward and socked the archer in the jaw, sending the tall man stumbling back. The thrower pressed his advantage and snatched Wee Johnson's bow from his hands. He smashed it into the man once, twice, knocking him to his knees.

Swift as a snake, Dunk slipped behind Wee Johnson and pulled his bow up under the tall man's jaw. He pressed it hard into the outlaw's throat and drove his knee into the man's spine. 'You son of a snotling!' Dunk hissed. 'That was my–'

'I'm okay!' Slick shouted, bouncing up behind his pony as if on springs. He pulled on a tear in the shoulder of his thick jacket. 'He just grazed me, son!'

Dunk froze, then looked down at Wee Johnson and realised that he'd almost killed the man in a blind rage, with his bare hands. Then he looked out at the other outlaws gaping at him, and he wondered if maybe he shouldn't have stopped.

The idea that he'd been ready to kill this man made Dunk ill. There had to be a better way out of this. He saw now that many of the outlaws had their bows trained on him. If he broke Wee Johnson's neck, as he'd been about to do, they'd fill him full of shafts before the tall man's body hit the ground.

Dunk glanced at the others. Most of them bore blades in their hands. M'Grash clenched his fists, forming them into hammers and staring at the heads of the outlaws as if they were nails.

'Hold it!' he said. 'Anybody else fires an arrow, and I'll snap Wee's neck.'

The tall man gurgled something at his fellows, and the bald man stepped forward, a hand raised in the air to ward the other outlaws off. 'Let's talk,' the man said. 'We don't want any trouble.'

'Ambushing people seems like a poor way to go about avoiding it,' Pegleg said, glaring at the outlaws all around them.

The bald man stared down at the pile of ashes. 'No one was supposed to get hurt,' he said. 'Robin there, he said no one would dare stand up to a gang like ours. "They'll trip over themselves to give us their money", he said.'

Dunk gaped at the man as he got a better look at him. He wore plain robes belted at the waist with a simple rope. A small religious icon carved from soapstone dangled from a string around his neck. 'You're a priest!'

The holy man nodded as he knelt down and made a small blessing over his friend's ashes. 'We like to say 'cleric.'' He rose and stood in front of Dunk, placing a hand on the bow still choking his friend. 'I'm called Brother Puck.'

Dunk let off some of the pressure on Wee Johnson's neck, and the archer swallowed deep gulps of air. The thrower had never had much luck with religious leaders, be they priests, brothers, or something more sinister. He remembered all too well the priest in Dörfchen who'd tried to trick him into feeding himself to the chimera living over their town.

'An outlaw priest?' Dunk spat into Robin's ashes, sending up another puff of steam. 'What were you thinking?'

Puck's eyes fell, and he pressed his hands together in a ritual of pleading. 'There aren't many in these parts who have the gold to spare for the gods, not to speak of the less fortunate. Our collection plate lay empty for many weeks. Robin – he was one of our church elders – he came up with the idea.'

'What idea?' Lästiges said from behind. The camra, which had been taking in the scene from high in the trees, floated down to focus tight on the cleric's face.

'Rob from the rich and give to the poor,' Brother Puck said, fat tears rolling down his pale, dirt-crusted face.

Slick tried to stifle a snort, but failed. Then Pegleg let loose half a cackle. Soon after, Lästiges giggled. Before Dunk knew it, every one of the Hackers beside him was bent double with laughter.

The outlaws surrounding the Hackers lowered their weapons, disarmed by this complete lack of respect for the basic principle upon which their merry band had been founded. Some of them shuffled their feet. One even started to laugh a bit himself before another of his compatriots smacked him in the back of the head.

'What?' Brother Puck said, confused.

'Son,' Slick said, wiping the tears from his eyes as he ambled toward the cleric, 'that has to be one of the stupidest things I've ever heard.'

CRESTFALLEN, BROTHER PUCK stared at the halfling as if he'd just blasphemed his mother. Sensing that Wee Johnson was too entranced by Slick's bravado to be a threat, Dunk let loose the bow, releasing the man's throat. Still, he kept a tight grip on it with his other hand, just in case.

'Think about it, 'brother,'' Slick said.

'Wait,' the cleric said. 'Don't you dare start up with the old, 'if you rob from the rich, they're not rich any more, are they?' bit. Or 'if you give to the poor, do you then have to rob them too?' questions. The plan was a good one. We were comfortable with it. And it worked.'

Brother Puck looked down at the pile of ash that had once been Robin. 'At least it did until today.'

Slick shook his head, pity overtaking his smugness. 'No, son. It's just the futility of what you're trying to do.' He looked back at the others, who'd all stopped laughing now. 'The rich are rich for a reason. It's one thing to come into money. It's something else entirely to keep it.'

'He's right, mate,' Simon said, lowering his sword.

'You may take my word on this,' said Guillermo. 'We piss through gold like it was beer.'

'You see,' Slick said. 'You give money to people who have never had money before – like just about any Blood Bowl player – and they don't know what to do with it. It runs through their fingers like water. Soon enough, they don't have a copper left to their name. That's how we get players to come back again year after year.'

Wee Johnson, still on his knees, goggled at the halfling, who he still towered over. 'I thought all players were rich. That's why Robin came up with the plan to get ahead of you after you left the pub and rob you.'

'Sure, they're rich,' Pegleg said, snorting. 'On payday. Maybe for a few days after. Most of them run through their cash before the next game rolls around.' He raised his eyebrows at his players. 'I've given out more than one payday advance in my time – for a vicious amount of interest, of course.'

'So if we give money to the poor, they'll just waste it?' Brother Puck looked as if he'd swallowed a hornet. 'I can't believe that.'

'Unless you teach them how to handle it,' Slick said. He swept his eyes over the assembled outlaws in their filth-stiff clothes. 'But I doubt any of you have those skills yourself.'

'I don't believe it,' Dunk said, surprising even himself as the words slipped from his mouth.

Slick nodded. 'Take yourself, son. What do you do with your money?'

'What do you mean?' Dunk didn't think he'd like where this was heading.

'What do you do with it? Do you spend it all every week?'

'Of course not. I spend a bit more than I should maybe, but I save a lot of it.'

'How?'

'I deposit at least half of each paysack in a bank backed by the Emperor.'

'Does that leave you enough to live on?'

Dunk nodded. 'More than enough.'

Slick turned to Simon. 'How much have you saved?'

'Saved?' The Albionman turned a bright pink.

'What about you, Guillermo?'

The Estalian shook his head.

'Cavre?' The dark-skinned man hesitated for a moment before dropping his eyes.

'What about Pegleg?' Dunk asked. 'Coach, you pay all of us. You have to know about handling money.'

The ex-pirate grimaced. 'I give just about every thin copper I must to my players. What I have left over goes back into the team's resources: the tents, the training camps, hiring an apothecary to stitch you dogs back together. Keeping a ship like the *Sea Chariot* isn't cheap either. Plus, there's Nuffle's tithe.'

Dunk gaped. 'You donate gold to the Blood Bowl god?'

Pegleg looked shocked. 'Of course, Mr. Hoffnung. How do you expect us to win a game if we set Nuffle against us from the start?'

Dunk stared at Pegleg for a moment, then at Brother Puck, then Slick. 'So that's how I manage to hold on to my money.' He turned his attention back to the cleric. 'See? There are far easier ways to part fools from their gold.' He threw down Wee Johnson's bow and backed away in disgust.

Brother Puck glared at Dunk for a moment. Then a window seemed to open in his head. He stepped toward Pegleg and the others, his arms spread wide. 'Friends,' he said. 'Can we impose upon your kindness for a moment?'

Dunk's friends glanced at each other for a moment, and then nodded at the cleric.

'I am a priest of the angry god of the Sure Wood. He has decreed that we should request a small donation from all who pass through his lands so that we may – in service to him, of course – maintain his wooded temple and alleviate the misery of the poor souls who nest beneath his boughs.' The cleric snatched a hat from the head of one of the other outlaws and turned it over and stretched it out toward the intruders. 'Can you find it in your hearts to help?'

Guillermo and Simon looked to each other. Simon spoke. 'It's like this, mate. As coach here told you, we don't have much to spare until we play another game, and that seems to be a fair ways off at this point.'

'You wouldn't want to anger the god of Sure Wood, would you?' Brother Puck asked, his face filled with concern. 'I ask only out of consideration for your own well being. Only this morning, I heard good Robin blaspheme our god, denying his existence, and well…' The cleric let his eyes fall and linger on the pile of ashes where Robin had last stood.

'Coach?' Guillermo said. 'Can you help us out?'

Pegleg sighed. 'I'm afraid I used most of the last of our cash to outfit this little expedition of ours. I don't have much left.'

'I must admit some admiration for brave souls like you,' Brother Puck said. 'To so blithely ignore the will of the gods, well, that's something few have the pluck to manage so well.'

'Mr. Merlin?'

'We'll have no truck with these dastards,' the wizard said. 'Faith! They're lucky we don't fry them all on the spot.'

'Mr. Fullbelly?' Pegleg asked.

The halfling pursed his lips. 'I'd do it, but I'd end up expensing it back to the Hackers. Would you be good with that?'

'Ms. Weibchen?'

The reporter snorted. 'If the Hackers won't pay for it, I don't think Wolf Sports would be interested in covering it.'

'But if we did, they would?'

'Then you'd have already paid for it,' Lästiges said, smiling wide. 'Rhett?'

Cavre opened his mouth to speak, but before any words came out M'Grash broke in. 'Coach,' he said. 'Here!'

The ogre reached into his pocket with a ham-sized fist. When he pulled it out and opened it, three bags lay in his palm. 'This enough?' he asked.

Brother Puck's eyes lit up like lanterns on a moonless night. The other outlaws brightened too, standing up straight, their attention riveted on the ogre's open hand.

'Ah!' said Slick. 'A new way to avoid blowing your wealth: being too dumb to spend it.'

'Hold it!' Dunk said. 'M'Grash, put that money away.'

'But Dunkel,' the ogre said, crushed, his shoulders and face sagging with sadness. 'Just want to help.'

'I know, big guy.' Dunk rubbed his chin. 'And maybe there's a way.'

'Surely there is,' said Brother Puck. 'You make a donation to the god of Sure Wood, and we all go away happy.'

Dunk shook his head. 'I have something more... equitable in mind.'

'THINK THEY WERE telling the truth, son, about where the cultists' hideout is?' Slick asked, back bouncing along atop his tubby pony.

'We paid them well enough for it,' Olsen grumbled back from his mount, positioned once again in the lead.

'You mean M'Grash paid them well enough for it.' Dunk stuck out his hand for a high-five from his large friend. Experience told him to roll with the blow when it came, and he did. Otherwise, he was sure he'd have been knocked clear from his saddle. 'Good job, big guy. You got us all out of there alive.'

'Not Robin,' M'Grash said, his voice choking just a bit.

Dunk smiled to himself. In many ways, the ogre was a large child – one who could rip your arms off in the middle of a tantrum. Still, the two had become good friends over the past year, and Dunk had come to admire M'Grash's honesty and loyalty and even his simplicity.

'As deaths go, it was a good one,' Dunk said. 'It was so quick, I'll bet he didn't feel a thing.'

Olsen turned around in his saddle and started to contradict the thrower, but Dunk cut him off with a steel-hard stare. The wizard shut his mouth for a moment, and then opened it again. 'We'd best be prepared for the worst with these cultists,' he said. 'They worship the Daemon Lord Nurgle, Prince of Pathlogy, Dark Duke of Disease, and Count of Corruption.'

'Sounds a real *sicko*,' Slick said with a grin.

'Joke all you like, our little friend,' Olsen said. 'See how well you laugh when your lungs fill with phlegm.'

'I think I can *hack* it.' The halfling chortled out loud.

Olsen reined his horse to a halt and turned to glare at Slick. 'This is a matter of the utmost seriousness, wee one. If you do not treat it as such, you may very well die – and threaten the lives of the rest of us in the process.'

'Come now, Merle,' Slick said, rolling his eyes. 'We're talking about a handful or two of tree-hugging wackos who've probably been chewing on the wrong kind of mushrooms found in this forest for the past twenty years. I saw how you toasted old Robin back there. With people like you and M'Grash on our side, how can these numbskulls pose a threat to us?'

'For such a wee person, you show a grand amount of ignorance,' Olsen said, his eyes blazing. 'I've seen such cultists control a horde of maggots once that stripped the flesh from a horse's bones in a matter of seconds. If they touch you, if they so much as breathe on you, you could find yourself bleeding from your ass and eyeballs in a matter of minutes. You'd consider yourself lucky if your innards didn't liquefy in the process, but you might beg for such a thing to happen to release you from other kinds of suffering they can inflict.

'Or is that not clear enough for you?'

'Like the blue sky.' The wizard's speech had snuffed the halfling's good mood.

'So,' Guillermo said, as they started around a wide bend in the trail, 'why is it that we are doing this again?'

'Stow that chatter, Mr. Reyes,' Pegleg said. 'We've set ourselves on this path, and we're not getting off it until–' The ex-pirate cut himself off for a moment, then continued in a low, awed voice. 'Whoa.'

Dunk looked up and saw a massive log blocking the way before them. The fallen tree had to over six feet across its middle – at least as tall as Dunk – and it stretched from one darkened part of the woods to another. The riders hauled their horses up short in front of the log and gazed up and over it, their mouths hanging open.

'Let's just go around it,' Simon said. 'It can't be that long.'

'We wouldn't recommend that, lad,' Olsen said. 'We smell a trap here. The cultists likely felled this rotting tree here to encourage intruders to wander off the path and into the danger beyond. Here, we are safe. There,' the wizards shuddered, 'wise men fear to tread.'

'I'll go,' M'Grash said brightly. 'No man here.'

'Belay that, Mr. K'Thragsh,' Cavre said. 'Even if you made it safely, the rest of us would still be stuck here.'

The ogre's face fell hard enough Dunk thought he heard it slam into the forest floor.

'We could jump the horses over it,' Dunk said. 'I used to make leaps taller than this back in Altdorf.'

'Even if you could teach us how to manage that, son, I don't think my pony here would manage it,' Slick said, still staring up at the log in awe.

'Couldn't our vaunted wizard do something about it?' Lästiges asked, her camra zipping around Olsen's head, looking for the best angle from which to capture his squirming.

'We could, lass. Aye, we could, but is that wise?' The wizard stroked his beard as he considered the log once again.

M'Grash stepped forward, squatted in front of the log, and shoved his maul-size hands under it. He grunted and groaned with all his might, snarling and growling at the fallen tree so loudly that Dunk thought any other attackers who might lay in ambush out there would have to be insane not to turn and run. Then again, they were talking about cultists who worshipped the evil god of rot.

'There's no way he can do that,' Lästiges whispered so that everyone could here. 'Can he?'

No one responded. Then, with a great roar from M'Grash, the log moved an inch. Encouraged, the ogre shoved his fingers in further beneath the log and redoubled his efforts. His biceps looked as big around at Dunk's waist, and the thrower feared the ogre might burst them with his heroic effort.

'Shouldn't we stop him?' Dunk asked. 'If he hurts himself, how can we haul him out of here?'

'Hush,' Slick said. 'Let him work.'

The tree must have lain there in the forest for years, perhaps decades. The soil of the forest floor had risen around it, almost as if the tree had cut into the land it had fallen on so long ago, like a sword through flesh. There it had stuck, probably forever, until the ogre came along.

M'Grash let loose a pealing howl that echoed throughout the forest. Dunk wondered if they could hear the ogre's cry back in the pub.

Then the tree came free of the earth. Dirt scattered everywhere, showering the riders with tiny pellets. The horses, already spooked by M'Grash's howling, scrambled backward, out of range of the log, which the ogre now stood holding over his head.

It turned out that the tree's top only extended a few yards to the left, and that now stabbed into the air. The right end, where the roots sat, still rested on the ground somewhere in the darkness beyond.

Dunk let out a cheer for his friend, and the others joined in. They let up only when the ogre shouted out, 'Hurry! It's heavy!'

The others stared at their companions, daring each other to go first. Dunk ignored them all and started down the path again, aiming to ride straight under the lifted log. Even on horseback, he saw there would be plenty of room for him under the ogre's outstretched arms. As he went, he reached down and slapped Slick's pony on the rump. The startled creature shot forward, moving under the tree ahead of the thrower, the halfling howling in dismay the whole while.

As Dunk passed under the tree to the left of the ogre, he heard a low, hollow voice say, 'Oi! Leave off, will ya!'

The thrower glanced up to see a set of glowing green eyes staring down at him from what he'd thought were a pair of knots in the bark of the tree. A rough stub of a branch stuck out beneath them, closer to M'Grash. Right over the ogre's head, between his hands, a horizontal crack that seemed like an old axe-wound moved like a set of lips.

Dunk's brain refused to understand this, and he stopped there under the tree to gape up at this strange face that had appeared in it.

'You there!' the tree said, snarling at Dunk. 'Tell this bloke to get his fingers out of me face!'

Lästiges screamed. The noise broke Dunk from his trance, and he spurred his horse forward just as M'Grash dropped the tree. The thing's branches brushed against his horse's tail as it fell down behind him.

Dunk brought his horse around next to Slick and his pony.

'I don't think I like this forest much,' Dunk said.

'Son, that's the smartest thing you've had to say all day.'

M'GRASH SAT THERE between Dunk and the tree, staring at the thing in horror. 'What *is* it?' the ogre asked, panic slicing through his voice.

The branches on the side of the tree started to move, and M'Grash crab-walked backward until he sat next to Dunk's horse. As he did, the branches pressed themselves into the ground, and the tree lifted itself up on them.

'Agh,' the tree said, raspier this time. 'That bloody hurt.'

The tree slowly rolled away from Dunk, Slick, and M'Grash until it could get a proper look at them through its eyes, which glowed as if lit from within. 'You lot really know how to cock things up.'

The tree collapsed back to the forest floor with a thud that Dunk felt through the horse beneath him. It closed its eyes as it did, and for a moment the thrower wondered if he'd just imagined it all. Perhaps this was some kind of sorcerous illusion or a hallucination brought on by breathing the foul air of the Sure Wood. Or maybe he'd hit his head on the bottom of the tree as he'd raced under it. Or possibly it had even fallen on him and crushed him dead. The last seemed the most likely at the moment.

'It – it's a treeman,' Slick said in the sort of tone that priests reserved for direct conversations with their god. Dunk had never heard such reverence in Slick's voice, but he'd never seen a talking tree until today either.

'Yer bloody right it's a treeman,' the treeman said as it opened its eyes and glared at the halfling.

Slick leapt backward as if someone had stabbed him. 'Remarkable,' he said.

'Maybe we should go,' Dunk said, pulling on his horse's reins as he prepared to urge it to flee. 'The others will catch up when they can.'

'Right!' the treeman said. 'Fine! Wake up a poor, sleeping bloke and then race off into the woods like a gaggle of frightened geese. It's all I expect from yer kind of chaps.'

Dunk shook his head. 'What kind of chap?'

'Breathers,' the treeman said. 'Axe wielders. Fire users. Scum.'

'You're mean,' M'Grash said, standing up now.

'You'd be bloody mean too if you'd just spent the last year face down in a dried patch of mud!' The treeman roared so forcefully in its hollow voice that the wind ruffled Dunk's hair.

A little, gold globe zipped up over the treeman and focused on its face.

'What in the sap-burning hells is that?' the treeman said. Startled, it swatted at the globe with its branches. One of them caught the camra on its side and batted it away into the woods. A squeal of protest that could only have come from Lästiges sounded from the other side of the treeman.

'It's not important,' Dunk said. 'We didn't mean to bother you. We just wanted to get by.'

The treeman frowned. 'Just like that black-robed lot that's always trooping through here at all hours of the night.'

'He means the cultists,' Olsen shouted over the treeman.

'Of course I mean your bloody cultists! If you can call them proper cultists. Nothing like the mean bastards that used to run the Sure Wood with an iron axe. These just want to gather in their clearing to screw under the stars. Pfaugh!'

Before Dunk could stop him, Slick dismounted from his pony and sidled his way toward the treeman, stopping just out of reach of the thing's branches. Dunk didn't know how much protection this offered, as they'd already seen the thing move. He put his hand on the hilt of his sword, ready to draw it in the blink of an eye. Perhaps he could lop off a branch before the thing struck, giving Slick enough time to break free. Would such a creature bleed – or just leak sap?

'How long have you been there, old boy?' Slick said. Again, his tone stayed so respectful that Dunk wouldn't have recognised it as coming from Slick if he hadn't been there to see it.

'Your bloody cultists, I–' The treeman cut itself off. It grimaced, and then continued on. 'They were chopping down some of my saplings for firewood. Can you bloody well believe it? This bloody place is full of dead and dying trees, and they have to go and cut down some tree barely past being a seedling, their branches almost as green as the bloody grass.'

The treeman fell silent then, until Slick prompted him again. 'What did you do?'

'I chased them out of there. That's what I bloody well did. I chased them out through the rain-soaked disaster of a forest. I almost had them too. If I'd have got them in my branches, I'd have turned them into fertiliser in just bare, bloody moments.'

'What happened?' Slick said.

Dunk flinched, anticipating another rant from the treeman, this worse than any of the rest. Instead, the creature cracked open its bark-lined mouth and said, it a voice soft but clear, 'I tripped.'

Slick didn't respond. Everyone else remained silent. Dunk could hear M'Grash breathing loudly next to him, the ogre enthralled by the treeman's tale. Eventually, the treeman continued on.

'I bloody tripped, and I fell face down in the muddy path. I–' Dunk saw a line of sap pour out of the treeman's eyes and roll down its bark. 'I got stuck. I've been lying here ever since, afraid that they'd come back for me with saws and axes.'

'They didn't,' Slick said. 'We're friends.'

M'Grash started to say something to deny that, but Slick stopped him with a hand on his shoulder.

'You're safe now, old boy,' Slick said. 'You're safe.'

'Bloody, bloody hell,' the treeman said. 'You're a dead good lot, you are, to be sure. It's about bloody, damned time.'

'Do you need a hand up?' Slick asked.

The treeman shook for a moment, and then pushed itself up on its branches. It rose high enough into the air that Dunk could see Olsen, Lästiges, and the rest of the Hackers gaping up at it as it trembled there in the air.

'You,' the treeman rasped at M'Grash. 'Give an old, thick trunk a hand, would you now.'

M'Grash leapt to his feet and charged over to cradle the treeman's face in his arms.

'Not in my bloody eyes, you damned beast!' the treeman shouted.

M'Grash yelped and leapt back. As he did, the treeman crashed to the earth again. The ogre turned to Dunk and held up a hand that bore a long, red mark around its thumb.

'He bit me!' M'Grash said.

Dunk dismounted and reached out to examine the ogre's proffered palm. It looked as if someone had slammed it in a rough-hewn, oaken door. The thrower started plucking the splinters out of the whimpering ogre's hand.

'That's gratitude for you,' Dunk said.

'Gratitude!' the treeman said, forcing itself up on its branches again. 'A bloody ogre pokes me right through my bloody eye, and I'm supposed to get down on my roots and kiss his bloody feet? Do you know how long it takes for me to grow back one of those bloody things? Besides, *it bloody hurt!*'

'He's only trying to help you,' Dunk said, flicking one of the larger splinters at the treeman's face. 'Maybe you'd rather we just left you here instead.'

The treeman shuddered along its entire length at that thought. 'No, nay, no,' it said. 'You seem like good blokes. Give an old tree your leave. It's the months in the mud talking, that's all. I appreciate all you've done, I do. Give a weary log another chance.'

Dunk looked up into M'Grash's eyes, each larger than a fried egg, as he pulled the final splinter from his massive hand. 'What do you say, big guy?'

The ogre wiped his nose with a long, thick finger and nodded. 'I try again.' He stood and walked back over to the treeman. 'But no biting!'

'Just grab him a little lower if you can,' Slick said, pointing to a spot well below the treeman's face. M'Grash went straight for it and started to lift the treeman up again.

'There,' Slick said, 'that's it. Now just work your way back along to his roots. Kind of walk your way under him with your hands.'

M'Grash did as the halfling suggested, and the treeman's upper end rose into the air, step by step. Once it was vertical, the creature looked down at M'Grash – at nearly twice his size, it towered over him – and said, 'You have my thanks, my – Hey! Wait! No!'

M'Grash had given the treeman just a bit too much of a push at the end. The treeman tipped back over the other way, spinning its branches wildly, then flapping them like a flightless bird doing its level best to defy gravity.

It failed and came toppling back toward the earth.

The treeman wrapped its branches around the bare trunk of a nearby tree as it fell, stopping it from crashing to the ground.

'Sorry!' M'Grash said. 'Can I help again?'

'NO!' the treeman shouted. 'Stay back, you bloody–!' It sighed deeply as it gathered its strength. 'You've done enough, chap. I can manage it from here, cheers.'

Dunk led M'Grash back to where the others stood and watched as the treeman righted itself. It brought its wooden legs closer to the tree it held like a long-lost brother. Soon, it pushed back, on its own roots again. It wobbled a bit, unsteady on its own legs for the first time in months, but it stood.

'Ah,' the treeman said with a deep sigh. 'That's much better. My thanks to you, you tame beast you,' it said, patting M'Grash on the head with a leafy branch.

Then the treeman surveyed the people standing around it, its great, green eyes scanning them each in turn. If it looked for some sign that these visitors to its forest could not be trusted, it seemed to come up empty. Other than its own suspicious nature, it had no reason not to treat Dunk and his friends with the utmost kindness.

'Now sod off!' it said, pointing the intruders back in the direction from which they'd come.

Dunk and the others all stared up at the wooden creature towering over them and stood there in shock. When M'Grash turned to Dunk, the thrower saw tears welling up in the ogre's eyes. Something snapped in Dunk at that moment, and he stepped up and stabbed a finger at the treeman.

'You ungrateful bastard,' he said. 'We almost literally stumble upon you in the woods and lend you a hand, and you're nothing but spiteful. M'Grash here, he helps you up despite the fact you bit his hand, and you practically spit at him.'

'Right,' the treeman said. 'Let me correct that.'

The treeman made a horrible noise in the back of its throat and then leaned forward, spitting something brown and sticky at M'Grash's feet. The ogre took a step back, trying to pull his bare toes from the mess, but the sap stuck to his skin like glue.

'That's it!' Dunk said drawing his sword and stalking toward the treeman. 'You're going to start treating us right, right now.'

'Or else what?' the treeman said. It took a single step, and its long stride carried it right in front of Dunk.

The thrower craned back his neck and looked straight up at the treeman, meeting the angry gaze in the thing's glowing green eyes. The creature wanted to intimidate him, but he refused to let it. He reversed his grip on his sword and stabbed it down through the tangle of roots that passed for the treeman's feet.

The treeman laughed. 'You can't hurt me that way. It would be like trying to hurt a fleshy thing like you by cutting your hair.'

'M'Grash,' Dunk said, beckoning his friend over with his free hand. 'Knock him back down.'

The ogre stepped up from behind Dunk as the thrower stepped back and out of the way. The treeman tried to walk away, probably thinking that its long legs would let it outrun the ogre, but it found that Dunk's sword had pinned its foot to the earth.

'Wait,' said the treeman. 'Let's be bloody reasonable about this.'

'Sure,' Dunk said. 'Give me a *reason* not to have M'Grash turn you into toothpicks.'

'I–' The treeman looked down at the ogre, horror growing on its bark-covered faced. 'I–' It cast its gaze wider, but Dunk met it with an impassive glare. The others showed it no sign of sympathy either.

'I know where the cultists are,' the treeman said, holding up its branches. 'I can lead you to them.'

Dunk raised a hand, and M'Grash stopped cold, his hands only inches from the treeman's roots. 'Seriously?' the thrower asked the treeman.

The creature nodded as best it could with its rigid trunk. It seemed more like a quick series of bows. 'For good friends like you blokes, I can point you right in their direction.'

Dunk waved M'Grash to commence the toothpicking of the treeman.

'Ah, I mean, take you right to them, of course. I could do no less for the fine gentlemen – and lady – who showed me such kindness as you lot have.'

The treeman ended on a hopeful note, and Dunk repaid him by signalling for M'Grash to stop, just as the ogre wrapped his fingers around the treeman's trunk.

Dunk turned to glance back at the others. They all nodded.

'And you'll guide us back out of this accursed place,' Olsen added.

'Of course,' the treeman said. 'I could do no less for such good folk as yourselves. I'll be happy to escort you straight from the Sure Wood, and to do my best to ensure that you leave in at least as good a condition as that in which you so elegantly arrived.'

Pegleg nodded. 'I can see how this one survived the great purge of the treemen from this forest.'

'Now that's hardly–' The treeman made to move toward Pegleg but found M'Grash's grip ripping at its bark, so it stopped itself short instead. 'Fine, fine, fine. Whatever you like. I've made you an offer, and I thought we had an agreement. There's no need to get personal about it now. I'll be happy to fulfil my end of the bargain if you blokes are willing to fulfil yours.'

'And why should we trust him?' Lästiges asked, her camra zipping about to get a close-up of Pegleg's face.

Slick answered instead. 'It's the quickest and easiest way to get rid of us,' he said, the earlier awe he'd had for the creature no longer evident. 'We get what we want, we leave, and it gets what it wants.'

'Which is?' Simon asked.

'We *leave*, son,' Slick smirked at the Albionman still gaping up at the treeman. 'Try to pay attention.'

'WHAT ARE THEY doing?' Dunk whispered as he stared down at the
mass of cultists in the hollow below. A massive bonfire burned in the
centre of the place, and in its light Dunk could see dozens of naked
bodies writhing among each other in strange rhythms he could not
decipher.

'Why, Dunk Hoffnung,' Lästiges said. 'Don't tell me you've never
witnessed an orgy before.'

Dunk blushed six shades of red. 'Um, sure I–' He shook his head.
'Wait, I mean, no.' He looked at the dark-haired woman out of the
corner of his eye. 'Have you?'

Lästiges giggled and flashed a hungry smile. 'A lady never tells.'

'So what's holding you up?' Slick asked.

Lästiges backhanded the halfling, and he tumbled back from the
crest of the hollow, down toward the trail that wound around it far
below. If M'Grash hadn't whipped out a hand to catch Slick, Dunk
might have found himself without an agent. The ogre cradled the
halfling in his palm like a newborn child for a moment before placing him back along the crest, this time out of Lästiges's reach.

Satisfied that the only part of Slick hurt was his pride – of which, as
an agent, he had little to harm – Dunk glanced over and saw the others watching the scene in the hollow below. Simon and Guillermo
had cocked their heads all the way to the right, trying to get a better

angle on some bit of the action. A knowing smile played across Cavre's face as he looked on. Pegleg wore a scowl as he squinted from the naked forms below to Olsen, who stood by his side, frowning and scratching his beard.

'Where's the cup?' Pegleg said, never one to be distracted from riches.

'Huh?' Olsen said, his mind leaping back from the hollow. 'Oh, yes.' He pointed at a tent hunkered down against the hollow's opposite side. 'My guess is that it's there. If we hurry, we might be able to get to it before they bring it out to use in their unholy ceremony.'

'Hrm,' the treeman rumbled behind them. 'That lot don't seem to be in much of a hurry, now, do they?' He tried to crank his head to the left, but the movement threatened to topple him over. 'You humans are a bloody messy sort.'

'How do treemen reproduce?' Lästiges asked. Her camra zipped up into the treeman's face, and he swatted it away with a leafy branch. Undaunted, it returned straight away, but this time it kept a respectful distance.

'Er...' The treeman's eyes turned a soft shade of red for a moment. 'It's all about pollination with us: blossoms, seeds, saplings – that sort of thing.' His eyes resumed their normal colour. 'This seems a bit more effort. Why do you bother with it all?'

A voracious grin split Lästiges's face, and Dunk blushed at just seeing it. 'That's not reproduction,' she said. 'It's sex, and it's incredible fun.'

A loud groan erupted from the base of the hollow, followed by two more similar noises. 'See?' Lästiges said, batting her eyes at the treeman.

The creature shook its branches. 'If you say so. Sounds bloody painful to me.'

The reporter reached out and caressed the treeman's bark. 'It's just the opposite.'

Olsen cut in, his voice and manner both fragile and edgy as he hissed at Lästiges. 'Can we put an end to the education of our treeman friend about human mating habits for–?'

'Edgar.'

The wizard craned his neck back to glare up at the treeman. 'What?' he spat.

'My name,' the treeman said. 'It's Edgar.'

Olsen stared at the creature for a moment, and then shook his head. 'All right, then, *Edgar*. We'd like to focus on our stated goal here for a moment, if that wouldn't trouble you over much.'

'Get on with it then,' Edgar said, unperturbed. If he'd heard the sarcasm in the wizard's voice, he gave no sign of it.

'I have a question I would like to ask,' Guillermo said. Beside him, Simon nodded along.

The wizard sighed through his nose. 'And?'

'I thought these people were supposed to be some kind of plague spreaders.' The Estalian pointed to the active folk in the hollow as more groans escaped from their pile of writhing bodies.

'And?'

'Well, they don't look so unhealthy to me.'

'Faith save us.' Olsen winced, and Dunk had the impression he was counting to himself under his breath. When the wizard opened his eyes again, he fixed his gaze on Guillermo and said, 'Have you ever heard of venereal disease, lad?'

The Estalian frowned. Lästiges leaned over and whispered something in his ear. Guillermo flushed so red that Dunk feared the cultists might see him like a signal fire.

'Really?' Guillermo said, glancing down at the front of his pants.

Lästiges patted him on the back and said, 'Let's just say you're better off enjoying the performances down there from a distance. A *long* distance.'

'Is that quite enough?' Olsen asked, frustration lacing his voice.

Guillermo swallowed hard and nodded.

'I have a plan, Mr. Merlin,' Pegleg said. He'd doffed his yellow tricorn hat. 'Simple, but serviceable.'

The wizard nodded for the ex-pirate to continue.

'A few of us set up a distraction on the east side of the hollow.' Pegleg pointed to the right, which meant they had to be on the hollow's south side. Dunk had turned around entirely during their time wandering in the Sure Wood, with no sun or stars to steer by.

'While the cultists investigate, we send our fastest runners into the tent to snatch the Far Albion Cup. We rendezvous back at the place where we found Edgar. Then we leave the wood with all due haste.'

'Who do you picture in each force?' Olsen asked.

'Mr. Reyes, Mr. Sherwood, and Mr. K'Thragsh will generate the distraction.' Pegleg stabbed his hook at each player in turn as he spoke. 'Dunk and Mr. Cavre, you two will go for the prize.'

'And what will the rest of you be doing while we're off risking our lives?' Simon asked, staring at Pegleg, Olsen, Lästiges, and Slick.

'Come now, Mr. Sherwood,' Pegleg said. 'Don't be a coward. This is a sound plan, and I've assigned the best people to each role. Would you rather Mr. Fullbelly here raced into the tent? Or myself?'

'We have a wizard with us,' Simon said.

'So we do.' Pegleg nodded. 'And if coaching Blood Bowl for so many years has taught me anything, it's that you leave your wizards in reserve until you need them – and you hope you never do.'

'What about me?' Edgar asked in a forlorn tone.

The coach stepped back and goggled up at the treeman. 'You'd care to help?'

'Sure,' Edgar rumbled. 'Why the bloody hell wouldn't I?'

Pegleg smirked as he twirled his moustache. 'You've fulfilled your "end of the bargain". You're free to go. We won't bother you again, Mr. Edgar.'

'But I'd–' Edgar fell silent for a moment. The others gazed up and him and waited. 'It's dead dull in this bloody forest since all the others have been gone.'

'You're bored?' Dunk said.

The treeman stabbed a branch at the thrower. 'That's it. That's it right in the heartwood. I'm bored. There's nothing like a full year face down in the bloody muck to make a body wish for a change.' He looked down at them all. 'You lot seem to be my best chance at that.'

'Are you certain, Mr. Edgar?' Pegleg said. Dunk could almost hear the gears whirring behind his coach's sparkling eyes. Or perhaps that was the ghostly sound of gold being scooped into a bag. 'If you come with us, I can guarantee you'll not be bored.'

The treeman's upper branches waved in a way that Dunk now understood to be his equivalent of nodding. 'It's either you bloody fools or those humping idiots down there.' He looked at them each in turn. 'You don't bother with all that sort of thing, do you?'

'Not often enough, honey,' Lästiges said with a dry chuckle. 'Not often enough.'

Not for the first time, Dunk wondered if this lady reporter had truly captured his brother's heart or just his loins. Perhaps Dirk wouldn't make such distinctions, but Dunk couldn't bring himself to not.

'Right then,' Pegleg said, scanning the faces of his players. Dunk could feel him sizing them each up, determining if they were all up for the jobs he had in mind for them. 'Let's go over this once again.'

Pegleg stepped forward and began to use his hook to scratch a diagram into the side of a nearby tree. Dunk had seen him do the same thing dozens of times before, although the coach usually used the wall of a locker room instead.

'Yowch!' Edgar howled. The treeman slapped the ex-pirate's arm away and stumbled backward. 'What in the bloody Chaos Wastes did you do that for?'

Pegleg took a step back. 'You can feel that?'

'I just *look* like a bloody tree! There's the "man" part of the word too. "Tree-*man*." The "man" part *hurts!*'

A silence fell over the hollow as Edgar bellowed down at Pegleg. None of the Hackers or their companions spoke a word. Then Dunk realised that the noises from the hollow had ceased too.

The thrower glanced down at the orgy and saw that its participants had frozen in their various, now-awkward positions, right in the middle of whatever pleasurable thing they'd been doing. One trio fell over onto each other, unable to maintain their balance any longer.

That seemed to break the spell Edgar's outburst had cast over the hollow. One of the cultists stood up and pointed at the towering forms of Edgar and M'Grash, just visible, Dunk guessed, on the fringe of the bonfire's light.

'Intruders!' the man shouted.

The people in the hollow scattered in a dozen different directions, each of them shouting for help or screaming for mercy. Some of them seemed to run in circles around the bonfire, gathering up scraps of clothing and wriggling into them as best they could. Many of the gatherers cared little whether the clothes were theirs or not, it seemed, as shown by one fat and hairy man who slipped into a corset in an instant. Dunk later wondered at how easily the man had performed that task, but he put that detail out of his head as something he'd rather not contemplate for long.

'I think we have our distraction,' Slick said.

Dunk and Cavre glanced at each other and then at Pegleg.

'What are you waiting for, lads?' the coach said pointing them off toward the west side of the hollow. 'Go, go, go! Head for the end zone! We'll keep them busy as long as we can!'

Dunk heard M'Grash say, 'End zone? Where?' as he and Cavre sprinted off through the darkness to the west. They curved around the edge of the hollow as they ran, and they soon came to the north side. Cavre cut to the right and raced up to the rim of the hollow.

Dunk caught up with the blitzer at the edge of the rim. Below in the hollow, the cultists seemed to be rallying. Most of them were clothed by this point, staring up into the darkness and pointing all around.

'What are they waiting for?' a balding man standing near the bonfire said. 'Why haven't they attacked?'

As if in answer, M'Grash and Edgar rose over the crest again. The treeman raised its branches tall and wide and let loose a horrible noise that seemed to shake every tree in the forest. At the same time, M'Grash hefted up a small boulder, a rock as large as a pirate's treasure chest, and flung it at the bonfire.

When the boulder hit the bonfire, burning bits of coal and wood exploded from it. These showered the hollow with glowing embers, some of which hung floating in the resultant smoke like angry stars in a murderous sky.

The cultists screamed like children and scattered like rats. The hollow's floor fell into total chaos as the cultists banged into and tried to climb over each other through the stinging smoke.

'Here,' Cavre said softly, handing Dunk a black bandana. The blitzer often wore one like this on the field, tied around his forehead or his biceps to absorb his sweat and keep his vision clear and his hands dry. He produced one for himself and tied it around his face, covering his nose and mouth.

Dunk followed Cavre's example and was happy to find the cloth dry and clean. He started to ask what it was for, but the blitzer raised a finger to cut him off.

Cavre signalled Dunk to follow him, and then plunged down the steep side of the hollow, toward the cultists' tent. As they reached it, Dunk saw that it bore strange symbols and patterns embroidered into the red fabric in black, green, and yellow threads. Dunk didn't look at them for long, but what little he did see made the inside of his head itch. After that, he avoided even glancing at them at all.

Cavre reached down and pulled up the tent's back wall and motioned Dunk inside. Before he could stop to wonder why it should be he who entered the place first, the thrower scrambled under the fabric and found himself inside the tent.

An awful stench stung Dunk's eyes and lungs and he tried to peer through the murky haze. At first, he thought that the flying embers in the chaos outside might have set the tent on fire. Or perhaps the noxious smell came from the too-sweet incense burning low in the brazier sitting in a far corner. Then he realised that the foul vapours in the air sprang not from any blaze but from the fleshy lump of a creature that sat in the centre of the place.

The sick thing that squatted there seemed like it might once have been a man, but it had long since left simple definitions of humanity behind. If it had any legs to stand on, it might have been taller than Dunk, judging by the size of its massive, flabby torso, but those limbs had been carved away, along with its arms. From the slick sheen of rot over an angry red rash on its pale, almost formless flesh, Dunk might have thought the once-man dead if it had not moved at the sound of their entrance.

As the creature rolled toward the intruders, gangrenous pus squished through the stitches where the limbs had once been, and the scent of rot grew stronger. Its blind eyes stared toward them through its red-rimmed, lidless sockets. Its nose had been removed, probably through some insane act of mercy, or perhaps to prevent it from constantly nauseating itself with its own stink. No stitches sealed that wound, though, which bore only the blistered marks of a cauterizing brand.

The thing's mouth was far wider than any human's could have been, its cheeks sliced wide with a jagged knife and stitched back to form ragged approximations of lips. As it smiled at him through its gaping mouth, Dunk could see that all of its teeth had been pulled

and its tongue bifurcated neatly down the middle, almost to its root.
The thing welcomed them softly in either gibberish or some ancient
tongue long since lost to all but sorcerers and madmen. As it did, it
thrust its groin at them, bursting a number of poorly laid stitches that
finally managed to escape its putrescent flesh.

Dunk stepped forward in a daze, his first instinct to kill the thing
with his bare hands. It would be a mercy killing, both for the creature
and himself – and perhaps for the kind of world that could produce
such an abomination.

Cavre's hand on Dunk's arm held him back. The thrower looked
back at his team-mate and saw him shake his head. His eyes drawn
away from the spectacle in the centre of the tent, Dunk realised the
blitzer was right. They needed to find the cup first, before the cultists
discovered them here.

Cavre pointed to the ceiling of the tent, right near the front flap.
There, nestled in a thin bit of netting, hung a golden cup studded
with emeralds and diamonds. Despite having been lost for over 500
years, the trophy – for that's what it was, no simple cup at all –
gleamed as if freshly made.

Dunk drew his sword, and the creature jerked at the scraping noise,
despite the fact that its ears had been removed. Steeling himself, the
thrower skirted past it to cut the trophy free with a single slice of his
well-honed blade. It dropped into his free hand, and for a moment
he cradled it in his arm and gazed upon it.

He could see why people had killed for this cup. It wasn't just the
money it was worth. Having seen it for just a moment, he couldn't
conceive of ever giving it up. He'd share it with his friends, sure – the
Hackers, Slick, people he trusted – but sell it? Never. He had to have
it, or at least a part of it, forever.

'Amazing,' Cavre said as he reached out to take the cup from Dunk.
The thrower hesitated for a moment before letting the blitzer take it.

Cavre never touched the cup itself. He had removed his shirt while
Dunk stood captivated by the sight of the cup, and he'd draped it over
his hands. As he took the cup from Dunk, Cavre wrapped his shirt
around it, hiding it beneath the dark fabric.

With the cup out of sight, Dunk remembered where he was. Before
he could turn to leave the tent though, he felt something strike him
in the feet. He looked down to see the rot-infested creature trying to
wrap itself around his boots. Disgusted, he raised his sword to hack
the thing to pieces, but once again Cavre stopped him.

'This poor, damned soul is ill, but he is also infectious – catching.
If you destroy it with your sword, you risk becoming ill as well.
Believe me,' Carve said, looking down at the creature with pity, 'this is
a fate you would not wish on your most hated foe.'

Dunk coughed once and nodded as he backed away from the creature. Then he strode to the glowing brazier and kicked it over with his boot. The coals lay on the rug for an instant before the carpet caught fire.

Dunk and Cavre watched as the fire licked along a trail of invisible slime the creature on the floor had left behind as it had squirmed across it. Soon, it caught up with the revolting sack of illness. It crept along its skin for a moment, and the creature stopped its insane, incomprehensible babbling and started to scream.

Cavre pulled Dunk to the back of the tent again and raised the flap for him to scoot under. Just before he went, Dunk looked back at the creature and saw its blistering flesh burst into flames.

'May Nurgle never find your soul,' Dunk whispered as he left the tent. Cavre, the covered cup tucked under his arm like a football, followed close on his heels.

'NOW WHAT?' DUNK asked, gathered with the rest of the Hackers around a table in the back yard of the nameless pub in which they'd first met Olsen.

'How about another round, lad?' Olsen said. The wizard had already downed more beer than Dunk thought he should have been able to hold in his frame, but he showed no signs of stopping. 'We'd like to toast the man who's finally given us the chance to end this cursed life of ours.'

'Again?' Dunk said, the contents of his stomach curdling at the thought.

'Again!' the red-faced Olsen roared. 'Aye! And again and again until there's no more toast – we mean, toasts! – to be made.'

Dunk tried to wave the gesture off, but a barmaid showed up with a fresh bottle of whiskey at that point. Olsen tried to grab the bottle to pour a fresh round of shots, but he knocked the bottle from the table instead. Cavre snatched the bottle from the air before it could smash against the ground, and he quickly poured the drinks himself.

Dunk noticed that Cavre had skipped over his own glass. 'Hey!' the thrower said. 'That's not fair! You're just as much to blame for getting that trophy as I am.'

Cavre grinned. 'Too true, Mr. Hoffnung, but someone has to stay sober enough to pour the drinks.'

Dunk turned to point at the barmaid, but his head swum around even faster. He had to reach back to clutch the table in front of him for fear of falling to the earth. 'Whoa!' he said, laughing. 'Are we back on the ship already?'

For some reason, the others at the table found his antics hysterical, especially Lästiges, who wrapped an arm around Dunk and leaned heavily against him.

'You're damned – damned – damned cute,' she said around her hiccups, smiling up at him with her dark eyes, ruby-red lips, and Cabalvision-perfect teeth. 'If I wasn't already with your brother –

Dunk became aware of Lästiges's breasts pressing against his shoulder, and he turned to gaze wobbly into her eyes. They seemed to be asking him – no, begging – to kiss those soft, red lips, the ones his brother–'

'My brother!' Dunk said, shrugging the reporter away. 'Wait until he hears about – whoa!'

Only intending to move a bit out of Lästiges's range, Dunk had overbalanced himself, and he tipped and fell backward off his seat. He landed flat on his back, which knocked the wind out of him for a moment, but the alcohol had numbed him so that the landing didn't hurt a bit.

The rest of the table went silent. Slick leaped up on the table, nearly slipping in a pool of spilled beer, and stared down at the young thrower. 'Dunk!' he said, his voice cracking with worry. 'Are you killed, son?'

When Dunk could breathe again, he started laughing harder than ever, and the others all joined in. After a moment, he stopped and clutched at the ground beneath him, dizzy enough to wonder whether he might spin out into the night sky should he let go. He closed his eyes and hoped that the vertigo would go away.

'So, wizard,' Edgar said, 'when will you end your life?'

That stopped the laughter dead.

Dunk pried his eyes open to see the treeman standing tall over him, his branches seeming farther away than the moon. Even from this angle, Dunk could see the creature wince, realising he had said something to spoil the mood.

'My apologies, mate,' he said. 'You seem like a good bloke, and I'm in no hurry to shove you off this mortal coil. I just – well, I haven't–' He stopped and mulled something over for a moment. 'Bollocks. Are you planning to die all at once – together, I mean – or in turns? And is this something I can bloody well lend a hand with?'

Dunk snorted at this but then realised no one else was laughing along. Embarrassed, he decided he had to do something to set this right. He sprang to his feet to launch himself into an impassioned speech about the sanctity of life, especially among friends, but he tipped over backward again before he could start.

Edgar caught him in his branches and set him upright. 'I'm sorry, mate,' he said. 'This is maybe a bit too human for me.'

'Not at all,' Dunk said. 'It's just, well, we're not all bent on killing ourselves – despite what it may look like on the gridiron. It's only Olsen here who's up for giving that a go, and only because we finally found the one thing that can kill him: the cup.'

'So you lot, as his friends, risked your lives to be able to help him kill himself?'

'Actually, we don't know him all that well. He paid us. With the cup.'

Edgar shook its upper branches. 'I don't suppose I might ever understand you lot.'

'This is a rare situation,' Olsen said to the treeman. 'Rare situations call for rare solutions.' He looked at the others around him. 'And this is about as rare a group of people as you'd ever want to find.'

A smile burst on the wizard's face. 'And we can't imagine wanting to leave such rare people behind tonight!'

A cheer rose, and many glasses clinked together at the announcement.

'A Blood Bowl team can always use a wizard on its side, Mr. Merlin,' Pegleg said with a grin. 'With your kind permission, I'd like to hire you as our full-time consultant on all matters sorcerous, magical, and otherwise unnatural.'

'Nothing could please us more, chappie, but we don't need your money.'

Pegleg's smile grew wider than ever. 'Better yet, Mr. Merlin. Better yet.'

The wizard leaned over the table and spoke directly into the coach's face before bursting into uncontrollable laughter. 'But I didn't say I wouldn't take it!'

The fact that Pegleg still kept his smile on his face indicated how drunk he must have been, Dunk thought. He knew that money was never a joking matter with the ex-pirate. Perhaps the smile wasn't as real or as strong now as it had been before, but maybe only because Pegleg knew better than to antagonise a drunken wizard.

'Now all we need are some more players to fill out our roster,' Slick said.

Olsen stopped laughing at this. 'How many players are you lot shy?'

'Eleven,' Cavre said. While the blitzer had been drinking with the rest of them, Dunk couldn't see that he'd suffered from it at all. He was as stoic as ever.

Dunk wished he could say the same for the team's other blitzer. M'Grash had washed down their celebratory feast with a personal keg of bitter ale, and now he lay sleeping like an elephant-sized baby curled up under the wide, round table.

M'Grash made for a friendly drunk at least. Dunk hated to think how bad it would be if strong drink turned the ogre surly instead. The last thing he needed was to spend his nights trying to keep M'Grash from picking a fight. As it was, he often just had to baby-sit as the ogre slept instead.

'Eleven?' Olsen said. 'Gods preserve us.' He looked around the table at the Hackers sitting there. 'We just assumed–' He stopped to count the players.

'Faith. Only five of you here?' The wizard gazed into the eyes of each of the Hackers. Dunk noticed the mirth had left the yard. 'You're all that's left then?'

Pegleg grimaced. 'The best of the lot too,' he said. 'The fittest survived.'

'Well,' Olsen said, 'there's only one thing for us to do then. We'll have to find another team to merge with in time for the Far Albion Cup tournament!'

'Wait.' Pegleg held up his hook to silence the wizard. 'We're in no shape to jump back into the game just like that. The Far Albion Cup tourney starts in less than a week.'

'Correct,' Cavre said. 'We're out of training, and even if we could manage to find enough players to fill out our roster, we'd never be able to work in enough practices to forge a team that could win a major cup.'

'But this isn't a major cup,' Slick said, nodding to Olsen and Simon. 'Apologies to our friends from Albion, but the competition here can't be anything like what we're used to back home. Even with just five players, we'd probably tear some of these local clubs apart.'

Simon pounded his glass on the table and spilled his beer as he pushed himself to his unsteady feet. His glassy eyes seemed like they might roll back into his head at any moment, but he still spoke, slurring out his words as best he could. 'Now, see here, Mr. Tiny Agent. We may not have the best football players in the world here in Old Blighty, but we're not nearly so bad as you... Wait... What was I on about?'

'Cheers!' Dunk shouted, raising his glass.

'Cheers!' everyone else replied, including Simon, who seemed pleased to be able to rid his mind of whatever it was that might have been bothering him.

After everyone had put their drinks back down, Olsen signalled the waitress for another round and said, 'Opinions of the relative strength of our local lads aside, you'll need to fill out the team with some warm bodies at least – or cold if you'd rather line up a willing necromancer. Not our area of expertise, we're afraid.'

'He's right,' said Slick. Even though the halfling stood less than half Dunk's height and had drunk at least as much as his client, he spoke in a steady voice, his eyes bright and strong. 'You have to start the game with at least eleven players. Otherwise, you forfeit automatically.'

'But where are you going to find any players willing to join a foreign team only days before the tournament starts?' Lästiges said. 'Who'd be so foolish?' She made a solid effort at a professional manner, but her hair rested cockeyed on her head from when she'd fallen asleep at the table during the dessert course. Dunk couldn't wait for her to see the Cabalvision images her camra was recording.

'I bloody well would!' Edgar said, waving about an empty wooden bowl. He'd been drinking a sweet, fragrant concoction made of warm, fermented maple syrup that Dunk could smell on his breath, even from half a table away.

'I'd be honoured to be a part of this team,' the treeman said. 'I've never seen such a great bunch of mates before in my life. If you lot say you can win this bloody game of yours, then I believe you, and I'll play by your bloody side.'

Pegleg and Carve looked at each other for a moment. Cavre hesitated for a moment, and then nodded. The coach shot to his feet, then, and raised his glass for another toast.

'Well, lads, here's to Edgar!' Pegleg said. 'A finer team-mate you could never want.'

Those able to stand did so and joined the ex-pirate in his cheers. Dunk looked over at Edgar, who jumped for sheer joy, and smiled. He'd already come to like the treeman a lot, and he could see how he would be a huge asset for the team. Even if Edgar had never played a game of Blood Bowl in his life, size and speed like his had to be good for something.

Sticky tears of sap rolled out of Edgar's great, green eyes. 'I've never been so – Whoa!'

As the treeman leaped once more, he landed off-balance and tipped over backwards. He seemed to fall in slow motion, as if the leaves in his upper branches dragged through the air like it was water. He came down flat on his back with a resounding thud that Dunk felt all the way through to his teeth.

Dunk leapt up on to the table to get a better view of the treeman where he lay. He couldn't tell if Edgar was breathing or not. Nor, he realised, did he know if Edgar ever breathed.

'Are you all right, Edgar?' Dunk asked.

'All right?' the treeman said. 'I'm bloody better than "all right", mate! I'm a bloody Bad Bay Hacker!'

* * *

'RISE AND SHINE, son!'

Dunk wanted to pry open his eyes, but the pounding in his head told him that if he tried the sun would kill him by frying holes through his retinas that would burn through his brain and burst out the backside of his skull.

'Go away,' he murmured. He wanted to shout at the intruder, but he couldn't muster the energy to speak so loudly, sure that it would shatter his eardrums if he tried.

'Come now, Dunk. It's past noon. Time to get a move on.'

It was Slick's voice, but Dunk didn't believe the halfling could ever be so cruel to him. It had to be an impostor, an evil doppelganger who had taken Slick's place in order to alienate all of his friends with his inhuman deviltry. Either that, or Dunk was going to need another agent when he recovered from this, as such a horrible act of intrusion was unforgivable.

'Here, son,' Slick said, as he helped Dunk sit up. 'Drink this.' The halfling shoved a mug of something hot into his client's hands.

The room spun around Dunk as he struggled to keep his back to the wall behind him. He put out a hand, trying to keep himself from tumbling from the bed beneath him. As he veered to the left, a bit of the scalding liquid spilled from the cup and landed on his lap.

That woke him right up.

'Yowch!' Dunk shouted, flinging off the wet sheet over him as his eyes flew open. The pain from the light stabbing into his eyes made them flinch closed again, and only his newfound respect for whatever it was in his mug made him careful enough to keep it from spilling on him again.

'For Nuffle's sake, can you keep it down!'

The voice next to him belonged to a woman. It was close, perhaps sitting in a chair at the side of the bed. Dunk reached out his free hand to push the woman away, but she wasn't where he expected her to be. He let his hand fall, and it landed on her breast.

'Hey!' the voice said. Her voice, Dunk realised, recognising it at last: Lästiges's voice.

'Gah!' Dunk leapt from the bed, flinging his eyes open again, even as he held the burning mug of liquid in both hands out of respect for the damage he knew it could do. Once he was standing, he looked down past the mug and spotted Lästiges's form in the bed, huddled under the dry part of the sheet with only her head and her unkempt hair sticking out.

'No, no, no!' Dunk said, the shock at what he saw causing him to forget for a moment the pain pounding in his temples. 'How drunk can a man get?'

'Oh, you're no catch either, I'm sure,' Lästiges said as she wrested open her own bloodshot eyes. 'Don't you–' Her eyes caught Dunk's and locked there in sheer terror.

Lästiges screamed.

Dunk screamed.

Slick screamed too. Then he started to laugh.

'I don't see what's so damn funny,' Dunk said.

'Perhaps he got a good look at your–' Lästiges started. 'Wait. You're still in your clothes.' She pulled down the sheet covering her and looked at herself.

'So are you,' Dunk said. Relief washed over him, with a wave of nausea quick on its heels. He staggered backward, and Slick guided him into a nearby chair.

'So we didn't…' Lästiges said.

'No, no, no,' Dunk said, smiling despite the fact his shrivelled brain seemed to be trying to force itself out either of his ears.

'You don't have to be so relieved about it,' the reporter said. Her camra rose from its resting spot near the door and began to hover near her again.

'It seems not even your daemon-infested device there could bring itself to bear witness to that potential horror,' Slick said. Lästiges whipped a pillow at his face, but he neatly caught it.

'Drink that,' the halfling said to Dunk. 'It's from Olsen.'

The thrower sniffed at the steaming mug in his hands as he wondered how he could hope to swallow something so hot. It smelled like week-old pig vomit.

'Something to put me out of my misery?'

Slick grinned. 'One way or the other. It's safe. I had one earlier myself.'

Dunk blew out a long sigh, and then tossed the drink back, swallowing it in one huge gulp. The hot liquid scorched him straight down his gullet and into his belly, where it seemed to take on a life of its own. He could feel it growling around in his stomach like a trapped badger trying to figure out the best route by which to claw its way free.

Dunk leaned over and put his head between his knees. He thought if he could just let loose the contents of his stomach, he'd feel much better, but he couldn't make it happen. Instead, after a moment he got tired of trying and sat back up.

'Hey,' Dunk said, 'my head doesn't feel like an overripe melon any more. And I can feel my tongue again.'

'See,' Slick said.

Dunk rolled his tongue around in his mouth and then made a horrified face.

'Olsen tells me that the taste should go away in a day or three.' Slick shrugged up at the thrower.

'I need something to eat,' Dunk said. 'Anything.'

'It doesn't help,' Slick said, patting his bulging belly. 'Believe me, son, I've tried.'

'Do you have any more of that junk?' Lästiges said, rolling out of the bed.

Dunk noticed that she still had on every bit of her clothing from the night before, right down to her shoes. He breathed a silent sigh of relief. He couldn't imagine cheating on Spinne, as much as he loved her, but to do so with his brother's girlfriend would have been even worse.

'Olsen has a kettle of it in the main room,' Slick said. 'I'd have brought you a cup if I'd known you were – Ah, who am I kidding? I wouldn't have bothered.'

Lästiges spat a bitter 'Thanks' at the halfling, and then scurried from the room.

Dunk remained silent for a moment after watching her go. 'What happened last night?' he finally asked.

'We all had a little too much to drink last night, son,' Slick said. 'All right: a lot. The last I saw of you, you had offered to escort that girl back to her room in a valiant effort to protect the honour of your brother's girlfriend.' He chuckled. 'A fool's errand if ever there was.'

'Fortunately, nothing happened. We must have just passed out here together.'

'Sure,' Slick said. 'Unless, of course, you managed to get your clothes back on after drunkenly violating the trust of your respective lovers.'

Dunk gave the halfling a sidelong glance. 'You can't be serious.'

Slick shook his head. 'No, I'm not, but Pegleg is. He sent me to find you for the team meeting.'

'What team meeting?'

'The one to meet your new team-mates.'

Dunk stared at the bed in the corner of the room. It called like a siren, offering the one thing he still wanted after that foul drink: the oblivion of a good, long rest. 'I've already met Edgar,' he said.

Slick frowned. 'Not him, son. The others.'

'Others?'

The halfling beckoned for Dunk to follow him as he strode out the door. 'Come and see,' he said.

'You must be Dunkel Hoffnung,' the man in the black clothes said as he extended his hand in greeting to the thrower when he entered the pub's courtyard. It looked far bleaker in the midday sun than it had the night before. 'A pleasure. I am Bavid Deckem.'

The sandy-haired Deckem stood an inch taller than Dunk, but massed a stone less. He moved with a dancer's grace, seeming to always be on the tips of his toes, every gesture a study in economy and grace. The thing that struck Dunk the most, though, was the shade of Deckem's eyes, which were the icy blue of an arctic sky.

'Mr. Deckem is the finest football player in all of Albion,' Olsen said.

'Ah, to be damned with such faint praise,' Slick said, sliding around from behind Dunk to take his place at the great, round table in the centre of the courtyard. He immediately started in again on a plate filled with half-demolished fruits and pastries.

Dunk glanced around and saw that the rest of the Hackers were there. Guillermo and Simon chatted on one side of the table, while Cavre sat quietly with M'Grash on the other. Behind the table, in the far corner of the courtyard, Pegleg stood talking to a group of fit-looking men dressed in clothes identical to Deckem's. Dunk didn't see Lästiges anywhere, but that suited him fine.

'Permit me to introduce you to my compatriots,' Deckem said, ignoring Slick's comment. With Olsen at his side, he led Dunk over to the men standing around Pegleg. The circle of the group parted without a word to admit the three newcomers.

Deckem spoke, pointing to each of his doubles in turn as he did. 'Mr. Hoffnung, I'm pleased to present your new team-mates: Oliver Dickens, Lemuel Swift, Long John Stevenson, and Victor Shelley.'

Each of the men shook Dunk's hand without a word, just the same hint of a smile on their faces.

'Team-mates?' Dunk asked, puzzled.

'Mr. Deckem and his friends here have come to fill out our roster,' Pegleg said with an unreserved smile.

'Really?' Dunk raised his eyebrows. 'How did you know we needed anyone?'

'Word about such famous Blood Bowlers as yourself travels fast,' Deckem said, 'at least among Albion's own aspirants.'

Dunk nodded. They'd only been in Albion for just over a day, but plenty of people had seen them arrive in the *Sea Chariot*. He'd been surprised at the absolute lack of any kind of reception then, so he thought he should be pleased to know that someone had finally recognised them. When he looked into Deckem's eyes, though, he couldn't conjure that emotion.

'I understand your surprise,' Deckem said. 'Under normal circumstances, we would have waited, given you some time to acclimatise yourself to your new surroundings. Time, however, is a luxury we no longer have.'

'The Far Albion Cup tournament starts in Wallington in less than a week,' Pegleg said. 'If we're to take part, we need to start practising today.'

'You really think we can manage this, coach?' Dunk asked. 'Even with our new recruits here, we only have eleven players. Isn't that cutting it a little close?'

Deckem put a hand on Dunk's shoulder. 'Do not fret, Mr. Hoffnung. My friends and I have promised not to hurt you. If we need more players at game time, we can procure them.'

'Does that work for you, Dunk?' Pegleg asked.

Dunk shrugged. 'Do I have a choice in the matter, coach?'

A toothy smile on his face, the ex-pirate slapped Dunk on the back. 'None at all! See, you are learning.'

'Ah, my little boy is growing up,' Slick said around a mouthful of jam-slathered crumpet. 'A rookie no longer. I'm so proud.'

THE WEEK SAILED past before Dunk could get his bearings. Pegleg and Cavre worked the team from dusk till dawn, with only short breaks between. These were mostly for drinks of water. In the evening, the innkeepers stuffed them full of bland, starchy foods served alongside large slabs of steak.

Over one lunch, Dunk noticed that the newcomers all ate their steaks nearly raw. 'Is that where the term "bloody" comes from?' he asked Simon later while waiting for their turn on the makeshift obstacle course Cavre had set up at their impromptu training camp. This was held in an open park nearest to the nameless pub the Hackers had adopted as their Albion home.

'Nah. It's just that many chaps around these parts prefer their meat to still be mooing when served. "The rawer, the better" they say.'

Dunk shook his head. 'Do they eat other meats the same way? Like chicken? Or fish?'

Simon snorted. 'Blood Bowlers make enough money that they don't have to eat anything but steak. Raw fish? Around here we call that "bait"!'

'Mr. Sherwood! Mr. Hoffnung!'

The two snapped their heads around to see Pegleg glaring at them. 'Yes, coach?' they said in unison.

'This isn't a knitting circle for little old ladies. You can blather on to each other in your own time. Right now, I want to see five laps around the park from each of you.'

Simon rolled his eyes.

'Make it ten!'

'Right, coach!' Dunk said, grabbing Simon and pulling him along after him before Pegleg increased their punishment again.

'So THIS IS Kingsbury,' Dunk said, craning his neck around from the deck of the *Sea Chariot* as it docked at the city's largest pier, within throwing distance of the largest palace the young man had ever seen. 'Impressive.'

'Sure,' Slick said, wrinkling his nose in disgust. 'There's an impressive amount of sewage floating in the river. And an impressive haze of soot in the impressively rain-filled air. And an impressive smell wafting from farther inland.'

'The Mootland I'm sure it's not,' Slick said, 'but that's what happens when you get so many people packed together in a single place.'

'We suppose you'd prefer we Albionmen all lived in dirty, little warrens like you wee folk,' Olsen said.

'Only because it would make it easier to bury you all alive,' Slick retorted. 'This town is an abomination.'

'What about the palace?' Dunk said. 'Look at those towers stabbing into the sky. Have you ever seen anything that tall?'

'Seems to me the sign of a sovereign who's overcompensating for some other shortcoming, if you follow me, son.' Slick hacked on the thick air. 'How are you going to be able to play in this stuff without losing a lung?'

'Don't you fret about that, Mr. Fullbelly,' Cavre said. 'The Buckingham Bowl where the Far Albion Cup games are held is enchanted to provide clear air and good weather at all times.'

'How'd they manage that?' Slick said. 'You'd think if they could afford to clean up the area around the stadium they'd at least do the same for the King's own palace.'

'The BBC paid for it, of course,' Simon said.

'BBC?'

'Boring-Brilliant Cabalvision. They broadcast all the games. If the air around the stadium was like it is here in the Smoke, their subscribers wouldn't be able to see a thing.'

'They're both boring and brilliant?' Dunk asked.

Deckem arrived at the railing and slipped into the conversation. It struck Dunk that he was the only one of the new recruits he'd ever heard speak. 'Those were the names of the founders: Billy Boring and Bobby Brilliant.'

'You have to be kidding,' Lästiges said. The camra circled her head at high speed, trying to fan the stench away.

'You can't make stuff like this up, Miss Weibchen.'

THE CROWD ROARED as the Hackers took the field for their first game in the Far Albion Cup. By this time, Dunk's sense of smell had already gone dead. The night before, at dinner, he'd realised that this was why the Albionmen ate such bland food. With their noses so effectively deadened, what was the point in making flavourful meals? No one could taste them anyway.

Here in the Buckingham Bowl, though, under its protective enchantments, his senses came alive again. He inhaled the crisp, clean air through his nose, and a smile spread across his face.

'I love the smell of Astrogranite in the morning,' Guillermo said as he trotted out onto the gridiron beside Dunk, stripes of black painted under his eyes, in the way of all of Nuffle's faithful. 'It smells like – hey, I can smell again!'

Dunk grinned under his helmet. He wore the war paint too, although for him it was purely a practical matter. The black paint cut down on the glare of the sun under his eyes, which made it easier for him to look for a catcher downfield. He didn't believe in Nuffle or any of the dozens of other gods worshipped across the Old World and beyond. He wasn't above using their best tricks for himself though.

A voice echoed out over the stadium's Preternatural Announcement system. 'And, all the way in from the Empire, please give a warm, Albion welcome to the Bad Bay Hackers!'

An image of a man dressed in a sheepskin coat stared down at the stadium from the Jumboball on the north end of the field. Dunk shuddered as he looked at the thing, not from the man's wild grin but the memory of his last encounter with such a device. Fortunately, this Jumboball weighed in smaller than the one in the *Spike! Magazine* Tournament, and it sat on a large, round pedestal instead of the easily sabotaged legs that had held up the one in Magritta.

'That's Mon Jotson,' Simon said proudly. 'He's a living legend around here. He's been commenting on our games for hundreds of years.'

Dunk looked carefully at the man and detected the telltale pointiness to his ears and other features that labelled him an elf. His brown hair looked like it had long ago formed into a helmet itself, as it stayed perfectly rigid in the winds that flapped the flags standing behind him. He wore a pair of wide, round spectacles with wooden rims that seemed to turn his face into that of an owl.

'Yessir,' Jotson said, 'it's not every day we get a visitor from out of town to play in the finest tournament in our land. The last one I remember was from just last year at this very event. The Evil Gitz, as they were called, only lasted a single round before our fine gentlemen from the Kent Kickers bought them a one-way ticket back home.'

Dunk laughed.

'That's no joke, Mr. Hoffnung,' Deckem said as he waved to the crowd. Even in a Hackers green-and-gold uniform, the man seemed to be dressed all in black. He exuded the colour in everything he did and said. 'The Kickers are the wealthiest team in the land. They paid off enough of the Gits that the visitors had to forfeit the game.'

'Aren't we playing them today?' Dunk asked.

Cavre nodded. 'They already tried to buy us off,' he said. 'Pegleg refused to talk with them unless they were willing to match the tournament's grand prize.'

'Why would they do that?' Dunk said.

Cavre slapped the thrower on his right shoulder pad. 'Now you're catching on, Mr. Hoffnung.'

As team captain, Cavre met the leader of the Kickers in the middle of the field for the coin toss. He called 'Eagles' and won. The Hackers swarmed down to the south end of the field to receive the kick-off.

The ball came sailing down the field toward Dunk, and he called for the catch. Before the ball reached him, though, Deckem dashed forward and plucked it from the air.

Dunk tried to protest, but Deckem sprinted up the field before Dunk could even open his mouth. All he could do was chase the new blitzer up the field and try to help.

As the first of the Kickers – dressed all in blue with a white helmet that featured a blue boot on each side – reached Deckem, the oncoming player launched himself into the air and aimed a vicious kick at the new Hacker's head. Deckem dodged the attack neatly, and drilled his opponent straight in the groin with a powerful jab of his free hand. The player dropped to the ground, writhing in pain.

Before the next Kicker could try to tackle Deckem, Swift and Dickens came at him from both sides, crushing him between them. Blood burst between the bars in the Kicker's face guard, and he fell to the Astrogranite and did not move again.

'Ouch!' Jotson's voice said. 'That sort of killing blow could really hurt someone!'

Another Kicker charged up and hurled a roundhouse kick at Deckem. Anticipating the attack, Deckem spun and pitched the ball backward to M'Grash, who bobbled it a few times before tucking it into the palm of his hand. Then he turned to block the Kicker still coming at him.

Deckem reached up and caught the Kicker's foot as it sailed through the air at him. In a single, smooth motion, he spun around, using the Kicker's momentum to slam him into the Astrogranite. Then he grabbed the Kicker's helmet and gave his neck a sharp, horrible twist.

At that point, Dunk lost track of the new Hacker. A trio of Kickers came straight at M'Grash, doing their level best to knock the ogre to the ground. M'Grash snarled at them, and Dunk noticed a dark, wet patch appear in the front of one player's pants.

'We don't see too many ogres in the Far Albion League,' said Jotson's voice. 'From the looks of Major's uniform, he may have just encountered his first!'

As they'd done in practice countless times, M'Grash swivelled back and handed the ball off to Dunk. The thrower tucked the ball under his arm and followed the ogre into the fray. There were few players as accomplished at blocking as M'Grash. He had a way of clearing a runner's path that none of the other Hackers could match.

While M'Grash made quick work of most of the Kickers who came his way, Dunk knew that one of them would eventually figure out how to get around the ogre and attack the ball carrier: him. He kept his eyes open downfield, hunting for a team-mate who was open for a pass.

To his surprise, a tree stood in the end zone. He'd seen a lot of strange things on the various fields on which the Hacker's had played, but most of them had gone to great lengths to remove large obstacles like that, especially in the end zone. The Athelorn Avengers' home field sat atop the Great Tree of the Greenwood, of course, but even that only had a few large branches that stuck through from below.

For a moment, Dunk wondered why someone had draped the tree in green and gold cloth. Perhaps a Hackers fan had gone to the trouble to decorate it. Then the tree waved its upper branches at Dunk, and the thrower realised he was looking straight at Edgar.

Dunk cocked back his arm to chuck the ball into Edgar's waiting branches. Just then, though, a Kicker dashed through between M'Grash's trunk-like legs and barrelled straight at him.

Dunk snarled at his challenger and tucked the ball under his left arm. With his right, he lashed out at the Kicker and smashed him in his exposed throat. The man collapsed, clutching his dented windpipe, and Dunk had to repress the strong urge to finish him off while he was down.

The feeling disturbed Dunk. He'd never been a dirty player. Sure, he knew the rules in Blood Bowl were more of a set of loosely followed suggestions, but he didn't believe he had to hurt people just to win games.

Right now, though, it was all he could do to pull himself away from murdering the hapless Kicker sprawled out before him. It would only take one, short move, and the Kickers would be down one more player. If that might help the Hackers win the game, wasn't it the right thing to do? If he really wanted to win, shouldn't he be willing to pull out all the stops?

Dunk pushed those thoughts aside and stepped back into the open area that M'Grash always left in his wake. He cocked his arm back and hurled the ball down the field. It spiralled smoothly through the air, arcing up into the sky like a shooting star and then landing square in Edgar's branches.

'Touchdown!' Jotson shouted. 'Our aggressive guests take the early lead from our proxy hosts, the Kickers. If things stay like this, there will be no stopping them!'

Somewhere, a referee blew a whistle and signalled the score. M'Grash scooped Dunk up in his arms and trotted back over to the Hacker bench, where he set the thrower down.

'Excellent work, men!' Pegleg said, almost crowing with delight. 'Perhaps it's true what they say about the team who owns the Far Albion Cup. You look unbeatable out there!'

'Oh, dear,' Jotson's voice said. 'A few of the Kickers would be more than just depressed about that last score if they weren't too dead to care. I count five casualties on the field, and a sixth – that's Clive Keegan, hometown favourite – being carted off the field with what looks like a crushed windpipe. We'll have to check in with the Kicker apothecary to see what his chances are for coming back into the game.'

Dunk's stomach sank at the news.

'Fantastic!' Pegleg said, happier than ever. 'Now they only have ten players left. The only thing better than taking the lead is doing it while crushing your foes' bodies and spirits!' The coach's face turned sharp. 'How are you all doing?'

Dunk knew what Pegleg was getting at. In games this bloody, it was rare for the damage to be one-sided. Once the initial victims figured out what kind of game they were in, they usually tossed all compunction out of the stadium and worked the bloodletting angle as hard as they could.

The thrower turned to see one of the new players, Shelley, cradling his left arm. When Dunk looked closer to see what was wrong, he noticed it was no longer attached at the elbow. Despite this, Shelley seemed able to ignore the pain.

'Are you okay?' Dunk asked.

Deckem answered. 'He'll be fine. Just give him a few minutes. He'll be set to play in time for the next kick-off.'

Dunk goggled at the new Hacker. 'You're kidding, right?'

'I never kid.'

DUNK SAID NOTHING to Pegleg, and no one else seemed to notice Shelley's injury. The thrower wanted to see how Shelley could possibly take the field again in this game. Despite what Deckem had promised, Dunk didn't think a player missing an arm would be much good to anyone.

By the time the Hackers were ready for the next kick-off, though, Shelley seemed fine. He even waved at Dunk with the arm that the thrower had seen detached just a moment before. He wondered if he could have been mistaken about the extent of Shelley's injuries. After all, Dunk always spent every Blood Bowl game pumped on adrenaline, and he guessed it might have made him see things that weren't there.

Then Cavre kicked the ball over the heads of most of the Kickers, and the game started up again.

The rest of the game was a blur for Dunk, who spent most of his time trying to avoid getting killed by the Kickers. The shock of losing so many of their players wore off fast, it seemed, and now they were determined to inflict even greater losses on the Hackers. Most of the players completely ignored the ball, setting out to break some bones instead.

'I'm going to tear off your arms!' a Kicker snarled at Dunk after planting a snap-kick straight into the thrower's gut. Lying on the

Astrogranite, gasping for breath, Dunk realised there wasn't a damn thing he could do to stop the Kicker from making good on his pledge.

Then Shelley smashed into the Kicker from behind and laid him out flat. They landed next to Dunk, close enough so he could feel the ground shake from their impact. The Kicker's helmet came off and dribbled away across the field, exposing him as a thick-cut man with short-cropped, dark hair and a series of scars on his face that made his face look more like a treeman's than a human's.

The Kicker reached back, grabbed Shelley by the arm, and pulled. The limb separated at the elbow once again, and the Kicker found himself holding Shelley's forearm in his fist. He screamed at the sight of the amputated arm before he dropped it and tried to scramble away.

Dunk saw that the arm had torn stitches running all the way around its elbow end. Stranger yet, while he'd expected to see blood pouring from the end of it, there was not a single drop.

Shelley picked up his forearm in his other hand and smashed it down on the Kicker's helmet like a hammer. The Kicker screamed in horror until Shelley smashed him with the loose arm again. It must have been like bringing a hammer down on the Kicker's skull. After the second blow, he fell silent, but Shelley kept beating the Kicker's face into a bloody mess. The whole time, he never said a word.

Jotson's voice kept up a steady commentary on the action, though it didn't seem to all be happening in front of Dunk.

'By all the stones in the henge, that's some serious killing going on down there. I haven't seen this kind of mayhem since – well, since last week, at least! Have you ever witnessed a tougher team than these Hackers? Shelley there is beating Percy to death with his own arm! That's one way to give a man a hand – into the grave!

'Of course, Stevenson's having his way with Silver on the other end of the field. He seems to be under the mistaken impression that Silver's head is the ball, as he's taken to spiking it in the end zone. Sorry, friend, but that's not going to score points with anyone but the fans!

'At midfield, it's Dickens and Swift having a go at Bantam, pulling his legs apart and cracking him like he was a wishbone. The Kickers can only wonder if the referee got a premium price for self-induced blindness during this game or if the Hackers robbed him as well!'

Something black and white and red all over came spinning through the air at Dunk. At first, he thought it might be the football, which he'd lost track of, and he threw up his hands to catch it. Then he noticed its strange colours, and he dodged out of the way instead. More than one Blood Bowl player had reflexively caught a bomb when he thought it was the game ball, and Dunk wasn't about to make the same mistake as Stumpy Kajowski.

The 'ball' sailed over Dunk's head and bounced three times before rolling to a rest on the Astrogranite behind him. When it came to a stop, he saw it for what it was: a human head wearing a black-and-white striped cap.

Dunk stared back down the field from where the head had come and spotted Simon standing over the referee's decapitated corpse, an insane grin on his face. The catcher's eyes flashed red at Dunk before he trotted away down the field.

'It looks like... It could be... Yes! He could... go... all... the... way!' Jotson's voice shouted. 'Touchdown, Hackers!'

The crowd roared, although whether with outrage or delight, Dunk couldn't tell. He was just thankful that the action had stopped for a moment and he could get his bearings again.

'Who scored that?' Dunk asked as he ran back over to the Hackers' bench.

'Deckem certainly hasn't lost any of his panache,' Jotson said. 'It's good to have him back out of retirement. I knew that fatal injury of his wouldn't keep him down!'

Dunk glanced back at the Jumboball to see an instant replay of the score. In the huge image, Deckem sprinted toward the goal line, the football tucked under his arm. As he neared the end zone, a large Kicker stepped between him and the goal. Deckem stuck out his arm and drove it into the Kicker's chest as he shoved him back over the plane of the goal line.

In the image, the crowd in the end zone seats behind Deckem went nuts. The new Hacker stood over the unconscious Kicker's form and hurled the ball up toward the cheap seats. Then he threw something else that landed even further up into the stands. A fight broke out in both locations as the fans trampled each other for a chance to claim Deckem's discarded prizes.

'Good work, Mr. Deckem!' Pegleg said. 'We're up two to nothing, and it's only halfway through the first half.'

Dunk turned to see Deckem trotting up behind him, still waving at the wild, adoring crowd. His hands were covered in blood, but not a drop of sweat marred his smooth, pale brow.

'Thanks, coach,' Deckem said with a smile. 'I don't believe in toying with my prey. It's an act of mercy to end things as soon as possible.'

'Great Nuffle's cooler of Hater-Aid!' Jotson said. 'Do you see what that second present Deckem sent to his fans is?'

The image on the Jumboball zoomed in tight on a tattooed dwarf with a bright-orange mohawk and more piercings than an archery target. He roared in triumph as he smashed aside the other treasure-hunters and thrust his prize aloft in a bloodied fist.

It was a battered human heart, still beating from the looks of it.

'Crikey! I have ten quid that says that ends up on B-BA tonight and fetches a princely sum!'

'Bee-bay?' M'Grash said, scratching his head.

'The Blood Bowl Auction network,' Slick said. The halfling stood on the end of the Hackers' bench, looking up at the Jumboball too.

'Yessir! Who wouldn't want to have that up on their mantel?' Jotson asked. 'But wait!'

The camra panned over to show a force of blue-uniformed knights in blood-spattered armour slashing their way through the crowd. Most of the fans parted before their wedge formation, and those that didn't tasted the knights' steel.

'It looks like the Kickers have sent their cheerleaders into the stands to get that vital part of Hartshorn's anatomy back. With luck, their team apothecary will be able to get it back into him in time!'

The dwarf clambered up on the shoulders of a nearby fan and held the heart aloft again, defying the armoured cheerleaders, daring them to take it from him. The crowd growled in anticipation of the coming fight, and the cheerleaders marched on undeterred by the dwarf's antics.

Just as the knights reached the dwarf, he tossed the heart back to a tall, thin, dark-haired man standing behind him, and then launched himself into the knights. Spreading his compact form out as much as he could, he bowled over the front two ranks of the knights. They might have all gone over if the crowd rushing in behind them hadn't been forced to hold them up for fear of being crushed themselves.

The man with the heart bobbled it for a moment, and then caught it tight. As he did, one of the cheerleaders broke free from the dwarf and pointed her sword straight at the man's neck. Terrified, the man pitched the heart farther up into the stands and then dived down over the gawkers standing below him.

The fans below caught the man and started to pass him toward the exit, overjoyed at the chance to foil the cheerleaders' efforts. At the same time, the fan who caught the slippery heart hurled it counterclockwise along the stands, straight into another section. The crowd cheered, and the noise went up time and again as fan after fan who found himself holding the heart tossed it on again.

Dunk stared at Deckem in disgust as the man grinned up at the images on the Jumboball. 'You would rip out a man's heart just to score a touchdown?' Dunk asked. 'He couldn't have stopped you anyway. You didn't have to kill him. What kind of player would do that?'

Deckem turned and looked the thrower straight in the eyes. The smile had left his face. 'A winner,' he said before he turned and headed for the locker room.

* * *

'THOSE GUYS SCARE me,' Dunk said before he took another pull from his ale.

'You're not the only one,' Slick said, gazing around the cosy pub – a well-appointed place called the Cock and Bull – every inch of which seemed panelled in dark, rich woods. 'I've never seen so many people blow off a victory dinner as I did tonight. I poked my nose into the dining room at the inn, and the only ones there were Pegleg, Cavre, and Deckem and his four stooges.'

'Not even Simon?' Dunk rubbed his chin as he gazed around the room. One of the first things he'd noticed about the place was that it had no Cabalvision. That alone had been enough to recommend the place. Dunk didn't feel like sitting though endless replays and joking commentary about that afternoon's game – or "wholesale massacre", as one of the BBC anchors had called it. 'I thought for sure he'd be whooping it up with his fellow countrymen.'

'Maybe he has other friends in town, folks who aren't so murderous.'

'We won, didn't we?' Dunk said. He waved for another beer, even as he polished off the one in his hand. 'Isn't that what it's all about? Win the tournament, grab the prize? The wealth of kings and the adulation of the fans?'

Slick nodded slowly, as if trying to convince himself of Dunk's words. 'That's the standard story, son, the one we all try to sell ourselves. Sad thing, isn't it, that it so rarely turns out that way?'

Dunk narrowed his eyes at the halfling for a moment. 'What do you mean?'

'Well, it's all just a big fairy tale, isn't it?' Slick leaned back in his chair, which was much too large for him, forcing him to bring his legs up so that his feet hung out over the edge of the seat. 'I mean, how many Blood Bowl teams are there?'

Dunk shook his head. He had no idea. 'Dozens?'

'More like hundreds if you count all those local club teams full of amateurs who play for the "fun" of it.'

Dunk accepted his next beer from the barmaid, a pretty, blonde woman dressed in a farm girl's clothes.

'Thanks,' Dunk said. 'Cheers, I mean.'

The barmaid smiled. 'You're not from around these parts, are you, love?'

Dunk shook his head, his thoughts drawn to the people back home he missed most: Spinne and his brother Dirk.

'Business or pleasure?' she asked.

'A bit of both,' Dunk said. 'We're here for the tournament.'

'Cor blimey,' the woman said, her blue eyes sparkling. 'It's been a cracking good tourney so far, hasn't it? That game this afternoon? What a bleeding bloodbath.'

Dunk's face froze. 'You like that sort of thing?'

The barmaid stuck out her bottom lip as she considered the question. 'I dunno, really. I don't normally care much for Blood Bowl. Too much going on, if you ask me. I'm more of a *real* football fan myself.'

'But you watched that "bloodbath" this afternoon?'

'Not really,' she said. 'I caught the replay on the chryssy. Just the highlights.'

'That's all you care for?'

'Well, I know there's a lot more to the game than fighting and killing, but that's all over my head, innit? It's like when you watch the chariot races. The only part anyone cares about are the crashes.'

Dunk hoisted his beer to the woman and said, 'Cheers.' She wandered off to find others in need of drink.

What the woman had said crawled around in Dunk's guts like a long-tailed rat. He knew all that most of the fans cared about was action, but were people really that bloodthirsty? Could they ignore the fact that real people were killed in front of them? And that they cheered to see it?

'What were you saying?' Dunk said to Slick.

'There are hundreds of Blood Bowl teams out there. Thousands of players. How many of them can be winners?'

'About half of them, every week,' Dunk said.

'No, no, no, son. I'm talking about real winners. How many can win one of the four major tournaments? How many have any kind of a shot at playing in the Blood Bowl, much less winning the trophy? Just a handful of teams.'

Slick moved forward in the chair until his legs dangled over the edge. As he spoke, he gestured with his hands to punctuate his points, warming to his subject. 'Maybe a dozen teams have a shot at the title every year – probably less than that. But how many of those teams *think* they're in that top dozen?'

Dunk shrugged.

'Dozens more. Maybe even hundreds. Half of the teams out there, at least. They think they can win it all, and they're dead wrong. Just ask the Gobbo next time you see him. Ask him how many teams have odds to win the title that are in the single digits.'

'I don't know if I'll see him again if I keep hanging out with you.' Dunk thought back to how the halfling had tried to beat the bookie up back in Magritta, and a smile flitted across his face. He washed it down with another swig of his beer.

Slick rolled his eyes. 'The *point* here – and I do have one, son – is that most Blood Bowl players spend their entire career chasing after a dream they have no real chance of achieving. They'd be better off shopping around for headstones instead. They're about ten times more likely to need one of those rather than a free spot on their hand for a championship ring.'

Dunk nodded, and Slick fell silent. They both worked at their beers for a moment, neither of them wanting to speak before the other. Finally, Dunk gave in.

'Are you telling me to quit?'

Slick looked across the table toward Dunk, a sad frown on his face. 'You're a big boy,' the halfling said. 'I can't tell you to do anything. Hell, I'm not sure what I want you to do myself. We've had a great ride with the Hackers over the past year. That bonus cheque we got at the end of the last season put quite a few good pies in me.'

Slick rubbed his belly at that thought. 'But money's no good to someone who's too dead to spend it.'

Dunk took another pull at his beer and considered this. After a while, he shook his head. 'I can't do it,' he said. 'I can't leave the team.'

'Why not?' The halfling asked the question as if he wanted to know what Dunk wanted for dinner.

'What would the team do without me?' Dunk said. 'They wouldn't have enough players to play. They'd have to forfeit.'

Slick snapped his fingers. 'You'd be replaced like that. There are always people desperate to get on to a decent Blood Bowl team. Just look at Deckem and his friends. Pegleg didn't even have to go looking for them. They came hunting for him.'

'But they're my friends,' Dunk said. 'What about Cavre or Simon or Guillermo or M'Grash? I can't leave them to fend for themselves.'

'Why not? They were there before you came around, and they'll manage well enough after you leave.'

'What's the first thing I told you about Blood Bowl?' Slick said.

Dunk had to think back about that one. 'When someone offers you a contract, get it in writing?'

'Yes! But that's not what I meant. What else?'

'Never shower with an orc?'

Slick nodded. 'That's a good one too, but it's not what I meant. What else?'

'It's only a foul if the ref sees it?'

'Wow, son. I am a positive fount of wisdom, but that's–' The halfling raised his hands to cut Dunk off. 'Here it is, the relevant secret: Never make friends with the other players.'

'What?' Dunk said.

'You never know when you might get traded or released. The people you're playing alongside this week could be your mortal foes the next. Don't get too attached to any particular team because you might find yourself having to play against them next week.'

'You never said that,' Dunk said.

Slick squinted at his client. 'Are you sure?'

'Yes.'

'Hm,' Slick said. 'Well it's good advice no matter when you get it. Sorry I skipped over it the first time around.'

'I think you're making things up as you go along.'

The halfling grinned up at the young man. 'You know, for a Blood Bowl player, you're pretty smart.'

'Such faint praise,' Dunk said.

'Hey, I can only work with what you give me. I'm an agent, not a miracle worker – your career rocketing toward the top aside.'

'I thought I was responsible for that.'

'See, son,' Slick said, reaching out a hand to pat Dunk's arm. 'That just goes to show how little it is you know.'

Dunk smirked. 'Thankfully I have you to watch out for me.'

'I think you could do better than that.' Deckem stepped around a pillar of polished wood. 'A player of your talents deserves a first-rate agent.'

Slick stood up on his chair. 'They don't get any better, pal!'

Deckem smiled at the halfling, and then pointedly ignored him. 'You are a fine player, Mr. Hoffnung. I admire your skills on the field. Even if they aren't as refined as my own, you have a great deal of natural talent for the game.'

'That's kind of you,' Dunk said, picking his words with care.

'I'd encourage you to stick around,' Deckem said. 'As Mr. Fullbelly points out, you could be replaced, but I don't think that would be in the best interests of the team. The more original Hackers on the team, the better. From a marketing point of view, at least. Otherwise, we become just another FA League team rather than the newest kids on the block. There is some mileage to be extracted from that if we are willing to squeeze hard enough.'

'I'll keep that in mind.'

'Of course, if you did leave, my friends might decide we were better off without the rest of the Hackers. I've done my best to convince them otherwise, but they are rather… single-minded.'

Dunk stood up at that. 'Are you saying you'll kill the others if I leave?'

Only Deckem's eyes smiled. 'I would never say that, Mr. Hoffnung,' he said as he turned to leave. 'But I would never say it couldn't happen either. You're a smart lad. Keep that in mind, would you?'

As Deckem left, Dunk slumped back into his seat, stunned. 'What? What should I do? What am I going to do?'

'Barmaid!' Slick said, motioning for the waitress to bring them another round. 'I think we're going to be here a while!'

THE KICK-OFF FOR the Hackers' next game went just as badly as the first – at least from Dunk's point of view.

'Cracking!' Mon Jotson's voice said over the PA system. 'Over the past week, fans, I've done some research on the new darlings of our little ball. The Far Albion Cup has been kind to the Hackers so far. Their Casualties Inflicted per Game has skyrocketed since they arrived in fair Albion. If that last play is any indication, they're on their way to bumping up their numbers once again!

'I see one, two, three – oh who can count them all? Some of them are in parts! There are at least five bodies in Mancaster Knighted uniforms scattered across the field. '

The news made Dunk feel sick. 'How many did we lose?' he asked.

'One of Deckem's men lost a leg,' Slick said. 'But he seems to be doing fine.'

Dunk followed the halfling's gaze over to where the team apothecary – a wizened old, woman with a swing-down monocle attached to a black band around her head – sat stitching Swift's leg back on at the knee. Even with it barely attached, the Hacker could still move the foot that had just been separated from him.

'Who are these guys?' Dunk asked. 'Could you learn anything about them?'

Slick shook his head. 'The whole country knows Deckem, but the rest of his contingent is a real mystery. Despite the fact they play great ball, no one's ever heard of them before.'

Dunk spotted Lästiges standing in the corner of the Hacker's dugout, behind Slick. He hadn't seen her since the morning she'd raced from her bed, almost a week ago. For his part, that had been fine. He knew he hadn't done anything wrong, but skating that close to the edge had upset him. If he hadn't seen anything of the reporter until the trip back to the Old World – or even later than that – he would not have minded.

She nodded at him tentatively, her usual aggressive bravado put aside, at least for the moment. He knew he should go over and talk to her, clear the air between them, but now wasn't the right time.

'How much longer do we have to put up with them?' Dunk asked.

'As long as we keep winning games, Mr. Hoffnung,' Pegleg said, slapping his starting thrower on the back. Dunk had never seen the ex-pirate happier.

'Coach,' Dunk said. 'Some of us are worried about our new team-mates. They're a little – well, violent.' As the words spilled out of Dunk's mouth, he regretted them. They sounded feeble even to his ears.

Pegleg laughed. 'It's a violent game,' he said. 'People die. Or don't you remember our last match in Magritta?'

Dunk nodded. He didn't think he'd ever forget it.

'It's a kill or be killed game, Dunk.' Pegleg's manner had turned softer now. 'If you're going to play, it's best to be on the side of the killers.'

'But it doesn't have to be that way,' Dunk said. 'We could just play the game – outscore the other team.'

'A win is a win. I spent enough years with nothing but losses. I'll take a win any way I can get it.'

'That's the kind of attitude I like to hear, coach,' Deckem said, strolling up to where Pegleg stood over Dunk on the bench. The new blitzer wiped his bloodstained hands off on his jersey as he spoke. 'A winning attitude.'

Dunk leapt to his feet and glared right into Deckem's eyes. 'If you're such a winner, why'd you ever leave the game in the first place?' he asked. 'Why'd you retire?'

Dark amusement danced in Deckem's ice-blue eyes as he smirked at Dunk. 'Strictly speaking, Mr. Hoffnung, I never did retire. I was killed.'

Dunk mulled that over. He'd long suspected that Deckem and his friends had long since felt the last beats of their own hearts. That wasn't too unusual in Blood Bowl players though. The Champions of

Death, the Erengrad Undertakers, the Zilargan Zombies, the Crimson Vampires – all of those teams featured all-undead rosters.

But they all had necromancers – sorcerers of death – as either coaches or owners too. Pegleg was many things – most of which he refused to share with his players – but he was no necromancer.

'Who brought you back?' Dunk asked. 'Or did you manage that all by your lonesome?'

'Now, now, Mr. Hoffnung,' Deckem said as he jammed his bright yellow helmet back on to his head. 'We all have our secrets. Let me keep mine, and I won't pry too hard into yours.'

The new Hacker turned and sprinted back out on to the field, and the crowd went wild. Dunk looked up and saw Deckem's grinning face on the Jumboball. The undead player spat something thick and black through the bars of his helmet, then winked right at the camra.

'What's this?' Jotson's voice said. 'I think we may have a new record for the shortest game ever in the Far Albion Cup! Four of the remaining Knighted players are refusing to take the field!'

Dunk glanced across the gridiron to see the Knighted coach screaming at his reluctant players, but they were already on their way to the locker room. The fans booed and hurled full steins of beer at the players, which bounced off one Knighted's helmet, but this only made the players who were left decide to join them.

'I've never seen anything like this,' Jotson said. 'What cowards! This will forever be a blight on the unimpeachable honour of the great city of Mancaster and its much-vaunted Knighted. But wait! What's this?'

Dunk stared off across the field at the Knighted coach as he tackled one of his own players. The crowd roared in delight as the coach tore the player's helmet off and started to strip him of his uniform.

'Feefa's spotted balls!' Jotson said. 'It looks like Coach Fergus Alexson has decided to take out all his frustration on Team Captain Neville Rooney, and poor Rooney's getting the worst of that match-up. Perhaps you'd have been safer on the pitch, Neville.'

'What is he doing, Dunkel?' M'Grash asked from over the thrower's shoulder.

Dunk shook his head, amazed. He looked back and saw that all of the living Hackers were lined up behind him, staring out at the spectacle too. Deckem and his crew still stood down near the Hacker's end zone, ready to kick the ball off again. None of the others had joined them yet.

'It looks like he's stripping his own player down to his briefs.'

'He's taking his uniform,' Carve said. 'For himself.'

'What?' Guillermo said. 'Why would he do something as insane as that?'

'The game's not over yet,' Simon said. 'Fergie hasn't forfeited yet, and the ref hasn't called it.'

'What ref?' Slick asked sarcastically.

Edgar remained silent, but Dunk thought he detected a guilty look on his wooden face.

'Dear Nuffle,' Pegleg said, his voice heavy with awe. 'He's going out there himself.'

The living Hackers all turned to goggle at their coach, and then went back to watching Coach Alexson kick his battered player away from him and start to put on the stripped uniform, starting with the pads. The crowd fell silent for a moment, unable to understand what it was that Alexson had in mind. When Alexson slammed Rooney's helmet onto his head and trotted out onto the gridiron though, they went nuts.

The Jumboball showed the Knighted coach charging onto the field and getting ready to receive the kick-off. When the roar of the crowd died down enough that Dunk could hear again, Jotson's voice spoke. 'This is inconceivable, yet not entirely unexpected. If you could ever expect any coach to stand up for the honour of his team, it would be Fergie. Even with all of his players abandoning him, he stands unwilling to surrender. He prefers death to dishonour.'

The image on the Jumboball switched to that of Deckem glaring down the field at Fergie and cracking his knuckles. The other Hackers on the field mirrored his actions.

'And if Deckem has his way, Fergie will get his wish. Oh, the drama! The Knighted coach – one of Albion's favourite sons – faces five of the killer Hackers – invaders from the Old World! While you have to admire such gumption, you can't imagine that old Alexson has a chance here. Farewell, Fergie, it is then! We'll remember you well!'

'No,' M'Grash said, frowning and shaking his head.

Dunk knew just what the ogre meant. 'We can't let them do this.'

'What's that, mate?' Simon said. No one but Slick and M'Grash had been able to hear Dunk over the roar of the crowd.

'We can't let them do this!' Dunk shouted. 'We have to stop it.' He looked to the others for support.

M'Grash bore a grin into which he could have stuffed a pig. The more restrained Slick nodded in approval. Guillermo and Simon goggled at Dunk as if he'd suddenly sprouted another head that had begun reciting epic poetry in a long-forgotten tongue. Edgar looked aghast. The unreadable Cavre's face remained impassive, betraying no thoughts at all.

In stark contrast, Pegleg was livid. His fiery glare forbade Dunk to do anything unusual here. 'Belay that, Mr. Hoffnung,' he snarled. 'If you take one step on to that field, you'll be warming the bench for the rest of the game.'

Dunk locked eyes with the ex-pirate. There was no doubt that Pegleg meant to threaten much worse than that. The game would be over here in minutes anyway, one way or the other. Then Dunk looked up at the Jumboball.

There, framed in the giant crystal, crouched Fergus Alexson. Dunk had never seen the man play before, but he'd heard about the man's reputation as a coach. Despite his greying hair, he had the fit and ready body of an athlete, someone who trained alongside his players. But there was no doubt in Dunk's mind that Deckem and his pals would tear Fergie apart in a matter of seconds.

Dunk strode out onto the gridiron and walked straight toward Deckem. The crowd – thinking that Dunk was going to help his teammates annihilate Fergie – booed.

'Hello, Mr. Hoffnung!' Deckem said over the noise. 'Come to take your place with the winners?'

'You can't do this,' Dunk said. 'This is pointless. That man doesn't need to die.'

'But he does,' Deckem said. 'Killing him sends a message to everyone that there's nothing the Hackers aren't willing to do to win.'

'You're not a Hacker,' Dunk said. 'I don't care if you wear the uniform. You're a disgrace to it.'

'I think that's up to Coach Pegleg,' Deckem said, 'not you. He seems to appreciate my efforts, no matter how crude my methods may be.'

'He's not here right now. *I'm* telling you to stop it.'

Half amused, Deckem raised an eyebrow at this. 'No. Now get out of my way, or I'll kill you too.'

Dunk had learned a lot of things in his misspent youth. As two sons of nobility, he and his brother Dirk had wandered through many of the slums of Altdorf, looking for trouble, for some excitement in their safe and placid lives. They'd found plenty of it, and sometimes a brawl came arm in arm with it.

Many times, Dirk had thrown the first punch, starting the whole fight – or so it seemed. This irritated Dunk for a long time, as he didn't care for fighting like Dirk did, so one day he confronted him about it.

'Why do you always start all these fights?' Dunk asked him one night over a bottle of Bugman's Best Ale in their favourite hole in the wall, a dive called the Skinned Cat.

Dirk just smiled. 'I don't start any of the fights. I finish them.'

'You know what I mean. You always hit the other guy first.'

Dirk sipped his beer and smiled. 'When I'm standing nose to nose with a guy like that, do you think there's going to be a fight?'

'There always is.'

'And who do you think is going to win that fight?'

'Usually it's you.'

'Always,' Dirk said, raising a finger. 'I always win. You know why? *Because* I hit first.'

'But you could just walk away.'

'You think that guy's just going to let me walk away? What about that orc in the Full Moon the other night. Think he'd have just let me traipse out of the pub?'

'But–'

'But, nothing. He'd have clocked me from behind, and you'd have ended up carrying me home that night.'

'I did.'

'Those victory celebrations do sometimes get out of hand.' Dirk smiled at the memory. Then he turned serious again. 'Instead, I hit him first. He starts the fight wounded, one good hit behind me. I may not be the biggest dog on the block. I may not be the best fighter. But give me an edge like that, and I'll come out on top every time.'

These thoughts shot through Dunk's head as Deckem stood nose to nose with him, daring him to try to stop him. Dunk reached out and put his hands on Deckem's shoulders. The new player glanced down at his arms and said, 'I'm really not in the mood for a hug.'

Dunk pulled the man to him and drove his head forward at the same time. His head-butt smashed Deckem's nose flat and cracked his head back so hard Dunk thought he felt the man' neck break. When he let go of Deckem's shoulders, the man collapsed to the Astrogranite.

The crowd cheered louder than ever.

As Dunk stepped back from where Deckem sat, the man's four friends started toward the thrower. Dunk knew he had no hope to take them all on at once. While he'd been able to surprise Deckem, these four were alert, ready, and not going to wait for him to attack.

'Now, guys, can't we talk about this?' he said, getting ready to turn and run. He thought he might be able to outdistance them in a short sprint to the Hackers' dugout. As undead, though, they wouldn't tire and would catch him if the chase went on for long.

Then Dunk felt the earth move beneath his feet, a low, thrumming he felt through his boots. He recognised it from dozens of games, and he grinned. He glanced over his shoulder to see M'Grash and Edgar stampeding toward him, rushing to his aid. Cavre, Guillermo, and Simon raced along behind them, unable to match their long-legged pace.

'Do not hurt Dunkel!' the ogre roared. 'He's my friend!'

'Incredible!' Jotson's voice said. 'Now it's the Hackers against the Hackers! Perhaps Fergie has a chance after all!'

The crowd cheered the thought, and Dunk saw an image of himself grinning, gazing out from the Jumboball. For a moment, seeing his head forty feet tall stunned him, but then Dickens lunged at him.

Dunk dived to the side. He refused to get into a fair fight with Dickens or any of the rest of Deckem's cronies. He'd seen them take apart nearly a dozen players already, and he had no desire to be the next notch on their collective belt.

Dickens flew past him and skidded along the ground. Before he came to a stop, M'Grash picked him up and hauled him into the air. The ogre held the man so that their noses almost touched. Dickens's feet kicked out wildly, hitting nothing, as he dangled in the air.

'Don't!' M'Grash shouted into Dickens's face.

Dickens twisted about like a hanged man trying to wriggle out of his noose. Then something popped loose, and he fell to the ground, leaving his helmet in M'Grash's meaty hand.

It took Dunk a moment to realise that Dickens's head was still in his helmet.

'Well,' Jotson said. 'Would you look at that? That's going to leave a mark.'

The crowd roared its approval.

M'Grash peered into the helmet through its faceguard and screamed in surprise. Without thinking – something the ogre rarely did – M'Grash flung the helmet away, and it went sailing into the stands.

Dunk stared in horror, but even before Dickens's occupied helmet landed something hit the thrower from behind. He spun around in the green-armed grasp to find Swift tackling him to the ground.

They hit the Astrogranite hard, and Dunk felt Swift's fingers reaching for his throat. He turned and smashed a spiked elbow pad into the man's forehead, and there it stuck for a moment before he could wrestle it back out.

'Crikey! You don't see a brawl like that every day,' Jotson said. 'Well, not between team-mates, at least. Ur, on the field.'

'Still, it's one cracking good fight! And wait! One of the Hackers has broken loose from the brawl and is racing toward Fergie!'

Dunk glanced up at the Jumboball and saw Deckem sprinting away down the field. The hapless Fergie stood there in his ill-fitting gear, fists balled, chin out, and ready to face his foe.

'No!' Dunk shouted. He was too far away, though, and Swift's death grip around his middle meant he couldn't even stand. The other living Hackers were too busy fighting with the dead ones to be able to stop Deckem either.

'This is it, blokes,' Jotson said. 'When – I mean, if – Deckem knackers Fergie, that's it for the game. If Mancaster can't field a single player for its team, the game is over!'

'No!' Dunk twisted Swift's head around hard enough that he was looking the other way. This didn't slow the undead player down at all, but it kept him from seeing what he was doing. Dunk pried himself loose from the effectively blinded Swift's fingers and scrambled to his feet. He launched himself down Deckem's path. He'd be too late to stop the new Hacker, of course, but maybe he could still avenge a good man's death.

In the Jumboball, Dunk saw Deckem stalking toward the Mancaster coach, who stood his ground, unwilling to run although he faced certain death. Deckem smiled so broadly that, even by way of the Jumboball, Dunk could see his too-white teeth behind his helmet.

As the undead Hacker came within reach, Fergie leapt at him, swinging both of his spiked gauntlets up at Deckem's face. It was a desperate ploy, for sure, but Dunk couldn't see the coach had any options left to him.

'No!' Dunk shouted, stretching out his hands to stop the massacre, even though dozens of yards separated him from the two combatants.

A flash of light blinded Dunk then, and a peal of thunder louder than even the noise of the crowd followed closer after. When Dunk's vision cleared, he saw Fergie's smoking body stretched out flat on the Astrogranite.

Deckem stood over the Mancaster coach's fallen form and spat something black at him through his faceguard.

'Feefa's blessed fife! What was that?' Jotson said. 'Fergie is down! He's down! Hackers win!'

The crowd booed louder than ever and started throwing things on to the field: empty beer steins, half-eaten rat-on-a-stick treats, hapless snotlings, even the remains of the missing referee. Dunk and the other Hackers had to sprint for their dugout, dodging flying debris every step of the way.

As Dunk ran, he spun about, his eyes searching the field and the stands, hunting for whoever or whatever had struck the Mancaster coach down. Anything that could strike out of the blue like that could attack anyone else as well, and there was no telling who or what its next target might be.

Of course, Dunk couldn't ignore the fact that the bolt had taken out Mancaster's last hope – however unlikely – just as Deckem had been about to kill him. Who would have bothered to kill a man already doomed to die?

When Dunk reached the Hackers' dugout, Pegleg stomped over toward him, smacking the tip of his wooden leg angrily on the concrete as he did. 'What in the name of Nuffle's dirty jockstrap were you thinking, Mr. Hoffnung?'

Dunk glanced about and saw all of the other players – both living and undead – staring at him, seeming as eager for an answer as the Hacker coach. Slick stood off to one side, watching his client from a safe corner but not stepping forward to help. Lästiges stood next to him, her camra zipping about the dugout, switching back and forth between focusing on Dunk and his coach.

When Dunk had sprinted across the gridiron to confront Deckem, he hadn't given much thought to the issue at all, but that wasn't going to be good enough for the ex-pirate, he could tell.

'I couldn't just let Deckem and his goons – or should I say 'ghouls' – kill that man. He didn't deserve to die.'

'No one deserves to die, Mr. Hoffnung,' Pegleg said. 'Yet our lives are littered with corpses. He was as deserving as anyone else.'

'More so,' Deckem said. 'He dared to stand against us.'

Dunk started toward Deckem, but Pegleg stepped between them.

'What if I *dare* to stand against you?' Dunk said to Deckem. 'Will you try to kill me too?'

Deckem smirked. 'I won't just "try".'

'No one hurts Dunkel!' M'Grash lashed out with one hand and shoved Deckem up against the back wall of the dugout. The blow might have killed a living man, but it just held Deckem in place. He stared up at the ogre with an odd smile on his face that sent a lance of ice up Dunk's spine.

'Belay that, Mr. K'Thragsh,' Pegleg snarled. 'Both of you back to your corners. This is a conversation between Mr. Hoffnung and me.'

'I don't have anything else to say,' Dunk said. 'I saw what the right thing to do was, and I did it.'

'Well, I'm not finished,' Pegleg said. 'You're fired!'

'What?' Dunk had been prepared for many punishments from his coach, up to and including death, but the thought that he might lose his position with the Hackers had never crossed his mind. To him, the Hackers weren't just a team. In many ways, they'd become his family, and you couldn't just kick someone out of a family.

Then Dunk remembered how his father had disowned Dirk when he'd run off to play Blood Bowl. He had no doubt the same fate would await him if he ever saw his father again, no matter how unlikely that may be. He had no intentions of ever running into his parents again.

'You can't do that,' Slick said, stepping forward. 'We have a contract!'

'Had!' Pegleg said. 'Mr. Cavre, cashier Mr. Hoffnung immediately. Give him his sentence, strip him of his uniform, and send him on his way.'

Dunk gaped at the star blitzer, the captain's first mate. Would he really do it? He couldn't imagine that Cavre would defy the coach as Dunk had.

'Captain Haken,' Cavre said, 'I believe Mr. Fullbelly has a point. According to the terms of the contract he negotiated with you, we must give six weeks' notice before cutting him loose.'

'Or else what?' Pegleg never took his eyes off Dunk.

'Or we're in breach, and he can sue. Given the fact he has Mr. Fullbelly as an agent, I assume that's a foregone conclusion. They would clearly be in the right and–'

'I don't care!' Pegleg said, frothing at the mouth. 'I will not stand for this. Disobedience! Mutiny!' He pointed his hook straight at Dunk's heart. 'It's either unemployment for you – or death!'

'Captain Haken,' Cavre said calmly. 'There's also the matter of the Far Albion Cup Final. Our victory puts us in the game, which is only a week from today. If we release Mr. Hoffnung, we will have to replace him or be forced to forfeit the game.'

'Then replace him! Use any warm body! Take Mr. Fullbelly! Or Miss Weibchen! Or maybe I'll take the field myself. Apparently, in this blasted country, other coaches do!'

'No,' M'Grash said. 'If Dunkel goes, I go too.' He let Deckem fall to the floor and then strode over to stand next to his friend.

'Aye,' Edgar said, stepping in behind the ogre. 'That bloody well goes for me as well. And next time I won't do you the bloody favour of taking out the referee by pretending to be a tree standing outside of his quarters, will I?'

Simon and Guillermo looked at each other, then shrugged and walked over to stand next to Dunk. They didn't say a word, just glared at Deckem and his compatriots, right along with the others.

'You can't replace us all,' Dunk said. 'You need us.'

Pegleg's eyes looked as if they might burst from their sockets. 'You cannot do this. You will not get away with this. This is my team! Mine!'

Deckem stepped up next to the coach. 'He can't replace you, but I can.' He tossed a thumb over his shoulder at the four undead players behind him. Dunk noticed that Swift had his head back on his shoulders, but he needed to hold it in place with both hands.

'You see those fellows?' Deckem said. 'I can come up with another dozen just like them in the space of that week. They'll be just as tough, strong, and unbeatable as me. And they won't question a single order.'

'Not one?' Pegleg raised an eyebrow beneath his yellow tricorn hat, still keeping his eyes locked on Dunk.

'They can't.'

Pegleg turned to shake Deckem's hand. 'You, sir,' he said, 'have a deal.'

Then the coach turned on his living players – all except Carve who stood off to one side of the argument still – and said, 'You bastards. You traitorous bastards. You're *all* fired.'

With that, he pivoted on his wooden leg and left the dugout through the underground passageway that led to the Hackers' locker room. After shooting Dunk a sympathetic look, Cavre followed close on the captain's heel.

Dunk and the others stared after them for a moment. As they did, Deckem snorted. 'Well done, my *former* team-mates.' He sneered as he spoke. 'I couldn't have planned this better if I tried. Within the course of a few weeks, I've gone from dead to complete control of an entire Blood Bowl team. You have my *undying* thanks.'

Before Dunk could reply, Deckem followed after Pegleg and Cavre. His four compatriots strode after him, Swift still balancing his head on his shoulders.

'He's right, you know,' Olsen said as he stepped into the dugout from the field. 'You've totally cocked this up.'

'Where have you been?' Lästiges asked. 'Isn't a team wizard supposed to stay in the dugout at all times?'

'Of course, our fair lass, unless said wizard wants to do something for which we wouldn't care to be fired.'

'It was you,' Dunk said. 'Wasn't it? You blasted the Mancaster coach with your wand.'

Outside the dugout, the crowd loosed a massive cheer followed by a long, loud ovation. 'I don't believe it!' Jotson's voice said. 'He's up!'

Dunk peered out over the lip of the dugout and saw Fergus Alexson getting to his feet on his own power, shaking off the outstretched hands of the Mancaster team apothecary as he did. A bit of smoke still rose from his body, particularly his hair, which now stood up on end and was scorched black at the tips. Still, he was alive and leaving the field without assistance.

'Amazing!' Jotson said. 'I've never seen such determination from a fellow who is not dead. Except for the *un*dead, of course. They always play like they have so little to lose!'

'If you mean, "Did we save the life of that foolhardy man?" then, yes, we did. The only way to do that seemed clear. We just had to win the game before he died.' He took his wand out and blew a bit of smoke off the tip of it. 'So we did just that. Notice that by our discreet measures, we never risked the wrath of our coach. Nor did we get fired.'

'Couldn't you have lit that thing off a few minutes earlier?' Slick said. 'You could have saved these boys here a whole lot of trouble.'

Olsen shrugged. 'Their antics provided us with the distraction we needed, wee one. Without that, we might not have taken the chance at all.'

'So thanks for bloody nothing, mate,' Edgar said. 'Only my second game as a Blood Bowler – as a part of a team – and I don't even make it out of the first half! I haven't played in a full game yet!'

'I'll bet you always got picked last for games as a sapling, too, didn't you?' Slick said, patting a sympathetic hand on Edgar's bark.

'How in the bloody Fire-Breathing Forest did you know that?' Edgar said, sap-like tears welling up in his glowing green eyes.

Slick looked toward Dunk and rolled his eyes. 'Just a lucky guess,' he said.

Dunk felt his heart slip down into his boots. He looked at the halfling – his agent, his friend – and slowly shook his head.

'What do we do now?' he asked. 'We're five Blood Bowl players without a team.'

'Six!' Edgar said.

'Six,' Dunk said. 'Slick, you're my agent. You're the one who directs my career. What should we do next?'

Slick came over and put an arm around Dunk's leg. 'Don't worry about it, son. Sometimes getting fired is the best thing that can happen to you. It gives you a chance to renegotiate your contract, which is great if you're in a position of strength.'

'And we are?' Guillermo asked, his voice filled with desperate hope.

Slick snorted. 'Not even close,' he said with a laugh. 'But that doesn't mean we can't get there from here.'

'What do we do next then?' Simon asked.

'I recommend we grab some grub, shoot around some ideas over a few beers, and then – as the Albionmen say – get "knock-down pissed".'

No one argued with that.

'HERE'S TO UNEMPLOYMENT!' Dunk said, raising the latest in a countless series of ales to his fellow ex-Hackers sitting at the table with him and Slick in the Cock and Bull.

A roar went up throughout the pub. As the Hackers had bought the first few rounds for themselves, they'd picked up drinks for everyone else in the place as well. They had soon found themselves surrounded by dozens of brand-new friends.

When the locals realised who their benefactors were, they'd cheered even louder. Their defence of the ever-popular Coach Alexson had made them national heroes, and the fact they'd lost their jobs over it only cemented the admiration the average Albion football fans felt for them. The bartender had refused to let them pay for another drink.

'Here's to sleeping in!' Simon said.

'Here's to getting soft!' Guillermo said.

'Here's to beer!' M'Grash said. That got the loudest cheer of all, and he grinned wide and sheepish at the applause.

'Here's to the Hackers,' Edgar said from his spot outside an open window.

While M'Grash had been just able to squeeze through the pub's door, it had proved too much of a hardship for the treeman. 'It's all right, mates,' he'd said. 'I can't bloody well sit down anyway.'

Dunk had felt bad for Edgar, but the treeman had kept his spirits up and joined in the fun by peering in a wide window in the front of the pub and occasionally reaching in for the bartender to refill his bowl of fermented maple syrup. Every now and then, someone on the street would remark on the fact that a tree had sprouted right there in the middle of a Kingsbury street, and Edgar would spin about and spit out a drunken, 'Sod off!'

This never failed to set off waves of laughter through the pub. When Edgar toasted the Hackers, though, the crowd fell quiet, as did the players at Dunk's table.

'Bollocks!' Slick said, jumping up on the table. 'Bollocks to the Hackers!'

Everyone in the bar roared at this, and Slick pranced proudly around the table at how well he'd sensed the mood of the place. When he slipped in a small pool of spilled beer, the roar changed to a sound of concern, but Dunk reached out and caught the halfling before he could crash to the floor. The patrons raised their glasses and cheered again.

'I don't like you talking about the team like that,' Simon said. 'It's not proper.'

'I guess you missed the part where we were fired,' Guillermo said. 'Hackers we are no more.'

'No more Hackers?' M'Grash said. He looked as if a tear might roll from his eye and plop into his barrel-sized tankard of ale.

'Don't you worry about it, big guy,' Dunk said. 'We're not done with the Hackers yet.'

'You dead sure about that?' Simon asked. 'I didn't see a doubt in Pegleg's mind.'

'He'll be fine once he calms down a bit,' Slick said. 'Cavre will talk some sense into him. Or we'll hit him with a big enough wrongful-termination lawsuit that *we'll* own the Hackers.'

'Now who'd want a washed-up team of losers like that?' Lästiges said as she strode into the pub, her camra zipping along behind her.

'They're only washed up because they no longer have us,' Guillermo said. 'We can repair that.'

'Don't kid yourself,' the reporter said. 'Your team has always got along more on luck and a prayer than any real talent. Your big run last year was nothing but a fluke.' She looked at Dunk as she said this. To avoid blushing at her, he turned away.

'Where have you been?' Slick asked, narrowing his eyes at the reporter.

'Following your former manager and team-mates around, of course,' she said. 'Captain Haken is still furious – mostly at you, Dunk.'

'Will coach be happy again soon?' M'Grash asked.

Lästiges gave the ogre a condescending smile and patted the back of his hand. 'Not today, I'm afraid. Cavre tells me that he thinks Pegleg will be in a better mood tomorrow – but that he'll still be willing to hire a fistful of snotlings to replace you rather than have you back.'

'He wouldn't,' Simon said in horror.

'He won't have to,' Lästiges said. 'Deckem has already offered to fill out the team's ranks with more of his clammy "friends".'

'Can he do that?' Guillermo said.

'He claims he can.'

'Where in all of bloody Albion did he come up with those creatures anyway?' Edgar shouted in from the window. 'They should be fertilising my bloody roots!'

'He doesn't know,' Lästiges said smugly.

'Wait,' Dunk said. 'You asked him?'

'See, that's why I like you,' she said, batting her eyes at him. 'You're one of the smart ones. Of course, I asked him. It's my job to ask questions.'

'Well?'

'Well what?'

Dunk choked back an urge to throttle Lästiges. 'What did he say?'

'He didn't know. After his retirement, he decided to travel the world a bit. The last thing he remembers is running into a crowd of irate fans of his former opponents. Then he wakes up in a shallow grave somewhere in the Sure Wood a couple of weeks back.'

'You're kidding.'

'He said that Wee Johnson almost keeled over from a heart attack when Wee and his friends heard Deckem trying to dig himself out of the ground. Brother Puck ran screaming off into the night. When they got over their terror, they started in helping with their bare hands and pulled him out.'

'That was right after we, um...' Dunk's voice trailed off as he realised that the other patrons in the bar might be able to hear him.

'Yes,' Lästiges said. 'It is.'

'They have to be connected,' Slick said.

'It could be a coincidence,' Guillermo said, visibly shaken. 'I mean, just because we happen to come upon an artefact of unearthly power and bodies of football superstars suddenly start pulling themselves up out of the dirt doesn't mean – oh, dear Nuffle...'

'What about the others, though?' Dunk asked. 'Where do they come from? They know how to play Blood Bowl, but – does anyone recognise them as retired players too?'

Everyone else at the table gave Dunk a blank look.

'I've followed Far Albion football ever since I was a lad,' Simon said. 'I used to be able to quote you every player's personal stats and on-field numbers for five years back. They don't look familiar to me. They sure do play like the greats of old though.'

'Did you ask Deckem about that?' Dunk said to Lästiges.

'Of course.'

'And...?'

'"No comment".' She scowled. 'I can't tell you how much I *hate* those two words.'

'He'll bloody well blab to me,' Edgar said, turning to leave. 'I'll strip the leaves from his limbs!'

'Hold it!' Dunk said before the treeman could stride away. 'I think I have a better idea.'

'WHY DON'T WE try the door, again?' Simon asked.

Dunk rolled his eyes as Slick shushed the Albionman for the third time. 'It'll be trapped,' Dunk whispered.

'And the window won't?'

Dunk looked down from where he, Simon, Guillermo, and Slick stood in Edgar's upper branches. M'Grash waved up at him with a smile from where the moonlit pavement beckoned far below. The window the treeman held them in front of sat in a sheer, plastered, whitewashed wall, with nothing to grasp onto nearby but the brown-painted frame itself.

'Would you expect an assault from this angle?'

'Why would anyone want to assault me?'

'I can think of a half-dozen reasons off the top of my head,' Slick said. 'Now shut up.'

'You're noisier than a scurry of bloody squirrels in heat,' Edgar said. 'It's a wonder he's not awake already.'

The treeman staggered a bit to the right, and all four of the people in its branches yelled out. M'Grash reached out and caught Edgar before he went over like a felled oak.

'Whoa!' said Dunk. 'How much of that maple juice did you have?'

'Not enough,' the treeman said, righting itself as it shook free from M'Grash, and licking its lips with a tongue the colour of heartwood.

407

'You don't get hooch that bloody good in the Sure Wood, I can tell you that.'

'For Nuffle's sake,' Simon said. 'You're noisier than the lot of us. Can't you keep it down.'

Dunk glanced up and down the darkened street in which they'd found themselves. It was late, and all the lights in the inn before them were out. In their target room, nothing seemed to stir.

'He must sleep like the dead,' Dunk said.

'I don't think Deckem sleeps very well,' Guillermo said. 'Or at all.'

'That's because he's *un*dead,' Slick said. 'He *un*sleeps.'

That sent Edgar into a titter, and the treeman nearly dropped all of its friends. 'Whoops!' it said. 'My apologies, mates, but that was bloody funny!'

'How are we going to get in there?' Guillermo said. 'It's closed.'

'We just open it,' Dunk said.

'And if it's locked?' asked Simon.

'Don't take your eye off the ball,' Slick said. 'One thing at a time.'

Edgar extended one of his branches forward, and Dunk crept along it until he could reach the window. There were two of them, actually, hung side by side on hinges so you could pull them into the room. Dunk pushed against them, hoping they would just give. They held firm.

'They're locked,' Dunk said.

'Here's your next thing,' said Simon.

'Let's just break the bloody things,' Edgar said. 'Then we drag him out of his bed and haul him into some dark corner of that wooded park we passed. No one will hear us – or him – there.'

'You don't think that this will wake him up?' Guillermo said. 'This breaking of glass?'

'Just throw the halfling through,' Simon said. 'We can follow right after.'

Slick gaped at the Albionman. 'First, no! Second, don't you think something like that would wake even the dead?'

'So what if it does?' Edgar said.

At that, the windows opened into the darkened room, and Olsen stepped forward, the moonlight catching him in the frame.

'Aye,' the wizard said. He looked older than Dunk had ever seen him, worn and on the verge of exhaustion – and not in a good mood. 'Whatever will you do?'

'Run?' Edgar squeaked in a tiny voice.

Olsen snorted, and a weary smile crept across his lips, leaving his tired eyes undisturbed. 'Come on in, lads,' he said, stepping back into the darkness. 'We think it's time we talked.'

Leaving M'Grash and Edgar out on the street to keep watch, Dunk, Simon, Guillermo, and Slick climbed into the wizard's room through the open window. By the time they all made it in, Olsen had lit a pair of lamps on either side of his bed and carried one of them over to a table on the opposite side of the room.

'Sit, lads, sit,' the wizard said, pointing to the four chairs arranged around the table. Dunk took one of them – the one nearest the door – and Guillermo and Simon each sat down too. Slick leaned up against the windowsill instead.

'So,' Olsen said, 'what can we help you with at this unusual hour?'

'You know why we're here,' Dunk said.

The wizard stared at the thrower in silence for a moment, a frown of regret on his face. 'Yes, we suppose we do. You want to know more about the Far Albion Cup.'

Simon, looking confused, said, 'We're here about Deckem and his deadboys, aren't we?'

'They're the same topic,' Olsen said. 'You can't talk about Deckem's lot without bringing the cup into it too.'

'What's going on?' Dunk asked.

'Ah,' Olsen said, settling back to sit on the end of his bed, 'now that's a simple question, but with a complicated answer.'

'We're unemployed,' Dunk said. 'We have plenty of time.'

'Right,' Olsen said. 'A long time ago, centuries before any of you were born, I was a great wizard.'

'Aren't you still a great wizard?' Guillermo asked.

'Perhaps. But back then, in the days of my youth, I *knew* I was a great wizard. I told everyone I knew that I was, and I set out to prove it. This was back before football of any kind had found our secluded isle, and fair Albion was sadly ignorant of such great discoveries. Without such a sport to play, I set out to make my mark by leading the effort to destroy the most dangerous and evil sorcerers of the day.

'My friends – compatriots, really – and I met with some successes. We ran off the Lizard-fiend of Loch Morrah, the Mole-master of Dro-gan Glen, and even the Black Oak of the Sure Wood.'

Dunk heard leaves rustle at this last name and glanced out the window to see Edgar shivering not in the breeze but stark fear.

'Then we set our sight on the greatest, most powerful evil in the land in those dark days: Tharg Retmatcher. That ancient crone ruled over most of Albion then, with the exception of the last bastion that was Kingsbury, and the king – King William I, in those days – bade us to take her down by any means necessary.'

Olsen bowed his head. For a moment, Dunk feared the old elf had nodded off. Then he raised his eyes again, red and puffy though they were.

'We were so sure of ourselves. We rode right out to Downing Castle and challenged her to show herself. Well, she did, and she destroyed us to a man. When – when I saw how the battle would go, I used my magic not to launch yet another futile attack, but to flee.

'I was the only one of us to survive.'

'What happened to Tharg?' Guillermo said.

'Hush,' Simon said, transfixed, never taking his eyes from the wizard. 'He's getting to that.'

Olsen nodded. 'I went into hiding after that, and Retmatcher's forces scoured the land for me. I was no longer here, though, having gone to hide in the Old World, in the majestic city of Altdorf.

'While in my exile there, I plotted for my return, for my chance to redeem myself and bring down Retmatcher once and for all. To that end, I constructed the ultimate weapon, an enchanted device so powerful that not even the dreaded Retmatcher could resist its power.

'When it was ready, I smuggled it and myself back to Albion aboard a pirate ship. I brought it to King William III, who now sat on the throne, and gave it to him to give to Retmatcher.'

'And she just accepted this 'gift' from her mortal enemy?' Slick asked.

Olsen raised finger to tell the halfling to be patient. 'William III had come to a sort of peace with this dictator. She let him remain on his throne, mostly as an impotent figurehead. In exchange, he retained control of Kingsbury and the surrounding area and paid her a regular tribute.'

'And he gave this weapon to her as part of his next tribute,' said Simon.

'Who's telling this story?' Olsen asked. The wizard waited in silence for an answer.

'My apologies,' Simon said. 'Please, continue.'

Olsen rolled his eyes but started talking again. 'William included the weapon in his next payment of tribute to Retmatcher.' The wizard ignored Simon's self-satisfied smile. 'When she saw it, she knew straightaway that she had to use it at once. I'd tailored it to fit her vanities and her taste. This might have made her suspicious, but she knew that King William had tried to do the same many times over the years, hoping to mollify her tempestuous nature.

'So, at dinner that night, she filled the cup with wine and drank deep from it.'

'The weapon was the Far Albion Cup?' Simon said, aghast.

'Not so clever as you think, eh?' Olsen said. 'Retmatcher was fooled as well.'

'So the cup killed her?' Dunk asked.

Olsen shook his head. 'Retmatcher was far too powerful for my magics to be able to kill her. Even though I invested a part of my own soul in the cup, the best I could hope for was to trap her. And that I did.

'The very night her tribute arrived from Kingsbury, Retmatcher hosted a feast in her own honour. At the height of the feast, she raised a toast to herself with my jewel-studded cup in her hands. As the sweet, red wine touched her lips, she fell over, dead to the world.'

'I thought you said you that it was not in your power to murder her,' Guillermo said.

'Despite appearances, she wasn't truly dead. Instead, the cup stole her soul as she drained that wine.'

Dunk narrowed his eyes at the wizard. 'Where did it go? Her soul, I mean?'

Olsen laid a hand on his own chest. In the wan light of the lamps, dressed only in his nightgown, the weary wizard looked older than ever. 'We have it,' he said.

Simon, Guillermo, and Dunk all gasped. Slick squinted at the wizard instead. 'You've been carrying this necromancer's soul around inside of you for all this time?'

'Nature – even magic – detests a vacuum. That's why I put a part of my soul in the cup. It created a conduit to the vacancy within me. That's how the cup could pull Retmatcher's soul from her flesh.'

Dunk considered this strange tale for a moment. 'How did that cup become Albion's national Blood Bowl trophy?'

Olsen nodded at the young thrower, impressed. 'Like all spells my magnum opus is not unbreakable. As you might have guessed by now, if we drink our own blood from the cup, the spell ends.'

'It would try to take your own soul from you and give it back to you.'

'Magic must follow its own rules – the internal logic that defies traditional logic. If it fails that test, it falls apart, and the spell ends.'

'But,' Simon said, 'isn't that what you wanted to do? You told us this would let you end your life.' ·

Olsen bowed his head and grimaced, then spoke. 'The spell had an unintended side-effect. The combining of my soul with Retmatcher's made me immortal. Her power is such that she refuses to let her soul's earthly vessel die – even if that vessel is her worst enemy: me.'

'So,' Slick said, 'you want to die and let this woman loose upon Albion again?'

The wizard's face sagged, emphasising the lines the centuries had graven there. 'We tire of this life. We have outlived everyone we ever knew. We long for the sweet oblivion of death. We are ready to pass into the great beyond and discover what awaits us in that mysterious country.'

'By "we",' Dunk asked, uncertain how to phrase his question, 'do you speak for both of you?'

Olsen nodded softly. 'We believe we do.'

The room fell silent for a moment as the Hackers considered the wizard's tale. When Dunk could take it no longer, he spoke. 'You still haven't answered my question – about how the cup became part of the Far Albion League.'

Rue filled the wizard's face. 'Just because Retmatcher was "dead" didn't mean she was defeated. We knew it would only be a matter of time before someone figured out what I'd done and tried to break the spell. Too many powerful people depended on her reign as ruler of Albion to let it end like that.'

Slick smiled his approval. 'You hid it in plain sight.'

'Exactly. When we learned of the founding of the new Far Albion Blood Bowl League, we made a gift of the cup to Bo Berobsson to serve as the travelling trophy for the league's annual champions. Who would suspect such a high-profile cup to be the same one as that which had been found near Retmatcher's hand as she lay sprawled dead on the floor of her dining hall?'

'And if anyone did, who better to protect it than a team of Blood Bowl players?' Guillermo said. 'What kind of thieves would be crazy enough to try to steal something that valuable?'

'Good question,' Dunk said, remembering how the cup had gone missing for five hundred years. 'So what happened?'

'We underestimated the greed of some Blood Bowl teams. Once word got out that the Far Albion League had such a handsome trophy, teams from the Old World swept into the tournament and tried to win it. We spent a few, harrowing years volunteering as the team wizard for any Albion team who would have us, doing our best to keep the trophy in the country, where we could keep an eye on it.'

'But one day your luck ran out,' Slick said.

'Aye. The Orcland Raiders joined the tournament and won, despite our best efforts to sabotage the bastards. They took the Far Albion Cup back with them to the Old World – they insisted on calling it "the Fah Cup" – and we never saw it again. Until now, that is. They said it was stolen, but we later learned they'd sold it soon after returning home.'

'They're orcs,' Slick said. 'What did you expect?'

'We spent some time trying to track it down and then gave up. If we couldn't find it, what were the chances that anyone else could? As long as it was well and truly lost, we were happy.'

'But that didn't last, did it?' Simon said.

'Not so much. As the years wore on into centuries, we decided that it was time to finally break the spell. But by then the cup was well and truly lost. It took us decades to determine it had somehow found its way into the Sure Wood. Then fortune finally smiled upon us when it brought you to help us recover the cup.'

'So what does all this have to do with Deckem?' Dunk said.

Olsen rolled his head back and looked up at the ceiling for a moment before loosing a deep sigh. 'Everything. It turns out we were wrong. We didn't get all of Retmatcher's soul. She was just too powerful. When the cup's magic tried to drag her soul through the cup to me, a good chunk of her soul stayed in the cup, along with the part of myself we'd stashed there.

'Over the years, the part of Retmatcher in the Far Albion Cup overwhelmed the part of me there. The cup slowly turned as evil as it could be, and it started to affect the world around it as best it could. It was likely the cup's influence that foiled our efforts and let the Raiders win that fateful tournament so many years ago, removing it from our influence so its evil could fester quietly on its own.'

'The cup brought Deckem back to life?' Dunk said, his eyes wide with horror.

'Aye, lad. He and all his friends. We suspect the others are ex-footballers too, but ones that Deckem, er, assembled from many bodies. Notably, he replaced each one's head with that of some random victim exhumed from any nearby grave, making it nearly impossible to identify them.

'Deckem and his cronies are nearly immortal, products of Retmatcher's enormous powers and her centuries of festering hate. If we destroy them, the cup will only create more of them. In fact, if what Deckem said after the last game is accurate, the cup may already be conjuring up more such creatures to replace you lot on your team.'

'No!' a voice outside the window hollered. Then the building shook with the force of three mighty blows.

'Bloody hell!' Edgar said, sticking his face in the window. 'You bastards have upset our wee ogre! Can someone have a bloody word with him before he shakes the building down and turns yours truly into so many toothpicks?'

Dunk dashed to the window and called down to the ogre, who sat in the gutter below, pounding his fist into the side of the building as he sobbed loudly. 'Hold it, M'Grash! I'm coming!'

The thrower leapt out of the window and slid down Edgar to land next to the weeping ogre. 'It's all right, big guy,' Dunk said. 'Don't cry. We can fix this.'

M'Grash raised his head as Dunk came over and wrapped an arm around one of the ogre's biceps as if he were trying to comfort a tiny child. 'How?' M'Grash said, wiping the tremendous tears from his face and tusks. 'How can we save the team, Dunkel? How?'

Dunk patted the ogre on the back as he watched flickering lights start to fill the windows all around them. They had overstayed their welcome here and had to leave right away.

'I don't know, buddy,' Dunk said to the ogre as he helped him to his feet. 'I don't know, but I promise you this: we won't let the Hackers go without a fight.'

'THE HACKERS SCORE again!' Mon Jotson's voice called out over the PA system, which echoed throughout the stadium and beyond, even into the depths of the visiting team's locker room. 'That makes five unanswered touchdowns against the scoreless Kingsbury Royals. If the Hackers can keep this up this pace, there will be no stopping them!'

The crowd booed and hissed at the news. Jotson and the rest of the press had spent the whole of the last week vilifying the Hackers – or what was left of them, anyway – every chance they'd had. Even Lästiges had chipped in, appearing on several Cabalvision shows on all five of the Albion stations to slag Deckem and his 'deadmen,' as they'd taken to called the undead linemen.

'They only have five stations?' Slick had said, stunned. 'How do they sell anything around here?'

'And two of them are owned by the King: BBC 1 and BBC 2. Then there's also the Itinerant Telepathic Visionaries network, and the innovatively named channels Four and Five. I've been on each of them twice already, and I'll go back for another round just before game time.'

'How many of them will show the game?' Dunk had asked.

'All of them?'

'*All* of them?'

'You think there's anything better to watch on a Sunday afternoon around here?'

At the time, Dunk had felt some strange sense of pride that the entire nation would tune in at once to watch the Hackers play in the Far Albion Cup final, even if he wouldn't be on the field. Now, the idea of an entire nation so fully focused on the game that there weren't any other activities scheduled for the day bothered him – especially given what he and his fellow ex-Hackers had planned.

Security around the game had been tight, but the guards – stuffy looking men in red uniforms and tall, furry, black hats – had recognised Dunk and the others as members of the team and waved them on through the gates. At Slick's insistence, they'd waited until just after the opening kick-off to get to the stadium, ensuring that Pegleg and his new-version Hackers would be out on the field when they arrived.

As predicted, the locker room lay empty, not even a straggling reporter poking through the team's gear skulking about. Everyone knew the big story was out on the field. Everyone but Dunk and his friends.

Slick strode into the room first, scouting ahead. When he signalled the all-clear, the rest tumbled in after him: first Dunk, then M'Grash, Simon, and Guillermo, with Edgar – bowing over the best he could to fit through the doorway – shuffling in at the rear.

'So,' Dunk said, 'where is it?'

Slick scurried about the place, peering into every nook and cranny he could find. 'Olsen said he'd leave the cup in his locker, but it's not there.' The halfling pointed over at a red door left flung open in the far corner of the room.

Indecipherable runes etched in gold, silver, and other, nameless inks glowed softly on the inside of the door and throughout the interior of the locker. Even in the dim light from the sigils, Dunk could see the locker stood empty. There wasn't even a bit of dust inside the thing.

'Isn't that just the way of things, lads?' Simon said, shaking his head.

Guillermo frowned, and Dunk noticed the man shiver. 'Then where bloody is it?' he snapped.

Edgar snorted. 'You can't use "bloody" like that,' he said. 'It's an adjective, not an adverb, except in some unique circumstances.'

'You can bloody well shut your mouth,' Simon said.

'Ah,' Edgar said with a laugh, 'like that.'

'Olsen must not have been able to leave the cup behind,' Slick said. 'Maybe Pegleg guessed what he might be up to and decided to put it under lock and key instead.'

'Would that work?' Dunk asked. 'Doesn't it have to be with Pegleg for the Hackers to always win?'

'Do I look like a wizard?' the halfling said. 'It's magic, son. It works like it wants to work.'

'Besides which,' Edgar said, 'with the way Deckem and his bloody deadmen are playing, who needs the bloody cup to assure a win?'

'Maybe that's how the legend manifests itself every time,' Dunk said. 'We don't know. We should have asked Olsen more questions.'

'What would you like to know?' the wizard said as he entered through the tunnel that led underground to the Hackers' dugout.

'Where did Merlin put the shiny cup?' M'Grash said, looming over the wizard. The ogre looked ready to hunt through Olsen's entrails for whatever clues he could find.

The wizard put a hand to mollify the ogre, but M'Grash took this as a threat. His meaty hand lashed out and wrapped around Olsen's neck. As the wizard clawed at the ogre's fingers, trying to pry them from his throat, M'Grash hauled the wizard up to his level so he could talk straight into his face.

'Where is the cup?' M'Grash demanded.

Olsen's feet kicked in the air below him as he struggled to maintain consciousness. He gurgled out a few syllables, but words were beyond him.

'Put him down, M'Grash,' Dunk said carefully. 'He can't talk like that, and he's no good to anyone dead.'

Dunk caught Olsen in his arms as the ogre dropped him. 'I'm sorry about that,' the thrower said as the wizard gasped fresh air into his lungs. 'He's a little on edge about stealing the cup from Pegleg.'

'That's bloody true of us all,' Edgar said, his leaves trembling as he spoke. 'Crikey, betraying your bloody coach isn't something any foot-baller should do lightly.'

'We're not betraying him,' Dunk said, setting Olsen down to sit on a nearby bench. 'We're saving the team – for him.'

'You think Pegleg would see it that way, son?' Slick asked. Olsen bent over double and sounded as if he meant to hack up a lung or two.

Dunk frowned as he checked to make sure that the wizard would survive M'Grash's interrogation. 'He will – eventually.'

Finished clearing his throat, Olsen sat back up with a wry smile on his face. 'You may get your chance to find out, lad. Your good coach stripped me of the responsibility of keeping watch over the cup. Apparently he feels I'll be far more useful to his cause if I spend my time zapping some of those poor, damn Royals off the pitch.'

'The deadmen haven't killed them yet?' Slick asked.

Olsen shook his head. 'They watched the DVDs of the last two games. Those Daemonic Visual Displays are bloody amazing, and they come out so fast these days. Anyways, their coach came up with a strategy to beat savage murderers like the deadmen.'

'And this strategy, it works?' Guillermo asked.

'So far. They haven't scored yet, but they're not dead either. They just flee whenever any of the deadmen get close to them, and they throw the ball forward as best they can.

'Sadly, the Royals aren't well known for their passing game. They tend to drop as many balls as they catch.'

'So,' Dunk said, trying to steer the conversation back to what they needed to know, 'where's the cup?'

'Pegleg has it sitting next to him in the Hackers' dugout.' The wizard sighed. 'He's planning to give it back to the Far Albion League at halftime.'

'What?' the others in the room all said.

'He believes that the team that controls the cup can't be beaten, right?'

The others nodded.

'Well, if the cup goes back to being the Far Albion Cup's travelling trophy, the Hackers get it right back. Legitimately too. And once that happens, the Hackers will never lose. They'll always get the cup back every year.'

'That's insane,' Dunk said. 'The legend can't be true then. Otherwise, how would the Orland Raiders ever have been able to win the trophy? Whoever had it before them would never have lost it.'

'Ah,' Olsen said ruefully. 'Here's where Pegleg's plan breaks down, just at it did for the Royals, who had it before the Raiders took it. You can only win the tournament if you show up to play. The Raiders made sure that the Royals never made it to the final game. Those damned orcs won the game by forfeit.

'It's hard to stop a team full of deadmen, though. If someone kills most of your team, you just conjure up a fistful more, and you're ready to go. They don't even have to be good players, right? You've got the cup, you don't really care about skills any more.'

'We have to get that cup,' Dunk said. 'How much time do we have?'

'And there's the two-minute warning!' Mon Jotson's voice said. 'This is the first time the Hackers have made it to one of these in a Far Albion Cup game!'

The crowd booed louder than ever.

'No time, son,' Slick said. 'No time at all.'

Dunk raced down the tunnel to the Hackers' dugout. He had no sort of plan in his head. He only knew that he needed to act, and now. He heard the others hot on his heels, including the thumping tromps of M'Grash and the scraping branches of Edgar as they forced their way through the too-small space. He hoped that the noise of the crowd's disapproval would be enough to mask their approach from Pegleg and Deckem, but he had little choice but to proceed either way.

When Dunk reached the end of the tunnel, he held up a hand to signal the others to stop, and he peered around the corner of the portal. To Dunk's relief, only Pegleg stood there in the dugout. The ex-pirate glared out across the gridiron, leaning on his wooden leg and tapping his booted toes against the cut-stone floor. Something sat on the bench behind him, wrapped in a burlap sack. From the size and shape of the thing, Dunk knew it could only be the Far Albion Cup.

'I'll get it,' Slick whispered.

Dunk glanced down to see the halfling peering around his leg, staring hard at the cup.

'Are you nuts?' Dunk asked. 'If he sees you, he'll gut you on the spot.'

'Shh,' Slick said. 'I'm a halfling. This is the kind of thing we do.' With that, the agent slipped past Dunk before the thrower could reach out to stop him.

Slick padded toward Pegleg, silent and smooth, and Dunk briefly wondered if Slogo Fullbelly had earned his nickname from his reputation as an agent or a thief.

For a moment, Dunk turned his attention to the field. Out there, he saw Deckem with his arms out, palms up, raising them up and down, exhorting the fans to be louder than ever. They obliged him by hissing and booing with insane fervour and tossing larger and larger things on to the field. A large chunk of a wooden bleacher seat – half of a long log cut lengthwise – bounced off the top of the dugout and rolled into the field in front of Pegleg, but the coach ignored it, steadfast as a sea captain sailing into a coming storm.

Dunk tensed for a moment, fearful that Pegleg might turn and see him in the darkened rear of the dugout, but the ex-pirate's gaze never wavered from the gridiron. Out there, Deckem continued to incite the crowd to an insane pitch as his deadmen trotted in circles around him. Some of them picked up the detritus the fans had thrown at them and hurled them back into the stands, where the tight packing of the fans guaranteed the junk would hit somebody.

Meanwhile, the Hackers' apothecary stood amid it all, stitching one of the deadmen – Dunk recognised him as Swift – back together. He'd somehow lost an arm, but it didn't bother him at all as the healer darned it back on to him with a thick, black thread.

Dunk understood Deckem's intentions. He wanted the field to be such a terrifying place that the Royals would refuse to go back on to it. No living creature in its right mind would want to dive into such a maelstrom, but few would accuse any Blood Bowl player of being entirely sane under even the best of circumstances. In his heart, Dunk rooted for the Royals to stand up to Deckem's attempt to intimidate them, no matter how foolhardy it might seem.

The crouched-over Slick reached out and put his hand on the sack-covered cup. He followed it with another. Then he wrapped his arms around the cup, cradling it from underneath its bowl and slowly stood up to his full height.

Despite the roaring noise outside the dugout, when Pegleg spoke, his voice seemed to cut through it all. 'What, Mr. Fullbelly, do you think you are doing?'

Slick looked up at the coach, who still hadn't torn his gaze away from the field. He shivered, but he did not drop the cup. Instead, he took one step backward, carrying the big burlap sack in his arms.

'Just thought she needed a little polishing, Pegleg,' the halfling said. 'You can't give it back to the league officials with it all dirty like this.'

'Your concern is touching, Mr. Fullbelly.' Pegleg's hook lashed out and pierced the top of the sack. Once the canvas was securely snarled in the hook, the ex-pirate turned about to stare into the halfling's eyes. 'But that won't be necessary.'

'Listen, my old friend,' Slick said. 'We're here to help you. This cup of yours, it's evil through and through.'

'Winning is never evil,' Pegleg said. 'Not in Blood Bowl. Not in life.'

'You see?' Slick said. 'That's just what I'm talking about. It's already got its hooks in you. You're a tough coach and a good one, one of the best I've ever had the pleasure of working with. I've known you for years, and I consider you not just a patriarch of the game but a good friend. Winning might have always been important to you *on the field*, but you've always been able to leave it there, on the field, when the game was over.'

Pegleg scowled. 'So you say. I was raised to be a gentleman, but this is not a gentleman's game. Still, I deported myself as best I could given my current vocation. And what did I get for my troubles?'

Slick shook his head, his mouth open but silent as he gaped up at the coach.

'Nothing. Unless you count poverty, hardship, and a bleeding ulcer. But I coached the way I wanted to, the way I thought I should, no matter how horrible the insults visited upon my team, no matter how many of them were *murdered* as I sat on the sidelines here and watched, helpless to do anything to stop it.

'And what did I get for that? The admiration of my peers? The accolades of the fans? The respect of our so-called reporters?'

Pegleg sneered down at the speechless halfling. 'No. None of that. Not one whit. Instead, we – me and my team – were branded losers. *Losers!* They *laughed* at us.'

Slick glanced out at the field, and Pegleg followed his gaze. 'Well,' the halfling said, having to shout to be heard over the noise, 'no one's laughing now.'

Pegleg nodded at this. 'I know. And, Mr. Fullbelly, it's about damned time.' Then he pulled the cup from the halfling's arms and set it down on the floor next to him. Once it was safely down, he freed his hook and brought it around to bear on Slick, who cowered from it as it glinted in the light.

'You can't do this,' the halfling said. 'We only came here to help!'

'We?' The coach turned toward the entrance to the tunnel toward the Hackers' locker room and spied Dunk peering around the corner. He coughed out a bitter laugh and beckoned toward the thrower with his hook.

'Come, Mr. Hoffnung,' Pegleg said. 'Why don't you join our conversation? I confess I'm learning a great deal about my so-called friends.'

Dunk stepped forward out of the tunnel, and the others emerged one by one behind him. Edgar stopped only halfway into the dugout, and even then his top branches nearly jutted out past the shelter's protective roof.

'So this is how it is,' said Pegleg as he watched his former players join Dunk and stand behind him. 'This is gratitude for you. After everything I've done for you.'

'Like fire us?' Dunk said. 'All of us? Come on, coach. Can't you see this is not like you? When have you ever fired a player before?'

Simon nodded. 'You always said firing was too good for me. It was worse punishment to keep me on the team.'

Pegleg smirked at this. 'That way you might actually get the beating you deserved, Mr. Sherwood.' He scowled again. 'But I grew tired of waiting for that. Better to cut you loose – to cut you *all* loose – and start over again.'

'Not all of us, coach,' a voice shouted out.

Everyone's head turned to see Cavre step into the dugout from the end nearest Pegleg. The star blitzer doffed his helmet and tossed it down on the bench with practiced ease. He wore a look of raw determination on his face. Dunk had seen this on the field many times, but never off, where Cavre's natural stoicism had become the stuff of legend. The fires in this man's soul burned hot, but he had kept them focused on the game – until now.

'I'm still here,' Cavre said, struggling to keep the anger from his voice. 'I've always been here. I've been with this team since I first played the game, and I'd always hoped they would bury me in my Hackers uniform. But not anymore.'

'Hold your tongue, Mr. Cavre!' Pegleg snarled at the blitzer, but Dunk could tell his heart wasn't in it. Here was a 'betrayal' from the one corner he'd never allowed himself to consider.

Pegleg's eyes flitted from Cavre to the others, then back again. Dunk felt he could read the coach's thoughts, so clearly did he wear them on his troubled face. If Cavre stood against him with the others, then perhaps he'd been wrong. Perhaps there was something to all this balderdash about the cup.

'No!' Pegleg growled. 'I won't let this happen! I'm so close! I'm about to win the whole damn thing!'

'There's no "I" in "team", coach,' M'Grash said hopefully.

'Arrgh!' the ex-pirate said. 'Who's been filling your empty head with such banalities, Mr. K'Thragsh? There's no "we" in "team", either! In fact, the damned word lacks an entire twenty-two letters from the alphabet, and none of them matter one damned bit!'

'There's no 'we' in this team any longer,' Cavre said, pulling off his jersey. He wadded it up into a ball and threw it at Pegleg's feet. 'Good luck with your new players, Captain Haken.'

Cavre shouldered his way past Pegleg and made for the exit tunnel. As he reached its portal, the coach called out after him.

'Wait!' Pegleg said. As a man who'd cultivated the image of a pirate legend he'd always taken great care with his grooming. Dunk had rarely seen him with a hair out of place. Now, though, the man looked dishevelled, rumpled even, and a dozen years older.

The coach looked down at the cup, which had somehow managed to find itself in Slick's arms again. The halfling flashed his most innocent smile up at the ex-pirate, fooling no one for even an instant. Pegleg ignored the gesture and reached down and tapped the cup with the curve of his hook.

'Get rid of it,' he whispered, his voice hoarse with raw emotion.

'What, coach?' M'Grash asked, cupping his massive ear in an effort to hear Pegleg over the still-roaring crowd.

'Take the cup,' the coach said, louder and more forcefully now. 'Take it and dispose of it. Do what you must.'

'What's going to happen to the game?' Simon said. 'It's the Far Albion Cup Final.'

Pegleg stared at each of his ex-players in turn and said. 'I don't care. The game and my new players can be damned.'

'What a stroke of luck for you, then,' Deckem shouted down into the dugout, his deadmen assembled behind him. 'We already are!'

DECKEM'S EYES GLOWED red as the undead player glared down at his coach and former team-mates. 'Look!' he said. 'A reunion of everyone I haven't got around to killing yet.'

Dunk looked to Slick, who hefted the sack-covered cup up in his arms and tossed it to the thrower. 'Run!' the halfling shouted before diving under the bench.

Without stopping to think, Dunk snatched the cup from the air and tucked it under his arm. He glanced up at the field and saw the deadmen had fanned out to block the way onto the gridiron. He dashed over to his right and hesitated as he stood before the grinning Deckem.

'Go on, mate,' Deckem said with an amused sneer. 'Give it a go.'

Dunk feinted a lunge up the steps that led out of the dugout, then spun on his toes and sprinted out through the locker room tunnel, ducking around Edgar, who still knelt there. As he went, Dunk heard Deckem snarl after him and then cry out, 'Get him!'

Then Dunk heard a horrible crack from the dugout, and a roar of frustration from Deckem.

'Would you look at that?' Jotson's voice said. 'Now they're throwing benches at the Hackers from *inside* their own dugout! I haven't seen that kind of team discord since the last time Khorne's Killers played here. Worshipping a god of Chaos can wreak havoc with team unity, it seems!'

Dunk just put his head down and ran. He knew it wouldn't be long until Deckem and his fellow deadmen came after him. While he might be able to outrun them all for a while, he would eventually tire. The living dead like Deckem had no such limitations. They'd just keep coming after him until they wore him down into the dirt.

When Dunk reached the Hackers' locker room, he skidded to a halt. There, right in front of him, stood Merlin Olsen, his wand at the ready.

'That the cup you have with yourself there, lad?' the wizard said.

Dunk nodded. Somewhere behind him, there was another loud crack, and an inhuman wail chased after it.

'That Deckem and his blokes pounding along after you like a herd of headless orcs?'

Dunk nodded again.

'Then get out of the way, lad.' The wizard snapped his wrist, and his wand began to crackle with bright arcs of golden power. 'This is about to get ugly.'

Deckem darted into the locker room then, a long, leafy branch in his arms. From down the tunnel, Dunk could hear Edgar wailing in pain. Seeing the power coursing through the wizard's wand, though, pried his attention away from that, and he dived to one side, flinging himself along the open floor.

'You old fool!' Deckem said. 'What do you think you can–?'

Every hair on Dunk's body stood on end all at once as the crackling sound from Olsen's wand zoomed to a quick crescendo. The sound reminded Dunk of when his brother Dirk had once thrown a hive full of bees at him while they'd been staying at the family's country home. As the enraged insects chased him over and into the lake, they'd made a noise something like that, except it had ended with a splash into the cool, protective waters rather than an eardrum-bursting peal of thunder.

When Dunk managed to scrape himself back up off the floor, blood trickling from his ears, he looked back and saw a long line of crispy corpses starting at the entrance and flowing back into the tunnel as far as he could see. They each stood flash-baked into the positions in which they'd been at the moment Olsen's spell had gone off, like some grisly queue of grotesque sculptures still smoking with the heat of their creation.

Olsen reached out with the end of his wand and gently tipped the lead corpse backward. It fell into the one behind it, knocking it back into the others in a horrible domino effect. As each of the bodies tumbled backward, it fell apart to ashes, leaving only fragments of charred skeletons behind.

As Dunk staggered to his feet, the wizard came over and mouthed something at him. The thrower couldn't make it out over the ringing in his head. After another attempt, the wizard realised what was wrong and stopped trying to talk. Instead, he clapped Dunk on the back and gave him a big thumb's up.

Dazed, Dunk wandered over to a nearby bench and sat down on it, still clutching the cup to his chest. The last thing he remembered was telling himself not to let go of it, not for any reason, not even death.

DUNK AWAKENED IN darkness with the distinct feeling that the world was swimming underneath him. He squeezed his eyes closed tight and fought against the vertigo for a moment, but it refused to go away. After a moment, he gave up and tried to open his eyes, but he discovered that something lay bound over them, keeping the light out.

For a moment, Dunk panicked, thinking to find himself bound, gagged, and blindfolded, but his hands, he found, were free, his mouth uncovered. He brought his fingers up and removed the eyeless mask of black silk.

He saw that he lay in a bed on one side of a low, cramped room lit only by a single candle that burned softly on a desk along the opposite wall. Dark, hand-polished wood panelled the walls, floor, and ceiling. A couch in crimson velvet sat against the wall nearest Dunk's feet, along which hung long, heavy, black curtains. Only the slightest hint of daylight peeked around them, but it was enough to show the outline of the man sitting at the desk across the room, staring at the flickering light before him.

Shelves filled with books and scrolls lined every available inch of open wall. Most of these were tucked neatly away, except for a set of navigational charts sprawled across a low table that squatted in front of the couch. A capped pot of ink and a pilot's compass served as paperweights for these on one side, ensuring they didn't slide or slip off the table with the slow movement of the room. A full set of silver tea service, along with a pair of fine, ceramic cups and saucers, perched on the table's far end.

As Dunk slipped out of the bed, he realised he wore only his breeches. He wondered where his clothes had gone, but at the moment that didn't seem as important as figuring out where he had landed. He stole over to where the man sat at the table, watching – as it turned out – a crystal ball. In its glowing depths, images of a Blood Bowl game flashed by.

The players stood in a familiar stadium – the one in Kingsbury, Dunk remembered after a moment's reflection – and they wore the purple and gold uniforms of the Royals. The man in the middle – the coach perhaps? – thrust a cup into the air in a gesture of victory.

The camra panned out over the cheering fans, then returned to a close-up of the Royals' coach kissing the cup. It was a cheap replica of the original Far Albion Cup, a battered piece of tin that wouldn't be used for more than catching spit in any but the toughest pubs in Albion.

'Welcome back to the land of the living, Dunk,' Pegleg said, never taking his eyes from the image. 'I'm glad to see that rather expensive apothecary's efforts weren't all for naught.'

Dunk tried to think of something to say, but his tongue caught in his mouth. He stared down at the back of his former coach's head and coughed.

Pegleg turned slowly to face the thrower, a faint smile on his lips warring with concern in his eyes. 'You can hear me, can't you? That scurvy dog swore up and down that your ears would be fine.' When Dunk didn't answer, Pegleg raised his voice to a shout. 'CAN YOU HEAR ME?'

'Yes!' Dunk said, covering his ears at the noise. 'I heard you fine the first time. I'm just a little… Where am I?'

'My quarters, Dunk, aboard the *Sea Chariot.*'

Dunk blinked, confused. 'We're… What happened? Where are we going?'

'One thing at a time,' Pegleg said, taking Dunk by the arm and moving him over to sit on the couch.

As the coach poured them each a steaming cup of tea, Dunk gazed over at the crystal ball on Pegleg's writing desk. 'We lost,' he said. 'I'm – I'm sorry, coach. I mean, captain.'

Pegleg frowned as he handed Dunk his tea. 'Don't concern yourself with it. It's all over with now.'

'What happened?'

Pegleg chuckled at this. 'Didn't you see what Olsen's spell did to Deckem and his crew? Incinerated every last one of them. We're just lucky the rest of us had stopped to help Edgar up before following them.'

'All of you?'

Pegleg blushed a bit, which shocked Dunk. He didn't think the captain had the capacity for embarrassment. 'Not all. Some were busy keeping me from chasing after you and ripping out your eyes.'

Dunk's gaze flickered to the captain's hook then back to his tired, resigned eyes. 'Don't worry yourself, Dunk. I've given up those plans.'

'For good?' Dunk worked up a little laugh that sounded weak even to his ears.

'For now, at least,' Pegleg said with a mischievous grin.

'So what happened after the big boom?' Dunk asked, eager to get off this topic of conversation. 'It looks like the Royals won.'

'By default.' Pegleg grimaced, the pain showing all the way through to his eyes. 'We didn't have any players left – except Mr. Cavre, that is.'

Dunk gaped. 'What about the other guys? The living ones, I mean. Weren't they willing to play?'

Pegleg chuckled again. 'They all volunteered to go back on to the field, just as I'm sure you would have, had you been conscious. But the rules on these things are clear. You can only field the players you start the game with. Otherwise, a coach could just keep flooding a game with fresh players, right? And where would the sport be in that?'

Dunk shook his head. 'I thought you'd already taken care of the referee. Who would have stopped you?'

Pegleg smiled again, this time wider than Dunk could remember seeing since they had first procured the cup. 'It's not always a matter of getting caught by the officials. If we had tried to send on anyone but Cavre, the Game Wizards would have been on us like carbuncles.'

Dunk had dealt with two such GWs during the last season, a paired dwarf and elf by the names of Blaque and Whyte. He knew from experience how tenacious they could be. The Cabalvision networks hired them to keep the game in line and give it some semblance of fairness. It was one thing to cheat – in the sense of trying to gain a small edge or get away with a cheap shot – and something else entirely to flaunt the rules in front of a game's entire audience.

'Some of the men wanted to suit up in the deadmen's uniforms, but these had been burnt to cinders along with their bodies. The GWs aren't always the sharpest blades in the body, but even they can read those great numbers on the backs of the players' jerseys.

'Cavre insisted on going out there alone of course.'

Dunk nearly choked on his tea. 'And you let him?' If any one of the Hackers could take on a team by himself, it would be Carve – or perhaps M'Grash. Cavre would employ his experience and finesse to stay alive, though, while the ogre would rely purely on brute force.

'No, no, no,' Pegleg said. 'It would have been a fool's errand, Dunk, and I'd already played the fool far too often that day. I wasn't about to let my best and most loyal player risk almost certain death on the off-chance that he could manage to make up for a ten-player deficit on the gridiron. He's good, but not that good.'

'So you say,' Cavre said as he entered the room, 'but I would have liked a chance to test that theory.' The bright light of the day spilled in behind him, blinding Dunk until his eyes adjusted to its intensity.

'Where are we?' he asked. 'Have we left Albion behind?'

Cavre smiled wide, his white teeth almost as blinding to Dunk as the sunlight. 'You might say that, Mr. Hoffnung. We left land behind two days ago, and the people of Albion were happy to see us go, as the scorch marks along our stern testify.'

'Is everyone okay?' Dunk pushed himself to his feet, which wobbled under him, and not just from the rolling of the sea.

Cavre nodded. 'You got the worst of it. We didn't want to have to move you, but if we'd have left you there the Albion fans would have torn you to pieces.'

'So that means we're back down to six players again: you, Simon, Guillermo, M'Grash, Edgar, and me.' Dunk rubbed his eyes. 'Barely better off than when we left for Albion. At least we don't have to worry about the Far Albion Cup anymore.'

Cavre and Pegleg traded a guilty glance.

Dunk's eyes flew wide. 'I said, "At least we don't have to worry about the-" Ah, damn it! You still have it don't you.' He glowered at Pegleg.

The coach put up his hands to placate his thrower. 'We went through a lot to get our hands on that bit of hardware. It would have been a waste to leave it behind.'

'Also,' Cavre said, 'Olsen warned there could be dire consequences if we left the cup behind. He wanted the time to deal with it himself.'

Dunk did a double-take. 'He's still here? On this ship? With us?'

'All three,' Pegleg said. 'There's no better expert on the subject of the cup than Mr. Merlin. If we want to crack how to best use it without repeating the events in Albion, he's our best hope.'

Dunk gaped. 'Here's our best hope: throw the cup overboard.'

'Now, Mr. Hoffnung,' Pegleg said. 'That would condemn that poor soul to wander this damned world until the end of time. That hardly seems fair.'

'Oh, no,' Dunk said, 'to be condemned to live forever? I can think of worse fates – like getting killed, which that wizard almost managed to do to me.'

'Now, don't get upset–'

'Why not?' Dunk asked. 'If there's ever been something for me to get upset about, I think this is it. Do we even know if Olsen's telling the truth? Maybe that was just some sob story to get us to help him find the cup. Maybe he knew what would happen when we did. Maybe we should try tossing him overboard and see what happens.'

'Mr. K'Thragsh already did.' Cavre smiled softly. 'When he found out who'd hurt you, it took three of us, including Edgar, to keep him from ripping Mr. Merlin's head from his shoulders. Once he calmed down, we thought things were fine until Mr. Merlin somehow offended Mr. K'Thragsh.'

'M'Grash threw him into the ocean?' Dunk fought the impulse to laugh. 'How'd Olsen get back on the ship?'

'Edgar went in after him,' Pegleg said. 'Did you know that treemen float, Mr. Hoffnung? They might have drifted all the way back to Albion if we'd not gone back for them.'

'You should have let them.'

'Mr. K'Thragsh was willing to give it another try. Edgar stopped him, but the treeman wasn't fast enough to keep the ogre from trying to rip off the wizard's head instead.'

'And he's still here?'

'Not through any lack of effort on Mr. K'Thragsh's part, I assure you. Had he been able to murder Mr. Merlin, we'd have had a lovely funeral at sea by now.'

Dunk frowned and sat back down on the bed, his head in his hands. After a moment, he looked up at Pegleg and Cavre. 'That cup,' he said, 'it's poison. You know that. Why do you keep it around?'

Cavre started to answer, but Pegleg stopped him. He leaned forward and stared into Dunk's eyes. 'The cup is but a tool, Dunk, albeit a very powerful one. If we can master it, think of what we could do with it.'

'Think of what could happen to us – what almost did.' He scowled. 'Is this one of those "sharp, pointy bits of metal don't kill people – people kill people" arguments?'

Pegleg smiled. 'Something like that, but there's more. If we can figure out how to harness the cup's power, imagine what it would mean for the team. We'd win every game. We'd never lose a player again.'

Cavre nodded. 'You have seen many of your team-mates die, Mr. Hoffnung, but you have not been with the Hackers for long. Of those we have left, only Mr. K'Thragsh and myself have managed to complete more than a single season.' He sat on the couch across from Dunk and reached out to him with his dark eyes. 'I've lost many a friend over the years, Mr. Hoffnung. In one sense, I'm used to it. I've been around long enough to know it's all part of this game. But if we could stop that – if there's even a chance to do so – then I can't imagine why we wouldn't take it.'

'There's a better way to avoid getting killed on the gridiron,' Dunk said. He got to his feet and staggered toward the door. When he reached it, he turned back to Pegleg and Carve and said. 'Just don't play.'

'I DON'T LIKE this,' Dunk said as he gazed out over the Hackers' practice field in Bad Bay. 'Not one bit.'

'I know, son,' Slick said, fanning himself. 'I've never liked tryouts much. It wears me out just watching these things.'

'Don't you have a chance to sign new players though?' Dunk asked.

Slick shook his head. 'I'm a one-player kind of agent. Unless I can get two or more players on the same team, it's too hard to follow them around and give them the kind of help they need. Even I can't be in two places at once.'

Dunk looked down at the halfling. 'Have you tried to recruit anyone else on the Hackers?'

Slick rubbed his hands together. 'Most of them already have adequate if lesser representation. However, as a complete novice to the game, I generously took Edgar under my wing and helped him negotiate his contract with the Hackers.'

'You didn't let Pegleg pay him in maple syrup, did you?'

Slick scoffed. 'And what would I do with my fifteen percent of that? I love syrup as much as the next halfling, but that's a lot of pancakes.'

'I thought you got ten percent,' Dunk said. 'That's what I pay you.'

Slick shrugged. 'Edgar's a treeman. He doesn't understand money at all and has little use for it – or so he thinks. He was happy to pay me a bit extra to work as his financial advisor as well.' He looked up at Dunk, a glint in his eye.

'I can handle that myself.'

'Of course, of course.'

'But I didn't mean adding new players to the team,' Dunk said. 'That's not what I don't like. We need new players – about ten of them – but I'd rather not do it while Pegleg still has his hands on that cup. I mean, have you seen some of the hopefuls?'

Dunk pointed out at the gridiron, where Cavre ran the latest round of prospects through a set of drills. Most of them were built like bulls, and some featured thick coats of fur and savage claws or tusks. They came in various shades of green, brown, pink, and grey, and they bore tattoos, piercings, and filings. One and all, they seemed barely more than savages, ready to disembowel their foes and then strangle them with their own intestines. In fact, two players had already been cut from the tryouts for doing just that to their nearest competitors.

'I admit they look like the rejects from the Chaos All-Stars training camp, but what do you expect? After Lästiges's Far Albion Cup special aired on Wolf Sports last week, just as many people think the Hackers are cursed as blessed. After all, we've lost twenty-one players already this year, cup or no. You'd have to be a pretty desperate sort to want to join up with such an outfit.'

'Or to stay with one.'

'You're not thinking of leaving the Hackers, are you, son? I could probably get you signed with another team, but not until the season's over. Pegleg's contracts are rock solid about that.'

Dunk shook his head. 'I don't give up that easily. It's just…'

'There are places you'd rather be.'

Dunk hung his head and nodded.

'Have you heard from Spinne again?'

'Not since we got back.' Dunk frowned. He could feel her letter in his pocket. He'd taken it out and read it at least three times a day since he'd got it. 'I can't believe they used that footage of me waking up in Lästiges's bed. You'd have thought she'd have more control over things like that.'

'The camra followed her around every second of that trip, son. Sadly, the little daemon inside doesn't have a discriminating memory. But if you had to be with that reporter woman every moment of your life, you'd probably be eager to ruin her life too.'

Dunk shrugged. Out on the field, one of the hopefuls snapped another prospect's arm in two with a sickening crack. The injured player kept right on running, though, leaping past another assailant and spinning his way into the end zone.

'Have you heard from your brother?'

Dunk frowned. 'Not at all.'

'I hear he broke it off with Lästiges too.'

'That's what ESPNN said on its *Best Damn Blood Bowl Show Period.* The Gobbo laughed so hard at the news I thought he'd choke on his own rancid spit.'

'We should be so lucky.'

Dunk sighed. 'I'm not looking forward to seeing him again.'

'I guess you're lucky we were still at sea when they announced the Blood Bowl would be in Kislev this year. There's something rotten about that though.'

'If Pegleg could have made the *Sea Chariot* grow wings, he would have flown us there in a heartbeat.'

'I heard he asked Olsen to try.' Slick laughed.

'And we would have done it too, given a bit more time.'

Dunk and Slick turned around to see the wizard standing behind them. Dunk felt his anger at the wizard start to rise, but he shoved it back down and bottled it up.

'So we could get there without enough players?' Slick asked. 'Or would you have just let the cup recruit them for us so we could duplicate our experiences in Albion?'

'We'd have worked it out,' the wizard said. 'Where there's a wand, there's a way.'

'You don't think sorcery's done enough harm to your life?' Dunk asked. 'Such as it is?'

'We lay in a bed of our own making, all of us, laddie. Don't think you're any exception.'

Dunk shot a hard look at the wizard. 'I'm just wondering why you're still here. Didn't you have a date with a cup of your own blood? For someone so weary of life, you seem to have taken a shine to it again.'

Olsen smiled as he bent over to pick a tiny white flower from the ground. 'There's nothing like staring the abyss in the face to make you long for the light.' He brought the bloom to his nose and sniffed it deeply. 'Aye. Everything suddenly seems much brighter than before.'

'If you like them so much, perhaps you'd like to gather a bouquet for yourself,' Slick said. 'I understand there's a real demand for ex-Blood Bowl players who know their way around a floral arrangement.'

Olsen smiled down at the halfling, then reached over and tucked the flower behind Slick's ear. 'Perhaps we will at that, my wee friend. The world has seen stranger things.'

With that, the wizard turned on his heel and strode off, smiling as he raised his face to the gentle rays of the sun.

'You know,' Slick said, 'that guy's really starting to get on my nerves.' He snatched the flower from his ear and threw it down to grind it into the dirt with his heel.

'WHAT'S WRONG?' DUNK said as he opened the door to his modest room above the FIB Tavern, which took its name for the opinion the owner held of the particular variety of Imperial Bastards ruling the Empire from distant Altdorf.

'Simon, he is sick,' Guillermo said. 'I think it is serious.'

Dunk rubbed his eyes. 'It's the middle of the night,' he said. 'Why bother me? Shouldn't someone get an apothecary?'

The Estalian nodded. 'Slick, he is already on his way, but I thought you might want to see this.'

Dunk paused for a moment, and then nodded. 'Let me get my boots and my blade.'

Moments later, Dunk and Guillermo stood outside Simon's room in the Hacker Hotel, the finest such establishment for at least fifty miles around. Most of the Hackers stayed here. In fact, at the moment only Dunk and M'Grash did not.

While the ogre didn't feel welcome at the Hacker Hotel – and rightfully so, given the way the staff always treated him like a lit bomb during his infrequent visits – Dunk had spent too much time worrying about money to patronise such a place. The FIB had everything he needed, and at a quarter of the price. As the son of a nobleman, Dunk had known great wealth in his youth, but his family had lost all that years ago. Having tasted both fortune and poverty, Dunk had the respect for gold that many of the other players lacked.

'His room is next door to mine,' Guillermo said. 'Tonight, we drank in the great hall downstairs with some of the new recruits. I had enough, so I excused myself and went to sleep. Later, I heard horrible moans coming from Simon's place, loud enough to wake me up. I got up to check on him, but the door was locked.'

Dunk saw where the frame around the lock's bolt had been shattered. 'You didn't let that stop you.'

'How could I? If you'd have heard the noises, you'd have–'

A plaintive groan interrupted the Estalian, emphasising the point he'd been about to make. It sounded like it could only have come from an animal that had lain dying for a long, pitiless time.

Dunk gave the door a push, and it swung wide on well-oiled hinges. Inside, a large, canopied bed with an airy mattress stood near the window in the far wall. A lamp flickered on the bedside table, showing something – someone, Dunk corrected – writhing in the once-crisp sheets now soaked with sweat.

As Dunk followed Guillermo into the room, the first thing that hit him was the sweet stench of decay. For a moment, he wondered if Simon had left a meal out in his room before they'd left for Albion. Only so much time with old meat left to rot could explain such a horrible smell, or so Dunk thought.

Then he saw Simon.

The catcher looked like he'd caught something horrible. An oily, grey sheen covered his skin and seemed to have stained through his breeches and soiled the bedclothes. He shivered as if adrift on an artic plain, although the night wind that breezed in through the open window was warm and humid.

Guillermo reached out to pull a cover over Simon. That was when Dunk saw the red rash crawling over Simon's skin. He snatched Guillermo's hand back before he could touch the soiled sheets.

'You see that?' Dunk asked the scowling Estalian. The rash seemed to be moving like a horde of insects along Simon's skin. 'I've seen that before – although it wasn't moving like that then.'

'Where?'

Dunk's mind flashed back to the horrible, maimed creature in the cultists' tent in that damned hollow in the heart of the Sure Wood. The rash on his skin had looked similar to this, although it hadn't crawled in the same way. Dunk wondered, though, if that was because it had already done as much damage as it could have to that poor soul.

'Just don't touch him,' Dunk said, giving Guillermo's hand back to him. Then a horrible thought struck him. 'Or have you already?'

'No,' Guillermo said. 'So I swear. When I first came in, he was thrashing about so much that it terrified me. I went for help right away. I found Slick in the hall, and he told me to watch over Simon while he went for help.'

'But you came to get me instead?'

Guillermo hesitated, and then seemed to make a decision. 'What you have not yet told me, that is what I feared.' He glanced down at his suffering friend as he loosed another pathetic moan for mercy. 'I had hoped this would not be.'

'Why didn't you just wake up Cavre? He's right here in the building.'

Guillermo grimaced. 'I know where his loyalties lie: with the captain. If Captain Haken had found out about this before I did, I am sure we would have only found an empty bed in the morning, with no explanation ever.'

Dunk put a hand on Guillermo's shoulder. 'I have more faith in Cavre than that, but I understand.' He looked over at Simon and winced. 'So, what should we do?'

'I had hoped that you might have an answer to that.'

Dunk knew immediately that the right answer was to kill Simon on the spot, to burn his body the way he'd immolated the creature back in the Sure Wood. That way, he could make sure no one else contracted the disease as well. But if he did that, he might never learn how Simon got sick.

'An illness like this doesn't come from nowhere,' Dunk said. 'We need to find out what happened to him.'

'But how?' Guillermo asked, terror creeping into his voice.

'Have you tried talking to him?'

The Estalian shook his head, his eyes bulging wide.

Dunk turned toward where Simon writhed on the bed and called his name once, softly, then again, louder.

Simon screamed as he sat bolt upright in his bed.

Dunk jumped back a step. He heard Guillermo let out a little squeak behind him, and when he glanced over his shoulder he saw the lineman back out in the hallway, peering around the frame of the door.

'Simon,' Dunk said. 'Listen to me. You're sick. Very sick. Do you know what happened to you? Can you tell me?'

Simon's eyes were wide but seemed to be watching something outside the room's four walls. Unfocused and bloodshot, they darted back and forth, searching for creatures that existed only in the fevered corners of the catcher's mind. Dunk called his name again. 'Simon? Simon Sherwood?'

The catcher screamed again. This time, he did not stop.

'You cannot do it like that,' Cavre said as he strode into the room in only a pair of long flowing pants, naked to the waist. 'You must be more forceful. Observe.' He stood at the end of the bed and glared down at the shivering Simon sitting there in his soiled sheets, stopping screaming only to take another breath before starting again.

'Mr. Sherwood!' Cavre said.

Simon's head whipped up, and his eyes snapped into focus on Cavre. His scream caught in his throat. For a moment, the only sound in the room was the Albionman's still-panicked panting.

'You are sick, Mr. Sherwood. If you do not listen to me and follow my instructions, you will die before sunrise.'

The catcher stared at Cavre with eyes as wide around as saucers. He said not a word, but his breathing slowed its pace, and he nodded at the star blitzer's words.

'Who did this to you?'

Simon shook his head as if not one word of the question made a bit of sense.

'You slept with someone tonight.'

Simon nodded.

'Who was it?'

'Ragretta,' the catcher croaked. 'She said her name was Ragretta.'

Guillermo moved a bit further into the room from where he'd been cowering behind the door. 'I saw him with a girl with long, curly hair,' he said. 'He disappeared with her about a half hour before I went to bed.' He stared down at his friend. 'I thought he'd got lucky.'

'He's lucky he's not already dead,' Cavre said. 'Have you sent for an apothecary yet?'

Dunk heard the patter of little feet out in the hallway, along with longer, steadier strides. Slick burst into the room, a lit lantern swinging in his hand and a bowl-shouldered old woman wrapped in a black shawl right behind him. The woman took one look at Simon and gasped.

'I – there is nothing–' she looked at the blade hanging at Dunk's side. 'Kill him,' she said, her eyes wild with fear. 'Cut off his head and burn his body. There is no other way.'

Dunk balked at this. 'There must be!'

The woman snatched at his sword, but Cavre caught her fragile wrist in his hand. 'He is not too far gone yet,' the blitzer said. 'I know something of this sickness. Work with me to save him.'

The woman shuddered for a moment, looking up at Cavre with wide, watery eyes. Then she lowered her head and nodded. 'It will be pointless, but I will try.'

'We could use you on our cheerleading team,' Slick said.

'What can we do to help?' Dunk asked, feeling as helpless as a child.

'Find this Ragretta,' Cavre said.

'And bring her back so you can force her to cure Simon?' Guillermo said hopefully.

Cavre shook his head gravely. 'Kill her and burn her body, but be careful not to touch her yourself. I'm afraid that for what Simon has there may be no cure.'

Dᴜɴᴋ ᴛʜᴏᴜɢʜᴛ Gᴜɪʟʟᴇʀᴍᴏ might fall to his knees right there and weep. Before that could happen, he grabbed the lineman by his shoulder and dragged him out of the room. Slick followed after them, closing the door behind them.

Dunk trotted down to the great hall, the others keeping up as best they could. When they got there, though, the place was dark but for the dying embers of what had once been a roaring fire in the main hearth.

'How will we find her now?' Guillermo said, his voice cracking with despair. 'She could be anywhere.'

'Well,' Slick said, 'if I were a wanton, Nurgle-worshipping harlot who passed on her dread lord's diseases through sex, where would I go?'

'Hush,' Dunk said, raising a hand as he cocked an ear. The hotel stood quiet at this hour of the night. The staff had all turned in for the night, and most of the guests were likely asleep in their rooms. If the cultist was still awake, they might be able to–

Dunk's head snapped up, and he beckoned for the others to follow him. He strode through the hall until he reached the door to the kitchen, under which a faint light flickered. A series of soft grunts and groans emanated from the room beyond. He drew his sword as silently as he could and motioned for Guillermo to quietly push open the swinging door.

Back in the Sure Wood, he'd seen the orgy from a distance, and he'd done his best to ignore it. Recovering the cup had been at the top of his agenda, and he'd refused to let prurient curiosity jeopardise his chances at that. Here, though, now, with the three participants right in front of him – lost in the throes of their disease-tainted ecstasy – he could not avoid it.

What the woman was doing with the men – who Dunk recognised as two of the more bestial prospects in the training camp that week – wasn't unbelievable, but her bare skin crawled with the same mobile, crimson rash that Simon had borne. As he watched, the rash slipped from body to body, transferring between the woman and the men where bare bits of flesh rubbed against each other, and then coming back again.

The trio turned at the sound of the opening of the kitchen door. The two prospects leaped away from the woman, surprised at having been caught with her. The woman, on the other hand, showed no sign of shame. She flashed Dunk a sly wink and licked her lascivious lips, beckoning for him to join them in their twisted tryst.

There was a moment – just a brief one, a fraction of a second – when Dunk considered joining the woman, knocking the others aside and taking her for himself. Her seductive eyes begged him to do so.

Instead, he brandished his sword at her. 'I know what you are,' he said. 'Plaguebearer.'

The prospects looked at the woman, as if for the first time, and gasped as they saw the rash writhing along her skin. Then they saw the same marks moving through their own flesh, and they screamed in horror.

The sound startled Dunk, and the woman took the opportunity to leap at him. He stumbled as he tried to avoid her, tripping backward through the door and dropping his blade. She leapt after him as he landed on his rump and tried to scramble away in a desperate crab-walk.

'Join us,' the woman hissed, her breath the sweet, fetid odor of a fresh corpse. She gathered up his sword in her hands and caressed its blade.

Before Dunk could respond, Slick threw his lit lantern at the woman. When it smashed into her, the lamp's oil burst and its flame set her ablaze. She howled, although whether in agony or fury, Dunk could not tell. Guillermo cut the horrible noise short when he stepped forward and brained her with a cast-iron frying pan.

Later – after Dunk had carted off the woman's burnt remains, and Slick and Guillermo had carefully brought the two prospects to see Cavre – the three sat around the glowing embers in the hearth, drinking from a flask of wine Slick had appropriated from the kitchen.

'Did anyone touch them?' Dunk asked.

'Just my frying pan,' Guillermo said, pointing at the weapon he'd tossed into the crackling fire, along with another log. 'They did not put a finger on me.'

Slick nodded along with the lineman. 'Careful you don't let Pegleg know you're that good with a frying pan,' he said. 'The next time we're on the *Sea Chariot*, he'll make you the ship's cook.'

'Leave it in the hearth,' Dunk said, jerking his chin at the pan. 'The fire should have cleaned it well enough, but why take the risk?'

'What about your sword?' Guillermo said. Dunk had left it wrapped in the same tarp they'd used to haul away the woman's charred body. 'It is a handsome blade to throw away.'

'It's just a thing,' Dunk said. 'I can always get another sword.'

'That's a good attitude, Mr. Hoffnung,' Cavre said as he walked into the great hall. 'It is far better to be cautious than cauterised.'

'How is Simon?' Guillermo asked. Dunk could hear a bit of guilt mixed in the worry lacing the lineman's words. 'And the others?'

'Simon will live,' Cavre said, 'although only Nuffle knows for how long. The two prospects killed themselves when they saw him and realised what lay in store for them.'

Dunk, Slick, and Guillermo gasped. 'Does he suffer so?' asked the lineman.

Cavre grimaced. 'Not as much as before. The old woman and I had to wrap him in strips of linen from head to toe and soak the wrappings in beer.' The blitzer stopped when he saw the others goggling at him. 'The alcohol helps to sterilise his skin. He has also consumed enough of it for it to have a sedative and anesthetic effect.'

'How long will he have to be like that?' Dunk asked.

Cavre shook his head. 'It is impossible to say. For now, the disease is under control, although I wouldn't share a bottle with him.'

Slick looked wall-eyed at the flask of wine now in his hands, then set it gingerly on the table before him. No one else reached out for it.

'It could take him at any time,' Cavre continued. 'Or he could live for years.'

'Can't you do anything about it?' Guillermo said.

Cavre shook his head. 'In my homeland, deep in the Southlands, such an illness is considered untreatable. The old woman knew it not at all.'

'What about Olsen?' Dunk asked.

'We're afraid not, lads,' the wizard said as he entered the great hall. 'Our skills go more to harming things than healing them. The best we could offer that poor sod is a quick release.'

'Will he ever play ball again?' Guillermo asked.

Cavre nodded. 'As long as he stays covered in his wrappings and keeps them wet, I do not see why not.'

Dunk looked over at Slick and saw that the halfling had his head down and his shoulders shaking. The thrower reached out and tried to comfort his friend with a hand on his shoulder.

Slick threw back his head, his face shining with tears. Dunk had never seen the halfling show such emotion before, and he felt his own grief over Simon's fate rising in his chest, threatening to break through as terrible sobs. He heard Guillermo already sniffling beside him.

'I'm sorry,' Slick said, wiping the tears from his face with the palms of his little hands. 'I'm so sorry!'

'No,' Dunk said. 'It's not your fault. You had nothing to do with it.'

'Or did you?' Olsen asked. 'Is there something you'd care to share with us, wee one? Secrets you need to slough from your soul?'

'No,' Slick said, his body shaking again. 'Not that. I'm sorry for laughing so damn hard.'

With that, the halfling doubled over, gasping for air.

Dunk stared at his agent for a moment, then at the others, all of whom goggled at the callous creature.

'What's so damn funny?' Dunk asked, pulling Slick back up to sit straight in his chair. 'What?'

'I know it's horrible,' Slick said. 'But all I can see in my head is Simon charging down the field in his wet wrappings, smelling of yeast and barley.' He put his hands out in front of him as if to frame a picture, then thrust his arms forward, his hands formed into claws.

'Imagine a drunk, diseased, living mummy staggering down the field at you like a walking bar rag.'

Olsen started to snicker. 'He'd be almost too drunk to stand, but everyone would be afraid to tackle him.'

'Talk about a mummy's curse,' Guillermo said, a wry smile on his face. 'He'll be fine – as long as stays away from the toilets. M'Grash might mistake him for an ogre-sized roll of toilet paper.'

Dunk had to laugh at this, despite himself, and even Cavre joined in.

'Thirsty ogres might be a hazard too. Jim Johnson might try to wring him out so he can drink all the beer.'

'Oh,' Slick said, 'if he did that in the announcer's booth in front of that bloodsucker Bob Bifford – now there's a cage match I'd *pay* to see.'

This set the entire group off, giggling like children until they were finally too tired to go on.

Dunk felt better about Simon for a moment, but he felt guilty too. 'I can't believe we're joking about a dying team-mate,' he said softly. That capped the laughter, and everyone fell silent.

Slick, solemn as the rest of them now, reached over and clapped Dunk on the knee. 'Laugh or cry, son,' he said. 'Laugh or cry.'

'THE HACKERS SURE have made a comeback since their devastating loss in the *Spike! Magazine* tournament, Jim. They look like a whole new team!'

'They practically are, Bob! As chronicled in the Wolf Sports' Cabalvision special *The Hackers Far Albion Cup*, they picked up a tree-man known only as Edgar during their time in Albion, the only survivor of the slate of rookies who joined the team while on that distant isle. Isn't that right, Lästiges?'

Dunk saw the lady reporter's smiling image appear in the monstrous Jumboball squatting over the east end zone of Emperor Stadium. This crystal ball was, if anything, larger than the one in Magritta, and just looking at it filled Dunk's head with thoughts of rolling, shattering balls again.

'It's anchored down tight, son,' Slick said, standing next to him on the edge of the Hackers' dugout. 'Don't give it another thought.'

'The Hackers are one of the most resilient teams I've had the pleasure to follow,' Lästiges said in a chipper tone. Dunk thought he could see something sad around her ten-foot tall eyes, though, and he wondered about his brother.

Dirk would be somewhere in Altdorf today too, along with Spinne and the rest of the Reavers. They were supposed to be playing a game later today in the Altdorf Oldbowl, their home stadium, against Da Deff Skwadd, a team of orcs, trolls, and goblins hailing from the distant Badlands, just west of the furthest end of the Worlds Edge Mountains. The oddsmakers – including the Gobbo – heavily favoured the Reavers, which comforted Dunk a bit. He didn't really care who won the game, though, as long as Dirk and Spinne came out of it all right.

'What else can you say about a team that only has two of the same players from two seasons ago?' Lästiges continued. 'They lost another fifteen players in the Far Albion Cup finals too in a tragic magical accident involving their own team wizard, the legendary – at least in the small media market of Albion – Olsen Merlin.

'Amazingly, the Hackers still have Merlin in their employ. This reporter can only speculate that this has something to do with the wizard's long history with the Hackers' new lucky charm: the original Far Albion Cup itself. The question in most fans' minds today, though, has to be: can a trophy, however pretty it might be, be enough to boost the Hackers out of the basement?'

'Now, Lästiges,' Bob said, 'the Hackers did make it to the finals of the Blood Bowl Open last year. What makes things so different this time around?'

Lästiges laughed. 'I suppose you must have been napping during the last game the Hackers played in the Old World. In the *Spike! Magazine* Tournament, the Chaos All-Stars handed the Hackers their heads – literally, in some cases. There's been rampant speculation since then that the Hackers might have somehow benefited – knowingly or not – from the machinations behind last year's Black Jerseys scandal.'

'Did you just use the word 'machinations' in a Blood Bowl broadcast?' Jim asked with a rude cackle. 'I think most of our viewers' eyes just rolled back into their heads. Let's get down to the action!'

Dunk tried to ignore the announcers for the rest of the game. The Jumboball made that hard though, and every time he heard Lästiges's voice he glanced up there and wondered if she'd managed to reconcile with Dirk yet. If there was hope for those two, then there might be some for Dunk and Spinne too.

Dunk hadn't allowed himself to think too much about Spinne since he'd got her letter. He'd written back to her three times, explaining himself, but he'd never received any response. He'd wanted to go to Altdorf to find her, but Slick had talked him out of it. Both the Hackers and the Reavers were in training for the Blood Bowl. His team needed him here.

More of a problem was the fact that, as this year's favourites, the Reavers had hidden themselves away in a secret camp for the entire month before the game. Their coach wanted no distractions, and he'd gone to great lengths to make sure that even people as dedicated as jilted lovers wouldn't be able to bother his players.

The Hackers lost the toss and set up down at the west end of the field to kick-off the ball. The Darkside Cowboys, a team composed entirely of dark elves dressed in black and blue uniforms, jogged down to the east end to receive.

'These Cowboys are mean bastards,' Pegleg had said in his pre-game talk to the entire team. 'They may not have the raw power of a team like the Oldheim Ogres, but they make up for it by playing the most vicious and ruthlessly efficient football I've ever seen. Their star blitzer – Raghib 'the White Rocket' Ishmael – once tore out two players' hearts and stuffed them into each others' chests, right in the middle of the game. And they played for the Cowboys!'

'Why do they call him 'the White Rocket'?' Dunk had asked Slick later.

'He's an albino, son,' Slick said. 'Skin whiter than the silver hair you see on most dark elves. And he's faster than just about anything else on two legs. He's got an amazing arm too. Used to be a whaler on a ship called the *Ahab*, and he hurls that ball like a harpoon.'

Dunk gritted his teeth as he waited for Cavre to kick the ball to the waiting Cowboys. He gazed around at the others players on the field and realised he didn't know but half of them well. He'd practiced with the new players, but they mostly kept to themselves. With all the death that had surrounded the team lately, Dunk hadn't felt like getting to know them. He didn't want to make more friends just to lose them too.

Besides which, they were a surly lot. Something about the new recruits put Dunk's teeth on edge. He had to admit they were good players, if not spectacular, but he wished they were all on someone else's team. They might be his team-mates but never his friends.

He told himself he was overreacting. The whole debacle with Deckem and his deadmen had left him with a foul taste in his mouth when it came to Blood Bowl. This was his first game since the Far Albion Cup Final. Once he got back into the zone, it would all be fun again.

Right?

The roar of the crowd rose as Cavre put up his hand, signalling to the others that he was about to kick the ball. As he ran forward, the noise reached a blistering crescendo, and then fell off as the ball sailed through the air toward the Cowboys.

Dunk raced straight down the field, following in M'Grash's wake as the ogre charged along the north side. Edgar cleared out the south side as he strode into and through the oncoming Cowboys, forcing the ball carrier back into the centre. Peering around the ogre's shoulder, Dunk saw that Ishmael, who stood taller than all of the other dark elves, had the ball.

'Oh, my, Bob! Did you see that move?'

'Barely, Jim, barely. The White Rocket is zooming along so fast I almost missed it. Too bad for the Hackers' rookie lineman Karfheim that Ishmael didn't miss him.'

'I wonder how the White Rocket gets out bloodstains when they fountain all over him like that. Perhaps Lästiges would know?'

'Just because I'm a woman doesn't mean I know one end of a laundry tub from another, girls,' Lästiges said. 'You're a vampire, Bob. Don't you know?'

'I know better than to get blood on my clothes,' Bob said. 'Oh! And there goes another player, the Cowboys' Meion Sanders. It's always sad to see a future Hall of Famer take a fall like that.'

'The only future Meion has is with an undead team now,' Jim said, 'if they can piece together enough of his corpse.'

Dunk spotted Ishmael jinking his way, and he spun out from behind M'Grash to launch himself at the Cowboy's star blitzer. Ishmael was ready for him and tried to stiff-arm him out of the way, but Dunk just grabbed the albino's white-skinned arm and spun him to the ground.

The ball tumbled free, and Dunk scrambled after it. Before he could reach it though, he felt a pair of wiry arms wrap around his lower legs and bring him to the Astrogranite.

'You dare to stand before the White Rocket, Hoffnung?' a voice rasped into his helmet. 'You should expect to pay.'

Dunk felt a blade cut across the back of his thigh, trying to hamstring him, but as the edge pierced his flesh, he wriggled away. The razor secreted in the edge of Ishmael's gauntlet missed its mark.

Dunk reached back and grabbed Ishmael's helmet by the face guard. The albino pulled away, slipping out of the helmet before Dunk could twist his head off. 'Well played, Hoff-Nung,' the not-so-dark elf hissed, 'but no one can stop a rocket.'

Dunk spun about, looking for the ball, and saw that Simon had scooped it up. As he ran for the end zone, many of the Cowboys seemed to be avoiding him, shoving their team-mates toward the diseased Hacker instead.

'Would you look at that?' Bob said. 'First the Hackers have an ogre on their team. Then a treeman. And now it's a mummy! Now that's diversity for you. Never let anyone tell you the dead and the living don't mix!'

'As we can testify ourselves, old friend,' said Jim. 'But according to the lovely Lästiges, that's no mummy!'

'Has anyone told the kids?'

'Ha, ha,' Lästiges said mirthlessly. 'That's none other than Simon Sherwood, the Albion native who joined the Hackers at the start of last season. Simon had a bit of a run-in with a ladyfriend who should have been playing groupie for Nurgle's Rotters instead. Now he's the poster child for safe sex.'

'And just how do you have safe sex with a Nurgle cultist?' Jim asked. 'An all-over body wrap like that? It seems Sherwood's trying to seal up the dungeon after the daemons are already out.'

'That's right,' Bob said. 'It seems like the secret to safe sex is the same as it is for comedy.'

'Is that so? Then tell us, what is—'

'Timing!'

Dunk felt a burning sensation across his back and turned around to see Ishmael standing behind him, his gauntlet running with blood. The albino grinned at him, showing a set of jet-black teeth behind his pale, white lips.

'You must be the sensitive sort, Hoff-Nung,' the albino said. 'Most people never feel the White Rocket's cuts until they're dead.'

'It's because your blade's just like you,' Dunk said, smashing the Cowboy over his unprotected head with his own helmet. 'Dull.'

The albino went down, crimson blood spurting from his shattered nose. Against Ishmael's white skin, the fluid looked redder than Dunk thought possible. As he watched it flow, he had to fight back a terrible urge to keep pounding at the helpless dark elf with his helmet until his head was only a bloody smear on the Astrogranite.

'Touchdown, Hackers!' Bob said. 'Simply amazing. Have you ever seen a score like that, Jim?'

'Not since the last time the Hackers played in the Old World, back in Magritta, but they were on the other side of the equation then. It seems they've learned how to play that kind of game. It's not often you see a body count that high on a team's first possession.'

Dunk looked back toward the Cowboys' end zone, where Simon was still letting loose with a complicated victory dance that threatened to unwind his wrappings. Between the thrower and the end zone, bodies in black and blue uniforms littered the field. In fact, by Dunk's count, not one of the Cowboys who had started the game still stood.

'Damn,' he swore, dropping Ishmael's helmet next to the albino's unconscious form. 'Not again.'

'IT'S THE CUP,' Dunk said to Pegleg. The coach's office attached to the Hackers' locker room was a cramped place made even more so by the large crystal ball mounted on the lone desk. It made the ex-pirate seem more dangerous than usual, perhaps because with the door shut behind him Dunk knew there was no place in the room that was out of the coach's reach. He wondered if the room had been built with that in mind.

'What, Mr. Hoffnung, is your point?'

'Coach, we can't go around killing off every team we face.'

'And why not?' Pegleg leaned back in his chair and ran a hand back through his long curls. Far more grey streaked them than had when they first met, Dunk noticed. 'Blood Bowl is a violent game. People get killed in it all the time.'

'We've already had this conversation,' Dunk said. 'You gave the cup up once before.'

'That was in a moment of weakness,' Pegleg said, leaning forward, his fingers splayed across the desk. 'I should never have given in. What did that do for us? We lost the Far Albion Cup tournament – including the purse, which would have helped defray the exorbitant expenses of the trip.

'A Blood Bowl team is not a charity. You expect to be paid, don't you? Your agent certainly expects you to, and the rest of the team would like to take their sacks of gold home, too, twice a month whether I have the cash or not.'

'Money isn't everything,' Dunk said.

'Spoken like a nobleman's son,' the coach said, scowling. 'You're right!' he continued as he leapt to his feet and stabbed his hook into the desk's mahogany surface. 'It's the *only* thing!'

'Coach.'

'Mr. Hoffnung. As long as I *am* the coach and you are the *player*, you will respect my decisions!'

Dunk noticed that Pegleg's hook was caught where he'd embedded it in the top of the desk. The ex-pirate tried to twist it free, but he was stuck. This took the wind from his sails, and he sat back down in his chair, the hook still jammed into the wood between them.

'Dunk,' Pegleg said, his manner softer, more reasonable. 'This isn't like the last time. Mr. Merlin has assured me of that. He believes he can control the cup and its effects.'

'But can he control our new players?'

'That is *my* responsibility, although he seemed to do a fine job of it last time.' He narrowed his eyes at Dunk. 'You might recall how it went.'

The door to the office swung open, and Dunk had to step aside to avoid it hitting him. There, framed in the entrance, stood the two Game Wizards who had stalked Dunk through much of the previous season: Blaque and Whyte.

Despite the fact that Whyte was an elf and Blaque was a dwarf, the two stood equally tall. As pale as Ishmael, but with white teeth and blue eyes, Whyte had never smiled that Dunk had seen. He didn't know if the elf even could.

Blaque, on the other hand, smiled all the time but in a wry, sarcastic way. He looked like he'd been carved from a mountain and covered with hair the colour of the coal mined from the range's roots.

Like Whyte, he wore a crisp-pressed GW uniform: a dark robe sashed with a crimson rope, a frothing wolf's head embroidered across the chest.

'What a happy reunion this is, don't you agree, Whyte?' the dwarf said with a smarmy grin. 'All of us back together again. It's just like old times.'

'I can't say I care for old times,' the elf said solemnly. 'They weren't all that good either.'

'What can I do for you, gentle wizards?' Pegleg said. He gave one last tug on his hook, subtly enough that the GWs might not notice, but Dunk saw that he was still stuck.

'The Far Albion Cup,' Blaque said. 'We're here to take it.'

'I'm afraid that's not possible.' The ex-pirate showed a savage smile that exposed his golden teeth.

'What do you think?' Blaque asked Whyte. 'Does he have much of an imagination?'

'I'd hazard not,' Whyte said. 'People with an imagination know that all sorts of things are possible.'

'It's not going to happen,' Pegleg said, the smile fading from his face.

'See, now this is where my imagination starts to kick in,' Blaque said. 'I can imagine all sorts of ways that this can happen.'

He stuck out one stubby finger. 'First, you can give it to us peacefully, and we'll quietly take it away.'

He stuck out another finger. 'Second, we can take it from your bloody corpse.'

The dwarf looked at the elf, concerned. 'Actually, that's it for me. I'm all out. You have any other notions?'

'You're the one with the imagination. Those sound like fine options to me.'

'You're not taking the cup, and you will not lay a finger on me.' The coach looked a lot more confident about his pronouncement than Dunk felt.

'Interesting,' Blaque said, chewing a chubby lip. 'Seems he does have a wild imagination after all.'

'That cup is the property of the Hackers, and its use falls within the rules as laid down by Sacred Commissioner Roze-El, directly from Nuffle's Book. If you take it from me – or lay a hand on me or any of my players to try it – I'll report you directly to Ruprecht Murdark himself.'

'Murdark's not here this time, is he?' Blaque said. 'By the time he asks us what happened, they'll be laying flowers on your grave. What kind do you think we should send?'

'Lilies,' Whyte said. 'I always like lilies.'

A wide grin grew on Pegleg's face as he looked past the Game Wizards and into the locker room beyond. 'Welcome, Mr. Merlin,' he said. 'Do you happen to know these two? Allow me to introduce–'

As the two GWs turned to see who Pegleg was talking to, the Albionish wizard bared his teeth at them in an unfriendly way. 'Only by reputation, laddie, but that's enough for us.' He glared at the two shorter wizards in turn, fingering the wand in his hand as he spoke. 'Listen to us, you two charlatans. Blackguards like you may be able to intimidate the ignorant with your parlour tricks, but we are not impressed. If we catch you talking with our employer again, we're going to assume you're up to no good and fry you on the spot.'

He paused for a moment to measure the looks on the other wizards' faces. 'Is that clear?'

Blaque jerked his head toward the door, and Whyte headed for it. Olsen stepped aside to let him pass, and the dwarf followed after him. Once he was out of the office, Blaque turned back and said, 'We're not through with this yet.'

Olsen barked a sharp, short laugh. 'Faith! Of course not, laddie. It won't end until you force our hand.' He stuffed his wand back into his robes. 'Then it'll be over before you know it.'

'HE SAID HE'D meet you here?' Slick asked, gazing around the Skinned Cat.

Dunk nodded, as he nursed his pint of Bugman's XXXXXX. It looked the same as ever: rough-hewn tables and chairs that looked like they'd been used more often as weapons than furniture, sawdust on the floor to soak up the spilled beer and vomit and blood.

It was the kind of seedy joint in which the patrons kept to themselves and minded their own business. The tourists in town for the Blood Bowl mostly stayed clear of this part of town, as it had a deserved reputation for being deadly dangerous. When Dunk had lived as a boy here in Altdorf, he would never have considered entering such a place, except in his most adventurous daydreams.

If anyone recognised Dunk as a Blood Bowl player here, they refused to admit it, and that was just what he wanted: a measure of anonymity. When the Blood Bowl Open came to town, a kind of madness invaded the city, carried in the hearts of the hundreds of thousands of fans in town for the games. Not all of them could manage to get tickets, but that deterred no one. Just being close to the stadiums when the games were being played was enough. That's why the Skinned Cat had become such a precious place to Dunk, a haven in which he could escape – at least for a little while – the insanity running rampant through Altdorf.

'There he is now,' Dunk said as he got to his feet. There, framed in the lamplight streaming in through the open doorway, stood Dirk

Dunk hadn't always got along well with his younger brother Dirk. They hadn't spoken much after Dirk left home to join the Reavers. That had only changed in the past year, when Dunk had followed in his prodigal brother's footsteps. Around this time last year, during the previous Blood Bowl Open, Dunk had felt like they really were *brothers*, in every sense of the word, for the first time since he could remember.

Now, looking at his brother's solemn face, he feared all that had been lost, perhaps forever.

'Dunk,' the younger man said as he approached. He looked well but worn, which was no surprise, as he'd played in a Blood Bowl game with the Reavers just hours before. A shallow cut under his left eye had been expertly stitched and looked to already be healing well. Still, he neither stuck out his hand nor opened his arms wide in greeting. He just took one of the open chairs at the table and sat down.

Dunk nodded and sat down as well, signalling for the barmaid's attention as he did. 'What'll you have?'

'Got any Hogshead in this hellhole?'

'Sorry,' the barmaid said without a trace of remorse. She was a hard-bitten woman who looked tough enough to play for the Hackers herself. 'They went out of business.'

'Really?' Dirk said. 'I thought they made the official beer of the GWs.'

'Used to be. They drink Green Ronin nowadays.'

Dirk nodded at that, and the barmaid sauntered off.

'So,' Dunk said.

'So,' said Dirk.

'Can we cut the chit-chat, boys?' Slick said. 'This is painful enough to just watch. You're brothers, for pity's sake. This is over a *woman* – *Lästiges*, for the love of Nuffle.'

'Hey!' Dirk said.

The halfling threw up his hands in surrender and then looked at both of the men in turn. 'Can't you just shake hands and make up.'

Dirk scrutinised Dunk. 'Can we do that?'

'I'd like that,' Dunk said.

'After what you did...' Dirk shook his head ruefully.

Dunk protested. 'This is all just a horrible misunder– '

Dirk cut off his older brother with a sweep of his hand. 'Oh,' he said, a grin spreading across his face, 'I know.'

Dunk paused in the middle of running through the explanation he'd been preparing ever since he'd got Dirk's message asking for this meeting. He cocked his head at his brother, looking deep into his so-familiar eyes, and said, 'What?'

'I know,' Dirk said, sitting back with a smirk on his face. 'Lästiges broke into my room earlier this week and forced me to watch the unedited footage of the night you ended up in bed together.' He shook his head and cackled. 'You weren't a threat to anyone's honour that night – not even your own.'

Dunk sat back in his chair, stunned.

The barmaid shoved a tall, greenish beer in front of Dirk. As opaque as a stout, it carried a thick, full head. Dirk grabbed the beer and took a huge slug of it into his mouth.

Dirk's eyes bulged out of his head, and for a moment Dunk thought he might spray the table with whatever swam around in his mouth. Dirk managed to keep it down, though, swallowing hard, and then gasping for air.

'This is *less* bitter?' he said, his eyes watering.

'You want me to get you something else?' Dunk asked, already looking for the barmaid again.

Dirk stared at the top of the beer for a moment, and then took another tentative sip. 'No,' he said. 'I actually like it. It grows on you fast.'

'I'll take your word for it.' Then he glared at his brother. 'But if you're okay with all this, why did you make me suffer for so long?'

Dirk made a face at his beer before taking another drink. He shook his head like a wet dog drying itself, then smiled at Dunk. 'Hey, just because nothing happened doesn't mean it couldn't have. You still needed to pay for it – if only just a little.'

'You son of a–'

'Yes, my brother?' Dirk said innocently.

Dunk tried to come up with something horrible to say, but as the words rolled around in his mouth, struggling to come out in the right order, a shout pierced the background noise of the tavern and drove itself straight into his brain.

'Dunkel Hoffnung!' the voice said. 'You've got a lot of nerve showing your face around here!'

DUNK'S HEAD SNAPPED around to see Spinne standing just inside the doorway, glaring at him with the intensity of an angry valkyrie sent down to haul his sorry carcass back up to the heavens for judgment. She had her long, strawberry-blonde hair pulled back in a warrior's braid, and her blue-grey eyes burned with a hellish intensity. She stomped over to him on her long, athletic legs and parted her wide, full lips to snarl down at him.

'What do you have to say for yourself?'

Dunk stood up in her face, took her into his arms, and planted a long, loving kiss square on her mouth. Her arms came up and wrapped around his neck, and to his delight they held him in a gentle, non-strangling way. For those precious seconds, the months they'd been apart seemed to melt away.

When they finally parted, moments later, she wore a wild, happy smile. 'What was that–?' Then she glared down at Dirk. 'You told him, didn't you?'

'I couldn't help it,' Dirk said, pointing at the greenish glass in front of him. 'It was the beer.'

Spinne narrowed her eyes at him and then at Dunk. 'I want you to know, I'm still mad at you. You never should have put yourself in that kind of position.'

'What kind of position?'

'The kind that lands you in bed with another woman so that it can be broadcast on a Cabalvision special.'

Dunk grinned. 'So, as long as there aren't any camras…?'

She cut him off with another kiss. 'Don't press your luck.' She broke free from their embrace then, and they sat down next to each other, with Spinne between Dunk and Dirk.

'So,' Slick said, 'one big happy family again, eh? That calls for another round.' He signalled the barmaid again.

'Add a Black Widow to the order if you don't mind,' Lästiges said, as she appeared from a darkened booth in a distant corner of the tavern's main room. She winked at Dunk, and he realised she'd been watching him the whole time.

'I spoke too soon,' Slick said with a wince. Despite this, he relayed Lästiges's request to the barmaid too.

'I'm so glad you're all here,' Dunk said, looking Spinne and Dirk in the eyes, measuring them up. 'I have a special favour to ask of you, and I don't know exactly how to put it.'

'Go ahead,' Spinne said, holding his hand. 'After this debacle, I think we can take it.'

Dirk nodded eagerly.

Dunk screwed up his courage and said, 'The Reavers need to drop out of the tournament.'

Everyone at the table froze, staring at Dunk. Only Slick seemed to understand what Dunk meant, and he hid behind his empty stein of beer rather than stand between Dunk and his friends.

'You're insane,' Dirk said. He turned to Slick. 'Did he get his bell rung in the game today? He's not making any sense.'

Lästiges didn't say a word. She just frowned at Dunk and drummed the long, red fingernails of one hand on the battle-scarred tabletop.

'What are you talking about?' Spinne said, her brow furrowed with concern.

Dunk took a deep breath. He knew this wouldn't be an easy sell, but he had to try. 'You two saw Lästiges's documentary.' Both Spinne and Dirk scowled at this.

'The whole thing,' Dunk added quickly. 'You know about the Far Albion Cup, right? Well, we – the Hackers – still have it. And it's just as dangerous here as it ever was in Albion, maybe more so.'

'What's your point?' Dirk said. 'With that fancy goblet, the Hackers are unbeatable, so we shouldn't even try?'

Dunk nodded. 'Yes! But that's not all. It's not just that we can't be defeated. It's that we'll kill most of the other players who make it on to the field. If the Reavers end up playing us in the finals like last year, you might both be killed.'

Spinne looked at Dirk, who scoffed with a bitter laugh. 'This is really pathetic,' he said to Dunk. 'Did Pegleg put you up to this? Or Slick?'

The halfling gave a too-innocent shrug. The drinks arrived just then, and he snatched up his fresh stein and hid his face in it. The others left their orders untouched.

'You can't expect us to quit our team because of some ancient legend,' Spinne said. 'We're Blood Bowl players. If we left the game every time there was some kind of threat, we'd never be able to take the field. Just being out there on the gridiron is one of the most dangerous things you can do.'

'But this isn't a legend,' Dunk said. 'It's real. I've seen it in action, both in Albion and during the game today. If you play against us, you'll be killed, and I don't want to see that happen.'

'So why don't you quit?' Dirk said. 'Or steal the cup? Or destroy it? Or sabotage the Hackers? Why should we have to forfeit our shot at the championship?'

Dunk frowned. He could feel the conversation slipping away from him. 'Don't you think I've thought of that? Pegleg has hidden the cup away, and he's got our team wizard, Olsen Merlin, guarding it for him. I've tried talking to them both, but it's no use. They want the championship, and they don't much care how many people have to die for them to get it.'

'You could say the same thing about any Blood Bowl coach,' Spinne said, unimpressed. 'Dunk, I wanted this to be a happy moment for us. Why do you have to ruin it like this?'

Dunk saw the disturbed look on her beautiful face, and he knew she wanted him to stop, to ignore the threat to her life and let her handle it herself, just like she always did. She was a Blood Bowl player. She lived with mortal danger every day, and they never talked about it. They preferred to ignore the threat of death that always hung over their heads, sticking to the moment instead, enjoying it for what it was, not what it might represent. To her, this threat of the Far Albion Cup was no different than any other – and a poor excuse for shattering the good mood.

But Dunk couldn't help himself. He couldn't sit here, finally reunited with her after so many months, and forget about the fact that the Far Albion Cup might make his team murder hers on the field. There was no way around it.

'You have to quit,' he said. 'Both of you. Or, if you care about your team-mates, you have to lose a game. Not right away, of course, but before the Hackers meet you in the playoffs.'

'What makes you think you scruffy bastards will make it to the playoffs again?' Dirk said.

Dunk snarled at him. 'Pay attention, would you? This isn't some joke. This is your life I'm talking about, and yours,' he said to Spinne.

She got to her feet. 'I've had enough of this,' she said. 'I thought you'd be glad to see me, to know that I'd decided to give you a second chance, but this…' Dunk thought he saw tears welling up in her eyes. 'I trusted you. I loved you, but this…'

He saw her reach down inside herself and clamp down on whatever it was that produced emotions in her. In an instant, she turned cold and distant. The woman he loved – correction, the woman who loved him – was gone.

'Let's go,' Spinne said to Dirk.

He stood up, shaking his head at his brother as if at a small child who hadn't learned to curb an insolent tongue. 'What are you think-ing?' he spat.

Spinne frowned down at Dunk. 'We'll see you on the field,' she said, 'if you're lucky.'

With that, the two Reavers turned and left.

As they walked out of the Skinned Cat, Lästiges rolled her eyes at Dunk. 'Well played,' she said. 'To get back the girl and lose her in the space of minutes, I'm impressed.'

'You know what I'm talking about here,' Dunk said. 'You have to talk to them.'

'We've seen just how much good that's done.'

'You can't just let the Hackers kill them.' Dunk strove to keep his desperation out of his voice.

Lästiges raised her perfectly sculpted eyebrows at Dunk. 'We're a long way from that point yet. We're still in the opening round, and there's no chance the two teams will meet yet. Wolf Sports is count-ing on a match-up at some point in the playoffs. If – *if* – that hits the schedule, I'll say something then, but not before.' Her eyes wandered toward the door, which Spinne had long since slammed behind her. 'Not before.'

'By then, it might be too late. The closer they get to the finals, the less the chance they'll listen to reason. The chance at being the repeat-ing champions will be too much for them.' Dunk buried his face in his hands and growled in frustration. 'Why will nobody help me?'

'Well, kid, just tell me what it is you need,' a greasy voice said, slith-ering into Dunk's ear. 'Maybe we can cut some kind of a deal.'

The thrower groaned, leaving his face in his hands. 'Leave me alone, Gunther.'

'Hey,' the slimy bookie said, 'would a good friend abandon another in his time of need?'

Dunk uncovered his eyes and shot the Gobbo an ironic look. The nauseating creature looked a shade greener than ever.

'Oh, whoops!' the bookie said dramatically. 'I guess that's what just happened here, isn't it? Well, when your friends abandon you, then who's left?'

Dunk glared at the Gobbo. 'What do you want?'

'What everyone wants: gold. To get that, I want to ask you the same question: What do you want?'

'I'll tell you what,' Dunk said. He regretted the words even as they left his mouth, but he didn't stop talking. 'If you can help me, I'll help you.'

'That's what I do,' the Gobbo said, phlegm flying from his rubbery lips as he chortled. He let loose a loud belch that smelled of old, fried meat. ''Scuse me,' he said. 'I'm a bit off my feed today. I think that last rat-on-a-stick at the game tried biting me back.' He tried to suppress another noisy burp and failed. 'Anyway, how can I help you?'

'Get the Reavers to lose a game so they don't meet the Hackers in the playoffs.'

The Gobbo rubbed his greasy chin. 'That's a tall order, kid. Last year, if you'd asked, I could have mobilised the Black Jerseys to make something happen, but someone,' he glared at Dunk here, 'caused me to fumble that little operation.'

Dunk nodded knowingly. 'What would you want in return?'

The Gobbo grinned. 'You don't like being on this side of it now, do you?' he said. 'Needing me? What I can offer? How does it feel?'

Dunk made a fist. 'Do you want to make a deal or not?'

'Sheesh!' the Gobbo said. 'Can you let a guy gloat a little?' Then he turned serious. 'I want you as the captain of my new version of the Black Jerseys.'

'Never,' Dunk said instantly.

The Gobbo showed even more of his teeth. 'You sure you don't want a bit more time to think that over, kid? What if I'm your only chance to keep your brother and your girlfriend alive?'

'There has to be a better way, son,' Slick said softly, his stein now on the table in front of him.

Dunk thought about this for a long moment, and then shook his head. 'All right,' he said to the Gobbo. 'If you can pull that off, I'll throw one game for you.'

'Just one?' the bookie looked distressed. For a moment, Dunk worried he might belch again – or worse. 'Aren't the lives of the two people closest in the world to you worth more than a single game?'

'That's the deal. And if you take it, I'll throw in a bit of advice about the Hackers for free.'

The Gobbo rubbed his chin until Dunk thought he might crack it wide open. 'All right,' he finally said. 'It's a deal.' He offered his clammy hand, but Dunk ignored it.

'How do I know I can trust you?' the Gobbo asked.

Dunk rolled his eyes. 'Of the two of us, who would you – even *you* – trust most?'

'Good point, kid.' the Gobbo said. 'So what's my "free" advice?'

'Consider it a down payment on the deal,' Slick said. 'If you don't produce, then you might owe us.'

The bookie sneered at the halfling, but before he could respond, Dunk spoke up. 'As long as the Hackers have the Far Albion Cup, don't bet against us.'

'That's it?' the Gobbo said. 'You're just going to repeat that tired legend from the lady's Cabalvision special?' He leered at her, and Lästiges squirmed away from him in her seat.

'It's no legend,' Dunk said. 'Didn't you pay attention? Everything in that show was real.'

'Everything?' the Gobbo said, trying to peer down Lästiges's shirt. She clasped a hand to her chest and scooted her chair farther away. Then his eyes snapped open and he sat bolt upright, a look of surprise on his face.

'It's a deal. Gotta go!' With that, he slid off his chair and waddled his way in the direction of the nearest latrine, holding his thighs together the entire time.

'WHAT A NIGHT!' Lästiges said, as she stumbled on a loose paving stone, nearly taking a spill in the dimly lit street. Dunk reached out and steadied her with an arm attached to a body only slightly less intoxicated than hers.

'You got that right,' Slick said as he scurried out of her way. 'You make up with your lovers, you run them out of the bar, and then you cut a deal with the slimiest creature this side of Nurgle himself.'

'By "you," I think he meansh *you*,' Lästiges said, wrapping an arm over Dunk's shoulder for support. Drunk, she'd developed a lateral lisp. '*I* wouldn't have done any of that. Well, maybe the firsht part – making up with our loversh – which was all my fault, thank you very much. But not the other two thingsh.'

'And thank you for that, by the way,' Dunk said. 'I'm just sorry I had to go and throw a wrench into that.' He hesitated for a moment, then continued.

'But loving someone doesn't mean much if you're willing to let them get killed, does it? It just frustrates me that they refused to listen. Isn't life more important than Blood Bowl?'

'Damned loser.'

Dunk spun about, nearly spilling Lästiges to the pavement as he did. They stood, he noticed, on the darkest stretch of street he'd yet seen on their stagger home. The voice – a low growl, really – seemed to have come from nowhere, as if the darkness itself had spat out the words.

'Slick?' Dunk said. 'Did you have something you wanted to get off your chest?'

The halfling, white as a sheet, shook his head. 'That wasn't me, son, not with my worst cold ever.'

A low, rumbling laugh emanated from the darkness overhead. Dunk snapped his neck back to glare into the clear night sky, but he saw nothing there, not even a wisp of a cloud scudding between the tops of the buildings on either side of the street.

Then Dunk felt a tap on his shoulder. He turned about and came face to chest with a huge person dressed all in black. He craned his neck backward and found himself nose to nose with a monstrous, pale orc staring down into his eyes.

'Boo,' Skragger said.

Lästiges unleashed a scream that Dunk thought might make his ears bleed. As she did, the orc grabbed her around her cheeks with a rough, hairy paw. His long, claw-like nails dug into her flesh as he forced her to stare into his glowing red eyes.

Lästiges stopped screaming.

'Sleep,' Skragger said, and the woman collapsed into Dunk's arms.

'You're dead,' Slick said, his voice constricting with terror. 'We saw you die.'

The massive orc stepped back from Dunk and Lästiges and snickered. 'I am dead.' He drew a long nail across his chest, pulling back his heavy, black cloak and revealing a white logo embroidered on his black shirt: a winner's cup made of human bones and a human skull.

'You're with the Champions of Death,' Dunk said. As the words left him, he realised their significance and recoiled in horror.

Skragger bared his jagged, broken teeth and tusks in a cold approximation of a smile. 'Von Irongrad found me. Made me this.' He opened his mouth wider, and a pair of fangs sank down from behind his thick upper lip.

'Tomolandry has the Impaler working as a vampire recruiter?' Slick breathed. 'Ingenious. How is the Champions' pay scale?'

'Sucks,' Skragger said, baring his fangs. 'But so do I.'

Dunk hefted Lästiges in his arms, wondering if he could outrun the vampire orc if he tossed the woman over his shoulder. When Skragger was alive, it would have been a close race, but give him the unending stamina of the undead, and Dunk didn't see how he had much of a chance. He couldn't just drop Lästiges and leave her to the merciless Skragger, although maybe the orc *would* just chase him instead. After all, he wanted to kill Dunk, right? But what about Slick too?

Skragger leaned forward into Dunk's face. 'Not here for revenge,' he said. 'Not for me. For Guterfiends.'

Dunk's jaw fell, and he nearly dropped Lästiges to the pavement. The Guterfiend family had been behind his family's downfall. They lived in the old Hoffnung estate now, here in Altdorf. Dunk had thought he'd be beneath their notice now. They'd beaten his father so thoroughly that the man had fled town without even bidding his son good-bye. What could they want with him?

'Guterfiends got gold,' Skragger said. 'Lotta gold.' He reached up and used a long fingernail to scratch a small cut in Dunk's forehead.

Dunk held still, terrified and trapped. He felt a rivulet of blood start to trickle down between his eyebrows and along the side of his nose. Skragger watched it as it went, and he licked his lips, catching his tongue for a moment on each of his fangs.

Dunk lunged forward and drove his forehead into the vampire orc's face. The impact stunned him as well, and he fell backward to land on the pavement, Lästiges still in his arms. Skragger looked down at Dunk and laughed, then used a pale finger to wipe the thrower's blood from his forehead. He stuck the finger in his mouth and licked it clean.

'Tasty,' Skragger said. 'Get it all tomorrow.'

Dunk stared up at the orc, his voice catching in his throat. 'What?' was all he could croak out.

'See you on the gridiron,' Skragger said, his eyes burning red as his too-pale form faded into insubstantial mist that blew away on an unfelt breeze. 'We got a game.'

'Nuffle's balls!' Bob's voice rang out over the PA system at Emperor Stadium, barely piercing the crowd's roar. 'Did you see that hit?'

Dunk hadn't seen a thing, but he'd sure felt it. Something the size and speed of a stampeding bull had smashed into him and sent him skittering across the Astrogranite. Only his armour had kept him from being crushed.

'Skragger's really giving it to Hoffnung today,' Jim said. 'You'd almost think it was personal. Oh, wait! It is!'

'Sure enough, Jim. This isn't just the first round of the Blood Bowl playoffs. It's a grudge match! Besides the fatal encounter Skragger had with Hoffnung last year, Coach Tomolandry's team is itching for a chance to avenge that bone-rattling loss at the Hackers' hands in last year's Dungeonbowl.'

'Another hit like that, Bob, and they might find themselves recruiting Hoffnung next! Maybe they can use him to replace Ramen-Tut, who turned to dust in that same game last year, in a pile-up beneath Hoffnung and the late Kur Ritternacht.'

Dunk scrambled to his feet and looked up, the ball still in his hands. He clenched his teeth, fighting through the pain, and wondered how many steps he could make before he got hit again. Then a sight rarer than an ogre with an education greeted him, and he froze in astonishment.

There, right in front of the thrower, stood a goblin dressed in a black cap and a shirt with black-and-white, vertical stripes. He had something silvery in one hand and something bright yellow in the other. As he threw the yellow thing – some kind of weighted hand-kerchief that sailed through the air – he brought the silvery thing up to his lips and blew a shrill blast.

'Penalty!' the goblin shouted.

Taken aback by this vision, Dunk stumbled backwards, a goofy grin on his face. Here, right in front of him, not only was there a referee but he had called a penalty on that cheap shot he'd just taken.

Then Dunk realised the ref was pointing at him.

'Unnecessary roughness!' the ref said.

'Can you believe it?' Jim said. 'The call is *against* Hoffnung. Talk about adding insult to injury.'

The crowd booed and hissed at the call. Dunk drew some small comfort from this, even though he knew it was only because Blood Bowl fans hated anything that slowed the pace of the bloodshed on the field.

'I don't know,' Bob said. 'I think Hoffnung had it coming. After all, he did get right in Skragger's way there. The all-star player almost tripped right over him.'

'But to get kicked out of the game for that?' Jim said. 'That seems more than a bit much.' The crowed booed in agreement.

Frustrated, Dunk dropped the ball on the ground and glanced back at Skragger. The snarling vampire orc drew his hand across his own throat in a cutting gesture. A sense of relief washed over the thrower.

'Ha!' he said to Skragger. 'This guy just cheated you of your revenge. You can't kill me in front of all these people if–'

The referee scurried past Dunk then, almost knocking him over. The thrower realised then that Skragger hadn't been making the signal at him but the referee.

'What's this?' Bob said. 'The ref is picking up his flag and waving off the call. There is no penalty!'

The crowd roared its approval.

'I don't know how much the Champions are paying that referee,' said Bob, 'but he sure seems intent on earning it!'

'No 'scape,' Skragger said, pointing a pale finger at Dunk. 'Not this time.'

Dunk scooped the ball back up, turned, and ran.

The Hackers hadn't had much of a game so far. The strategy that Pegleg pursued these days, under the auspices of the Far Albion Cup – killing enough of the opposing players to force them to forfeit the game – crashed against the shoals when it came to the Champions of Death. The Champions were already dead, which made them impossible to kill. To get them out of the game, you had to tear them apart instead, a much more involved process.

For once, Dunk wished his new team-mates were *more* destructive. As it was, he needed to do something fast or Skragger would be collecting his fee from the Guterfiends before halftime.

There was no way for him to stand up to Skragger toe to toe. When the orc had been breathing, he'd been more than enough to handle Dunk. Now that he had the hellish powers of a vampire as well, he'd be able to pound the thrower into a sponge, and then use him to soak up the spilled blood and wring that out into a nice brandy snifter to enjoy later with a good book.

Of course, vampires had their weaknesses as well: sunlight, running water, holy water, and wood. But where could Dunk find any of those? The sun shone brightly overhead, and it didn't seem to bother Skragger at all. Dunk suspected the vampire orc had one of those Sun Protection Fetishes that von Irongrad was known to use. Dunk didn't know what an SPF looked like, though, or if he'd be able to destroy it if he found it.

Could Dunk find an aqueduct somewhere and route the water onto the field? He might as well ask for one of those spiked steamrollers the dwarf teams used to magically show up with in the end zone. He didn't know if crushing Skragger with a machine like that would put an end to him, but Dunk would have been happy to give it a shot.

Maybe there was a priest in the crowd?

Dunk spotted an open Hacker downfield – Edgar, who was busy stomping the stuffing out of 'Rotting' Rick Bupkiss while Matt 'Bones' Klimesh tried to chew through the treeman's bark – and he had his answer. In mid-stride, he cocked back his arm and rifled the ball toward Simon, who had just broken free from Gilda 'the Girly Ghoul' Fleshsplitter.

The ball sailed high, but this presented no problem for the treeman, who reached up and snagged the ball with his upper branches. Dunk looked back to see Skragger still dogging his heels, not caring at all if the thrower still had the ball or not. This wasn't about the game anymore. At least, it wouldn't be until one of them had to be carried off the field in pieces.

'Edgar!' Dunk yelled as he sprinted toward the treeman. 'I need a hand – a branch, actually.'

'Sure thing, mate!' Edgar said. 'Just as soon as I get rid of these bloody bits of walking fertiliser!'

With the zombie under his feet pounded into paste, Edgar swung a mighty branch at the skeleton gnawing at him and scattered the creature's bones across the field. Then he turned to face Dunk and the vampire orc steaming up his wake.

'Literally,' Dunk said as he neared the treeman, 'can you break me off a branch?'

Edgar recoiled in horror. 'You're a bleeding loon! Give up one of me own limbs? What would you say if I asked that of you?'

Dunk dashed around Edgar, putting the treeman between himself and the angry, undead orc. 'I'd say, "How badly do you need it?"'

'Move!' Skragger bellowed as he circled around the treeman, trying to catch Dunk, the thrower always two steps ahead of him. 'Move, or I'll crush you to toothpicks!'

'Just you bloody well try it!' Edgar said. It swatted the vampire orc back with a swing of a long, solid branch. The effort laid open Skragger's cheek.

Skragger reached up and felt the hole in his face, then gazed up at the treeman, his eyes wide with terror.

'Tackle him!' Dunk shouted.

'I'm not really built for such things, mate,' Edgar said, 'not being able to bend at the – Whoa!'

Knowing he only had split seconds to act, Dunk barrelled into Edgar from behind. Already overbalanced from leaning forward to smack Skragger, the treeman toppled on top of the vampire orc and pinned him to the ground.

The scream Skragger let loose would have been enough to curdle Dunk's blood, but the roar of the crowd drowned it out. The thrower knew he didn't have much time to act. In moments, the orc might figure out he could turn to mist if he wanted to. Maybe he couldn't when he was pinned under a fallen tree. Maybe he could. But Dunk didn't want to find out the hard way.

Dunk leaped over Edgar and found himself face to face with Skragger. Blood surged from the orc's pale lips as he tried to find enough air in his lungs to curse each and every one of the Hackers to their last dying days.

Dunk reached down and grabbed the vampire by his helmet. He tried to pull it off, but the damned thing was strapped on tight enough to be like an extension of Skragger's skull.

Skragger finally cleared his throat enough to spit a mouthful of someone else's blood into Dunk's face. The thrower nearly gagged, but instead he gritted his teeth, grabbed Skragger's helmet by the face guard and started to twist.

'Think you're tough?' Skragger howled. 'Think you can kill me? I'm already dead!'

Dunk ignored the vampire orc's ramblings and kept twisting the helmet as hard as he could to one side. Skragger fought him every inch of the way, but Dunk had the position and the leverage he needed. He put one last burst of strength into his effort, and the report of a loud crack from Skragger's neck rewarded him.

'Won't stop me!' Skragger growled as Dunk continued to twist. 'Can't kill the dead!'

Dunk knew Skragger was right, that what he did here would only be a temporary measure, but he didn't care. As long as he stopped Skragger from killing him today – and collecting his fee from the Guterfiends – he didn't mind a bit.

Dunk twisted the head around until Skragger faced him again. The vampire orc spit blood at him again. Dunk gave the vampire orc's head another twist, then another, and more, until the inevitable happened. With a final wrench of Skragger's black helmet, Dunk felt the creature's torn and shattered neck finally give. The helmeted head snapped free of Skragger's body.

Dunk bobbled the head and almost lost it. When he came up with it again, Skragger still stared back at him. 'Think this stop me?' he said. 'Nothing can stop me!'

'Not from talking, at least,' Dunk said. He got to his feet and thrust Skragger's head aloft.

The crowd loved it.

'Sensational!' Jim's voice said. 'So rarely do you get to see such a powerful rivalry end so badly for the vampire.'

'It's horrible!' Bob said, his voice heavy with emotion. 'The orc had barely been blooded. To see eternity cut so savagely short… I… I…' He sobbed for a moment, and then shouted, 'Just what is immortality for if you can't enjoy it?'

'Uh, right,' Jim said as Bob's microphone went dead. 'I think this one might have hit a little too close to home for our old friend here, folks.'

Dunk didn't care. The crowd kept roaring for him, sounding like a never-ending peal of thunder. When the noise finally started to ebb, Dunk heard a high-pitched noise piercing through it. He glanced around to find it and saw the referee standing next to a flag thrown on the Astrogranite, his face a bright red from blowing his whistle so hard.

When the ref caught Dunk's eye, he pointed a thin, green finger at the thrower, then threw his thumb back over his shoulder, toward the cheap seats in the stadium. Dunk was being tossed out of the game. This time, though, he didn't mind. He tucked the still-cursing head of Skragger under his arm – the face guard keeping the vampire orc from being able to bite him, no matter how hard he tried – and trotted over to the Hackers' dugout, smiling the whole way.

'So, son, how do you feel about your new team-mates now?' Slick asked.

Dunk sighed, and then took a sip of his Killer Lite – after all of the blood in his face today, he wanted something smooth and easy –

before he answered. After the Hackers' victory, they'd run off to the Skinned Cat again, where Dunk had rented a private room in which he and Slick could watch that night's game, a match-up between the Reavers and the Evil Gits. While there may not have been any crystal balls in the main room, the Skinned Cat's management was savvy enough to keep a few on hand for their customers with the heaviest purses.

'It's hard for me to feel bad about anyone putting down the kind of monsters you find in the Champions of Death,' Dunk said. 'Most of them will be up and running about again the next day anyway.'

'Too true,' Slick said. 'And, hey, the Hackers made it to the Blood Bowl finals for the second year in a row. Not too shabby!'

'Only with the help of the Far Albion Cup. I can't feel much pride in that.'

Slick sighed. 'It's part of the game, son. Every team does everything it can to tip the scales in its favour. You think the Champions of Death would do any different? Or the Gits? Or the Reavers?'

Dunk frowned. 'I don't object to the cup helping us win so much as how it does it. It turns us into a team of merciless killers. I feel it when I'm out there on the field too: a whispering in the back of my head urging me to kill any foe in my path.'

'Is that so bad?'

'It's a game, not a battle. According to the teachings of Commissioner Roze-El, Nuffle sent us the rules for Blood Bowl to end the eternal series of wars that once wracked this world. Now, instead, of fighting those wars, we play Blood Bowl, and the people who would have been the foot soldiers in those battles cheer us on.'

'I thought you didn't believe in any of that stuff.'

Dunk raised his eyebrows and glanced down at the table. 'I don't. But whether I believe the godly bits about the story or not, it's true, isn't it? We don't send thousands of troops to war against each other any more. We just watch Blood Bowl on Cabalvision. Maybe it satisfies some deep need for violent conflict we all have. Maybe it just distracts us so we can't be bothered with other things like border skirmishes or invasions. Either way, it works out the same in the end.'

He rubbed his chin a moment before he continued. 'But the Far Albion Cup, it doesn't want that. It digs into your head and screams for total annihilation. If it could, it would find a way to lead us all into war instead, leading an undefeatable army to conquer the entire world.'

'Seriously?' Slick said, his eyes wide.

Dunk took another sip of his beer.

'Well then, son,' Slick said. 'Maybe getting the Reavers to lose a game isn't really enough, is it?'

Dunk drank deeply this time. 'No,' he said, 'not really.'

'What did you end up doing with Skragger's head, anyway?' The halfling shuddered as he tried to change the subject. 'I'd rather he never reported in for the Champions' line-up again.'

'I know what you mean,' Dunk said, grateful to talk about anything but the Far Albion Cup for the moment. 'Even decapitated, the cruel bastard just wouldn't shut up. He kept threatening me. "Just wait till I heal.", "Put me down so I can bite you.", "Scratch my nose".'

'So, did you?'

Dunk grinned. 'I gave him to Cavre.'

'You thought he wanted a talking trophy to put on his mantel?'

'I don't know. He came to me and asked for it.' Dunk shrugged. 'Why not?'

'Why not, indeed!' the Gobbo said as he slid into the room.

Slick scowled. 'The sign on the door says, "Private".'

'Does it now?' the Gobbo grinned as he pulled up a chair next to the halfling and sat down. 'I never did learn how to read or write. Nasty habits that waste your time and tend to leave evidence lying around all over the place.'

'What do you want?' Dunk asked.

'A woman who truly understands me.' The Gobbo's grin told Dunk this was far down on his list of desires. 'Or at least one who could suck the fire out of a dragon's belly through its nose.' He cackled at his own joke.

'Really, though, I came here so I could brief you on your mission.'

'What mission?' Slick asked, standing up in his chair so he could stare the Gobbo straight in the eyes.

'The game the kid's going to throw after the Reavers lose this match.' The Gobbo laughed in Slick's face. 'I always collect my winnings.'

The halfling started to protest, but Dunk cut him off. 'He's right. If he manages to pull it off, I'll keep my end of the bargain.'

The Gobbo grinned at Slick as he sat back in his chair. 'It's always a pleasure to do business with such a gentlemen. With some of the others, I have to resort to blackmail to get them to hold up their side of a deal. I can see I won't have to do that with your client.'

'Right,' Slick said sarcastically, giving Dunk a disappointed look the young thrower managed to ignore. 'I'm so proud.'

'So who's your plant?' Dunk asked, keeping his eyes on the crystal ball. 'I'd guess Breitzel from the way he's been playing.'

'And you'd be right, kid.' The Gobbo clapped Dunk on the back. 'I've been grooming him for years. When the GWs cleaned house at the end of the last season, they only got about half of my guys. Breitzel hadn't done much of anything for me up till then, and he slipped right through their fingers.'

'How fortunate for you,' Slick said.

'Hey,' the Gobbo said, 'joke all you want, but that little scandal almost put me out of business. I considered going back into defence contracting for the Empire instead, but hey, I gotta have some sense of decency left.'

Dunk stared at the bookie for a moment before he realised he wasn't kidding. He decided to ignore the implications. 'You really think Breitzel can sway the game? He's not exactly the Reavers' star player.'

The Gobbo snorted. 'It doesn't take much to tip a game one way or the other, kid. All he has to do is fumble the ball at the right moment. Just like that!'

Dunk looked at the crystal ball and saw Breitzel drop the ball deep in the Reavers' own territory. An ogre with the nickname 'Kill! Kill! Kill!' emblazoned across his back scooped it up and zoomed into the end zone. Breitzel made a feeble attempt to tackle the creature but got knocked flat on his rear for his trouble.

'Don't you guys have the sound up on this thing?' the Gobbo said. 'I want to hear the play-by-play.' He reached out for the ball, but Dunk intercepted his warty hand and pushed it away.

'I hear enough of Jim and Bob while I'm on the field,' he said. 'I don't need more of them while I'm off it.'

The Gobbo gloated as the score flashed up on the ball. 'It doesn't matter. That's the only stat that counts. Gits: 3, Reavers: 1.'

'It's only the first half,' Slick said. Dunk couldn't believe it, but he found part of himself rooting for the Reavers too. Even though he knew it would destroy his plan to save Dirk and Spinne from death at the Hackers' hands, he hated the thought that he would owe the Gobbo a favour – and he shuddered to think what he might have to do to pay it off.

'Look, kid,' the Gobbo said to Dunk as the thrower stared into the crystal ball. 'This is your last chance. If the Reavers win this one, they'll face the Hackers in the finals. What will you do then?'

Dunk groaned, and then buried his face in his hands. 'It looks like I'm going to get the chance to find out.'

'How's that, kid?' the Gobbo said. 'This game's in the bag. And once it's over and official, you and me will need to talk.'

Dunk reached out and tapped the crystal ball's base. Sound burst out of it then, carrying Jim and Bob's voices over the crazed roar of the crowd.

'Did you see that, Jim? Absolutely amazing!'

'How could I miss it? I haven't seen that much blood since – well, since we had lunch!'

'If I was a Reaver, I think I'd be careful about how hard I played from now on – nothing but a hundred and ten percent! Otherwise, just look what could happen.'

'Too true, Bob. We've heard reports from the Reavers' camp that team captain Dirk Heldmann was struggling with some discipline problems, but it looks like those might be over.'

'What happened?' the Gobbo said, elbowing Slick out of the way so he could get a better view of the crystal ball.

'Let's see that again, Jim! This is one for the highlights tonight!'

As Dunk, Slick, and the Gobbo watched, the camra panned from Kill! Kill! Kill! celebrating his touchdown in the end zone to just a few feet away where Spinne stood beating the tar out of Breitzel. Then the traitorous Reaver stripped off his helmet and started using it as a weapon to bash Spinne over the head.

Spinne went down trying to defend herself from the helmet with her arms, but Breitzel kept hammering at her. Then, just as the traitor was about to start kicking in Spinne's ribs, Dirk came out of nowhere and smashed Breitzel into the Astrogranite. Then he crawled on top of the traitor's back and used both hands to smash the man's unprotected head into the ground until the fight left him for good.

'I think,' Slick said, turning to the Gobbo, whose face looked greener than ever, 'you just saw a flaw develop in your master plan.'

'HERE'S TO THE Hackers!' Pegleg said, raising a glass to the team assembled around the long table he stood at the head of. 'And here's to the Blood Bowl championship!'

Dunk joined the others in clinking their glasses together, but he remained silent as the others cheered. Looking around, he knew that some of his friends felt the way he did, but they all somehow managed to put up a better front. Normally, everyone enjoyed a Monday-evening feast after a victory. Even the players nursing injuries wore irremovable smiles. Tonight, though, the grins pasted on the faces of the new players were savage ones, and the old guard – which Dunk thought ironic to find himself in – wore their smiles as masks.

'So, mate,' Simon said, clapping Dunk on the back, 'how about those Reavers? What do you think about going up against your brother and your girlfriend again, just like last year?' The Albionman still wore the bandages that kept the disease he'd contracted from advancing any further. So far, they seemed to be doing all right, even though Simon's eyes looked like he'd been drinking almost constantly since the game had ended the night before.

'Not much,' Dunk said, not bothering to keep his voice down. 'I don't care to see strangers get killed, much less family and friends.'

Simon grinned, and his breath stank of liquor and rot. 'Well, that's what it's all about, though, in'nit? Beating down the other team? By *any means necessary!'* He staggered forward, and Dunk put out a hand to steady him. 'In'nit that what happened to me? It's all part of Nuffle's damned game.'

'Maybe,' Dunk said. He glared around the room at the new players, and then at Pegleg and Olsen, who sat chatting at the far corner of the table, enjoying their goblets of wine. Dunk noticed that Pegleg didn't seem to want to be anywhere near him at the moment, and given the sourness of his mood he could understand why. 'Maybe. But I don't have to like it.'

Simon put a wet-wrapped hand on Dunk's shoulder. 'You don't have to like it, though, do you? You just have to get the job done. Make the money for the team. For our investors. Earn that pay cheque. And we're paid well indeed, aren't we?'

'I suppose so.'

'Don't you think that'd take the sting off it? You know, dull the edge of the knife a bit as they keep digging it into you week after week? I used to think it would. I did.'

The catcher sat back and hugged his arms across his chest. 'But look at me now. A prettier picture you'll never find, eh? All my money, and what good does it do me now. If I get killed out there...' Fat, hot tears rolled out of Simon's eyes, but the wrappings on his face instantly soaked them up. He choked back the raw emotion in his voice. 'Well, what good will all that gold do me then?'

Dunk put a hand on Simon's shoulder to steady him, to lend his friend some strength. Before he could say a word, though, a voice rang out in what Dunk realised was a silent room, but for Simon's soft, muffled sobs.

'Mr. Hoffnung,' Pegleg said. 'I wonder if I might have a word with you before our first course arrives.'

'Please,' Dunk said, gesturing for the coach to talk.

'In private, if you don't mind,' Pegleg said, an uneven smile on his face.

'Can't we speak openly in front of my team-mates?' Dunk asked. 'Let's be honest as we can about this. I have nothing to hide.'

Pegleg shot a glance at the wizard sitting next to him. Olsen nodded at him grimly, and the ex-pirate grimaced at the thrower. 'All right,' he said, but he hesitated to continue.

'What is it?' Dunk asked.

'Can I ask what it is you've said to turn Mr. Sherwood into a sobbing mess?'

Dunk started to respond, but Simon put a gauze-swaddled hand on his arm. The Albionman gawked at the coach for a long, painful moment, then spoke. 'He said nothing to me. Nothing. What would anyone have to say to a creature like myself to set me off, whimpering like a battered schoolgirl?' He sprang to his feet so fast Dunk feared he might burst through his wrappings. 'Look at me!' he screeched. *'Look at me!'*

Guillermo came up behind Simon then and grabbed him by the shoulders. The catcher spun into his friend's arms and let him lead him out of the room, his sobs still wracking his frame, his feet squishing along the floor as he walked out.

Dunk glared across the table at the ex-pirate and the wizard hunched over next to him, whispering something in his ear. Edgar and M'Grash stared back and forth at them both, waiting for something to happen. Cavre gave Dunk an appraising look, his face betraying nothing.

The others – the new players who'd joined the team in Bad Bay – all looked to Pegleg for direction. Dunk knew that they'd turn on him and tear him to pieces at a word from their coach.

Olsen refused to meet Dunk's glare.

'Can you explain that, Mr. Hoffnung?'

'Explain what, coach?'

Pegleg leaned forward in his chair. 'Just why a game-hardened veteran like Mr. Sherwood might dissolve into tears like that in your presence.'

A dozen snappy answers rolled through Dunk's brain: the body odour of the new team-mates; the fact that the bar was out of Killer Lite; the godlike presence Dunk exuded that made all lesser men reconsider their manhood; the fact that M'Grash had asked Simon if he could borrow a tissue. But he cast all those aside. It was time to tackle the truth.

'It's the Far Albion Cup,' Dunk said. 'We need to get rid of it.'

Pegleg rolled his eyes theatrically, and the new players all began to mutter murderous somethings under their breath. 'Are we on to that again, Mr. Hoffnung? Honestly, it's become tiresome. The cup is staying with us, and that is that.'

Dunk got to his feet. 'Coach, you can't tell me that you don't see what that thing has done to us. Maybe you don't feel it when we're in the middle of a game – you're in the dugout, not on the field – but it's turned us into a pack of killers, a bunch of murderous thugs.'

Pegleg laughed maliciously at this. 'And how am I supposed to tell the difference between that and a regular Blood Bowl team?' he asked. Then realisation spread across his face. 'Oh, yes! I know now. It's that we've finally started *playing* like a regular Blood Bowl team.'

The new players and Olsen all laughed along with Pegleg's mirthless joke. Only M'Grash, Edgar, and Cavre did not join in.

'The cup was behind Simon's disease too,' Dunk said. 'He has the same illness as those cultists we took it from.'

'Mr. Sherwood should consider that an abject lesson in taking care in picking his flings – and his friends.'

Dunk shook his head. 'Don't you remember Deckem and his crew? The cup brought us those recruits. What makes you think this lot here isn't just as tainted?'

The new players all scowled at Dunk then, and a shudder ran through him as he realised just how outnumbered he was. This wasn't a time for him to think about his personal safety though. He had to convince Pegleg to give up the cup.

'This is about your brother, isn't it?' Pegleg said. 'Him and that Schönheit woman you've been seeing.' He shook his head. 'Were we in the navy, I'd have you flogged for consorting with the enemy.'

'They're players on another team.'

Pegleg smashed his hook into the table at that. 'They are the *enemy!*' he thundered. 'We must do everything we can to *crush* the enemy. That's the difference between winners and *losers!*'

'You didn't have a problem with that before,' Dunk said.

'We lost before, didn't we, Mr. Hoffnung? I let my urge to be a good coach – a friend to my players – blind me. I don't want to be a *good* coach any more.'

'Congratulations,' Dunk started. 'You're well on your–'

'I want to be a *great* coach! I want to lead my team to win *championships!* The Bad Bay Hackers have been losers for the *last* time! And I will kill anyone who stands in my way!' Pegleg snarled at his star thrower before he lowered his voice to a menacing whisper. 'Including you.'

'Ah, gee,' Blaque said as he strode through the door, Whyte walking alongside him. 'What's the chance of him being named coach of the year with an attitude like that?'

Whyte shook his head as they stood next to each other at the foot of the table, just to Dunk's right. 'Not good,' the pale-skinned elf said. 'Not good at all.'

'Faith!' Olsen said, standing up at the other end of the table, a little rickety from too much drink. 'We don't believe anyone invited you two blackguards to this party. Leave, or we'll throw you bastards out ourselves.'

'We're here for the cup,' Blaque said. 'And we're not leaving until we get it.'

The sound of chairs scraping backward as every player in the room rose to his feet filled the otherwise silent air. The two Game Wizards stared down the table at the assembled Hackers, and Dunk wished, not for the first time tonight, that he was someplace else.

'Stand down, men,' Pegleg said to the players and to Olsen as well. 'Stand down. It's far too late for the GWs to do anything about the cup at this point – or for anyone else.' He glared directly at Dunk and just down behind him.

Dunk turned to see Slick peeking in around the edge of the dining hall's doorway. He waved a little hand at the thrower, than disappeared before Pegleg could snarl at him again.

Pegleg looked at the Game Wizards, his gaze flicking back and forth between the two. Then he gestured for the players to all sit. The new ones sat without further comment. Edgar and M'Grash waited to see what Dunk would do. When he sat down too, they complied as well. Cavre was the last to take his seat.

Olsen remained standing. When Pegleg nodded at him, he turned to the GWs and said, 'Once a team has taken full possession of the cup, there is nothing that can be done to break it, short of disbanding the entire team.'

'You think that can be arranged, Mr. Whyte?'

'Certainly, Mr. Blaque. Mr. Murdark tells me he's behind us a thousand percent. Something about how killing off one team after another could be construed as harmful to the long-term prospects of the sport.'

'You wouldn't dare,' Pegleg said. 'We're just about to play in the Blood Bowl finals. You'd rob us of that? The fans would scream foul for decades to come. Anyway, you can't do it. It's not your choice.'

Blaque grimaced. 'True enough, but we don't have to disband the team to stop you. We just have to refuse to let you play in the game.'

'Or else what?'

'Or else Wolf Sports won't broadcast it.'

Pegleg snorted at this. 'Blood Bowl has a dozen networks lined up to take your place.'

'Just give us the cup, Captain Haken,' Blaque said. 'It doesn't have to go down this way.'

'It won't do you any good,' Pegleg said. 'It's been *attuned* to us – to me. And it can only be destroyed if Olsen here drinks his own blood from it.'

It was Blaque's turn to snort as he drew his wand. 'We'd be happy to make that happen. What would you think about that, Mr. Whyte?'

'Icing on the cake,' the pale elf said, pulling his wand from his robes as well.

'We'll fight you lot to our dying breath,' Olsen said, his wand appearing his in hand. 'Destroying the cup would kill us dead. You two only have your jobs on the line. For us, it's our life.'

'Sounds like more icing to me,' Blaque said.

'Hold it,' Dunk said, surprising even himself. 'Wait. It doesn't have to happen like this.'

'We don't mind,' said Blaque. 'Really.'

'Belay that,' Pegleg said. His soft words carried throughout the room. 'If you destroy the cup, you'll seal my fate as well.'

'Come on, coach,' Dunk said. 'It won't be that bad. We made it to the finals last year on our own, without the cup. We can do it again, and we can *win*.'

The ex-pirate shook his head sadly. 'Aye. Maybe we could at that, Mr. Hoffnung, but I've made my choice and bound myself to the cup in every way possible.'

A shiver ran down Dunk's spine. 'What are you talking about, coach?' He knew he didn't want to hear the answer. He didn't want to, but he had to anyway.

Pegleg held up his hook and used his good hand to pull back that sleeve, baring the maimed arm. There, in the crook of his arm, he wore a large, white bandage, a few dark spots on it where the blood had seeped through.

'With Mr. Merlin's help, I bled myself into that damned cup of his, and then I drank my fill.'

'Bloody, bleeding hell,' Edgar said. 'That's not like someone tapping a tree, mate. You could have lost your life.'

Pegleg wore a sad smirk on his lips. 'It wasn't my life I lost, Edgar, but a part of my soul. That special piece of me now resides in the cup, right alongside the spirits of Mr. Merlin and Miss Retmatcher.'

Dunk wanted to vomit. 'Why, coach? Why would you do that?'

Pegleg arched his eyebrows. 'A cup – even one as magnificent as that one – is a thing. As such, it can be lost, stolen, or otherwise go missing, just as it once did for over five hundred years.' He bowed his head for a second before continuing on. 'I – I couldn't let it just leave me. I couldn't take the chance it might be taken from me. It's been a long, hard road to find myself standing just outside the winner's circle, waiting for you mates to pour the cooler full of Haterade over me. I just couldn't let it get away.'

'You are terrified of water, coach,' Cavre said quietly.

'For that, Mr. Cavre, I think I might have been able to make an exception. Just once.'

'So, if the cup is destroyed?' Blaque said.

'I'll die, along with Mr. Merlin here,' Pegleg said. 'And you'll have our deaths on both of your heads.'

'What do you think about that, Mr. Whyte?' Blaque said.

'Sounds like cherries on top.'

The two wizards levelled their wands at Pegleg and Merlin.

Without a word, the players all got back on their feet. The threat was clear. If the GWs made a move, the Hackers would make sure they'd pay.

Dunk's mind flashed back to his last up-close encounter with battle magic, when Olsen had flung that lightning bolt down the tunnel and fried all those deadmen. He didn't know what it would be like to be in a room with three powerful wizards letting loose their worst on each other, but he didn't want to find out.

Dunk smashed Blaque in the face with his elbow, and then spun past him to drive his fist into Whyte's gut. Both wizards went down hard, and before they could realise what – or who – had hit them, he snatched their wands from their hands.

'You'll regret that,' Blaque said, his nose bleeding freely. Whyte sat on the ground, still struggling to catch his breath.

'The only thing I regret,' Dunk said, 'is not doing it sooner. This doesn't have anything to do with you two or Wolf Sports. It's a Hacker matter, and the Hackers will handle it – alone.'

Blaque's fists started to crackle with raw power. 'We don't need the wands, you know. They only help us to focus our spells. We could still bring the roof of this place down around your – urk!'

With the GW still in mid-threat, M'Grash plucked him from his feet and held him dangling in the air. Edgar did the same with Whyte, who struggled not at all, still trying to get air back into his lungs. The treeman held him out at arm's length, dangling him there in his smaller branches as if the wizard might somehow be toxic.

'Listen to Dunkel,' M'Grash said directly into the dwarf's face. 'Dunkel, Dunkel, Dunkel smart!'

Blaque nodded, then spat in the ogre's face. 'You and your barking mad friend there had better put us both down, or I'll–'

M'Grash dropped the dwarf, who landed with a hard thud. Edgar did the same with Whyte.

'Toss them out of here,' Dunk said. 'If they come back, toss them farther – like into the Reik.'

'I hear they have forty-foot-long, carnivorous, mutant eels that glow in the dark living in that river,' Slick said, poking his head back in the room.

'They'd be lucky to have those find them first,' said Dunk as M'Grash and Edgar stormed out of the room, toting the GWs under their arms like a couple of footballs come to squirming life.

'So, Dunk,' Pegleg called out from the far end of the table, 'are we good then?'

Dunk glanced back over his shoulder at the ex-pirate standing there next to Olsen. 'Not by a million yards,' he said. 'I'm trying to make sure we don't all get killed, because you know that's what it'll come to next, right? As soon as word gets out that we have some kind of magic goblet that keeps us from losing, someone else is going to want it. Even if they can't get it, they'll settle for killing us, just so their team can have a fighting chance.'

'How can you be so sure?' Olsen asked.

'It's what we would do.' With that, Dunk strode out of the room, leaving Pegleg alone with Olsen, Cavre, and their murderous new recruits.

'WHAT IN ALL the hells did you do?' Lästiges said as she stormed into the Hackers' practice.

Dunk held up his hands, both as a gesture of innocence and so he could defend himself if the reporter decided to attack him. She looked angry enough to chew through both M'Grash and Edgar to get to him, and Dunk noticed that his two gigantic friends had scurried out of the way when they had seen the woman coming.

'I'm not sure what you mean,' Dunk said slowly, trying to calm Lästiges down.

'With Dirk and Spinne!' she said. 'Are you out of your walnut of a mind?'

Dunk winced and glanced up at the golden camra hovering over the reporter's head. 'Is this on the record or deep background?'

'What were you thinking, talking to the Gobbo?' A vein in her normally flawless forehead pulsed so hard and fast that Dunk feared it might burst.

'Ah, that,' Dunk said, putting an arm around the woman and gathering her to him as he walked her off the field. None of the Hackers knew about Dunk's attempt to cut a deal with the bookie, and he wanted to keep it that way. 'Let's talk somewhere more private.'

Lästiges let the thrower escort her from the practice field. He waved at the other players, and said, 'I'll be right back,' to Cavre. Pegleg and

Olsen, who'd been chatting at the other end of the field stopped to watch the two leave, but they said nothing to stop them.

Dunk steered Lästiges through an open doorway in the high, stone wall that surrounded the place, which Pegleg had paid an exorbitant fee to rent. Most of the money went not for the field itself, which was fine enough, but to pay for the strict security surrounding the place. With the Blood Bowl finals looming ahead, Pegleg wanted to make sure his players didn't have to worry about angry rivals or overexcited fans. Dunk wondered for a moment how Lästiges had got through, but he realised that other reporters wandered in and out of the place all the time. Her press pass must have been enough.

As they strode into the empty locker room, Lästiges jabbed an elbow into Dunk's ribs and strode away from him while he rubbed his injured side.

'What was that for?' he asked.

'You deserve a lot worse,' she said, spinning to wag a long, crimson-nailed finger at him. 'Making a pact with the Gobbo to get Breitzel to ruin the Reavers' game? You might as well have cut a deal with Khorne himself!'

Dunk put his hands up in front of him again, just in case. 'I only meant–'

'It doesn't – that doesn't – I don't *care* what you *meant* to do. "I just wanted to save my little brother and my little girlfriend". Well, you screwed that up and everything else too!'

'Hey, at least I tried. I did *something*. You were with us when we found the cup. You know how it works. You know what's going to happen in the finals. We're going to systematically *murder* the Reavers on the gridiron.'

'I know,' Lästiges said, putting a hand to her forehead, perhaps trying to hold that pulsing vein back from bursting. 'I tried to tell them that. I know you did too, but what you did…'

'It didn't work anyway,' Dunk said, surprised at his own bitterness. A part of him had been relieved to not end up beholden to the Gobbo, but he would have gladly been so if it would have saved Spinne and Dirk's lives. 'It doesn't matter.'

'So you think,' Lästiges said. 'They know all about it.'

Dunk felt a chill in his gut. 'Who?'

'Spinne and Dirk! Once Breitzel came to in the infirmary, they really put the screws to him. He gave them the Gobbo's name.'

Dunk closed his eyes and shook his head.

'They found the Gobbo in the Skinned Cat, and he skavened you out. Then they came looking for me.'

Dunk opened his eyes again and stared at Lästiges. 'Why? You had nothing to do with that.'

'I *know!*' she said, frustration marring her picture-perfect face. 'But do you think they believed that? They thought I was in on it with you from the beginning.'

Dunk frowned. 'I'll talk to them,' he said, more to himself than Lästiges. 'I'll set this right.'

'How?' she asked. 'How? They told me they never want to talk to you again. If it weren't for the finals, they'd never want to *see* you. Or me either!'

'I just wanted to keep them safe.'

'Then you should have quit the game and got them to do the same! Do you know what the average life expectancy of a Blood Bowl player is? Two and a half seasons. And all the immortals who have been playing for hundreds of years throw off that curve! Most players never make it past their first season, either from injury or death or post-traumatic stress.'

'What's your point?' Dunk didn't like where this was going.

'It's a dangerous game. Lethal.' She was screaming now, tears flowing, and makeup running down her face. 'If you were so damned worried about living forever, you should have stuck to something easier – like fighting dragons!'

Neither of them said anything for a moment, letting the heavy silence hang between them. The only sound came from Lästiges's sniffles.

'Are you through?' Dunk asked.

Lästiges nodded, wiping her face and nose with a handkerchief she pulled from her pocket.

'I will make this right,' he said. 'I will make sure Dirk knows you had nothing to do with it. I don't know how to make up for what I did – best intentions aside – but there's no reason for him to be mad at you. I'll set him straight.'

'You'd damn well better,' she said. She'd stopped crying now, but her voice was still raw. She opened her mouth to add something else, but it seemed – for the first time since Dunk had met her – she had nothing to say. She gave him a wan smile, then turned and left through the locker room's back door.

Dunk rubbed his face with his hands and turned around to get back to practice. Cavre stood in the doorway, watching him, an easy smile on his face.

'You are having a difficult time, Mr. Hoffnung.'

Dunk started to say something flippant, then just nodded and said, 'Too true.'

'This is a hard time for us all. The captain isn't himself these days. The grip of the cup on him is strong. It gets stronger all the time. If we do not break this grip before the end of our season, I fear it may have him for all time.'

'You don't think it's already too late? Didn't he give the cup part of his soul?'

Cavre nodded. 'But the cup has yet to live up to its end of the bargain: to give the captain a Blood Bowl championship. There is still a chance, although it is small.'

Dunk looked into Cavre's deep, brown eyes. For a man as tough as the veteran was, they were soft and filled with hard-won wisdom.

'I wondered which side you'd come down on,' Dunk said. 'Pegleg's or mine.'

Cavre smiled at that, his teeth glaring white against his dark skin. 'I'm on our side, Mr. Hoffnung, the Hackers. That includes us all.'

'Does that mean I can count on your help.'

The blitzer reached up under the right spaulder on his practice armour – the Hackers only used the spiked variety during official games – and withdrew a small pouch made of finely worked links of steel. He tossed it to Dunk, who snatched it from the air.

'I thought you might find this entertaining if not useful,' he said. Then, before Dunk could open the pouch, he turned and trotted back onto the practice field.

Dunk hefted the pouch in his hand. It felt heavier than he thought it should. He opened it and dumped the contents into his other hand.

Out tumbled a miniature Hacker helmet, green and gold with the crossed blades forming the well-known Hacker H. Dunk smiled, thinking the team captain had made him a souvenir, a symbol that showed he would always be part of the team, a handy charm for good luck.

Then the helmet moved in his hand.

Dunk bobbled the helmet for a moment, but he managed to fight his first instinct: to drop the helmet on the floor and stomp it flat. If it had come from anyone other than Cavre, he might well have, but he trusted the veteran as much as he did anyone.

He held the helmet carefully between his index finger and thumb to inspect it. Other than its size, it seemed an exact replica of a Bad Bay Hacker helmet, right down to the chinstrap, which was fastened and seemed to be holding something inside.

Dunk turned the helmet around so he could peer in through the faceguard, and he saw a pair of tiny, eyes staring back at him out of a pale green face. The level of detail on the face stunned the thrower. How could anyone make something look so real? The face looked so lifelike, so real, so... familiar?

Then Dunk placed the face. 'Skragger?' he said.

The face opened its mouth and snarled, in a squeaky, high-pitched voice, 'You're dead, Hoffnung! Dead!'

Dunk froze, staring into the tiny eyes that shot daggers of hatred at him.

'You hear me? Get my hands on you, you're dead!' Even in a voice strung higher than that of a tiny child, the bile in the tone could not be mistaken.

Dunk blinked at the shrunken face in his hand and then threw back his head and laughed. He laughed loud and long and in a way he didn't think he had since he'd first laid eyes on the Far Albion Cup back in that damned camp in the cursed Sure Wood. Fat, happy tears rolled down his reddening cheeks until he realised he could barely breathe and had to sit down on the locker room floor. He coughed and hacked some air back into his lungs until he could start to laugh again, and he did.

'Ah, Cavre,' he said as he stuffed the little helmet back into its pouch, which muffled the tiny voice until it fell silent. 'I don't know how anyone could top that.' He wiped his face dry as he pulled himself to his feet, and then shook his head as he trotted back out onto the practice field. "Hands," he chuckled. 'That's priceless.'

'I'M SO GLAD you agreed to talk with me,' Dunk said.

Spinne shut the door to her suite of rooms behind him as he entered. 'A little voice in the back of my head tells me this is a bad idea, but I never did listen to that when it came to you.'

Dunk smiled his thanks at her. She gestured for him to take an over-stuffed chair in a sitting area near the room's bay window, and he did. She sat down on a matching couch opposite him, a low, empty table between them.

'Lästiges came to see me,' Dunk said. 'She was pretty upset.'

'So was I.' Spinne looked out the window. The sun shone bright over the rooftops of Altdorf, glinting off the spires of the Emperor's castle in the distance.

'But you're not anymore?' Dunk tried to keep the hope in his heart from creeping into his voice.

'I've had some time to reflect.'

'I'm sorry,' Dunk said. 'I just wanted to say that. I really am. I didn't mean to – I don't know. I just wanted to keep you safe.'

Spinne nodded. 'I get it. I understand what you were trying to do.' She shook her head. 'You just picked one of the worst possible ways to do it.'

Dunk started to speak, and then snorted softly. 'I don't want you to die on me. Every other team we've faced while we've had the Far Albion Cup has suffered seventy-five percent or more casualties. I couldn't bear to watch that.'

'Then don't. Quit the Hackers. Leave it all behind.'

'That's not much of a solution – unless you leave the game too.'

Spinne gave Dunk a thin-lipped smile. 'I like playing Blood Bowl. How many other women do you know who can say that? I'm a bit of a freak, I'm afraid.' She looked out the window again. 'It's the only thing I'm really good at.'

'Aren't you going to ask me why I did it?'

Spinne looked confused. 'What do you mean?'

'Why I made the deal with Gobbo? Why I tried to rig your game against you? Or don't you care about any of that?'

She smirked in a not unkind way. 'Go ahead. Tell me.'

'I love you,' he said. 'I don't want to lose you.'

'Is that right?'

'You don't believe me?'

Spinne lowered her head. 'Oh, I believe you, Dunk. I love you too. But for two people who love each other so much, we haven't seen much of each other lately.'

The conversation had taken a right angle from where Dunk had thought it was headed.

'I – I guess you're right about that, but after the massacre in that game in Magritta, Pegleg decided to take the team to Albion.'

'And you decided to go along.'

'Yes.'

'Even though you knew it would mean we might not see each other for months on end.'

Dunk sighed. 'Spinne, we often go for weeks at a time without seeing each other. We live in different cities. We play games in different parts of the world. About the only time we can guarantee we'll see each other is during one of the four major tournaments.'

'Two of which, you missed this year.'

'I couldn't do anything about that,' Dunk said. 'I was in Albion. We got stuck there longer than I'd hoped. I – I almost died trying to get us out of there.'

'That's your excuse? "I almost died". That's supposed to make me feel better.'

Dunk groaned inwardly. 'I'm just trying to tell you what happened and why.'

Spinne nodded. Dunk could tell she was getting reading to say something big, so he kept quiet. When she spoke, she held her voice even and calm. When she looked at him, though, he could see her eyes were red and swollen from struggling to dam the flood of tears behind them.

'I don't know if we should be together anymore.'

Dunk sat back in his chair, stunned. 'What?'

'I don't know if we should be together anymore.'

'I heard what you said. I meant, why?'

'We're not really together as it is, are we? We've seen each other only a handful of times in the past nine months.'

'I write to you all the time.'

'And I love your letters,' she said. 'I really do, but they are cold comfort on a lonely night. I can't curl up next to your letters.'

'But–' For a moment, Dunk couldn't think of anything with which to follow that up. 'Are you just trying to get back at me for what happened in your last game?'

Dunk hoped the answer would be yes. If so, maybe Spinne would change her mind when the season was over and she'd had a chance to calm down. Maybe all he needed to do was to stall, to get her to wait breaking it off with him a week or so more, until she had time to forgive him in her heart.

'No,' she said, and Dunk's heart cracked.

'I've had some time to think about this,' she said. 'At first, I wasn't sure. I mean, I was angry with you, really angry, and that was hard to separate out from how I feel about you.

'But I've been having these thoughts for a long time. When you didn't make it to the Dungeonbowl, I understood. After all, the Grey Wizards went with the Reavers again, so your slot was gone. And you were still stuck in Albion.'

'I heard about what happened in the Far Albion Cup Final just as we were getting ready to leave for the Chaos Cup. I thought maybe I'd finally see you then, but when you got back to Bad Bay, you just stayed there. Then I saw that Cabalvision special with you in bed with Lästiges, and I had all these horrible feelings toward you. I hated you then – at least as much as I could.'

'But that was all innocent,' Dunk said. 'You know that.'

'Sure,' Spinne said, 'but it didn't change how I felt. In the end, I realised I wasn't jealous of Lästiges so much because she'd been found in bed with you but because of how much time she'd got to spend with you. She was with your team throughout that entire trip of yours to Albion, and I didn't get to see you once. Not once.'

'But, Spinne,' Dunk said, 'I'm back now – for good. All that stuff – going to Albion, disappearing for months at a time – that's all over with now. It won't happen again.'

'You can't know that,' Spinne said. 'You could have said the same thing to me this time last year. Would it have made a difference in what you did?'

Dunk swallowed hard as he considered the question. He knew, just looking at Spinne, that he had to be as honest as possible. She'd see straight through any lie he might tell, and not giving enough thought to the issue would be just as bad.

'I don't know,' he finally said. 'I'd like to think that I might have done things differently, but I didn't expect things to work out that badly back then. I don't suppose I would if the same situation came up again either.'

Spinne gazed at him solemnly, and all Dunk could think about was how much he just wanted to lose himself in her blue-grey eyes and leave the rest of the world behind.

'Thank you,' she said. 'If you had lied or dissembled or...' She put her hand to her mouth to cut off a sob.

'I think you should leave now,' she said.

'Oh. Okay.' Dunk got up to go, unsure what he should do. He wanted nothing more than to put his arms around her, to comfort her, to tell her everything would be all right, but he couldn't tell if that was what she would want. He took a tentative step toward her, and she turned away.

'Just go,' she said, pointing at the door as she gazed out the window at the wide world beyond. Outside, a flock of white birds caught the rays of the evening sun flaring through their feathers.

'Can I come to see you again?' he asked. 'There's a team dinner tonight, but I could–'

'No. Never.'

Dunk gaped at her as his heart crumbled into bright, sharp shards in his chest.

'Good-bye, Dunk,' she said. She never took her eyes from the window.

Dunk started to reach out to touch her strawberry-blonde hair, but then pulled his hand back. Without a word, he turned and left. He heard her begin to sob as he closed the door behind him.

'NUFFLE'S CODPIECE,' SLICK said as he poked Dunk in the shoulder. 'I was afraid I'd find you like this.'

Dunk tried to raise his head to respond to the halfling, but he only succeeded in turning his face to the side instead. He spotted his agent standing there, a stern look on his face, but sideways – and more than a little blurry – and the image made him laugh.

'Hi, Slick!' Dunk said. 'Glad you could make it! I'm a...' He fumbled for the right word for a moment, and then held up his hand with his thumb and index finger just a little bit apart. He tried to adjust them to the right distance apart, but they just kept moving about. Or were they? He decided to not worry about it any longer. 'Weeeee bit drunk.'

'Oh, really, son?' Slick said. 'Is that why M'Grash here sent word for me in the middle of the night? I thought perhaps you might be hosting a surprise birthday party for me.'

Dunk sat back in his chair and grinned as the world swam around him. 'It's your birthday? Why didn't you say so? Hey, bartender!' He swung his arm up to signal for another drink, but he lost track of it somewhere between where it started and where he wanted it to end. He looked down and saw Slick's hand holding his arm down.

'It's not my–' Slick shook his head. 'Never mind. I hear you've had a rough night.'

'What do you mean?' Dunk said. 'I'm having a *great* time. I'm just out here celebrating the Hackers' success with my biggest friend and my smallest one.' He put his arm around M'Grash here.

The ogre looked down at the halfling and shrugged as innocently as he could. 'Dunkel drunkel.'

'You got that right, big guy!' Dunk said, chucking M'Grash in the shoulder. 'Living large and loving it!'

'You're breaking training, son,' Slick said. 'If we get you back to your room soon, Pegleg might be none the wiser. I know an apothecary who has a hangover remedy that will keep you from wanting to commit ritual suicide tomorrow morning to end the pain. It's expensive, but you can afford it.'

'What do I care about Pegleg?' Dunk asked. 'He's gonna fire me right before the big game? His star thrower? Ha!'

'Dunkel not happy,' M'Grash said, with a frown big enough to bring down the entire room. 'He very sad.'

'I can see that,' Slick said. 'What in the Emperor's name has he been drinking?' The halfling peered over the rim of Dunk's stein.

'Tastes great!' M'Grash said.

'Less filling!' Dunk answered.

'Now, you two, don't start up with that!'

Dunk and M'Grash laughed so hard they had to hold each other up for fear of falling off their stools. Then M'Grash started to tip over backward, and there was nothing that Dunk could do about it. They toppled over and landed hard in an area behind them that mysteriously had no tables in it.

'All that's holy!' Slick said, climbing up on the table so he could look down at the two friends tangled on the floor. 'You two better be more careful. You're going to kill someone.'

'Don't worry about that,' the barmaid said as she righted the steins that had fallen over along with Dunk and M'Grash. 'After the first time, we got smart and moved the other tables away to give them some space.'

Slick looked aghast. 'How long have you two been at this?'

Dunk glanced at M'Grash, the crash to the floor seeming to have sobered him up just a bit. 'What day is this?' he asked.

'Beerday!' M'Grash shouted in reply.

'Beerday?' Slick said. 'When's beerday?'

Dunk grinned at M'Grash, and the two answered in unison. 'Every day is beerday!'

Slick slapped a hand over his face and groaned.

Dunk continued on. 'A wise man once said… he…' The thrower stopped and turned about, looking all around him. 'Hey,' he said, a note of true concern in his voice. 'Where'd my little friend go?'

'I'm right *here*,' Slick said, exasperated.

'No.' Dunk stopped hunting for a moment to look at the halfling and giggle. 'Not you. The *little* guy. M'Grash? Have you seen him?'

'Uh-uh, Dunkel.' The ogre set his heavy stool – more of an iron-bound bench, really – back into position and recovered what was left of his drink. He threw back the dregs in one clean move, and smiled wide, showing his tusks all the way down to his teeth.

Then he started to gag.

M'Grash's hands went to his neck as he coughed and hacked, searching for some way to clear his throat. Dunk swept around behind him and started to beat him on the back with a barstool. Thunk! Thunk! Thunk!

On the fourth or fifth thunk, the ogre hacked hard, and something small and slimy came flying out of his throat to land on the table in front of him. Dunk scooted around from behind his friend to see what it was.

There, lying in the centre of the table, lay Skragger's shrunken head.

'You bastards!' Skragger's squeaky voice railed at Dunk and M'Grash. 'Good thing I don't breath, or I'd be dead! Stuck in a beer and can't damn drink!' He howled in despair.

M'Grash kept coughing through it all. The barmaid brought him another keg-sized stein on a wheeled cart, and he snatched it up, draining half of it in a single draught.

'Ha!' Skragger said. 'Almost killed you, didn't I? *That* woulda been worth it!'

Dunk picked the shrunken head up by the sides of its helmet and peered into its eyes. 'So,' he said, 'what was it you said before, wise man?'

'Beer is proof the gods love us and want us to be happy!'

'Right,' a new voice said, 'and hangovers are proof they hate us and want us to wish we were dead.'

Dunk's head snapped around, and his eyes struggled to focus on the speaker. 'Funny,' he said, dropping Skragger's head in the middle of the table, 'that sounded just like my old teacher.'

The man standing before Dunk was shorter than him and slighter of frame. He wore his silver hair cropped short over sparkling, grey eyes. His cloak was the same drab colour as the stone walls of the buildings in Altdorf's ancient quarters. He shook his head as he looked at Dunk, a mixture of disapproval and understanding blended in his face.

'Lehrer?' Dunk said, unsure his drunkenness wasn't leading him astray.

'Hey, kid.' The man's raspy voice made Dunk feel like a child again, and he felt aware of how silly he'd been acting. 'I'd ask you how you're doing, but it seems pretty clear.'

'Sit down,' Dunk said, signalling the barmaid to bring them each a drink. 'Stay a while.'

'I don't have long,' Lehrer said, even as he took the offered seat. 'The Guterfiends will miss me if I'm gone for too long.'

'Who?' Slick asked. 'What's this all about?'

Dunk, far more sober now, pointed at Lehrer and said. 'This man was in charge of security at my family's estates since before I can remember. He taught me everything I know about fighting, with weapons and without.'

Dunk put a hand on Slick's shoulder and his other on M'Grash's arm. 'This is Slick Fullbelly – my agent – and M'Grash K'Thragsh, one of my best friends. And that,' he pointed to the miniature helmet in the centre of the table, 'I believe you may already know.'

'Is that…?' Lehrer leaned over to peer in through the tiny helmet's faceplate. 'Skragger?'

'Help me, you bastard!' Skragger squeaked.

Lehrer gaped at Dunk and his friends. 'How? Did one of you manage this?'

Dunk shook his head. 'It was Cavre. Something he learned how to do during his childhood in the Southlands. He says his father was some kind of witch doctor.'

'You lead an interesting life,' Lehrer said, staring at the thing inside the little helmet.

'You don't know the half of it,' said Slick.

Lehrer grunted at this. 'Sadly, I don't have the time to sit here and catch up the way I probably should. The Guterfiends – who now occupy Dunk's family home *and* who cover my wages each week – have apparently decided to give up on their little vendetta against Dunk here. At least, for now.'

'Why's that?' Dunk asked, hoping he didn't sound as drunk as he still was.

'After you knocked Skragger's head off, they went nuts. Would have been ready to burn down half the town if they could've guaranteed you'd be in it. They hadn't said anything to me or anyone else on the old staff up till that point, but they were hopping mad and started screaming how much they wanted you dead.'

'So why don't I have a dozen assassins chasing me through town?'

'Wiser heads prevailed. Someone who knows you well convinced them that targeting a Blood Bowl player during the week before the final game wasn't such a bright idea. Said you would all be on high alert, and there was no way a killer could get through such tight security.' He looked around the Skinned Cat and then back at the drunk Dunk. 'Sorry to see I was so wrong.'

'What happens after the game?' Slick asked.

Lehrer nodded at Dunk. 'The Guterfiends declare open season on him. This time around, they might just put a price on his head and let all comers take a shot at it. Hiring the best guy for the job didn't work out so well for them last time.' He looked down at Skragger's head. 'Did it?'

Skragger cut loose with a string of curses so evocative that they made Dunk blush. Unperturbed, Lehrer reached over and picked up the head, then dropped it into his beer, where it sank to the bottom, the liquid instantly muffling the creature's complaints.

Then Dirk walked in. He strode through the front door of the bar as if he owned the place. The regulars in the crowd hailed him, shouting, 'Dirk!' in unison. He waved back at them all, not cracking a smile, despite the adoration in the room. When his roving eyes found Dunk, though, he made straight for him.

'Spinne told me she broke it off with you. I thought I might find you here,' Dirk said, looking around the room and then down at Dunk with a hint of disgust. 'And maybe like this.'

Dunk waved at his brothers – all three of them.

Dirk scanned the faces of the others at the table. When his gaze lighted on Lehrer, who sat looking straight ahead, stone-faced as ever, his face fell into a sneer. 'But I never thought I'd find you with *him*.'

'Hey,' Dunk said, his head clearing again as he picked up on the implied threat of violence in his brother's voice. 'Aren't you happy to see an old friend?'

'Friend?' Dirk said, his eyes wide in disbelief. He looked down at Lehrer and bared his teeth as he took a half a step back. 'You can't be that drunk, can you?'

'Hey,' Dunk said, getting a little offended himself now. 'What's the matter with you? Don't you know who this is? He's one of the good guys.' Then he pointed at Dirk. 'You, I'm not so sure about. I try to save your life– '

'By trying to arrange for my team to lose in the semi-finals!'

'–and do I see any gratitude? A word of thanks? Maybe my methods were bad– '

'Try "the worst ever".'

'–but my heart was in the right place.' He shook his head which started to swim again at the movement. 'All I wanted was to keep you and Spinne safe, and what do I get for that? My girlfriend dumps me, and my brother won't talk to me!'

'I'm talking to you now,' Dirk said, barely containing his anger. For a moment, Dunk wondered if his brother might launch himself across the table at him.

'So,' Dunk said, mustering every ounce of seriousness he had in him, 'what do you have to say?'

Dirk glanced down at Lehrer and edged away from him again before stabbing a finger at Dunk. 'You are an idiot! This is the same kind of crap you used to pull when we were growing up. "Dirk's too young. I need to protect him"'.

Dunk started to protest, but Dirk cut him off.

'I'm not finished.' He grimaced and took a deep breath before starting again.

'I'm not a kid any more. I was never that much younger than you. I'm a Blood Bowl star with more seasons under my helmet than you.' He leaned over the table and stabbed his finger into its surface to punctuate every word. 'I don't need your help.'

Dunk looked into his brother's eyes and saw how badly he'd hurt him. The two had grown closer over the past two years than they had been since they were children racing around the ramparts of the family keep. Until then, Dunk hadn't realised how much he'd missed that, the connection, and the sense of brotherhood that nothing could sever.

And now he'd done something that seemed like it might cut that bond forever.

'Look,' Dunk said. 'I was only trying to help. I tried to warn you and Spinne about the Far Albion Cup. Damn it, I've been trying to warn Pegleg too, and nobody seems to want to listen. But this isn't some kind of game. We're not playing knights and orcs back in the keep anymore. It's deadly and real.

'If you had just listened to me–'

'Maybe if you'd stop telling me what to do–'

'Maybe if you didn't need it so badly–'

'That's it!' Dirk roared, stepping back. 'It's bad enough that you colluded with the Gobbo to harm my team. That I can forgive. Other teams do it all the damn time. Why shouldn't you, no matter how "noble" your reasons?'

'See,' Dunk said, 'that's all I was trying to say.'

'But to come in here and see you sitting at a table with *him*…' Dirk glared over at Lehrer, who still stared off into space, ignoring him. 'That's just beyond the pale.'

Dunk narrowed his eyes at Dirk. 'What are you talking about?' He glanced at Lehrer, then back at Dirk. 'That's our teacher, our mentor. One of our oldest friends. He was best friends with our parents since before we were born.'

'And now he works for our family's most hated enemies, the Guterfiends,' Dirk said. 'Doesn't that tell you something?'

Dunk stared at his brother. 'So do most of the old staff. What else could they do? In case you don't recall, our parents abandoned the place. All those people needed to eat, Lehrer included.'

Dirk cocked his head at Dunk. 'You don't find it the least bit odd that the Guterfiends would keep on our "loyal family friend" in any capacity? Much less putting him in charge of their security?'

Dunk couldn't believe what he was hearing. 'He just came here to warn me about how the Guterfiends plan to put a price on my head after the Blood Bowl finals. They paid Skragger to try to kill me in the semis.'

Dirk stared at Dunk. 'And who do you think hired Skragger in the first place?'

Dunk's eyes snapped toward Lehrer, but the man had already bolted from his seat and started sprinting for the door.

'Stop him!' Dirk shouted.

Dunk stood up to take after Lehrer. He wanted an explanation for all of this as much as anyone. His legs wobbled beneath him as he did, but he refused to let that stop him.

M'Grash overturned the table as he stood up and started after Lehrer. Only a step later, though, he tripped over the chair that Dirk had left behind as he raced ahead of them.

As the ogre stumbled toward the door, he flailed his arms wildly to try to regain his balance. When it became clear this wouldn't work, M'Grash leaped for the door instead.

Getting in and out of the Skinned Cat had always been a challenge for M'Grash. Despite how much he liked the place, which always surprised Dunk, it wasn't built for ogres. The chairs were too small – he'd broken three before the innkeeper had supplied him with a wide bench instead – the tables too fragile, and the steins too small. He'd taken to ordering his drinks by the cask and prying one end off with a battered nail.

So, when M'Grash's off-balance bulk smashed into the door that he'd had to so carefully navigate in the past, he didn't fit through it smoothly. In fact, he didn't fit through it at all. He only got his head and shoulders through the frame before he became stuck.

As the ogre howled in pain and frustration, Dunk clambered over his back to see what had happened to Lehrer and Dirk. When he reached the street, though, by sliding down over M'Grash's massive head, they had already disappeared.

Dunk cursed as he peered down both directions on the long street, which wound like a snake through the worst part of Altdorf. He couldn't even tell which way they'd gone.

In his frustration, Dunk roared up at the distant sky. 'How can this day get any worse?'

Then a small strange voice came from behind. 'Dunkel help?'

Dunk turned to see M'Grash struggling to free himself from the doorway. The ogre had landed hard enough to wedge himself in good, though, and at such angle that he couldn't find the kind of leverage he needed to force himself free.

'Don't worry!' Slick called from inside the tavern. Dunk could just see his eyes peering over the top of the fallen ogre. 'I've already got an order placed for every bit of butter they have in the place.'

The halfling cocked his head and grimaced as he evaluated M'Grash's plight once again. 'I might have to ask for every bit of cooking oil and rendered fat too.'

Dunk groaned, then reached out and patted the whimpering M'Grash on the top of his head.

'AND THERE'S THE kick-off to start the championship final in this year's Blood Bowl Open!' Bob's voice echoed out over the stadium, barely audible over the cheers of the crowd.

Dunk raced down the field with three goals in mind. Winning the game came last, he realised, which he felt odd about. Before that, he wanted to survive the game. He'd never been one of those 'team first' players, and if there was ever a sport meant for people to watch out for themselves Blood Bowl was it.

In last year's game, he hadn't felt that way at all. Back then, he'd cared about everyone on the team, with one exception: Kur Ritternacht. Given that Kur had wanted to kill him, Dunk couldn't see how he should feel bad about that.

This time around, though, he only gave a damn about M'Grash, Edgar, Simon, Guillermo, and Cavre. The rest could all go back to rotting in whatever hell they'd come from, as far as Dunk was concerned. He was pretty sure the new players felt the same about him, if they gave him any thought at all.

Dunk slammed into the first Reaver he saw, knocking him to the ground. The thrower had learned a lot in the two seasons he'd been playing the game. Things like, 'Hit lower than the other guy,' stuck with you once you'd been trampled a few dozen times.

'The Hackers are in rare form tonight!' Jim said. 'They've become a truly brutal team. Most of the credit has to go to team coach Captain Pegleg Haken. Can this really be the same team the Chaos All-Stars tore to pieces nine months ago?'

'Not really,' Bob said. 'Only five players survived that rout. Even though they all started the game tonight, there's more fresh blood on the Hackers' side of the field than old.'

'That, and their new team wizard, of course. He's been in the Hackers' dugout since day one of their return. His wand and a little item known as the Far Albion Cup seem to have turned the Hackers' fortunes right around. Perhaps our roving reporter can tell us something more about it. Lästiges?'

Dunk spun out of the grasp of one Reaver and straight into another. He hammered at his foe twice with his fists, and then rammed the crown of his spiked helmet at the man. The Reaver let go of Dunk's spaulder then, and the thrower ran back into the thick of the game again. As he did, he saw Lästiges's face appear on the Jumboball. She stood next to Pegleg and Olsen in the Hackers' dugout, the Far Albion Cup itself on display behind them.

'Thanks, Jim! I'm down here with Captain Haken and his team wizard, the legendary Olsen Merlin. What can you gentlemen tell us about the Far Albion Cup and the effect it's had on the team?'

'Bugger off,' Olsen said. 'We're working here.'

Pegleg stepped between the wizard and the camra, a nervous yet charming smile on his face. 'What my esteemed colleague means to say, Miss Weibchen, is that the cup is more of a symbol of what our team has gone through over the past season rather than any kind of an object of raw, magical power. Our players have become fond of it and look on it as a mascot more than anything else.'

'So this cup is your team mascot?'

'Well, yes, I suppose it is.' Pegleg's smile widened, becoming both more charming and more nervous.

'I think that says more about their off-field antics than I ever could.' Lästiges gave the camra a savage smile, while Pegleg blustered in the background. 'Back to you, Jim!'

Dunk smiled behind his faceguard as he jinked to the right, dodging past a Reaver intent on slamming him into the Astrogranite. He spotted Dirk upfield from him, the ball tucked under his arm as he scrambled away from M'Grash.

Dunk hadn't talked to Dirk since his younger brother had chased Lehrer from the Skinned Cat. When Bob had called Dirk's name out while introducing the Reavers before the start of the game, Dunk had sighed with relief. At least Dirk was all right, although Dunk still wondered about Lehrer. Was he really the traitor Dirk said he was? After the game ended, he knew that he had to find out, even if it meant digging through the darker parts of his family's history.

Dunk charged towards where he thought Dirk would end up if he managed to elude M'Grash. Sure enough, his brother burst out of the pile-up in the middle of the field and swung right, looking downfield for a target. As Dunk closed in on him, he cocked his arm back to throw.

Dunk lowered his shoulder and smashed into Dirk's middle. As he did, he knew that Dirk would get the pass off, but Dunk wanted to make him pay. Also, he thought if he tackled Dirk that might get the new Hackers to leave him alone and go after other prey.

'What an amazing throw!' Jim said. 'As Hoffnung takes him down, Heldmann hurls the ball downfield in a perfect spiral. Schönheit reaches out for it under double coverage and pulls it down! She stiff-arms Schmidt and races into the end zone. Touchdown, Reavers!'

'First blood,' Dirk shouted over the roar of the crowd. 'So much for your damned cup.'

'What an amazing play!' Bob said. 'The Reavers state their case to be crowned champions by picking up a quick score.'

'But they seem to have bought their point with blood,' Jim said. 'I count one, two, three Reaver casualties on the field already, and they don't look like they're getting up.'

'What about Hoffnung and Heldmann? The two brothers seem to have taken each other out. If so, that would be an anticlimactic end to their sibling rivalry!'

'Dunk?'

'Yeah, Dirk.'

'You can get off me now.'

'Oh, right!'

Dunk scrambled to his feet, and the crowd saw that he and Dirk were all right. He stuck out his hand at Dirk, and his brother took it.

'Brothers forever,' Dunk said.

Dirk grinned despite himself.

The fans roared in approval.

Some of those roars, though, soon turned to screams.

'It seems something's happening in the cheap seats on the south side of the stadium,' Jim said. 'Most times the fans are happy to watch the action unfold on the field, but it looks like that might not have been enough for that crew. But, wow, I don't think I've seen that much blood spilled in the bleachers since, well, when was your last birthday party, Bob?'

'I stopped celebrating them decades ago, but even in my youngest years the festivities never looked much like that. What's going on over there?'

As Dunk trotted back to the Hackers' end of the field, he looked up at the Jumboball, which showed the view from a camra focused on the top of the stadium's south side. Dozens of people had stripped off their clothes and were going at each other in an amorous way. Each person's skin had a greyish cast, except for the red rash that seemed to crawl along under the flesh.

In the centre of it all stood a rat-on-a-stick vendor with a particularly bad rash and a wild look in his yellowing eyes. He stood flinging his product into the stands, yelling for people to eat the free grub, despite the fact that – other than his food harness – he was buck naked and, from all appearances, thrilled about it.

'You know, Bob, I don't think those are your standard rats-on-sticks there.'

Dunk raced back down the field to the Reavers' side. A few of the players getting into position there tried to slow him down, but he slipped past them until he reached Dirk, who was preparing to kick off the ball.

'Hey,' Dirk said. 'How long have you been playing this game? You're not allowed back – Hey!'

Dunk snatched up the football and then raced back toward the middle of the field. When he reached it, he slung his arm back and then unleashed a powerful throw that sailed through the air and caught the rat-on-a-stick vendor square in the chest. The spike on the tip of the ball pierced the vendor's heart, but he stood there for a moment, shocked at his imminent death and raging against it. Then his heart burst from his chest, showering all those around him in bloody gore.

'That's one way to handle an unruly fan,' Bob said. 'Remind me to never get Hoffnung angry at me – or to have ball-proof glass installed in the announcers' booth.'

'Maybe our new friend Olsen Merlin could tell us something about what's happening here. Lästiges?'

'Yes, Jim, I'm here in the Hackers' dugout with–' The reporter cut herself off with a horrified scream.

Dunk looked over at the dugout and saw that all of the new Hackers had dashed into it. One of them dashed out of the place with the Far Albion Cup tucked under his arm. A few others chased after him, Lästiges stretched out among them, struggling to free herself with all her might.

Then something in the dugout exploded, and the other new Hackers came flying out of the place, some in more pieces than they'd been in while entering.

The fans in the stands behind the Hackers' dugout started to scream. Then they stampeded away from the field, trying to escape whatever horrible thing they expected to issue forth from the dugout. Their path took them up and south, directly toward the fans in the higher stands, whose skin writhed faster and redder now than ever. Most of them had stripped off their clothes, and either set to scratching at their rashes, heedless of the amount of blood they drew, or started to copulate with any vaguely compatible person they could find, whether infected or willing or neither.

'Lästiges!' Dirk shouted. 'Lästiges!'

Dunk watched his brother call for his fellow Reavers to follow him and then chase after his woman, who the new Hackers were dragging into the stands.

Dunk did not see how this could end well. All he knew was he had to put an end to it – now. He sprinted toward his team's dugout. As he did, he bumped into a Reaver he almost ran over. When he turned to snarl at the Reaver, he recognised her instantly.

Spinne.

'Come with me,' he said as he grabbed her hand.

'Let me go!' she shouted, pulling her arm free. 'I need to help Dirk.'

'He doesn't stand a chance!' Dunk spun back and held Spinne by her spaulders. 'You can't fight a sickness like that. You have to kill it at its cause.'

'And where do you think we could find something like that, Dunk?' Spinne's tone told Dunk she'd lost all patience with him. Despite that, he needed her to trust him just a minute more.

'Follow me!' he said, offering her his hand once again. To his amazement, she took it.

When they reached the dugout, Dunk planned to skirt around it and take off into the stands after the traitor Hackers carrying away the Far Albion Cup. Instead, Slick charged up the stairs at them, a Hacker helmet on his head.

'We need to get the cup!' Slick shouted at Dunk. 'Olsen says it's the only way.'

'Figures,' Dunk said, glaring up into the stands. The players absconding with the cup were already a few rows into the seats. If they reached the exit only a handful of rows ahead of them, they could disappear in the tunnels beneath the stadium and beneath Altdorf itself. If so, Dunk might never be able to find them.

Simon and Guillermo sprinted for the stands, hoping to catch the other Hackers on foot. The crowd parted before the diseased Simon, seeming to identify him as a mummy and fearing such a creature's legendary rotting touch. Dunk could tell, though, that the two would never catch up with the other Hackers in time.

'M'Grash, Edgar!' Dunk shouted, pointing up to where the cup moved through the stands. 'I need to get up there fast!'

'How the bloody hell do you propose we manage that, mate?'

'Throw me?'

Edgar looked at Dunk. 'I don't think I could. You're a bit bloody large for a trick like that. The wee one here,' he pointed at Slick, 'sure, but you're full grown.'

'Not you alone,' Dunk said, gesturing to Edgar and M'Grash with open hands. 'Both of you. Pick me up and swing me up there – together.'

'That's a bloody long way, mate. Could kill you dead.'

Dunk glanced up at the cup as it neared the exit. 'No other way,' he said, putting out his arms for the two giant creatures to grab. 'Let's do it!'

'On three,' Edgar said as it picked up Dunk's left arm and leg and M'Grash got the right.

'Three?' the ogre said. He nearly dropped Dunk as he tried to scratch his head, but he recovered in time to keep the thrower from hitting the dirt.

'You know: one, two, three?' The treeman narrowed its glowing green eyes at M'Grash. 'Oh, bollocks. Just throw him when I say "Go". Ready?'

The two swung Dunk back and forth.

'Set?'

Back and forth.

'Go!'

Back and gone.

Dunk held his breath, waiting for something horrible to happen, for Edgar to let him loose and M'Grash to keep his hold, for someone to pull his arm from its socket. Instead, he zoomed off, arcing high into the air over the stands.

When he reached the apex of his flight, Dunk realised he had no way to steer himself. The best he could do was keep his arms out and his legs together, like a diver reaching for the water of a pool. At that moment, far too late to do himself any good, he questioned how desperate he must have been to get the cup that he not only let someone throw him through the air like a stone from a catapult but had actually asked for it.

Fortunately, M'Grash and Edgar had excellent aim.

As Dunk came soaring in at the Hackers with the Far Albion Cup, he brought his armoured arms and knees to his front and bore down hard on his targets. He slammed into the back of the bestial Hacker holding the cup, a black-furred man-shaped thing with crimson horns shaped like those of a ram. His helmet had been carved back to expose these horns while still offering some protection to the back and sides of his head. His face, however, stood unguarded.

The ram-horned Hacker never saw Dunk hit him. One moment, he was dashing for the exit, gloating at how easy it had been to wrest the cup away from Pegleg and that old wizard. The next, he'd been knocked unconscious as Dunk's full, armoured weight slammed into him from behind and drove his face into the last of the cut-stone steps he'd been about to top. The impact cracked his horns off near their bases and forced the jewel-encrusted cup to go flying from his hands.

While Dunk's target absorbed most of the momentum from his fall, Dunk still had to roll past the ram-horned one, tumbling end over end like a football dribbling along the gridiron after a kick-off. He came to a halt in the frame of the exit, the cup there next to him, within arm's reach. His every bone aching, he snatched up the trophy and scrambled to his feet.

Dunk stared down the stairs behind him and saw five of the new Hackers gaping up at him. 'Hi, guys,' he said, hefting the cup in his hands.

He glanced around and saw that the fans in this part of the stadium had all fallen silent in shock. While the stands to the south were filled with people screaming for their lives – images of Dirk and the Reavers closing in on Lästiges and her kidnappers flashed across the Jumboball – here everyone stood in shock at how Dunk had taken out his ram-horned team-mate, staring with open mouths at him and his bejewelled cup.

Dunk pointed down at his five team-mates and shouted to the crowd, 'Are we going to let those cowards get out of here alive?'

The fans roared in glee and converged on the bestial Hackers like a school of sharks on bloodied prey. One of them, a wolf-faced man with a snout full of vicious teeth that he'd somehow already bloodied, squirted free from the crowd and charged Dunk.

The thrower considered throwing the cup back toward the field, but he doubted he'd be able to manage it with its unwieldy shape. Instead, he grasped the cup's neck with both hands and brought it down on his attacker's green and gold helmet with all his might.

The cup dented the crown of the wolf-faced Hacker's helmet, knocking him to the ground. When Dunk brought the cup back up to strike again, though, only the cup's base and neck came back. The bowl of the cup had snapped off its mooring with the impact.

Dunk winced and held his breath as he waited for the sky to open up and for the magical energy stored in the cup to strike him down for destroying it, but nothing happened. It seemed it would take more to break the cup – and its curse – than that.

The wolf-faced Hacker staggered to its feet and snarled at Dunk with a sound that wasn't human, its reddish eyes glowing with evil and hate. The thrower pulled back his arm, the cup's neck still in it, hoping he could use it to bash the Hacker's helmet in even farther.

Instead of charging, though, the wolf-faced Hacker reached down and scooped up the rest of the cup. It glittered in his hands as he let loose a jackal's mad cackle of triumph.

Dunk steeled himself for the creature's attack. The wolf-faced creature lowered itself on its powerful haunches and launched himself straight at the thrower. Dunk went low, hoping to knock the creature back, just as he would have on the field. As he did, he saw his attacker sail straight over his head.

At first, Dunk felt relieved that he'd avoided the assault, but he wondered how he'd been able to do that so easily. Then he realised that the wolf-faced Hacker hadn't been coming at him at all. The cup in his hands, he'd been trying to escape, and Dunk had let him.

Dunk spun around and saw the Hacker sprinting for the exit, about to reach the tunnel that led through the stands to open daylight beyond. Then something green, yellow, and white burst out of the crowd and tackled the creature, knocking the both of them tumbling down into the tunnel.

DUNK RECOGNISED THE new assailant right away: Simon Sherwood. The diseased catcher had made good time through the crowd and caught up with the bestial Hackers and the cup at just the right moment.

Forging his way through the fans had been rough on Simon. He bled from a dozen cuts, and his beer-soaked wrapping had begun to unravel, exposing his greyish skin. The red rash there seemed worse than ever, red as blood and thrashing about under his flesh like a wild animal trapped in a bag of skin. His eyes were wild with madness, far worse than those of his wolf-faced foe.

As Simon tore at the bestial Hacker with his bare hands, the creature's jaws snapped at his face and throat. An unintelligible roar sprang from his lips, and Dunk knew that the illness now had him entirely, body and soul. He moved only on instinct and the final coherent thoughts that had driven him to pursue the cup and bring down anyone who held it.

Dunk wondered if Simon would have attacked him if the catcher had arrived a moment earlier and found the thrower with the cup still in his hands. Such thoughts didn't bear more consideration at the moment. He sprinted down the tunnel after the two, but before he could catch up with them, the wolf-faced man clamped his teeth around Simon's throat and tore it out.

Simon's blood exploded from his neck as if every ounce in his veins had been under pressure. The wolf-faced Hacker choked on it and tried to sputter it away, as the rush of fluid nearly drowned him.

Dunk pulled Simon's corpse off the blood-soaked Hacker and stabbed the creature in the chest with the jagged stem of the Far Albion Cup still in his hand. The wolf-faced man clawed at Dunk as he shoved the makeshift weapon further in through the creature's ribcage, its tip hunting for his heart.

When Dunk found the pulsating muscle, he gave the broken stem a hard shove and burst the creature's organ. As the wolf-faced Hacker's life spilled out of him, Dunk snatched the bowl of the cup from under his arm and shoved him back to the ground.

When Dunk turned around, he saw Simon's corpse lying there in the tunnel, its throat somewhere else. The pallor of its skin contrasted sharply with the quarts of blood that had covered it and soaked through the wrappings and splashed across the pavement around it. Still, the skin was clear now and rashless, and Dunk could see a savage, satisfied smile poking through the unwrapped parts of Simon's face.

Dunk tucked the cup's bowl under his arm and raced back up the tunnel and into the stadium. The fans around the entrance cheered as he held up the bit of the Far Albion Cup he'd recovered. Dunk didn't see any of the other bestial Hackers, as if the crowd had simply and permanently swallowed them up. He spotted an official Hackers helmet on one fan's head, and a couple of fresh jerseys on some others, and he wondered whether or not they'd been there just minutes ago.

'I need to get down to the Hackers' dugout!' Dunk shouted.

The fans nearby roared their approval and held their hands high over their heads, chanting something Dunk didn't understand. He cocked his head to the side and listened, and it became clear: 'Jump! Jump! Jump!'

Dunk remembered all too well what had happened the first time he'd been given up to the tender mercies of the crowd. At last year's *Spike! Magazine* Tournament, he'd been chucked into the stands after scoring his first touchdown, and the fans had body-passed him up to and over the top edge of the stadium in Magritta. He'd survived the fall but been beaten half to death by the owner of the food cart on top of which he'd crashed.

'Jump! Jump! Jump!' The fans kept chanting at him, and the words took on a hypnotic beat, encouraging him to discard caution and experience and trust them, to comply.

'Jump! Jump! Jump!'

Dunk peered down at the field and wondered if he could hurl the Far Albion Cup all the way down to the gridiron, where perhaps Edgar or

M'Grash could catch it, but he couldn't spot them anywhere. When he looked over to where the Reavers had leaped into the stands to save Lästiges, though, he saw the two gigantic players forging their way through the sea of people to lend Dirk and his fellows a hand – or branch. Someone rode on the ogre's back, beating away infected fans with what looked like a long, thin fragment of a bench. It was Spinne.

Dunk stared back down the aisle that led through the bleachers to the field below, and fans crammed it from one end to the other. If he wanted to get down to the dugout before the entire stadium succumbed to the threat of the Sure Wood cultists, he had only one choice, only one chance.

'Jump! Jump! Jump!'

Dunk wrapped both arms around the bowl of the Far Albion Cup and made a mad dash for the fans standing right in front of him, chanting and stomping their feet so hard he could feel the vibrations through the ground around him. When he reached them, he launched himself into the air and gave himself over to their will.

Half-a-dozen sets of hands snatched Dunk from the apex of his jump and hoisted him farther into the air. Once he lay level upon them, or nearly so, the fans started to pass him around, from one set of outstretched hands to another.

Dunk closed his eyes rather than succumb to the vertigo that threatened to overcome him as he spun about over the heads of the crowd at terrifying speed. He clutched the cup to himself as hard as he could, keeping it from the occasional hand that grabbed at it and tried to tear it from his grasp. Then he felt the hands near his feet disappear, and he felt as if he were sliding off a cliff of ice, and into the great, wide unknown.

Unable to restrain himself any longer, Dunk opened his eyes, which gave him just enough time to bend his knees before he hit the ground. To his astonishment, he knelt crouched on the Astrogranite of Emperor Stadium instead of lying crushed and dying on the pavement just outside. He leapt to his feet, holding the cup over his head, and raced toward the dugout.

The crowd cheered.

'Can you believe it?' Bob's voice said. 'Hoffnung has the cup!'

'That's what I called dogged determination,' Jim said. 'Here the Reavers – including his brother – and two of his team-mates are fighting to the death to rescue our roving reporter from a breakout of a lethal disease that causes madness in all it touches, and Hoffnung's busy making sure the Hackers still have the magic artefact they need to ensure victory.'

'Too true! You just don't see many competitors that cold-hearted these days!'

Dunk dashed into the dugout and saw Cavre and Slick talking with Pegleg as Olsen railed at them all.

'This is *not* going to happen, laddies,' Olsen said. 'Not as long as we–' The wizard cut himself off as Dunk entered. 'Ah, and here's the grand prize now, come to us in the arms of the reluctant hero. We're impressed you managed to recover it.'

'What can we do to stop this?' Dunk said, holding what was left of the Far Albion Cup before him. 'There are hundreds of people dying out there!'

'Faith, lad!' the wizard said, a strange cross between a smile and a scowl on his face. 'More like thousands. Soon, the entire stadium will succumb, we're sure.'

'You're the great wizard around here. Can't you do something about it?'

'Aye, lad, we could,' Olsen said, deadly serious now. 'But we won't.'

'What?' Dunk nearly dropped the cup.

'We could stop all this in an instant, cure the disease in even the worst of the cultists, and make everyone sing camp songs together all night long – if we wanted to. But we'd have to drink our own blood from that cup you're carrying.'

Dunk's jaw dropped. 'You're too much of a coward to face death to save thousands of people?'

'More like we don't give enough of a damn about them. If it comes down to us or them, well, it looks like it's us.'

Dunk goggled at the wizard. 'When we found you, you were ready to kill yourself as soon as you could.'

'Aye, we were. Ironic, isn't it? We suppose it's one thing to talk tough about it when it seems it could never happen.'

Olsen's wand appeared in his hand. 'And don't you go getting any bright ideas about making us change our mind. You're a good lad, Dunk, and we'd hate to see you get incinerated.'

Dunk held the cup between him and the wizard. 'You wouldn't dare. You might destroy the cup.'

Olsen snorted at this. 'That wee cup is far tougher than you give it credit for. You can bust off the base like you've already done, and still it works. You can try to break the bowl, but it can't be done, not by man nor god.'

The wizard nodded proudly at the aghast Dunk. 'When we work magic, lad, it's built to last.'

Dunk glared at the wizard. He only saw one option left, but he couldn't imagine how he might pull it off, and with each tick of the clock more and more people died – including, maybe, Dirk, Lästiges, M'Grash, Edgar, Guillermo, and even Spinne.

Then Slick hurled himself at the wizard. 'Get him, son!' the halfling said as he wrapped his arms around Olsen's leg. 'We'll force him to drink his own blood!'

The wizard swung his fist down and smacked Slick in the nose. The halfling spun backward and landed in a corner of the dugout. When he looked back, Dunk saw blood dripping from his face.

Dunk stepped toward Olsen, bringing up the cup to brain the wizard, but Olsen raised his wand and pointed it straight at him. 'Ah-ah-ah, lad. Don't think you can catch me out so–'

A helmet smashed into the side of Olsen's head, one of the spikes on the crest catching him in the temple. He slid to the floor, dead before his skull cracked against it. Cavre stood over him, the helmet's faceguard still in his hand.

'Sadly, that will not be permanent,' the catcher said, examining his handiwork. 'Unless we manage to destroy the cup before he rises again.'

'Oh, the humanity!' Jim's voice rang out.

'Don't forget the dwarves, elves, orcs, ogres, goblins, skaven – oh, hell with it! It's a bloodbath out there!' Bob said in a voice raw with emotion. Then, quieter: 'Makes me miss the old days that much more.'

'So how can we destroy it?' Dunk said. 'Any ideas?'

Slick shrugged. Cavre grimaced. Pegleg whistled innocently.

'What, coach?' Dunk said suspiciously. 'What is it?'

'Well,' Pegleg said, wincing, 'I hate to even mention it, but Olsen did suggest that, if someone whose soul was attached to the cup drank his own blood from it, well, that would destroy the cup.'

'I think we're clear on that, Pegleg,' Slick said.

'By 'someone,' I think he may have meant 'anyone,'' Pegleg said. 'Including me.'

Dunk's eyes flew wide. 'You can do that? Stop all this? What's the hold up?'

Cavre spoke low and serious. 'But, captain, won't that kill you?'

'I don't believe so,' Pegleg said, shaking his head. 'I won't live forever anymore, I suppose, but I'm not yet on borrowed time like Mr. Merlin here. He may crumble to dust, but I think I'd be just fine.'

Dunk stared at the ex-pirate. 'So what's stopping you?'

Pegleg sucked at his teeth before he spoke. 'The answer to your dreams doesn't come along every day, does it? Immortality *and* an unbeatable team? That's a dynasty built on a winning streak that could last forever.'

Cavre put a hand on Pegleg's shoulder. 'Captain,' he said, 'where's the challenge in all that?'

Pegleg bowed his head for a moment, then doffed his yellow tricorn and came back up with a rueful smile. 'Mr. Cavre, I can always count on you to set my sails in the right direction.'

With that, Pegleg drew the cutlass he always kept at his side. At a nod of his head, Carve pulled back the man's sleeve on his maimed arm, exposing the skin beneath. In a swift, sharp move, Pegleg drew the blade across his arm, and then held it over the bowl of the cup, which Dunk held under his wound.

The coach's blood dripped from his arm and pooled in the bottom of the cup. When it seemed like there was enough, Cavre used some gauze from the kit of the missing apothecary to bind the cut and stop the bleeding. Meanwhile, Dunk raised up the cup and helped Pegleg bring it to his lips.

'Prepare yourself, my friends,' the coach said. 'This could be one hell of a squall.'

Dunk tipped the cup up, and Pegleg drank deep from it, swallowing every last drop.

Dunk lowered the cup, and the ex-pirate licked the blood from his lips. For a moment, nothing happened. Then Pegleg opened his mouth and belched.

'I beg your pardon,' the coach started to say, but before the word 'beg' had left his tongue, the cup began to glow.

Pegleg stared at it and said, 'I think, Dunk, you might want to get rid of that as quickly as possible.'

Dunk leapt up the dugout's steps and looked for some place to put the cup where it had the least chance of hurting someone. Since the centre of the field was empty, he hurled it there. It bounced once on the midfield line, then rolled a short way before coming to a rest. With each passing second, it glowed brighter and brighter, until it became difficult to look at directly.

'Well, that's one way to get rid of a cursed trophy,' Bob said. 'In most parts of the stadium, leaving something like that on the ground wouldn't last–'

The cup exploded, and the noise drowned out everything else in the stadium. The force of the blast knocked Dunk to the back wall of the dugout, and for a moment everything went black.

When Dunk's vision cleared, he saw that everyone else had been knocked down but was unharmed. He stood up to peer out onto the field and saw a massive crater where the cup had last been. Out in the stands, the fans seemed mostly unhurt, slowly picking themselves up and dusting themselves off.

'Congratulations, Mr. Merlin,' Pegleg said solemnly. Dunk turned to see him poking the tip of his cutlass through the wizard's robes, which lay in a pile of ancient dust. 'You finally got your wish.'

'Nuffle's leathery balls!' Jim said. 'Have you ever seen anything so appalling in your life? Bob? Bob, where are you?'

Dunk poked his head out of the dugout to gaze up at the Jumboball looming over the stadium. The image in it panned over the higher sections of the south side of the stadium.

Only a few people stood there: a handful of Reavers, a few more fans, all of them drenched in blood. Dunk saw Edgar and M'Grash towering over the others. The camera pulled in tight on one particular Reaver who carried someone in his arms: Dirk and Lästiges for sure. But where was Spinne?

Dunk dashed out of the dugout and leapt on top of it so he could get a clear view at the stands above. 'Spinne!' he shouted. 'Spinne!' But he was too far away for anyone in that area to hear.

Then M'Grash turned around, and Dunk spotted Spinne still hanging from his back. His heart jumped back up out of the bottom of his boots and lodged itself in his throat. He vaulted over the restraining wall that kept the fans off the field and charged straight up to her, taking care not to slip in the gore as he went.

'We have some good news, Blood Bowl fans! Our roving reporter not only survived her kidnapping but is in the centre of that amazing mess down there. Lästiges, what can you tell us about what happened up there?'

The image in the Jumboball switched to show Lästiges and Dirk locked in a deep, probing kiss. It took her a moment to realise she was on camra, but when she did she pulled back from Dirk and flashed the viewers a winning grin. 'Hi, Jim!' she said. 'It's good to be back on the air.'

Dirk set Lästiges down gently, and the camra pulled back. 'It seems that the incident here in the stands was started by a cult of Nurgle related to the one in Albion's Sure Wood, to provide a distraction so that their agents on the Hackers could steal the legendary Far Albion Cup. Little did we know how tightly their fate was tied to that of the trophy itself. When the cup exploded, so did every one of the cultists infected with the dread disease they passed among themselves. Sadly, they managed to infect a number of the fans during the game, too, along with a few of the Reavers who gallantly came to my rescue. Those brave souls were lost as well.'

'Thanks for that update, Lästiges. Um, you haven't seen Bob anywhere down there, have you?'

The camra panned to the right and focused on a vampire with thick sunglasses and slicked-back hair, dressed in a Wolf Sports jacket. He knelt in the bleachers, scooping the blood from the benches and into his mouth in wild handfuls. When he noticed the camra was on him, he turned toward it and smiled, showing his vicious fangs, and said, 'It just doesn't get any better than this!'

When Dunk reached Spinne, she slid down from M'Grash's back and landed in his arms. He started to say something to her – he wasn't sure what – but she kissed him long and hard instead. He responded in kind, and it was a long time before anyone dared to interrupt.

'It's like kissing your sister,' Slick said.

Dunk chuckled loud and long as he sat at the same, familiar table in the Skinned Cat again. It had been a long time since he'd felt free enough to enjoy a laugh like that. He put his arm around Spinne, who giggled too, and leaned over to the halfling and said, 'Like kissing *your* sister, maybe.'

'You leave Loretta out of this,' Slick said. 'You know what I'm saying. A draw! A tie! In the blasted Blood Bowl finals!'

'Well, we only had five players left,' said Dunk. 'And so did the Reavers.'

'So? You keep playing. Neither of those numbers are zero.'

'And there was that huge crater in the middle of the field.'

'That just makes the game more interesting.'

'And all those dead people in the stands.' Dunk peered into his friend's eyes, looking for a hint of compassion. He knew it was there, just as he also knew that Slick didn't want to show it.

'Professionals never let what happens in the stands–' The halfling scowled. 'Ah, forget it. It's over and done with, I suppose.'

'We'll get you next year,' Dirk said around Lästiges, who sat curled up in his lap. 'You were just lucky this time.'

'Lucky?' Dunk gaped. 'You call ending up in possession of a cursed trophy that nearly gets you killed time and time again "lucky"?'

'It got you into the championship game, didn't it?' Lästiges said with a grin.

Dunk sighed. 'Hey,' he said to Dirk, 'you never told me what happened with Lehrer.'

'Got away,' Dirk said around a sip of his beer. 'He's like a ghost when it comes to hiding in this city.'

'Think he's serious about the Guterfiends putting a price on my head now?'

'Do you really have to ask?'

Dunk rolled his eyes.

'Well,' Slick said, 'it's a good thing we're headed back to Bad Bay tomorrow then. We're ten players short of a full squad again, and the *Spike! Magazine* tournament is coming up just around the corner.'

'Ten?' Dunk said. 'There's only M'Grash, Carve, Guillermo, Edgar, and me left. That's five. We need eleven?'

Slick arched his eyebrows at Dunk and then at Spinne. 'You haven't told him yet?'

Dunk's heart stopped. 'Told me what?'

'Meet my newest client,' the halfling said. 'I just got her a new contract with–'

'I'm playing with the Hackers!' Spinne said, her eyes sparkling.

Dunk's jaw fell open, and he stared at Spinne as if she'd just sprouted horns from her head.

'What?' she said. 'You're not happy?'

'No,' Dunk said, shaking his head. 'To say it like Edgar would, I'm bloody ecstatic!' He leapt to his feet and dipped Spinne back in his arms for a long, lingering kiss.

All of the pain and horrors of the year melted away from Dunk in that moment. Thoughts of Deckem and his deadmen, of diseased cultists, of vampire orcs out for revenge, and even of the Guterfiends and their unknown plots all faded from his mind. As his lips parted from Spinne's, he looked deep into her eyes and said, 'This is going to be the best year ever.'

DEATH MATCH

DEATH MATCH

THE LAST THING Dunk Hoffnung remembered was the ogre trying to knock his helmet off his head with a bench torn from the first rows of the end zone. Dunk had just scored a touchdown for his team, the Bad Bay Hackers, and the crowd had gone wild. From hard-won experience, Dunk had avoided letting those battle-crazed, blood-thirsty bastards pull him into the stands. He knew that even fans who liked you often got carried away once they got their hands on you.

That's probably why he hadn't seen the ogre coming up behind him. He couldn't remember which one it was anymore. All of the Oldheim Ogres looked the same under their cauldron-sized helmets and with their tent-sized jerseys draped over their massive plates of spiked and sharp-edged armour: like gigantic servants of death with mean hangovers.

The ogre had picked Dunk up with one hand and held him dangling in the air by his ankles, like a bad daemon baby in need of a fatal spanking. Then the creature reached into the stands with its other hand and pried the bench off one of the bleachers there, sending the fans who had been sitting on it scrambling for their lives.

Dunk remembered one snotling still clutching one splintered end of the bench as the ogre hoisted it into the air as a makeshift club. The hapless thing had got its Hackers fan jersey snagged on the splinters.

It started to try to gnaw through the fabric with its wide, flat teeth, but there hadn't been enough time.

Dunk had heard the green-skinned midget squeal in horror as the bench came swinging down at him, but he couldn't muster any pity for the thing. He was too busy trying to angle himself out of the way of the ogre's mighty swing.

As the blue painted plank came at him, Dunk reached for his toes, which hung high above him, still in the ogre's grasp. The weight of his own armour made this nearly impossible, but the terror-fuelled adrenalin coursing through him inspired the heroic effort.

The board went sailing underneath him, right through the space where his head had once been.

'Jim, I haven't seen a swing that feeble since you tried to dismember that dwarf for dinner last night!' Bob Bifford's voice rang out over the Preternatural Address system, echoing across the stadium and throughout the nearby streets of Magritta.

'I still enjoy a bit of sport with my meals,' Jim Johnson grumbled. The retired ogre player's massive, battle-scarred mug flashed across the gigantic crystal ball perched at the far end of the stadium. Then it cut straight back to Dunk, squirming in the Oldheim blitzer's grasp.

'It seems Gr'Nash down there shares your passion for a good fight,' said Bob, 'and your skill!'

The crowd erupted in laughter, and the sound drove Gr'Nash even madder than before. The ogre swung at Dunk again, but the Hackers' star thrower managed to angle himself out of the way once more.

Dunk wondered where the rest of his team could be. They wouldn't just leave him up here forever, would they? M'Grash K'Thragsh – the Hackers' own ogre – was Dunk's best friend. Spinne Schönheit shared his bed. Edgar – the treeman they'd picked up in Albion last season – was as solid as his trunk. And Dunk had played alongside Cavre and Reyes for two years now.

Of course, the other players had only been on the team since the start of the tournament. Few of them had set boots on a Blood Bowl field before, and none of them had ever faced down an opposing team of eleven angry ogres.

Dunk barely knew these new players at all. If it weren't for the fact that their names were stencilled across the backs of their green and gold armour, he didn't think he'd have been able to pick them out from each other in the game. Still, they were on his team, and he expected them to come to his aid.

A glance at the Jumboball – which piped the Cabalvision broadcast to the fans in the stadium via the most advanced mass communications magic of the day – showed Dunk that the other Oldheim Ogres had formed a wall of armour-plated flesh between Dunk and his team-mates. He knew that the wall couldn't stand forever. Sooner or later his friends would get around it. M'Grash would just plough right through it. But it would take time, something he didn't have.

Gr'Nash raised the busted bench up for another swing, and the snotling on the end broke free and went sailing off into the stands. The fans there batted the poor creature into the air again, bopping it back and forth like a beach ball, the pathetic beast squeaking like a living chew toy with every blow.

'It's always great to see the fans working together to entertain themselves,' Bob said. 'That just might be our Bloodweiser Beer play of the day.'

'I don't know about that, but keep your attention on that end zone,' Jim said. 'It looks like Hoffnung has a great, early shot at being named the game's Most Violated Player.'

Seemingly to prove the point, Gr'Nash lowered his arm and slammed Dunk headfirst into the Astrogranite below. Stars flashed before Dunk's eyes, and his head felt like the muscles in his neck had turned to rubber.

'I thought the MVP went to the 'Most Violent Player,' sad Bob.

'It's a double-edged acronym,' said Jim, 'and here's Gr'Nash to stake his claim for the other side of the award.'

Stunned, his arms flailing about, Dunk swung his head around to his left. He saw a flash of blue and smelled fresh-cut lumber. Then everything went black.

THE NEXT THING Dunk knew, he was lying flat on his back. This didn't seem so unusual, what with the savage blow to the head he'd just taken, but he couldn't see or hear a thing. He started to panic, then realised his eyes were closed, which at least explained why he was blind.

His eyes felt like they might have been glued shut, but he finally managed to peel them open. He instantly regretted it.

He stared up at the ceiling above him, the light of a number of lanterns flickering across its rough-finished surface. He recognised it as belonging to one of the team locker rooms in Magritta's Killer Stadium, for which the legendary brewing company had bought the naming rights. The holes in the plaster from when M'Grash had leapt with joy after their last victory told him that this was the locker room in which the Hackers had started the day.

'How's your head?' The voice sounded like it had been forced through the chewed end of a halfling's pipe: smoky and distant.

Now that the speaker mentioned it, Dunk realised that his head felt like his brains were beating away at the inside of his skull with spiked warhammers. 'Not good,' he rasped through a mouth coated with an all-too-familiar flavour: dried blood.

The speaker leaned over into Dunk's field of vision. He was an old elf with a bloodstained patch of white fabric slung over his right eye, his lips curled in a disgusted sneer. 'You'll live,' the elf said as he shook his head, his voice dripping with disdain. 'I've seen little halfling girls take punches better than you.'

'There was a board and an ogre involved,' Dunk said. He started to get angry, but the rush of blood to his head made his brain switch over to using steam-powered jackhammers. To placate them, he let out a deep sigh instead of the string of curses he'd been preparing.

Then the elf slapped him in the jaw, and the stars started swirling around his vision again. 'Sit up,' the elf said.

'Take it easy on him,' another voice said, one that Dunk knew as well as any. It belonged to his agent, a tubby halfling by the name of Slick Fullbelly.

'Don't worry,' the elf said as Dunk used his wobbly arms to shove himself halfway up into a sitting position. 'I won't punch your meal ticket here.' The elf fitted a bulging monocle over his good eye and squinted through it at Dunk. 'Looks like the ogres nearly took care of that for you already. If they'd succeeded, maybe a scumbag like you would finally have to go and find some honest work.'

'Like gathering illegal substances to concoct potions designed to get players back on the field?' Slick asked. Dunk saw him flittering around the elf's feet, trying to get the apothecary's attention, but the elf ignored him as if he were nothing more than a fly hunting for carrion. 'Do the Game Wizards know about the little operation you have here, Dr. Pill? Maybe Wolf Sports would be interested in running an exposé.'

The elf removed his monocle and started to rummage through a wooden rack filled with iron flasks. Some of these looked fresh while others rested under thick layers of dust. The elf scratched his chin, and then selected a flask, possibly at random. He turned towards Slick and blew the dust off the bottle and into the agent's face.

As Slick tried to hack the dust from his lungs and rub it from his eyes, the elf pulled a rusty scalpel from a sheath on his belt and worked it around the red wax seal covering the flask's cork. 'Who do you think supplies me with those truly hard-to-find ingredients?' the elf asked, ignoring Slick once more. 'Do you think ratings go up or down when an injured player manages to hobble back onto the field for a few more plays?'

Dr. Pill stabbed his scalpel into the top of the broken seal and used it to pry the flask's cork free. It came loose with an explosive pop that sent it and the scalpel flying into the ceiling, where they embedded themselves next to one of the holes M'Grash had made.

A green and slimy substance bubbled forth from the flask's open top, spilling down over Dr. Pill's hand, which Dunk now saw was covered with a rubber glove. Where the stuff plopped on the floor, it hissed and sizzled like water on a hot, greased griddle.

'Drink this,' the elf said, shoving the potion at Dunk. The flask smacked him in the face and knocked him back to the table again.

Dunk growled and sat right back up again. The elf grimaced at him, shamefaced. 'My apologies,' he said, pointing at his eye patch with his free hand as he offered up the bubbling flask again. 'No depth perception.'

Dunk crossed his eyes to stare at the flask of frothing gunk, which hung too close to his face, but at least it hadn't smashed into him this time. He felt the sharp scent of it scorch the hair in his nostrils right off.

'How does he know that's not some kind of poison?' Slick squeaked out between coughs.

'Oh, it's a poison, all right,' Dr. Pill said, staring at Dunk with his one good eye, 'arsenic, to be precise. Smell the bitter almonds in it? That's always a dead giveaway.'

'What?'

'But it has an antidote mixed into it, along with some other things, the so-called 'secret ingredients.' This volatile combination can strip the paint off your armour, but it'll put your head right too. Otherwise, it's weeks in the sickhouse. You'll miss not only this game but the rest of the tournament too.'

From somewhere above, Dunk heard a low, muffled roar. The plaster shook loose from the ceiling, and the cork and scalpel came tumbling down, barely missing Slick's feet as they stabbed juddering into the floor. The agent leapt back in dismay.

Dunk reached out with an unsteady hand and snatched the potion from the leering elf's hands. Before his other arm could give out and send him collapsing back on the table, he tipped the flask back, opened up his throat, and swallowed its noxious contents in one determined gulp.

Slick looked up at Dunk as if the thrower had promised him another beer, and Dr. Pill glared at him, his good eye seeming as dead as the other. Dunk felt the potion swirl its way down into his belly where it began its work. Warmth spread out from his stomach to his head, fingers, and toes until he felt like he wanted to jump into a sauna to cool off. Sweat poured off his skin, streaming down from his hairline and into his eyes. His eyeballs started to burn from the inside, and his teeth felt like glowing coals in his mouth.

'Water,' Dunk rasped. 'Please.'

'Here,' Dr. Pill said. He handed Dunk a wide funnel attached to a long, rubber hose that wound its way under the table on which the rack of flasks rested.

Dunk squinted into the funnel, unsure what to do with it. Would it fill with water for him to drink? Should he hold it over his head and let a cascade of water shower him? He needed something to drink so badly that he thought of sticking his face into the funnel and sucking on it until the water came out.

Then his stomach turned on him hard, flipping and flopping like a fish on a dry dock, gasping for water, drowning in air. Dunk's eyes flew open, as wide as the zeroes on a scoreboard.

'What's happening?' Slick asked. 'Son, are you all right?' The halfling turned on the elf, 'I swear to every bastard god that ever sinned I'll turn you over to our own team's ogre if he dies. Dunk's like a brother to M'Grash. He'll take it hard – and he'll take it out on–'

Dunk interrupted Slick's tirade of threats by unleashing the contents of his stomach into the funnel. It started with a savage roar, travelled through the gush of a flooding river, and trickled off into a sickly whimper punctuated with a hack and a spit.

'Nuffle's leathery balls!' Slick said as he rushed to Dunk's side. 'What have you done to him? Son? Son!'

Dunk wiped his mouth on the back of his sleeve and sat up, ready to be knocked over by the tiny force of the halfling's breath. Instead, as he shook his head, he realised it felt fine. The throbbing that had been there was gone, his brains having dropped their excavating tools and called it a day.

'I'm good,' he said, bounding off the apothecary's table, 'better than ever, maybe. I feel great!'

Slick squinted up at Dunk suspiciously. 'When we brought you in here, son, you were half-dead. I thought we'd have to go with a closed coffin at the funeral. How's this quack manage–'

'It's customary to thank those who save your life,' Dr. Pill said, 'although I'm accustomed to not receiving such pleasantries from primitives.'

Dunk smirked at the apothecary. He wanted to be angry at the man and his sour attitude, but he felt too damn fine to be bothered with such things. 'Thank you,' he said sincerely.

'Just doing my job,' the elf said, the sneer back on his face. 'And at the rates I charge I suspect your employer would prefer it if you ceased joining in this riveting knitting circle here in the locker room with your agent and me and got back out on that pitch to do your job.'

Dunk bounded off the table and cracked his neck back and forth. 'On my way,' he said as he headed for the door.

As he left, he heard Slick ask Dr. Pill a question, trying to curry his favour. As an agent, Slick found it his duty to work every possible angle on Dunk's behalf, and being able to call on someone who could heal an injured player like that might come in handy.

'That's an amazing contraption you have there to catch your patients' illnesses. Does it just vent into the sewers?'

The elf snorted. 'Do I just throw it away? Of course not. Do you have any idea how much those materials cost? I find they can last for three or four applications at least.'

Dunk raced out through the tunnel that led to the Hackers' dugout, certain he didn't want to hear any more.

WHEN DUNK EMERGED into the dugout, he saw Pegleg glaring out at the open field beyond. The former pirate had his good leg planted on the top step and his wooden prosthetic stabbed right into the Astrogranite that edged the dugout. He braced his fleshy hand against the dugout's roof, designed to keep out bad weather and 'gifts' hurled by furious fans. His hook scratched at the wide-brimmed, yellow tricorn hat that already bore a score of holes from such abuse.

'Reporting for duty, coach!' Dunk said as he strode past the benchwarmers that lined the back of the dugout, supposedly the safest place in the entire stadium. A couple of them glared at Dunk with jealous eyes, but the others trembled as he walked by, fearful not of him, but of anyone who made sudden movements.

'Thank Nuffle you're here, Hoffnung,' Pegleg said. 'Dr. Pill's magic never fails.'

Dunk rubbed his head again, amazed that it didn't still feel like an axe through the kindling of his skull. 'It was worth whatever you paid him.'

Pegleg spat on the field. 'I'm glad you feel that way. I'm deducting his fee from your pay.'

'What?' Dunk goggled at the captain. The man hadn't fallen too far from his piratical roots, it seemed.

'It's the least you can do,' Pegleg said. 'In the grand scheme of things, I'll end up paying more for it than you.'

'How's that?' Dunk asked. As he spoke, he watched the ball sail downfield with something that looked like a long branch jammed atop one of the spikes.

Pegleg growled. 'We're going to have to teach that treeman of ours how to hold the damned ball.'

Dunk pointed down to where Spinne had caught the ball and pulled off the branch to use as a club against the pair of ogres trying to capture her. Even encased in her helmet and armour, Dunk could see how beautiful she was. She moved with a dancer's grace, but struck with the trained savagery of a born warrior.

Dunk smiled, glad that the two of them were finally on the same team for once. Dating Spinne, back when she'd been with the Reikland Reavers, had been trouble for them both. The fact that his brother Dirk played for the Reavers too and had once shared Spinne's bed hadn't made it any easier.

'Do you think maybe Edgar planned that?' Dunk asked. 'It looks like it's working.'

'Edgar's brains are composed of wood, Mr. Hoffnung. What do you think?'

Somewhere on the field, a whistle blew. A russet-coated minotaur dressed in a black and white striped shirt charged out on to the field and scooped up a yellow penalty flag.

'Ooh!' Bob's voice said over the PA. 'That's going to be "illegal use of a weapon on the field" against Schönheit. Bool's going to kick her out of the game for that!'

'Amazing!' Jim said. 'You hardly ever see that kind of solid, fair officiating in a game of Blood Bowl, and clearly the fans don't like it.'

A rousing howl went up from the stands, punctuated with hisses and boos.

'If anyone can take that kind of abuse, though, it's a player like Rhett Bool. It's too bad he chose to play for Nurgle's Nits during this tournament.'

'Too true, Bob! I think Nits' management must have blown its whole stake on his salary, considering the rest of the team was made of up Chaos-tainted halflings. Where do they find these players?'

'I don't know, Jim, but they're going to have to keep looking if they want to try it again. They may have won their first game against the Darkside Cowboys, but Bool was the only player to survive!'

'It didn't help that he trampled half of his own team's starting line on that first-half kick-off runback!'

Dunk scowled. 'I though you paid off the referee,' he said to Pegleg. Dunk didn't like the idea of distracting the ref's eyes with a stack of shiny gold coins, but he knew it was an established and respected part of the game.

'Oldheim paid him more – and he kept our own booty too!' The ex-pirate turned on Dunk. 'Get out there if you like and tell him how wrong he is to do that.'

Dunk stared up at the minotaur as he charged into the stands and gored an unfortunate section of fans that had come to cheer on the red-uniformed Ogres. He swallowed hard.

'Would you give him his money back for Dr. Pill's treatment?' Slick asked as he emerged from the tunnel in the back of the dugout.

Pegleg shook his head, 'Only if he could get me out of my part of the bargain with that blackguard as well.'

'What did you promise him, coach?' Dunk asked.

Pegleg spat on the ground. 'A guest appearance on his bloody Cabalvision show.'

'The one where he heals people in front of a live audience?' Slick asked. 'I thought that was fictitious.'

Dunk gazed up at Pegleg. 'Hand or foot?' he asked.

'Neither!' The coach snarled, stabbing his hook at Dunk.

A roar erupting from the crowd told Dunk something was up. 'What happened?' he asked, unable to hear the announcers over the hullabaloo.

'The Ogres scored,' Slick shouted. He could project his voice well from his tiny frame. 'That evens up the score at two touchdowns apiece.'

Dunk frowned. 'They didn't stop the game for the penalty.'

'You've been playing this game for two years now,' Pegleg said. 'Haven't you ever seen a bloody penalty called?'

'Sure,' Dunk said. 'There was that game against the Chaos All-Stars last year. They called penalties against both me and M'Grash, but then that Jumboball came crashing down.'

'Yes,' Slick nodded, 'and you were called for excessive celebration after your first touchdown.'

'But I was unconscious for that.'

'Ah, yes,' Slick said, stroking his chin. 'Well what about when you got booted from the game for killing Schlitz 'Malty' Likker?'

'That was during halftime, and Zauberer had ensorcelled him to be possessed by the spirit of Khorne. It wasn't in the middle of the game.'

'Actually, since it was halftime, it was exactly the middle of the game.'

'You know what I mean. The game wasn't going on at the time.'

'Well, the game's stopped now, Mr. Hoffnung,' Pegleg said in a voice laced with menace. 'If you'd care to join it instead of taking this sweet jaunt down memory lane, I'd surely appreciate it.'

Dunk blushed with embarrassment, 'Sure thing, coach. Whatever you say.'

Pegleg flashed a gold-toothed grin at the thrower. 'Good lad. Now get out there to take Spinne's place, and try not to get yourself spanked like a wee child this time!'

Dunk nodded, then grabbed his spare helmet from the rack in the back of the dugout and trotted out onto the field. As he reached the sideline, he met Spinne coming off. She stopped for a moment and butted her helmeted head against his. Grinning at him through their faceguards, she blew him a kiss and said, 'Make them pay.'

Dunk grinned when she turned to smack him on his butt, and he hustled out onto the field. The crowd roared as he raced to the end the Hackers were protecting. He raised his hand to acknowledge them, and the noise grew so loud he could barely hear.

When Dunk had first decided to become a Blood Bowl player, the adulation of the fans was the last thing on his mind. As a washed-up dragonslayer – more of a never-was than a has-been – he'd just wanted to put his past behind him and try something new, something entirely different. Taking up a career on the gridiron seemed like just the thing.

He'd resisted the notion at first. After all, his family had disowned his brother Dirk when he'd gone off to join the Reavers. In response, Dirk had even changed his last name from Hoffnung to Heldmann.

Of course, the disgrace and dissolution of the Hoffnung family had been what had spurred Dunk to take up dragonslaying in the first place. He still felt responsible for what had happened in those dark days, even though he'd done his best to put them behind him. Living as a Blood Bowl star player made forgetting his old life a whole lot easier.

'Dunkel!' M'Grash shouted, bounding towards the thrower in joy. 'Dunkel okay!'

Dunk had long since learned not to deny the Hackers' ogre his happy moments. He let the huge lug haul him up in his arms and give him a hug that could have crushed a bear. Once Dunk was back on his feet, he felt thankful he'd been wearing his armour. The ogre had cracked his ribs more than once in the past.

Edgar came up and ran a branch along the back of Dunk's helmet too. 'You're a bloody hard nut to crack,' the treeman said with a gentle rap.

'Good to have you back!' Guillermo Reyes called from his position towards the front of their formation. The Estalian lineman's accent always seemed thicker here in his homeland, and he played harder too. Because of how he'd left Altdorf, the capital of the Empire and his home since birth, Dunk envied Guillermo his hometown hero status, which he never imagined he could enjoy.

Then Rhett Cavre, the legendary blitzer and the Hackers' team captain, trotted up. 'Are you all right, Dunk?' he asked. Despite the chaos surrounding them, the man's demeanour was as soft and solid as ever. True concern for Dunk as a friend, not just a player, showed in his wide, dark eyes. Cavre saw the players on his team as people, not just bodies to fill positions, and for that he'd earned the respect of each and every one of his team-mates.

'Dr. Pill fixed me right up,' Dunk said, nodding.

Cavre winced. 'Did he use one of the dusty bottles or one of the clean ones?'

'Dusty. Why?'

Cavre smiled, his brilliant white teeth shining like a crescent moon against his ebony skin. 'Those haven't been 'recycled' as often.'

Dunk felt his stomach turn again, empty as it was. 'Think we'll have any more trouble with the ref?' he asked, eager to change the subject.

Carve laughed warmly. 'Not after what she threatened to do to him after the game if he made any more calls like that.'

Dunk glanced down the field at the minotaur in the striped shirt. He noticed that Bool moved with a bit of a limp as he trotted the spiked ball out for the Ogres to kick it off.

'She mentioned something about having him for a steak dinner,' Carve said. Then he knocked Dunk on his pauldron. 'Get into position before that ball comes our way.'

Dunk turned and sprinted off to the end of the field, right in front of the end zone, and then turned around to face the Ogres. Their kicker had booted the ball right into the stands twice so far this game, but if it came down anywhere near Dunk, it was his job to catch it. Then, as the team's thrower, he had to hurl it downfield to anyone he could find open.

This sort of play could be risky. If the Ogres intercepted the ball, they could be in the end zone in a matter of seconds. However, it was the best way to move the ball down the field. Trying to run it past the Ogres was almost impossible. With arms as long as Dunk was tall, the creatures just grabbed any of the Hackers that tried to dash past them.

The crowd hushed for a moment, and then started out with a low, collective moan that rose to a roar as the Ogre kicker approached the ball. When he booted it down the field, the fans burst into bloodthirsty screams, sure their desires would soon be sated.

The ball arced high into the air, and for a moment Dunk thought it might go right over his hands and into the stands – maybe even over the top of the stadium and into the streets beyond. Then a freak wind sprang up and blew the ball back towards the field.

As Dunk tracked the ball's progress, he noticed that dark clouds had raced in to block out the sun in the last few minutes. It seemed strange, but he couldn't worry about that at the moment. If he didn't catch the ball and get rid of it as fast as he could, he risked far worse than a few drops of rain on his helmet.

The weather didn't matter anyway. Blood Bowl games never stopped or even paused on account of rain, sleet, snow, frogs, beetles, locusts, ashes, or even fresh flows of volcanic magma. Any team that left the field before a game was over automatically forfeited the match, and with the amount of money on the line, few teams valued their health more than their share of the gold.

The ball sailed right down towards Dunk. He took two steps up, spread his arms and hands into a basket and caught the ball against his chest, just like in practice. He'd learned the hard way not to catch a ball with any unarmoured parts of his body, and he'd had his breastplate reinforced just so he could receive kick-offs like this.

'Hoffnung has the ball, and he's off! He races towards the side-line, trying to find some blockers and hunting for a receiver downfield.' Dunk tried to tune out the PA system when playing, but Bob and Jim's voices were so amplified that it usually proved impossible.

Dunk saw a wall of angry Oldheim Ogres coming his way and knew that he had to get rid of the ball fast if he didn't want to end up right back on Dr. Pill's table. He wasn't sure what would be worse: being left to mend on his own if Pegleg wouldn't pay the fee this time, or having to 'recycle' the potion he'd just used.

He jinked to the left, and then sprinted to the right, angling forward and towards the sideline as he ran. The Hackers linemen forged a wall of their own in front of him, backed by M'Grash and Edgar. Just as the two lines were about to clash, the linemen scattered to the left and right, leaving only the two tallest Hackers standing between Dunk and the onrushing Ogres.

Some of the Ogres chased after the Hackers linemen. The brain of an ogre is smaller than that of a human, but has to motivate far more flesh. This doesn't leave the ogre a great deal of leftover grey matter with which to do things like make simple decisions, taste its food, or develop emotionally beyond the level of a five-year-old human child. When an ogre starts chasing something, it usually keeps after it – unless something else distracts it. Then it chases that instead – until the whistle blows, and sometimes it ignores that too, a lesson Dunk had just learned in the hardest way possible, barring a messy death and sudden resurrection.

Many of the Ogres followed the linemen as they scrambled out of the way, but most of them were running so fast that they couldn't eas-ily change their momentum. Some of them tried and tripped over their own feet, creating obstacles for those behind them to stumble over too. The resultant crash shook the Astrogranite enough that Dunk almost fell as well.

A few of the Ogres ignored the linemen, concentrating on Dunk instead, or perhaps on Dunk and Edgar. The Hacker ogre and treeman charged straight at the four Ogres who hadn't been fooled by the ploy and lowered their armoured shoulders.

Edgar managed to knock one of the Ogres to a standstill. M'Grash – who was large, even for an ogre – managed to shove two of the Old-heim players back on their rumps, but the last Ogre made it through unscathed, and thundered straight at Dunk.

Dunk peered around the oncoming Ogre and spotted Cavre down-field. When the Ogres had charged after the ball, he'd slid through their line and dashed most of the way down the field. Now he leaped up and down, waving his arms, signalling that he might never be more open for a pass for the remainder of his career.

Dunk cocked back his arm to let the ball fly, but even as he did he realised he'd misjudged the last Ogre's determination. The towering creature seemed to have put on a burst of speed once he got past Edgar and M'Grash. Now, with the Ogre's arms raised high and wide over his head, Dunk didn't see how he could get a clear throw off at Cavre.

On the other hand, if he held onto it, he knew the Ogre racing at him would grind him into dust. He pumped the ball once in an effort to fake out the Ogre, and it worked. The Oldheimer left his feet to try to block the pass.

Still, the Ogre was so large, its reach so wide, that Dunk didn't see any daylight around him. Instead of trying to slip between the Ogre's arms, he took one step back, and hurled the ball downfield towards Cavre.

Dunk looked up and saw the Ogre's long arms coming down over him like a tidal wave, and the ball heading right for the creature's out-stretched fingers. Not only was he going to get crushed beneath this beast's mighty bulk, his pass would be intercepted too. Considering he'd already woken up from a head injury in the locker room once that day, he didn't see how this game could get any worse.

Then the world disappeared in a flash of blinding light, followed almost instantly by a boom so loud that Dunk thought he might never want to hear anything ever again.

UNABLE TO SEE past the afterimage still flashing before his eyes, Dunk stumbled and fell flat on his back. As he did, something that felt like a sack of hot sand hit him and then broke apart. Cloying clouds of some dry substance stuck to his sweaty skin and caught in his nose, throat, and lungs. He spun over onto his hand and knees and tried to hack it out of his chest until it all finally came free.

By the time the thunderous clap finally stopped echoing in Dunk's ears, he could wipe the gunk off his face and out of his eyes to try to see just what had happened. He stared up at the Jumboball towering over the end zone behind him, and his jaw dropped.

'Let's see that one more time, Jim!'

The image on the screen showed the Ogre racing towards Dunk, captured in a slow-motion replay. Just as the creature was about to land on Dunk, the image froze.

'Right there, Bob. Do you see it?'

'See it,' Bob said. 'If I wasn't wearing my Sun Protection Fetish, I think it might have fried my grave-delicate skin from here. As a vampire, I owe my life to my Coppertomb SPF 1,000.'

'The bolt of lightning, Bob. It's right there. Advance that forward just a hair.'

The image on the Jumboball moved almost imperceptibly, and Dunk saw the flash that had only been a tiny spot before stretch into

533

an explosion of light that crossed the massive crystal, stabbing straight through the Ogre as it went.

'See, there's the bolt. Now just a little bit more.'

The image changed again. The bolt was gone, and the Ogre had disappeared too. An Ogre-shaped pile of ash hung in mid-air in its place.

The image moved forward once more, and the pile of ash fell to the Astrogranite. Some of it had already started to blow away as it dropped, but the bulk of it crashed down to the earth.

As he watched this, Dunk realised he had flash-fried ogre all over him. He stood up and screamed.

Then M'Grash dumped an entire keg of Killer Genuine Draft beer on top of him. The force of the falling liquid knocked him to his knees and left him gasping for air. On the other hand, it did exactly what it was supposed to do. It rinsed the remnants of the ogre from his hair, armour, and skin. The hop-scented residue it left behind made Dunk think more than anything that he needed to get himself something pure and clean to drink to wash the taste of ogre ashes out of his mouth.

'I've never seen anything like this,' Jim said over the PA. 'I mean, death, maiming, even dismemberment, but for the game to stop for it is truly strange.'

'Well it's hard to play when you're missing the ball,' Bob said. 'Most times if the ball gets blown up or just flattened the players can at least scoop up the pieces and play with those until the next break in the action. When it just disappears like that, it's hard to see what you might do with it.'

'Gr'Nash, the Ogres' team captain sure showed some initiative, scooping up a handful of those ashes and running them into the end zone.'

'True, although I think Bool made the right call by nullifying the touchdown. After all, it's impossible to tell if any of those ashes came from the ball instead of poor Ch'Brakk.'

'You gotta admire a competitor like that. Even the death of his cousin isn't enough to slow him down for a second.'

'Well, with the clock winding down here, Bob, it looks like this game might end up in a tie.'

'I hate ties. They're like kissing your sister.'

'I told you to stop dating her.'

'Hey, I said I hate kissing her, but she seems to love it. I can't get her to respect the restraining order!'

'Hold it, Jim. Our roving reporter on the field, the lovely Lästiges Weibchen, would like to check in.'

The image on the screen shifted to a beautiful woman with long, auburn hair and black eyes, who smiled out at the viewer like she had always been your best friend. She stood down on the sidelines, somewhere near the ogre's dugout from the look of it. As she spoke, she glanced up behind her from time to time.

'Thanks, Bob! Eyewitnesses here on the field and in the stands claim that this mysterious thunderbolt did not come from the sky, but from right here in the stadium.'

M'Grash helped Dunk to his feet, and then picked him up and shook him like a wet dog, flinging beer and beer-soaked ash everywhere. Just when Dunk had started to wonder if M'Grash might accidentally kill him, the shaking stopped, and Dunk could watch the Jumboball again.

'There he is, Bob!' Lästiges said, her voice ringing out over the PA system, even though the image on the Jumboball was that of a gaunt, middle-aged man in midnight-blue robes. As the camra zoomed in on the man – picking out his wispy white beard, his silver skullcap, and his watery, green eyes – Dunk recognised him instantly.

Lästiges gasped and said 'It's Schlechter Zauberer!'

The crowd echoed the reporter's sharp intake of breath.

'Blood Bowl fans may remember Zauberer's involvement in the death almost two years ago of the mutant minotaur captain of the Chaos All-Stars, Schlitz 'Malty' Likker. Rumour also has it that he was the motivating force behind the tragic Jumboball accident here in Magritta last year that ended in the messy and permanent death of Krader, the troll player who had showed so much promise up until that point. To make matters worse, Zauberer was on the All-Stars' payroll at the time, ostensibly hired to help them, not murder their star players.'

As Dunk watched, Zauberer – who had been standing among a group of passed-out drunks in the nosebleed section of the bleachers, right under the announcers' box – lifted his arms over his head and took off into the air. Dunk wondered for a moment if the fans the wizard had left behind were really sleeping at all or just not moving under their own power forever. Before he could ponder the issue much longer, an idea struck him, and he turned and sprinted off towards the Hackers' dugout.

'As you might remember, Hoffnung and Zauberer have clashed several times before, both on the field and off. Since the wizard is not listed as an official employee or freebooter for either team, I can only guess that Zauberer has decided to take their rivalry to a new, deadlier level.'

When Dunk was only twenty yards or so from the dugout, another lightning bolt came scorching out of the sky to carve a crater in the ground right behind where Dunk had been, proving Lästiges's words right.

'A ball,' Dunk yelled at his team-mates in the dugout. 'Toss me a ball!'

All of the players in the Hackers' dugout just stared at Dunk in some odd mixture of astonishment and fear. Lined up in their green and gold uniforms, the Hackers' three-sword H logo emblazoned across the sides of the helmets they held on their laps, they seemed like little more than children brought together to play a game. Unfortunately, Blood Bowl was a game of life and death.

Spinne stepped out of the dugout and pitched a ball to Dunk underhand. He caught it neatly in his left hand and swapped it to his right. Then he cocked his head back and searched the sky over the stadium for any sign of the wizard who meant to fry him to ashes in moments.

A third bolt of lightning passed close enough to Dunk to stand his hair on end. The clap of thunder that followed deafened him again, but since it passed behind him he could still see. He spun around, looked directly above him, and spotted Zauberer diving closer, cursing in some language Dunk had never heard, a long, silver wand waving in his hand.

Dunk cocked back his arm and threw the football like a bullet at the wizard. Zauberer tried to dodge the spiked missile, but instead he only managed to put his shoulder forward. This caused the tip of the ball to slam into the wizard's right arm rather than his chest.

Zauberer shrieked like a little girl from the pain. Clutching at the ball still embedded in his flesh, he fluttered towards the ground like a wounded duck, clawing desperately at the air with his fingers, but finding no purchase.

Dunk took one long step to the side, and the wizard crashed to the Astrogranite in front of him with a dull thud. Dunk reached down with one hand and pulled Zauberer to his feet. He needed to know what was going on. He hadn't seen the wizard in over a year, and now he'd tried to kill him for no reason Dunk could discern.

Zauberer's head slumped down between his shoulders, and a thin line of bloody drool trickled out of his mouth. He groaned when Dunk lifted him to his feet, but his feet wouldn't bear his weight, and his eyes only opened long enough to roll back into his head before closing again.

Dunk yanked the ball from the wizard's shoulder, planning to use it to jab him back to consciousness. The open wound bled freely, and what little colour the pasty-faced wizard had drained from him, leaving him whiter than the lines painted on the field.

'Speaking of competitors, Jim, what do you think about Hoffnung there? It seems he's found himself a ball!'

Startled, Dunk peered around the field and saw everyone staring at him. For just a moment, no one in the stadium breathed. Then Gr'Nash, the Oldheim Ogre who'd cracked his skull earlier in the game, threw a long, broken, sausage-sized finger in Dunk's direction – it must have come from one of the other Ogres – and bellowed, 'Kill him!'

Dunk dropped Zauberer and heard the wizard's skullcap crack against the Astrogranite. Then he started to race towards the Hackers' dugout.

'That's a damned shame,' Bob's voice said. 'One little assassination attempt by a wizard tossing lightning bolts around like snotlings in a bar fight, and Hoffnung loses his nerve. He had such potential too.'

'Not to mention the fact that we only have a few seconds left in the game. Looks like you'll be puckering up for my baby sister Bertha tonight!'

'Not today, Jim. Since this game is part of the *Spike!* magazine tournament finals, no ties are allowed. We'll go into sudden-death overtime instead.'

'If those Ogres catch Hoffnung, I think I know whose death we'll see first!'

Dunk ignored the commentators and scanned the Hackers' end zone. He saw Cavre racing towards it now, breaking away from the Ogres eager to carry out Gr'Nash's death sentence.

Dunk brought his arm back one more time and tossed the ball high and long into the air. It arced up and then down like the smooth parabola of a rainbow. At the end stood no pot of gold, just Cavre's outstretched, wide open hands.

Cavre pulled the ball in just as time ran out, but Dunk couldn't tell where the catcher's feet were. Had he scored, or had they been too late?

Bool blew the whistle, but Dunk couldn't tell if it was to signal a touchdown or the end of the game – maybe both?

'Touchdown! The Hackers win the game!'

Dunk started to throw his arms up in the air to cheer, but he saw the Oldheim Ogres still racing towards him. Remembering how well Gr'Nash had treated him after the last touchdown he'd scored, Dunk decided to dive into the Hackers' dugout rather than celebrate their victory within arm's reach of the angry ogres.

THAT NIGHT IN the Bad Water – a sports tavern located in the worst part of Magritta, right down next to the wharf – Dunk raised a tankard of Killer Genuine Draft to toast the Hackers and their advancement to the *Spike!* magazine tournament finals. 'Here's to the finest bunch of hard-bitten killers I've ever played alongside!' he said.

The other Hackers – all of them, including Pegleg – roared in approval, as did the assembled crowd of regulars and hangers-on tough enough to work their way into the main room that night. They clanked their mugs together and drank deeply in approval of Dunk's sentiment.

'Another round of Killers, Sparky!' Slick called. 'Put it on the Hackers' tab.'

Pegleg started to protest, but everyone else in the bar shouted him down, including his own players. He raised his hook to slash the throat out of the nearest of those who'd failed to respect him, but Cavre stepped forward to grab him by the wrist and sit him down before anyone could get hurt.

The dwarf bartender raced along the high foot rail behind the bar – which boosted him up high enough so that he could reach out over the bar – towards a fresh keg of beer. A cheer rose up, and at first Dunk thought it was for the beer. Then Spinne elbowed him in the ribs and pointed up at the set of crystal balls hanging over the bar.

Each of the crystal balls showed a sporting event of one kind or another. These ranged from professional snotling tossing (an event favoured in dwarf taverns around the Old World) to dragon wrestling (dragon vs. ogre, dragon vs. troll, dragon vs. dragon, etc.) to witchball (played by scantily clad women straddling flying broomsticks). On the largest crystal ball, the Reikland Reavers faced off against the Darkside Cowboys, a dark elf team with a reputation for cruelty, even among Blood Bowl players.

The Reavers had just scored the go-ahead touchdown as the time wound down in the half. As the Wolf Sports team cut over to the Gods-Damned Blood Bowl Halftime Show – hosted by Barry Hacksaw and No. J. Pimpson – Spinne nuzzled up under Dunk's arm and kissed him on the cheek, a forlorn look on her face.

'Are you okay?' he asked.

A frown marred Spinne's beautiful face. Here in the bar, her strawberry-blonde hair and blue-grey eyes gleamed in the lanterns' light. The set of her jaw showed the strength she had to have to be one of the few female Blood Bowl players, but her eyes had softened tonight for some reason.

'I don't know whether to root for the Reavers or their opposition,' she said with a sigh.

'I know what you mean,' Dunk said, wrapping his arm tighter around her shoulders. 'I want Dirk and his team to win, but if they do we'll have to face them in the finals. That could get... messy.'

'Their starting thrower may be your little brother, but I played on that team just a couple of months back.'

'Are you worried you'll have to play against your old friends? Maybe hurt them?'

Spinne stood up straight and scoffed at Dunk, his arm falling from her. 'Not at all. They're a bunch of jackasses, Dirk included. Why do you think I'm playing for the Hackers?'

'Because Slick forced Pegleg to make you a great offer?' Dunk smiled behind his tankard as he took a long pull from the fresh beer that Sparky had slid in front of him.

'Okay, that was it.' Spinne grinned at him.

'So what's the problem?'

'Well, if we play against the Reavers, I know them backwards and forwards, every strength and every flaw. The downside is they know mine too.'

'Your flaws? That's a short list.'

'You have a list?' Spinne narrowed her eyes at Dunk.

'It's just a metaphor.' He held up his hands in mock surrender.

'Is that something like a dikphor?' She raised an eyebrow at him.

'What's a dikphor?' Dunk asked, regretting the words as they left his mouth.

Spinne leaned in close and whispered in Dunk's ear. 'Play your cards right, and I'll show you later.'

Then Spinne froze in his arms.

'What?' Dunk asked. He held her at arm's length and stared into her eyes, which were focused on something behind him. 'What is it?'

'Look,' she said, jerking her chin at the wall over the bar.

Dunk turned to see Lästiges interviewing Schlechter Zauberer on Wolf Sports' Cabalvision. The wizard lay sitting up bare-chested in a sickhouse bed, fat and slimy leeches hanging from his wounded shoulder, which looked like it had been stitched up with a dirty shoelace. Without his robes, the man seemed skeletal, his papery, white skin stretched thin over his jutting bones. The dark circles under his red-rimmed eyes made him seem like he might soon be hammering on death's door with his silver skullcap.

Lästiges asked the wizard a question, and he started to rant out the answer. With the celebration in the tavern as loud as it was, Dunk couldn't hear a thing. He grabbed M'Grash by the arm and signalled for the ogre to quiet down the crowd.

M'Grash turned to face the people gathered in the bar and put a finger to his lips. Then he shouted out, 'Shhhh! Be quiet! Dunkel wants to hear the evil wizard talk!'

Dunk blushed as all eyes turned to him, but he ignored the attention and focused on the large crystal ball instead. Everyone followed his example without saying another word.

'So you attack in broad daylight because you like the attention?' Lästiges asked.

The camra focused on the clammy-faced Zauberer. 'This is just the start of everything,' he said, a line of drool hanging from his bottom lip as he spoke. 'Soon the world will know my name. Soon emperors will tremble at my feet. The ultimate power will soon be m-mine!'

Lästiges leaned into the camra's view and said, 'Uh-huh. So, just how does your attempt on Dunk Hoffnung's life earlier today fit in with your plans for world domination?'

A sly smile played across Zauberer's purplish lips. He gazed so intently into the camra it seemed he could see everyone watching back at him through their crystal balls.

'I have friends – acquaintances, really – in high places with low intentions. In return for their favours – their infernal influence – they have requested that I bring them the head of one Dunkel Hoffnung, formerly of Altdorf and now part of the Bad Bay Hackers.'

'That doesn't seem to have gone so well for you.'

Zauberer ignored Lästiges's sarcastic tone and kept staring into the camra, his eyes growing wider, and his words more urgent.

'These noble people have authorized me to place a price on Hoffnung's egg-fragile head.'

Dunk heard Lästiges nearly choke at this news. Once she cleared her throat, she asked, 'And how much would this reward of yours be worth?'

Zauberer's eyes focused off-camra, in the reporter's direction, for just a moment, a horrifying leer on his face. Then he looked back into the camra, which zoomed in tight on his red-rimmed, bloodshot, slime-green eyes.

'One million Imperial crowns.'

Everyone in the bar caught their breath at once. No one moved. Dunk's heart froze in his chest. He wanted nothing more than to rewind that moment and shut the crystal ball off before those words went out again.

Then Zauberer threw back his head, exposing his pale gums and his awkward rows of chipped and stained teeth, and he laughed.

Dunk looked to Spinne, then to Slick and the rest of the Hackers. He could see by the looks on their faces that they stood with him.

It took a lot to bribe a Blood Bowl player, but that kind of money was enough to start a whole new team. Still, the Hackers had become Dunk's family over the past two years, and he knew he could trust them to have his back under any circumstances. Even the new players had trained and practised with him long enough for him to rely on them during a game. This could be no more dangerous than that.

Then Dunk saw the rest of the Bad Water's rough and tumble patrons eyeing him, some of them counting up the odds and figuring how much they'd each get by splitting the reward up that many ways. It wouldn't take them long to realise it would be worth chancing a horrible beating at the Hackers' hands.

'Guys,' Dunk said, his voice serious and low as he clutched Spinne's hand, 'I think it's time to go.'

THE FIRST OF the bounty hunters – for that's what everyone in the bar had transformed into with the mad wizard's announcement of an impossible reward – launched himself at Dunk with the neck of a broken bottle in his hand. Dunk dodged the drunken man's clumsy slash, and then smashed his nose back into his head with his fist.

Before the first attacker even hit the floor, a pair of other hopefuls charged forward. Dunk knew that he wouldn't be able to get his arms up to defend himself in time, so he gritted his teeth and waited for them to hit him. Instead, Spinne knocked one of them flat with a spinning kick while Guillermo dropped the other in his tracks with a roundhouse that landed square in the man's overflowing gut.

Dunk righted himself from his own swing and saw that the Hackers had to be outnumbered five to one. While he knew that he and his team-mates still had the upper hand, he didn't see how this could end well. The Hackers had to play in the *Spike!* magazine tournament finals in just a few days. If they lost a few players in a bar brawl, that could throw off their whole game.

Since the bar's patrons were all after him, the best thing he could do for everyone, he realised, was disappear. He glanced around for a way out.

The front door was too far away, he knew, and too many people stood between him and it. To get there, he'd have to harm and maybe kill at least a half-dozen of the bounty hunters, if not more.

People blocked his way to the back door too. Plus, Dunk knew such an escape would be too obvious. Even if he managed to make it out to the street, he'd probably find another dozen people there ready and waiting for him to emerge.

He eyed the nearest window. At the moment, it seemed like his best bet. If he managed to crash through it without killing himself, he might be able to disappear into the maze of alleys and barely standing shacks that formed Magritta's seaside district.

Then Dunk spotted Sparky standing on top of the bar and waving like a marooned sailor trying to signal a passing ship. He'd done everything but set the bar on fire, and he looked as if that might be next on his list.

Dunk nodded at the dwarf, who pointed at Dunk and then back down behind the bar. His intent was clear. If Dunk could make it over there, he'd do what he could to protect him, which, given the fact he ran the place, might be a good deal.

Sparky was a great bartender, always friendly and respectful and ready to drive off anyone who gave the Hackers any trouble, which was why they always came here to blow off steam after every game. People in the area knew this, and it had started to drive up business for Sparky – even when the team wasn't in town – and Dunk knew he was grateful for it.

Was that enough of a bond for Dunk to stake his life on? At the moment, it seemed it would have to do. Knowing the eyes of every bounty hunter in the house were on him, Dunk stood atop the bar and shook his fist down at them.

'If any of you think you're tough enough to take me on without all your friends around you, then let's have a go!' Dunk bellowed. 'The one who beats me first can have the entire reward!'

The patrons in the bar paused for a second to stare at Dunk and then at each other. Then they started swinging at each other instead.

Dunk knew that the distraction wouldn't last long. As soon as he moved back onto the tavern floor, the bounty hunters would forget their differences and return their attentions to him. So he took one step backward and fell down behind the bar in a crouch, dropping straight out of sight of anyone beyond.

'Quick!' Sparky pressed at Dunk in a stage whisper. With one hand, the dwarf held up a low, wide hatch set in the floor directly under the bar. The index finger on his other hand jabbed straight towards the dark hole under the hatch.

'Where does it lead?' Dunk asked as he scrambled over to the hatch on his hands and knees.

'Anywhere's better than here right now,' Sparky said. 'Once you go, I can break up the fight quick, but you better move. They'll fill the streets looking for you right after.'

'Thanks,' Dunk said, shaking the dwarf's meaty hand.

Sparky grinned at Dunk through his beer-soaked beard. 'Just add in a hefty tip once I send you your bill.'

Dunk dived into the darkness beyond the hatch. It clicked shut behind him, cutting off all light and leaving him in pitch blackness. For a moment, panic gripped him, and he wondered if Sparky had trapped him in here so he could claim the reward for himself.

Dunk told himself that he'd already made the decision to trust Sparky. Now he'd have to explore the results.

He felt around with his hands and discovered he was in a long, low, and narrow passageway. The sides and bottom of it were lined with bricks, and the roof appeared to be the bottom of the tavern's floorboards. There seemed to be only one way to go, and so that's the way he went.

Dunk found out the hard way that the crossbeams under the Bad Water's floorboards cut through the top of the tunnel. After he banged his head the first time, he resolved to move more slowly and carefully.

As he worked his way further along, the dull thumps and muffled bangs that sounded above his head stopped. For a moment, he hoped the fight was over, but he realised he'd probably just moved out from under the tavern's floor. He tried to picture where the tunnel might lead him, but he couldn't. He'd kept clear of the alleys that ran behind the Bad Water, and it came to him that if the passageway had been slowly turning in one way or the other he'd never have been able to tell. There was nothing to do but keep crawling on.

The tunnel might have been comfortable for a dwarf, but Dunk found it claustrophobic after a while. He yearned to be able to stand up or just stretch his arms out to the sides. He doubted he could even turn around in the passageway, even if he wanted to. It was just too tight.

Then something bit him on his thigh. He fell on his shoulder as he spun around in the tight tunnel and grabbed at it, but he couldn't find anything there. He gasped in horror and began shoving himself down the tunnel with his heels, sliding along on his seat.

A muffled laugh echoed through the tunnel, and Dunk knew what had happened. He sat up in the tunnel – it was just tall enough for him to do so without bumping his head – and stuffed his hand into his pocket. There he found his leather purse. He pulled it out and untied it from his belt and then swung it hard, smacking it against the wall.

'Yowch!' a tiny voice said from within the bag, 'Knock it off!'

'You bit me, you little bastard,' Dunk said.

The thing in the purse sniggered. 'Gotta make my own fun.'

'Do it again, Skragger, and I'll smash you flat.'

'Better than being a shrunken head,' Skragger said in his high, tiny voice.

Dunk swung the purse around fast. 'Are you sure about that?'

'Respect me!' Skragger said. 'Had season scoring record once.'

'Before Dirk broke it.' Dunk said. 'You're lucky to even be a shrunken head after what you tried to do to me. If Cavre hadn't worked his magic on you, you'd be just one more dead orc rotting in the ground.'

Dunk considered crushing Skragger's head into paste right there and then, but he couldn't bring himself to do it. If living as a shrunken head in Dunk's purse wasn't punishment enough, what was? Killing the orc would be too good for him.

If Dunk could have figured out a better fate for his old nemesis, he'd have made it happen. He hadn't asked Cavre to make the old orc into a squeaking caricature of his former self, although Dunk had to admit the little guy was a ton of fun to break out at parties. He felt responsible for him now though. He couldn't just give him to someone else.

Or could he? Either way, that wasn't something he could devote any time to ponder now. He tied his purse to his belt again with its leather strings and let it dangle there. Skragger wouldn't be able to bite him while he swayed about in mid-air, and that would do for the moment.

'What's the big idea biting me?' Dunk asked. 'Don't you think I have enough trouble on my hands?'

Skragger snorted. 'Get me that reward, buy me new body. Maybe use yours, get me stitched to your neck.'

Dunk smacked the purse hard and started crawling again, trying to shut the old blitzer's snickering out. After a while, Dunk smacked his own head into something again, but not nearly as hard as the first time. He reached out with his hand to see how far down it ran, and he found that the obstacle ran from the top of the tunnel to its bottom and all the way across.

Dunk took a deep breath to steady his nerves, and when he exhaled it sounded like a shout in the closed-off tunnel. He reached out and felt along the wall in front of him until his fingers found a latch. Letting loose a sigh of relief, he undid the latch and gave the little door in front of him a push.

Dunk saw lanterns flickering in the distance, but the world outside the doorway stood shrouded in shadows. He heard the familiar sound of water lapping up against a reinforced shoreline, and somewhere above him people shouted something he couldn't make out.

He moved out through this hatch and glanced around to get his bearings. The tunnel had brought him out underneath the base of one of the piers that stabbed out of Magritta's wharfside district. Boots tramped along the wooden planks above him, moving in all directions. He heard his name shouted a few times, but never in alarm. He believed, for the moment at least, that he was safe.

'Fancy meeting you here, kid,' said a high-pitched voice that seemed as if it might break into a wicked cackle any second.

Dunk recognised the voice immediately. He'd never heard anyone else talk like that, and he hoped he never would. In fact, he'd have been thrilled if he hadn't been hearing this exact person's voice.

'Gunther the Gobbo!' Dunk said, keeping his voice at a harsh whisper. 'What are you doing here?'

The thought that Sparky had sold him out to the unscrupulous bookie thrummed in Dunk's mind. It made him want to strike out and kill the greasy creature right there and then. He could just let the body fall into the waters of the harbour below, and no one would be the wiser. No one would miss the bookie anyway, least of all his clients.

Gunther crept out from behind a nearby piling, and Dunk realised he was standing on a narrow, wooden walkway that ran directly under the hatch out of which he was leaning. The bookie had the same wild, green eyes, long, wide nose, and horrible, wart-and-lesion covered skin that Dunk remembered. He swept the long wisps of his forelock back onto his balding scalp and grinned at Dunk with his tiny, child's teeth.

'Waiting for you, of course. You're suddenly a lot more popular than you used to be.'

Dunk crawled out of the tunnel and crouched on the walkway, ready to pounce at Gunther in an instant.

'Where are they?' Dunk asked, glancing around.

'Who?' Gunther jumped as if startled, and almost fell off the walkway as he scanned the darkness for whomever Dunk might have expected.

'Your henchmen, your hired muscle, your thugs, your business associates – whatever you're calling them these days. Trot them out and let me kill them.'

Gunther chuckled softly, and Dunk knew he'd seen through his bluff. Despite the fact that he played Blood Bowl for a living, he was no cold-blooded killer. 'I'm no bounty hunter, kid. I'm a businessman.'

Dunk narrowed his eyes at the squat bookie. 'You're alone?'

'Have you ever known me to want to share my profits?'

Dunk scowled at the piggish bookie, and then said, 'How did you know where to find me.'

'Kid.' Gunther looked at Dunk as if he must be shamming being a moron because no one could really be that thick. 'Sparky's a friend of mine. In my line of work, I've had occasion to make use of that secret passage of his myself. I knew you'd be at the Bad Water tonight celebrating your victory, just like you always do. You're a creature of habit.'

The thought that his actions were so predictable disturbed Dunk. If Gunther could figure out where he might end up, then anyone else could too. Due to his time with the Hackers – and that documentary Lästiges made about their voyage to Albion in search of the Far Albion Cup last year – anyone with access to Cabalvision knew what he looked like. With a million-crown reward on his head, how would he be able to live?

'I was just a few doors down from here myself when I saw that half-time report. That's a bad break, kid. You're going to need all the friends you can get.'

Dunk saw where the Gobbo was going. The man had long made a living as an influence peddler. He saw a wealthy player on a popular team in need of his services, and he pounced on it like a snake on a rat.

'I already have all the friends I want,' Dunk said. 'Besides, I thought you'd shut the Black Jerseys down.'

Gunther smiled, and his teeth seemed to glow in the shadows. 'Let's just say I've learned my lesson about keeping a low profile. Who needs such colourful names and complicated plans when it's so much more effective to just help guide the right players in the right directions?'

'Get out of my way,' Dunk said.

Gunther pointed to where the walkway ran off behind Dunk. 'You'd be better off going that way.' His grin grew wider. 'Take my word for it.'

'I owe you nothing,' Dunk said. He turned and padded off away from the bookie as fast as he could without making too much noise.

'It's on the house, kid,' Gunther called after him, far louder than he would have liked. 'I'm already setting up a pool for when you'll get caught. I'll make a killing!'

DUNK SPENT THE next few days in hiding. That night, he rolled a drunken sailor on the edge of the wharf and stole his clothes for a disguise. He smudged his face with grease he found in a barrel at one dark end of the wharf. Then he made his way through the back alleys near Magritta's wharf until he found a pub that rented out a few rooms in the back, mostly by the hour. Then he collapsed until the sun rode high over the city the next day.

Dunk knew that Pegleg would want him to take part in the team's practices, but he didn't see how he could manage it without starting a riot. So he stayed away, exercising in private to keep himself in condition and to force his mind away from concentrating on his troubles. He would deal with Zauberer and his mysterious employers soon, but right now he just needed to concentrate on getting ready for the game.

The morning of the *Spike!* magazine tournament final match, Dunk slunk through Magritta's predawn streets and found his way to the Hackers' inn. He entered the place through the kitchen, blowing past the workers, who thought he was trying to steal a meal. He took the back passages up to Cavre's room and knocked gently on the door.

'Come in,' Cavre said, looking like he was ready to start the day's match already, even though the sun had just risen over the horizon.

'Were you expecting someone?' Dunk asked as he stepped into the room. 'You're already dressed.'

547

Cavre closed the door behind Dunk and gestured for him to take one of the chairs in the suite's parlour. 'You, of course,' the blitzer said. 'People have been camped out in front of your and Spinne's room for days. Even M'Grash has a contingent of hopefuls who believe you will go to him first. For myself, I chased every one of them off with a long knife, and so the way is clear.'

'Isn't the fact that we're staying here supposed to be a secret anyway?' Dunk asked. Before the big matches, teams often checked into new inns or stayed in remote areas to prevent their upcoming opponents – or opposing fans – from trying to sabotage them before the game even started. The Hackers stayed only with trusted innkeepers renowned for their discretion, and they paid handsomely for the treatment. With as much gold on the line as there was in top-level Blood Bowl tournaments, even a cheapskate like Pegleg considered the cost a wise investment.

Cavre gave Dunk a smile that said the thrower already knew the answer. 'We pay for our privacy in gold, so gold can penetrate it as well. With a million Imperial crowns at stake, our privacy looks like a used archery target.'

'So I'm not safe here,' Dunk said, glancing at the door.

'You are not safe anywhere, my friend. As long as there's that price on your head, you're fortunate to find any space where you can rest it.' Cavre took a long look at Dunk. 'Take a nap in my bed. I'll have some food brought up later, and when you're ready we'll gather the team to make a try for the stadium together.'

'I'm surprised some of the new players haven't tried to sell me out.' Dunk lay back on the couch, surprised to realise how tired he was.

'Who's to say they didn't?' Cavre said. 'Captain Pegleg has held team meetings every day in which he emphasises loyalty and team-work. I doubt any of them would move against you directly, but someone might decide that selling information about your where-abouts would be harmless enough.'

'So it's good I kept away,' Dunk said. 'I thought Pegleg would be furious about me missing so much practice time.'

Cavre laughed. 'I never said he was happy. He's spoken to Mr. Full-belly about docking your pay, but I believe your agent has convinced him that you're acting in the team's best interests.'

'Let's hope he's right,' Dunk said with a yawn. 'Maybe it would be better for the team if I quit.'

This time Cavre didn't laugh a bit. 'Do you think that throwers with your talent and skill can be found on any street corner? Do not fool yourself, Dunk. The Hackers' fortunes have turned around since you joined our team, and the timing is no coincidence.'

'Why, Cavre, that almost sounded like a compliment.' Dunk's eyes closed of their own accord as he spoke.

'Do not become arrogant about it. Those who let such things go to their heads often have their brains dashed out on the field.'

Dunk thought he had a snappy response to that, but before he could utter it he fell fast asleep.

WHEN DUNK WOKE up, he found himself laid out on a bench in the Hackers' locker room, already dressed in his Blood Bowl armour. He opened his eyes to find Slick staring down at him, a self-satisfied grin on his face.

'Welcome back to the land of the living, son. You're just in time to make your mark on Blood Bowl history.'

Dunk tried to sit up right away, but found that his head felt woozy. Spinne jumped over an intervening bench to give him a hand and get him up on his feet. 'Thank you,' he said before sitting back down again. He considered it a personal victory that he hadn't lain down on the bench once more.

'What happened?' he asked as he tried to shake the cobwebs from his head. 'I don't think I've ever slept that hard before.'

'Well,' Spinne said putting an arm around Dunk and kissing him on his unshaven cheek, 'Pegleg figured that we couldn't be seen walking into the stadium with you. It would have caused a riot, and – as much as I'd be happy to defend you to the death – we have a match to play today.'

'So?' Dunk said, still confused.

'So he called in Dr. Pill who slipped you a little something to help keep you asleep.'

Dunk glanced across the room and spotted the elf watching him, nodding approvingly at his own handiwork. He flashed Dunk a grin and gave him a big thumbs-up. 'You'll feel fine in no time,' he called over.

The other players in the locker room paused for a moment to give Dunk a cheer, which he waved off with a sheepish grin. 'Thanks, guys,' he said before they each returned to their own pre-game preparations and rituals.

'How did you get me here?' He ran a hand through his hair and realised it was wet.

'Well, we had to pack you away in something that no one would notice us carrying through the streets of Magritta. We couldn't trust anyone else to transport you, especially since you were unconscious, so it had to be something we regularly had with us. If there had been anything out of the ordinary, people after that bounty on your head would have tried to stop us immediately.'

Dunk cracked his neck, working the stiffness from it. He saw M'Grash coming over to greet him, the ogre's regular, goofy grin on his face. Some people mistook it for an evil leer, but Dunk had known M'Grash for far too long to make that mistake. 'So how did you get me here?' Dunk asked again.

'It really was the only way,' Spinne said, looking up at M'Grash.

The ogre put down the keg he was carrying, and then leaned over and laid a heavy hand on Dunk's shoulder. 'Did it for you, Dunkel. My friend, Dunkel!'

The ogre's breath reeked of beer, and lots of it. M'Grash drank regularly and often, but rarely this early in the day and never before a game. If Pegleg had thought it would help make the ogre mean, he'd have forced the alcohol down M'Grash's throat himself. Unfortunately for the coach, beer just made M'Grash sweeter than ever. He was – unlike any other ogre Dunk had ever met – a happy drunk.

Why M'Grash was drunk now, he could only guess. Then he noticed that when M'Grash had set his keg down on the ground it had thumped with a peculiarly hollow noise. It was empty.

Dunk leapt to his feet, aghast. 'You brought me here in that?' He pointed at the keg, the top of which he could now see was missing.

M'Grash grinned and nodded at Dunk so much that Dunk feared the ogre's head might roll off and crush his legs. Spinne winced in sympathy as she put an arm around him. 'It was the only way,' she said, 'and we knew it wouldn't be comfortable for you. We didn't want to have to worry about you getting cramped or scared in the keg, so...'

'So you had our hired quack slip me something to keep me out.' Dunk shook his head in disgust. As he did, he realised the cobweb inside his skull had disappeared. As creepy as the apothecary was, Dunk had to admit the old elf knew his potions.

Spinne held him tight and cocked her head low to peer up into his eyes. 'Are you all right?' she asked. 'They had to fold you in half to get you to fit in the keg. I begged them to stop, but they promised me it wouldn't hurt.'

'Of course he's fine,' Slick offered as he strode up to stand in front of Dunk. 'Look at him. He's the picture of health. Looks like a million crowns – I mean – oh, never mind me. You look great!'

Dunk scowled down at the Halfling, who beamed back up at him, undeterred by his client's attitude. 'You seem pretty happy for an agent whose top client got his last three days' pay docked.'

'Ah,' Slick said, his grin broadening. 'That might have been the sad fate of an ordinary player with an ordinary agent, but there's nothing at all so pedestrian about you and me, son.'

'So you talked him into forgetting about me ditching practice?'

Slick pursed his lips. 'It's more like I made a little wager with him. If we win today, he'll pay you every dime for those lost days – plus we'll get our share of the championship purse!'

'And if we lose?'

Slick glared at Dunk as if he'd been slapped. 'Shut your mouth, son! We're not going to lose this game.'

Dunk raised an eyebrow at Slick, and then knelt down to whisper at him. 'You convinced Pegleg to bet against his own team?'

'He looks at it this way: If we should – through some horrible twist of fate – happen to lose the game, he gets some of his money back. When, instead, we win, he'll be happy to pay the properly owed amount out of the winner's purse.'

Slick gave Dunk a smug smile. 'Don't think of it as a bet. It's more like we offered your employer a money-back guarantee.'

Dunk laughed quietly as he stood up and looked down at his agent. 'Only you could sell that angle, Slick.'

'That's why you pay me to be your agent.'

Dunk just sighed. Then a thought struck him. 'Who won the game the other night?'

'You don't know?' Spinne asked, concerned.

Dunk shook his head. 'I was busy running for my life. I haven't seen a crystal ball or a broadsheet since. So, who are we playing?'

Spinne stared straight into Dunk's eyes. 'The Reikland Reavers,' she said with a twisted smile, 'of course.'

Dunk put his hands over his face, and then pulled them down past his chin. 'Of course.'

'You SHOULDN'T BE here,' Dirk Heldmann said as he shook Dunk's hand for the camras. As team captain, Cavre had asked Dunk to accompany him to the centre of the field for the opening coin toss. With Dirk as the Reavers' captain, this would be the only chance for the two brothers to talk before the game began, and Dunk thanked Cavre for the opportunity.

'I'm just here to play Blood Bowl,' Dunk said.

Dirk glared up at Dunk. It often struck Dunk how different the two brothers looked, seeing as how they'd undeniably come from the same two parents. Dunk had a thick build and his hair and eyes were so dark they were almost black. Dirk, on the other hand, was lean and wiry, with white-blond hair and bright blue eyes, and stood at least an inch taller than his older brother. When the pair stood next to each other, people could see the resemblance, but only then.

'You're going to get killed,' Dirk said.

'That's sweet that you're concerned for me, but I know how to handle myself on a Blood Bowl field.'

Dirk grabbed Dunk by the side of his helmet and pulled him close. 'You're not listening to me. You never listen.'

Dunk sighed. They'd had this fight countless times before, and it had long since become old. 'Okay. Speak.'

'The Reavers – the players, at least – have decided that collecting the reward on your head is more important than winning the game. The first chance they get, they're going to kill you, snatch your body, and load you on the fastest boat to Altdorf.'

'You really know how to make a guy feel wanted.'

'Stop being cute.' Dirk sneered down at Dunk. 'You *are* wanted – dead or alive.'

Dunk scowled. 'Hasn't anyone bothered to consider that Zauberer might be lying? What makes anyone think they can take his word on anything? He's a wizard of the blackest kind.'

'With that amount of money possibly on the line, people are willing to take the chance. Besides, Lästiges's sources say its real.'

'I can't believe you're still dating her.'

Dirk rolled his eyes. 'You need to leave here. Now. Before the first play. You're a fine player, Dunk, but even you can't beat ten-to-one odds–'

'Orcs or Eagles,' the referee – Rhett Bool again – grunted as he presented Dunk and the team captains with a commemorative coin cast just for the game.

'Never bet against the Emperor,' Dirk said. 'Eagles!'

The minotaur flipped the coin into the air and let it bounce to a stop on the Astrogranite. 'Eagles!' he announced before he turned to Dirk. 'Kick or receive?'

'Receive.' Dirk glared at Dunk with desperate eyes. 'Don't let them do this to you,' he said. 'Meet me after the game. We can figure this out.'

'North or south end?' Bool asked.

'South,' said Cavre.

Dunk grimaced at his brother, and then reached out and pulled their helmets together for an instant. 'I'm sorry,' he said. 'I can't.'

With that, he turned and trotted down to the south end of the field.

Soon after Edgar kicked the ball, Dunk knew Dirk had been right. The ball went sailing right over every one of the Reavers and landed in the stands behind the end zone. The bloodthirsty fans – eager for the game to get started in earnest – tossed the ball back onto the field, but the Reavers ignored it. Instead of going for the ball, they went straight for Dunk.

'Have you ever seen anything like this, Bob?' Jim's voice boomed out over the PA system. 'The Reavers seem to have decided that taking out Hoffnung is more important than playing the game!'

'With a million crowns on the line, can you blame them?' said Bob. 'Maybe they hope to stake their claim in Hoffnung's valuable chest and then go on to destroy the Hackers to put the froth on that blood money.'

'Hoffnung's a contender though. I don't think he'll go down without a fight.'

'Your money's better than mine already, Jim. In the Gobbo's pool, I had him being found floating in the harbour last night!'

Dunk let the commentators' banter fade into the background as he concentrated on the task at hand: staying alive. He raced towards M'Grash, who was already trotting in his direction.

'They want to hurt Dunkel!' M'Grash said, dismay painted on his face. For a moment, Dunk thought the ogre might weep.

'Let's see that doesn't happen, big guy,' Dunk said. 'Give me a ride?'

M'Grash's fear for his friend's life evaporated in an instant. Child-like joy danced in his eyes instead. 'Piggyback?'

'How about on your shoulders?' Dunk said. He scrambled up the ogre's outstretched arms and wrapped his legs around the ogre's tree trunk of a neck.

Just then, the first of the Reavers hit M'Grash in the legs. The line-man speared the ogre in the thigh with the line of spikes that ran along the crest of his helmet.

M'Grash howled in pain. For all his size and strength, Dunk knew that he was a bit of a baby when it came to being hurt.

Most teams respected M'Grash for his superhuman strength and gave him as wide a berth as possible on the field. He spent most of his time chasing them down and breaking them apart like a series of desert-dry wishbones. Sure, he had to take on the big bruisers on the other teams, but he was ready for that. To have a human attack him directly surprised the ogre, and he didn't like it one bit.

M'Grash reached down and plucked the money-mad lineman from his thigh. He hauled the Reaver into the air by his helmet, the strap of which held tight, choking the man as his feet thrashed in the empty air below them.

'You hurt me!' M'Grash bellowed into the front of the man's hel-met, raw spittle drenching the terrified lineman's face. 'Me hurt you!'

With that, the ogre swung his arm in a wide arc and pitched the hapless lineman high into the air. The Reaver sailed through the sky over the field and landed in the stands behind the Hackers' dugout. The fans there – at least the ones that weren't crushed – cheered and set to taking their revenge on the Reaver for having the nerve to fall on top of them.

Downfield, Dunk saw that one of the new Hackers, a Brettonian catcher by the name of Singe de Fromage, had scooped up the ball and was making a mad dash for the end zone. A moment later, Rhett Bool blew the whistle and stuck his arms up to signal the Hackers' first touchdown.

Dunk and the rest of the Hackers were too busy battling with the Reavers to pay any attention. Despite the score, which should have stopped the game for a moment, the Reavers refused to end their assault.

M'Grash tried to avoid the Reavers, but there were just too many of them. They grabbed at his legs and ankles, trying to trip him up or drag him down. Dunk watched Spinne tear the helmet off one of the Reavers and start to beat him senseless with it, and Guillermo was in the process of breaking the arm of one of the Reavers' throwers. Still, Dunk knew it wouldn't be enough.

Then he saw Edgar standing in the middle of the field, waving his arms. 'I'm open!' the treeman hollered. 'I'm bloody well open!'

Dunk tapped M'Grash on the top of his bald skull and pointed towards Edgar. The ogre might have had the smarts of a five-year-old, but he understood Blood Bowl well enough to know what Dunk wanted. He plucked his friend off of his neck and pitched him towards Edgar's waiting branches, a dozen yards away.

Dunk flung his arms and legs wide, trying to make himself as large a target as possible for Edgar to catch. As he hung in the air at the apex of the throw, he realised that M'Grash had hurled him a bit long. He was going to land on the treeman's far side.

Edgar spotted this and spun around, stretching his branches out towards the north end of the field. When Dunk flew over his leafy top, he reached out as far as he could and caught the thrower like a baby in a basket.

'Thanks!' Dunk said, amazed not to be lying flat on the Astrogranite with a crushed spine. Then he glanced back around Edgar's trunk. 'Now run!'

The Reavers had happily given up on M'Grash as soon as Dunk left the ogre's hands. M'Grash lumbered after them with a roar, his flying tackle smashing three of them under his bulk. The rest of the Reavers – a half-dozen of them – kept right after Edgar, ignoring their fallen team-mates.

'Just more for the rest of us!' said one of the Reavers – their fastest catcher – as he clawed onto Edgar's back with his spiked gauntlets and began to climb towards where Dunk sat in the treeman's branches.

Then another Reaver reached out and pulled his teammate off Edgar, smashing his helmet into the ground. Dunk cheered as he saw Dirk pounding away at his own teammate.

'I'm *still* the captain of this team!' Dirk said as he picked up the Reaver catcher and bodily flung him at the other Reavers stampeding up behind them.

'That's just the kind of old-school discipline missing on most teams these days,' Bob's voice said, 'I remember back when Griff Oberwald was the Reavers' captain. He'd have never let his players disobey him like that.'

'True enough,' Jim said, 'but with a million crowns at stake, Oberwald would probably have led the charge. What we have here is less a case of needed discipline than blood being thicker than Hater-Aid.

'Really?' Dunk could hear the vampire licking his lips. 'The Hater-Aid I drink comes with blood in it!'

The Reavers chasing Edgar pounded to a halt in front of Dirk, who stood between them and his brother. Dunk grabbed Edgar and pointed for him to turn around so they could see what happened next. Somewhere in the distance, he heard the protesting screams of de Fromage as the fans pulled the celebrating rookie into the stands and started to pass him up and over the stadium's outer wall.

'Stand down,' Dirk snarled at his team-mates. 'The play is over. If we want to win this game–'

'Sod the game,' said one of the Reavers' linemen, a bearded, bear-like man with a belly that probably weighed more than Dirk. 'And if you stand between us and that reward, sod you!'

As the lineman spoke, he stepped up closer to his captain and stabbed his finger at Dirk's face. Dirk reached out and grabbed the finger, and then snapped it, in one, quick motion. The lineman retracted his mangled digit, screaming at it in disbelief.

Dirk lowered his shoulder and charged into the astonished lineman, driving him backward into the other Reavers. 'Game on!' Dirk shouted, and the brawl started up again.

Seeing how his captain had betrayed the team, the Reavers' coach cleared the team's bench, and another four players in their blue-and-white uniforms raced on to the field. Never one to let another coach get an edge on his team, Pegleg did the same.

With Dirk in the middle of the brawl, Dunk refused to keep out of the fight anymore. 'Toss me in there!' he ordered Edgar.

'A bloody 'please' wouldn't hurt,' the treeman grumped.

'Please!' Dunk said. 'Now!'

A moment later, Dunk found himself arcing through the air again. This time, he came down hard in the middle of the action, spiked knee guards first. As he smashed into one Reaver's back, he lashed out with his fist at another and felt a satisfying crunch.

Joining in the brawl felt right to Dunk. He'd been running from his problems for too long. It was time to take his destiny in his own hands and stop letting others fight his battles for him.

Then all other concerns except the fight dropped away, and Dunk gave himself over to punishing the Reavers for their collective attack. Every time he saw a blue-and-white helmet or armour, he punched, tore, and kicked at it until it went away. He couldn't tell for how long he fought – it could have been seconds or hours – but he kept swinging, determined to put an end to this on his own terms or to go down fighting.

'Wow!' said Bob. 'You don't usually see that much violence until the post-game parties!'

'I think it's refreshing,' said Jim. 'Players these days are all about the money. They don't show any passion for the game.'

'I don't think this is about the game anymore.'

'That's my point! If it was, they'd be more concerned about scoring than surviving. Too many of these pansies want to live forever.'

'I don't think that's going to be a concern for most of the Reavers after today. Look! There's only one of them left standing!'

Dunk dropped the Reaver blitzer he'd been beating and spun around to defend himself. He grabbed at the only Reaver he saw on his feet, and smashed his helmet into the other player's.

'It's me, you idiot!' Dirk snarled as he punched Dunk away, his blow knocking his brother's helmet askew.

Dunk ripped his helmet from his head and stared at his brother, huffing and puffing for breath. He nodded his thanks to Dirk wordlessly, but Dirk ignored him.

Dirk turned around slowly, surveying the human wreckage on the Astrogranite. Dunk followed his brother's eyes and saw that only a few of the players on the field could still stand under their own power. A number of them were clearly dead, including, Dunk guessed, whoever owned the better part of an arm lying near midfield.

Players from both teams counted among the dead, and even more of them were injured. M'Grash bled from a half-dozen wounds he didn't seem to feel. Edgar had sap running out of a hole in his trunk. Guillermo and Spinne were battered and bruised, with their share of minor cuts, but no worse than they would have received in the course of a game. One of the Hacker rookies lay whimpering to one side, cradling a mangled hand.

Now that it appeared the fight had come to an end, a squad of stretcher bearers from the stadium's staff swarmed onto the field. As the orange-uniformed men lifted the dead and wounded onto their litters, some of them glanced at Dunk with a familiar hunger in their eyes. He snarled at the one closest to him, and the man wet himself. As he scurried off the field, the others returned to their jobs, carefully avoiding Dunk's gaze.

A determined Reaver reached out for Dunk's ankle, and Dunk kicked him in the arm for his troubles. He thought about making sure the man had been knocked senseless, but Dirk grabbed him by the shoulder before he could strike again.

'That's enough,' Dirk said. 'He's had enough.'

Dunk shrugged his brother's hand off him. 'If you'd keep your animals on a proper leash–'

'These are good players,' Dirk said, tearing off his own helmet and getting in Dunk's face. 'Who could resist that kind of reward? You think any of us play this game for the exercise?'

'They tried to kill me.'

'Just like they might during any given game.'

Dunk stared straight into his little brother's bright blue eyes. 'You think maybe you can take that reward all for yourself now?' he asked.

All the frustration of having to run and hide over the past few days had boiled over during the fight, and Dunk hadn't stuffed it back in the bottle yet. If Dirk wanted a piece of him, he'd give it to him.

Dirk raised his fists as if he wanted to throttle the life out of Dunk, but before he could make his move, Rhett Bool stepped between them. He had a ball in his hand, and he shoved it into Dunk's hands.

'It's your kick-off,' he said to Dunk. Then he turned to Dirk. 'You need to get back to receive.'

Dunk and Dirk stared at the minotaur as if he'd grown a second head between his horns. He just gazed back at them with his large, bull's eyes, unblinking and silent.

'You can't be serious,' Dunk said. 'Who's left to play?'

'There's six of you still capable,' Bool said. 'And the Reavers still have one player left.'

Dunk felt sick as he looked over at Dirk, who just glared back at him. 'You can't… Forget it. I won't do it.'

The Reavers' coach stormed onto the field. Dunk had never met him before, but Blitz Bombardi's reputation preceded him. He dressed like a businessman, in a suit of the finest silk, under an over-large bear-fur coat, purportedly made from the skin of a beast he'd killed with his own hands in his youth. He stared out at Dunk for a moment through a pair of black-rimmed spectacles that legend had it were fashioned from the black horn of a chaos daemon. If so, Dunk thought that might explain the way the man's eyes blazed at him.

'What's the problem?' Bombardi asked Dirk. He held his voice steady, almost quiet, but no one could mistake the menace carried in every syllable he uttered. This man expected his players to execute his orders efficiently and without question. He refused to show his irritation, but Dunk could feel it simmering beneath his placid surface.

'No problem, coach,' Dirk said, keeping his eyes locked on Dunk. 'The game's over.'

Bombardi shook his head. 'The game isn't over as long as there is one Reaver standing.'

'You can't be–' Dunk started to speak, but Bombardi snapped his head in the Hacker's direction and cut him off with a glance that Dunk thought could have stopped a starving troll.

Bombardi turned back to Dirk. 'Get down that field and prepare to receive that ball. We are in the final match of this tournament, and we will not forfeit the game under any circumstances.'

'Coach,' Dirk started.

'That's correct. I am the coach. You are the player. You will follow my lead, or you will be fired.'

Dunk watched Dirk struggle with his emotions. Dirk had been part of the Reavers ever since he'd left home. The team had become his new family, and every member of that family had betrayed him today when he'd stood up to them to defend his brother.

'It's okay,' Dunk said. 'We'll forfeit too. We'll call it a draw.'

Bombardi spun on Dunk. 'You can't do that. This is a tournament. The final game. There is a fortune at stake. There will be a winner. It will be the Reavers.'

M'Grash leaned forward and put a gentle hand on Bombardi's back. 'Pegleg always tells me...' He rolled his eyes back for a moment to concentrate, smiled when he found the thought he'd almost lost, and then continued. '"Just 'cause I say it don't make it real."'

Bombardi looked like he might shoot flames out through the lenses of his glasses. Instead, he shrugged off the ogre's hand and glared at Dirk. 'Get in the game, or go home.'

Dirk chewed on his bottom lip for a moment. Then he tossed Bombardi his helmet. 'Screw you and this screwy game,' he said. Then he walked off the field to the boos and hisses of scores of thousands of angry fans.

'Hackers win!' Bob's voice said. 'Hackers win! The Hackers have won the *Spike!* magazine tournament!'

Dunk stared up at the scoreboard and then at his own baffled face as it appeared on the Jumboball. He raised his arm in victory and tried to offer up a smile, but he just couldn't make it happen.

As Dunk, Spinne, and Slick strolled down the hall of the Hackers' 'secret' inn, the halfling seemed like the only one pleased with the day's results.

'It's wonderful, son, wonderful!' Slick said. 'Do you have any idea what the winner's purse for a major tournament like this is? Why, my percentage alone will be enough to keep me solvent for the rest of the year.'

Neither Dunk nor Spinne cared to respond, but this didn't give Slick any pause. He just stabbed his finger into the air and kept talking.

'Just think what this will do for the Hackers' reputation too. We'll have hopeful rookies crawling out of their burrows.' Slick rubbed his chubby, little hands together. 'And they'll all need representation.'

'I'm just happy you were able to find us another room here in the hotel,' Dunk said. 'I thought they were all sold out.'

'They were,' Slick said, grinning. 'But, because you two are my best clients, I decided I would swap rooms with you to give you a break until we leave this town behind.'

'Thanks,' Dunk said, impressed by the halfling's generosity. 'When do you think we'll be leaving?'

'Pegleg doesn't see any reason to stick around here, especially with you having to deal with this bounty nonsense. He wants to be out of here on tomorrow morning's high tide.'

Dunk couldn't wait to be out on the wide-open ocean on the *Sea Chariot*, the Hackers' team ship. The chances that someone would manage to find him out there and try to grab the reward were far less than they were here on land. He'd grown tired of having to glance over his shoulder every moment he was in Magritta. Leaving the town behind would not sadden him a bit.

'Here we are,' Slick said, turning to present the couple to a round door that stood only five feet tall.

Dunk stared at the door for a moment, then at Slick, and then back at the door.

'This is the halfling part of the inn,' Spinne said.

'Exactly!' said Slick. 'Who would think to look for you two here?'

Dunk had to admit that the halfling had a point. He wouldn't have thought to hole up here himself. He turned and gave Spinne a kiss. 'Will you mind if I don't carry you across the threshold?' he asked. 'It would be hard on my knees.'

'As long as you let me sleep in the bed,' she said with a grin. 'I can't imagine there will be room for us both – for sleeping, at least.'

'That's where you're wrong,' Slick said. 'I had the staff move a standard-sized double bed in here for me. There's enough room on it for a handful of halflings. I think they thought I was some kind of swinger.'

'You think of everything,' Spinne said, laughing as Slick produced a key and used it to open the door.

'After you, my friends,' the halfling said, sweeping his arm wide to usher them into the room.

With no lanterns burning inside the room, Dunk couldn't see a thing. That was his first clue that something was wrong. He reached towards his belt for his sword, but it wasn't there. They'd come to the hotel dressed as monks, and there hadn't been a place for a blade under the hooded robes. He'd insisted on slipping a knife under the costume though, which Slick had razzed him about when they'd slipped out of the robes after leaving the inn's main room behind.

Dunk had felt silly at the time, but now, as the blade's handle filled his hand, he was glad he had it.

'You don't need that,' a gravelly voice said from somewhere in the darkness. Dunk recognised who it belonged to instantly: his old teacher Lehrer.

A match blazed in the far corner of the room, and Dunk saw the old man set the flame to a lamp sitting on a low table next to the low chair in which he crouched. He looked the same as ever, perhaps a bit more careworn. His silver hair had grown out a bit and threatened to fall into his sparkling, grey eyes. His drab clothes stood out in the brightly decorated room, the muddy colours of the cloth clashing with the primary colours that halflings with money seemed to love so much.

'Here to collect the reward?' Dunk asked as he moved into the room, crouching over to make sure he didn't bump his head. He peered left and right, hunting for some sign that Lehrer was not alone. He didn't think the old man would have brought someone else into their business together, but all sorts of strange things had happened to him that week.

Spinne slid into the room behind Dunk, and Slick marched in after her, closing the door behind him. 'Fancy meeting a scumbag like you in a nice place like this,' Spinne said to Lehrer as she moved to check and then cover the curtained windows.

The old man smirked. 'I don't believe I've had the pleasure, Miss Schönheit, although I almost feel I know you from all the news reports I've seen.' He glanced at Dunk. 'The ones from that Weibchen woman are always so deliciously mean.'

'Get out,' Dunk said, pointing the knife at Lehrer. Even though the old man seemed to be unarmed, Dunk knew better. He'd never known his old teacher to go anywhere without at least two weapons on his body – usually more.

'Now, now,' Lehrer said. 'There's no call to be like that. Just consider this a friendly visit from an old fan of yours.'

'You work for the Guterfiends,' Spinne said. 'They destroyed Dunk's family.'

Lehrer threw up his hands in mock surrender. 'I work for the people who occupy the Hoffnung's old estate, just as I worked for the Hoffnungs before that. Hey, a man's got to eat.'

Dunk dug into his purse, fished out Skragger's shrunken head, and tossed it to Lehrer. 'You hired this bugger to kill me – after he'd been brought back as a vampire – once we stopped him from killing us the first time.'

Lehrer caught Skragger's head neatly and spun it around so he could look into the creature's eyes. 'You've seen better days,' he said to the head with a wry grin.

Skragger snapped at Lehrer with his tiny teeth, but the old man just held him by his temples and let his jaw swing wildly through the air.

'Pathetic,' Lehrer said so softly Dunk could barely hear him. He set Skragger's head upside down on the table next to him, pointing its eyes towards the lamp.

Then Lehrer looked back up at Dunk, who still stared at him, waiting for an explanation. 'Yeah, that's all true,' Lehrer said. 'Guilty as charged, although I was just following the Guterfiends' orders.'

'That's not much of an excuse,' Slick said as he sat down in an overstuffed, halfling-sized chair in the far corner of the room from Lehrer.

Seeing the halfling in his chair, Dunk realised that Lehrer had to be sitting in a halfling couch, as it was three times as wide as Slick's seat.

'If I hadn't done it, they would have just got someone else to hire Skragger. As it was, I could keep tabs on this bugger and even try to warn Dunk if he got too close to him.'

'Which you never did.'

Lehrer smirked. 'You didn't need my help, kid.'

'And I don't need it now,' Dunk said, jabbing his knife in Lehrer's direction. 'Get out.'

Lehrer grimaced as if trying to suppress his temper. Dunk remembered that look on the man's face all too well. He'd frustrated Lehrer to the point of losing his cool all too often. Eventually, he'd figured out the signs that he was about to trigger such an outburst, and he'd learned how to step back until everything was fine again.

Now, he didn't care.

'You're wrong,' Lehrer said. 'Again.' He blew out a long sigh and narrowed his eyes at Dunk. 'Who do you think put that price on your head?'

Dunk's jaw dropped. 'You?'

'No,' Lehrer said, disgusted. 'Think, kid, if I'd done that, would I have shown up here alone? I'd have just waited for the bounty hunters to bring you to me.

'So,' Dunk said. 'Who was it then?'

'The Guterfiends,' Slick said from the couch behind Dunk. 'It has to be. They wanted you dead enough to send Skragger after you.'

'Give the little guy a pipe full of weed,' Lehrer said. 'They want your boy here dead in the worst way.'

'Do they really have a million crowns to spend on my death?' Dunk asked. He looked down and noticed the mattress Slick had mentioned, sprawling right there on the floor before him. He sat down on it and laid his knife across his thighs. If there really was someone willing to offer that kind of money to bring him down, how could he stop it?

'They seem to have a bottomless treasury,' Lehrer said. 'How do you think they managed to break up your family business? It wasn't done with mirrors.'

Dunk sat there in silence for a long moment, just staring down at the knife in his hands. This was it, he realised, the shoe he'd been waiting to drop. And now it had.

'Kid,' Lehrer said. 'I'm sorry to have to be the one to break all this to you. You know how the reward is for you dead or alive. Well, that pretty much means dead. If you show up to the old keep still breathing, they'll take care of that quick.'

Dunk let loose a low growl in his throat.

'What about Dirk?' Spinne asked.

Dunk looked up at her, confused.

'What about Dirk?' Spinne asked again, looking straight at Lehrer.

The old man smirked. 'I can see why the Hoffnung boys like you, girl. You're sharp like a knife.'

'What about Dirk?' Dunk asked.

'Once you're dead, they'll come for him.'

Dunk fought the urge to be sick. 'They want to wipe us out, don't they?' he said. 'And they're doing it in order, one at a time. First it was my parents. Now it's me. Then it'll be Dirk too.' He stared at Lehrer. 'What happens once we're all gone?'

'Then the Guterfiends have a free and clear claim to your family's holdings, uncontested by any heirs who might crop up.'

'Is that so important?' Slick asked. 'They already have those things. Why bother with wiping out the Hoffnung line?'

'You don't know these people,' said Lehrer. 'They're thorough. If they think there's even a chance they'll lose what they have, they'll go to any lengths, track down every possibility and eliminate them.'

'Why are you telling me this?' Dunk asked. 'This all smells like some sort of set-up.'

Lehrer sighed. 'Believe it or not, kid, I'm fond of you. I've been with your family since before you were born, and I've watched you grow from a little infant to a superstar.'

'Then why did you help the Guterfiends destroy my family?'

Lehrer cocked his head at Dunk. 'Who told you I did that?'

'Dirk has some pretty hard words for you.'

'He's just jealous. He always thought I favoured you.'

Dunk thought about that for a moment. 'Did you?'

Lehrer smiled. 'By default. You weren't the one who kept stuffing horse dung in my codpiece.'

'Do the Guterfiends know you're here?' Slick asked.

Lehrer grimaced at this question, and Dunk wondered if a squad of trained killers might erupt from the wardrobe now that someone had finally asked the worst sort of question: one which only had bad answers.

'They think I'm here to kill Dunk myself.'

Slick nodded. 'And if they find out you've been trying to warn him away?'

'Let's just say I won't be welcome back in the family keep – and they won't have to pay anyone to kill me.'

'Why's that?' asked Spinne.

Lehrer winked at her. 'There are plenty of folks ready to do that for free.'

'So,' Dunk said. 'You've delivered your warning. Now what? Just what do you expect me to do?'

Lehrer rubbed his chin as he talked to the thrower. 'If you had a lick of sense, you'd hightail it out of the Old World. Maybe go back to Albion. You might be safe there. Or head someplace even farther away: the Dark Lands, the Chaos Wastes.'

'You don't think they'd be able to find me there?'

'Out of sight, out of mind. These days, they see you every few weeks on their crystal ball – more often if that Weibchen woman covers you the way she likes to. If you quit the game, dropped out for a bit, they might forget.'

'Or they might not.'

Lehrer raised his eyebrows at that. 'True enough, kid. I did say they were thorough.'

Dunk sat with his head in his hands. Maybe Lehrer was right. As long as he continued on as a Blood Bowl player, he was a prime target. His constant presence on Cabalvision would drive the Guterfiends nuts, and his high profile would mean that anyone greedy enough to go after their reward would know where to find him.

It would be easier to give all this up, everything he'd worked for the past two years. After all, he'd never had any burning desire to become a Blood Bowl player. If he hadn't run into Slick in Dörfchen, he probably never would have even considered taking up such a career. He'd made plenty of money. He could live on it for the rest of his life. Spinne might even come with him if he asked her to.

'I don't know,' he said, looking at her. 'Would you join me? If I left all this behind, I mean. Would you come with me?'

Spinne furrowed her brow at Dunk and crept over to sit next to him on the mattress lying in the centre of the cosy halfling room. She reached up and took his face in her hands.

'Blood Bowl is my career,' she said. 'For the past five years, it's been my passion and my life. I can't imagine my life without it.'

Dunk's heart fell into his stomach. He let his head hang low. Could he go on without her? If he was a target, then she was in danger too. Bounty hunters rarely cared who got hurt when they chased after their prey. He couldn't stand the thought that she might get hurt because of him.

'All right,' he said. Before he could continue, she pulled up his chin and looked into his eyes.

'But when I try to imagine my life without you,' she said with a wan smile, 'it's even worse.'

Dunk leaned forward and kissed her soft and tender lips. He hoped their embrace would never have to end.

'Oh, for the love of the game,' Lehrer said. 'How trite can you get? Could you two at least get a room?'

Dunk extricated himself from Spinne's arms and raised his eye-brows at the old man, then glanced about at the ceiling, floor, and walls.

'Oh,' Lehrer said. 'Right.'

Dunk put an arm around Spinne and felt her melt into his chest. With her at his side, at least, he knew everything would be okay, no matter if he stayed or left.

'It's okay with me too, son,' Slick said.

Dunk peered over Spinne's reddish hair at the halfling. In the light of the room's single lantern, Slick looked a bit older than Dunk remembered ever seeing him. He and the halfling had started out at arm's length, but they'd quickly come to trust each other, to depend on each other for the truth. They'd formed a deep and abiding friend-ship based on mutual respect and need for each other's invaluable skills.

To leave Blood Bowl behind would mean leaving Slick behind too, and M'Grash and Guillermo, and Cavre and Edgar, and even Pegleg.

The only thing Dunk could think of to say to Slick was, 'What?'

'If you must know, I've been thinking of retiring myself. After all, what better time to go out than at the top of your game, right? Why hang around until you're a feeble old fool bumming ales from young fools in exchange for tired tales of the glories of your past?'

'What?' Dunk's brain couldn't digest the feast of foolishness Slick was trying to feed it.

'Don't worry yourself about me, son,' Slick said, piling it on. 'I'll be just fine. I've had my eye on a tavern in Greenfield for a year or so now. I might even help out with the Grasshuggers a bit while I'm there, just to keep my hand in, you know.'

Dunk couldn't help it. He started to laugh. At first, he tried to hide it. Slick had delivered such a serious speech to him, after all, and he thought he should try to give the halfling his due. The more he thought about Slick retiring from being an agent to take up owner-ship of some tavern in a halfling backwater, the harder it became to ignore the humour in it.

When Spinne joined in, Dunk had no way left to resist. He threw back his head and laughed loud, hard, and long until tears streamed down his face and he turned red from lack of breath. Spinne held him tight, her own jiggling frame spurring him to wilder howls of humour. Eventually, they collapsed on top of each other, too worn out for even one more giggle.

'Nuffle's holy balls!' Slick said. 'The least you could do is wait until I've left the room before you fall about yourselves in hysterics.'

The thought that Slick might truly be angry with him struck fear into Dunk, but when he opened his eyes to take a look he saw the halfling smiling down at him and shaking his head. 'I take it you're sticking with the team,' Slick said with a chuckle of his own.

Without thinking another second about it, Dunk nodded yes. 'It's strange, I know, but this game, this team, has got into my blood.'

Dunk wiped his face dry and spoke seriously. 'After my family's fall from grace, I wandered around lost and alone for a while. I didn't know how to get back the life I once had, and truthfully I didn't know if I wanted it.'

He put his arms around Spinne once more. 'With Blood Bowl, I found everything I ever wanted: good friends, true love, and a purpose in life. What more could I want?'

'You're insane, kid,' Lehrer said. He hadn't laughed with the others. He hadn't even cracked a single smile.

'I may have tumbled backward into this life,' Dunk said, 'but it's my life. I'm not going to let the Guterfiends or anyone else take it away from me without a fight.'

Dunk heaved the last remnants of his breakfast over the gunwale of the *Sea Chariot* as it churned onward through the open seas to the south of Estalia. He'd never cared much for ocean voyages, but he seemed to be getting worse about them as he got older. He knew that once he finally got rid of everything he'd eaten, he'd be fine. It would be a long trip to Barak Varr, and he'd have lost a few pounds by the time they got there, but he'd survive.

Spinne handed Dunk a skin of Hater-Aid. Dunk didn't normally care much for sports drinks, but they seemed to be the only thing he could keep down when onboard. He thanked her for it, taking care not to assault her with the scent of his breath as he did so.

'Dr. Pill says he has something that can settle your stomach,' Spinne said as she rubbed a comforting hand up and down his back.

'Somehow, I don't find that news reassuring,' Dunk said. He looked over his shoulder and saw the skinny elf raise the eyebrow over his white patch at him with an expectant grin. 'I think I'll take my chances with the seasickness. I can't believe we brought him along.'

'After how much good he did for our team in the *Spike!* magazine tournament, Pegleg became his number one fan. He offered him a year's contract after the finals.'

'You're not making me feel any better,' Dunk said, remembering what the apothecary had done to him to get him back on his feet during the game against the Oldheim Ogres.

Slick strode up next to Dunk and leaned next to him on the gunwale, which rose to the top of the halfling's head. 'What luck, eh?' Slick said.

Dunk retched again, and then wiped his mouth on his sodden sleeve. 'I don't feel lucky,' he said.

'Not that, son. I'm talking about the Dungeonbowl. When we destroyed the Reavers – or rather as they self-destructed – I hadn't thought that it would cost the Grey Wizards their chosen team for their upcoming tournament.'

'I thought for sure that Bombardi would just rebuild the team in time for the start of the games,' Spinne said. 'I'm surprised he let the sponsorship get away from him.'

'More likely it was summarily yanked from his clutches,' Slick said. 'The Grey Wizards may have a lot of faith in the Reavers' management, but they like to think their team should have a shot at winning the tournament. It's hard to rebuild a top-ranked team from scratch in less than three months. If Dirk had stuck with Bombardi, they might have had a chance, but to literally lose every decent member of your team…'

'Did we really kill all of the Reavers?' Dunk asked. 'We must have got more carried away than I'd thought.'

Slick shook his head. 'Some of them died at our hands, true, but the fans took care of the rest. They were furious that the Reavers made the best game in the region not get past the first five minutes of play. Seats for a game like that aren't cheap, you know.'

'No one hurt Dirk, did they?'

Slick snorted. 'A few of them tried, but he made quick work of them.'

Spinne leaned over to look at Dunk, who still had his head and arms hung out over the gunwale. 'You still haven't talked to him?'

Dunk shook his head. 'I couldn't find him before we left Magritta. You'd think he was the one with a price on his head. I left a message for him at the Bad Water, though. Sparky said he'd deliver it if he saw him.'

'Good idea,' Spinne said. 'That was always his favourite watering hole in town. If he hasn't left town already, he's sure to end up there.'

Dunk slumped down with his back against the gunwale, sitting next to where Slick stood. 'He told me something else funny too. Sparky, I mean. He said he hated Gunther the Gobbo with a passion.'

'Who doesn't?' asked Slick. 'He's as loved as the plague.'

'But Gunther was waiting for me that night Sparky showed me the secret tunnel out of the Bad Water. He said Sparky was his friend. That's why he knew about the secret tunnel and where it let out.'

'So the Gobbo's a liar now?' Slick said in mock horror. 'Quick, someone get me Lästiges! This is big news!'

'One of Sparky's real friends probably owed Gunther some money,' Spinne said.

'Maybe,' Dunk said. 'It just seems strange. I mean, he was right there waiting for me.'

'I wonder how Lästiges is doing,' Spinne said. 'She and Dirk seemed to be getting fairly serious.'

'You think she'll dump him now that he's quit playing Blood Bowl?'

Spinne shrugged. 'She's always been a glory hound. Dating an ex-player isn't nearly as glamorous as being seen with someone who's still in the game.'

'Yet another good reason for me to stay with the game myself,' Dunk said. He fended off a half-hearted punch in the arm from Spinne. 'Don't you find professional athletes intriguing?' he asked her playfully.

'I spend far too much time with them,' Spinne said. 'They mostly bore me to tears.'

'I guess I'll have to try harder to entertain you,' Dunk said.

'Don't bother,' Spinne said. 'You're the exception that proves the rule.'

Cavre walked across the deck of the ship towards the trio at the gunwale, a wooden bucket swinging in one hand. He moved with the surety of a man who'd spent many an hour on the sea, a broad smile on his face.

'Dunk,' said Cavre. 'The captain would like to see you.'

Dunk's stomach twisted again at the idea of having to chat with Pegleg. They hadn't said much to each other since the victory ceremony and trophy presentation at the end of the *Spike!* magazine tournament. Dunk had spent all his time avoiding the public eye while his coach had basked in it.

Pegleg had worked a long time to forge a championship team, and he seemed determined to make the most of it. Every time Dunk sat near a crystal ball, it seemed that one reporter or another was interviewing Pegleg about the Hackers and their victory. Some of the questions inevitably centred on Dunk and the price on his head.

'What's it like when your star player has a massive price on his head? Doesn't a million crowns seem a bit excessive?' one goblin asked on ESPNN (the Extraordinary Spellcasters Prognosticated News Network).

Pegleg smiled and said, 'We're very proud of Mr. Hoffnung and his contributions to the Hackers, so we understand why this mysterious malefactor would value him so highly. However, I'd like to question the authenticity of this mad wizard's bounty. It's clear he doesn't have the kind of treasury required to back up such an amazing offer.'

'Are you saying Schlechter Zauberer is a liar?'

'He's clearly insane. Is he a liar if he's mad enough to believe his own ludicrous tales? Let's just say I doubt there's a reward of any kind and leave it at that.'

Pegleg had hammered at the same point over and over, on every show that would have him: CNN (Corpse-Necromancer News), CBS (Crystal Ball Service), NBC (Nymphomantic Bardic Casters), ABC (Auguristic Bestial Clairvoyants), and even Albion's ITV (Itinerant Telepathic Visionaries). The most incredible spot had been on the 'Impaired and Unbalanced' Cox News, which aired live the night before the Hackers set out from the port city of Luccini on the south-west side of the Tilean Peninsula.

'Don't you think that this Dunk Hoffnung placed the reward on his own head as a means of distracting the people of the Empire from noticing the fact that no one in power in Altdorf has any clothes?' asked anchorman Dill O'Really.

'Are you saying nudity is now in fashion in Altdorf?' Pegleg said with a leer.

'By avoiding my question, you're tacitly acknowledging Hoffnung's part in the vast daemon-winged conspiracy that operates politics in the Old World these days.'

'Nothing of the sort, Mr. O'Really, such accusations sound like they might have come only from the mind of a madman like Mr. Zauberer himself.'

The interview had gone sour when O'Really consulted an unfurled scroll on his desk. Then he glanced over his spectacles at Pegleg and asked, 'Are you aware of Dunk's family history?'

'Tryouts for the Bad Bay Hackers don't involve taking a detailed biography of prospective players. I just care whether or not they can play the game.'

'According to this report published three years ago in the Altdorf Augur, the Hoffnung family was part of a vast scandal involving organised crime, mutant skaven, and the blackest sort of magic.'

'I don't judge a man by the members of his family.'

'Well, maybe you should. It seems that the Hoffnungs were all run out of town with torches and pitchforks after your friend Dunk got in a fight at a party celebrating his engagement to Lady Helgreta Brecher.'

Pegleg looked like a halfling caught in a battle train's headlights. 'Of Brecher International Conglomerated Holdings?'

'Exactly!'

'Well, Blood Bowl teams are filled with killers and worse. That's what we pay them for, after all. I don't see how a simple brawl would be any of my concern.'

O'Really held a painting up for Pegleg to see. 'This is an artist's rendition of what happened that night. Do you see all the daemons flying around, tearing and rending flesh?'

'That's appalling, Mr. O'Really. I didn't know that B.I.C.H. employed daemonic help at their galas.'

A smug grin festered on the commentator's face. 'Those daemons you see came to help your Dunk kill a man, Helgreta's older brother Kügel.'

'Well,' Pegleg said with an uneasy smile. 'At least he got the job done right.'

'So you condone the use of daemonic forces in disputes? Can we expect to see you employ such resources in your next game?'

'Only in the finals.'

O'Really didn't laugh.

'Can't the captain come out here to talk to me?' Dunk asked. 'I'm busy communing with the open sea air.'

Cavre shook his head. 'You know it doesn't work like that.' He handed Dunk the bucket he carried. 'Try not to make too much of a mess. His mood is worse than usual.'

Dunk rolled his eyes as the next wave caught the ship's bow. 'How much worse can it get?'

'That's the kind of question a wise man never asks.'

Dunk got to his feet, clutching the bucket before him in both hands. He nodded his goodbyes to Spinne, Slick, and Cavre before heading to the captain's cabin. 'If I'm not back in ten minutes, dive overboard and save yourselves,' he called back.

Dunk knocked on the captain's door and heard the man call, 'Enter!' Then he slipped inside the cabin and shut the door tight behind him.

Dunk had been on many other ships, but he'd never seen a captain's cabin like Pegleg's. The windows and portholes had all been painted black and covered over with thick, red curtains, which made the place as dark as a cave. Scrolls, furled and unfurled, filled every nook and cranny of the room that didn't have a bit of furniture crammed into it or a framed picture hung on it. These featured scouting reports on all of the teams the Hackers might have to play, including rosters, health reports, playbooks, and even the kinds of dirty tricks each team had historically favoured or was known to have in production.

A massive crystal ball sat perched on a low table in one corner of the room. A scene from the *Spike!* magazine tournament finals played within it, sending a ghostly light flickering around the room. The only other light came from an oil lamp that hung from the ceiling over the red velvet couch on which Pegleg sat hunched over the low, wide table before him. Papers of all sorts covered the table, held in place by the *Spike!* magazine trophy, a mithril spike held in a mailed and spiked fist thrust upward in victory.

'Sit, Mr. Hoffnung,' Pegleg said, gesturing towards a chair across the table from him.

Dunk did as he was told. He folded his hands atop the bucket in his lap and waited for his coach to speak. When, after several minutes, it didn't seem like that would ever happen, Dunk opened his mouth and said, 'I want to thank you for sticking up for me, for telling everyone that the reward was a hoax. I think it–'

'Daemons, Mr. Hoffnung?' Pegleg used his hook to push back his yellow tricorn hat. He had worn so many holes in it that it was in tatters.

'I can explain.'

'There are many things I can abide in a player, Mr. Hoffnung, but even I have to draw the line at consorting with daemons. If that's how you intend to conduct yourself, I'll speak with Slick about selling your contract to the Chaos All-Stars.'

Dunk perched on the edge of his seat. He thought that maybe Pegleg would be upset with him, but he hadn't expected to be traded away – especially not to the Chaos All-Stars. That was a team with a reputation for forcing players to stick to the letter of its contract by unspeakable means.

'But, coach, I didn't consort with daemons. Don't tell me you're going to take O'Really's word for it.'

Pegleg leaned back in his couch and brushed his long, dark curls from his shoulders. 'Of course not, Mr. Hoffnung, if I had, you'd have already found yourself on your way to meet with your new employers. Why do you think I called you in here?'

Dunk looked down at his bucket. 'Some kind of cruel torture for having to answer questions about the reward on me while you'd rather have been crowing about our victory?'

Pegleg allowed himself a thin smile. 'Perhaps under happier circumstances. As it is, I need you to explain yourself.'

Dunk closed his eyes and felt the motion of the ocean in his stomach. He'd hoped that he'd put that part of his life far behind him, but he knew better. As the price the Guterfiends had put on his head illustrated, you carried every bit of your history with you wherever you went.

'I DON'T REALLY know what happened,' Dunk said. When Pegleg scoffed at this, Dunk raised his eyes and continued. 'Okay, I know what happened to me, but I'm still not sure why.

'You've been to Altdorf, so you've probably heard of the Hoffnungs. We were one of the wealthiest and oldest families in the city. I can trace my ancestors straight back to the place's earliest days.

'Over the centuries, our influence waxed and waned. In my grand-father's day, we hit one of our low points and had to sell almost everything. He hanged himself in disgrace when my father was just twenty years old.

'From the family's point of view, that was one of the best things that could have happened to us. My father and grandfather had often butted heads. Grandfather stuck hard and fast to the old ways, while my father advocated moving into new businesses and investing what little money we had aggressively while we still had it. With Grandfa-ther gone, the reins of the business fell into Father's hands, and he made the most of it.

'By the time I was born, the Hoffnung fortune had been revived and the family had become a vital part of Imperial culture once more. Father proved to be an excellent businessman and a cunning student of Imperial politics.

'When I came of age as a young man, my father arranged a match between myself and Helgreta Brecher. Our wedding was meant to join far more than ourselves. It would marry the city's largest fortune with its sharpest entrepreneurs.'

'Didn't you have any say in this?'

Dunk snorted softly. 'Not much, but I didn't much care either. Helgreta was pretty enough – a sweet young lady, really – and I was willing to do whatever Father asked of me. He impressed upon me how important this merger of our two families would be, and I was ready to play along.

'It all seemed to be going well until the night of our official engagement party, which the Brechers held in their family keep, right in the heart of Altdorf. Although we'd been betrothed to each other for years, the party signalled that we would be married within the year.'

Dunk stopped speaking for a moment, his eyes focused on something far beyond the confines of Pegleg's sealed cabin. 'She was so beautiful that night. She gave me a scarf of the finest silk as a symbol of our impending union.' He raised a hand to his neck where he had worn it.

'Towards the end of the night, Helgreta's brother Kügel accosted me. He'd had a great deal to drink, so I tried to give him his space. He pursued me though, accusing me and my family of worming their way into his family over nothing but gold.'

'Wasn't there a bit of truth in that?'

'Of course. We all knew it. These sorts of marriages happen all the time in Imperial society, and if Helgreta and I didn't have any problem with it, I didn't see what Kügel had to get angry about. And I told him so.

'He didn't take that well at all. He went and found a ceremonial sword hanging in the front hall of their estate, and he came back to the ballroom with it. Everyone stopped and stared at him. The band's instruments froze in their hands.

'The guards – who worked for the Brechers, of course – stayed right where they were. They weren't about to stop the heir to the Brecher fortune from doing whatever he wanted. Nüsse Brecher, the patriarch of the clan, stood up and told Kügel to sit down before he made more of a fool of himself, but Kügel attacked me instead.

'As a rising nobleman, I hadn't been in too many real fights, but I'd been trained in the arts of war since my childhood. Kügel had spent his days writing poetry and swilling wine. When he came at me with the sword, I snatched it from his hand, shoved him away and then held the blade to his neck.

'Now, keep in mind that this is the brother of my fiancée. Although he'd attacked me in his own home, I could see that he was drunk and upset. I had no desire to humiliate him further, much less hurt him.

'Then the most amazing and horrible thing happened. A trio of armoured daemons wielding burning whips and swords smashed in through the skylights over the ballroom and brought the massive chandelier hanging there crashing down to the floor. It crushed several people to death.'

Dunk glanced back at Pegleg and saw that the man was holding his breath.

'They stood eight feet tall on their cloven hooves, not counting the tops of their large, leathery wings. They bore crimson tattoos on their charcoal-coloured skin, which glowed like burning embers in a hot breeze. Their eyes were black, polished marbles, like those of a shark. Long horns thrust from the fronts of their skulls, curling back on themselves again and again. They stank of sulphur, and it hurt to stand in the heat of their presence.'

'How terrible,' Pegleg said. He'd inched away from Dunk as the story unfolded, and now he sat curled up in the far corner of his velvet couch.

'The worst part was how they claimed to know me. One of them pointed his burning sword at me and said, "Do not fear, Dunkel Hoffnung. We will protect you."

'With that, the others used their blades to slice Kügel into bite-sized portions. He was dead before he could scream about it. I blinked, and the floor in front of me was filled with wet pieces of Kügel.

'Helgreta screamed. A lot of people screamed, actually. I think I screamed. Then everyone ran.

'With one daemon standing in front of me, I didn't see a clear path from the hall, so I hacked at it with the sword I'd taken from Kügel. I stabbed the creature clean through the heart, and it howled in pain and then disappeared in an explosion of hot ash.

'I couldn't see a thing. Then someone knocked the blade from me, and two sets of hands grabbed me by my arms and hauled me into the air.

'When I emerged through the shattered windows and into the night sky above, I saw the remaining daemons had me. They laughed as I screamed at them in protest. A few moments later, they deposited me just inside the gates of my own family's keep. Then they flew off into the night, and I never saw them again.'

'By Nuffle's sacred rulebook,' Pegleg said. 'That's an amazing story, Mr. Hoffnung. Is any of it true?'

Dunk stared at the ex-pirate. For a moment, he considered throwing something at him, perhaps the bucket in his hands. Then he realised that telling the story had distracted him so much that his body had forgotten to keep being seasick. He felt fine.

'Every word of it, Coach,' Dunk said.

Pegleg shook his head. 'I'm so sorry to hear that, Mr. Hoffnung.'

Dunk didn't know what to say. He couldn't read the captain at all, even as the man unfolded himself from the corner of the couch.

'Do you believe me?' Dunk asked.

Pegleg arched his eyebrows at Dunk. 'I take it no one in Altdorf did.'

Dunk shook his head. 'My parents did. My father knew what was coming though and started packing to leave right away. My mother just sat there in shock. She couldn't understand what had happened and how it would affect us all.

'When the mob showed up on our doorstep – led by a platoon of Imperial soldiers – she went to open the door. I'd been helping my father pack, and we'd lost track of her.'

Dunk closed his eyes. He didn't think he could go on. He'd got this far through the story that he'd never told anyone since he'd left Altdorf – not Slick, not Spinne, not even Dirk, who'd left the Hoffnung home a year before the incident. He had to finish it.

'The mob tore my mother apart. We had no idea what she'd done until we heard her screams. By then, it was already too late.

'Father showed me a secret passage out of the estate. It opened up near a public stable, and he purchased us a pair of horses there.

'"They'll be looking for two men riding together," he said. "Best if we split up for now. Meet me at the summer estate near Marienburg when you can."

'That was the last I saw of him. The city's gates were locked at night, so I hid in the alley behind the Skinned Cat until dawn. Well after midnight, a drunken sot stumbled into the alley to look for a place to sleep. I paid him to trade clothes with me and keep his mouth shut, which he did as soon as he passed out again.

'As dawn broke over the city, I mounted up again and rode for the northern gates. I heard some people in the street gossiping about the daemonic attack, but no one recognised me. Once I left the city behind, I rode hard until Altdorf – my birthplace, the only real home I'd ever known – disappeared in the distance.'

'Did you ever see your father again?'

Dunk shook his head. 'I went to the summer estate, but word of the incident at the Brecher keep travelled fast. I couldn't stay there long. I rode into Marienburg in disguise and took work as a warehouse guard there, down near the wharf.

'Every day I had a break, I rode back out to the estate to hunt for a sign of my father. One day when I got there, I found a host of people using the place. Some of them I recognised as our servants.

'I rode into the place, hoping to find my father taking some sun in the gardens, this whole nightmare over. When the servants spotted me, they turned white as sheets. One of them raced into the house, shouting for help.

'"What is it?" I asked the ones still left. "Where is my father?"

'Lehrer emerged from the estate then and strode out to talk with me. "Your father is not here," he said.

'"Fine," I said. "I'm glad you came ahead to prepare the place for him. It's a terrible mess."

'"Your father is dead," he said. Just like that. I nearly fell off my horse.

'"Our new employers – the Guterfiends – are here," he said. "If they find you, they will kill you. You must leave. Now."

'When I tried to protest, Lehrer grabbed the reins of my horse and turned it around. Then he slapped it on its hindquarters and sent it – and me – galloping off.

'"Don't come back – for your own good!" he shouted after me.'

Dunk sat there in silence for a moment, watching Pegleg's impassive face. 'Do you have anything in here to drink?' Dunk asked. 'An afternoon of vomiting and talking dries a man out.'

PEGLEG RETRIEVED A bottle of wine and a pair of glasses from a cabinet near the still-glowing crystal ball. He removed the cork with the tip of his hook, decanted the wine into the glasses and handed one of them to Dunk. Then he raised his glass in his good hand for a toast.

'To living with our daemons,' Pegleg said. He took a large mouthful of the wine and swirled it around his tongue before swallowing it. 'And to grinding the bastards into bloody paste.'

'Hear, hear.'

Dunk drank deeply of the wine, and then shoved his glass forward to be topped up. Pegleg obliged him, and then re-corked the bottle with his hook.

'So,' Dunk said, 'do you believe me?'

Pegleg arched an eyebrow at Dunk. 'Why wouldn't I, Mr. Hoffnung? Have you shown yourself to be less than trustworthy in the more than two years you've been with my team?'

Dunk waited for his answer.

'I am haunted by daemons of my own, Mr. Hoffnung, and I don't mean the metaphorical kind. I've seen the kind of creatures you describe. In fact, I once worked for them as their slave.'

Dunk's eyes opened wide.

'Given your own experiences, do you find this so hard to believe?' Pegleg stroked the back of his hook with his good hand as he spoke.

Dunk shook his head, and then nodded. 'Yes – I mean, no. I don't doubt that someone who travels as much as you do has encountered daemons before, but I would never have guessed they'd enslaved you.'

Pegleg swirled his red wine in his glass and took another sip. 'I wasn't always a coach, you know – or a pirate, for that matter. In fact, I was never much of a pirate.

'I used to be a fisherman, like my father before me and his father before him, back as far as we knew. My family lived on the south shore of the Sea of Claws, in a little town so small that no one had ever bothered to give it a name. Those who knew where it was lived there, and few others cared about it at all.

'Now, of course, it's not there at all. Nothing more than the burnt skeletons of a few buildings standing along that distant stretch of shore.'

'What happened to it?'

Pegleg gave Dunk a thin smile. 'Mr. Hoffnung, will you allow me to tell my own story at my own pace, to make my own decisions about how to present the facts as I saw them?'

Dunk flushed red and nodded his apology.

Pegleg stared into the wine sloshing about in his glass for a moment before he continued. 'I was little more than a boy, but I'd served on my father's boat from the moment I could tie a sheepshank. We'd taken in a good haul that day and were sailing home with the harvest of our nets when I saw the smoke rising from our little seaside hamlet.

'At first, we didn't know what to do. If someone had destroyed the town already, there seemed little profit in racing in to add our souls to the pyre. On the other hand, if any were still alive, we knew we could not abandon them there. Soon enough, we decided to drop anchor a hundred yards out and swim in, hoping we could slip in unnoticed.

'When we reached the beach, the sun hung low in the west. My father and I slipped forward into the nearby forest and then circled around to the back of the hamlet. We entered the settlement near our home, where we'd left my mother and sister that morning.

'As we crept closer, we heard screams coming from the house. Before I could stop him, my father dashed from the safety of the leafy cover and charged into the house, holding his filleting knife before him like a cutlass. I followed straight after him, my own knife out and at the ready.

The shingles on our house caught fire just before we entered the place. Smoke filled the main room to the rafters, but we forged our way into it anyway, following the sounds of my sister's screams. Coughing on the smoke, we reached my parents' bedroom and thrust open the door.

'I will not describe the scene we found therein. I can see every detail of it whenever I close my eyes. The mercy of sleep never takes me far from it, and I cannot escape it in my waking hours.

'My mother was already dead, and my sister followed soon after. The daemons we found in that room with them – crimson skinned monsters with snakes for eyes and limbs – smashed consciousness from us.

'My father and I awoke in chains in the lower hold of a massive ship I later discovered was called *Seas of Hate*. We lay huddled there for I know not how long, recovering from our wounds. There were others in there with us – some from our hamlet but many from parts unknown. Not all of us were human, but we were all imprisoned together.

'From time to time, someone would lower a bucket of boiling gruel or filthy water into the hold, and we would squabble over it. We had to eat the food with our bare fingers while it was still scalding hot or it would have disappeared before we could even have taken a bite.

'Sometimes they would come for us. A noose of barbed wire snaked through the hatch above and ensnared some hapless soul and hauled him up and out of our lives. Then the hatch slammed shut again, leaving us in the darkness once more.

'They caught my father first, perhaps a few days after we were captured. Maybe weeks. I thought I might never see him again, but I refused to weep before my fellow prisoners. Instead, I began to plan my escape.

'I had lost everything that had ever meant anything to me – all but my life. I intended to hold on to that with everything I had, and I swore to myself I'd kill whoever I must to keep myself alive.

'When they finally came for me, I went willingly. I actually grabbed the noose and held it with my hands, letting them pull me up by my wrists rather than my neck.

'The same sorts of daemons I'd seen in my family's home set me down on a bench, shackled my left hand to an oar, and put the oar in my hands. They used the whip on my back straight away to impress their will upon me, but they didn't need it. I knew what they expected of me, and I planned to deliver it without pause or complaint – at least until I saw my chance to escape.

'As I set to building up the blisters that would turn to calluses on my hands, I peered around. There were at least two dozen rows of oars working to move that hateful ship through the water, with three men – or creatures – dedicated to each oar.

'At least two of us would row at a time, with the third sometimes lying collapsed at our side, sleeping from sheer exhaustion. We were never all allowed to rest all at once, and if our reptilian masters wished for more speed, we would all set to our oars with respite for none.

'A pair of daemons licked their long lashes out over the oarsmen, one to the fore and one aft, while a third kept beat on an ogre's skin stretched over the mouth of a deep kettle drum.

'I spotted my father rowing three rows ahead of me and on the other side of the aisle. I tried to speak to him once, and I had my back laid open for my troubles. But I knew that he'd seen me, and for the moment that was enough.

'After countless weeks under those conditions, I still hadn't seen my chance to make my break. A few others had tried it, and they had been struck down before they reached the gunwale. The snakeheads on the daemons' limbs bore terrible venom. A single bite was enough to kill a man within minutes, leaving him a shaking, frothing wreck, bleeding out through his liquefied eyes.

'Some of the captives sought that 'blessed bite,' as they called it, their chance for final release from that horrific life. The daemons were sparing in their use of it, if only because they didn't want to lose too many of their slaves in one go.

'My father's strength eventually gave out. One day, he slumped over his oar and did not move. When the overseers lashed his skin, he did not cry out in pain or even flinch. One of the daemons ran him through with a spear to make sure he was dead. Then they drew up his body and tossed him overboard to feed the school of sharks that many of the prisoners claimed constantly followed in our wake.

'I knew then that I could not stand another moment. As night fell, I spied a nearby shoreline through my oar's hole, and I set to work on my chains in the darkness. I knew I could not remove them, but in the madness of my grief an option came to me that I had not considered before.

'If I could not break my chains, then I would leave behind that which they held.'

The captain held up his hook and watched it shine in the lamplight, a sad but proud expression on his face. Horror ran through Dunk's gut as he gaped at his coach.

'You took off your own hand?' Dunk asked. 'With what?'

Pegleg laughed bitterly, exposing his teeth. The ones up front were made of gold, and they seemed as sharp as razors now in his mouth.

Despite the cabin's warmth, Dunk shivered.

'Once I was free,' Pegleg said, 'I charged for the gunwale. As I cleared it, I felt something sharp sink deep into my ankle. I reached back with my hand to grab the snakehead I found there, and I pulled it and its daemonic owner after me into the briny deep.

'The tales of the sharks proved to be no legend. Once I fought my way back towards the surface, I could see a dozen fins circling in the lantern light that the daemons on the ship shone out at us, laughing at their sport.

'Knowing the wound on my arm would draw the sharks to me, I swam hard for the shore. I could barely see it in the darkness, just a strip of grey caught between the dark of the sky and the sea, but I knew it had to be there, so I pulled myself towards it.

'As I went, I could feel the daemon's venom working its way into the wound from its bite, numbing my nerves as it crawled upwards from my ankle. I didn't know what would kill me first: the sharks, the poison, or the daemon pursuing me through the waves.

'The daemon struck out at me again, its snake-arm tagging me on the same foot as before. Having found purchase in my flesh, it tried to pull me back towards it. Before it could bring me within reach of its other limbs, something pulled it back down into the water, and its grip on my ankle was gone.

'The creature emerged a moment later, screeching and howling in a way I'd never known. I could smell blood in the water, which began to churn beneath the daemon, just before it was hauled down one last time.

'I put my back to the scene and swam for my life. As I went, I could feel my poisoned leg starting to grow cold. Despite this, I kept swimming as fast as my limbs would carry me.

'The first time I felt the shark, it hit me in the side, just with a glancing blow. The massive beast seemed to have decided that the feeding frenzy going on behind me was too much trouble – or that human flesh tasted better than the daemonic variety.

'Perhaps the shark was a daemon itself, or maybe it had just been living in the wake of daemons for too long. Either way, something had gifted it with a sharp malignance I'd not seen in any animal before or since. It didn't just want to eat me; it wanted me to know who was doing it.

'The beast hit me again, this time in my leg. As it came around for a third pass, I saw its entire head emerge from the water, and it looked me straight in the face with its dead-black eyes. I was only yards from the shore, and yet I knew I would never make it – and so did that thing.

'I watched the shark as it circled me and came in for the kill. As it did, I curled my legs under me. When it struck, I kicked out with my poisoned leg and jammed it as far into the bastard's gullet as it would go.

'The damn thing nearly choked on the limb. As it chewed on my flesh, I thrashed about, trying to kick out its brains from its insides.

'Soon enough, I felt myself become a great deal lighter. While the beast gnawed on my limb, I set to dragging myself through the last bit of surf and onto that sacred shore.

'A wave came along and carried my bloodied carcass all the way to the sand. I hit the ground hard, and it almost knocked me senseless. For a moment, I feared the riptide would sweep me back out to sea, but I managed to find purchase in the waterlogged sand for long enough to hold out.

'I hauled myself out on to that shore and bound my wounds with torn strips of my tattered clothing. I thought for sure I'd die during the night, but my will to live was too strong. I made it through to the dawn.

'Some fishermen found me then and carried me back to their village. Their wives tended to me there, nursing me back to health, although I would never be whole again.'

Pegleg tapped the end of his wooden leg on the floor, as if for luck, and gazed down at his missing parts. When the captain raised his eyes again, Dunk realised he must be staring at his coach in horror, and he looked away.

Pegleg sat there in silence, his story apparently done. Dunk couldn't stand the quiet and had to speak.

'And from there you went on to coach the Hackers? What about you being a pirate? Is that all just a sham?'

The coach smiled, wider this time, and picked up the bottle of wine to fill their glasses again, emptying it. 'My Blood Bowl career is a tale for another time, Mr. Hoffnung. I think we've bared enough of our souls for one day. As for me being a pirate, I often find it's easier to let people believe what they like – especially if it can be turned to your advantage.'

Dunk nodded and got up to leave. 'Now I understand your fear of water,' he said. 'Don't get me wrong. You're one of the bravest men I know. I don't think you'd ever get me on a boat again if I'd gone through that.' He glanced around the sealed-up cabin. 'Even like this.'

'Yes,' Pegleg said. 'I'm not one to let my limitations limit me any more than they must. Dr. Pill has been working with me on that detail as well. He seems to think I'm ready to try a short stroll on the main deck. I think I'll take his advice.'

Pegleg rose to his feet. He seemed a bit unsteady, but whether that was from the sea, the wine, or his nerves, Dunk could not tell.

'Could you get the door for me, Mr. Hoffnung?' Pegleg said as he limped towards the thrower.

'Aye, captain,' Dunk said. He unlatched the door, pulled it open and held it wide for the man.

Pegleg nodded his thanks and then stumped his way on through, out into the crisp, night air of the open sea. Dunk waited for a moment, seeing the captain's cabin empty for the first time since he'd known the man. Then he left as well, shutting the door behind him.

'DUNKEL? WHO ARE the bad guys?' M'Grash asked for the third time.

'The Dwarf Giants,' Dunk said, just as he had each time. He knew that pre-game stress often destroyed what small powers of concentration the ogre had, and there was little use in getting steamed about it. If anything, it kept his own mind off his fears.

'Dunkel? Who are the good guys?'

Dunk smiled. 'The Hackers. The guys in green and gold, just like you.'

'Not enough!'

'True,' Dunk nodded. 'Normally we'd play with the full team in the Barak Varr Bowl, but remember the 75th anniversary game two years back? We beat the Champions of Death?'

M'Grash grinned, and not for the first time Dunk gave thanks that this was not his foe, but his friend.

'That tournament had gone so well that they decided to keep using the original rules for Dungeonbowl. There's only six players on a side, and we move about using magical teleportation pads.'

'Dunkel? How those work?'

Dunk grinned. 'You just step on them and – poof! – You're gone.'

'Gone?' M'Grash clutched Dunk in fear.

'Gone somewhere else, big guy. The wizards of the Colleges of Magic set up for the game in the dungeon. The dwarfs built it for them.'

That seemed to calm the ogre's nerves a bit.

'Dunkel?'

'Yes?'

'Who are the good guys?'

Dunk put his face in his hands.

Spinne jumped in to help out. 'It's okay, M'Grash. There's you, me, Dunk, Edgar, Guillermo, and Cavre. That's all six. That's all we get for this game.'

M'Grash smiled at Spinne. It had taken him a while to realise she was with the Hackers and not a 'bad girl' anymore, but once he had he'd taken a real shine to her.

'Spinne? Are others dead?' Tears welled in the ogre's eyes. He could dismember a troll without blinking, but the thought that his friends might be killed sometimes put him into hysterics.

'No. They're right behind you.'

M'Grash turned and saw the other five Hackers, Pegleg, Dr. Pill, and Slick looking up at him from a sitting area on the far side of the locker room. He gave them a nervous, little wave, and they all waved back with the same level of enthusiasm.

'What about him?' M'Grash asked, pointing at Dunk's neck. Before the game, Dunk had taken Skragger's shrunken head and hung it around his neck on an iron chain. He'd paid a handsome coin to make sure that the necklace's mounting would keep Skragger from biting him in the neck. The last thing he needed was for the black orc to take a gouge out of his throat. A steely ball gag forced between Skragger's tiny fangs provided another layer of insurance against that.

'Slick thought I needed something to make me seem more fearsome on the field. I thought this would do the trick,' Dunk said. 'He doesn't count as a player – or much of anything else.' The thrower turned the tiny head around to look at its face, and its wide, white eyes glared at him from its wrinkled, black eye sockets. Skragger growled something at him, but the gag muffled it.

'Are you ready?' Dunk asked the ogre as he dropped Skragger's head back into place on his chest. 'The game's about to start.'

'Dunkel?'

'Yes?' Dunk shouted, finally pushed far enough to show his frustration with his massive friend.

'Why so tense?'

Dunk closed his eyes. Before he could say anything, he heard the sound of a piercing whistle over the PA system, and the game was on.

Cavre led the way, dashing on to the glowing circle on the floor in front of him. Once he disappeared, Edgar charged after him, followed by Guillermo and Spinne.

'Go, M'Grash!' Dunk said, shoving the ogre from behind.

'Don't have to shout,' M'Grash said as he crept towards the teleportation pad. He put his big toe on it like he was testing the water in a dark and chilly pool, and then he disappeared.

Dunk chased right after the ogre. When he popped into the dungeon, he ran right into M'Grash's back.

'I move,' M'Grash said, jumping out of Dunk's way and heading for the sole exit from the room.

Dunk picked himself up off the floor, which had been painted with the Hackers' logo and name, with gold letters on a green background. The letters seemed to have been done in real gold leaf, which Dunk knew fitted with the level of dedication the dwarfs had to the game.

Drawing the lot to face the Dwarf Giants – the most popular of the dwarf Blood Bowl teams – in the opening round of the Dungeonbowl tournament had put the fear of the gods into the Hackers. Pegleg had taken to walking about the practice area, muttering and grumbling, since he'd heard the news, and it had put a scare into all of the players.

The rookies were glad to not have to play, it seemed. Once when Guillermo had bruised his knee during practice, one of the more promising new recruits had burst into tears. Fortunately, Dr. Pill had been able to make the lineman as good as new in no time.

Having played in the tournament two years ago, Dunk knew exactly what the Hackers were in for, and that had terrified him even more. The dwarfs were renowned for using strange – sometimes crazed – devices in their games. They'd come up with a new dungeon this year, just for this event, and knowledge of its arrangement had been kept protected like a state secret.

Of course, everyone suspected the Dwarf Giants were in on the new layout. Lästiges had even aired an investigative report on it for Wolf Sports. Blaque and Whyte, the two Game Wizards that seemed to have been assigned to her, led her around the labyrinthine halls and tunnels of Barak Varr to show her viewers that any such suspicions were unfounded.

In one segment, unchaperoned by the GWs, Lästiges had interviewed a dwarf by the name of Dimlet. They'd met in a secluded booth in the House of Booze, a legendary watering hole in the dwarf city. The dwarf had a white stripe that ran right through his black hair and beard, making him look something like a walking skunk, and his seedy clothes and weasely demeanour only added to the impression.

'Yeah,' the dwarf said, 'it's all a sham, isn't it? The good lords of Barak Varr would never do anything to help out their own boys for a game as vital as this now, would they? Never happen in a million years, right?'

Lästiges leaned in close to the dwarf for a moment, and then leaned right back, her eyes watering from his scent. 'Are you saying,' she said through her coughs, 'that the Dwarf Giants were given the plans for the new Dungeonbowl dungeon?'

'Do you know that dwarfs is all related? We breed like rabbits, and the orcs is the only things keeping us in line. Every one of us is someone's brother or sister or someone else's cousin. You think it's easy to keep secrets in a family, do you? Even one the size of that?'

'But do you have any proof that this is so?'

Dimlet scoffed, and then one of his eyes rolled back into his head. The other stayed riveted on Lästiges. 'What's "proof"? What's good enough? If I said I'd seen this happen, would it matter? If I had a letter from the Council of Barak Varr to the Dwarf Giants, would that help? If I could show you a meeting of these blackguards on a Daemonic Visual Display, would that be good enough for you?'

Lästiges's eyes shone with lust for the big scoop she scented, or maybe from Dimlet's stench. 'I think our viewers would find such evidence compelling,' she said.

'I can have those things forged for you in a day,' Dimlet said. 'Less if you can double the standard rate.'

The interview had ended there, but the debate had continued. Was Dimlet some kind of crook, or had the Dwarf Giants sent him to Lästiges to throw her off their track?

In the end, Dunk decided it didn't matter. There were some things about the game he could control, and this wasn't one of them. He ran through the door, chasing after M'Grash.

'All the players are in the dungeon now, Jim, but we still don't have a ball. Where do you think they're hiding it?'

'Well, Bob, if you hadn't made a pre-game snack of that young dwarf you found passed out on Bugman's XXXXXX, you'd be conscious enough to remember that the ball's hidden in one of the six chests scattered throughout the dungeon.'

'Does that mean there are six balls?'

'Just one ball, Bob; if the players open a chest that doesn't have a ball in it, it explodes! What more fun could you ask for from a game?'

'Gee, that sounds dangerous, Jim. Has anyone warned the players?'

'Go back to sleep, Bob.'

The next room featured a river of lava that cut across it, disappearing underneath the walls at both ends. A high bridge went over it, and Dunk saw M'Grash just coming off the other end of it and trying to decide which of the two facing doors he should go through.

'Stay here, M'Grash!' Dunk called as he topped the bridge himself. The last time the Hackers had played Dungeonbowl, the Champions of Death had put a few of the players right in the Hackers' own end zone, and getting past them had been horrible. 'You're on defence. If you see a dwarf come through here, stop him. If he has the ball, take it.'

M'Grash nodded at everything Dunk said, but Dunk knew that didn't mean he had understood all of it. M'Grash could only remember an order or two at a time. Anything more complicated risked him losing track of it all.

'Scratch that!' Dunk said. 'Just stay here and knock down any dwarf you see!'

M'Grash grinned at that and gave Dunk a big thumbs-up.

Dunk glanced around and saw something glowing up at him out of the lava below. Shielding his eyes against the heat, he picked out the edges of a teleportation pad right there in the molten rock. To get to it, he'd have to leap off the bridge. He reasoned that the wizards who designed this place would only ask someone to take a risk like that if there was a correspondingly worthwhile payoff.

On the other hand, some of those wizards had a wicked sense of humour.

'Can't win the game without taking some chances,' Dunk muttered, repeating the words that Pegleg and Cavre had tried to hammer into the Hackers over the past few months. They hadn't played any official games since the *Spike!* magazine tournament, and the coach had worried about the players getting rusty. He hadn't wanted to risk any injuries before the Dungeonbowl tournament, but that didn't mean he couldn't browbeat the players into being mentally tough – although that seemed to have backfired with M'Grash.

Dunk vaulted over the bridge's low railing. The heat from the magma nearly flash-roasted him as he neared it, but before his feet even touched the teleportation pad he found himself somewhere else.

After the blazing light from the lava, it took Dunk a moment to adjust to the darkness around him. When his eyes finally cleared, he clamped them shut again. Then he peeled them open slowly.

Dunk looked down first and saw the teleportation pad through which he'd passed. It took up the entirety of a slab of rock that seemed to be floating in midair, four torches ringing it around its base. Pitch blackness yawned below it.

Looking up, Dunk saw the same thing: nothing. The light from the pad and the torches never reached the ceiling – if there was one.

The only thing Dunk could see was a series of stones just like the one he was on, stretching ahead of and behind him like a string of steppingstones. A yard or two separated each of them. Had it not been for the torches ringing them, Dunk didn't know if he'd have been able to pick them out of the darkness.

In the distance in either direction, Dunk spotted a portal leading out of the room. It seemed to hover in midair, like a doorway cut from the fabric of night.

'Look, Bob! Hoffnung's found the Bottomless Pit Room. What luck for the Hackers! As first on the scene, he'll have first shot at that chest hovering below him. Amazing!

'Bob?

'Bob?'

Dunk laid down on the rock hovering beneath him and peered over the edge. There, only a couple of yards below him, hung another rock. This one had no torches around it, which is why he'd missed it the first time he'd glanced down. It did, however, carry a small, wooden chest.

'Oh, and look! Here comes Helmut Krakker, the Giants' new captain. Sure was a shame what happened to his predecessor – Gurni Rockrider – during the *Spike!* magazine tournament, eh? I've never seen just a beard left behind like that before. Usually there's at least some part of the chin attached to it!'

Dunk glanced up just in time to see a dwarf in navy and gold armour leap from the doorway to the first of the floating rocks in the string. If the thrower didn't move fast, the dwarf would be on him in seconds.

Dunk lowered himself over the edge of the floating rock he was on. His boots dangled just a foot over the chest below. It would be a good drop for a dwarf, but Dunk didn't hesitate to let go. He landed squarely on the chest and then slid off it to the rock below.

Dungeonbowl chests were never locked, Dunk knew that, but he hesitated for a moment. There was a good chance the chest would explode, and if that happened he'd be lucky if the blast was the only thing that hurt him. If he got knocked off the rock, there was no telling what might happen to him.

Then Dunk noticed a handle sticking out of each side of the chest. He got down on his knees and grabbed the one on the left. As he did, he heard Krakker land on the rock next to the one above him.

Dunk drew a deep breath, held it, and then opened the chest.

It exploded in his face.

Dunk couldn't see, hear, or feel anything for a moment – nothing but the pain and shock of the explosion. Once his head started to clear, he discovered the handle of the chest still in his hand, and he smiled. When he looked down at the handle, though, he saw nothing attached to it but his fingers. Then he noticed how windy it seemed to be. That, coupled with the fact that he didn't see anything below him, told him he was in deep trouble.

He screamed.

11

DUNK KNEW HE was dead. Any second now, the unseen ground below him would rush up and crush him into paste…

…Any second now.

His voice became hoarse from all the screaming, and he stopped to clear it.

Any second…

Something popped into view below him: a series of lit spots stretched like a string of pearls across the darkness. As he approached them, he realised that they looked just like the set of rocks he'd just fallen from.

The pearls grew into rocks, and Dunk wondered just how deep this bottomless pit was. If he could fall so far and then come upon another set of stepping stones like the last… It seemed impossible.

Dunk zoomed up to the rocks, and then past them. As he did, he saw someone moving along the stepping stones far to his left: a dwarf in navy and gold armour.

A suspicion popped into Dunk's head, and when he zipped past the remains of an exploded chest on a rock hovering just below the line the others made, he knew what had happened.

'Help!' he yelled. 'Heeelllppp!'

It did him no good.

'Hey, Bob! Bob? Ah, never mind,' said Jim's voice.

'Well, folks, it looks like Hoffnung has finally twigged to what's happened to him. While a bottomless pit is impossible, of course, the Colleges of Magic built the largest simulation of such a tired old cliché that I've ever seen. They set up a wide matrix of overlapping teleportation pads at the bottom of this massive chasm. Their pairs are set up on the ceiling of the chasm, upside down. When a victim – I mean, player! – gets within a few inches of the bottom of the chasm, he teleports to the ceiling before he hits the floor, and thus he never stops falling.

'That's my favourite kind of trap: clever *and* cruel!'

If Dunk hadn't been so terrified, he might have been able to admire the inspiration and craftsmanship that had gone into torturing him so effectively. It seemed like a lot of trouble to go to just to remove a player from a game, but Dunk had long ago learned never to under-estimate the public's hunger for its sports stars to find new ways to be destroyed. He could almost hear the audience cheering now.

Dunk had no idea how he could get himself out of this. Even if he managed to get one of the Hackers to help him – he knew the Giants would just laugh at him – what could they do? If they tried to catch him, the impact would probably kill them both. Even M'Grash wouldn't be able to rescue him from falling what seemed to have already totalled up to a couple hundred feet.

The line of rocks appeared in front of Dunk again, signifying that he'd been teleported back up to the vast chamber's ceiling. He noticed that his stomach flipped every time that happened, and he seemed to hover for a moment just before he started falling again. That meant, he thought, that the teleportation killed his downward momentum. When he reappeared at the ceiling, it was like he'd just been dropped from that height for the first time. Otherwise, he'd have kept acceler-ating downward until he passed out.

At first, Dunk didn't know if this meant anything to him, either for good or bad. This time, when he zipped past the stepping stones, the glow from the teleportation pad that covered the rock in the centre of the line gave him an idea.

If he could somehow angle himself towards that rock and hit the teleportation pad, it might safely teleport him someplace else. If it killed his downward momentum, like the other teleportations seemed to, he'd land gently on the ground wherever he happened to end up.

Of course, if he was wrong, he'd wind up as a large red splash in that same spot.

Coming up with the idea was one thing. Putting the plan into action was something else entirely. Dunk stuck out his arms and tried flapping them like a bird.

'Look, folks! The pressure seems to have caused Hoffnung to crack. He thinks he's playing for the Eagles!'

Dunk snarled at the joke, but he couldn't let it distract him. He didn't know how many times the teleportation pads would keep working for him. It was possible that they'd all shut off once someone won the game, and unless one of the Grey Wizards saw fit to save a member of the team that had just lost the tournament for them, he'd be doomed.

As Dunk neared the bottom of the chasm, he readied himself. The moment his stomach flipped, he reached up and swatted his arms above him. His hands slapped into the ceiling, and propelled him backward, towards the rock with the teleportation pad.

'Dunkel!' M'Grash said as he barged into the room. 'Save Dunkel!'

'No!' Dunk said. If M'Grash tried to grab him, they'd both be hurt, maybe killed. 'Go get the ball! Leave me!'

The ogre didn't seem to hear a word Dunk said. He charged forward, leaping from one steppingstone to the next. As he went, Dunk saw the rocks sag and bounce in midair. The sorcery that kept the stones hovering in space seemed barely strong enough to hold M'Grash.

Dunk knew that this would be his last clear shot at the teleportation pad. After this pass, M'Grash would officially be too close for comfort. He angled towards the rock, putting his hands in an arc over his head like the cliff divers he'd once seen leaping into the ocean from insane heights on the southern shores of Tilea.

'Save Dunkel!' M'Grash shouted as he sprinted towards his friend.

'No, M'Grash!' Dunk said. 'No!'

M'Grash dived for Dunk just as he hit the teleportation pad. Dunk tried to roll away from him at the last moment and only succeeded in turning his back on the ogre. Then he felt his body slam into the ogre's arms, and everything disappeared in a flash.

Dunk and M'Grash popped into another place. Dunk looked about, and at first glance he knew that they hadn't died and ended up in some kind of afterlife – at least not any of which he'd ever heard. Every surface of the room had a mirror polish, and it seemed there were lots of them.

'Dunkel not dead!' M'Grash said as Dunk pulled himself off the ogre. 'Huzzah!'

Dunk smiled down at his friend. Despite the fact that the ogre had almost ended up getting them both killed, Dunk couldn't get mad at someone who'd tried to save his life. Then he remembered what he'd told the ogre when they'd split up.

'Why aren't you back in the room with the river of lava?' Dunk asked. 'Didn't I tell you to stay there?'

M'Grash's face fell as he nodded at his friend. 'Then Dunkel said, 'Help!' I heard Dunkel. Dunkel says, 'Help!' very loud.'

Dunk slapped himself on his forehead as M'Grash got to his feet. 'You're right,' he said to M'Grash. 'I need to be more careful about what I ask for.'

'Mama tells me that too,' said M'Grash. As the ogre spoke, his voice trailed off to nothing. 'Who are they?' he asked.

Dunk looked around them and saw what had confused M'Grash. The room had been set up as a chamber of mirrors. There didn't seem to be many things in it beyond the mirrors, other than Dunk and M'Grash – and an unopened chest. However, the reflections they saw made it seem like there might be a dozen of each of those things, and that made it nearly impossible to tell which image might be real.

'They look like friends,' M'Grash said, although he seemed unsure of his judgement.

Dunk stepped forward and put his foot out at a chest. His toes struck a mirror instead. He moved back a step and then spat at the mirror. His saliva ran down its slick surface, marking it. As he looked around, he saw the mark on another nearby image, so he could rule that one out as real too.

'M'Grash?' Dunk pointed at where he'd spat on the mirror. 'Think you could do that to every other mirror in this place?'

'Dunkel want me to spit on people?'

'No. Don't spit on us.'

'Dunkel just did. Look!' The ogre pointed to where Dunk's spit ran down his own face.

'That's just...' Dunk arched an eyebrow at M'Grash. 'Never mind. Can you just spit at the chests – and hurry.' Dunk thought he heard someone coming. Instead of the stomping feet of a human or dwarf, it sounded something like the stamp of metal-booted halflings, distant now, but coming closer.

M'Grash hocked up something evil from deep inside his chest and then began to spew it about in all directions. Not wishing to depend on the ogre's sense of what constituted a 'chest' – Dunk had a chest of his own on the front of his upper body, after all – he worked hard to stay behind the ogre, where the creature's spit could not reach.

That's when one of the Dwarf Giants rolled in – literally. The dwarf player sat in the saddle of a monstrous steam-driven machine fronted by a steel-spiked cylinder of stone that stood almost as tall as Dunk.

'Uh-oh,' said Jim's voice. 'It looks like Zam Boney has found a dwarf death-roller, and he's not afraid to use it!'

Dunk and M'Grash stared at the machine as Boney forced it through the doorway and onto the mirrored floor. The glassy material there cracked and crumbled as the death-roller moved across it, shattering it into countless thousands of pieces. The dwarf riding the machine shouted something – a threat, no doubt – but Dunk couldn't hear it over the engine's noise. Then the thing came straight at them, picking up speed as it went.

'Run!' Dunk said, turning and grabbing M'Grash's hand, and hauling the ogre along behind him.

'Devices like the death-roller are strictly against the rules, of course,' Jim's voice said, 'but who cares when they're so much fun! Besides which, what are the chances of the referee stumbling into the right room to spot it – especially when two of the Giants are busy drowning him in the merdwarf room!'

As the two Hackers took off across the room, Dunk felt grateful that M'Grash had managed to mark as many surfaces as he had, no matter how disgusting the method. Otherwise, he knew, they'd have bounced into one mirrored wall after another until the death-roller had crushed them under its tremendous, spiked mass.

'Dunkel!' M'Grash shouted.

Dunk glanced back over his shoulder and saw that the death-roller was almost on them. Boney cackled so loudly that Dunk could hear him, even over the roar of his accelerating machine as it bore down on him and M'Grash.

The ogre grabbed Dunk and thrust him to one side as he dived for the other at the last instant. Boney seemed to have a hard time deciding which of the Hackers to go after, perhaps hoping to take them both out at the same time. Instead, he missed them both, but only by bare inches.

As Dunk scrambled to his feet, he watched Boney race past and then put the death-roller into a controlled slide that ended with the machine swivelled around and pointing back in his direction. The Giant pointed at M'Grash and held up an index finger. Then he pointed to Dunk and held up two fingers, indicating the human would go down last.

Dunk held up his middle finger in response, and then howled in dismay as the machine took off after M'Grash. Despite its size, the death-roller moved so fast that Dunk knew he could never catch it on foot, not in a straight-up race. He needed something to even the odds.

He scanned the area around him, hoping to spy something – anything – that could help. Then his eyes fell on what he'd been looking for before: a small chest.

Dunk dashed over and picked up the chest. At that moment, he was less interested in how it could help the Hackers win the game than he was in how he might use it to stop Boney dead.

'Hey, you sawed-off, half-pint, runt of a litter of dwarf-orcs!' Dunk shouted at Boney. As the Giant turned to look at the thrower over his shoulder, Dunk raised the chest over his head and waved it about like a red flag in front of a bull.

Boney reached over and hauled on a lever as he wrenched the steering wheel to the left. This sent the machine into a hard spin that nearly threw the dwarf from his seat, but it put the death-roller on a path towards Dunk, still moving at top speed.

Dunk glanced left and right, and discovered he'd found the chest in a mirrored cul-de-sac. There was nowhere for him to go. When Boney realised the thrower's predicament, he tossed back his head and loosed a loud cackle that rang out over the engine's noise.

'Well, folks, it looks like the Hackers better put in their order for a Dunk Hoffnung-sized coffin,' Jim's voice said. 'Boney has the thrower dead to rights, and he seemed like he had such promise too.'

Dunk thrust the chest up over his head and then hurled it straight into the death-roller's path. It bounced once, and then landed squarely in front of the machine's spiked roller.

When Boney saw Dunk start to throw the chest at him, the dwarf knew what the Hacker meant to do, and he hauled back on the death-roller's brakes and yanked the wheel to the right. The thing's forward momentum was too much for it to stop that quickly, though, and the machine skidded right into the chest.

Dunk held his breath and waited for the explosion. Instead, all he heard was a loud crunching noise, followed by a muffled pop.

The death-roller smashed into one of the cul-de-sac's walls, and Boney catapulted out of his seat and crunched into the wall right after it, leaving a wet, red streak on the mirrored surface as he slid down it. Dunk raced forward and spotted the remnants of the chest poking out underneath the machine's rear wheels. The death-roller had reduced it to little more than splinters, but Dunk spied a few shiny spikes sticking up out of the wreckage.

The Hacker scrambled underneath the death-roller and snatched the flattened football out from beneath it. The heat from the boiler that drove the machine's steam engine threatened to bake the skin from the back of his arm, but he gritted his teeth and ignored the pain. As he pulled the pancake of a ball free from the wreckage, he heard a high-pitched whistle start to shriek from the steam engine.

A rivet shot out of the engine's casing and zinged over Dunk's head like a bullet from a sling. A fine spray of scalding water and steam followed it, and the pitch of the whistling rose to an ear-splitting crescendo.

Dunk tucked the flat ball under his arm and sprinted away from the machine. He didn't get ten feet before he ran past M'Grash. As he did, he grabbed the ogre's hand and tugged the big guy after him, shouting, 'Run!'

Just then, the steam engine exploded. The shockwave knocked M'Grash and Dunk flying across the room, skidding along the floor's silvery surface to come to a crashing halt in a pile against the far wall.

'M'Grash?' Dunk asked as he mentally took inventory of his body parts. Although a bit squished, everything seemed to be there.

The ogre nodded. 'Dunkel alive!' he shouted with glee.

'Hey, buddy,' Dunk said. 'Are you all right?'

The ogre nodded again.

'Then can you get off me so I can breathe?'

M'Grash leapt off his friend and helped him to his feet. 'Sorry, Dunkel,' he said, blushing.

'It's all right.' Dunk plucked the flat ball up from the ground and held it up for M'Grash to see. 'It was worth it.'

'THE HACKERS HAVE the ball!' Jim's voice said. 'The Hackers have the ball. Now all they need to do is get it back to their end zone to score. Remember, folks, in Dungeonbowl, the first to score wins the game!'

Dunk cursed the camras scattered throughout the dungeon. If he'd been thinking, he might have tried to hide the ball from them – and everyone else – a bit longer. Sure, Jim would have eventually figured out that if the chest hadn't exploded then it must have had a ball in it, but as an ogre Jim wasn't the sharpest knife in the corpse.

'Let's get to the end zone,' Dunk said to M'Grash. 'How did you get in here?'

The ogre pointed to the door through which he'd come.

'Then lead the way, big guy,' Dunk said with a grin.

M'Grash lumbered forward like a galloping elephant, and Dunk paced after him, stuffing the flat ball underneath his breastplate to keep it safe. In the confines of the dungeon's passages, M'Grash's head and pauldrons scraped the ceiling and walls. Unlike the other players, the ogre rarely wore a helmet. They were hard to find in his size, and his skull was harder than any helmet could be.

The hall ended in a wall of water. It stretched from floor to ceiling, and it splashed as M'Grash thrust his right arm through it.

'Hold breath, Dunkel,' the ogre said. Dunk did as he'd been told, and M'Grash scooped him up and charged into the water.

Dunk opened his eyes in the water, which was as clear as that in a nobleman's pool. He wondered for a moment if it was all just an illusion, and he thought about testing it by trying to breathe. Then he saw the corpse of a dwarf dressed in a Giant's uniform float by, and he decided against it.

Dunk couldn't tell where they were going, but M'Grash seemed to know. He moved without hesitation, pushing himself and Dunk through the water on his powerful legs.

In Dunk's limited experience, ogres weren't much good at thinking, but if you gave them a clear task – like 'let's get to the end zone' – they put everything they had into completing it. M'Grash set to his job like a starving dog to a fresh steak. Dunk had no doubt they would get through the water in record time.

As the doorway on the opposite side of the room came wavering through the rippling water, Dunk spotted something large and grey coming towards them like a rocket. The face full of huge, vicious teeth told Dunk that this was the largest shark Dunk had ever seen. It looked like the thing might have been able to swallow him alive, and he had no doubt it would tear M'Grash's flesh to tatters with its trap-like maw.

Dunk tapped M'Grash on the shoulder and pointed towards the shark. The ogre shouted out in fear, losing most of the air he'd held in his lungs. A warm, yellow cloud formed around the ogre's waist, but thankfully M'Grash kept moving forward and left it far behind.

Before the shark could strike at them, something thick and brown charged into the water through the doorway and met the prehistoric monster head on. The shark snapped at it with its massive jaws, but Edgar's trunk was too wide around for the creature's teeth to find purchase on it, and his bark protected him from the deepest scratches.

Dunk and M'Grash burst out of the standing wall of water and into the room beyond, the ogre hacking and gasping for air. While Dunk's lungs held far less than M'Grash's, the thrower hadn't panicked when the shark had appeared, and he was the better off for it.

'Hold it right there,' Dunk said after helping pound the water out of M'Grash's lungs. 'I think I spotted something back there.'

Dunk stuck his head back into the water and opened his eyes. He was right. There, just off to the left of the doorway, a wooden chest rested among a stand of seaweed. If M'Grash hadn't made such a wake behind him, shoving aside the weeds as he went, Dunk doubted he'd ever have seen it.

Dunk peered around and saw that Edgar had shoved one of his branches straight down the shark's gullet and was flinging the hapless creature all around, as if his own arm was just a shark from his elbow down. Since Edgar didn't need to breathe in the way that the other players did, the water posed no threat to him. This meant he could tackle the shark with an aplomb any other player had to envy.

Seeing no other threats, Dunk shoved his way into the wall of water and plucked the chest from the weeds. Then he turned and hauled it back into the airy room where he'd left M'Grash.

When Dunk broke through the water, a horrible roar assaulted his ears. He blinked the water out of his eyes and saw a Dwarf Giant standing across the torch-lit room. Unlike the other Giants, this one wore a large pack on his back and dark goggles over his eyes. His black beard, which bristled like a chimney brush, had been cropped short, and he carried a torch in his hand, from which ran a hose that attached to the bottom of the tank.

'Nuffle's smoky joe!' Jim's voice said. 'Weber 'Toasty' Grilmore has caught up with Hoffnung and K'Thragsh. Let's see how they handle him and his legendary flamethrower!'

The dwarf pointed the torch at Dunk – who now noticed that the end of it hissed at him – and said, in a voice that came from lungs that seemed to breathe through a burning pipe, 'Give me that chest. You have until three.'

Dunk hesitated.

'Three!' the dwarf yelled as he pulled a lever on the bottom of his torch. Fire leapt from the tip of the torch like a hungry dragon, reaching for Dunk and the chest in his hands.

The heat singed Dunk's skin and hair. If he hadn't already been soaking wet, he might have gone up in flames right there. Being water-logged gave him an extra moment to live, and he used it to do the only thing that came to mind: he shoved himself back into the watery room.

The fires that had been starting to smoulder on Dunk went out immediately as the cool waters enveloped him. He glanced backward to see that Edgar had split the shark in half and left the carcass float-ing in the water. Other, smaller sharks, which Dunk hadn't noticed before, dived into the tendrils of blood as they curled out from their massive cousin and churned the water with their maddened feeding on the fresh-made chum.

Dunk knew he had to stop Edgar from walking into the airy room. He didn't want to face a flamethrower himself, but it turned him pale to think about what such a weapon would do against a treeman like Edgar, waterlogged or not. Being underwater, he could not speak and would somehow have to signal his warning, and perhaps some kind of plan.

Before Dunk could attempt this, M'Grash came splashing in from the room beyond, his skin ablaze, the water turning to steam as it smothered the fires on the ogre. Edgar caught M'Grash before the ogre could float to the ground, but when the treeman turned the blitzer over, Dunk saw that the ogre's face was already turning blue. In his haste to get away from the flames, M'Grash must not have taken a breath before leaping into the water. If Dunk didn't do something soon, his humongous friend would die.

Dunk sprinted out of the water and into the room, where he found Grilmore working a pump handle that came out over his shoulder from the tank on his back.

'Back for more, eh?' the dwarf growled. 'I'll be right with you.'

'Don't!' Dunk said. 'If you want this so badly, you can have it.' With that, he tossed the chest high in the air. It bounced once, and then rolled to a stop under Grilmore's raised boot.

'Wise for a beardless one,' Grilmore grunted. 'Now git!'

The flamethrower spat fire at Dunk once more, and he dived backward into the water behind him to avoid it. Once safe in the cool liquid, he glanced back and saw M'Grash grasping at his throat, strangling on a lack of air. The ogre only had seconds left.

Dunk pressed his nose up to the edge of the water and peered through it into the room beyond. There he watched as Grilmore leaned over and opened up the chest.

The first explosion smacked into the dwarf and sent him flying backward. He landed on his tank, hard, and it sprang a leak, but Grilmore was as tough a dwarf as they came. The blast only stunned him, and he shook it off before he'd even stopped rolling.

Dunk cursed his luck. All the dwarf had to do now was camp out there in the room and wait. In scant seconds, M'Grash would have to charge back into the room for a breath, and Grilmore would flash-fry him that same instant.

But it seemed as if the dwarf was a bit more stunned than he had let on. As Grilmore pushed himself to his feet, he used the hand that held his torch on a tube. It touched the black, viscous fluid leaking from the tank and raced along it until it hit the reservoir.

The second explosion filled the room with raging fire. The shockwave smacked into the water and drove Dunk flipping backward and deeper into it. The water actually receded from the doorway from the force of the blast. When it rebounded back, it overwhelmed the magic keeping the water from plunging through the portal, and it surged through and into the room beyond.

The coursing water dragged Dunk, Edgar, and M'Grash into the room where Grilmore had just been. There was nothing left of him, from what Dunk saw, but a few shreds of his armour attached to the flamethrower's burst-open tank.

The flood carried the three Hackers through that room and into the next. There, Dunk spied Spinne, who had been facing off against a white-bearded dwarf racing along on a steam-powered bicycle. She had managed to grab onto a torch sconce as the waters raged through the room in a flash flood, but the dwarf hadn't been so lucky. The wall of water had knocked the bike flat, and since he was strapped to it, the dwarf had been sucked under the swirling mess.

'The river of lava is next!' Spinne said. 'Then the end zone!'

'Thanks!' Dunk said as the water dragged him past her. 'I love you!'

'Isn't that just too damn cute, folks?' Jim's voice said. 'It just makes you want to gag yourself with a snotling's toes.'

Dunk cursed at the announcer as the new-made river dragged him from the room. Before he could even complete his sentence, he found himself in the room with the lava river – or at least in the room where it had been.

When the water hit the lava, it transformed into steam that curled into the air and filled the room until it was thicker than any fog. It might have been hot enough to parboil anyone nearby when it first hit, but by the time Dunk and the others got there, the lava was submerged three feet below the water line.

The water carried Dunk straight over the river – which still glowed through the cracks forming in the dark crust of cooler rock that had formed on the lava's surface – and deposited him on the other side. When he regained his feet, he turned back to see M'Grash and Edgar stuck on the river's other side. Being heavier than Dunk, they would have scraped the skin right off that river of lava and maybe been burned to death. Edgar had figured this out and managed to catch himself in the hallway leading into the room, and he had caught M'Grash too before the ogre went sailing past or through him.

Dunk waved at the others, and then dashed towards the end zone, just on the other side of the portal ahead of him. Before he could reach the room, another dwarf stepped out into the now-receding waters and stood his ground in front of the doorway.

'Give me the ball,' the dwarf snarled at Dunk. He had no strange weapon in his hands, he sat astride no vicious vehicle, but he didn't need any of these things to exude danger.

The dwarf stood taller than any dwarf Dunk had ever seen – and nearly as wide. He wore his beard in a forked braid, and his head had been shaved, leaving behind only a high-crested, bright orange fan of hair straight down the centre. He bore tattoos on nearly every inch of his body, and he wore no armour, only leather straps fitted with spikes, wound around his arms, chest, knees, and fists.

Dunk yelped, and threw his arms wide to show that his hands were empty.

'Where is it, manling?' the dwarf asked, stalking closer to the thrower.

Dunk stepped to one side and pointed back at Edgar and M'Grash standing on the other side of the river of lava. They'd already started for the stone bridge that arced high over the river, and they would be there in seconds.

The dwarf raced off to take on the others, and Dunk didn't care to lay odds against him, despite the fact he faced an ogre and a treeman together. Something in Dunk rebelled at leaving his friends to face such a foe on their own, but he had a job to do as part of the same team on which they played.

Dunk spun on his heel and dashed into the room where the Hackers' end zone sprawled. Once there, he reached under his breastplate and pulled out the flattened football. He held it up to the camra standing in the corner, and smiled for the viewers at home.

'Hoffnung scores a touchdown!' Jim's voice said. 'Wake up, Bob, you ancient sot! You just missed one hell of a game! The Hackers win!'

THAT NIGHT, DUNK settled into a cosy corner of the House of Booze with Spinne, Slick, and M'Grash. The place hadn't changed much since they'd been there two years ago, although Spinne hadn't been with them then. She'd just survived a cave-in during a Dungeonbowl game, which had killed four of her team-mates.

Dunk had later learned that M'Grash had been responsible for that cave-in, something he didn't think he'd ever share with Spinne. He glanced at the two of them chatting happily with each other over their drinks, and decided that perhaps it was for the best.

Dunk had visited a number of taverns in Barak Varr – the dwarfs took great pride in their drink and sampled and shared it often – but the House of Booze was still his favourite. He like Ye Olde Trip to Araby – the oldest tavern in the dwarf kingdoms – too, but he and Dirk had been banned from it two years ago when they'd torn the place apart in a brotherly brawl.

The carved stone ceilings of the House of Booze arched higher than those of a cathedral, and Dunk realised that the place served as a church in a sense. The patrons who came here worshipped no gods, but good friends, food, and drink – and not necessarily in that order. From the clouds of smoke that collected under some of the highest arches, Dunk knew that some of the people were here for a good pipe instead.

The best thing about the place was the way it welcomed people of all stripes. The private booth at which the four sat stood open at one end, but each of the benches on the other three sides could be adjusted to different heights. Slick sat up high on one wing, Dunk and Spinne sat at a standard height in the back, and M'Grash sat down low on the other wing. None of them had to hunch over or stand on a stool, and they could enjoy their fare and each other in comfort and peace.

Dunk raised his stein of Torin Oakencask's Deep Shaft, a black brew concocted in the farthest depths of the dwarf lands. Rumour had it that the brewmeisters used actual ore in the drink's production. Dunk didn't know if that was what made it thick enough to stand a knife in, but he liked it.

'To the Hackers,' he said. 'And to victory.'

The others all joined in, clanking their steins together. Here, even M'Grash had a stein of his own, instead of his usual barrel with the top torn free. It was so large that Slick could have bathed in it – and later in the night might have been tempted to try.

'Winning,' M'Grash said. 'It beats losing.' The skin on his arms and face had already started to heal over. Dr. Pill had given him something to help the process along and to take care of the pain, and it seemed to have worked. M'Grash had been nothing but smiles all night. Nothing fazed him for a moment. Even when he'd tripped over that group of orcs on the way in, he'd just kept walking, not even noticing that he'd crushed one under his heel.

'I like that,' Slick said. 'I think I'll have that put on a T-shirt with your face on it. I'll give you ten percent.'

'Deal,' M'Grash said. He grinned so hard the skin on his face split again, but he didn't seem to notice.

'Shouldn't he have had his agent negotiate that for him?' Spinne asked the halfling.

'Of course!' Slick nodded to Spinne and Dunk, and then turned back to M'Grash. 'As your duly appointed representative in all matters financial, I urge you to take the T-shirt deal, M'Grash. It's a good bargain for you, and I can vouch for the licensee's honour and integrity personally.'

M'Grash furrowed his brow and then looked at Dunk for advice. The thrower smiled gamely and nodded. The ogre reached out to shake hands with Slick, a grin on his face. 'Deal!' he said as the halfling's hand and forearm disappeared in his fist.

'Isn't that a conflict of interest?' Spinne asked. 'I'd like my agent to be more independent than that.'

Slick put on a look of mock dismay. 'Sweetheart,' he said, 'first, you're talking about agents. Honesty and agency are not synonymous.

'Second, what could be more honest? I proposed and executed the deal here in the presence of my client and gave both him and his good friends the chance to comment and even intercede. How many other agents do you think bother going to that kind of trouble?

'Most agents would just set up the T-shirt deal with an old pal and never let their client know who they were really negotiating with. Not so with Slogo Fullbelly! I'm as above board as an agent can get.'

Spinne squinted her eyes and frowned at Slick, but Dunk and M'Grash laughed along with the halfling. After a moment, she joined in with them as well.

Dunk took a pull from his stein. As he savoured the rich, bitter flavour, he smiled. Here he had the three people who mattered most to him in his life – except Dirk, of course, who seemed to have cut himself out of Dunk's life. Despite that, Dunk felt happy, and he wanted that feeling to last.

Then someone pushed a tall stool up to the far side of the table. Stuck in the back of the booth, Dunk couldn't see who it was that meant to join them. He heard whoever it was climbing the ladder built into the back of the seat.

When the newcomer's head cleared the table, Dunk dropped his beer. Fortunately, this happened often enough in the House of Booze that the dwarfs had designed the steins to right themselves if possible, and this one did, letting only the barest dribble of the Deep Shaft spill over its edge.

The man who sat in the stool across the table from Dunk looked older, but no wiser. His clothes looked as if he'd been sleeping in a nest of hungry rats, and he smelled something like that too. Somewhere along the line, his nose had been broken, and it had healed poorly, leaving it with a downward bend. His hair might have been greyer – a great deal more white showed in his scraggly beard – but Dunk couldn't be sure of its colour under the layer of filth the man wore with a comfort borne of long companionship.

'Hello, Dunkel,' the man said, his voice a bit rougher too. 'How have you been?'

Dunk didn't say a word. He couldn't. His tongue refused to work. All he could do was sit and stare at this ghost from his past come back to haunt his present.

Spinne and Slick stared at Dunk for a moment, waiting for him to say something, anything. M'Grash, ever oblivious, took a long draught from his beer and then waved at the man.

'Hi,' the ogre said. Then he pointed at himself. 'M'Grash!'

The man wiped his hand on his soiled tunic. Realising that it wasn't any cleaner, he reached out and performed the same task with a napkin instead, leaving a grimy residue on the cloth. Then he stuck out his hand to M'Grash.

'I've seen you play,' the man said as he shook the ogre's hand. 'You're very good.'

'Since when did you ever watch Blood Bowl?' Dunk asked. The question blurted out of him without him even thinking to ask it, and now it lay there between them.

The man recovered his hand from M'Grash and gave Dunk an easy smile. 'Since you and your brother started playing it. I never saw much use in it before that myself. It's not the stage or the opera, but I've come to appreciate it at its own level for what it is.'

'Which is?'

'An alternative to war, of course.' The man waved down a waiter and said, 'Bring a bottle of your finest Montfort, and I'd like to see a menu too, please.'

Dunk slumped back in his seat, stunned.

'I'm Spinne,' the catcher said. 'I don't think I caught your name.'

'There's not much you don't catch, miss,' the man said. 'I've seen you play too. I'll consider it a compliment to have got anything past you.'

'You haven't yet,' Spinne said, wearing a smile that barely covered a bulldog's snarl. 'I'd like to know who you are.'

The man shook a finger at the woman. 'I like that. I really do; sharp, direct, and unafraid of confrontation. Unusual in a woman, especially in these parts, but I find it unnervingly attractive. I see what Dunk finds exciting about you. You'll go far, miss.' He put out his hands in a wide shrug. 'Hey, you already have.'

Spinne's smile closed, and she turned to Dunk. 'Perhaps you could identify our dinner guest for us.'

The man raised his eyebrows and shrugged at Dunk. 'That's your call, Dunkel. We have a lot of catching up to do. Whether you care to share that with your friends is up to you.'

Dunk shook his head at the man. He didn't know how he felt about this yet, but it surprised him how easily the man could still push his buttons.

'Spinne, Slick, M'Grash,' Dunk said looking at each of them in turn and then at the man again. 'I'd like you to meet Lügner Hoffnung, my father.'

Spinne gasped. M'Grash stared back and forth at Dunk and Lügner, confused as ever. Slick reached across the table as best he could and offered his hand, which Lügner took.

'A pleasure, sir,' the halfling said. 'I've often wondered who could have had a hand in raising such a fine boy as you have in your son here.'

Lügner flashed a grin, which grew wider as his drink appeared. 'I'm afraid you'll have to blame most of Dunk's upbringing on his blessed mother, gods rest her soul.'

'Oh, you're just being modest.'

'No,' Dunk said, staring at his father through sunken eyes. 'He's not.'

Lügner looked abashed. 'Come now, Dunkel,' he said. 'Is that any way to speak to your father?'

'How would I know?' Dunk asked. 'I haven't seen you for over three years. We never did have much to say to each other.'

Lügner nodded as he glanced down the menu. 'All too true, I'm afraid,' he said. 'All too true.' Then he turned to the dwarf waiter who stood ready to take his order. 'I'll have the steak Bordeleaux, medium rare, light on the blue cheese, but heavy on the onions.'

'Excellent choice, sir,' the waiter said before gliding off towards the kitchen on a set of tall, metal stilts.

'What are you doing here?' Dunk asked. 'I thought you were dead.'

'You thought wrong,' Lügner said with a devilish grin, 'but you can take comfort in knowing you weren't the only one. I wanted the world to think I was dead. Life, I find, is much easier that way.'

'What are you doing here?' Dunk repeated. He didn't bother to ask his father if he knew about the Guterfiends and Lehrer and all the rest. He knew he did.

Lügner took a long draw from his stein and smacked his lips in satisfaction. 'Well, I usually prefer to leave business for after the meal. I find it aids in the digestion to put such things off until then. But I can tell from your demeanour that you're anxious to get started. Where would you like me to begin?'

'How about with the angry mob killing my mother and sister, and running us out of town?'

Lügner's smile faded. 'Yes. You would want to know about that, wouldn't you?'

'What happened to you?' Dunk asked. 'I went to the summer house. I checked in there for you every day for weeks. Then Lehrer ran me off the property because someone else had taken it.'

'The Guterfiends,' Lügner said with a grim nod. 'I'd heard they'd ended up with the place, but I hadn't guessed they'd take ownership so soon.'

'I thought you were *dead*,' Dunk said, his voice cracking on the last word. He grimaced to hold his emotions in check.

'I can see why,' Lügner said. 'I wanted everyone to think I was dead. Even you.'

'Why?'

Lügner snorted at himself. 'Face it, Dunkel. You were better off without me. I'd never done anything but put you and the rest of my family in constant danger just by living with me. You saw what that did to your mother and sister. I didn't want to have that happen to you too.'

'So you did it for my own good?' Dunk asked. 'You just wandered away and let me think you were dead and gone for three years out of your concern for my wellbeing?'

Lügner winced. 'Well, that was what I thought would be a pleasant side-effect of my central reason, which was to escape the people who wanted me dead.'

'It looks like that worked well,' said Slick. Dunk shot him a murderous look, and the halfling sat back in his seat again.

'Why did the Guterfiends want you dead?'

Lügner let a wry smile play on his lips. 'They didn't, really. They didn't even know me. Oh, sure, they knew of me, and they wanted me out of their way, but it wasn't anything personal.'

'Not personal?' Dunk couldn't believe his ears. 'They killed your wife and daughter, ran you off your estate, took everything you owned, and 'forced' you to arrange for everyone to think you were dead.'

'No, Dunkel,' Lügner said. 'You're jumping to conclusions. You've got it all wrong. The Guterfiends didn't care about me or anyone else who lived in our keep. They just happened to work for the same people. Once we were out, they were in. It was that bloodless and simple – at least to them.'

Dunk stared at his father. 'Then who did all that to us?'

'Khorne,' Lügner said.

Dunk felt Spinne recoil next to him.

'You mean 'Khorne' as in 'Khorne's Killers'?' Slick asked, his eyes wide in disbelief.

'Yes.'

'Khorne, the Blood God?'

'Yes.'

'Khorne, one of the Lords of Chaos?'

'Yes!'

Conversation around the table ground to a halt, and Lügner tried to use a smile to mask his irritation. Soon enough, the dull roar of others talking nearby resumed.

'Why?' Dunk asked. 'What would Khorne want with us?'

'Besides the fact that the Hoffnungs were one of the oldest and most influential families in the Empire?'

'There are other families with the same credentials.'

'True,' said Lügner, 'but none of them were in such rotten shape as ours was when I took over the family business.'

Dunk narrowed his eyes at his father and tried to understand where he was heading.

Seeing that Dunk wasn't about to hold up his end of the conversation with anything but prompts, both verbal and otherwise, Lügner continued to speak.

'Your grandfather was a great man: a patron of the arts, a good friend, and kind to all who knew him. Someone who put the 'gentle' in 'gentleman' and the 'noble' in 'nobleman.' But he was a horrible businessman.

'In the twenty-five years my father was in charge of the Hoffnung family holdings, he managed to piss away hundreds of thousands of crowns – maybe even enough to pay for the price that's on your head.'

Dunk winced at that.

'You see, that's why I'm here. I wanted to tell you that the Guterfiends are the ones backing this Zauberer fellow's mad claims. You've done a fine job debunking the man and making him look like the lunatic he is, but he made too big a splash.

'Even if you no longer have every joker with a sword in his closet coming after you for the reward, the professionals – the killers who really know what they're doing – are going to figure it out. They're going to go to that crackpot, and he'll tell them who's offering the money, and then they'll go after you harder than ever. And the worst part is that you won't even be expecting it.

'Or at least you wouldn't, if not for me.'

Dunk smiled finally. 'I already knew.'

It was Lügner's turn to be surprised. 'Really? How? Did you track it down through Zauberer yourself? Smart boy! I always told your mother you'd get over that head wound.'

'No, I heard it from – Wait! What head wound?'

Lügner grimaced. 'Um, the one you got as a child when you were dropped.'

'Who dropped me?' Dunk asked. 'You?'

Lügner nodded, his cheeks turning pink. 'You were just a few months old, and Lehrer had tossed me a skin full of wine. I just – well, I wasn't used to carrying a child around quite yet.'

Dunk slapped a hand over his eyes. 'You dropped your infant son in favour of a wineskin.'

Lügner nodded, a pathetic look on his face. 'It was some really good wine.'

Dunk put his head down on the table and wrapped his hands over it. For some reason, it seemed to be throbbing.

'So who told you the Guterfiends were behind the reward money?' Lügner asked, clearly hoping to change the subject.

'Lehrer,' Dunk mumbled.

'Who?'

'Lehrer,' Dunk said, raising his head. 'He tracked me down in Magritta to let me know.'

'Lehrer?' Lügner's voice was barely more than a whisper. 'He's still around?'

'He's been with the Guterfiends ever since we left the keep. They came in and hired our whole staff on the spot, it seems.'

'He's been with them far longer than that. He started up with them soon after I signed on with Khorne.'

Dunk blinked. 'You did what?'

15

Lügner scowled at Dunk. 'Don't you dare judge me, Dunkel. The house was floundering. Your grandfather had not only lost everything we had, he'd also run up a horrendous debt. The people who held those markers were ready to take everything we had and then hang our skins from our flagpoles to make their point.'

'You made a deal with one of the Ruinous Powers, and you didn't think that would come back to bite you?' Dunk stared at his father, stunned. He'd known his father had done some pretty horrible things in the course of building the family business back up over the years, but he'd had no idea that it had involved pacts with the forces of darkness.

'Of course I did!' Lügner scowled. 'I knew the deal would go sour eventually – I did – but eventually can be an awfully long time. It got me through your entire childhood. Yours and Dirk's.'

'But it killed Mother and Kirta. Does that seem like a fair trade?'

'That's not fair, Dunkel. You know I would have done anything to save Greta and your sister from that mob. They came on so quick…

'As it was, I was thrilled to be able to save your life at least. That day was the first time I felt glad that Dirk had left home.'

Dunk just gaped at Lügner. The horror of the notion that his father had tied his family fortunes to the whims of the Blood God staggered him.

'You thought you could cheat him, didn't you?' Slick said.

Dunk stared at the halfling, and then back at his father, who was squirming in his seat.

'Go on,' Slick said. 'Admit it. I know what it's like. Someone presents you with a deal you just can't bring yourself to refuse, even though you know you should. You go back and forth on it, but eventually you convince yourself that there's a loophole in it somewhere, some way for you to wriggle out of your end of the bargain – at least if something in the deal goes sour, which it will, especially for something that's supposed to last forever.

'So you make the deal, and you regret it every day after that, knowing that some day the executioner's axe will drop, and you have to be ready to try to dodge it at any second.

'I understand all this. I'm an old wheeler and dealer myself. Sometimes the temptation seems too great. I've seen it break many a desperate man in my time, but you just have to resist.

'It's no way to live.'

Lügner nodded along with Slick, and said, 'It's an even worse way to die. Do you know what part of the deal was? Eternal damnation. Khorne owns my soul. When I die, it becomes his plaything for the rest of time.'

'I take it back,' Slick said. 'You're an idiot.'

'Hey,' Lügner said, becoming indignant, 'I didn't think souls were real back then, and if I did have one I wasn't doing a damned thing with it. I was young. I was naïve. I was–'

'An idiot,' M'Grash said, shaking his head in pity.

Lügner sighed. 'I can't win. Even the ogre thinks I'm an idiot.'

'What did you promise them?' Dunk asked.

Lügner waved his son off. 'You don't want to know,' he said. 'It's not important.'

'As unimportant as your soul?' Dunk felt his anger at his father rising again.

Lügner closed his eyes for a moment. When he opened them again, Dunk could see that he'd been beaten. Given the look of his hair, skin, and clothes, he'd been that way since he'd left Altdorf three years ago. Dunk guessed that the man had lapsed into his old, enthusiastic ways only because of the encounter with him. Now that he'd had the wind taken from his sails, he'd reverted to the worn, tired, old man he'd become.

'I can't say.'

'Can't or won't?'

'It comes to the same thing.' Lügner hung his head low and spoke so softly that he could barely be heard.

'*Tell me!*' Dunk roared, slamming his fists onto the table.

Once again, all nearby conversation froze. It started up again a moment later, but Dunk knew that his table had just about worn out its welcome. The managers of the House of Booze traded upon their willingness to leave their patrons alone, but that included keeping them from upsetting each other.

Lügner raised his sunken, red-rimmed eyes. Dunk could smell the man's fear.

'My bloodline,' Lügner said in a soft, horrified breath. 'I – I sold you all.'

Dunk's heart froze in his chest. He didn't want to believe what his father had just said, but at the same time he knew that it was true.

'Forgive me, Dunkel,' Lügner whispered.

Dunk bit his lower lip so hard he tasted blood in his mouth. He gripped the edge of the table in front of him so tight he could hear his knuckles crack. Then he shoved out hard and flipped the table over in front of him.

Lügner's chair tipped over hard, but the old man managed to scramble out of the way, squeaking clear before the table's heavy top could crash into him. Dunk leapt down after the table before anyone could stop him. He landed crouched on the table's upper edge and stared down at his father like a vengeful god come from the mountaintop to smite down the most offensive of heretics.

'Forgive you?' Dunk said. 'You're lucky I don't tear out your heart and send you straight off to Khorne here and now!'

Lügner cried out in horror and threw his arms up over his head and face for protection. He whimpered in a soft voice, 'I did it all for you.'

The pathetic display triggered something in Dunk's head. One moment he wanted nothing more than to rip the man's life from him in large, bloody chunks; the next, he couldn't stand the thought of laying his hands on the man, for fear that some of that creature's weaknesses might rub off on him. Then Dunk remembered that this was his father and that it might already be too late.

'Isn't that Dunk Hoffnung?' a lady dwarf asked from the other side of the tavern's main hall.

Dunk knew he shouldn't have been able to hear the dwarf's question. Any other time he'd been in the House of Booze, the general background noise would have drowned it out. Now, it rang out in the silence that seemed to have smothered every other conversation to death.

'Get out of here,' Dunk said to his father as the man squirmed away from him along the tavern's cold, stone floor. 'If I ever see you again, you're dead.'

* * *

'So, DUNK,' LÄSTIGES said through the crack in the door, her floating golden camra arcing over her shoulder to get the best shot of the thrower's reaction. 'Tell our viewers just how long you've been worshiping at the altar of the Blood God?'

'Don't do this to me,' Dunk said, trying to rub the sleep from his eyes. 'Not now.'

'So you're not denying reports of you threatening a harmless old man in the House of Booze last night and threatening to sacrifice him to Khorne?'

Dunk slapped both of his hands over his face. Of course, that's what it must have looked like to an outsider, and plenty of them had seen him come within inches of killing his father. He wondered how many of them had tried to sell the story to Wolf Sports, especially considering that no one outside of his friends had moved more than a finger to try to stop him from carrying out his threats.

'Leave him alone,' Spinne called from inside the room. 'He had a rough night.'

'I'm just happy to hear your voice, Spinne,' Lästiges said. 'After the old man got away from Dunk last night, some of the witnesses wondered if he might be desperate enough to try to sacrifice you instead.'

Dunk arched an eyebrow at the reporter. They had spent a lot of time together the previous year. She'd come along on the Hackers' trip to Albion and made a documentary based on how they'd found and captured the original Far Albion Cup.

'Your concern is touching,' he said. 'Now go away.' With that, he shut the door in her face.

'Dunk,' Lästiges said. 'Dunk! You know this story is going to be airing on every major Cabalvision network by the end of the day. I'm giving you a chance to head off the negative publicity and tell your side of the story!'

'Let her in,' Spinne said as she tossed on a fresh shirt and skirt.

'Are you nuts?'

Spinne shrugged. 'She's got a point. Besides, do you think she's going to go away?'

'Not without an exclusive,' Lästiges said through the door.

Dunk sighed and pulled the door open, holding it wide and gesturing for the reporter to enter.

'Thank you,' she said as she strolled past him, her camra hovering around her shoulders, its eye taking in everything at once. She gave Spinne a little wave and then curled up on the couch near the room's bay window, through which the morning sun streamed. Dunk could hear the calls of sea birds riding the gentle breeze across the bay, which stretched out towards the horizon beyond.

'So,' Lästiges said, 'what can you tell me about this man you assaulted? Crazed fan? Jilted lover? Evangelist for Khorne?'

'None of the above,' Dunk said, rubbing his unshaven chin. 'I'll talk to you about it if you like, but you have to turn that camra off.'

Lästiges frowned. 'But what if you say something interesting for once?'

'That's a chance you're just going to have to take.'

Lästiges peered up at him from the couch for a moment before making her decision. 'All right,' she said. At her signal, the camra dropped from the air to land neatly in her hand. She polished it on her sleeve and then stuffed it into a pocket on her Wolf Sports jacket.

Satisfied for the moment, Dunk looked down into Lästiges's deep brown eyes. 'It was my father,' he said.

'Lügner Hoffnung?' The colour drained from Lästiges's face. 'I thought he was dead.'

'No one could have been more surprised than me,' Dunk said. 'I hadn't seen him since the night we were run out of Altdorf.'

'What – what's he doing here?' The news of Lügner's return had shattered the woman's concentration.

'He came back to warn me about who's behind the price on my head.'

Lästiges shook her head. 'But how can you believe a word he says? He's one of the most evil people to ever walk the planet.'

'That's a bit harsh, I think,' said Dunk.

'Do you know what he did to my family?' the woman asked, her eyes welling up with tears of rage and frustration as she spoke. 'Do you know why I ended up taking a job as a Blood Bowl reporter? He ruined us – entirely! The only way I could deal with that was to know that at least he was dead.'

Lästiges's eyes shone as she looked at Dunk's impassive face. 'And now you tell me he's alive? What do I do with that?'

Dunk shook his head. He knew his father had done some horrible things with the family business, but up until now he hadn't realised just how bad they might have been. For the first time, he truly felt sorry for Lästiges.

'How's Dirk?' he asked. He knew his brother would want to know about their father, but he had no way to reach him. He'd be able to commiserate with the lady reporter at least.

'I – I don't know,' Lästiges said, pouting out her red lower lip. 'I've been dreading you asking me that. I haven't seen him since he quit the Reavers.'

Dunk frowned. Dirk and Lästiges had been dating for a while and becoming a serious couple. If he had cut off all ties with her as well, it couldn't be good. He could understand Dirk being mad at him, but staying away from Lästiges didn't make sense.

'So why did you attack him?' Lästiges asked, her reporter's instincts kicking in. 'Your father, I mean. I would think you'd be thrilled to see him.'

Dunk snorted at that. 'I'd love to tell you, but only as a friend and as the woman dating my brother.'

'Have you done something to be ashamed of?' Lästiges asked. Dunk could tell she smelled blood. If she had to spill that of a few innocents to take her revenge on Lügner, he didn't doubt she would.

But Dunk and Dirk weren't just innocents to her, were they? Dunk had come to know and grudgingly respect Lästiges over the past couple of years, and Dirk had shared more with her than just her bed.

'Do you think I can trust her?' Dunk asked Spinne.

The catcher mulled it over for a moment. 'I think you have to.'

'This has to be off the record,' he said, turning to the reporter.

'Of course,' Lästiges said, leaning forward to catch his every word.

'When the family business was bad, before Dirk and I were even born, my father made a deal with Khorne. He sold the Blood God his soul and the souls of all his heirs.'

The reporter's face went white, and she sat back in the couch, horrified. 'Are you... He told you this?'

Dunk nodded.

'Then what happened?'

'We got rich,' Dunk said, confused by the question.

'Sure, and then you got run out of town. Why?'

Dunk stopped. 'I don't know,' he said, mystified. 'I never asked.'

'You didn't *ask*?'

'My head was still ringing from the "I sold your soul to Khorne" thing.'

Lästiges nodded as she stared out of the window. 'Amazing,' she muttered. 'I should have known.'

'You need to find Dirk.'

'What's that?' she asked; raising her eyebrows at Dunk.

'You need to find my brother and tell him about this. He needs to know.'

'Then what?' Lästiges asked. She felt most comfortable when asking questions. It put her back on familiar ground.

'Then find us, and we'll figure out what we need to do about this.'

'Why did your father come forth now?' Lästiges asked. 'He's been missing for years.'

'The Guterfiends are the ones who put up the reward for my head. He wanted me to know – and know why they want me dead.'

'Zauberer!' Lästiges said. 'I almost forgot. That's the reason I'm here!'

'You didn't come just to ask me awkward questions about that encounter in the House of Booze?'

She dismissed him with a wave of her hand. 'That was just for fun. This is serious.' She reached into her pocket and pulled out her camra. With a little toss, it rose into the air under its own power and hovered near her shoulder again.

'I said, no camra.'

Lästiges gave him an irritated smile. 'I'm not going to record anything. I need to show you something.'

The reporter snapped her fingers twice, and the eyehole on the front of the camra grew wider. Then a ray of light stabbed out of the hole, shining on a blank wall at one end of the couch.

Dunk blinked his eyes, and stared at the brightly lit spot on the wall. There he saw an image of Schlechter Zauberer frozen in a sneer. It looked like a painting that the light had somehow revealed, as if it had always been there, just waiting for the camra to point it out.

'These Daemonic Lidless Projectors are incredible,' Lästiges said, 'and they just keep getting smaller every year.'

'A DLP?' Spinne asked. 'You can make a moving image without a crystal ball with one of those.'

'Give the girl a clean shirt,' Lästiges said. 'These things are great for playback. It used to be I couldn't see what I'd recorded until I got back to the studio.'

'So what's on the marquee tonight?' Dunk asked.

Lästiges reached out and touched something on the floating camra, and the image on the wall sprang to life. It showed Zauberer slinking down a dark hallway.

'Wolf Sports got this footage from the camras we had set up at the Orcidas Stadium in the Badlands.'

'Isn't that where the Gouged Eye play?' Dunk asked.

Spinne nodded. 'They beat us – the Reavers – in the finals for the Chaos Cup last year.'

'Funny you should mention that,' said Lästiges. 'Watch.'

In the image, Zauberer snaked his way down the hallway until he reached a room in which a couple dozen orcs lay scattered about. From the sounds – which also emitted from the camra – they were all sleeping off a great deal of drink.

'Yesterday, the Gouged Eye beat the Marauders in their annual grudge match. They play it during the Dungeonbowl tournament every year that neither team is invited to the main event.'

'So they play every year,' said Spinne.

'Without fail,' said Lästiges. 'When the Gouged Eye wins, they have a massive party to celebrate. Most of them survive it. Not this year though.'

Zauberer tiptoed through the orcs towards an oak table in the centre of the room. On it sat a large trophy – the Chaos Cup itself, Dunk realised – fashioned from what looked like the skull of a many-horned daemon squatting atop a pile of tiny skulls with equally vicious fangs. As the wizard approached, an eye appeared in one of the daemon-skull's sockets and rolled around to focus on the intruder.

Zauberer froze and said something to the trophy. It opened its toothy maw and began to laugh. The wizard tried to shush it, but it only laughed louder and louder until the orcs nearest to it started to wake up.

Zauberer dashed forward and plucked the cup from its stand. He clutched it to his chest, and the thing bit through his clothes and flesh. His blood ran red on its ivory-bleached bones. He screamed.

The nearest orc – Dunk recognised him as Da Fridge, the Gouged Eye team's best blocker – leapt up and grabbed the wailing wizard. The massive monster stretched up to his full height and held Zauberer out at arm's length, his feet flailing a full yard off of the floor.

Then Da Fridge burst into flames.

The orc dropped Zauberer, who landed nimbly on his feet. The other orcs around him leapt to their feet. Some of them had woken when Da Fridge had started laughing at the wizard, and his screams had jolted even the most intoxicated of them from their sleep.

Da Fridge tried to run, but he only made it a few feet before a blast of ebony lightning lanced out from the cup and ran him through. He collapsed at Zauberer's feet without another sound.

Some of the orcs charged the wizard. Others tried to escape, scurrying in every direction.

Zauberer cackled in evil mirth. With each laugh, another ebon bolt shot out of the Chaos Cup, skewering another screaming orc. Within seconds, the wizard stood alone in the room, surrounded by nothing more than the corpses of charred orcs.

Zauberer stalked around the room like a victorious conqueror surveying a smoking battlefield. No one else moved.

Then the wizard spotted the security camra that had been recording the entire event. He strutted up to it, a wicked smile splitting his face. He held the Chaos Cup up before the device, and the thing's eye swivelled about and focused through it as if it could see right through the camra's lens to Lästiges, Spinne, and Dunk.

Dunk reached out and held Spinne's hand as she stifled a gasp. Lästiges sat unmoved, solid as a rock. She'd witnessed this scene at least once already. It wasn't until he glanced at her chin that he saw that she was shaking.

'Tell the world,' Zauberer said. 'The power I have sought for so long is finally mine.

'Tell everyone you meet. Soon they will all worship me as their emperor-god.

'For anyone else, if Dunk Hoffnung is hurt before I get my hands on him – if anyone even scratches his armour – I'll destroy you and everyone you hold dear.

'And be sure to tell Hoffnung this for me when you see him: Dunk, my old friend, you're next.'

'Byufell Triehugger has the ball!' Bob's voice said. 'The Elfheim Eagles are on a roll!'

Dunk swore under his breath. This game hadn't gone well at all.

When the Hackers had first lined up against their all-elf opponents, Dunk had thought that the wizards who had sponsored the Eagles must have owed their coach some kind of favour. He hadn't had a lot of experience with elves, but these didn't look like any Blood Bowl players he'd ever seen.

Each of the Eagles was physically perfect with stunning good looks. That they enhanced their appearance with make-up and designer orange-and-purple armour had surprised Dunk. Apparently helmets were out this year, although Dunk couldn't say if this was a fashion decision or that the elf players just refused to mess up their perfectly coiffed hair.

All of this made Dunk think that the Eagles were a team composed merely of poseurs who had showed up simply to display how good an elf could look on the field. He expected that the rough-and-tumble Hackers would tear them apart before they had to break a sweat – something he suspected the Eagles themselves would have refused to do for any reason short of torture.

He'd been sorely mistaken.

The immortal elves had a different kind of strategy than Dunk was used to. Instead of focusing on raw power, or even the elegant use of skill, they excelled at the use of rotten tricks that were technically within the rules. Apparently Nuffle had never written anything in his sacred rulebook about using a herbicide in the middle of a game, for instance, despite the fact that it had sent Edgar into an itching fit that made it impossible for him to do anything during the rest game.

The Eagles had made good use of the dungeon's terrain too. They had drawn M'Grash into the room with the bottomless pit and then knocked him off one of the string of floating rocks. The poor ogre had been falling for over ten minutes now, wailing in terror at the top of his lungs the entire time.

Cavre had been the most successful in dealing with the elves, but he'd had a chest explode on him. While he was stunned, the Eagles had stuffed him into the chest and bound it tight with something Dunk could only guess was an elf's excuse for a jockstrap.

That left Spinne, Guillermo, and Dunk as the only Hackers still in the game. Outnumbered two to one, they were bound to have a hard time of it. The most frustrating part for Dunk was the fact that he'd not even been able to tackle anyone yet. The Eagles had studiously avoided having any contact with him. Whenever he entered a room, they left.

'What's going on?' he'd asked Guillermo. 'Why won't they come after us?'

The Estalian had used the back of his arm to wipe some blood from his eyes. 'I think you mean, why don't they come after you?'

Dunk realised the lineman was right. Word of Zauberer's capture of the Chaos Cup and his subsequent threat against anyone who might hurt Dunk had saturated the Cabalvision networks almost immediately after Dunk had seen it himself. In the middle of talk shows like Bloodcentre, player after player had gone white at the thought of being forced to play against Dunk while the sorcerer's edict against harming the Hacker stayed in effect.

Not so for Lassolegs Gladhandriel, the Eagles' captain. 'As you know, we always play strictly by the rules,' he'd said. 'We do not fear that we might hurt Mr. Hoffnung accidentally.'

Of course, that left a lot of room for things the Eagles might try to do to Dunk on purpose. So far, just isolating Dunk had worked well. Unless he or his team-mates found the ball, the Eagles had no need to get anywhere near him.

Now that the ball had been found, Dunk hoped to turn the tables. He gave up trying to figure out how to rescue M'Grash without getting killed in the process, and bounded across the floating rocks in seconds. When he reached the room with the mirrored walls, he closed his eyes and felt his way through the place, taking care to listen hard for any attackers approaching him while he was blind.

Once through the mirrored room, Dunk found a teleportation pad in the hallway beyond. He didn't know where it would take him, but since he needed to get ahead of the ball carrier fast, he jumped on it and hoped for the best.

He popped into a room filled with rabid, three-headed, seven-tailed cats that smelled of carrion and looked as if they'd been starved half to madness. He moved off the glowing circle, and then jumped back onto it again. It blinked him away.

Dunk landed in another golden circle, and promptly skidded off it, out of control. The floor in this high-ceilinged chamber was a smooth sheet of ice, and his boots could find no purchase on it.

As Dunk slid, he started to pick up speed. The room seemed to go on forever. As he stared around, he realised he wasn't in a room at all. The teleportation pad had transported him to the top of a snowy mountain peak, and it had been engineered to send him slipping along its face at top speed.

Although he had managed to maintain his footing, he could do little to change his course. Peering ahead, he saw the land in front of him disappear into thin air. Then he knew where he was. He'd seen the place from a distance as they'd sailed in to Barak Varr. The dwarfs called it Khalakazam, which had no equivalent in the Imperial tongue. The best that one of the bartenders at the House of Booze had been able to come up with was, 'Mount You-Must-Be-Joking.'

'They call it that because of the steep drop-off on its front face,' the bartender had said. 'If you happen to slip off it, it's nearly a mile down before you hit anything else. They say you'd probably pass out and die long before that happened, but me, I think they just say that. More likely you flounder there screaming in the air every damned second until you smash into the rocks below. I hear most people bounce near twenty feet in the air after an impact like that.'

Dunk and Spinne had paid their tab and gone to find another bar after that.

'Oh, no! Hoffnung's found his way on to Mount No-Freaking-Way!' Jim's voice said from somewhere off to the left. 'He's doomed for sure.'

'If that's true, I'd hate to be the dwarfs who built that death trap – or the wizards who commissioned it,' said Bob. 'I can't imagine that watching this happen on live Cabalvision – *only* here on Wolf Sports! – will make a certain wizard very happy. I can only guess where he'd begin to take his revenge.'

Dunk threw himself down on the ice and tried to grab on with his entire body, but no part of him could find purchase. He clutched at the ice with his hands, hugged it with his body, and kicked at it with his feet, but it ignored his every attempt to cling on. He wound up on his rump, stomping the heels of his cleated boots into the ice zipping past underneath him, but he couldn't even manage to slow himself down.

Dunk looked up and saw a trio of birds circling overhead, carrion eaters waiting for their next meal, no doubt. He turned over on his belly and tried to ram the spikes on the various parts of his armour into the ice too, but the slick surface proved impenetrable. Nothing worked.

Then the ice disappeared, and he found himself sailing out into open space, nothing beneath him but a mile of crisp, cold air. He looked down and saw how the wall of the mountain curved away from the precipitous edge. About a quarter of the way down, the snow and ice gave way to bare rock. Near the bottom – still far away, but already rising fast – the rock plunged into a lush and fertile valley. Down there, Dunk could see tiny white dots moving about, and he realised they were cattle.

An eagle's cry split the open air, cutting through the sound of the wind rushing through Dunk's ears. He tried to look behind him to see what might have made the noise, but he only succeeded in sending his body into an uncontrolled spin.

It took Dunk a full ten seconds to re-stabilise himself. Once he did, he was too dizzy to understand anything he could see. Then a great fluttering of wings surrounded him, and he found himself clinging to a feathered tree trunk.

Dunk peered around the side of the trunk and saw a giant eagle's head staring back at him over its shoulder. 'Relax,' the creature said. 'I'll have you back on the ground in no time. You didn't think they'd just execute you like that, did you?'

Dunk decided that this would be the perfect time to pass out. The last words he heard were, 'By the way, you lost.'

'Is IT TRUE?' DUNK woke up with the words on his lips. He was in his room in the Hackers' official inn again, in bed, alone, but not as alone as he'd hoped.

'Yes,' said Dr. Pill, who leered at Dunk as he stood up from where he'd been sitting on the couch at the other end of the large room.

Dunk stared at the apothecary. 'What happened?'

'You slid off the tallest cliff in the world. A giant eagle rescued you. Your team lost.'

Dunk groaned.

'Really, what chance did Spinne and Guillermo have all by themselves? As it was, they tried so hard that I had to put stitches into both of them.'

'Stitches? Is Spinne all right?'

'She's fine,' Dr. Pill said with a bemused grin. A few minor slashes on her upper right bicep. She'll be back at full capacity in no time.'

'What about the others?'

'Cavre bruised himself trying to get out of that chest. He took some splinters when he succeeded, but it was already too late.

'I got to Edgar in time to save most of his bark. You might see him wearing a long sheet like a toga for the next few weeks, but don't comment on it. It makes him self-conscious.

'Once the game ended, M'Grash finally figured out that he should grab on to something. He nearly pulled one of the floating rocks out of its spot when he hit it. Nothing but minor bruises for him, though. He's tougher than a bag of rocks and nearly as smart.'

'And Guillermo?'

'Took six stabs from elf armour spikes and nearly bled to death, but I got to him in time. He'll be fine soon enough.

'Now, how do you feel?'

'Dunk ran his hands over his body, taking inventory as he went. 'I feel fine,' he finally said. 'Nothing damaged but my ego.'

Dr. Pill nodded. 'I'm afraid I don't have a potion powerful enough to help with that.'

The door to the room opened, and Spinne and Slick came in. 'Dunk!' Spinne said as she dashed over to the bed and took him in her arms. She held him for a long time without saying a word. Then she sat back and caressed his face as she spoke.

'Thank Nuffle I couldn't watch you falling off that cliff while it happened,' she said. 'I think my heart would have stopped dead.'

'Mine almost did,' said Dunk. 'I'm just glad those eagles were there.'

'I've already filed a protest with the Colleges of Magic's Dungeonbowl Steering Committee,' Slick said. 'They shouldn't be able to do something like that to a professional player like you. Sure, it makes for great Cabalvision, but it's hardly fair, is it?'

'I didn't realise Blood Bowl had to be fair,' said Dr. Pill.

'Life's not fair,' Slick said. 'We play games to make it better. We can't just abandon that whenever the mood suits us.'

'So will anything come of your complaint?' Dunk asked.

'Not a chance,' said Slick, 'nothing directly, at least. It might make us look less pathetic to sympathetic members of the Grey Wizards' sponsoring team, though, and that might mean getting invited back next year.'

'I don't know,' Dunk said, shivering as images from sliding down the mountain flashed through his head. 'I could give it a miss, I think.'

'Bollocks!' Slick said. 'Now, son, that's no way for a champion to talk.'

'Champions win games,' Spinne said, holding Dunk's hand. He could see the stitches on her upper arm. They looked clean and well matched, healing already. 'We lost.'

'But you'll all live to play another day,' Dr. Pill said. 'That's more than most teams can manage, especially in Dungeonbowl. That's how I lost my last job. I was working for the Moot Mighties when they lost every single player in just one game against the New Albion Patriots.'

'Don't the Mighties have a total loss at least three times a year?' asked Slick.

'This one was worse. Their coach and manager were killed too, along with about half the fans in the stands.'

'The Patriots did that?' Dunk asked.

Dr. Pill shook his head. 'It was Free Spiked Ball Day for the first five hundred fans. It all went downhill from there.'

Dunk winced. Then he looked to Slick. 'What's the plan from here?' he asked. 'Do we stick around for the final round of the tournament?'

'No, son, we're heading home. Back to Bad Bay as soon as you and the others are fit to travel.' He looked to Dr. Pill.

'We can leave with the next tide,' the apothecary said.

'Any truth to the vicious rumour going around that we'll see Pegleg at the wheel of the *Sea Chariot* as we pull out into the bay?' Spinne asked.

'As many truths as you care to seek,' Dr. Pill said with a mysterious grin.

'Can you translate that for the less enlightened?' Slick asked.

'Yes.'

'Yes, you can translate or – oh, never mind!'

'I am hopeful that Captain Haken has overcome his irrational fear of water,' Dr. Pill said. 'However, I must caution that the relief he experiences from this may cause him to experience an overwhelming sense of confidence that may not be entirely grounded in reality. We should take great care to keep watch over him to ensure that he does not overextend himself and expose the entire ship to danger.'

Slick glared at the apothecary. 'Just in time for a long ocean voyage.'

'Come on, Slick. We've made this same trip many times before,' Dunk said. 'What could go wrong?'

'JOLLY ROGER OFF the port bow!'

Dunk shaded his eyes to peer up at Guillermo in the crow's nest, tipping back and forth high above the *Sea Chariot*'s main deck. The lineman's arm stabbed off to the left of the ship's nose. Dunk brought his head down in that direction and saw what Guillermo had spotted first from his higher vantage point: a ship sailing towards them from the horizon, a black flag flapping from its mast.

Dunk couldn't make out the flag's design, but if Guillermo – who had a spyglass up there with him – said it bore a skull and crossbones, Dunk believed him.

Dunk climbed up to the bridge where Pegleg stood, squinting through his own spyglass at the oncoming ship. Cavre, who had the wheel, craned his neck to look back at the captain, waiting for his orders.

'Are those really pirates, coach?' Dunk asked.

'Aye, they are, Mr. Hoffnung,' Pegleg said. Try as he might, Dunk couldn't read the man's tone. Instead of fear, it bore something else. Anticipation?

'Orders, captain?' Cavre asked.

'Steady as she goes, Mr. Cavre.'

'But captain, she'll catch us for sure at this rate.' Dunk checked the other horizon and saw that they weren't far from Estalia's western coast. A wide, sandy beach beckoned from that direction, and Dunk pointed towards it. 'If we hurry, we can reach dry land before they catch us. Then we might have a chance.'

Pegleg brought down his spyglass, collapsed it, and stuffed it into one of the pockets of his long, green, velvet coat. He adjusted his bright yellow tricorn hat, which seemed to be mostly made of holes now. 'I'm aware of where the shoreline is, Mr. Hoffnung. Steady as she goes.'

With that, Pegleg limped off the bridge and disappeared into his cabin. Dunk stared after him, hardly noticing when Slick and Spinne climbed onto the bridge next to him.

'What's happening, son?' Slick asked.

'I don't know,' Dunk said. He looked to Cavre, whose face carried a world of worry. 'Shouldn't we do something? That ship looks like it could eat the *Sea Chariot* alive.'

'The captain knows what he's doing,' Cavre said.

'Are you sure about that?' Spinne asked. 'This is the first time any of us have seen him outside of his cabin anywhere but at dock or on dry land.'

'Dr. Pill's treatment seems to have been effective, wouldn't you say?'

Slick frowned. 'Are we certain that the treatment doesn't have any side-effects like, perhaps, insanity?'

Cavre kept silent, his mouth a thin, grim line.

As the pirate ship grew closer, Dunk could make out some of its details. It was huge, twice the size of the *Sea Chariot*, and it had a row of oars sticking out from either side. These were held up from the water at the moment, but Dunk could see how they could be put into service at a moment's notice.

When Dunk got a good look at the ship's masthead, his stomach shrank into a tiny knot. It had been carved to resemble a bloody daemon with snakes for limbs and eyes. Dunk squinted at the crimson lettering just under that, running parallel with the rail. It read '*Seas of Hate*.'

'We have to get out of here,' Dunk said to Cavre. 'We have to outrun them or we're all doomed.'

'I have my orders.'

Dunk grabbed the wheel, testing Cavre's grip on it. 'You can't follow those orders. The captain's gone mad.'

'Do you hear that?' Slick asked, a hand cupped to his ear, which he'd cocked in the direction of the pirate ship. 'It sounds like hissing.'

'Look,' Spinne said to Cavre, 'I understand your loyalty to Pegleg. He's our captain and our coach, but now is the time to question those orders. Forcing himself out of the cabin has clearly unbalanced him. We need to turn tail and see if we can outrace that ship.'

Cavre gave hard looks to all three of the others in turn. Then his shoulders slumped and he nodded gently. 'All right,' he said. 'What do you propose we do? No one knows this ship better than Captain Haken. We need him and his support.'

'We'll have to live without it,' Spinne said.

This talk of mutiny made Dunk uncomfortable, but he couldn't see any other way around it. Unlike the others – except perhaps the now-haggard Cavre – he knew what hungered for them on that ship and what would happen to those who were captured. To risk meeting such daemons seemed to be insane.

'Belay that, Mr. Cavre!' The captain came stalking out of his cabin, shoving a wheeled rack of cannonballs before him. 'Mad or not, I have a plan. We'll never outrun that ship. Once you see the *Seas of Hate*, your fate is sealed. Your only chance is to fight.'

'With what?' Dunk called down at the ex-pirate. 'We may be a great Blood Bowl team, but half us of don't know how to handle a sword and even fewer have ever fought on a moving ship.'

Pegleg doffed his tricorn hat, exposing his long, black curls to the sun. With a wink and a grin, he waved the hat at the rack of cannon-balls squatting next to him. 'Why, with these, of course! You don't think I'd jeopardise the safety of my team without a plan, do you?'

Spinne gaped at the man. 'You did this on purpose?'

Pegleg grinned. 'Suffice it to say, Miss Schönheit, that I knew that there was a significant chance that this particular ship full of dae-monic pirates might take a stab at procuring for themselves the substantial reward placed on Mr. Hoffnung's head.'

Dunk's eyes popped wide open. 'How's that? I thought that's why we sailed out of Barak Varr under cover of night. You had us under strict orders not to tell anyone our schedule, our route, or our desti-nation. How could they have found us?'

'They are daemons, Mr. Hoffnung. I suppose it's not beyond them to use magic.'

Slick peered down at the captain from over the bridge's railing. 'But they didn't, did they?'

Dunk stared at his agent, not understanding what the halfling meant to imply.

'No, of course not,' Pegleg said. 'They didn't have to. I *told* them.'

Spinne gasped.

'Don't be so shocked,' Pegleg said. 'I did what I had to do to get those devils right where I want them.' He rubbed his chin, bemused. 'I'll admit that I didn't expect to see them until we were closer to Bad Bay, but no matter. I'm as happy to send them into the briny deep here as anywhere.'

'Dr. Pill told you to do this,' Dunk said. 'Didn't he?'

'All part of the solution to my hydrophobia. In order to surmount your fears you must confront them, after all.'

'Or inflict them on others at least,' said Slick.

The hissing from the other ship grew louder. Dunk peered out at it again and saw that the masthead had come to life. It looked as if someone had taken one of the snake-daemons Dunk could now see gathering on the foredeck, grown it to the size of M'Grash, and then lashed it to the ship's prow. The long snake-arms whipped before it in the wind, reaching out for the *Sea Chariot*.

Dunk had no doubt that when they finally found purchase on the ship's deck the other daemons would use those arms as part of a boarding action. The Hackers would then find themselves fighting for their lives against a well-armed crew of daemons.

Images of the daemons crashing his engagement party flashed through his head. Dunk felt like he might vomit, but he clamped down on his stomach and went to go find his sword.

'Where do you think you're going, Mr. Hoffnung?' Pegleg reached out with his hook and snagged Dunk by the sleeve as he tried to walk past.

'To get my blade. I'm not going down without a fight.'

Pegleg shook his head. 'That won't be necessary.'

Dunk glanced back at the onrushing *Seas of Hate*. 'I think they might disagree with you.'

Pegleg tapped one of the cannonballs with his hook. They were covered with strange runes arranged in odd patterns. Each of them seemed to have three thick holes bored into one side.

'With these enchanted cannonballs on our side, Mr. Hoffnung, we have the advantage.'

The captain's calm demeanour irritated Dunk. Seeing the creatures that had killed his father and tortured him for so long – badly enough that he'd chewed off his own hand and lost his leg in the escape – how could he be so placid?

'You forgot one thing, coach,' Dunk said, panic creeping into his voice. 'We don't have a cannon on board!'

'Ah,' Pegleg said, holding up his hook, 'but we don't need one.' He glanced up over Dunk's shoulder. 'Ready?' he asked.

'Ready, coach,' said M'Grash.

Dunk turned and gaped at the ogre. M'Grash grinned down at Dunk as he cracked his knuckles. Did Pegleg think that the ogre could take on an entire ship full of daemons with nothing but his bare hands?

'Fire at will,' Pegleg said. The captain took Dunk by the elbow and steered him to the gunwale facing the *Seas of Hate*, close to the stairs leading up to the bridge and out of M'Grash's way.

The ogre reached down and hefted one of the cannonballs in his hands. Then he stuck his two middle fingers and his thumb into the three holes drilled in the ball of enchanted, cold iron. This left his other two fingers splayed out along the surface of the ball, where they fit perfectly along the symbols engraved there.

'See the formation of the hand, Mr. Hoffnung? Some call a hand held like that a mark of Chaos. It's an integral part of the activation of the ball's magic.'

Dunk just stood there stunned. He couldn't believe what he was seeing.

M'Grash stretched his arms out above him, the cannonball perched in his monstrous mitt. Dunk couldn't recall ever seeing such concentration on the ogre's face. It made him seem more dangerous than ever.

M'Grash took a huge stride forward and swung the ball down and back behind him as he did. The players crouching behind the ogre on the other side of the ship, watching the scene play out, suddenly scattered, fearful that the ball might come back at them.

Then M'Grash took another smooth stride towards the *Seas of Hate*. As he did, he swung his mighty arm forward and released the cannonball.

The massive piece of iron sailed into the air, arcing like a rainbow. As it went, it fizzled and hissed as if angered – no – as if hungry.

The snake-daemons on the *Seas of Hate* all watched the cannonball in unison. They'd been laughing at the ogre and the others in the *Sea Chariot* up until then, contributing to a mad symphony of hisses. Now, they fell silent as they stared at the missile of cold iron coming straight towards them.

The ball landed in the middle of the foredeck. Dunk had expected it to bounce or maybe roll a bit, perhaps to knock some of the daemons into the sea. Instead, it smashed right through the decking, tearing through it as if it were little more than paper.

Dunk wondered for a moment just how far down the ball might go. Where would it stop? Then a geyser of seawater gushed up through the hole it had created.

Pegleg cackled with glee as the snake-daemons scrambled about the deck, looking desperately for some way to seal the hole. Then a second ball crashed down among them. This one caught a snake-daemon square in the back as it fell, and it dragged the creature down into the new hole it made before it could even hiss in protest.

A third ball smashed down a moment later, and the ship's nose started to tilt forward as she took on water. The snake-daemons started leaping over the ship's rail and paddling for the shore. Unfortunately for them, the snakes didn't make particularly good swimmers, and they made poor progress against the outgoing tide.

The monstrous masthead on the *Seas of Hate* let loose a horrendous hiss as it reached for the *Sea Chariot*. The viper's head on one of its arms smashed down in front of Dunk and Pegleg, sinking its fangs into the gunwale's wood. Pegleg pulled Dunk back from the railing and turned him to watch M'Grash's response.

The ogre wrapped his hands around the cannonball this time and stood sideways to the *Seas of Hate*. Then he kicked up his front leg as he brought the ball over his head. He transferred the cannonball into one hand as he thrust his front leg forward. Dunk could see the ball glowing white in an outline around his hand.

M'Grash hurled the cannonball forward with all his might, and it left his hand as if fired from a real cannon. It shot straight towards the living masthead and smashed into its chest. Then it exploded in a blast of noise, heat, and light.

Bits of the snake-daemon masthead went everywhere. Some of them landed on the deck next to Dunk. He kicked one with his foot and saw that it was nothing more than splinters of badly scorched wood.

The rest of the snake-daemons gaped in astonishment at the large hole where their masthead had once been. The only thing left was the one snake arm still attached to the *Sea Chariot*. It held on to where the shoulder had been on the *Seas of Hate*, stretched taut almost to the point of snapping.

The snake-daemons pitched themselves over the side of the ship and swam desperately for the shore. Some of them tried to climb up onto the *Sea Chariot*, but a well-aimed crossbow bolt through the cranium of the first two or three put their ambitions to rest. Dunk glanced back and saw Cavre grin at him from the back railing of the bridge as he loaded his crossbow once more.

Over the hissing of the creatures in the water, Dunk heard a chorus of pathetic wails rise up. At first, he couldn't tell from where they came. Then he figured it out.

'The prisoners!' Dunk grabbed Pegleg by the shoulders. 'The people rowing that ship, they're all chained to it. They'll go down with it!'

Pegleg grimaced. 'They would have all died under those daemons' tender mercies anyhow. It's a small price to pay to rid the seas of the taint of those bastards.'

Dunk cursed. He couldn't just let all those people die. He stared over at the *Sea of Hate*, and then did the only thing he could think of. He leapt upon the masthead's remaining arm.

18

Now that the masthead lived no more, the arm had become a plank of well carved wood. With the ship's nose already starting to sink, Dunk could slide down the plank, right to the deck of the *Seas of Hate* – and he did.

Once Dunk reached the ship, he pulled himself up over the gunwale and onto the main deck. There, in the open hold below, he saw a few dozen bruised and battered men straining desperately against their shackles. None had managed to free themselves yet.

'The keys!' Dunk shouted down at the prisoners. 'Where are the keys?'

A few of the slaves stood up and pointed at the rhythm-keeper's drum at the edge of the deck overlooking the hold. Dunk dashed over to it and found a single rusty key hanging from a vicious hook. He snatched it up and dived into the hold below.

Insane with panic, the water already sloshing around their ankles, the men grabbed at Dunk and tried to take the key from him. After he smashed the first few attempts down with his free fist, they held up their iron-cuffed wrists instead and pleaded with him to let them go.

Dunk worked that key into every lock he could find. In, twist, out. In, twist, out. In, twist, out.

A few of the freed muttered their thanks to the thrower, but most scrambled free and dived over the gunwale without a word. Dunk could hardly blame them. The water was rising fast.

Just as Dunk reached the final row of oarsmen, something in the front of the ship gave way, and the sea came rushing into the hold. In, twist, out. In, twist, out. In, twist, out.

Dunk thought he just might make it, but the last prisoner refused to show Dunk his shackles. Instead, he snarled at the thrower and tried to bite him. Dunk considered knocking the man out and then freeing him, but the hold chose that moment to slip beneath the waves.

The water hit Dunk in the back and shoved him up and free. He reached for the shackled madman, but his grip slipped away. As he bobbed on the surface for an instant, he looked down and saw the man struggling with his irons, the air bubbling from his lungs.

Dunk grabbed a good breath and then dived down towards the man. He wasn't going to let this poor soul drown if he could help it. The more people he could rescue from daemons of any kind, the better, and if he had to risk his own life to do it, then so be it.

When Dunk reached the man, his impending death by drowning seemed to have washed his madness away. He presented his shackles and waited for Dunk to work the key into the lock.

Once the man was free, he kicked away towards the surface. Dunk made to follow him, but found that the sleeve of his shirt had caught on the man's irons. Before he could separate himself, one of the last escapee's desperate kicks caught Dunk in the side of the head.

Stunned, Dunk hung there in the water for a moment. As his head started to clear, he heard a loud, horrible creaking noise, and the irons dragged him deeper into the water. The entire ship was going down.

Dunk wanted to curse, but he saved his breath, as he had precious little of it left. He tried to tear himself away from the irons again, but with his feet now dragging along above him he couldn't find the leverage.

The world around Dunk began to spin and close in around the edges, and he felt his consciousness leaving him. Looking up through the water, he saw the sunlight above getting further and further away. Then something huge splashed into the water next to him, knocking the last of the air out of his lungs.

Dunk thought for sure that he was dead. Then he felt his sleeve tear loose from his shirt at the shoulder, and a strong hand yanked him up towards the light.

The next thing Dunk knew he was flat on his back, stretched out on M'Grash's torso, with Spinne shoving on his chest and belly, forcing the water from him. He sat up, coughing and spluttering, choking fresh air back into his lungs. For a moment, he didn't know where he was. Then he saw that M'Grash was lying in the open sea, floating on his back to give Spinne a surface to work on Dunk.

'Thanks,' Dunk croaked, both at M'Grash and Spinne. A cheer went up from the deck of the *Sea Chariot* and from the newly freed men swimming around them in the water.

Spinne pulled Dunk to her and held him tight. Although he'd nearly drowned, she was the one who was shivering.

'You're the bravest, most amazing man I've ever known,' she whispered in his ear. 'And if you ever do something like that again, I'll kill you myself.'

THE REST OF the trip to Bad Bay wasn't nearly so eventful. Pegleg ordered the freed slaves to be brought onto the ship, and the Hackers deposited them safely in Valhallaholic, a resort town founded by the Estalians to cater to the frequent Norscan raiding parties that always seemed to wander a bit off track after spending too much time pillaging. The ex-prisoners treated Dunk like a conquering hero the entire time they were on the ship, and many of them wept for him when they had to leave.

Once the Hackers arrived at Valhallaholic, Pegleg declared an evening of shore leave for them all. They swarmed into the port town, right behind the refugees.

'I need a drink,' Slick said as he, Spinne, and Dunk strolled into the town. M'Grash had stayed behind with Pegleg to guard the ship. Now over his fear of water, Pegleg seemed never to want to leave the *Sea Chariot* again. In fact, he'd threatened to hold practices on the main deck – or at least on a beach right next to the boat so he could call out instructions from the crow's nest during scrimmages.

'I think we all do,' Spinne said, holding Dunk's arm. Ever since she and M'Grash had pulled him from the sinking *Seas of Death*, she'd clung to his side. Dunk knew he'd scared her badly – he'd scared himself – but he didn't see what he could do to make it up to her. Perhaps an evening hanging out in a tavern over a few cold drinks would be the best thing for everyone.

'Wait,' Dunk said, as he scanned the street, looking for a sign of a welcoming inn. 'Is that who I think it is?'

Someone who looked exactly like Gunther the Gobbo had poked his nose out from between two buildings and was peering up and down the street.

'Is that the Gobbo?' Spinne asked, squinting at the figure standing half in the shadows.

'It couldn't be,' said Slick. 'What would he be doing here?'

Then the figure turned towards the trio and spotted them. Even from this far away, Dunk could see Gunther go white. Then he turned and scurried back down the alley from which he'd come.

Dunk took off at a sprint, chasing after the figure. 'Hold it!' he shouted after the Gobbo as he finally reached the mouth of the blind alley. Two doors let out into it. Both of them must have been locked, as Gunther was hanging from the latch of one of them, trying to open it with all of his might.

'Hello, Gunther,' Dunk said as Spinne came pounding into the alley behind him. He could hear Slick's tiny feet padding slowly after her as well.

The clammy-faced bookie let go of the locked door's latch and turned to show Dunk what he probably thought was his best, crooked-toothed grin. 'Hey there, kid. What brings you to this back-water hole?'

Dunk squinted at Gunther. 'Something tells me you already know.'

The greasy bookie laughed nervously. 'No,' he said in false surprise. 'Don't tell me that I somehow stumbled upon the Hackers' new secret training camp.'

Spinne snorted. 'Try again,' she said with a growl.

'Did Pegleg decide to treat the whole team to a holiday here? You really should try the mead and the mulled wine. They're excellent.'

Slick entered the alley, sweating and puffing for breath. 'It is you,' he said, 'you petty little bastard. You sold us out to those pirates.'

'Hey, I don't know what you're talking about,' Gunther said, hold-ing his hands up. His beady eyes darted all over the place, trying to spot some way out of this. 'If a bunch of daemons happen to find you out in the middle of the ocean and attack you, how am I supposed to be responsible for that?'

'Who said they were daemons?' asked Dunk.

Gunther froze. 'It's, um, a figure of speech?' he said weakly.

Dunk and Spinne stalked towards the Gobbo, with Slick bringing up the rear.

'I'll scream,' Gunther said. 'They don't look kindly on killers in this town.'

'How about scum who cut deals with daemons?' asked Dunk. 'We'd be happy to explain everything.'

'If you're lucky, they'll just kill you on the spot,' said Spinne. 'I hear the Norscans like to spit-roast anyone caught trafficking with such creatures.'

'That's a nasty way to die,' Slick said. 'Takes forever, I hear. On a windy day like this, out near the sea, there's no chance that you'll choke on the smoke before the fire reaches you. Your legs will proba-bly burn to a crisp before the fire reaches your vitals.'

'I'll bet they'd hear you screaming in Altdorf,' said Dunk.

'All right!' Gunther said, nearly sobbing, his eyes wide in terror. 'I did it. I did it.' He looked up at them as he started to whimper. 'What are you going to do with me?'

* * *

'THAT WAS YOU?' Gunther said to Pegleg as he clapped his warty hand over his pimply forehead. The bookie sat on the deck of the *Sea Chariot*, too stunned to get back on his feet. 'I had no idea.'

'You weren't supposed to.'

'But you were dressed up as a Chaos All-Stars fan, all in leather and spikes – and with a chainsaw in place of your hook!' Gunther gaped at the coach, and Dunk, M'Grash, Spinne, and Slick each took a half step away from the ex-pirate.

'It's called a disguise, Mr. Gobbo. It's not very effective if you can see right through it.'

'But-but-but…' Gunther just couldn't wrap his head around something. 'Why? Why would you sell out your whole team – including yourself – to me?'

'All part of a personal self-improvement project,' Pegleg said with a smile.

'What?'

Dunk shook his head. 'You came here expecting to get some evidence of my death, didn't you?'

'Hey, you can't prove that.'

Dunk leaned over, almost putting his nose in Gunther's face. 'This isn't a court of law. I don't need proof. I know what you did. I just want to know why?'

'He asked me to!' Gunther said, stabbing a fat finger at Pegleg.

'So?'

'He told me that I'd get a share of the reward on your head.' Gunther glared at Pegleg. 'You *lied* to me.'

'And you set up a deal with a boat of daemons to kill a couple of dozen people,' Slick said.

Gunther shut his trap and swallowed hard. 'What are you going to do with me?'

'Nothing,' Pegleg said.

'Nothing?' everyone else in the room said.

The captain grinned. 'Why would we want to do anything to harm the Hackers' newest employee?'

Dunk rubbed his eyes. Everything about this confused him.

'That's right,' Pegleg said, leaning over the Gobbo. 'You work for me now. Secretly and off the books.'

'But I'm a bookie, not a Blood Bowl player! I don't have the ability or the skills. And I bleed easily.'

M'Grash nodded at that. 'He sure does.'

'You're not our latest player,' Pegleg said. 'You're our first scout.'

'No way,' Gunther said. 'Uh-uh. No way, no how, no time.' He folded his arms across his chest as if that settled the matter.

'You act as if you had a choice in the matter,' Pegleg said. 'There's a reason I chose you to act as my go-between with the daemons, you know. After your work with the Black Jerseys went public, you've been in shallow waters. Do you think anyone would do business with you ever again if they knew you'd tried to wipe out an entire Blood Bowl champion-calibre team with the help of your daemon friends?'

'Hey,' Gunther said, 'they got over me fixing games, didn't they?'

'On some level, people admired that. It took smarts, organisation, and a bit of vision to pull that off. Trucking with daemons, that just takes a complete lack of morals or ethics.'

Gunther sighed deeply, and looked Pegleg in the eyes. 'All right,' he said. 'I work for you.'

Dunk stared at the Gobbo and then at Pegleg. 'You planned this from the start, didn't you coach?' he asked.

The ex-pirate just smiled. 'You win games by concocting a plan and then executing it to the letter. We hit this plan perfectly.'

'So we just let him go now?'

Pegleg nodded. 'He's agreed to work for us, but in secret. The less he's seen with us, the better.'

'I'll be leaving right now then,' Gunther said. 'I'll send my reports to you in Bad Bay.'

Dunk reached out and put a hand on Gunther's shoulder. 'I have one last question for you,' he said. 'That night that Zauberer put that price on my head, how did you know where to find me? You're no friend of Sparky's.'

'Did he tell you that? He would. Just because he owes me a little money, he goes and disowns me like that.'

Dunk just glared at the bookie.

'All right,' Gunther said. 'It was Zauberer. He told me where to find you.'

Dunk couldn't believe it. 'Why would he do that?' he asked. 'That was right after he put that price on my head.'

'He said it had something to do with forcing you into the hands of your enemies, forcing you to trust people who would later betray you.' The bookie shot Pegleg a dirty look. 'I suppose you'd know something about that.'

The ex-pirate smiled down at Gunther. 'Just admit you were well played and move on,' he said.

'So you've been in contact with Zauberer?' Dunk asked.

Gunther started to nod, and then shook his head. 'Oh, no,' he said. 'It's one thing to act as your team scout and pass you information. It's something else entirely to ask me to cross a wizard like that. I won't do it. He'd kill me in a heartbeat.'

'What makes you think we won't?'

Gunther snorted. 'I've seen you play, kid. You don't have that instinct.'

'What about M'Grash?' Dunk asked. The ogre made a good show of cracking his knuckles.

'Don't, kid,' Gunther said, his voice quavering. 'Just don't.'

Dunk frowned. 'I still don't get it though. How did Zauberer know where to find me? And how did he know about the tunnel coming out of the Bad Water?'

'Who knows,' Gunther said with a shrug. 'Wizards work in mysterious ways.'

'You could say the same about Blood Bowl coaches.'

WHEN THE HACKERS finally made it back to Bad Bay, tucking into a natural harbour on the Empire's north shore, overlooking the Sea of Claws, they headed straight for the room they shared at the FIB Tavern. Although the place had been named for an obscene variety of Imperial Bastard – a shot at the occasional visitors from Altdorf who sometimes vacationed there – the staff had always treated Dunk like family, and Spinne had come to enjoy the place too. They could have taken a suite in the Hacker Hotel, the poshest place for miles around, but since they spent so little time there Dunk preferred to remain with people he'd come to trust.

The winter snows had come to the place, and the sky had turned its seasonal steel grey. When Dunk and Spinne barged into the tavern, the only thing on his mind was a hot drink and a warm bed that he hoped to not have to get out of for a week. Instead, they found company waiting for them: Dirk and Lästiges.

'You took your damned time getting here,' Dirk said as he gave his brother and then Spinne a hug. 'I thought we might have to send out a search party.'

'We had a bit of a delay near Valhallaholic,' Spinne said. 'Once we got through that, it was smooth sailing.'

'Spending time in a tourist trap while there's a price on your head?' Lästiges said to Dunk. 'That has a certain kind of mad style to it.'

'I thought you debunked that on Cabalvision,' Dunk said.

'To the public, sure, but we all know that what you hear on Cabalvision isn't often even a close cousin to the truth.'

Dunk couldn't help but grin at Dirk as the quartet took a private table in the back corner of the main room, far from anyone else in the place. The people of Bad Bay were used to seeing the Hackers around and had long since become impervious to their fame. They gave the four a wide berth out of respect for them and the kind of money the Hackers brought into town on a regular basis.

'I'm just glad to see you alive and well,' Dunk said to his brother. 'You look good. Not playing Blood Bowl agrees with you.'

'It's just the lack of cuts, bruises, and other injuries,' Dirk said. 'You'd be surprised what that can do for your outlook on life. For the first time in years, I don't hurt every time I move.'

'So,' Spinne said once they'd signalled for a round of beers – Hacker High Life, of course – 'what are you two doing here?'

'It's a crime to want to see my brother?' Dirk asked, taking mock offence.

'Traditionally, it's not been high on your list,' Dunk said with a wry smile.

'Dirk's turned over a new leaf,' Lästiges said. 'Family's important to him these days.'

Dunk frowned as he nodded. 'She told you about Father.'

Dirk nodded too. 'I can't believe the old bastard's still alive. Lästiges told me about your meeting with him in the House of Booze. I've been doing some poking around about him and the Guterfiends since I left the game. It's one hell of a twisted tale.'

'Tell me about it,' said Dunk. As Dirk laughed, Dunk repeated himself. 'No, seriously, tell me about it.'

'All right,' Dirk said, as their drinks arrived. He hoisted his tankard for a toast. 'To the Hoffnung brothers, no matter what their names may be now. May their blood always run thick.'

Dunk grinned. 'You're just trying to put off having to tell me what you know.'

'Not so,' Dirk said. He took a large swing of his beer, leaned forward with his elbow on the table and began to talk in a conspiratorial tone. 'I just want to make sure you're ready to hear it.

'I checked in to what Father told you. It seems like most of it's true.'

'What's not?'

'Well, there seems to be some disagreement among some of the people who were there about how Mother and Kirta died.'

'I always thought the angry mob got them.'

'Sure,' Dirk nodded, 'that theory makes some sense, but I tracked down one person in Altdorf who'd been a part of that mob. He says that Mother and Kirta were already dead when they opened the door.'

Dunk frowned. 'That doesn't make much sense. Who inside the keep would want to kill them? You don't think Father had something to do with it?'

Dirk shrugged. 'It's possible. Maybe he wanted to make a last-second attempt to keep his daemon lords satisfied with his performance. Or maybe he wanted to cheat them of the chance to kill Mother and Kirta and banish their souls to the Realm of Chaos.'

'But he didn't kill me.'

'Maybe he didn't care so much about your soul.'

'It doesn't add up,' Spinne said. 'Why kill them if the mob was about to do that anyhow?'

'Who knows if they would have?' asked Lästiges. 'Maybe they knew something dangerous, something that Dunk wasn't aware of.'

Dunk shook his head. 'I just don't believe it. Father got into trouble with Khorne for refusing him the souls of his children. That included Kirta. If Father loved us enough to squabble with the Blood God over us, I don't think he'd kill any of us the first time things looked bad. You don't defy Khorne without bringing down misery on yourself, after all.' He narrowed his eyes at Dirk. 'What else do you have?'

'I went to Altdorf and spoke with Chiara.'

'The head maid?' Dunk was impressed. Chiara had never cared much for him, but she'd doted on Dirk all his life – up until he'd run away from home. After that point, she'd refused to even speak his name, referring to him as 'that other boy.'

'She wasn't happy to see me at first, but I soon had her eating out of my hand. She didn't want to talk about our family at all when I arrived. 'Better to let the dead stay dead,' she said.

'Eventually she confessed that Father's bargaining with Khorne was an open secret among the keep's senior staff. There's only so much you can do to hide the pentagrams and other things you need to communicate with gods in their far-off realms, after all.

'Some of the staff just ignored it. Lehrer, for instance, never paid it any mind. He only cared that the people who were supposed to dole out his pay actually did. He didn't care how they came up with it in the first place.'

'Ever the practical soul,' Dunk said.

'So what happened?' Spinne asked. Dunk wasn't sure why she felt the need to prod the conversation along, but she clearly wanted to hear everything Dirk had to say – and fast. 'Why did your father turn against Khorne?'

'It seems that his deal with the Blood God stated that Khorne got the souls of his children as well as his own. You can't just sign away someone else's soul though. They have to be given freely. However, Father had promised he could make that happen as part of his own bargain.

'He had until the day one of his children became betrothed.'

Dunk's breath froze in his chest.

'At that point, it seems that the child would be considered to be an adult. After all, if you can pledge yourself forever to a mate, you can certainly do the same for a daemon lord.'

'But Father never mentioned any of this to me,' Dunk said. 'Ever.'

'And what would you have done if he did?' Spinne asked. 'Would you have sold your soul to Khorne to keep your family's fortunes safe?'

Dunk considered this for a moment. 'My first instinct is to say, "No, of course not". However, if it would have saved my mother and sister, I don't know. At the least, I'd have known what was coming our way. I could have helped him fight against it.'

'You'd have been killed as well,' Spinne said, placing her hands on his arm.

'We could have run away and kept everyone safe. Or I could just as easily not got engaged. It was an arranged marriage, for the love of life. Father arranged it himself.'

Dirk frowned. 'Could be he never thought Khorne would try to hold him to the letter of his agreement. Or maybe he thought he could convince Khorne that an alliance with the Brechers would be more valuable than just handing you over. Either way, it seems he meant to protect you from what he was doing.'

Dunk glared at Dirk. 'Did you know what he was doing? I mean, you had all those fights with him, and then you left home without ever telling me why. I thought you two just kept butting heads because you were too alike, but – did you learn something you shouldn't have known?'

'Do you have to ask me that?'

'At this point, I think so. So?'

Dirk screwed up his face for a moment. 'Yes,' he said. 'I stumbled into Father's den once while he was speaking with a daemon.'

'Was it Khorne?' Lästiges asked, suddenly all ears. It seemed Dirk hadn't shared this with anyone else before.

'What did you do?' Dunk asked.

Dirk looked away. 'I – I turned around and left before he could see me. The daemon saw me though. He looked straight at me through the crack in the door that I'd peered through. He caught me with those glowing red eyes, like a fly in amber. For a moment, I couldn't move out of sheer terror that I might send the daemon into a rage. It took everything I had just to shut the door and run away as if I had a horde of daemons on my heels.'

'Did you ever talk with Father about it?'

Dirk shook his head. 'But it came between us anyway. I wanted to demand an explanation from him, but I couldn't conceive of anything he could say that could possibly justify what he was doing – and I hated him for it.

'I finally did say something about it, but not until the night I left the keep for good. I told him not to come after me, or I'd let Mother and the rest of the world know about his sins.'

'He told me he'd had to disown you.'

Dirk smirked. 'It came down to the same thing. Neither of us wanted to have anything to do with each other, and we both got our wish.'

Dunk stared at his younger brother. 'Why didn't you tell me any of this back then?'

'So you could let your guilt over your complicity in Father's plots tear you apart too? No thanks. It was bad enough I had to deal with it. I couldn't drag you into it too.'

Dirk took a long drink of his beer, polishing off the last of what was in his tankard. When he finished, Dunk could still see the hurt hanging in his brother's eyes. Dunk reached across the table and shook Dirk's hand. 'Thanks,' he said. 'I wish you hadn't done it – but thanks.'

'You're welcome,' Dirk said in a dry tone. 'Anyway, according to Chiara, my leaving the keep seemed to be the turning point for Father. I think that's when he realised what he'd be missing if he kept to his deal with Khorne.'

'You think as highly of yourself as ever,' Spinne said.

Dirk ignored her and kept his focus on Dunk. 'That's why when everything went wrong on your wedding day, he was ready for it.'

'Ready?' said Dunk. 'Mother and Kirta were killed, and we had to run for the hills.'

'More ready than he would have been. Honestly, when I heard what had happened that day – weeks after the fact – I was shocked. I thought for sure he'd be better prepared than that. I – well, I thought you were all dead, of course.'

Dirk lowered his head and took a deep breath, then let it out slowly. 'I mourned for you all, but – through that – the one thought I held on to was that if it had happened then at least Father had finally stood up to the daemons and gone back to being his own man.'

Dunk hadn't thought of it that way. He hadn't understood much of what had happened, and he'd blamed himself for it for a long time. He'd thought that he must have done something to bring the wrath of all those daemons down on the night of his engagement party.

Now, although he hated what his father had done, he could respect how he'd refused to sell out his family in the end, no matter what it might cost him. And it had cost him everything he had.

Dunk raised his tankard for a toast, and Dirk joined in. 'Here's to him,' Dunk said. That was enough.

'What about the Guterfiends?' asked Spinne, pulling her hands back to herself. 'Who are they, and how did they end up in your keep?'

'We couldn't find out too much about them,' said Lästiges. 'It seems they were a middle-class family of travelling merchants, supposedly hailing from Nuln, although I couldn't confirm that.

'As for their rise to power, it looks like they were just in the right place at the right time. The day after the Hoffnung keep was nearly burned down, the Guterfiends were there laying claim to the place. They paid off the right people and secured the deeds to all of the Hoffnung holdings, and they moved in soon after. A few months later, it was like nothing had ever happened, except the name over the gate had changed.

'Of course, they could only purchase these things because everyone in the Empire thought that the Hoffnungs were all dead, their line extinguished. In such cases, the property goes to the Empire, and the bureaucrats there were only too happy to sell the Hoffnung estate in one large block to the Guterfiends for a monstrous lump sum. If the gold they paid with smelled a bit like brimstone, no one seemed to notice or care.'

'What about Dirk?' Dunk asked. 'He may have changed his last name to Heldmann, but his real identity was an open secret.'

'Father disowned me, remember?' Dirk said. 'It may have come after I'd removed myself from the family, but it meant I had no legal claim to the property as far as Imperial law was concerned.'

'So when I started playing Blood Bowl…'

'The Guterfiends aren't fans of the sport,' Lästiges said, 'but they heard soon enough that you'd come back. They feared you might come forth to claim your inheritance and strip them of everything they'd paid so much for.'

'That's why they put up the money for Zauberer's ludicrous reward,' Spinne said. 'But where would they get that much money?'

'Gold isn't anything to a Lord of Chaos, assuming Khorne's backing the Guterfiends like he did Father,' Dirk said. 'Of course, it's easier to kill those who come to claim the reward than to pay them a million crowns, so I wouldn't count that out either.'

Spinne started to speak, but she choked on her words. Dunk reached out his hands to her, but she pushed them away. 'You need to quit the Hackers,' she said, her voice low and raw. 'You need to leave Blood Bowl behind and get as far away from the Empire as you can.'

Dunk stared at her, trying to understand her distress. 'Hey, now. People try to kill me all the time. It's part of my job.'

'Orcs, elves, ogres, sure,' she said, 'but not people like this. These Guterfiends have real power, and you're a direct threat to that power. They'll do anything they think they must to make sure you're dead.'

Dunk reached out to caress Spinne's flushed cheek, but she pulled away. 'I'll be fine,' he said. 'We can handle this.'

'We can't.' Spinne said. Her chin dropped to her chest. 'I can't.'

Dunk started to ask what she meant, but decided to keep his mouth shut. He knew.

Spinne sat there for a moment, no one saying anything. When she looked back up, her eyes were red and wet. 'We're talking about people who have as much gold as the Emperor. Who have Khorne – the bloody Blood God – backing them.

'We're just people. Sure, we play Blood Bowl in front of hundreds of thousands, and we make a good living at it, but it's just a job. It's not worth death and eternal damnation.'

Dirk stared at Spinne. 'I've known you for years,' he said. 'I've never heard you talk like this. We defy death during every game. What's so different about this?'

Spinne ignored Dirk and Lästiges and gazed into Dunk's eyes instead. 'I never cared much about living before.' Then she frowned and wiped her eyes. 'Besides, we're not talking about my life here. It's Dunk's life and his *soul*. And yours too, damn it. Just because the Empire doesn't see you as an heir to your father – who deserves to burn for all time – doesn't mean Khorne has given up his claim on you.'

Dunk peered into Spinne's eyes. 'I can't walk away from this,' he said.

'Then run!'

'I have to see this through.'

'I know you do,' Spinne said as she stood up to leave, 'but I don't.' She reached down and gave Dunk one last, passionate kiss. Then she walked out the tavern's door.

Just before Spinne shut the door behind her, she turned back and said, 'I can't watch you do this. Tell Pegleg I quit.'

'WELCOME TO SPIKE Stadium here in beautiful downtown Praag for the something-or-other annual Chaos Cup Tournament!' Bob's voice said, ringing out over the snow-covered field. 'We'd tell you how many years it's been, but no one knows. That's Chaos for you!'

'You said it, Bob!' said Jim. 'If you want to see some Chaos around here, look no further than the Hackers. They've lost ten players since their appearance in the Dungeonbowl Tournament – including star standout Spinne Schönheit.'

'Still, they had the guts to accept Da Deff Skwad's invitation to play here in the first round of the Chaos Cup. How many teams would be that stupid? – I mean, desperate? – I mean, brave?'

'Who's the brave team here, Bob? With the edict against harming Hoffnung still hanging over his head, who's going to be crazy enough to try to tackle him?'

The crowd's roar started out low and built to a deafening crescendo as the wall-sized orcs who made up Da Deff Skwad prepared to kick off.

'Well, Jim, I think we're about to find out!'

Dunk rubbed his hands together for warmth, and cursed the cold. To get to Praag from Bad Bay in time for the tournament, the Hackers had been forced to make a mad dash, both by land and by sea. They hadn't had any time to pick up warm underclothes for their armour, and when they got to Praag they found that the other teams had cleaned out what stock there was in the city. The Evil Gits, for instance, had bought ten sets of warm underclothes for each of their players – far more than they needed – and then burned them in the courtyard of their hotel for their first pre-game rally.

'Don't worry about the cold,' Dr. Pill had said to the Hackers in their locker room before the game. 'The cold is your friend. It helps to deaden the pain from all the injuries you're going to sustain. It slows the loss of blood too.'

These thoughts comforted Dunk little as he stamped his feet on the snow-covered Astrogranite, trying to beat some sensation back into his toes. He almost hoped that he would get hurt early in the game. At least then he could spend the rest of the day in the heated confines of the Hackers' locker room.

Dunk looked up into the snow-filled sky, felt the falling flakes melting on his exposed skin, and shivered. Then the ball arced down at him out of the ice-grey, and the game was on.

'Looks like Da Deff Skwad aren't shy at all,' Jim said. 'They kicked the ball straight at Hoffnung!'

'Well,' said Lästiges's voice, 'according to their coach, Yeevil Gut-snatcher, their stated goal is to take out Hoffnung fast and demoralise the rest of the Hackers. Once they see that Da Deff Skwad's monsters can dismember whoever they like, it may make the surviving Hackers shy of the ball – not to mention their opponents!'

The ball cascaded out of the sky and into Dunk's waiting arms, and he took off running. If a bunch of illiterate orcs wanted to tear him limb from limb, they were going to have to work for it.

Dunk zigged to the left, zagged right, and angled for the sideline. M'Grash and Edgar put up a wall between him and the onrushing orcs, but it wasn't enough. The cold made the treeman sluggish, and a speedy pair of goblins snaked around his trunk to sprint right for the Hackers' thrower.

Dunk cocked back his arm and looked for a catcher downfield. He would have been thrilled to see Spinne waving her arms at him right then, but he hadn't seen her since that night in the FIB Tavern. Most of the rookies had seen her departure as a bad omen, and had left the team soon after.

The new recruits were so green that Edgar took to calling them shoots. Eager as kids on the last day of school, they worked hard, but none of them had the level of skill gained only by being blooded on the Astrogranite. Today, they'd pick up those skills, or die.

But none of them were open.

Then Dunk spotted Cavre breaking free from an orc lineman he'd left clutching a broken nose. Just as the two goblins came at him,

Dunk loosed the ball at the blitzer and watched it sail through the air.

He never saw it come down, though, as the goblins hit him hard. They wrapped their arms around his legs and brought him down. One of them sunk his teeth into Dunk's thigh and only became dislodged when Dunk used the other goblin's head to club him away.

Even then, the two creatures kept coming at Dunk. Harming a player who didn't have the ball was a flagrant foul – one that would get the goblins kicked out of the game. But as Pegleg often said, 'It's only a foul if the ref catches it, and if he's been paid to look the other way, that won't happen.'

Still on his back, Dunk couldn't find the leverage he needed to throw the rabid pair of goblins off him. They kept tearing at him with tooth and claw, trying to find the soft parts under his armour or the skin exposed to the bitter-cold air. If the thrower didn't do something to stop them soon, they'd succeed – mortally.

Then the goblins disappeared, and M'Grash stood over Dunk, holding out his hand to help his friend up. 'Dunkel okay?' the ogre asked, concerned. His frown changed to a grin as Dunk leapt to his feet.

'Thanks, big guy,' Dunk said as he scanned the field, searching for where the twinned goblins might have landed. They weren't the kind to give up. He knew they'd be back.

Then black lightning cracked down from the sky, and two smoking holes appeared only yards away. The ashes in them swirled around in the flash-melted snow, forming a boiling, grey paste in which pieces of spiked armour smouldered.

'Wow,' Jim said. 'I haven't seen anything like that since, well, ever!'

'Did you notice how that bolt split into two as it neared the field? You hardly ever see skill like that in a wizard. Most are perfectly happy to use two bolts when one will do, but that's the sign of a true craftsman, someone who takes real pride in his killings!'

'Let's see that in slow motion!'

Dunk looked up at the Jumboball framed under a gothic arch at the end of the ancient field and watched the two goblins smacking each other a high five before moving to attack him again. As they turned towards him, a single bolt of black energy slipped out of the sky. Then it split into two and arced into the helpless creatures, lancing through them and turning their flesh to ash.

Dunk just stood there on the field, stunned. To think that he had such powerful protection humbled him, and he wondered if Spinne had been right all along. After all, it wouldn't take much for Zauberer to turn such power on him. If that happened, what hope would Dunk have?

Then Dunk noticed a Deff Skwad troll racing down the field at him, dragging a rookie Hacker from each of his legs as it charged for the end zone. Dunk had almost forgotten he was still playing a game. He sprinted towards the troll, angling to get between the creature and the goal line.

When the troll spotted Dunk, it skidded to a halt, sliding several yards on the snow-slick field. The skid sent the troll straight towards Dunk, and the thrower braced himself for the impact from the tackle he planned to throw at the creature. But before he could launch himself at the troll, the creature flipped the ball into the air, straight at Dunk.

Surprised, Dunk did the only thing he could think of. He stood up straight and caught the ball. He snapped his head left and right to see who might be coming at him, but seeing no one he pivoted on one cleated boot and sprinted towards his own end zone.

As Dunk ran down the field, he saw Da Deff Skwad players, not chasing towards him, but scurrying out of his way, terror shining in their eyes. Seconds later, he stood in the end zone, untouched.

'Touchdown Hackers!' Jim announced over the PA system.

Dunk thrust the ball up into the air in triumph, and the crowd went wild. The Hackers fans – a growing contingent at any game these days, all dressed in green and gold jerseys and replicas of Pegleg's perforated, tri-corn hat – loved the ease of the score, and even the orc rooters in the crowd had to admire the authority with which Dunk had scored.

'Did you see that?' said Bob. 'Not a finger laid on him. Amazing!'

'Of course no one with any sense of self-preservation wants to get anywhere near him,' said Jim. 'At this point, I don't think his own team-mates would be willing to slap him on the back!'

Dunk just grinned as he trotted back down the field. He might not like having Zauberer's threats hanging over him, but Blood Bowl was an odd game that seemed to change with every match. He'd take touchdowns any way he could get them.

When the Hackers kicked the ball off to Da Deff Skwad, Dunk ran right towards the ball. The orc who had it tossed it away in a hurried pass and then raced off in the other direction. Guillermo intercepted the throw and started to run it back. As he went, Dunk lined up next to him, ready to block anyone who might come their way.

No one did. Every player on Da Deff Skwad kept a respectful dis-tance from Dunk, and Guillermo trotted into the end zone untouched.

'Thanks!' Guillermo said after he tossed the ball into the stands. 'Linemen don't get to score too often.'

'Whatever I can do to help,' Dunk said, holding up his hand for a high five.

Guillermo avoided the extended hand with a sheepish grin. 'Ah!' he said with a grin. 'You almost got me.' With that, he jogged off to get back into his position.

Dunk frowned. Having his foes fear him was wonderful. He wondered if he could get Zauberer to threaten his life on a regular basis. But having his team-mates – his friends – nervous around him made him uncomfortable; he relied on these people to be his support system, and if they couldn't rally around him when he needed them, who could?

Maybe they thought he didn't need them anymore. Maybe they had a point.

In the next play, the Hackers went for a squib kick, knocking the ball only a few yards forward in an effort to get it closer to Dunk's hands. The kicker – another rookie, of course – gave it a bit too much leg, though, and the ball bounced up into the stands.

Losing the ball in the stands was a long-standing tradition in Blood Bowl. The fans loved it, as it made them feel like a bigger part of the game, and the players respected their fervour. More than one over-eager rookie going after the ball had been torn apart by a crazed mob of fans.

In Dunk's first game, for instance, he'd let one of the Reavers knock him into the stands while he celebrated his first touchdown. The fans had body-passed him up to the nosebleed seats and right over the stadium's top edge. Fortunately, a series of awnings had broken his fall, or he might have been killed. Unfortunately, he'd fallen on the stand of a sausage-on-a-stick vendor who'd beat him nine-tenths to death.

When the ball went into the stands, the smart players always waited for it to be kicked back out of the crowd. The game clock kept rolling while the fans had their fun. Blood Bowl had no 'out of bounds' rule. The game only stopped for halftime or for scores.

This time, the fans tossed the ball straight back out at Dunk. As he caught it, they cheered, and he waved back at them with a smile.

Dunk walked all the way down the field and into the end zone. When he got to the goal line, he put the ball down for a moment so he could tie his shoe. One of Da Deff Skwad players reached for it, but the orc snatched his hand back as if burned when Dunk raised his head to glare at him.

When the Hackers set up to kick the ball again, Dunk could sense the crowd starting to get ugly – well, uglier than usual. They'd paid good money to see a brawl of a match, and here they were watching a game in which no player had hit another for minutes. They wanted blood, and someone had denied them that.

'Squib it again,' Pegleg had ordered the kicker. 'We're going to stay on Mr. Hoffnung's free ride for as long as we can.'

The crowd had started booing as soon as the Hackers lined up. That and the rocks, tankards, and other things they started to throw shook up the kicker. He booted the ball just a bit too hard again, and it ended up in the stands.

This time, the crowd refused to give the ball back. Instead, they held onto it, bouncing it back and forth among them like a beach ball.

The crowd roared with delight as they realised that they now controlled the match. They started to chant, and the noise quickly drowned out the general boos. As the volume of the chant grew, Dunk made out the words roaring out over the field.

'Play the game!

'Play the game!

'Play the game!'

'Amazing!' said Jim. 'The fans are refusing to let the game go on until – well, until what?'

'What do you think?' asked Bob. 'There's only one solution to this problem. Hoffnung has to leave the game!'

'Hey, hey, ho, ho, Hoffnung has to go!' the crowd started to chant in agreement.

Dunk flushed red under his helmet. He understood how the fans felt, but he hadn't broken any rules. This was the first time, in fact, that his problems with Zauberer had managed to work out well for him. Still, he trotted over to the Hackers' dugout to talk with Pegleg.

'What in Nuffle's name are you doing, Mr. Hoffnung?' Pegleg asked.

'I just wanted to check in with you, coach,' Dunk said.

'About what?'

Dunk looked up at the crowd. 'The fans, they're pretty mad about all this.'

'Mr. Hoffnung? Do you play for the fans?'

Dunk shook his head.

'I can't hear you.'

'No!' Dunk said.

'Do the fans pay your salary?'

'No.'

'Who does?'

'You do, coach.'

'Right, Mr. Hoffnung. I hired you to win games for me, something I've had cause to regret on some days.' He put his hook on Dunk's shoulder. 'Today is not one of those days.'

'Go home, Hoffnung!

'Go home, Hoffnung!

'Go home, Hoffnung!'

Dunk frowned, upset, but he looked at Pegleg and said, 'Just tell me what you want me to do, coach.'

Pegleg grabbed Dunk by the shoulders, spun him around towards the field, and gave him a push. 'Get in there and win this bloody game!'

As Dunk trotted back into the middle of the field, the crowd's chanting broke down into general boos. He tried to ignore it, but couldn't. The noise made it hard for him to think.

Cavre beckoned Dunk over to where he stood near the sideline in front of the section where the ball bobbed along atop the fans like a bit of flotsam in a rough sea. 'Still in the game?' Cavre asked, leaning in close to Dunk's ear so the thrower could hear him.

Dunk nodded.

'Good,' Cavre pointed up into the stands. 'Now get in there and get that ball.'

Dunk gaped at the team captain, but didn't say a word.

'If a bunch of professional killers like Da Deff Skwad won't come near you, Dunk, I don't think the fans will either.' Cavre patted Dunk on back.

'Are you sure about this?'

'No,' Cavre grinned, 'but there's only one way to find out.'

With a slap on the back of his helmet, Dunk started towards the stands. At first, the crowd kept on jeering the thrower, but when he made it to the restraining wall, the people in the front rows grew silent. He reached up and pulled himself onto the top of the restraining row, and all of the angry fans bundled up in their winter gear turned as white as the snow that had fallen on their furs.

'Boo,' Dunk said.

The fans shoved away from him, parting as if he had the plague or was made of something both unstable and explosive. They pushed each other aside, making room that wasn't there in the sold-out stadium. Then, once he'd passed them, making his way farther up into the stands where the ball was still in play, they closed around him again, forming a bubble of solitude around him in a mass of people.

The person who had the ball – a tall skaven with glowing green eyes – held on to it, unwilling to give it up to anyone else. Whether that sprang from arrogance or paralysing fear, Dunk couldn't tell, but he kept on climbing up towards the creature, taking long steps from one bleacher to another.

When Dunk reached the monstrous rat-man – who'd drooled something chunky onto the ball – the creature put the ball down on the bench beside him and stepped away. Dunk picked up the ball by grabbing an un-slimed spike, nodded at the creature and said, 'Thanks!'

By the time Dunk made it back down to the Astrogranite, the crowd's booing had grown to a deafening level. The other Hackers had formed a knot near where he came out of the stands, and they formed a cordon that stood ready to escort him to the end zone. At first, he thought it strange that they offered him extra protection that he obviously didn't need. Then he realised that they just wanted to keep close to him to avoid anyone attacking them instead.

Dunk started towards the end zone, and then changed his mind and swept out towards the cluster of Deff Skwad players huddled together by their dugout. Their coach stood at the edge of their dugout, snarling and screaming at them. He'd gone so far as to hurl an axe at them, which had landed in one player's leg, but they refused to move any closer to Dunk.

When they noticed Dunk coming closer to them, they panicked. Dunk rushed at them, the other Hackers spreading out behind him like a phalanx of warriors ready to bring down the ultimate doom. The troll, who towered over the others, squealed like a little girl and then turned and ran towards Da Deff Skwad's dugout. The other Deff Skwad players chased after him as fast as their shorter legs would carry them.

Coach Gutsnatcher railed against his players as they flooded into his dugout, threatening to disembowel each and every one of them if they didn't turn and fight. They ignored him, shoving him aside and trampling each other in a mad race to get down the tunnel that led to their locker room. After a short commotion, the entire dugout stood empty, except for Gutsnatcher.

'You!' the black orc said. He towered over Dunk and reminded him a bit of Skragger – whose head still dangled on the chain around his neck – back when the star player had been alive. 'You can't do this to my team!'

Dunk grimaced. 'It's not me,' he said, 'blame Zauberer. In the meantime, you might as well chase after your players and see if you can help them find their backbones. This game is over.'

'It's not over until *I* say its over!' Gutsnatcher said.

On the field, a whistle blew. 'That's the game, folks,' Jim said. 'It's over! The Hackers win by forfeit!'

'That's what happens when you can't get any of your players to stay on the field! I haven't seen something like this since the last time the Greenfield Grasshuggers took on the Oldheim Ogres in the opening round of last year's Blood Bowl tournament!'

'Don't knock that game! The Grasshuggers used that to establish themselves as the first halfling team with a survival rate of over fifty percent that year. They've had the best halfling players flocking to their banner because of that – well, that and the pies their manager's mother makes!'

'If this continues, it can only herald the start of a long winning streak for the Hackers,' Bob said. 'The only question is, how long will Hoffnung's luck hold out?'

DUNK DIDN'T KNOW how long someone had been pounding on his door. He just wanted them to leave him alone. Pegleg let his players sleep in on game days to get as much rest as they could, and Dunk was determined to take full advantage of that today.

'Go away!' he said, and pulled the extra pillow over his head, sandwiching his ears between the two.

Mornings like this, on the road and alone, he missed Spinne more than ever. He sometimes found it hard to believe that she'd left not only him, but the team as well. As her agent, Slick had tried to talk her out of it, but she'd refused to listen. According to him, she didn't even want Slick to try to sign her with another team.

Dunk knew any team would be lucky to have her. The Reavers, for instance, would probably have knocked themselves out trying to get her back on their team, but she wasn't even willing to talk to them.

'This is your fault, son,' Slick had said, 'and you've cost me a good chunk of my income for it. Fix it.'

'She wanted us both to leave the game. How much of your income would that have cost you? You're just lucky I decided to stick around,' Dunk said, 'and how is this my fault?'

'Take it from me,' said Slick, 'it's always the male's fault. And even if it isn't, the only thing that can fix it is for the male to apologise as if it is.'

Dunk stared at the halfling. 'Is this kind of advice why you're so lucky in love?'

'Don't be unkind, son. It doesn't suit you.'

So when the pounding on the door continued unabated, Dunk buried himself further in his bed. Unless it was Spinne knocking at the door, he didn't want to be bothered, and he knew it wouldn't be her.

'Wake up, lazy bum!' Skragger's head screeched from its spot on the mantel. 'Get damn door!'

Dunk pulled the pillow from under his head and put it on top of the others.

Then the door flew open so hard it slammed into the wall next to it.

Dunk leapt out of bed dressed only in his underwear. His head was still a bit fuzzy with sleep, but he thought he was ready for anything: Slick, Dirk, Pegleg, M'Grash, maybe a horde of angry fans. He held up his fists, ready to fight if he had to.

Two people dressed in black robes emblazoned with the Wolf Sports logo strode into the room, each holding a wand before him: the Game Wizards Blaque and Whyte. The first was a tall, stocky dwarf with soot-black hair and a swarthy, rough-hewn face. The second was a short, thin elf with white-blond hair and a proud, angular face. Despite their differing races, they stood at exactly the same height.

'What?' Dunk asked, confused but still keeping his fists at the ready. 'What do you two want?'

Blaque sniggered. 'That's cute,' he said. 'Can you help out Hoffnung here, Whyte? Perhaps you can enlighten him as to why we're here.'

'Allow me to hazard a guess, Blaque. Could it be because of his performance in his last game, the one against Da Deff Skwad?'

'Yeah, Whyte, I think that could be it. You see, Hoffnung here forced one of the dullest games of Blood Bowl ever upon the public. More specifically, the part of the public paying to see the games in the stadium and over Cabalvision networks like our own sponsors at Wolf Sports.'

The dwarf glared at Dunk. 'You see, that kind of game is a direct threat to the livelihoods of our employers. That means it's a direct threat to our livelihoods as well. We don't take kindly to that, of course, and neither do they.'

'Get out,' Dunk said.

'Are those the kind of manners they teach a man who was once heir to one of the largest fortunes in the Empire? It's a crying shame how politeness seems to have fallen off with the younger generation, isn't it, Whyte?'

'A damned shame,' the elf said. 'Happens all the time in humans, of course. Too short-lived to develop a true appreciation for their elders.'

'Good point, Whyte. Good point.'

Dunk took a step towards the pair of wizards and pointed at the door. 'I said, "Get out."'

Blaque tapped the tip of his wand into his open palm in a way that Dunk could only see as a threat. 'You'd think a player like this – MVP of his last game – would be kinder to GWs like us, given the kind of authority we have over him and his game, wouldn't you?'

Whyte stared at Dunk with ice-white eyes. 'I certainly would.'

Dunk dived for Blaque's wand. The dwarf tried to avoid the thrower, but failed. Dunk snatched one end of the wand and then punched the dwarf in the nose. Dunk felt something crunch, and Blaque let go of the wand.

Dunk spun towards Whyte, the wand in his hand. How could he make something like this work, he wondered? Instead of trying to cast a spell with it, he flipped it in his hand into an overhand grip and stabbed it down at the elf's neck. For some reason, though, his arm caught in mid-stab and refused to come down any farther. Dunk tried to growl in frustration and pull the wand free from where it had become stuck in midair, but he realised that it wasn't the wand that was stuck. It was him.

Blaque stood up from where Dunk's blow had knocked him to the floor. He wiped the blood from his nose and scowled at it. Then he cleaned off his fingers in his mouth. 'Was that really necessary?' he asked.

'I don't see how,' said Whyte.

'I was speaking to Hoffnung,' Blaque snapped. He walked over to the bed and used one of Dunk's pillows to wipe his face clean. The blood stained the pillowcase the red of a bright rose.

'He, um, he can't answer you.'

Blaque shuddered with frustration. 'It was a rhetorical question,' he said. He wiggled his nose. If it was broken, Dunk couldn't tell from its shape. It looked like it had been broken a dozen times before. It seemed to be swelling up around the sides though.

'Your room or mine?' Blaque asked.

'Perhaps the main suite,' said Whyte. 'He might like to watch the game.'

'You're far too kind.'

Blaque grabbed the paralyzed Dunk and threw him over his back. While Dunk stood at least a foot taller than the dwarf, Blaque was built like a boulder, and he hefted the thrower as if he was a small child.

Whyte stood by the door while Blaque toted Dunk out into the hall. As they passed through the doorway, Blaque turned and smacked Dunk's skull against the frame. Then Whyte shut the door behind them, and they strode along the hallway, heading for the back stairs.

'Do you think I should apologise to Hoffnung for that?' Blaque asked as they reached the stairs and headed up to the next floor. 'Tell him I'm sorry for that lump on his noggin?'

'I believe your mother taught you not to lie.'

'Perfectly right.'

As they left the stairwell, Blaque knocked Dunk's head against a doorframe again.

'Clumsy me, eh, Whyte?' Dunk could hear the smile in the dwarf's voice.

'Is that a lie, Blaque?'

'You need to work on your sense of humour, Whyte.'

Whyte strode ahead of Blaque and opened one of the doors that lined the hallway. He held it open for Dunk, as Blaque carried him in, clipping the top of his head once more.

The dwarf chuckled as he brought Dunk over to a couch in the centre of the room and set him down on it. He moved Dunk so he had a good view of a large crystal ball mounted atop an iron stand against one wall.

'He looks a bit awkward like that, doesn't he?' Blaque asked.

Dunk's arms and legs were still bent at the same angles they'd been in when Whyte's spell had frozen him. If not for the pounding pain in his head – which he found far more distracting – he'd have probably thought this uncomfortable.

Whyte waved his wand at Dunk, and the thrower felt his body relax into the couch. Then the two wizards worked together to prop him into a sitting position, slouched low on the couch so they could arrange his head so he could see them instead of the ceiling.

'You bastards,' Dunk said. When he realised he could talk, he tried to stand up again so he could attack the wizards and make them pay for treating him this way. But his body wouldn't work. Everything below his head was dead to him. Not only could he not move it, he couldn't feel it either.

He wondered if this was what it was like to be Skragger.

'Let me go!' Dunk said.

'All in good time,' Blaque said. 'We just wanted to have a private conversation with you without you trying to smash our faces in. I think this fits the bill well, don't you, Whyte?'

'Perfect,' the elf said as he holstered his wand inside his robes.

'What do you want?' Dunk asked. It hadn't occurred to him until now that maybe he should be afraid.

'We just want to talk,' said Blaque, 'about you and your performance in your last game.'

'Wolf Sports named me the MVP.'

Blaque nodded as if that had been an unfortunate mistake. 'True. It was spectacular. We watched the whole thing, didn't we?'

'Every minute,' said Whyte. 'Transfixing.'

'It was an amazing victory,' Blaque said, staring deep into Dunk's eyes. 'But it wasn't great Blood Bowl. Fun to watch the first time, but if that keeps up every game, it'll get – what did you call it, Whyte?'

'Bloody boring.'

'Right. Boring is not good. Boring means people shut down their crystal balls and go do something else instead of watching the game. So, as I said, it's not good for Blood Bowl, for the game itself.'

'Take it up with Zauberer,' Dunk said. 'I can't help it if he wants to kill anyone who tries to harm me.' He glared up at the ceiling and then at Blaque. 'And how come you aren't a pile of ashes yet?'

Blaque smiled. 'That's because your wizard friend and we are on the same side. We both want the same thing, don't we, Whyte?'

'To keep Hoffnung safe.' The elf nodded at Dunk.

Dunk rubbed the sore spots on his head against the pillow the wizards had stuck behind it. 'You're doing a hell of a job of it,' he said.

'You're a Blood Bowl player,' said Blaque. 'A few bruises on that thick skull of yours are nothing. We're out to keep you from dying.'

A chill ran down Dunk's spine, but his paralysed body couldn't shudder along with it. 'How?'

'By keeping you out of the game, of course,' said Blaque. 'Until you work out your issues with Zauberer.'

'I don't have any "issues" with him,' Dunk said. 'He wants me dead. He just wants to kill me himself. If I could find him, I'd challenge him right now, but no one knows where he is.' He narrowed his eyes at Blaque, and then Whyte. 'Do you?'

Whyte shook his head. Blaque frowned. 'Not yet. Believe me, we'd like to. Players get threats all the time, but I've never heard of anyone threatening everyone else but the player. This Zauberer's a crank, not much of a wizard as those things go.'

'But he has the Chaos Cup.'

Blaque smiled. 'Exactly. I was worried those knocks had rattled your brains a bit, but you're as sharp as ever. He had the Chaos Cup, which somehow gives him a staggering amount of power. And we can't find him, either, so we can't stop him, but we can stop you.'

'Okay,' Dunk said, 'I won't play.'

Blaque snorted. 'Didn't your mother teach you not to lie, Hoffnung? After how you assaulted me in your room, we're supposed to take you at your word?'

'Whyte, if we let Hoffnung go, what do you suppose he does first?'

'Runs whining to Pegleg to protect him until the game starts.'

'And do you suppose he might renege on our deal and play in the game anyway?'

'Of course, for three reasons: first, Pegleg will force him to; second, any deal he makes with us at this point is under duress, and he can't be held to it; and third, he wants to.'

'Hey!' Dunk said.

'Those all sound like solid reasons to me, Hoffnung. With any one of those on your side, I don't think we could trust you. With three, there's no way we can risk it.'

Dunk closed his eyes for a moment, and then opened them again, resigned. 'So what happens now?'

Blaque smirked. 'Now I send Whyte out for a cask of ale and some munchies. We're going to be here for a while.'

'How long?'

Blaque glanced over at the crystal ball in front of Dunk. 'It's still four hours until game time,' he said.

'THIS LATE IN the second half, the Hackers better have a platoon of priests praying for them,' Jim's voice said as the image on the crystal ball showed four of the Champions of Death tackling M'Grash at once.

'That's right,' said Bob. 'Only a miracle could save this game for them now. What a turnaround for the Hackers' fortunes! To go from untouchable to losers in the space of one game!'

'Too true. This loss should knock them right out of tournament, and only yesterday they were the heavy favourites to win! Does anyone else smell the Gobbo's touch here? Gunther?'

'Very funny,' Gunther's voice said. 'Under other circumstances, I might suspect myself too, but I have an airtight alibi. I spent all morning stuck in the stadium with you!'

'I'm convinced!' said Bob, 'but how about all those gamblers who placed money with you on the Hackers? How are they going to take this?'

The image shifted to Gunther, who stood next to Lästiges on the sidelines. 'Fortunately, I'm in the clear there too. With Hoffnung on the team, the Hackers were such clear favourites that I declined to take any bets on the game. See, I lack opportunity *and* motive!'

'True!' said Jim. 'What a difference Hoffnung's absence has made for this team though.'

'Don't forget that Schönheit left just before the tournament too,' said Bob.

'Yes! It's been a hard few weeks for Captain Haken and his merry crew. Can the Hackers do anything to recover from this?'

'Well, Jim,' Lästiges cut in, standing between Gunther and the camra, 'I have an exclusive report that Dirk Heldmann – Dunk

Hoffnung's younger brother – has agreed to join the Hackers after the end of the Chaos Cup!'

'Wow!' said Bob. 'That's amazing news. I suspect if Heldmann could have played in this game, the outcome might have been very different.'

'Unfortunately, since he didn't start the tournament with the Hackers, he cannot join in the middle of the competition,' Lästiges said. 'But this should set them up nicely for the Blood Bowl Tournament.'

'Especially if they can manage to turn over whatever rock Hoffnung crawled under!' said Jim.

'Or got stuffed under!' said Bob. 'Even so, if they can recover the body, I'll bet that Coach Tomolandry the Undying would pay a high premium to add Hoffnung to his Champions of Death!'

'I think he coined the necromancer coach motto that says it best, "Blood Bowl players never die. They just end up playing for me!"'

Dunk growled in frustration. 'Can you shut that thing off?'

'Why?' Blaque asked. 'Could it be that you've given up faith in your team? How could that be, Whyte?'

'The Hackers are down by three touchdowns with only a few minutes left, and they've lost four of their players to either lycanthropy or mummy rot.'

'Yeah. A mummy werewolf, or is that a werewolf mummy? Either way, I didn't see that one coming,' Blaque said.

'There was that cloud of blackness that covered the middle of the field just before halftime. That's probably what blocked your view. I think Hugo von Irongrad must have been behind it.'

'The Impaler?' Blaque nodded. 'Seemed like his style. I especially like the way he stuck one of the Hacker linemen on the end of the football after scoring that last touchdown. That's what I call spiking.'

Dunk growled again, louder this time, and Whyte shut off the crystal ball.

'So what happens now?' Dunk asked. 'Are you going to keep me like this forever?'

'I don't see a need for that,' said Blaque. 'Do you, Whyte?'

The elf shook his head. 'The Hackers are out of the tournament. We should be good until the Blood Bowl starts. If Hoffnung decides to play in any games between now and then, Wolf Sports will just refuse to cover them.'

'Why didn't you just do that here?' Dunk asked.

'It's the Chaos Cup,' Blaque said. 'Do you know how much money goes into these tournaments? Do you think those game purses just pop up out of the centre of the field? Most of it comes from Cabalvision fees; money our employer pays to the organisers. They want to recoup some of those costs, and they can't do that if they don't show the games.'

'What happens if I show up for the Blood Bowl?' Dunk asked.

'Gee, you seem a lot smarter than that. Don't you think, Whyte?'

'I do think, but those kinds of questions make me think Hoffnung does not.'

Blaque reached out and patted Dunk on the shoulder. Dunk considered trying to bite the dwarf's hand, but he just wanted to have this all over with. Instead, he glared at the wizards and asked the question that had been burning in his mind for the past six hours.

'How did you find me?'

'See,' Blaque said, waving his finger at Dunk, 'now there's a good question. Can you answer that Whyte?'

'We are the Game Wizards, part of the crew in charge of security for the tournaments. We know every hotel in this city, and we have people happy to talk to us in each of them.'

'And?'

'Everyone in the city wanted us to find Hoffnung and persuade him not to play. For the sake of the game.'

'And?'

'Despite all that, the Hackers' security is surprisingly good. If Zauberer hadn't sent word to us with Hoffnung's location, we might never have found him in time.'

'Zauberer?' Dunk said. 'He told you?'

'Of course,' said Blaque as he got up to leave and motioned for Whyte to follow him. 'He knows your every move. How do you think he keeps track of who's trying to harm you?'

'Where are you going?' Dunk asked. The thought that the two wizards might abandon him, paralysed still, in this room terrified him.

'Our work here is done,' said Blaque. 'The spell on you should wear off in another fifteen minutes or so.' He rubbed his nose, which showed a good bruise on both sides. 'We'd rather not be here when that happens.'

As the two wizards walked out of the room and locked the door behind them, Dunk hurled curse after curse at them. He wished that he'd studied magic so that he could have put some real hurt behind them. As it was, they were only words.

'Lord Guterfiend will see you now, Mr. Hoffnung.'

Dunk stood up and followed Lehrer from the foyer and into the main house. 'Surprised to see me?' he asked as he dogged the older man's footsteps.

'Do you mean me or the Guterfiends?' Lehrer didn't turn back to look at Dunk as he spoke. In fact, he'd studiously avoided meeting Dunk's eyes since the guards at the keep's gate had first presented his old student to him.

'Either. Both.'

'I knew you might try this someday. I had hoped I'd taught you better than to try something like this.'

'Like what? I don't have a weapon on me. I'm here alone.'

'You'd have been an idiot to come any other way.'

'I'll take that as a compliment.' Dunk glanced around the place as they wound through the halls that led to what had been his father's office. Most of the decorations were the same, although the family portraits had been replaced with paintings of a group of people that Dunk presumed were the Guterfiends.

They were a pale, gaunt people with wispy, greyish hair, one and all – even the children – and something burned in their eyes. Whether this was hunger, anger, ambition, something else, or a combination of many things, Dunk could not tell, but the burning looked like it hurt.

'Don't,' said Lehrer. 'You're still an idiot. I tried to warn you away on my own, and you had to come here to push their buttons instead.'

'How do you know what I'm here for?' asked Dunk.

'I know *you*, kid. Better than your parents did, maybe.'

Dunk lunged forward and blocked Lehrer in the back, hurling the older man into a nearby wall. He heard a satisfying thunk as Lehrer's forehead bounced off the plaster.

Lehrer spun around, a knife flashing in his hand. 'Not bad, kid. You surprised me. I didn't think you had it in you.'

'Don't ever compare yourself to my father,' Dunk said. 'He did what he did to help my family. You betrayed him.' He walked forward until the tip of Lehrer's knife pressed against his shirt, right over his heart, daring the man to use the weapon. 'You betrayed us.'

Lehrer pulled his knife away and put it back in its sheath. He glanced up at the sky through a nearby window. 'Still have that wizard looking out for you?'

Dunk flashed a savage grin as Lehrer pushed past him and started down the hall again. They soon reached the main office, and Lehrer stopped and opened the door of polished oak. Dunk preceded him through it and then waited for the man to close the door behind them.

A gaunt man with even less hair than Dunk had seen in the portraits, sat in a tall, leather chair behind the vast mahogany desk that had once belonged to Dunk's father. In Lügner's day, Dunk had almost never seen the top of the desk. Papers, scrolls, and maps of all sorts had always covered it. Today, though, it stood empty but for the hands of the man who sat before him. They were long, thin, and white, with nails that seemed to be sharpened to points.

'Rutger Guterfiend,' Lehrer said, 'may I present Dunk Hoffnung.'

The man behind the desk rose and gave Dunk a stiff bow. 'I wish I could say that this was a pleasure, Mr. Hoffnung.'

Dunk spat on the polished marble floor.

Rutger gasped. 'Is this how you behave as a guest in my house?'

Dunk stepped forward. 'I figure I can spit on anything here I like.'

Rutger narrowed his eyes at Dunk. 'And how do you "figure" that?'

'It's not your house,' Dunk said. 'It's *mine*.'

Rutger's eyes smouldered at Dunk for a moment. Then the man threw back his head and laughed. Dunk had never heard a sound so lacking in humour.

'We will have to agree to disagree,' Rutger said. 'I think you'll find that the Emperor will side with me on this.'

'The Emperor is man enough to admit when he's made a mistake,' Dunk said, 'like selling a man's property out from under him.'

Rutger snorted through his long, bent nose. 'It is not yours, and it never was. It was stripped from your father when his association with daemons was discovered.'

'It should then go to the eldest son,' Dunk said. 'Me. I've never known the Emperor to punish sons for the sins of their fathers.'

'You've been gone a long time.'

'Perhaps the Emperor would be interested to know how you backed Zauberer's pledge of a million crowns for my head. Being accused of dealing with daemons was enough to have my family run out of this place. I suppose it would be enough for you too.'

Rutger screwed his face up at Dunk. 'Your father,' he said softly, 'was a gutless coward. He had the throne itself at his fingertips, and he threw it all away over something as ephemeral and useless as his soul.'

'And those of this family,' Dunk said. 'I suppose you were only too happy to put those of your children on the block.'

Rutger snorted. 'If you knew the things I've done – and had my children do both for and with me – you wouldn't imply such things. You'd shout them from the rooftops. One of my few regrets,' he said with a sneer, 'is that I didn't get to perpetrate some of my favourite atrocities on your family. For cowards, the Hoffnungs are a speedy lot, it seems.'

Dunk launched himself across the desk and wrapped his hands around Rutger's throat. As he did, he felt the tip of Lehrer's knife cut into the back of his neck.

'If you don't put him down in three seconds, I'll cut your throat,' Lehrer said. 'If Zauberer's lightning strikes me now, it'll electrocute you too.'

Dunk felt the pulse of Rutger's pounding heart coursing past the palm of his hand. All it would take would be a firm flick of his wrist and he could snap the man's scrawny neck. Lehrer would kill him and likely be killed in turn. They'd all lie there dead together until someone came to find them, and this would all be over with.

The image had its appeal.

Dunk shoved Rutger away from him. The man staggered back into his chair, clutching his throat and coughing and hacking for breath.

Dunk turned to deal with Lehrer, but the man already stood against the far wall again, his knife in one hand, his arms folded across his chest. Dunk's blood trickled down the knife's blade and into Lehrer's fist.

'State your reason for darkening my door and then be gone!' Rutger said. 'You've wasted enough of my time today.'

Dunk ignored the blood that seeped down his back from the wound on his neck, and walked back around the desk towards the door. The cut was only superficial. He'd sustained worse in almost every kick-off return on a Blood Bowl field.

'Call off Zauberer,' Dunk said.

Rutger stared at Dunk and then laughed. 'If that was in my power, don't you think I'd have done it by now?'

Dunk squinted at the Guterfiend patriarch. 'You sent him after me. You gave him the reward money.'

'I gave him nothing – nothing but a hollow promise, one that he believed and sold to the world with an authority that I could not have mustered myself. Do you really think that if I had a million crowns on hand I would trust them to that madman?'

Dunk grimaced, and then glanced around at the walls and ceiling of the office. 'Look, I don't really care about this place or the fact that you're the filthy, daemon-worshipping bastard who lives in it. Apparently my father was a filthy, daemon-worshipping bastard too, and I've been trying to put all that behind me.

'That's all I want: to put this behind me. Get Zauberer off my back. Rescind that reward. After that, I won't cross the street to piss on this place if it's on fire.'

Rutger leaned forward in his chair. 'If I could somehow manage that, nothing would give me more pleasure, but I'm afraid it's not as easy as calling Zauberer into my office and sacking him. He never was a stable man to begin with. Too many encounters with daemons can drive a man headlong towards madness, and he went charging off that cliff a long time ago.'

'It got worse after he got his hands on the Chaos Cup,' Lehrer said. 'Until then, we had some control over him – especially if we dangled the chance of your death in front of his face. He'd always had this obsession with the Chaos Cup, and we never did know why. The first chance he got to grab it, he did, and we haven't seen him since.'

'The power that the Chaos Cup bestows comes with a price. It saps away the holder's sanity until that price is paid.'

'How long did you hold it for?' asked Dunk. 'Seems like you must have passed it around the table at dinner parties here.'

Rutger ignored him. 'The cup can only be sated with the blood of your worst enemy, the one who has caused you the most pain, the most frustration, the most humiliation.'

A sick feeling grew in Dunk's gut.

Lehrer put a hand on Dunk's shoulder. 'Kid, for Zauberer, I'm afraid that's you.'

Dunk shrugged off his old teacher's hand and stared at Rutger. 'And you don't have any idea where he is?'

'I'd give him up to you if I could. I'd be just as happy to be rid of him as you would, and if the two of you could somehow manage to kill each other… Well, the walls of this keep would ring with a feast the likes of which it has never seen.'

'I wouldn't worry about looking for him, kid,' said Lehrer. 'Now that you're in Altdorf and the Blood Bowl tournament is about to begin, I'd say he'll come looking for you.'

'WHAT A ROUT!' Bob's voice said. 'I haven't seen a massacre this bad since that scheduling accident last year pitted Mother Superior's School for the Blind against the Underworld Creepers!'

'I think those blind kids put up a better fight than the Halfling Titans have against the Hackers today!' said Jim.

'Well, they were the only professional team that would accept a match against the Hackers in the opening round of this year's Blood Bowl tournament. Given the fear that most players have of the Hoffnung Curse, you have to admire the Titans' pluck.'

'They're getting plucked, all right, like chickens! I can almost see the feathers!'

'You're not seeing things, Jim. Those are from the pillows that Berry Butterbeer strapped underneath his armour to help cushion the blows. That last tackle from Edgar knocked the stuffing out of them!'

Dunk loved playing Blood Bowl, but after the walkover that his last game had been – the one against Da Deff Skwad – even he had to admit that this had quickly become dull. The Hackers had scored ten touchdowns in the first half of the game and another in the opening minute of the second.

Over half of the Titans had stayed in the locker room when the ref blew the whistle to start the second half of the game. By Dunk's count, only a few of them had been hurt badly enough to keep them out of the game. Word was that the rest of the slackers had barricaded themselves in their lockers and refused to come out. That left only eight of the little guys to take on the Hackers, who were as fresh as they had been when the game had started.

'Boy, those Titans have taken a real battering today!' said Bob.

'Coincidentally,' said Jim, 'that's just how I like those little morsels: battered and with a side of chips!'

Dunk clapped his hands together as he got ready for the kick-off. At least he'd got to play today, even if it hadn't been much of a game. He wondered how they'd find another team to take them on after this. No truly competitive team would be willing to accept a challenge from them, and this game would likely warn off any of the second or third stringers.

'Enjoying the game?' Dirk asked as he stepped up next to Dunk.

Dunk still couldn't quite wrap his head around seeing his brother in Hacker green and gold. They had been rivals since they were kids.

To play on the same team with Dirk just seemed wrong, like it wouldn't be fair to anyone who tried to take them on. This first game against the Titans had driven that home perhaps a bit too hard.

'An auspicious debut for the Brothers Hoffnung,' Dunk said.

'If you consider beating up children before you take their candy auspicious.'

The noise of the crowd rose as Cavre came forward to kick the ball, but the relatively quiet sound spoke volumes about how even the most bloodthirsty fans felt about the game. The ball arced high up into the air and came down like a spear, in a tight, perfect spiral. A Titan stood right underneath it, his arms reaching for it, ready to make a doomed dash towards the end zone.

M'Grash and Edgar raced ahead of Dunk, and he couldn't see what happened next. He expected the halflings to make a valiant attempt to run the ball up the field, just like the last time, and have one of the Hackers pick him up and race into the end zone with him and the ball under his arm – just like last time.

Then the crowd let loose a collective gasp, and everyone on the field stopped – except for Dunk, who still hadn't seen what had happened. Still running, he veered around M'Grash and almost tripped over the halfling on the ground.

Dunk started to reach down for the ball when he realised that it had stabbed right through the halfling, pinning the ball and the Titan to the ground. The gritty little guy lay there trying to pry the ball out of his midsection while his lifeblood spilled out onto the ground around him.

'Oh, no!' Bob's voice said. 'Mofo Waggins, the Titans' long-time captain, looks to be out for the count – and maybe out forever!'

Dunk knelt down next to the Titan and put his hand on the ball to pull it out.

'And where do you think you're going with that?' Waggins asked, clutching the ball to himself. 'That's my damned ball! I earned it with my damned life, and if you try to take it from me I'll ram it down your damned throat and then drag your bloated carcass across the end zone by your damned thumbs!'

Dunk pulled back, surprised by Waggins's vehemence. 'I just meant to–'

'To take the damned ball from me and score another damned touchdown! I know your kind. I've been playing against you for years. I've buried more team-mates than you'll ever have.

'You damned biggies always think of us folk as just speed bumps on your way to the end zone. Well it stops here, damn it!'

With a terrible growl, the Titan pried himself up off the Astrogranite, the surface of the fake field crumbling behind him and leaving a large chunk of it still attached to his back where the spiked tip of the ball had gone clean through him. The Hackers huddled around the little guy, admiring his refusal to let his mortal wound bring him low.

'Hey, Mofo,' Dunk said to Waggins, 'do you have any last words? A final request?'

The Titan staggered forward, his face ruddy with pain as he coughed and hacked out his words. Dunk couldn't make them out, so he leaned closer. All the other Hackers gathered around too, straining their ears.

'What was that?' Dunk asked softly.

'Eat. My. Dust.'

'What?' Dunk pulled back, but too late. Before he could shout a warning, a net spun from the finest mithril dropped down over him and the other Hackers. Waggins dodged between M'Grash's legs and out the other side, where he had nothing but daylight between him and the end zone.

'Get him!' Cavre shouted, but he, along with all of the other Hackers, were caught in the fine-spun net.

Dunk snapped his head about and saw the other Titans at the edges of the net, pounding stakes into the ground. Then someone – another Titan, for sure – hit him behind the knees and knocked him off his feet. He tried to stand back up, but found he could only make it to his hands and knees. The netting over the Hackers had been pulled tight enough so that none of them could stand up. Even Edgar and M'Grash had been brought low.

'I can't believe this,' Dunk said. 'That little bastard is about to score a–'

'Touchdown, Titans!' said Jim. 'Mofo Waggins scores!'

'I can't believe it!' Bob said. 'I never thought I'd see such a historic moment as this! Oh, those of you who have seen this will forever have gloating rights over your friends who missed it. To think that we might see the Titans score their first touchdown ever against a human-based team – a *top-ranked* team – like the Hackers. It's just… I'll say it again: unbelievable.'

Dunk buried his face in his hands and wondered if the ref would make the Titans free them before the kick-off. Could he expect to spend the rest of the game in this position, watching the Titans roll in to the end zone for score after score?

Then the net came up off him, the spikes holding its moorings twanging as they popped free from the Astrogranite. Dunk turned on his back to see Edgar standing up, the net now tangled in his upper branches. The treeman leaned over to offer him a branch up.

As Dunk dusted himself off, he glared up into Edgar's glowing green eyes. 'You could have done that any time you liked,' Dunk said.

Edgar smiled down at him. 'Helped you up off the bloody field? Sure thing.'

Dunk narrowed his eyes at the treeman. 'What did they do for you?'

'Well,' Edgar said, 'we tree-men have always had a soft spot in our hardwood for those bloody little buggers, haven't we? It's painful to watch them have such a hard time in a game like this – they're so out-matched – and they had this bloody wonderful plan. I was the only hitch in the bloody thing.'

'So you gave them a pity point?'

Edgar raised his branches towards the mithril net now tangled hopelessly in his upper branches. 'How do you think it looks?' he asked. 'They said I could keep it.'

'GOOD NEWS, BOYS,' Slick said as he hoisted himself up onto a chair at Dunk and Dirk's table at the Skinned Cat. 'Based on our record, our chances of winning, and our thorough thrashing of the Titans, we've made it to the final round!'

'Who are the poor victims this time? The Association for the Revolution of Self-Euthanasia?' Dirk asked as he sipped at his Bugman's XXXXXX. He'd already had a couple of draughts of the potent ale and was riding high in his cups.

'No. We tried to get them in the opening round, but those ARSEs complained that we wouldn't kill them with the dignity they deserved. The Galadrieth Gladiators apparently dispatched them in an appropriate manner though.'

'So? Don't keep me in suspense.'

'It's the Bright Crusaders!'

'Wait,' Dunk said. 'That isn't some band of flower-tending fairies, is it? This massacring the helpless bit gets old fast.'

'Spoken like someone who's never been helpless,' said Slick as he gratefully accepted a pint of Potter's Field Lager from the waitress, a woman who looked like she might have played on the line for the Vynheim Valkyries several generations back. 'Thanks, love,' he said as he tossed her a stiff tip.

'No, son,' Slick said, smacking his lips once he'd had a sip of his beer. 'The Bright Crusaders is a human team that includes some of the best players in the league.'

'How come I've never heard of them?'

'Because, you pay attention to the part of Bloodcentre where they rattle off the scores for the top-ranked teams; the Bright Crusaders, beloved as they are among the fans, hardly ever win.'

Dunk frowned. 'I don't get it. If they're that good, why don't they win any games?'

Dirk gave Dunk his 'you're *so* naïve' grin and said, 'Because they're too good.'

'How can you be *too* good,' Dunk asked. None of this made sense to him yet.

'Because,' said Slick, 'they don't cheat.'

Dunk's jaw dropped. 'They don't? Not at all? I thought that was part of the game.'

'To those of us who love and play the game well, the way Nuffle meant it, cheating is an integral part of the game. Why, between two well-matched teams, sometimes cheating is the only way for one team to win!'

'Do the Bright Crusaders *ever* win?'

Dirk snickered. 'What team do you think gives teams like the Titans hope?'

'The Bright Crusaders,' Dunk said softly. 'This doesn't sound fair.'

'Who said anything about fair, son?' asked Slick. 'I thought we were talking about Blood Bowl.'

'Maybe I can help you change the subject.'

Dirk turned as white as a sheet, staring at someone over Dunk's shoulder. Slick grabbed his pint and sat it in his lap, ready to dive under the table with it should it be required. Dunk turned around, already aware of who was there.

'Hello, Father,' he said. 'Won't you join us?'

'For Nuffle's sake,' said Dirk, 'they'll let anyone into this place these days.'

Dirk glanced around. All sorts of tough and seedy types filled the tavern. At one table, a pair of minotaurs butted heads over a fresh steak that had just been brought to them, rare. At another, a flock of naked fairies frolicked in a bowl of mead large enough to serve them as a swimming pool. Over by the bar, a man in a cowled robe sold some eager young adventurers a map to a hidden dungeon. Behind the bar, a troll in a bloodstained apron sliced off one of his fingers to pay a bar bet and then watched as a new one grew to replace the old.

'Give me one good reason,' Dirk started, snarling at Lügner as he rose from his seat. Then the drink spinning in his head sat him back down again before he could fall to the floor. 'Aw, never mind.'

Lügner sat down in the empty chair between Dunk and Dirk, opposite Slick, and signalled for another round. 'Make mine a Bloodweiser Dry,' he said.

'Dear Nuffle,' said Slick. 'It's true. Only someone who deals with daemons could drink that pale-spirited excuse for a drink. Have some water instead; at least that's an honest drink.'

'Then it would burn his lips off,' Dirk said.

Lügner put a hand on Dirk's arm. 'It's good to see you too, Dirk.' The younger son stared at the fingers on his forearm, but he left them there.

'All right,' Dunk said. 'I'll ask. What in the Chaos Wastes are you doing here?'

'Excellent question, Dunkel,' Lügner said. 'Direct and to the point.'

When Lügner reached for Dunk's arm, Dunk pulled it away. 'Quit glad-handing me and answer the question.'

Lügner turned serious. 'I came here to see you both and to apologise to you.'

'Apologise?' Dirk said, getting half out of his chair. 'You think that's going to get you off the hook here? We're talking dealing with daemons, getting our mother and sister slaughtered at the hands of an angry mob, and making our lives a living–'

'Sit down,' Dunk said, reaching across the table to push Dirk back into his seat. 'It's bad enough all that's true. Don't announce it to the entire bar. Besides, what harm did any of that do you? You'd already left the keep and declared the rest of us dead to you.' He couldn't keep the bitterness from his voice.

Dirk glared at Dunk, his eyes glassy from the drink, but his fury managing to burn through. 'What harm? I was a kid when I left home – more than a little naïve. I said some stupid things back then, but I never stopped caring about you – any of you.' Dirk looked over at his father, tears brimming in his eyes.

Lügner put an arm around his younger son, and this time Dirk didn't push it away. He just laid his head down on the table and wept into his sleeves. 'I'm sorry, Dirk,' Lügner said. 'I'm so sorry. I'll do anything to help you forgive me.'

'Anything?' asked Dunk.

'Hold on just a minute, Dunkel. I'm having a moment with your brother here. He's finally–'

'Passed out?'

Lügner glared at Dunk, and gave Dirk's shoulders a little shake. 'It's all right, Dirk,' he said. 'It's all right.'

When Dirk didn't respond, Lügner brought his head down nearer to Dirk's face to listen to him breathe. When he didn't hear anything, he grew concerned and put his face closer.

Dirk let loose with a humongous belch right into his father's face. Then he rolled over onto one arm, sprawled across the table and began to snore loudly.

'Damn, damn, and damn,' Lügner said. 'Yet another chance just slipped through my fingers.'

Dunk tried to smother his laughter, but couldn't manage to mask it entirely.

'And you think this is funny?' Lügner asked, turning on Dunk.

'You have to admit,' Slick said, 'the whole burping up your nose thing was fairly hilarious.'

'I didn't think so,' Lügner said, seeming to see the halfling for the first time.

'Well, of course you wouldn't,' said Slick as he started to giggle, a mischievous sparkle in his eye. 'It was your nose. For those of us who maintain noses that have not gathered a snootful of a Bugman's belch, rest assured, it was damned funny.'

Lügner struggled to maintain his anger at Slick, but he failed and broke out into a sheepish smile. 'I suppose it was, wasn't it?'

Dunk took a pull from his bottle of beer, which was filled with Spotted Minotaur. He'd picked up a taste for the mellow brew in Bad Bay, a region filled with the black and white cows that resembled the bull-headed creature on the label. For some reason, it had come to remind him of a place he now thought of as home more than he ever had of Altdorf.

'So,' Lügner said once Dunk put down his bottle, 'you still want to take a shot at me?'

'I've been thinking about it.'

'Here's what I think, Dunkel.' Lügner leaned across the table at Dunk, neatly avoiding the puddle of drool starting to form under Dirk's head. 'If you really wanted to give me the beating I deserve, you'd have done it back in Barak Varr. I know you. You're not violent by nature.'

'Really?' Slick said. 'Have you seen him play?'

Lügner ignored the halfling. 'You might have been able to hurt me in the heat of the moment, but not here, not now after you've had months to think about it. You must know that I never meant you or anyone else in the family any harm.'

'You should try telling that to Mother and Kirta,' Dunk said.

'I would if I could, Dunkel. I miss them as much as anyone. You lost a mother and sister. I lost a wife and daughter, but at least I managed to keep you alive.' He looked down at Dirk and then back at Dunk. 'We still have the three of us. Isn't that worth something?'

Dirk grimaced at his father and shook his head. A part of him still wanted to reach out and twist the man's neck until his head separated from his shoulders. He could hear his mother and sister crying out for retribution, for vengeance, just as he'd heard them every day for nearly four years.

Now he heard other words, too, in his mother's voice: 'He loves you, you know.'

Dunk knew it, but he wasn't sure it mattered one damn bit. Weren't some things unforgivable?

Then he saw Lehrer coming through the bar towards their table.

'What?' Lügner asked, staring at Dunk's face. 'What's the matter?'

Slick started to kick Dirk under the table. When that didn't seem to rouse the man, he moved on to slapping him in the face instead.

'Keep your hands off my son,' Lügner said, blocking the halfling's open hand. 'I won't put up with anyone abusing my–'

Lügner caught sight of Lehrer and his tongue froze. When Lehrer spotted Lügner, he didn't recognise him at first. He smiled at Dunk and Slick as he approached, and then slapped Dirk on the back and grabbed his shoulders as he came up behind him.

Dirk raised his head, his eyes still focused on some place far away. He saw Dunk and Slick and flashed a goofy grin. When his gaze wandered over to his father, he scowled at the man's blood-less face.

'What's wrong with you?' Dirk asked Lügner, his words slurring only a little. He craned his neck around to see who was helping to hold him up, and he saw Lehrer smiling down at him.

Dirk's eyes snapped into focus. He stared at Lehrer for a moment, and then looked back at his father, a wide, mean grin on his face. 'Oh,' Dirk said, 'I'm so glad someone woke me up for this.'

Lehrer shot Dunk a quizzical look. Dunk put a hand towards his father to reintroduce the two old men, but before a single word left his mouth, Lügner stood up and smashed Lehrer in the mouth with a white-knuckled fist.

All conversation in the bar stopped as the patrons turned to see what was going on. No one looked inclined to intervene, instead just craning their necks around towards the two old men. Fights took place in the Skinned Cat all the time. The regulars just wanted a clear view of the action.

'You son of a harpy!' Lügner said as he stood over the fallen Lehrer, pointing down at the man with one hand and waving a fist at him with the other. 'Stand up so I can knock you down again!'

Lehrer glared up at the man as he pushed himself up on to his elbows, and then his eyes went wide and all colour drained from his face. 'Lügner,' he whispered. 'How – how...? You're a ghost.'

Lügner kicked Lehrer in the ribs, and the tavern's patrons cheered. They'd been afraid this bout might end with a single punch, which wouldn't have been nearly enough for them. Most of them hadn't even seen that punch, and they would have hated to miss out on the fight entirely.

'Does that feel like a ghost?' Lügner asked. He followed up the first kick with another to Lehrer's belly. The air rushed out of the servant's lungs. 'Does that?'

Dunk stood and grabbed his father by the arm. 'Stop!' he said. 'You'll kill him.'

'I think that's the point!' the troll behind the bar shouted. The crowd erupted in laughter.

Lehrer pulled himself to his feet and lunged for the door. Before he got two steps, Dirk leapt from his chair and laid a perfect tackle into the man's legs. Slick slid down from his chair and went over to grab Lehrer by the ear and haul him back to the table with Dirk's help.

'See,' Slick said proudly as he and Dirk sat Lehrer down in Slick's chair, 'that boy's a natural at defence. Even near-dead drunk he can still hit you in the back of the knees. Sheer poetry, I tell you.'

Dunk guided his father to the chair across from Lehrer. Then he and Dirk sat back down in their own seats, between their father and their old teacher. The men flung daggers at each other with their eyes as they smouldered in grim-faced silence.

Most of the other patrons in the tavern went back to conversations or fights-in-the-making of their own. Dirk glared at the others until they looked away.

Slick signalled for another round of drinks. 'We're either going to be here for five seconds or a long while,' he said to Dirk. 'Either way, I'll need a drink.'

'Traitor,' Lügner snarled at Lehrer.

'What did you ever do to deserve my loyalty?' Lehrer asked, his lips curled in an angry sneer as he cradled his injured ribs with his arms.

'Besides pay you handsomely for more than two decades of service?' Lügner rolled his eyes and then snapped them back at Lehrer. 'We were friends once, you and I.'

Lehrer snorted. 'A friend doesn't steal another man's woman.'

Lügner's nostrils flared and his eyes grew so wide that Dunk feared they might pop from his head and roll off the table. 'Steal…? She *chose* me.'

'She was too young.'

'We *all* were. That was thirty years ago.'

Lehrer flinched at that. 'It's still fresh in my mind.'

'I'd be happy to solve that for you – by removing that mind from your skull. You as much as killed her, opening the front gate for that mob.'

'Wait,' Dunk said. 'Are you talking about Mother?'

'Kirta didn't deserve to die like that,' Lügner said, 'and Greta never did you a bit of–'

'She–!' Lehrer bit his tongue and tried again, his voice a harsh whisper this time. 'She was a trollop who played with the hearts of men good and true. She–'

Lehrer doubled up over the table, his eyes watering in pain as he grabbed his privates.

Slick pulled his fist out from under the table and then turned and shrugged at Dirk. 'Does anyone here think he didn't have that coming?'

Dirk gave the halfling a bitter grin, and then grabbed Lehrer by the shoulder and hauled him up so he sat straight again. 'Now,' he said. 'Let's talk about this some more, but this time without the cracks about my mother. Next time, I'll let Dunk have his way with you instead of the halfling.'

Dirk glowered at Lehrer and cracked his knuckles. The barmaid brought their drinks and placed one each in front of everyone but Lehrer.

'What'll you have?' she asked.

'Nothing,' said Lügner. 'He won't be living that long.'

She shrugged and left. As she did, Dirk hoisted his mug by its handle as if to take another drink. Instead, he brought it down on the edge of the table and shattered it, leaving only the handle in his hand, with several jagged shards still sticking out of it.

'That's extra!' the barmaid said. When she saw the look in Dunk's eyes, she gave him a nervous smile. 'I'll put it on your tab.'

Dirk shoved the makeshift weapon into Lehrer's face, stopping bare inches from his eyes. 'Let's try that again.'

Lehrer's shoulders slumped, and the fight left him. He released a deep sigh. 'I never meant for your mother or sister to get hurt,' he said. 'Your father,' he glared at Lügner, 'he crossed the wrong people. They decided to destroy him that night.'

'But you helped them?' Dunk asked. He still found this hard to believe, although glancing around the table it seemed like he was the only one. 'Why?'

Lehrer squirmed in his chair.

Dirk jabbed the broken mug into the man's cheek. 'Why?'

Lehrer flinched away, but not fast enough. Blood trickled from a small cut on his face. 'It's his fault. He betrayed Khorne. You can't just do that and hope he won't notice. If I hadn't stayed loyal to the Blood God, I would have shared his fate.'

'So you chose Chaos over your old friend,' Slick said to Lehrer. Then to Lügner, he said, 'and you trusted him not to. I don't know which one of you is a poorer judge of character.

Dunk put his head in his hands. 'What are we going to do with you?' he asked Lehrer.

'Kill him,' said Dirk.

Dunk ignored him. 'We can't let him report back to the Guterfiends. If they find out that Father's alive... Well, you saw how far they'd go to get me, and I'm just the heir to their troubles.'

'Kill him,' said Lügner.

'Just like that?' Dunk asked. 'In cold blood?'

'My blood is boiling,' Lügner said.

'We can't,' Dunk said. 'This is Altdorf, not the wild. They have laws against that sort of thing here.'

'We kill people every game,' Dirk said.

'That's different,' said Dunk. 'Just by getting on the field, they're asking for it. That act alone is considered an assault. Any killings during the game are considered self-defence – at least in places where they care about such things.'

Dirk pulled the broken mug from Lehrer's face. The old teacher looked at him askance.

'Let him run then,' said Dirk. 'We can catch him in hot pursuit.'

Lügner stood up and placed his hands on the table. Then he leaned over and put his chin in Lehrer's face. 'Go ahead,' Lügner said. 'Give me your best shot.'

Lehrer glared up into his old employer's eyes and shook his head. He refused to say a word.

'Come on,' Lügner said. 'You know you want to.' He reached out and took one of Lehrer's hands and placed it around his throat.

'Do it,' Lügner said. 'Kill me.'

Lehrer smirked through trembling lips. 'Your sons will drop me before your body hits the table.'

Lügner nodded. 'And then we'll both be dead, and this entire horrid affair will be over. Don't tell me that holds no appeal for you.'

Lehrer squeezed Lügner's throat with a touch that surprised Dunk with its tenderness. Then the old teacher's hand fell to the table with a thud. 'You may hate yourself. You may think you deserve to die,' Lehrer said. 'But I don't feel that way about myself.'

'You're in the minority then,' Dunk said as he stood and hauled Lehrer up by his elbow.

'Where do you think you're going with him?' Lügner asked, standing up behind the table. Dirk shoved himself away from the table and tried to stand, but fell back in his chair. Slick followed after Dunk.

'Somewhere no one will find him,' Dunk said, 'until I want them to.'

'THE BRIGHT CRUSADERS score!' Bob's voice said. 'That puts them in the lead, one to nothing!'

Dunk swore. He hadn't brought his best game to the field today. The meeting between his father and Lehrer had him preoccupied, and he just couldn't seem to keep his mind on the action.

'That so-called Hoffnung Curse hasn't been much help to the Hackers today,' said Jim. 'I don't think Hoffnung has even touched the ball yet!'

'That's one way to avoid a mad sorcerer's wrath!' said Jim. 'Personally, I've found that burying yourself underground for a century or so works fine. You'd be surprised how short the memories of mortals can be.'

'I prefer tearing them limb from limb, myself,' said Jim. 'But as you know, that's just not always possible. Every news organisation in the Empire has been scouring the land, hunting for Zauberer, hoping to score an exclusive interview with the man, and so far we've all turned up zilch. It's not hard to see why Hoffnung might just have to live with the curse – at least until the wizard comes for him!'

'Tell me, Jim. Do you think it's better to confront your fate as soon as possible, or to avoid it for as long as you can?'

Jim laughed. 'I've always thought it best to put off for now what you can face another day!'

'Well, then you might want to get a head start out of here, my massive friend. According to our security camras, I see your mistress's husband stomping up the aisle in Section 30 and heading our way!'

Dunk trotted back to the Hackers' side of the field to wait for the kick-off. He stared down the field at the Bright Crusaders, resplendent in the dazzling sun; the light reflecting off their suits of armour, which had been polished to a mirror finish.

At first, Dunk had wondered how the Crusaders managed to keep their armour so clean given how hard a game Blood Bowl could be. Then he noticed that the team's coach – Father E. A. 'the Padre' Matten – kept substituting the dirty players off the field so that a team of cheerleaders dressed in black and white habits could restore the soiled players' shine.

The first time the Crusaders had taken the kick-off, they had squibbed it into the stands. The fans had squirted it back out at the Crusaders, and they had driven it all the way down the field and into the end zone. Every time Dunk had come near the ball, the Crusader holding it had thrown it away. He hadn't been able to get within ten yards of the spiked pigskin.

This time, he refused to let the same thing happen again. When the Crusaders lined up to kick the ball, he raced forward instead of hanging back. The kicker squibbed it again, but when the ball popped back out of the stands and into the field, Dunk was right there, ready and waiting for it. He leapt up and snagged the ball from the air.

'Hoffnung has the ball!' Bob's voice said. 'Now we'll see how well the Padre's plan stacks up!'

Dunk tucked the ball under his arm and ran for the end zone. He expected the Crusaders to dive out of his way. They might have wanted to play by the rules, but that didn't mean they wanted to be turned to ash on the spot.

When the first Crusader came at Dunk, he almost stopped and let himself get hit. He thought, on first blush, that the Crusader was a man, but the armour had large bumps on the chest, presumably to protect large breasts, and the back fringe of a wimple hung out from under the back of its helmet. The fuzzy moustache on the lady's lip, and the shoulders that many a lineman would kill to have, threw him off.

'Leave it to Sister Mary Mister to break the tacit injunction against harming Hoffnung!' said Lästiges's voice. 'I've been following her career for years, Bob, and she's never been one to let something like a daemonic curse stand in her righteous way.'

'Repent, sinner!' Sister Mister bellowed as she thundered after Dunk. Her stomping treads shook the Astrogranite beneath her so hard that Dunk wondered if she were somehow half-ogre – or maybe full. 'Hold still, and I will send you directly to Nuffle for judgement!'

Dunk dodged left, and the large lady lurched right past him. Then he saw an open hole and cut right to surge down the field. M'Grash got in front of him to provide blocking and smashed down two line-men who came his way. Unfortunately, those Crusaders tripped M'Grash up as they went down, and Dunk found himself without protection again.

'It looks like only Brother Mother stands between Hoffnung and the goal line now!' said Bob. 'Will Mother martyr himself for the cause?'

To Dunk's mind, there was no question Mother would try to tackle him. Instead, he needed to smack this Crusader down hard and fast. Perhaps then Zauberer wouldn't need to zap him to smithereens.

Brother Mother was the skinniest Blood Bowl player Dunk had ever seen, a young man with a figure that could only be described as girl-ish. As they grew closer, Dunk marvelled at the man's lips and eyes, which looked as if they'd been abused. The eyes were sunken into dark, shaded holes, and the lips shone redder than fresh blood. It took Dunk a moment to realise that Mother wasn't hurt. The man wore make-up – and lots of it.

Mother stretched his arms wide, and Dunk wondered if he should stiff-arm the weakling out of the way or just spin out of his grasp. Then an image of the last person who'd tackled him filled his mind, and he found that he just couldn't do it. He couldn't let Mother even touch him.

Dunk jinked to the right and then ran to the left, hoping to find daylight. Mother followed his every move, not fooled for even an instant. Seeing that he couldn't get past the Crusader, Dunk looked for an open Hacker, but he couldn't see a single one.

So Dunk did the only thing he could think of. He turned and ran away from the end zone.

'Has Hoffnung turned coward?' Bob's voice asked. 'Are the Hackers' new colours yellow and yellow?'

'I don't think so, Bob,' said Lästiges's voice. 'In his own twisted way, I think Hoffnung is trying to save the Crusaders' lives.'

'On a Blood Bowl field?' Bob said. 'Now *that's* blasphemy!'

Dunk shut all the chatter out and looked for some way, any way, to get rid of the ball. That's when Brother Mother hit him.

The tackle caught Dunk just behind the knees and brought him down clean. As he bounced off the fake stone surface, the ball bounced free from his hands. Not caring what happened to it next, Dunk reached back and grabbed Mother by the helmet.

'You moron!' Dunk said. 'You just killed yourself!'

'Yea, though I sprint through the Darkside Cowboys' Stadium of Darkness, I will fear no evil,' Mother said. 'Nuffle does windsprints by my side. Where there is only one set of footprints on the Astrogranite, that's where he carried me!'

'He should have carried you to the nearest asylum and left you there!'

Mother tried to pull himself from Dunk's grasp, but the thrower kept his death grip on the Crusader's faceguard. Mother kept pushing away anyhow, somehow hoping that the far stronger Hackers would give up before he did.

'Don't you get it?' Dunk asked. 'As soon as you walk away from me, you're dead.'

Mother gave Dunk a serene smile with his ruby-painted lips. 'My faith is my shield and my armour.'

'All the other victims wore armour too,' Dunk said. 'None of them made it to the sidelines.'

'You are faithless,' Mother said. 'Those of us who have accepted Nuffle into our lives as our own personal saviours do not fear death. When this game is over, can I discuss the emptiness in your soul with you? Perhaps I can leave you with some literature?'

'Crusaders score!' Bob's voice said.

'You see,' Mother said. 'It's not too late to join the winning team – at least in spirit.'

'Would you just listen to me?' Dunk asked. 'Pull your head out of your damned sacred rulebook for one minute so I can get through to you?'

'Pull my head out?' Mother said with a satisfied grin. 'That's an excellent idea.'

Before Dunk realised what Mother meant, the Crusader reached up and undid the strap on his helmet. His head slipped free from Dunk's grasp on his faceguard, and the rest of his body followed along right after it.

'No!' Dunk shouted as he fell backward, Mother's helmet still in his hands. 'Come back!'

'There's no reason to go back,' Mother said as he started towards his dugout. 'With Nuffle on your side, you're always on your–'

The crack from a bolt of ebony lightning drowned out Brother Mother's last words.

Tears of utter frustration rolled down Dunk's cheeks as the wind blew Mother's ashes back at him. The Crusader's blackened armour hung there in the air for a moment, held together by little more than memories. Then it came crashing down into a clanging heap.

'Dunkel okay?' M'Grash asked as he trotted up behind Dunk, who sat there on the Astrogranite, hugging his legs to his chest.

Dunk shook his head. 'No, big guy,' he said. 'I'm anything but all right.'

'Okay, Dunkel,' the ogre said. He reached down and scooped Dunk up in his arms like an infant. Looking down at the man cradled against his chest, M'Grash said, 'Dr. Pill make everything all right.'

'I DON'T SEE anything wrong with you,' said Dr. Pill.

'You are the worst quack excuse for a physician I've ever seen,' said Dunk, clutching his back. It felt fine, but he wasn't about to let the apothecary know that.

The gaunt elf with the eye patch scowled at Dunk. 'If I tell Pegleg that you're faking an injury–'

'Then I will tear out your spleen and stuff it down your throat with my bare hands,' Dunk said. 'If I can somehow manage to work my way through the pain.'

Something banged away in a large locker in the corner, one of those custom-made for gigantic players like Edgar or M'Grash. Dunk ignored it.

'What in Nuffle's re-broadcast warning is making that noise?' Dr. Pill asked, scratching his chin.

'It's nothing,' Dunk said. 'Leave it alone.'

'I think it's coming from the ogre's locker.' The apothecary crept towards the locker's red, steel door as if he could sneak up on it.

'He likes to leave livestock in there for an after-game snack.'

Dr. Pill turned to sneer at Dunk in disgust.

'Hey,' Dunk said. 'He gets hungry after a big game. Are you going to be the one to tell him to wait until dinner?'

'Pegleg isn't that much of a savage.'

'He doesn't eat any of it.' Dunk said.

Dr. Pill turned back towards the banging locker. The noises coming from inside it grew louder, faster and more insistent. A sign on the front of it read 'KEYP OWT – DAYNJER!' in M'Grash's crude scrawl.

'However,' Dunk said, 'Pegleg does believe in giving the food a fighting chance. He picks out the meanest, nastiest critters he can to give M'Grash a challenge. Sometimes the vicious little buggers manage to get out and run wild through the place. A few of them even get away.

'Some aren't so easy to deal with though. There was that massive, rabid badger Pegleg stuck in there one time. That bugger killed two rookies and maimed a third before M'Grash finally crushed its skull.'

Dr. Pill looked at Dunk as he reached the locker and cocked his ear so that it almost rested against the metal. 'You're lying,' he said.

'Okay,' Dunk said, 'you got me.'

Dr. Pill hesitated for a moment, his hand on the locker's handle.

'It was a wolverine.'

Dr. Pill scowled. Before Dunk could stop him, he yanked open the locker in one swift move.

For a moment, nothing happened, and Dunk breathed a sigh of relief. Then a bound and gagged Lehrer toppled out of the locker and landed on his face. The prisoner looked up at Dunk and Dr. Pill and let loose a muffled scream.

'Oh, dear,' said Dr. Pill. 'This won't do at all.'

'Hold on a moment,' said Dunk. 'I can explain.'

'I certainly hope so. You and your accomplices have done an awful job of this.' The apothecary stared down at Lehrer with a critical eye.

'That's true. I – What do you mean?' Dunk was confused.

Dr. Pill pointed down at the ropes holding Lehrer's limbs. 'These are tied all wrong. In another hour or so, he'd have been able to wriggle out of them all by himself.'

Dunk blinked. 'Ah,' he said. It was the most intelligent thing he could think of at the moment.

Dr. Pill went over to a black leather case on a nearby bench and unfolded it. His back to Dunk, he rummaged around inside it. First, he snapped on a pair of rubber gloves. Then he grabbed and shook something hard.

'Ropes are such crude devices anyhow,' he said. 'I prefer a proper hog-tying for restraints myself, when pressed to rely on such measures. However…'

The apothecary turned around and displayed a large syringe in his hands. He watched the sharpened tip of its wide-bore needle as he pushed a drop of clear, but pungent fluid through it. 'There are such excellent chemical alternatives that one need hardly ever bother.'

Dr. Pill walked over to Lehrer. Tears ran down the man's face as he whimpered into his gag. 'Hold still,' the apothecary said. 'I'm afraid this is going to hurt a great deal.'

'HERE'S TO THE Hackers!' Slick said, raising his tankard in a toast. The others gathered around the table in the Skinned Cat cheered in accord.

'And here's to making the final match of the Blood Bowl Tournament!' said Guillermo. More cheers followed.

'Ah, it's not that big a deal,' Dirk said with a grin.

Dunk put one arm around his brother's neck and ruffled his hair with the other. 'Just because the Reavers do it every year doesn't mean it's not great for us. And you're a *Hacker* now!'

'Go Hackers!' M'Grash crowed. The ogre leaned back and downed the rest of the keg of Killer Genuine Draft he'd been powering through. By Dunk's count, this was the ogre's third.

M'Grash leaned back further and used the heel of his hand to pound the last drops of ale out of the keg. Then he set it back down on his lap and grinned from ear to ear. Had Dunk not been the best of friends with the ogre, he might have fled from the table right then. As it was, a few of the others clutched the backs of their chairs as if they might toss furniture behind them in an attempt to trip up the ogre as they fled.

Then M'Grash unleashed a monstrous belch that shook the tavern's walls. After that, his grin was, if anything larger and happier. It faded only a bit as he tipped back over in his chair and landed with a thud that made the building tremble.

'Out cold before he hit the floor,' Edgar said. The treeman stood next to the table instead of sitting, as his body would not bend in the middle. Fortunately, the main room of the Skinned Cat was tall enough to accommodate him, although his upper branches brushed the ceiling. 'Bloody ogres can't handle their bloody drink for bloody anything.'

'It's just good that you're here, old friend,' Slick said to Edgar.

'Of course it is.' The treeman scowled down at halfling. 'I'm the only one of this bloody pack of tree-swinging mammals that has a bloody prayer of hauling his gargantuan carcass home, ain't I? What in hell did you lot bloody well do before I came along?'

'Mostly we left him where he fell,' said Dunk.

'It is not like we had much choice in the matter,' Guillermo said.

'Oh, who'd dare to not "let a drunk ogre lie"?' asked Slick.

'Do we know who we're playing yet?' Dirk asked. Sometimes Dunk's younger brother surprised him with how seriously he took his job – and the game.

'Right here, Mr. Heldmann,' Pegleg said as he limped into the room, Cavre at his side. He waved a scroll in his good hand and gave it to his team captain to read.

Cavre unfurled the scroll and read its contents silently. Then he spoke. 'The other semi-final game was between the Chaos All-Stars and the Badlands Buccaneers.'

'We know all that. What happened to the broadcast?' Dirk asked. 'We were watching it here on the giant crystal ball when it went black.'

Pegleg nodded. 'Since it was a game that Mr. Hoffnung wasn't involved in, Mr. Zauberer took the chance to destroy every camra in the place.'

'Nuffle's masticated mouth guard,' Slick said. 'Why would he do that?'

'Apparently it was an attempt to get each and every one of the game's sponsors up in arms,' Pegleg said. 'The tournament organisers were nearly crucified in front of the stadium on those nice new lights the Guterfiend family paid to have installed after the post-game riots last year. They made scores of other improvements to the place as well.'

'The Guterfiends?' Dirk and Dunk said together.

Pegleg nodded. 'I know about the troubles your family's had with them, but they did something good with their money there at least.'

Dunk shook his head. 'I don't believe it for a second. The lamps are probably all filled with explosives.'

'Or death rays,' Dirk said, nodding his head.

'Or a bunch of bloody fairies trapped in those bloody, little glass balls and forever forced to shed bloody light on their evil masters' command.'

Everyone craned their necks to stare up at Edgar.

'What?' he said. 'Now don't tell me you lot are a bunch of bloody fairy lovers.'

The others all decided to ignore him.

'So that's all that happened?' asked Dunk. 'Just a bunch of ruined camras?'

'To you, Dunk, those are "just a bunch of ruined camras,"' said Cavre. 'To Ruprect Murdark, that's the loss of hundreds of thousands of crowns in advertising dollars.'

'I have heard that the commercials during the final match can go for a million crowns a minute,' said Guillermo.

'Too true, Mr. Reyes,' said Pegleg. 'Now stretch your imagination if you will and think about what would happen to Wolf Sports if Murdark had to refund all that money because no one ever saw the commercials.'

Everyone fell silent for a moment. Then Edgar started to giggle, a low and hollow sound that tickled the ears. Slick joined in soon after, and then Dirk, Dunk, Guillermo, and even Cavre. The laughter grew from snickers, through guffaws, to full-blown belly laughs. In the end, even Pegleg had cracked a wry smile.

'We don't need to worry about that, though,' Cavre said. 'We just need to play the best we can, no matter who is watching.'

'Well said, Mr. Cavre,' said Pegleg. 'However, I have it on good authority that Murdark is paying a fortune to have every camra in the Emperors Stadium replaced and reinforced so that no magic – however strong – can damage them or interrupt their signals.'

Slick let out a low whistle. 'That'll cost him a small fortune.'

'He'll make it up with the ads, Mr. Fullbelly. Word is that he's getting premium rates for this game. After all, it's a grudge match.'

Dunk frowned. 'A grudge match?' He glanced at the other players, each of whom seemed just as mystified as he – except Cavre, of course, who always seemed to know what the coach was talking about. 'I don't think any of us like the All-Stars, coach, but they're no worse than any other rival team.'

'Oh, really, Mr. Hoffnung?' Pegleg said. 'I would have thought you'd have been able to understand the spin on this game better than anyone.'

Dunk narrowed his eyes at the coach. 'Why?'

'Who is the most renowned team wizard the All-Stars have ever fielded?'

'Didn't Olsen Merlin help them out for a year about fifty seasons back?' asked Slick.

Pegleg moved to backhand the halfling with his hook, but Slick slinked behind Edgar's trunk before the ex-pirate could land the blow. 'You always remind me of a saying, Mr. Fullbelly,' Pegleg growled.

'Which is?'

'Agents aren't necessary, just evil.'

Slick turned red, but managed to say, 'So, Zauberer's back working for the All-Stars, is he?'

Dunk gasped. He'd wondered when the wizard might finally show his hand. Now, during the championship game of the Blood Bowl Tournament, seemed like as good a time as any. Dunk wondered how he could ever defeat Zauberer now that the man had his wormy hands on the Chaos Cup. Any wizard who could incinerate anyone who tried to hurt Dunk could flash-fry him in an instant too. Still, there had to be a way. At least during the game, he might finally have a chance to try to take the wizard out and put an end to the hated Hoffnung Curse.

The nasty snarl on Pegleg's face faded to a simple frown. 'That he is, Mr. Fullbelly.' He gave Dunk a sympathetic look. 'We'll do everything in our power – such as it is – to help you take him out. We can assume that his edict against killing you is only in effect until the game begins. After that, all bets are off.'

'Now who would be so heartless as to say something like that?' said Gunther the Gobbo as he shouldered his way close to the table.

Dunk's eyes grew wide. 'What are you doing here?' he asked as he leaned over and whispered at the bookie. 'I thought we agreed you couldn't be seen with us.'

'Leave now?' Gunther said a bit too loudly. 'But you guys are my favourite team – unless you lose, of course. The odds are already three to one against you.'

'Against us?' Dirk asked. Dunk felt ill.

'Of course. The All-Stars were the heavy favourites beforehand, but when someone leaked their roster for the championship game…' Gunther winked at Dunk. 'Well, now everyone knows you're going to get your ashes handed to you – or to your next of kin, at least!'

'Has he…?' Dunk asked Pegleg.

'He's been quite helpful so far, Mr. Hoffnung.'

'It doesn't hurt that I've made a mint so far at it.'

'How's that?' asked Dirk, ever suspicious of the Gobbo.

'If there's one thing I've learned in this business,' said Gunther, 'it's that you never bet against your team. I've been betting with the Hackers since just after the Dungeonbowl, and it's been easy money.' The Gobbo leered. 'Of course, starting a rumour that Zauberer's been known to miss his targets with those lightning bolts from time to time helped out with putting the odds more in my favour too.' As an aside, he whispered to Dunk. 'Not true. Don't believe it.'

'Should you really be seen in our presence?' Guillermo asked. 'At least out in such a public place?'

Gunther snorted, and then replied with a fake grin pasted on his face. 'Kid, I'm the most notorious odds maker in town. The two teams that'll compete in the Blood Bowl championship game just got announced. If I don't track you guys down and chat with you, *that's* going to look suspicious. So just shut your trap and try to tolerate my company for a few more minutes so we can make this look good.'

'Have you been doing anything to help, other than just lining your pockets?' Dunk asked.

Gunther shook a finger at Dunk. 'See, now that's the kind of question I can respect: full of the suspicion and the derision I've earned. Well done, kid!'

'Have you?'

'It's just that kind of doggedness that's going to lead the Hackers to victory in the championship game. Go Hackers!'

Gunther raised his arm to lead a cheer in which no one else joined. 'Give me an H!'

Silence.

'Go to *hell*,' said Guillermo.

'There's an H! Give me an A!'

Dunk leaned towards the bookie. '*Answer* my question.'

'Hey,' said Gunther. 'I got you that match against the Titans, didn't I?'

The eyes of the Hackers turned towards Pegleg.

'Aye,' the coach said, 'that he did.'

'And how about how I brought Dunk's old flame here tonight, to help him celebrate?'

Dunk's heart went cold. 'You did what?'

'Well,' Gunther said, wincing. 'She's been after me for a while to tell her where you are, but I wouldn't say a word! I absolutely refused to let her know where the Hackers are staying during the tournament. She gave me a few notes to pass on to you, but I refused those too. I didn't want her to bother you. I was protecting you.'

'But now that Dunk's in the championship, you think it's all right to shake him up a bit?' asked Dirk. He'd ended up on the other side of Gunther from Dunk, and the bookie now stood sandwiched between them.

'Well,' Gunther said, 'with Schönheit gone and Zauberer on the loose still, I… Well, I figured…'

'If I'm facing certain death I might as well get this out of the way?' Dunk said.

Gunther grimaced. 'I'd have put it better than that, of course, given a bit more time, but sure, that's the gist of it. Thanks, kid!'

Dunk glanced around the room, peering over the shoulders of his team-mates. 'Where is she?' he asked.

Gunther's face lit up. 'I figured you two lovebirds would want a little privacy, so I arranged for a sheltered booth in the third room back.'

'I left her, Gunther.'

'Is this Helgreta?' Dirk asked. He glared at the Gobbo. 'This is Helgreta Brecher, isn't it?'

Gunther nodded as if his neck had been replaced with a loose spring.

'I thought she tossed you out on your chin,' Dirk said to Dunk.

'That's the official story,' Dunk said. 'That's what the Brechers told everyone. I never saw her after that... incident during our engagement party.'

'So you call fleeing town with an angry mob of daemon-hunters on your tail "leaving her"?'

'She wrote me letters,' Dunk said. 'They found me somehow. She said she wanted me back. No matter what people said about Father, she knew I was innocent. She still wanted to go through with the marriage.'

'Daemons, weddings,' Slick said. 'All the reasons I left my little halfling home in the Moot far behind.'

'And still she wishes to speak with you?' Guillermo asked, astonished.

'Amazes me too,' said Gunther. 'I don't know what you've got in that codpiece, kid, but I'd be careful with it if it inspires that kind of loyalty.'

Dunk fought the urge to smack Gunther across the room. 'Where did you say she is?'

'Back booth, third room back.'

Dunk stood up and noticed that everyone at the table was watching him. 'If I'm not back in five minutes, send a search party for me.'

'If you're not dead within the first minute, you may need longer than that,' said Cavre.

Dunk nodded. 'Make it twenty.'

With that, Dunk turned and walked towards the open doorway in the back of the Skinned Cat's main room. He scooted through the room beyond, in which a number of Bright Crusaders players nursed their wounds and their pride. Dunk didn't know if any of them recognised him – he saw Sister Mister weeping into a trough of ale that M'Grash would have appreciated – but he took comfort in the fact that he could rely on them to stick to the rules and leave him alone off the field.

The second room back felt smaller than the first because of the draperies that could be pulled across the faces of each booth. About half of these had been drawn, and in the others the occupants shot Dunk dirty looks for glancing in their direction. Six people – a goblin, an elf, three orcs, and a dwarf – sat around a table in the middle of the room, playing a low-stakes hand of pogre. Dunk had tried to play the game with M'Grash a few times, but they stopped when Dunk realised the game was designed to start fights.

The door to the third room back stood closed. It took Dunk a while to find it. At first, he thought it was an exit to the place's outdoor privy. Seeing no other option, though, he tried it. The latch rose easily, and the door pushed inward on oiled hinges.

'Hello, Dunkel,' a voice said. 'I've been waiting for you for a long time.'

26

Dunk slipped into the room, but left the door open behind him. The sounds of the pogre players and of the rooms beyond comforted him somehow. The thought of cutting them off, of leaving him alone in this room with Lady Helgreta Brecher, terrified him.

'Please,' Helgreta said, motioning to the chair next to her at the lone table in the room. 'Have a seat.'

The room was, in fact, a booth all to itself. Two stuffed leather chairs crouched next to a small, circular table made of clean, polished wood, all of which were of exquisite make. The place smelled of fresh cedar – which Dunk saw lined the walls – and an enticing perfume, which he recognised as Helgreta's favourite scent.

Helgreta looked as stunning as ever. Her auburn curls had straightened a bit as she'd let her hair grow out, but her wide, dark eyes issued the same strong invitation to him that they always had. She carried a few more wrinkles around her eyes and mouth, and to Dunk's chagrin they seemed to have been caused by frowning.

A pair of golden goblets sat on the table in front of her, next to an uncorked bottle of wine – an excellent vintage by Dunk's memory. He hadn't bothered to keep track of such things since fleeing from his home four years ago. The cups stood empty, but somehow Dunk caught the scent of spirits from somewhere else.

'You look well,' Dunk said as he took the seat offered to him. He found he could not relax in it. Instead, he perched on its edge, his hands on the table in front of him. 'The years have been kind to you.'

'You flatter me,' Helgreta said with a sly grin. As she spoke, Dunk knew from where the smell of alcohol had come: her breath. She batted her eyes at him, 'But you always did have a way with words.'

Dunk blushed at this and lowered his eyes. 'I must apologise,' he said, 'for not answering your letters. By the time they reached me–'

'No need,' Helgreta said, placing a hand on his. 'Those were trying times. I understand that you needed to take care of yourself then and couldn't possibly have spared time for me.'

'It's not that I didn't–'

'Hush,' Helgreta said, pursing her soft, red lips. 'Let's not insult the memory of what we once had with such words.'

Dunk smiled at her softly. This was going better than he could have hoped. The sense of dread he'd felt since Gunther had announced Helgreta was here slowly sloughed away. 'You're far too kind,' he said.

Helgreta breathed in through her nose, her smile now thin and brittle. 'Adversity builds character, or so they tell me.'

Dunk glanced down at her hand on his. It bore no ring. 'You never married?' he asked. 'I find that hard to believe.'

Helgreta frowned. 'I– Since you insist… After the incident in my family's home, we were tainted with suspicions of dealing with daemons as well. Arranging another marriage for me proved…'

'Difficult?'

'Impossible.' She sighed. 'But I never minded. I'd already given my heart away once. Since it was never returned to me, I didn't have it to bestow on another.'

Dunk felt ill. He glanced at the wine, but his appetite for such things had left him.

'How is your family?' he asked, hoping to change the subject she'd claimed to wish to avoid.

Helgreta smiled pleasantly. 'Well, for the most part. My father still soldiers on, despite the way half of his body was paralysed by a stroke following that horrid, fateful night. Sadly, we lost my mother soon after that. Some say she died of sheer shame.'

'How about your cousins?' Dunk asked. Helgreta had always been close to them, and he had enjoyed carousing with them in more carefree days.

'With the taint that followed us, we were forced to ever more desperate measures to retain our holdings and position. Karl disappeared while leading a caravan over the Grey Mountains to Parravon. Kurt, though, decided to follow in your footsteps.'

'He was chased from his family home by an angry mob?'

The bitter look Helgreta shot Dunk was as far from the smile he'd hoped for as he could imagine.

'He took up Blood Bowl. He said, 'If Dunk and Dirk can do it, then why not me?' Did you know you two set off quite a trend among the disaffected sons and daughters of the Empire's elite? For a while, there was even an all-nobility team called "the Imperial Counts".'

Dunk thought hard on this. 'Whatever happened to them? I don't think I ever heard of them.'

'They became embroiled in a trademark dispute with a team of vampires from the Dark Lands over the "Counts" name. They submitted to binding arbitration over it, and the vampires bound them and bled them dry.'

Dunk gasped. 'Was Kurt on that team?'

'No, sadly,' Helgreta said. 'That would have been far easier for him, I'm sure.'

'What happened to him?' Dunk wasn't sure he wanted to know the answer, but he couldn't keep from asking.

'He started to question his sexuality. Then, while he was at his most vulnerable, he fell in with a team – more a cult, really – called the Bright Crusaders.'

Rivers of ice ran through Dunk's veins. 'You can't be–'

'He became a "brother" in their organisation. He took on the new name "Mother" to show how he'd channelled his maternal urges into helping the team and furthering the cause of good and fair play, both on the field and off. They raised thousands of crowns for poor children through their charity matches alone, and Karl donated all but a small portion of his wages to keeping the homeless off the streets – via a euthanasia program he started before he joined the team.'

'The Association for the Revolution of Self-Euthanasia?'

'You've heard of them?' Helgreta smiled warmly. 'Karl would have been so pleased. I understand they've started a Blood Bowl team of their own. Karl said he often scrimmaged against them and dispatched at least one opponent each game – with the dignity they deserved, of course.'

Dunk put a hand over his mouth.

'Helgreta, I–'

'I know,' she said. 'It was your job to kill him, and I don't begrudge you that. He'd lost so much weight over the past few years, I wouldn't be surprised if you hadn't recognised him at all.'

Dunk nodded. Between that, the armour, and the man's caked-on make-up, he couldn't possibly have known who Brother Mother had once been – or so he told himself. Still, he had to set the record straight.

'I didn't kill him though,' he said. 'I tried to save him. I didn't want for him to tackle me.'

'Oh, you weren't the first player to flee from Karl's embrace,' Helgreta said. 'He scared more than one macho man off the field with his aggressive yet feminine ways.'

Dunk shook his head. 'That's not it. I didn't know who he was, other than another innocent Blood Bowl player.'

Helgreta failed to stifle a giggle. 'Is there any such animal as an "innocent Blood Bowl player"?'

'I just wanted to keep from having Zauberer kill him,' said Dunk.

'Ah, yes,' Helgreta smiled, but Dunk felt no warmth behind it, 'the wizard who's threatening your life. Aren't you getting tired of using that excuse?'

Dunk stared at her. 'What do you mean? It's not imaginary. So far, he's struck down anyone who's managed to tackle me on the field.'

'And yet you keep playing. Why is that?'

'I…' Dunk had wrestled with this question a great deal on his own. 'It's complicated.'

Helgreta picked up the bottle of wine and proceeded to fill the two glasses sitting in front of her and Dunk. 'We have the whole night ahead of us.'

That thought made Dunk shiver, but he decided to take a shot at explaining himself anyhow. When he looked at Helgreta and saw what had happened to her family and her life, he knew she deserved at least that much.

'There are a number of reasons, and they all get mixed together in my head. First, my coach demands that I play. I've signed a contract with him to play. If I don't play, I get fired.'

'You don't think you could find work elsewhere?'

'Sure. Maybe. I don't know if I'd want it. The Hackers are like my family now, especially since Dirk joined the team. I don't think I'd want to play for anyone else.'

'There is a world out there beyond Blood Bowl, you know.' Helgreta sipped from her glass. Her smile pronounced the wine delicious.

'I've been in that world. I was trying my hand at slaying dragons when Slick found me and convinced me to try out for the team. I didn't know much about Blood Bowl back then, and I thought it would have taken a team of wild horses to drag me to a try-out. As it turns out, it took a hungry chimera and a town full of angry citizens to push me into it.'

'Can one get used to being run out of a town?' The way Helgreta asked made Dunk wonder if the wine had gone to her head already.

'I don't think so. The last time was enough to get me to try something new, to put my old life behind me entirely.'

'But that hasn't really worked, has it?' She tossed back the rest of her wine in one, long drink.

Dunk pondered that. 'No. At least not the way I did it. Every day, it seems like my past comes back to haunt me in different ways. First it was Dirk. Then Lehrer and the Guterfiends. Then my father, and now–'

'Your father is alive?'

Dunk nodded. He reached for his wine, but Helgreta grabbed it before he could, and dumped the contents of his cup into hers. 'How could that be?' she asked as she set his empty goblet back in front of him.

'He and I both managed to get out of the keep before the mob came and tore my mother and sister to pieces. I lost track of him after that and figured he was dead. It seems I was wrong.'

Helgreta looked at Dunk through lidded eyes. 'And how do you know this? Have you heard from him?'

'I had a drink with him in this very bar earlier this week.'

Helgreta gasped. She sipped the wine she'd taken from Dunk and curled up in her chair like a contented cat. 'Do you know where he is? I always liked him.'

Dunk shook his head. 'He shows up when he wants to. You know, when I first saw him, I wanted to kill him.'

'What kept you from doing it? You've killed lots of people, haven't you?'

'Not that many.' Dunk frowned. 'This is my father we're talking about. I... Well, if the reason why I keep playing Blood Bowl with a wizard's curse over my head is complicated, then my reasons for not killing my father are right up there with the rest of the great mysteries of the world.

'I wanted to kill him, especially when I found out what he'd done, how he'd been responsible for so much of the misery in my life, for Dirk leaving home, for the deaths of my mother and sister. But he didn't mean any of it. He'd been trying to do right by his family, and somehow it all got messed up.'

'So you think you should judge people by their intentions, not by the results of their actions?'

'I – I suppose that's right. After all, there are so many things that can go wrong with a plan; so many awful, stupid things. It seems harsh to only account for an action's results without considering what the actor meant to happen.'

Helgreta smiled, and then sat up and poured Dunk some more wine. 'You see,' she said, 'it's probably better that we never got married anyway. That's a huge point on which we differ.'

Dunk shrugged. 'After everything you've gone through on account of me and my family, I can understand that.'

Helgreta raised her goblet. 'Here's to putting the past behind us,' she said with a savage grin.

Dunk picked up his own goblet and clinked it against hers. 'And here's to second chances,' he said.

As Dunk brought the goblet to his lips, he knew something was wrong. The scent of the cedar, of Helgreta's overpowering perfume, of his own nervous sweat had all drowned out something else he'd sensed there, something more subtle and more dangerous. He sniffed at the wine, and there it was.

Bitter almonds.

Dunk choked on his own spit and dropped the goblet to the floor. As he hacked and coughed until he was red in the face, Helgreta gazed at him and laughed.

'When I first heard you'd come back to town two years ago, Dunkel, I ignored it. I satisfied myself with watching that championship game you played against the Reavers, and I hoped and prayed that someone would tear your head off in the middle of the match. When that didn't happen, I cried myself into a stupor. By the time I'd recovered, you'd left town once again.

'Last year, when you played the Reavers again, I prayed that a horrible plague would destroy you and everyone you held dear, all your friends from your new life. A new beginning denied to me. My petitions went unanswered again.'

Dunk finally managed to bring the coughing under control. He shoved himself back in his chair and clutched at his throat and stared at Helgreta with wide-open eyes.

'This year, I prayed again. I prayed so hard. When I heard about the reward on your head and then the Hoffnung Curse, I thought my prayers had finally been answered.

'Then you killed Karl, and I knew I had to take matters into my own hands. Like the saying goes, "the gods help those who help themselves".'

Helgreta crept from her chair and stood over Dunk. 'Can you feel the poison working its way through your veins? Has it reached your lungs? Your brain?' She reached over and rubbed her hand against his chest. 'Has it stopped your heart?'

Dunk's hand snaked out and caught Helgreta by the throat. Then he shoved her back into her chair. 'This charade is over,' he said. 'You're insane.'

'You?' She stared at him, her eyes wide as zeroes on a scoreboard, her voice rising to a screech. 'Why can't you ever seem to die?'

Dunk clenched his hands into claws. He wanted to strike back at Helgreta, to kill her for trying to kill him, but he couldn't.

'The poison's not affecting you; that liquor I smelled on your breath when I came in-'

'Was the antidote,' Helgreta said. 'You always were the clever one.'

'If anyone in the world deserves to kill me,' Dunk said, 'it's you, but I won't just roll over and die.' He shook his head in amazement at the lengths to which this woman had been willing to go to end his life.

'Who gave you a choice in the matter?' Tears streamed from Helgreta's dark eyes, forming rivers of black that streaked down her face from the ebony smudges of make-up surrounding her eyes. 'No one asked me!'

'You took your best shot,' Dunk said. 'It didn't work out. Let it go.'

'Never!' Helgreta launched herself at Dunk and clawed at him with her long, sharp nails. He caught her by the wrists and held her away from him at arm's length. 'Somehow, some way, you will die!'

Dunk shoved the woman back into her chair again. 'Someday,' he said, 'but not today.'

Helgreta shrieked at Dunk in frustration, snatched the bottle from the tabletop and hurled it at him. He ducked beneath it, and it shattered against the wall behind him.

By the time Dunk had stood up again, Helgreta had already dashed out of the door of the tiny room, screaming the entire way. 'He's evil!' she said. 'Evil!'

'No!' Dunk lunged for the door and into the room beyond. There he saw the pogre players standing between him and the door. 'You best leave 'er alone,' one of the orcs said. The rest of them nodded in agreement.

Dunk charged at the group, cutting his way between the elf and the goblin as if they were linemen he'd caught flat-footed on the field. With one move, he grabbed the end of the table closest to him and overturned it, shoving it forward against the orc and the dwarf on the far side of the table. They tried to duck under it, and the table started to roll right over them.

Dunk went with the momentum and somersaulted across the bottom of the flipping table. This put him on its far side, with the table between him and the angry players.

He charged into the next room, and he could see Helgreta's back as she fled past the Hackers' table in the main hall. 'No!' he shouted. 'Stop her!'

The Bright Crusaders had leapt up from the chairs and stools at which they'd been drowning their sorrows. They closed ranks around Dunk, forming a human wall between him and the doorway as they linked their arms together.

'Get out of my way!' he shouted at them. 'Or she's dead!'

'We won't let you kill again, Hoffnung,' Sister Mister said in a voice as rough as an ogre's beard, 'especially not Karl's cousin.'

Dunk stared at the woman in horror – and not just because he could finally get a good look at her without her helmet on. Then he dived straight at her. She rebuffed him with a push of her belly, and he found himself on the floor.

'She attacked me,' Dunk said. 'She's going to die!'

'How dare you threaten that lady?' the dwarf called from the other side of the room. Dunk glanced back and saw that a line of Bright Crusaders had closed that doorway off too.

'Don't worry, Hoffnung. You have nothing to fear from them. We won't allow anyone else to come to harm because of your so-called curse,' Sister Mister said, the menace in her voice unmistakable. 'As a charter member of ARSE, Helgreta has already come to terms with her fate. You can do nothing to stop it – nor to save yourself.'

With that, the circle of Bright Crusaders began to tighten around Dunk. He searched for a way out, a hint of daylight between his attackers, but he could find none. It looked like he was just going to have to kill his way out of the situation. The Crusaders outnumbered him ten to one, though, and had absolutely no fear for their lives. They'd come here to martyr themselves for their cause: his death.

A large hand shot out from behind Sister Mister and grabbed her by the head. With a quick twist of her neck, she fell down to the floor, dead. She bore a wide smile on her face.

M'Grash stuck his head through the door after his arm and said, 'Dunkel okay?'

Somewhere outside the Skinned Cat, thunder rolled across what Dunk knew to be a crystal clear sky. Grim frustration marred Dunk's face as he grimaced at the ogre and said, 'All right, big guy. Let's give these bastards what they want.'

'Welcome, Blood Bowl fans, to the championship pre-game show for this year's Blood Bowl tournament. I'm Jim Johnson!'

'And I'm Bob Bifford! This should be one humdinger of a match, Jim, featuring the Bad Bay Hackers versus the Chaos All-Stars!'

'True enough, Bob! Due to the now infamous Hoffnung Curse the wizard Schlechter Zauberer placed on star Hacker Dunk Hoffnung, the Hackers were heavily favoured going into this game. Let's talk to our able odds-making consultant, the legendary Gunther the Gobbo, to see what happened. Gunther?'

'Thanks, Jim! It's simple. In a nutshell, Zauberer's backing the All-Stars. As long as he has the power of the Chaos Cup behind him, he's the heavy favourite.'

'And what are the chances that the Hackers might be able to find Zauberer and take the Chaos Cup away from him, thereby evening the odds?'

'That of a snotling's snowball in an ogre's pitcher of hot blood.'

'Excellent,' said Bob! 'Now lets check in with our roving reporter Lästiges Weibchen to set up this burgeoning rivalry for us.'

'Thanks, Bob! Traditionally, the Hackers and the All-Stars haven't had much time for each other. Remember, just a few years back, the Hackers weren't considered contenders for the championship games for any of the majors, despite the leadership of Captain Pegleg Haken and of team captain Rhett Cavre, not to mention the brute force of M'Grash K'Thragsh.

'That changed three seasons ago when then-protégée Dunk Hoffnung joined the team. Something about the chemistry of the team gelled strongly around a central group of players that has survived to this day, despite dozens of casualties to the Hackers' roster.

'The modern-day Hackers have faced the All-Stars twice in the past three seasons. The first time was in the Chaos Cup two years back. In that game, Hoffnung killed the All-Stars' team captain Schlitz 'Malty' Likker during a half-time ceremony set to honour former All-Star captain Skragger.'

'Didn't Hoffnung claim at the time that the Blood God had possessed the minotaur with Zauberer's help?' asked Jim.

'He certainly did, and that seems to have been the start of the conflict between Zauberer and Hoffnung. This flared up whenever the two met, but it usually ended up with the humiliation of Zauberer, who sometimes served as the All-Stars' team wizard.

'Still, the All-Stars won that game, as they did in their only match against the Hackers the following year in the *Spike!* magazine tournament. That's the game with the infamous Jumboball incident, when the gigantic display at the end of the field came off its mount and crushed hundreds of fans to death as it rolled onto the field.'

'I remember that,' said Bob, licking his lips. 'I almost couldn't restrain myself from getting down there and helping to, ah, clean up.'

'That game ended with several players dead on both sides, including the All-Stars' new team captain, Macky Maus. In the end, though, the All-Stars prevailed when Coach Haken threw in the towel. With only three players left on the field, he knew the Hackers didn't stand a chance.'

'How many players are still left from the original team that Hoffnung joined just three years ago?' Jim asked.

'Only four: K'Thragsh, Cavre, Reyes, and Hoffnung himself. That's a hard-bitten, battle-tested core, and to that they've added Edgar – a treeman from Albion – and Dirk Heldmann, Hoffnung's younger brother and long-time fixture of the Reikland Reavers. Up until this year, at least.'

'So this is a grudge match to beat all grudges,' said Bob. 'Just the way it should be!'

Pegleg shut off the Cabalvision feed to the crystal ball in the Hackers' locker room. He gazed out at the players sitting on the benches in front of him, staring back, and he let loose a grim sigh.

'I know you've been watching that crap every day since we beat the Bright Crusaders,' Pegleg said. 'I want you to ignore every word of it. All that analysis, all those stats they throw at you, everything, all of it.

'It's all crap. Sophisticated fairy tales they feed to the emotionally stunted excuses for sentient creatures we call fans. The fans need this stuff. They feed on it. They have to have a story woven around the game, some kind of framing device to give the match more purpose than it really has to them.

'Honestly, what does a fan care about Blood Bowl? Even when it comes to a championship game like this? Anyone?'

'Whatever they bet on it,' said Erhaltenes Spiel, one of the more promising rookies the Hackers had seen this year. He'd joined them back in Magritta, so just the fact that he had survived this far spoke volumes about his ability to play the game – or at least to find ways to collect a cheque while warming the bench.

'Exactly right, Mr. Spiel,' said Pegleg. 'Anyone else?'

'Bloody pride,' said Edgar, who stood in the back of the rows of benches, towering over all the other players, even M'Grash, who sat at one end of one of the middle rows, next to Dunk.

'Well put,' Pegleg said with a grin. 'We thank those rabid fans who stake their pride on our success. They wear our jerseys, come to our games and buy the things we endorse. In a real sense, they pay all of our salaries, and I love them for it.'

Pegleg held his hook in the air. 'But the only things they have at stake in this game are money and pride. That Cabalvision crap caters to them and their needs.'

'But coach,' Jammernder Anfäger – another rookie, but with far less promise than Spiel – said, 'don't we have money and pride on the line as well?'

Pegleg smiled. Dunk knew that smile. The ex-pirate reserved it for when some fool walked straight into one of his rhetorical traps. Pegleg lived for straight men like this, the ones who handed him the set-ups for his punch lines, but he showed them no pity. He always made them pay.

'True, Mr. Anfäger. We have even more to lose, in those senses than any but our most rabid fans. Our jobs are on the line, and our professional reputations. That's something to fight for, isn't it?'

Anfäger nodded, pleased with himself for having triggered this portion of the coach's pep talk. Then the ex-pirate lunged forward and brought his hook up under the rookie's chin, pressing there just enough to break the skin, but not to catch the man by his jawbone like an unlucky, warm-blooded fish.

'I suppose then that you don't much value your life,' Pegleg said as he glared deep into the rookie's frightened eyes.

Anfäger swallowed hard, but didn't move, for which Dunk was thankful. Right here before the game, they wouldn't be able to replace the rookie if he made a stupid decision. Pegleg's glare dared the man to try to escape the hook threatening him, but Anfäger remained frozen.

Pegleg dropped his hook and stepped back to the front of the benches. He gazed out at the players, all staring at him, and wiped the blood on his hook on his bright, white shirt, where it left a crimson trail.

'That's what's really at stake for you, my hearties. Not fame, not fortune, not the way people will remember you. Sure, all those things are there, and more, but they're nothing more than phantoms striving to distract you from the most vital thing you each possess: your very lives.

'This is no idle threat on my part. Only four Hackers are still left here from our game against the Chaos All-Stars last year, and they remember the mayhem from that fateful day all too well.'

Dunk nodded at that, as did M'Grash, Guillermo, and Cavre. He missed the friends he'd lost during that game and since. So many Hackers had died last year – although a good number of them had been the creatures brought to the team by the Far Albion Cup. Those he wouldn't miss at all.

The deaths that surrounded the game – permeated it – didn't bother Dunk most days. He'd come to Blood Bowl from a failed career as a dragonslayer, so this had seemed to be a step up.

Now, though, he had things to live for. He'd reconciled with his brother. He'd found his father. He had more money than he'd ever dreamed of since he'd left the family keep in the hands of an angry mob, and there was Spinne, whom he loved. The only thing keeping them apart, it seemed, was this damned game.

Dunk considered standing up and leaving the team, the stadium, and the game behind there and then. After all, he was sure that Zauberer would kill him shortly after he stepped onto the field. The wizard would only want to wait for the right moment, something that fit his quirky sense of drama.

But Dunk knew he couldn't leave all this behind. He couldn't abandon his friends, his family. He glanced at Dirk, who flashed him a cocky smile. Dunk could see past it to how nervous the man was underneath the façade. He couldn't leave him behind.

And, of course, Pegleg would murder him on the spot if he tried to go now.

'This is kill or be killed,' Pegleg said. 'We have the All-Stars outmatched in every position. We play better ball than them. We can score on them at will.

'But that's not how they win games. They don't care about touchdowns. We could be ahead ten to zilch, but if the game ends under their terms, they won't care.

'All they have to do to win is murder every damned one of you. Once we can't put any players on the field, they win by forfeit, no matter what the score.

'Now, that's not a very big field out there as battlefields go. There are no forests to hide in, no hills to skulk behind. In short, there's nowhere you can hide.

'The only thing you can do is face up to the bastards the best you can – and kill them before they kill you!'

The Hackers stood up and cheered at the top of their lungs.

'Are you with me?'

'Yes!' the Hackers shouted as one.

'What?'

'*Yes!*'

'I can't hear you!'

'*YES!*'

'Then get on out there and kill! Kill for your fans! Kill for your family! Kill for your team! *Kill for yourselves!*'

'Go! Go! Go!' Cavre took up the chant, and the others joined in straight away. 'Go! Go! Go!'

Pegleg stamped over to the door to the tunnel that led to the Hackers' dugout and to the field in the centre of the Emperors Stadium, where a hundred thousand fans waited to watch them prove themselves the champions they knew they could be. '*Let's GO!*' he bellowed.

The Hackers' voices devolved into a cacophony of howls that would have sent a tribe of wild wolves fleeing, their tails between their legs. Then they charged after Cavre as he led them down through that dark tunnel and towards the chances for life and glory that awaited them beyond.

DUNK STOMPED HIS feet and jumped up and down in the dugout as he waited for the game to begin. They'd already introduced the teams and gone through all the pre-game nonsense. All that was left was the coin toss and the kick-off.

Trotting out onto the field to the deafening roar of the crowd had been a rush. After a moment, his ears had adjusted to the noise, and he could hear the people chanting, 'Dunk! Dunk! Dunk!' He'd grinned wide and waved at them and listened to them roar their approval.

No amount of gold could buy a feeling like that.

'Hold still,' Dr. Pill said as he approached Dunk and waved a wand at him that looked like it had been constructed with leather straps and chicken bones.

'What's this?' Dunk asked. 'Some kind of blessing?'

The apothecary shook his head. 'Big game like this, it pays to check everything. The All-Stars like to slip cursed contraband into their foes' kits. I already found a mouth guard that would have turned into a snake.'

Without another word, Dunk stretched out his arms and legs, and let Dr. Pill wave the wand over them. It whined like a stuck snotling as it approached his throat, rising in pitch as it got nearer and then lowering as he moved it away.

'What's this?' Dr. Pill asked, pointing at the shrunken head. The thing twisted on its chain under the apothecary's glare.

'You ever hear of a player named Skragger?'

Dr. Pill nodded. 'Black orc, star player for the All-Stars, set all sorts of records.' He cocked his head at Dunk. 'Killed while attacking you and then came back as a vampire player for the Champions of Death. I heard you ripped his head off in the middle of a game.'

Dunk gestured towards the shrunken head. 'Cavre made it for me.'

'Is it a replica? Some kind of memento?'

Dunk shook his head. 'It's the real thing. Cavre shrunk it.'

Dr. Pill leaned over and peered at the tiny head closely, getting within inches of it, but never touching it. Then he strode over to the other side of the dugout to chat with Cavre. A moment later, the two of them came back to talk with Dunk. Dr. Pill had his black bag with him.

'I'm so sorry, Dunk,' Cavre said.

'How do you get this thing off?' Dr. Pill asked, pointing at the metal ball gag in Skragger's mouth. 'Can you remove it?'

'Sure,' Dunk said. He reached down and released the gag, letting it fall into his hand.

'Sons of witches!' Skragger's head said in its squeaky voice. 'Gonna grow my head, get my body back, and kill every damn one of you!'

'I can see why you had him gagged,' said Cavre.

'Hold still,' Dr. Pill said as he rummaged about in his bag. He produced a small silver vial and uncorked it. Then he tapped a small amount of bright red powder from the vial into the palm of his hand.

'I hear all your records were fakes,' Dr. Pill said to Skragger's head.

'Who said?' Skragger screeched. 'Lies! All lies! Earned every–'

Dr. Pill blew the red dust into the shrunken head's face. Skragger inhaled most of it, and it set him off on a coughing fit.

'How is that possible?' Dunk asked. 'He doesn't have any lungs.'

'You're toting around a talking shrunken head on a chain around your neck, and now you want to debate its physiology with me?' Dr. Pill permitted himself a smirk.

'Whoa!' Skragger said. 'That's good stuff.'

'What's going on?' Dunk asked.

Dr. Pill re-corked his vial and then stuffed it into his bag. As he did, Cavre spoke. 'My most sincere apologies, Dunk. If I'd known this was possible, I never would have allowed it.'

'Known what was possible?'

Cavre pointed at Skragger's head as the thing mumbled on about all the pretty orc cheerleaders in its path. 'That thing,' Cavre said. 'It's telepathic.'

Dunk's eyes flew wide. 'You're kidding.'

'I'm afraid not. It makes sense when you think about it. How could someone as dense as Skragger be such a great Blood Bowl player? Simple. He reads his opponents' minds. He could tell what they were going to do as soon as they thought about it.'

'He knows everything they think?' Horror gripped Dunk's heart.

Cavre shook his head. 'He's a simple orc who can barely construct a sentence. Even if he could read your mind, he probably wouldn't understand most of it – beyond the violence. That he understands, and that's what he's been communicating to Zauberer.'

Dunk felt like he might fall over. He stabbed his finger at the thing hanging on his chest. 'This is how he's been doing it? How Zauberer knows where I am and when I'm in danger?'

Cavre raised his eyebrows and nodded.

Dunk reached for the head. 'I'm going to stomp this thing into tiny pieces.'

'No!' said Dr. Pill. 'I just went to a great deal of trouble to drug that little bugger before Zauberer would be able to notice it. Don't you dare wash my work down the drain.'

Dunk narrowed his eyes at the apothecary. 'What did that stuff do to him?'

'It's a powerful hallucinogenic. It makes him see things that aren't there.'

'And things that are?'

'He can't distinguish between reality and fantasy at the moment. He's also highly suggestible.'

'What exactly does that mean?'

THE HACKERS WON the opening coin toss – handled by the only referee both teams could agree on: Rhett Bool – and elected to receive. Dunk trotted down to one end of the field and waited for the All-Stars to kick the ball.

The more he thought about it, the more he knew that Zauberer would probably wait until the worst moment to attack him. He also knew that the wizard had a traitor's soul. He saw anyone and anything as expendable in the race to achieve his goals. He'd zap Skragger in an instant.

He wanted to kick himself for not figuring out about the connection between Zauberer and the black orc. Zauberer had been such a horrible shot in that game against the Oldheim Ogres back in Magritta. How had he got to be so deadly accurate? He had a tiny little spotter working for him, helping him call down his ebony bolts from the blue.

Dunk rattled Skragger's chain just for fun and heard the head howl in protest. 'Yer gonna die!' he said. 'Zappity-zap-zap!'

Then the crowd started in on the rising shout that told Dunk the ball would be coming his way soon. When it reached its climax, it ended in a massive, unified shout and then shattered into thousands of cheers.

Dunk spotted the ball spinning end over end through the crisp, afternoon air, arcing right towards him. He spread his arms, and it landed right between them and his chest with a satisfying thump. He turned his head to the right and spotted Rotes Hernd, the Hackers' back-up thrower, standing near the sideline, waving her arms at him. Dunk snapped a quick pass to Rotes, who stood behind the protective wall of M'Grash and Edgar, and then sprinted upfield.

The first few All-Stars ignored Dunk and chased after the ball instead. Then Dunk heard a chorus of horrifying barks, and he knew that he'd attracted the attention of Serby 'Dawgy-Dawg-Dawg' Triomphe, the All-Stars' new team captain.

Dunk glanced to his right and saw Serby sprinting after him. The mutant beastman's three canine heads – each with its own black and red helmet, but none with a muzzle – growled in harmony, their eyes blazing red, blue, and green. Drool dripped from each head, slicking down Serby's jersey. Dunk had heard that he had to change jerseys at least four times a game, which close up, didn't seem to be often enough.

'Mine!' the green-eyed head said. 'Mine! Mine! Mine!'

'Catch!' the blue-eyed head said. 'Catch! Catch! Catch!'

'Kill!' the red-eyed head said. 'Kill! Kill! Kill!'

Any one of the heads looked like it could rip one of Dunk's arms clean from its socket. He'd seen just that happen in the scouting report Pegleg had prepared before the game too. Serby had taken hold of a doomed orc blitzer playing for the Underworld Creepers. In one blood-soaked blur, the orc had gone from four limbs to a single arm, which still held on to the ball as Serby's three heads scurried off into the dugout to enjoy their hard-earned snacks.

Dunk's legs pounded against the Astrogranite, propelling him downfield. He gave thanks that Serby's stride wasn't much faster than his, and that the creature's three heads made him top-heavy. When the beastman got too close, Dunk jinked to one side or the other, and Serby's helmets clashed against each other as he tried to follow Dunk's moves.

Dunk knew he couldn't keep this up forever. There was only so much open field around him. Sooner or later, Serby would corner him or get some of the other All-Stars to team up on him, and then Dunk would be doomed.

'Look at Hoffnung run!' Jim's voice said. 'That's one way to walk the Dawgy-Dawg-Dawg!'

'Let's see if Hoffnung has it in him to curb that canine!' said Bob. 'If he can't somehow collar that mutt, he's going to end up having kibble made from his bits!'

Dunk spun away from Serby's snapping jaws once again and sprinted towards the end zone. As he did, he glanced back and saw the ball spinning down out of the sky towards him. He reached out his gauntleted hands and caught the pigskin between them.

The crowd cheered. With Dunk scant yards from the goal line, he had a touchdown in the bag – or so it seemed.

Dunk reached up and pulled Skragger's chain from around his neck. As he did, he turned and stopped, standing a mere yard in front of the end zone. 'I can't believe I'm about to score,' he shouted. 'I can't wait to hear the crowd cheer when I do!'

'Cheer!' Skragger said, his tiny eyes focused on something far away. Froth filled his miniature mouth. 'Make 'em cheer!'

Dunk wrapped the chain around the ball, winding it fast around the spikes. Then he held it up in front of him and waved it at Serby. 'Here, Dawgy-Dawg-Dawg!'

All six of Serby's eyes flashed red at the insult. Their words devolved into nothing more than rabid barking. The beastman charged straight at Dunk with the speed of a runaway mining cart sliding on its way down to hell.

Just as Serby reached him, Dunk said, 'Here it comes.' He gave the ball a little flip into the air and then dived to the side. The ball hung there for a moment, right where he had been. Then Serby crashed into it at full speed and wrapped his arms around it.

'Amazing!' Jim said, the crowd's cheers drowning out his voice. 'Just as Hoffnung was about to score–'

A crack of black lightning cut off the announcer's comments. The noise sent Dunk's ears ringing, and the flash blinded and dazzled him. He smelled something that reminded him of the sausage-on-a-stick vendor just outside the stadium.

He grinned. The plan had worked.

'Nuffle's gnarled nads!' Bob's voice said. 'Triomphe is gone! Blasted to ashes by a freak bolt of lightning that seemed to come from nowhere! Do the Hackers have a wizard on their side who's not listed on their roster?'

'We'd better check the replay on that!' Jim said. 'That colour of bolt has been a trademark of Zauberer's ever since he stole – I mean, apprehended. No that's not right either. He – ah, forget it!'

'What was your point again, Jim?'

'Just this: Since Zauberer *stole* the Chaos Cup, he's been blasting all of Hoffnung's foes with bolts just like that one, with the same dramatic and messy results.'

'Does this mean that Zauberer's somehow switched sides?' Bob asked. 'How could he have killed Triomphe instead of Hoffnung?'

'Hold on a moment. We have a report coming in from our intrepid correspondent on the front lines – I mean, the sidelines. What's up with the All-Stars, Lästiges?'

'Total chaos, Jim!'

'Well, that's nothing new. How about we check in with–'

'Wait, Jim! The All-Stars' dugout is even more chaotic than normal. As usual, their dugout is shrouded in an impenetrable cloud of blackness, but bodies and parts thereof have been appearing from it ever since that bolt passed through Triomphe, hot enough to blast his shadow onto the Astrogranite beneath him.'

'Have you been able to get a word in with the coach?'

'You well know, Bob, that no one has ever interviewed the All-Stars' coach – at least not without either dying or falling into a gibbering heap on the spot. Whoever he is, he likes his privacy and has protected it for decades. Even under such unusual circumstances, it seems that he will maintain that secrecy for now.'

'So, if you can't get into the dugout, and you can't ask anyone any questions, what can you tell us?'

'Not much, I'm afraid. Back to you, Jim!'

'Thank you, Lästiges, for that confuzzling report!'

While the announcers blathered away over the PA system, Dunk shoved himself to his feet and poked around through Triomphe's ashes, helmets, and bits of armour, for the remains of the ball. All he could find were a few blackened spikes, a couple of which had melted into steaming lumps of metal.

Dunk discovered even less of Skragger's shrunken head: nothing at all, not a single trace. Wherever the black orc vampire was now, Dunk hoped it hurt.

Bool whistled the play dead when he came to the same conclusion that Dunk had. There was no ball left to be found. The ref signalled for a fresh ball to be thrown in from the sidelines, and one was.

Cavre conferred with Bool and the newly appointed captain of the All-Stars, a squid-headed woman with ink-black eyes, by the name of Kathula Lustcruft. Dunk trotted over to join with the other Hackers on their side of the field, and the All-Star players congregated together on the other.

'What's going on?' Dunk asked.

'They're trying to figure out what to do about the missing ball,' Dirk said.

'Last time we just had another one thrown in.'

'The Blood Bowl Tournament organisers got an interpretation of Nuffle's Rules that made that illegal,' Rotes said.

'What's their bloody alternative then?' Edgar asked. 'Call it a bloody tie only two bloody minutes into the bloody game?'

Spiel shook his head. 'According to the latest dispatch from the Church of Nuffle, ancient scholars delved deep into the apocrypha and came up with a new rule for what to do if such a thing ever happened again.' The rookie noticed everyone staring at him. 'What? Don't you people read what they send you?'

'Read?' M'Grash said, scratching his head.

'So what's going to happen?' Dunk asked. 'Give us the short version.'

'That was,' Spiel said, scowling. 'It's called a death match. They put two players in the middle of the field, ten yards apart. Everyone else has to be twenty yards back. Then the ref drops the ball between them and runs for his life.'

'Nuffle's jolly jockstrap,' said Guillermo. 'That will be a mess. How do they decide who enters this match of death?'

'That's what I just spent the last minute figuring out, Mr. Reyes,' Cavre said as he trotted over from the conference. He looked over at the ogre. 'Mr. K'Thragsh, you're up!'

THE ALL-STARS put their largest, meanest player up against M'Grash: a headless, slime-skinned troll by the name of Ichorbod. The green-slick thing carried an All-Star's helmet around under his arm like a mother cradling an infant – a starving, undead infant. It stood as tall as M'Grash, even without a head atop its shoulders, and its mass was at least equal to the ogre's.

As M'Grash lined up in his designated spot, the other creature did the same and let loose with a horrifying bellow that made Dunk wish he'd taken up a safer sport, like daemon baiting. Cavre stood by the ogre, calming him with a pat on the arm and some words shouted into his ear over the roar of the crowd.

'If he has no head, how does he yell like that?' Dunk asked.

'See that helmet under his arm?' Dirk said. 'It's not empty.'

Dunk did a double-take. 'You mean he carries his own head around in that thing? That's insane.'

'Strong words from a man who toted a black orc vampire's head about on a chain around his neck for the past year.'

'Good point.'

Cavre trotted back from the centre of the field, where he'd left M'Grash. He lined up in the centre of the rest of the Hackers, all exactly twenty yards away from the middle of the field. This put him right between Dunk and Dirk.

'Get ready, Hackers!' Cavre shouted. 'As soon as that ball drops, it is live! Grab it and go!'

'What did you tell M'Grash?' Dunk asked.

'To kill the troll. It's not called a Hug Match. Now keep your eyes on that ball. When it squirts out of there, we need to grab it.'

'You think he can follow those directions?'

'Kill. Troll.' Cavre smiled and shrugged. 'It's M'Grash. I don't know.'

Dunk nodded and focused on the new pigskin. He hoped that his stunt with Triomphe had disrupted Zauberer's plans enough that he'd be able to play the rest of the game without interference from the wizard. At the very least, by getting rid of Skragger, he'd removed the bright, red target on his chest.

Bool walked to the centre of the field and held up the new ball. He showed it to the two monstrous players flanking him. A humongous image of it played on the Jumboball looking down on the stadium from the wall behind the northern end zone.

Bool tossed the ball straight up in the air and then galloped out of there as fast as his boots would take him.

Ichorbod ripped the faceguard off his helmet while the ball was still in the air, and then hurled his head straight at M'Grash. Distracted by the ball, the ogre didn't see the head coming at him until it hit him in the face, smashing flat a nose that had been broken countless times before.

As M'Grash howled in pain, a long, pink tongue lashed out of the helmet and wrapped all the way around his throat. Then it pulled tight, constricting around his windpipe as he tried to claw it off with his thick, stubby fingers.

While M'Grash struggled with Ichorbod's head, the troll's body lumbered forward and blindly lashed out at the ogre. Its hands found M'Grash's arm and locked on. Acrid vapours rose from where the troll's flesh touched that of M'Grash, and the ogre howled in pain.

'Get that ball!' Cavre shouted.

The pigskin thudded in the middle of the field and took a bounce towards the Hackers. Dunk lunged forward, closest to it of anyone, but the choice between grabbing the ball and helping his friend tore at him as he went. In the end, he decided to do both.

Dunk plucked up the ball. It felt good in his hand – clean, a good heft, nicely balanced – the perfect weapon.

Dunk cocked back his arm and leapt up at M'Grash, who'd staggered backward towards him and the rest of the Hackers' line. He grabbed the ogre's pauldron and used it to lever himself up high enough that he had a good shot at Ichorbod's head. He brought the ball down hard, and the spike on its tip slammed right through the troll's helmet.

Ichorbod's body shivered and fell back a step as it released its grip on M'Grash's arm, leaving red blisters behind. The creature's head, though, roared around its still-extended tongue. It did not let go.

'Wow, Jim! You have to admire a player who's willing to use the ball like that.'

'You sure do! Too bad it doesn't seem to have done any good. Hoffnung was probably aiming for Ichorbod's brain. Those are darn small things to have to find in a skull the size of a troll's!'

Dunk yanked the ball from the troll's helmet and cocked back his arm to have another go at lobotomising Ichorbod. If he kept at it, he knew he'd strike grey matter soon.

Ichorbod's body slammed into M'Grash, which sent Dunk toppling to the ground. He tucked the ball under his arm and tumbled away. When he rolled to his feet, he saw that two ram-headed beastmen had knocked the troll into the ogre, and then leapt away before the creature's skin could harm them as well.

M'Grash tried to howl in pain, but he couldn't get enough air past Ichorbod's tongue. He marched a few tremendous steps and then fell backward, the troll clutching its toxic skin to him.

'Over here, Dunk!'

The thrower turned and saw Dirk sprinting towards the right sideline and waving an arm at him. No All-Stars had bothered to cover him. When Dunk glanced straight up field, he saw why. They were all coming for him.

Dunk hurled the ball towards Dirk and then turned to run before he even saw if his brother caught it. As he did, he saw M'Grash on the ground between him and the other All-Stars, struggling for his life.

Although it seemed like suicide, Dunk charged forward, lowered his shoulder, and dived into M'Grash's neck, headfirst, using his helmet as a spear. It smacked into Ichorbod's helmet, and something gave way with a wet sound. The head popped free and twirled off towards the onrushing All-Stars.

One of the All-Stars, an orc with a giant crab's arms and pincers, stopped to catch the screaming troll's loose head. The others came at Dunk like an ebony-jerseyed wave.

Dunk braced himself for the impact, but he couldn't have imagined how bad it would be. The two ram-headed All-Stars smashed into him first, sending him flying back and to the ground. Then a man with the body of a bear landed on him, crushing the air from his lungs.

As spots floated before Dunk's eyes, Kathula dived at him, the tentacles that dangled from her face wrapping around his helmet, creeping in underneath it, and gripping at his skin. Unable to move his arms or even cry for help, all he could do was watch in panicked terror as her beak-like mouth appeared from among her tentacles and made its way towards his face, its sucker-surfaced tongue flicking out at him like a slaver's lash.

One side of the tongue slapped wet and warm against Dunk's cheeks and stuck there. Then it started to pull him in towards the black beak, which flexed in anticipation of biting into his flesh. The tip of the tongue flailed free, searching, pressing for a way between Dunk's lips and into his mouth.

Then Kathula's tongue pulled free from Dunk's face, pocking his skin as it left. The rest of her tentacles followed along with her tongue, and then the two ram-headed linemen disappeared as well. Still flat on his back, Dunk saw M'Grash grinning down at him and offering him a hand up.

'Thanks, big guy. I thought the ram-men and noodle-face there were going to make a cheap lunch out of me.'

'S'alright.'

Dunk glanced around and saw his attackers getting up and starting to circle him and M'Grash again. 'Doesn't anyone around here ever play the ball any more?' he asked.

'Touchdown, Hackers!' Jim's voice said. 'What an amazing play. Dirk Heldmann's pass to Rhett Cavre put the ball way down the field, and then Cavre worked his foot magic to break three tackles – and a couple of arms – to get into the end zone!'

'It's that kind of attention to basics – things like scoring points – that has always served the Hackers well. If they can avoid the All-Stars' Total 'Ponent Kill strategy, they should be able to win this game.'

Lästiges chipped in at that point. 'I just finished talking with Dr. Shnahps Magillicutty, the team apothecary for the All-Stars. He says he thinks the team will abandon the TPK tactics now. With Dr. Pill on the Hackers' side, it's likely the team could manage to outlast the All-Stars. If so, the game would come down to points, and with the Hackers already up by a touchdown, the All-Stars have some catching up to do.'

'Good point, Lästiges. It would be great to see a game based upon the classic 'scoring' strategies rather than total annihilation. Call me old-fashioned if you like–'

'You're six hundred years old, Bob!' said Jim. 'Of course you're old-fashioned.'

'Maybe. And maybe I just like yelling, "Touchdown!"'

'Well, you have to admit, it does have a certain ring to it.'

Dunk trotted back to the Hackers' end of the field to line up for the kick-off, a grin on his face. Cavre's score couldn't have come at a better time. For the first time all day, he started to think about more than just surviving the game. If things continued to go this well, they might just win.

'Don't go thinking about victory yet,' Cavre shouted out to the other players as they got into position, almost as if he could read Dunk's mind. The thought made the thrower nervous for a moment. He hadn't suspected that Skragger was telepathic. Could he have missed something with his team's captain too?

'No,' Cavre called over to Dunk. 'You just wear every emotion you have on your face.'

'Remind me not to play pogre with you.'

Cavre held up his arm to signal the others to get ready. Then he charged up to the ball and booted it towards the distant end zone. It arced through the sky and came down in the arms of a lizardman called Tzun Su, who had a bright orange crest that ran along the top of his skull.

The lizardman reminded Dunk a bit of Sseth Skinshucker, who'd played for the All-Stars last year. His career had ended after M'Grash had tossed him into the stands in Magritta. The fans there had skinned the creature alive and made, from later accounts, five sets of quality boots from his scales. Sseth had survived the incident and later claimed one of the pairs of boots for himself as a memento of his playing days.

Dunk hung back to cover the All-Star catchers who raced down the field. As they raced towards him, M'Grash and Edgar led the charge against them. On their way towards the lizardman, they trampled a beetle-headed man – one Kanz Frafka – under their feet as if he were nothing more than a giant cockroach caught unwillingly in a game not of his own design – and then paying the ultimate price.

An eagle-headed creature with wings for arms flapped towards Dunk, his feet almost leaving the ground as he sped along. The thrower threw himself forward to check the catcher, whose uniform read 'Sam,' but the birdman skirted away from Dunk's check and left him clutching air.

Downfield, Edgar put his branches in the lizardman's face, giving him nowhere to throw the ball. As the treeman started to gloat, Tzun Su darted his head forward and spit fire from deep in his gullet.

The flames incinerated some of Edgar's leaves and ignited his smaller branches. The treeman let loose a terrified scream that made Dunk think he might never care to go into a forest alone again. Then he began to dash back and forth across the field, looking for some kind of relief.

Under Cavre's direction, M'Grash slammed into Edgar from behind and knocked him over. As the treeman toppled to the ground, the ogre yelled, 'Timberrrr!' This did nothing for the bug-eyed goblin caught underneath Edgar's bulk as he fell.

The poor creature chattered madly as its legs were crushed. This rose to a fevered pitch as M'Grash began to roll Edgar back and forth on the ground like a rolling pin, trying to put the flames out. By the time he succeeded, the goblin was little more than a nice, flat sheet of reddish paste that had been baked solid by the burning treeman's heat.

'Cookie?' M'Grash asked as he scooped up the hot goblin/baked goodie.

Dunk didn't see what happened next. He saw the ball appear in the air high above the field, and he angled towards Sam to try to intercept the pass.

It wasn't a good throw, but the kind Pegleg liked to call a 'wounded parrot,' and Dunk had the angle on it. All he had to do was jump up a little at the last second, and the ball would be his.

The sound of a massive bird cry from behind him almost sent Dunk diving to the Astrogranite instead. He managed to keep his composure long enough to jump for the ball as he'd planned, but as his fingers reached up, a taloned foot reached down and snagged it as the beating of wings sounded in Dunk's ears.

Dunk looked up and cursed. Sam's wings were more than just for looks. The creature had made it into the air and was now winging back around for a shot at his end zone. Dunk leapt up to try to grab Sam, but his fingers closed only on air. A moment later, the eagle-man, having gained enough height, went into a power dive that deposited him and the ball right in the middle of his end zone.

'Touchdown, All-Stars!' Bob said. 'Yep, I never do get tired of that word! Touchdown!'

'That hardly seems fair,' said Jim. 'The birdman there was flying! Blood Bowl isn't one of those sissy games wizards play on the backs of broomsticks. It's down and dirty action! Three yards and a cloud of dust! Ploughing divots out of the Astrogranite! It stays on the ground!'

'Spoken like someone who can't fly!' Bob said.

THE ALL-STARS and the Hackers stymied each other for the rest of the half. Sam kept his flying to a minimum, but only when Rhett Bool wasn't looking his way. During one harrowing play, the eagle-man dived into Edgar's upper branches in an effort to strip the ball from the treeman. He only ended up coming away with some bark, but ever after that Edgar chased the creature around the field, ignoring the ball unless it happened to cross his path.

When the whistle blew and the Hackers trotted back down the tunnel to their locker room, no one said a word. Ever since their early score, the game had been one frustration after another for them, and the Hackers were worn and tired.

'What in Nuffle's nine original divisions is going on out there?' Pegleg demanded as the players sat down on their benches once again. 'These scurvy dogs finally decide to give us a real ball game, and you bilge rats can't be bothered to make them pay for it?'

'We're down to only ten players,' Dirk said as he poured a tankard of water over his head. 'Plus, it turns out the All-Stars aren't all that bad when they actually play.'

'"Not all that bad"?' Pegleg's eyes grew large and showed whites all around. 'These are the Chaos All-Stars we're talking about here! They're nothing *but* bad! We need to go out there and punish them like the evil beasts they are!'

'Coach?' Dunk said. When Pegleg turned his furious eyes on him, he instantly regretted saying a word, but this game was too important for him to back down. 'Are you just going to yell at us, or do you have a plan?'

Pegleg's face turned bright red, and spittle sputtered from his lips. He raised his hook as if looking for something soft and yielding to plunge it into – like a beating heart. Then he managed some small amount of control over himself, just enough to speak. He spat each word out with a precision that said that to do otherwise might cause him to explode.

'What, Mr. Hoffnung, would you have us do?'

'I have some ideas.'

THE HACKERS KICKED the ball off to start the second half. It arced down towards the All-Stars, and Sam the eagleman leapt into the air and snatched it.

Dunk stood right where he was, not making a move, while he watched Cavre, Edgar, and M'Grash stomp down the field after the ball. The rest of the Hackers gathered around him.

Dunk peered over their helmets and saw that the two ram-headed All-Stars had challenged the referee to a head-butting match right after he'd blown the whistle to start the half. As an ex-player himself, Bool managed to gore one of the creatures with his horns before the other laid him flat on his back.

With the ref out of the picture, Sam beat his wings and gained altitude. M'Grash jumped up and made a grab at the eagle-man, but fell short.

'Sam takes the kick-off, and he's got nothing but daylight in front of him!' Bob's voice said. 'The All-Stars seem to have come up with a spectacular plan during halftime. If they keep this up, we can put this game into the record books right now.'

'The All-Stars are turning this into a game of broomball!' Jim said. 'I don't like it, and the fans don't either!' A rousing chorus of boos and hisses confirmed the commentator's opinion. 'Drop the airborne routine, All-Stars! We came here to see Blood Bowl!'

Cocky from his clear shot at success, Sam performed a barrel roll, spinning his wings as an insult to Jim and the fans. This put him straight on course for Edgar, who raised his branches up high over his head.

The eagle-man let loose the screech of a predator bird spotting its prey. He dived straight for Edgar, planning to skim the tops of the treeman's branches and prove that literally no one could touch him.

As Sam zoomed in hard and fast, Edgar flung a shimmering something between his arms. It glinted like a spider's web in the clear sunlight.

Sam spied the thing at the last second and tried to pull up, but it was too late. He hurtled straight into the mithril net the Halfling Titans had given to Edgar.

The net engulfed the eagle-man, and the momentum of his sudden stop knocked Edgar to the ground. The treeman kept his grip on the net and brought it and its occupant down along with him.

The net rolled into a tight ball around Sam as he struggled to break free. He failed to do so before the net slammed into the Astrogranite and knocked him senseless.

'That's one way to ground all flights in and out of Emperor Stadium!' Bob said.

The ball squirted free from the net and took a Hacker bounce. Rotes dashed forward and scooped it up. Standing alone in the middle of the field, she saw the rest of the All-Stars charging at her, and she froze.

'Stick to the plan!' Dunk shouted. 'Throw the ball!'

Rotes broke the hold her terror had on her, spun and hurled the ball back towards the other players, who still stood huddled in the middle of the field. Anfäger reached up and dragged it down into the scrum like a frog snatching and swallowing an errant fly.

'All right,' Dunk said. 'Break!'

The Hackers burst out of the huddle, each in a different direction. They left only one player still standing there, clutching something under his arms.

The All-Stars ignored the other players and went for the stationary one, who seemed to be just standing there with the ball, daring them to try to hurt him. They were happy to oblige.

'I smell something up here, Jim. Do you have any idea who number 18 is for the Hackers? He looks like he's pleading for a quick death!'

'I don't have him listed on my roster. Lästiges?'

'Coach Haken tells me he's a last-minute addition to the roster, a new rookie who's never seen a minute of play!'

'It looks like our man of mystery might *only* see a minute of play!' said Jim. 'Here come the All-Stars!'

Dunk glanced back over his shoulder and saw three of the Chaos players slam into number 18 at once. They knocked him flat on his back and piled on top of him, trying to crush the life from him with the weight of their bodies. A moment later, they leapt to their feet, howling.

'Can you see what's going on down there, Lästiges?'

'It's a huge mess, Bob. Whatever number 18 was holding down there, it wasn't a ball! When the All-Stars hit him, it burst, and the contents of – it looks like a canvas sack – went everywhere. Oh, gods! The smell is awful!'

Dunk grinned as an image of number 18 flashed up on the Jumboball above the end zone before him. Inside the spare set of armour, Lehrer had just been awakened by the horrible scent of the gunk that had coated nearly every part of him. As the old man tried in vain to wipe away the cast-offs of Dr. Pill's overused healing potions, he started to scream.

'Amazing!' Bob said. 'But if that wasn't the real ball in number 18's hands, then where is it?'

'Look!' said Jim. 'Hoffnung's heading for the goal line, and there's only one All-Star who can stop him!'

'Where you goin'?' Ichorbod asked as he stomped between Dunk and the end zone.

Dunk skidded to a halt, nearly sliding into the acid-skinned troll. 'Nowhere special,' the thrower said, putting up his hands to show they were empty. 'I don't have the ball. I'm just decoy number two.'

It took Dunk a moment to remember the troll's voice couldn't have come from the area above his shoulders. He looked straight ahead and saw Ichorbod's face grinning at him from where his slime-covered body held it right between his outstretched hands.

'Don't care,' Ichorbod said. 'Yer dead.'

Dunk reached out and grabbed the troll's helmet by the edges of the rim that framed the creature's face. 'Don't!' he said, falling to his knees. 'Please! You can't kill me! I have too much to live for. I have five kids back home! I'm – I'm *pregnant!*'

The troll stared out at Dunk, dumbfounded, which wasn't a big mental leap for him. The thrower's outburst had confused it so much it didn't hear the thunderous footsteps approaching over the crowd's raucous cheers.

'Touchdown, Hackers!' Bob's voice said. 'Heldmann strolls into the end zone untouched! I *love* this game!'

Before Ichorbod could turn to see the replay on the Jumboball, M'Grash's spike-cleated boot came rushing at him. At the last second, Dunk snatched his arms back, and M'Grash punted the troll's severed head up and away.

Dunk scrambled backward away from Ichorbod's body, eager to escape its final efforts at senseless violence. As he did, he watched the troll's head soar past the fans in the nosebleed seats and nearly knock a circling gull from the cloudless sky. It arced out over the stadium's upper edge, and was gone.

Ichorbod's body tripped on something and toppled to the Astro-granite. It lay there for a moment, and then started to beat its fists and feet against the ground like a massive, acid-skinned toddler in the middle of a monstrous tantrum.

'Thanks, big guy,' Dunk said to M'Grash as they trotted back to their end of the field for their next kick-off.

'Dunkel safe!' the ogre said with a tusk-filled grin. 'We win!'

'Not yet,' Dunk said. Above them, the scoreboard changed to show the new tally: All-Stars 1, Hackers 2. 'But it's a good start.'

When Dunk got into position, he turned and saw the All-Stars leading Ichorbod's body into the dead centre of the field. As they did, a figure in black robes strode out onto the field, bearing in his arms a massive, fanged skull mounted atop a short stand covered with smaller skulls.

Dunk stared for a moment. He recognised Zauberer, but he couldn't imagine what the wizard could be thinking, walking right onto the field in the middle of the biggest game of the year. Whatever it was, it couldn't be good.

'Stop him!' Dunk said as he dashed ahead. 'We have to stop him!'

Ten of the All-Stars stepped forward between the Hackers and Zauberer. They formed a wall through which the Hackers would have to fight to stop the wizard's plot. Dunk led the charge, launching himself at the crab-armed man who stood closest to him.

Zauberer set the Chaos Cup down on top of Ichorbod's chest and withdrew a pair of black-bladed knives from the sleeves of his robes. As he did, the two ram-headed men leaned over the cup to peer into it. The cup's handles lashed out and snared the beastmen, holding them fast. They bleated in terror and tried to pull free, but they could not manage it before Zauberer ducked in with his blades and slit their throats.

As the lifeblood of the ram-men flowed into the cup's main bowl, the skulls around the base rolled off and began to burrow into Ichorbod's torso with their vicious, sharp teeth. The troll flailed about, trying to keep itself from being devoured alive, but it couldn't seem to shake a single one of the skulls from its flesh. Each of them had found an unbreakable purchase and continued to gnaw at the troll's sinews until long after it had stopped fighting them.

One of the crab-armed man's claws caught Dunk around his left bicep and started to pinch. The thrower shoved down hard and wedged his pauldron into the claw to keep it from clipping his arm in half. Still, the pressure started to bend the armour, and Dunk howled in pain.

Desperate, Dunk began pounding the crab-armed man in the face. Each blow seemed like it should have been enough to knock the All-Star senseless or dead, but the man's mutated arms kept holding on.

Dunk stopped punching the man for a moment and realised that he was unconscious or worse, but his claw had not unclenched. He pulled and yanked at the claw in frustration, but it refused to give. M'Grash reached over and tore the claw from the All-Star's arm, then jammed his fingers into the pincer and pried it loose.

Dunk rubbed his arm as he sprang free. 'Thanks!' he said, staring at the ogre as he looked down at the monstrous crab claw in his hands. 'I owe you a tub of butter!'

Dunk spun around and spotted Zauberer standing over a skeleton, holding the Chaos Cup aloft in his hands. Even as Dunk watched, the troll's flesh started to re-grow on its bones, knitting them together once again. He wondered what had happened to the smaller skulls, since none of them were around the trophy's base, or attacking Ichorbod's torso any longer.

Then he spotted the last of the small skulls emerge from the troll's ribcage with something pulsing between its savage teeth. Defying gravity, it tumbled up the wizard's robes and over the rim of the Chaos Cup.

'We are ready, o mighty Khorne, for your sacred embrace!' Zauberer shouted.

The sky turned to blood, and everyone screamed.

ONE MOMENT, DUNK stood in Emperor Stadium in Altdorf, in the heart of the Empire, the seat of power and culture in the Old World. The next, he and everyone else in the stadium – including the entire building – were somewhere else.

Dunk didn't know how he knew that it wasn't just that the sky had changed colour. Perhaps it was the hot, humid air, or the stench of blood and brimstone, or the foul taste of ashes in his mouth. Or perhaps it was the screams of the more than one hundred thousand people in the stadium with him, who all sounded as if their souls had been ripped from their flesh.

Whatever it was, he knew he was somewhere else, and he couldn't stop screaming about it either.

In the entire stadium, only Zauberer's voice wasn't screeching in horror. Instead, the wizard had thrown back his head and started to laugh.

Dunk thought he'd never heard anything so evil in his entire life. He covered his ears and cringed at the sound.

As he did, he saw Ichorbod's body pull itself to its feet, only it didn't look anything like Ichorbod any more. Its skin had the same wet sheen, but it was crimson coloured now, and it had a head.

Dunk had never seen the face on that head before. He'd heard it described, and he'd known there and then that he preferred to know

735

nothing more about it. He'd tried to do many things to remove those descriptions from his head, but nothing, not sleep, not drink, no oblivion but death could help. And now that face stared down at him and smiled as it opened its mouth and took a deep breath.

Next to the creature's laugh, Zauberer's seemed little worse than the giggles of a happy child.

Khorne. It could only be Khorne.

'By all that's unholy,' Bob's voice said, 'the Blood God has come to life in Ichorbod's corpse!'

'I think that's an illegal substitution,' said Jim, 'but since Bool's cowering under the Hackers' bench, I don't see how he's going to call it!'

The All-Stars gathered around Khorne – or at least his avatar brought to life in Ichorbod's flesh – and fell to their knees before him. The Blood God waved his hand over each of them, and they transformed. Their armour writhed around them, as did their flesh.

One by one, the All-Stars rose once more. Their black armour glistened as if with wet paint, but Dunk knew without touching it that it now seeped ebony-coloured blood. Their skin all mirrored that of Khorne himself, shining red as if their epidermises had been stripped away. Their eyes glowed as if lit from within by the fires of hell.

Beyond the stadium's rim, Dunk saw dark mountains gathered round the place. These towered over the people, like dead gods forced to bear witness to the atrocities that would be carried out within. Red-gold lightning lit the roiling crimson clouds that scudded overhead as if carried by a hurricane bringing a storm of blood.

Between the flashes of lightning and the terrified rolls of thunder that seemed like the moans of a million cursed souls, Dunk realised he could see, high above the highest seats, a ring of floating lights illuminating the stadium with a hellish glow. Dunk recognised these as the new lamps that had once surrounded the arena in a tremendous circle – the ones paid for by the Guterfiends.

'What's that Lästiges?'

'I said, according to Hacker apothecary Dr. Pill, it seems that Schlechter Zauberer has transported the entirety of Emperors Stadium to the Realm of Chaos, home of such legendary chaos lords as Nurgle and Khorne!'

'Stunning!' said Bob. 'Just like we told you before the game folks, this is one Blood Bowl final you cannot afford to miss!'

'Are we still broadcasting via Cabalvision?' asked Jim. 'I know I'm an ogre, but that doesn't seem possible!'

'It's all done with the latest in camra magic,' said Bob. 'Remember that Zauberer destroyed the old camras in the semi-final game that pitted the All-Stars against the Badlands Buccaneers. Wolf Sports had them replaced with the finest camras available! These babies can transmit our Cabalvision feeds across unlimited distances, even to hell and back it seems!'

Dunk fell back and found himself standing with the other Hackers on the field in an impromptu huddle. Looking around to see his friends by his side helped to calm his pounding heart. He reached out and put his hand on Dirk's shoulder. His brother glanced back at him, and Dunk saw the fear ebb in his eyes. Then he gave Dunk a reckless grin, and the two clasped hands. No matter what they had to face, they'd face it together. Dunk only wished that Spinne could be there too.

Khorne raised his hands and brought them down in a cutting motion. Every scream in the stadium stopped, and an eerie silence reigned over the entire place. Even Bob and Jim had quit their chattering.

'People of Altdorf,' Khorne said. Although the Blood God didn't raise his voice, Dunk could hear him perfectly, and he had no doubt that everyone else in the stadium could as well. In the absence of the deafening screams, Dunk was surprised that everyone couldn't hear the blood rushing through his veins as well.

'My servant Zauberer has completed the ritual that activates the Chaos Cup. My followers placed this with your people centuries ago. It is now carrying out its true purpose.

'My champions will play your champions in this sacred game handed down to you by means of Nuffle and his writings. If your champions win, you and your stadium will return to your home realm.'

Khorne gestured to the ensorcelled All-Stars. 'If my champions win, your realm will become mine.'

'No,' Dunk whispered.

'Wow!' said Bob. 'That's the deal of a lifetime – for Khorne!'

Dunk stepped forward. 'No way!' he said, the words leaping from him before he could pause to consider the creature at which they were directed. 'You can take your deal and shove it!'

The crowd cheered.

'We won't do it,' Dunk said. 'We won't play!'

'It seems that Hoffnung has lost his mind!' said Jim. 'He's refusing to go along with the Blood God's deal!'

Khorne stared down at Dunk with his glowing, unblinking eyes. Dunk wondered if the Blood God would bleed him dry there on the spot. Then Khorne threw back his head and laughed. The sound felt like knives in Dunk's ears.

'If you refuse to play, you will be my guests here in my realm forever,' Khorne said. Then he crossed his arms on his chest and stood as still as a statue.

Pegleg ran out onto the field, with Slick and Dr. Pill trailing in his wake. 'Mr. Hoffnung!' he said. 'When the Blood God says, "play ball," you play ball!'

'Coach,' Dunk said. 'We can't. They'll kill us either way. If we lose, Altdorf and maybe the whole of the Empire – possibly the world – becomes Khorne's. This way, he only gets a stadium full of souls instead of everyone alive.'

'That's a fine theory,' Zauberer said, calling over from where he stood in Khorne's shadow, 'but sooner or later, some of you will crack, and then we will have a game!'

'He has a point,' said Dirk. 'I'd rather play them while we're still fresh. A few days from now, we may be too weak to have any hope.'

'We don't have any hope now!' Dunk said. 'Look around you! Have you seen where we are? Do you see who we have to play? We are doomed!'

Someone wrapped her arms around Dunk from behind. 'No, Dunk,' said Spinne. 'There is always hope.'

Dunk gasped, spun around and took the woman in his arms. 'What are you doing here?' he asked, half thrilled and half terrified. Hugging her tight, he saw his father standing behind her, nodding his support.

'I held out hope,' Spinne said, 'for you. I hoped that if you won this game, you might consider retiring. I wanted to be here to see that happen, to cheer you on, even if you might never have known I was here.'

Dunk gaped at the woman for a moment, and then kissed her tenderly. 'You are the most amazing person I've ever met.'

'Ditto,' Spinne said with a toothsome grin. 'Now what do you say we kick that Blood God's ass?'

'Hey,' said Slick, 'if you're going to rejoin the team, I'd like to renegotiate your contract!'

'Belay that,' said Pegleg. 'We'll renew our old agreement, or I'll toss you into the arms of Khorne as a blood sacrifice before the game begins.'

'We're still short some players, captain,' Cavre said. 'We lost a few in that last drive.'

'Who do we have left?'

'Hoffnung, Heldmann, K'Thragsh, Reyes, Edgar, Spiel, Anfäger, Hernd, now Schönheit, and myself.'

'That's ten,' Pegleg said, scratching yet another hole in his yellow tricorn hat. 'We only need one more for a full team.'

'I'll give it a try if you don't mind,' Lügner said.

'Father!' Dirk and Dunk said at the same time.

'Thanks, my sons, for pointing out that I'm old enough to make these sorts of decisions on my own. I used to be one hell of a brawler back in my day, and I've had the occasion to put those skills to use over the past few years.'

'Who else would be mad enough to give it a go?' asked Pegleg. He stuck out his hand towards Lügner, who shook it. 'Welcome aboard, sir!'

Slick stuck up a hand to say something about negotiating a salary, but a scowl from Pegleg shut him up.

'All right,' Dunk said. 'That's eleven players, but I still don't like our odds. We're talking about playing against a Chaos Lord. How can we even tackle him? What else can we do to even things up?'

'How are the All-Stars doing?' asked Spinne. 'They were down to nine players before Khorne took over Ichorbod.'

'Is that nine with or without Ichorbod?' asked Guillermo.

'Without.'

'Does that make sense? He never did leave the field – most of him, at least.'

Spinne arched an eyebrow at Guillermo. 'Given that M'Grash kicked his head so hard that it's probably now floating down the Reik, I was comfortable counting him out.'

Guillermo nodded, and then noticed that all the other players were staring at him. He shrugged. 'I just wanted to be sure.'

'They're putting someone into a uniform,' Rotes said. 'It's that man we propped up here at the start of the half.'

'Lehrer?' Dunk said. He peered around the Blood God and saw Kathula and the bear-bodied All-Star stuffing Lehrer into a black suit of armour. As they cinched the straps around him, an evil grin grew on his face.

'It makes sense,' said Lügner with scorn. 'The Guterfiends have worshipped Khorne for decades, and he was in their pocket.'

Dirk stared at his father in disbelief. 'That's a glass castle you're standing in there.'

'Hey, I gave it up.' Lügner gazed up at Khorne. 'Look what it got me.'

'They're still short a player,' Anfäger said. 'Think we can get them to forfeit?'

Pegleg shook his head. 'They'll find someone they can press into service, have no doubt.' He glanced down at his hook. 'Daemons excel at that sort of thing.'

'Look at this!' said Jim. 'The Game Wizards are coming in to break up this shindig! They'll set things straight!'

'Jim,' Bob said, 'I don't know what it is you've been smoking over there since we ended up in the Realms of Chaos, but you'd better damn well share it!'

'That's not me!' said Jim. 'That's the network's Censer Wizard, who's in charge of keeping our broadcast clean. The smoke is coming out of his ears!'

Dunk spotted Blaque and Whyte running across the field towards them. 'Right!' the dwarf said as they trotted up. 'You didn't have a team wizard. Now you have two.'

Dunk coughed in surprise.

'You can't do that,' Dirk said. 'It violates the GWs' neutrality.'

Blaque glanced over at Khorne, who still stood waiting. 'Can anyone blame us if we ignore a few picky regulations at this point?' he asked Whyte.

'I don't see how,' said the elf.

'Fair enough, then,' said Blaque as he turned to Pegleg. 'We're with you now.'

'We're still going to get slaughtered,' Dunk said. 'We can't play against a Chaos Lord.'

Spinne and Lügner started to protest Dunk's lack of faith, but Pegleg cut them off. 'The young Mr. Hoffnung has a point.'

The ex-pirate pivoted on his wooden leg and strode out towards midfield. He stopped ten yards short of Khorne. 'Ahoy, the Blood God!' he said.

Khorne bowed his head to look down at the man. 'You are ready?'

'The Bad Bay Hackers accept your challenge and will play on your terms – with one exception.'

'Which is?'

'You must sit on the sidelines and not interfere with the game, except as a coach.'

Khorne unfolded his arms and cracked his knuckles. They made a sound like claps of thunder. 'Why?'

'We are but mortals and can barely tolerate your mighty presence. If you are on the field, you cannot play.'

'Plus,' Dr. Pill said, strolling up behind the coach, 'the Chaos Cup's spell requires your champions to beat ours. If you play, you technically cannot be considered a champion. You run the risk of negating the spell and everything you've worked for.'

Khorne stared down at the two men. For a moment, Dunk thought he might smite them dead right there.

Instead, an evil smile played across his face. 'Standard rules. Sudden death,' he said.

'Done,' Pegleg said without hesitation.

A moment later, Ichorbod's body fell away from Khorne as if the Blood God's own form – which then revealed itself – had turned as insubstantial as that of a ghost. It crashed to the ground at an awkward angle, leaving Khorne floating there in the air in all his gory glory.

Khorne slowly settled to the ground. He snapped a salute at the Hackers and then stomped back to the All-Stars' dugout. The ground shook as he walked, and he left wide pools of blood behind in every footstep.

'Wow, folks!' Bob's voice said. 'It looks like we have a game here!'

'And not just any game,' said Jim. 'The only game I've ever been to where the fate of the Empire rests on its outcome!'

'Not to mention all our lives!' Lästiges chipped in.

'Always looking on the dark side, aren't you?' said Bob. 'I've been dead for centuries!'

As Khorne left the field, Zauberer strode up to Ichorbod's headless form. Once there, he removed something from a pocket deep within his robes and waved it over the stump of the creature's neck.

'What's that bastard doing?' asked Dirk.

'I don't know,' Dunk said with a sick feeling in the pit of his stomach, 'but it can't be good.'

Zauberer pulled out a knife with his other hand and sliced open Ichorbod's neck stump. As the blood flowed hot and free from it, he jammed the thing in his hand into the wound. He chanted a few words over it, and then stepped back to admire his work.

One of Ichorbod's legs twitched, then the other. Soon the entire body convulsed to a spastic beat no one else could hear. Then it stopped.

The body pushed itself up on its arms and then climbed to its feet. As it did, Dunk saw a small sphere sticking up out of the centre of the neck. From this distance, he couldn't make out what it was, but he had the awful feeling it was staring right at him.

Then he heard a pitiful squeak, and he knew what Zauberer had done. Despite the stifling heat in this horrible realm, he shivered.

'Can we get a close-up on Ichorbod's neck there?' asked Bob. 'Thanks!'

The image on the Jumboball zoomed in at the top of the troll. Dunk watched it until he could pick out a confirmation of his fears. There, stuck atop the stump of Ichorbod's neck, sat Skragger's shrunken head. The vampiric orc's skull must have gone flying in the blast from the bolt of lightning that had incinerated Triomphe, and Zauberer had used his magic to locate and collect it.

'Dear Nuffle's nasties!' Jim said. 'It's Skragger, the black orc legend and former captain of the Chaos All-Stars! He's back!'

'And looking better – if far stranger – than ever!' Bob said.

Skragger flexed the muscles on his huge, new, acid-skinned body and grinned up at his image on the Jumboball.

'That's right!' Skragger growled with an insane grin. 'And the Hackers are dead!'

RHETT BOOL LIMPED into the centre of the field. One of his horns had been snapped in half, and the end of it was missing. 'Captains!' he said, his voice carried over the PA system. 'Please meet in the centre of the field for the coin toss!'

Cavre trotted over to the minotaur referee, while Skragger stomped there from the other side of the field. Cavre offered his hand, but Skragger refused to take it and snarled at him instead.

'We are playing by the standard rules, but the game will be sudden death. The first score wins the game.' Bool glanced up at the blood-red, lightning-traced sky. 'Here, the All-Stars are considered the home team. The visiting team calls the coin toss in the air.'

Bool pointed at Cavre. 'Orcs or Eagles?' he said, and flipped the coin into the air.

'Eagles!' Cavre called out.

'Orcs!' said Bool.

The crowd groaned as one.

'Do you wish to kick-off or receive?' Bool asked Skragger.

The creature showed his fangs with a horrible grin. 'Receive.'

'We will take the south end of the field,' Carve said, pointing back to where the Hackers already stood. He glanced at the mountain faces leering down at the game. 'If that means anything here.'

Cavre called the Hackers to him before they scattered to their positions.

'This is bad,' he said, 'but not insurmountable, as they will have the ball first. The good thing is that they will start deep in their own territory. We cannot let them score.

'This is no time to settle old fights. We must take the ball from them as fast as we can. Once we have it, we must put it in the end zone.'

Cavre gazed at each of the Hackers in turn. 'This is no ordinary game, but you are no ordinary players. I am proud to have served as your captain. Now, let's kick some ass!'

'Go Hackers!' the players shouted in response.

The Hackers trotted out to their positions. Dunk showed Lügner where to stand, in a spot just ahead of his own and to one side. While Pegleg had parlayed with Khorne, Lügner had borrowed a suit of armour from a fallen Hacker and donned it with Dirk's help. Spinne had done the same.

'You do this for a living?' Lügner asked, a worried smile on his face. 'I thought I raised you better than that.'

'Mother raised us,' said Dunk.

'Right,' Lügner said. Dunk noticed his hands shaking.

'It's okay, Father,' Dunk said. 'We'll get through this.'

Lügner tried to smile. 'You're a good son, Dunk.'

'Hey,' Dirk said from a few yards away, 'what about me?'

'Your problem,' said Dunk, 'is you're too much of a suck-up.'

Dirk stalked over and pulled both his brother and their father into a quick embrace. 'It's good to be back in business with you two,' he said before jogging back to his position.

Spinne, who had the spot in front of Dunk and opposite Lügner, turned and blew Dunk a kiss through her helmet. 'See you after the game,' she said.

Then Bool blew the whistle, and Cavre signalled for the Hackers to get ready. The crowd watched in silence, too terrified to bother with their long-standing traditions.

Cavre laid into the ball, and it sailed far down the field. He led the charge after it, with the Hackers running in his wake.

The ball tumbled into Skragger's hand, and the blitzer spurred his new body into action. M'Grash headed straight for him, while Edgar hung back a bit, hoping to intercept any pass the All-Star captain might attempt.

Dunk raced along behind his father. He appreciated his father's valiant offer to take the field with his sons, but he knew he didn't have the experience they did. If he got into trouble, Dunk wanted to be able to help him.

Of course, taking the ball and winning the game ranked far more important than Lügner's life. After all, if the Hackers failed to manage those things, far more people than Dunk's father would suffer.

Still, Dunk kept an eye on Lügner anyhow.

M'Grash roared as he slammed into Skragger, and the All-Star captain bellowed in response. The noise echoed throughout the stadium, and the fans screamed, although whether in terror or excitement Dunk could not say.

A sleek skaven raced through the Hackers, hunting for a clear part of the field so he could get open for a pass. Lügner charged at the rat-man, whose eyes glowed red, just like those of the rest of the All-Stars.

'While K'Thragsh mixes it up with Skragger near the All-Stars' end zone, Morty Maus makes a break for daylight near the other end of the field,' Bob said. 'Morty is new to the All-Stars this year, having been drafted to fill the shoes of his cousin, Macky, the All-Stars' captain who was killed in a game against the Hackers in last year's *Spike!* magazine Tournament.'

'Amazing! How can you say all that without taking a breath?' Jim asked.

'I don't breathe at all!' the vampire said.

Morty seemed faster than Dunk remembered him. He moved with a surety the rookie hadn't shown earlier in the game, and he showed no signs of exerting himself, despite sprinting up the field at top speed.

Lügner threw himself at the skaven, and Morty stiff-armed him for his trouble. Lügner fell back as if he'd hit a brick wall, and lay there, unmoving.

Dunk knew he was the only player standing between Morty and the end zone. He couldn't stop to check on his father. He had to concentrate on the skaven.

As Dunk closed with Morty, he looked into the skaven's eyes, which glowed red under his helmet. Right then, Dunk knew that Morty wasn't there any more. Just as Khorne had taken over Ichorbod's frame, a lesser daemon had possessed Morty's body and made him stronger and faster than ever.

At the last instant, Dunk dived under Morty's outstretched claw and slid along the Astrogranite at the creature, lashing out at him with his feet. The move surprised the skaven, who failed to even attempt to leap over Dunk's legs.

Morty tripped over Dunk at full speed and cartwheeled into the ground. The impact knocked off his helmet, and Dunk heard the tell-tale, sickening sound of at least one of the skaven's limbs snapping.

The Hacker thrower rolled to his feet and looked back to where he'd been. His father was already standing up, and staggering towards the next All-Star coming at him.

'Lower your shoulder!' Dunk shouted at him. 'If you stand straight up, they'll just–'

Dunk cut himself off when he spotted the ball arcing out over the field at him. Skragger had clearly meant the throw for Morty, but with the skaven down and possibly even out, Dunk had a clear shot at it. He leapt up into the air and felt the ball bend back his fingers and then stick between then.

Dunk hauled the ball down and landed in a crouch. When he did, he saw the bear-bodied All-Star slam into Lügner. Dunk's father either hadn't heard his son's advice or hadn't bothered to heed it. When the All-Star hit him, he'd not only been standing up, but he'd been back-pedalling to get in front of his opponent.

Lügner went flying backward and landed near Dunk's feet.

Dunk wanted to help his father, but he couldn't just hand the ball over to the All-Stars. He scanned downfield and couldn't find a single Hacker open for a pass.

Cavre had become embroiled in a mass pile-up in the centre of the field. He couldn't possibly break free in time.

Spinne had managed to get past the jam in the middle of the field, but Kathula was covering her like a blanket. Dunk didn't even know if Spinne could see through the tentacles the squid-headed woman was waving in her face.

Dunk thought about tucking the ball under his arm and making a run for it. Chances were good he'd get stuck in the middle, just like Cavre, though, and it would mean leaving his father to the tender mercies of the bear-bodied All-Star, and another who'd just broken out of the mess: Lehrer.

The sight of his family's former servant made the decision for Dunk. He cocked his arm back and fired the football off like a bullet. It skated over the heads of the players in the scrum and angled straight for Spinne, but when she reached up for it, it kept on going. It was far too high for her or Kathula to catch. In the end, it disappeared into the stands, where the fans swallowed it behind their bodies.

'It looks like the Hoffnung family reunion is about to be over!' Jim said. 'Bik Dutkus is about to lay a bear-style body slam on the senior Hoffnung's chest.'

'I've seen Dutkus burst open chests with that move before. It's a real heartbreaker!'

Dunk charged forward just as the bear-bodied All-Star raised his arms and leapt from his feet, aiming to land flat atop the stunned Lügner, and put a quick end to his short career. Dunk hit Dutkus right in the ribs as he came down, knocking him clear of his fallen father.

'What a hit!' Bob said. 'The last time I saw someone get knocked around like that was when I had dinner at your house last Friday, Jim!'

'My baby girl's usually much more gentle than that with our guests, I swear!'

As Dunk scrambled to his feet, he noticed where Dutkus had sliced open Lügner's exposed forearm, splattering blood everywhere. Before he had the time to wonder why, Lehrer came at him.

Dunk took his own advice and bent low and came up under his old teacher's attack. He shoved his forearm up under Lehrer's helmet and hit him with everything he had.

Lehrer's helmet went flying off, leaving his head still attached to his shoulders, and the man flipped over onto his back. Dunk piled on top of him, determined to finish him off as fast as he could, before Dutkus could recover and kill Lügner.

'Good hit, kid,' Lehrer said. 'I taught you well.'

Dunk didn't say a thing. He just laid into the man with his fists, smashing his spiked gauntlets into his face. After three solid blows, the fight flushed out of Lehrer, and he went limp.

Dunk grabbed the old man by the top of his breastplate so he could get in a good, solid hit. Then he cocked back his arm for the killing blow.

Dunk hesitated. He'd wanted to kill Lehrer for months, but faced with the chance to do it with his bare hands, he found it hard to follow through. Killing other players on the field was one thing. It was all part of his job. But to kill the man who'd taught him to fight, who'd raised him as much as his father had – maybe more – gave him pause, no matter how much Lehrer deserved it.

'Go ahead, kid,' Lehrer said. 'I got it coming.'

Dunk realised that the old man hadn't been possessed like the other All-Stars. He'd joined the team after the daemons had taken over the roster – which meant he'd taken up with them of his own free will.

Dunk shook his head. As he did, he spotted Dutkus getting to his feet. If he wanted to kill Lehrer, it had to be right now. Even so, it might take too long and doom Lügner to death at the bear-man's claws.

Dunk let the old man drop to the ground. 'This isn't over,' he said as he charged Dutkus again.

This time, the bear-man stood ready for Dunk. This wasn't some old man who'd never suited up for a game before. Dutkus had played Blood Bowl for years – a lifetime for an All-Stars lineman – and Dunk's last hit had driven him – and the daemon inside him – furious.

Dunk lowered his shoulder and rammed straight into Dutkus's chest. Too late, he realised that this had been exactly what the All-Star had wanted him to do.

Dutkus wrapped his arms around Dunk and managed to keep his feet. With the strength of the daemon possessing him, the bear-man worked Dunk up against him and started to squeeze, forcing the air from his lungs.

Dunk tried to break free, but Dutkus had pulled him from his feet to prevent him from getting any leverage at all. The bear-man's embrace proved impossible to shrug off. The only thing left to do was to head-butt the bear-man, but his helmet kept him too well protected. Dunk's efforts only bounced off Dutkus's faceguard.

For a moment, Dunk hoped that his own breastplate would protect him from suffocating. If Dutkus couldn't squeeze him any further, he'd get tired eventually, and then Dunk could make his move.

But the breastplate started to give. The middle bent in towards Dunk's sternum, threatening to break his ribs and crush his lungs. Dunk flailed about with his helmet and hands, looking for some opening – anything – but nothing he did had any effect.

Dunk started to black out. Somewhere impossibly far away – maybe in a dream, he thought – he heard Lügner say, 'Let go of my son!'

Then Dutkus let loose a horrible howl right in Dunk's face. The thrower screamed back, both in pain and terror, and then he was free. He staggered backward gasping for breath, and saw his father stabbing the spikes on his gauntlet up under the bear-man's custom-made breastplate, over and over again. Each blow made a hard, meaty sound and produced gouts of blood.

Dutkus reached out and slapped Lügner away with a rough backhand, but instead of following up on the blow, the All-Star fell hard to his knees, keening in pain.

Lügner picked himself up off the ground and looked towards Dunk, worry flaring in his eyes. 'Are you okay?' he asked.

Before Dunk could shout a warning, Lehrer hit Lügner from behind. The two of them went down in a tangle of tired limbs.

'I've never seen anything like this before, Jim! The fans are refusing to give up the ball!'

'Would you want to give it back to a team who would condemn you and the entire world around you to eternal damnation, Bob?'

'That's a delicious idea! I'll have to get back to you on that one!'

'This is for Greta!' Lehrer said as he used a sharp edge on the side of his gauntlet to slice through the chinstrap on Lügner's helmet.

Dunk found that he couldn't shout because he still couldn't breathe. His crushed breastplate pressed so hard on his lungs, that even without Dutkus's help, he'd pass out if he didn't get some relief soon. He clawed at the straps that held his armour together, but they were trapped under the bent metal, and he couldn't quite reach them on his own.

'She was mine!' Lügner said to Lehrer as he held the other man's arm at bay. Lügner's helmet had fallen off, exposing his head. Blood flowed from a half-dozen small cuts on his face and neck.

'She loved me first!' Lehrer said. 'You stole her from me, and because of you, she's dead!'

Lügner shoved his free hand up under Lehrer's faceguard and wrapped his fingers around the man's throat. 'You think you grieve for her more than me? I know it's my fault that mob stormed the castle. There's not a day goes by that the guilt doesn't crush me!'

Lehrer started to laugh, low and strained, as Lügner's choking of him made anything louder impossible. 'You don't understand,' he said, 'but then you never did.

'I let that mob in,' Lehrer said. 'I gave Greta the chance to escape with me, to take Kirta and run away with me to start a new life somewhere else.'

'You–!'

Lehrer spat down into Lügner's face. 'She spurned me – again – because of you. She slapped my face.'

Dunk strained against his armour with all his might, but it just wouldn't give. He fell forward on his knees and started to crawl forward, but he could not get enough air in his lungs to proceed. He collapsed onto his face.

'I killed her,' Lehrer rasped as Lügner's fingers crushed his windpipe. 'I killed them both, and I let the mob in to cover my sins.'

Lügner let go of the hand Lehrer had poised near his own neck and drove both of his hands into the other man's larynx. As he did, Lehrer punched up under his old master's jaw with his spiked gauntlet, piercing the soft flesh there and tearing open his throat.

As Dunk watched, unable to do anything to prevent the horrors before him, a blade slipped between the halves of his breastplate and sliced through the straps holding them together. He ignored the pain that flared in his side as the blade cut through the flesh in his haste. He drew in a large gulp of air and bellowed, 'No!'

'FORGET THEM,' DIRK said as he hauled Dunk to his feet and helped him shrug off his crushed breastplate. 'It's too late for them, but maybe not for the rest of us.'

Dunk growled in frustration, and turned to see the ball bouncing around in the stands. Skragger had waded in after it, slaughtering helpless fans left and right, causing a general stampede away from him, but every time he got near the ball, the fans would toss it away from him again towards another part of the stadium.

Now some of the other All-Stars, emboldened by Skragger's success, were venturing into the stands too. Eventually, the fans would make a mistake – or one of them would decide to buy his own life with the ball – and the All-Stars would get the pigskin back, unless the Hackers did something fast.

Dunk and Dirk sprinted towards the end zone, where they saw Spinne sparring with Kathula. They looked like they'd been at it for a while. Each of them had lost pieces of armour and bled from a handful of superficial wounds. Kathula's helmet had gone missing, but she made up for it by lashing out harder and faster with the unrestrained tentacles that made up the lower half of her face.

One of the tentacles wrapped around Spinne's bare forearm and started to pull her in towards Kathula's snapping beak. Spinne braced her feet and spun around, swinging Kathula after her by the tentacle attached to the catcher's arm.

The squeals of pain that spouted from Kathula's face only encouraged Spinne, and she began to turn faster and faster, pulling the squid-woman from her feet. The soft tissue of the attached tentacle began to stretch, and this caused the tentacle's grip around Spinne's arm to tighten until it started to cut off the circulation to her hand.

The Hackers' catcher spun faster and faster. She screamed from the pain in her arm as the tentacle stretched thinner and thinner and began to slice into her bare flesh like a length of sharp wire.

'That's one way to dance!' Bob said. 'Looks like Schönheit's the one calling the tune!'

'I think Kathula is regretting extending the invitation now. She looks like she – or her face, rather – might snap at any second!' said Jim.

A moment later, that's exactly what happened. The tentacle around Spinne's arm pulled free from Kathula's face, and the squid-woman went flying towards the stands. She landed against the restraining wall, and the fans in the first row caught her. She screamed again as they pulled her into the bleachers, blood spouting from her face. The people there tore her to pieces with a dozen sets of hands at once, and they kept at her until long after she stopped screaming from the pain.

'What happened to you?' Spinne asked Dunk as she unwrapped the length of tentacle from her arm. It left a deep cut behind, but it had not gone through the muscle to the bone. She glanced at his bare chest. 'I like the new look.'

Dunk wanted to smile at her, but found he couldn't. 'We need to get that ball,' he said. 'Do you think we'll survive if we go into the crowd?'

Spinne nodded. 'The trick is that the All-Stars will then use you as a shield so they can get in too. At least, that's what they've done twice so far, and when the shield fails, they'll kill you if they can. We've lost Anfäger and Hernd that way already. I think I even saw Slick disappear in there.'

Dunk glanced around. M'Grash and Cavre were trying to get into the crowd, but a trio of All-Stars had blocked them. Spiel had climbed into Edgar's upper branches to get away from an orc whose arms seemed to have become axes. Guillermo had made it ten rows up into the stands and was waving and hollering for the fans to throw him the ball. Skragger was working his way towards the Estalian, slaughtering fans as he went.

Up in the stands, Dunk saw a Hacker helmet bouncing along atop the heads and upraised hands of the fans, but there didn't seem to be anything but a jersey beneath it, somehow snagged inside the helmet.

It turned his stomach to think whose head might be in it. Oddly, it seemed to be heading for the ball, as if the fans wished to bring the two together.

'We'll have to chance it,' Dunk said. 'I'll distract Skragger. You two get that ball!'

He charged towards the worst part of the devastation, a section of stands cleared out entirely but for a couple of handfuls of dead or dying fans. 'Skragger!' he shouted. 'You damned coward! Come on down here and fight someone your own – fight me, you wuss! I'm looking forward to keeping your tiny head in the bottom of my chamber pot from now on.'

'You!' Skragger said as he turned to see who had insulted him. 'Kill you!'

Dunk stood his ground in the end zone, waiting for the crazed troll-bodied, vampire-headed orc creature to make his way down to him. They were going to end this here, one way or the other, he was sure.

As Dunk braced for Skragger's attack, a bolt of red lightning cracked into the Astrogranite next to him. He turned around just in time to see a pillar of ash that had once been a dark elf in an All-Stars' uniform crumble into a pile of dust.

'That Chaos Cup must have made Zauberer a better shot,' Jim said, 'because without it he doesn't seem like he could hit the backside of an ogre!'

'He can't even do that!' said Bob. 'He's missed K'Thragsh three times already today!'

Dunk spotted Zauberer floating high over the stadium, cursing as he pointed his wand in Dunk's direction again. The thrower stared up at the wizard and wondered just how someone could try to dodge a lightning bolt. As he watched, Zauberer's robes transformed into a writhing sheet of vipers.

'Got 'em!' Blaque shouted from the sidelines near the Hackers' dugout. He turned towards Whyte. 'Do you have something about snakes? Why not just kill the bugger?'

Dunk never heard the reply. As he laughed, watching the snakes strike at the wizard in an effort to keep from falling to their deaths, a shadow fell over him. He had just enough time to glance over and see Skragger coming down at him – and maybe to wonder just how he could possibly survive this.

Acting on instinct instead of conscious thought, Dunk dived forward. Most of Skragger sailed over him, but the creature's boot tagged Dunk on his pauldron and knocked him spinning to the ground.

When Dunk got up, he found Skragger standing over him. 'You're dead!' the creature snarled, spreading its arms wide and gathering Dunk into its fatal embrace.

Contact with Skragger's skin burned Dunk's bare chest, but just barely. At first he fought it, but having gone through that just moments ago with Dutkus, he knew that he was doomed to fail. Instead, he began to claw at Skragger with everything he had.

As Dunk clawed at Skragger with his fingers, he realised that the creature wasn't all there. His fingers passed right through Skragger's flesh, striking bone instead. When Khorne had remade the body, it seemed it had only been an illusion, not real at all. The bits that had burned Dunk's skin a bit were the bare remnants that were left: not much more than a skeletal frame underneath it all.

Confused, but still determined, Dunk kept pulling at Skragger. His efforts became more desperate as the bony Skragger increased the pressure on him, squeezing the breath from him, realising that the skin he thought would burn Dunk wasn't doing a thing. Dunk's digging hands found a set of ribs and started yanking on them, pulling them out and tossing them over his shoulder.

'Crush you dead!' Skragger growled as Dunk continued his grisly work. Once through the ribcage, he stabbed his hand into the creature's chest, hoping to find a vital organ, or maybe to snap Skragger's borrowed spine.

Instead, his fingers struck something hard and gnarled. He felt for purchase, and then it bit him hard, straight to the bone. Dunk pulled his bloody fingers back for a second and then dived back in with both arms. This time the thing inside didn't put up a fight. But the creature it was inside of did.

'No!' Skragger screeched in his high-pitched voice. 'You can't! I won't let you!'

Skragger went from crushing Dunk to his chest to desperately trying to shove him away. He wedged an arm between himself and Dunk and pushed with all his might.

Dunk had found the grips his hands needed, and he refused to let go, no matter what happened. He gritted his teeth and pulled with both his arms, using Skragger's strength to reinforce his own.

'No!' Skragger said, bashing at Dunk with his free arm. The blows smashed into Dunk's helmet and rattled his brains in his skull. Still he held on as best he could. He worked his knees up between himself and Skragger and pulled as hard as he could on the thing in the creature's chest. Soon, he knew either the thing would give out or he would. Soon it would all be over, one way or another.

Then Bob said, 'Touchdown, Hackers!'

'No!' something inside of Skragger screamed. At first, Dunk thought it had come from Skragger's head, but the voice had been far too deep. Then, with one last pull, the thing inside Skragger yanked free from his ribcage, and Dunk went tumbling backward off the beast.

Dunk landed in the end zone, right next to Slick, who stood over him, grinning and holding the ball. The halfling wore a Hacker helmet that fit him like an umbrella, and a Hacker jersey that tumbled past his knees like a dress.

'Good work, son!' Slick said. 'That's an astonishing prize you have there.'

Dunk glanced back to discover what he held in his hands, and he saw the Chaos Cup staring back at him. It screamed at him, its beady, black eyes blazing red fire.

Another, more horrible scream, echoed that of the Chaos Cup. It came from the All-Stars' dugout, still shrouded in blackness. It didn't remain in there. A moment later, Khorne's blood-soaked form burst from the dugout and sailed high into the sky over the stadium.

'The preparation of a thousand years gone to waste!' the Blood God shouted in disgust. 'I was so close! It was almost mine!'

With that, the blazing hot air around the stadium shimmered and gave way to crisp, cool weather. The sky turned clear and blue once more, and the leering mountains disappeared from the distance. The scent of brimstone faded away, and Dunk's mouth tasted not of ash, but of his own tongue again.

The crowd stood up and cheered.

'Hackers win!' Bob said, even happier than when he'd announced the touchdown. 'The world is saved! We all get to live! Hackers win!'

'LET'S SEE THAT replay again,' Slick said. The image on the crystal ball leapt backward and showed the halfling standing alone in the stands with the ball in his hands. Then Dirk appeared next to him and lifted him up over his head. With a two-handed throw, Dirk hurled Slick down the field, where Spinne caught him just before his head smacked into the ground.

Dunk listened from the doorway for a moment and smiled. Seeing everyone together like this made all the strange, horrible, and sometimes even wonderful adventures of the past three years seem worthwhile.

'I think that's enough,' Lästiges said. 'You'll wear out my Daemonic Visual Display.'

'I thought you could run a DVD forever?'

Lästiges smiled as she leaned back into Dirk's arms in the plush couch. 'After what we've all been through, I thought you'd know that daemons don't last forever.'

'Show what happens to Skragger instead, then,' Slick said. 'I love seeing justice served.'

'Must we suffer through that again?' Guillermo asked with a shiver, from the other end of the couch. 'It is bad enough we have to watch his tiny head torn from the skeleton time after time, but to see the sad

757

little thing disappear into the stadium's communal bog... I can do without that.'

'Are you getting soft, Mr. Reyes?' Cavre asked with a smile from his overstuffed chair across the way.

'Just on myself,' Guillermo said with a wry smile.

'That bloody bastard had worse than that coming to him,' said Edgar. Here in the private courtyard, he could stretch his branches high into the open sky, which tended to put him in a much better mood than when he was forced indoors just to be near his team-mates, his friends. 'He's just lucky I didn't get my bloody twigs on him, or I'd have crushed him under my roots.'

'He got off easier than that accursed wizard for sure,' Pegleg said. The coach reclined on a divan, his good leg up on the furniture while his wooden one rested, removed, on the floor.

'Still sorry,' M'Grash said with a frown. He sat on the floor, too morose still to permit himself anything more comfortable. 'Didn't know.'

'It's okay, M'Grash,' Spiel said. 'The way you don't like snakes, it's easy to see why you'd want to stomp all those vipers to a bloody paste. It's just unfortunate that Zauberer happened to be underneath them when you did.'

Dunk took this as his cue to stroll back into the room. The best thing he could do for M'Grash would be to help keep his mind off that accidental, but convenient killing.

'Did you get rid of it, Mr. Hoffnung?' Pegleg asked.

Dunk nodded. 'The Champions of Death were pleased to get their trophy, and I was happy to get rid of it.'

'We could have won that game if not for the Game Wizards,' Pegleg said. 'The Chaos Cup should be ours.'

'That's one honour I think I can do without,' Dunk said.

'Besides, captain, we do have the Blood Bowl trophy to help assuage that pain,' said Cavre. 'I can contact Dr. Pill if you need anything stronger.'

'That one-eyed elf gives me the willies,' Spinne said from an overstuffed love seat that bore scorch marks from a wayward torch. 'I'll be happy to not see him for a couple of months.'

'Careful,' said Pegleg. 'Just because we've won the greatest trophy in the land doesn't mean we can rest on our laurels. Now we have a title to defend!'

'Right,' said Dunk, 'but for my part I'm looking forward to a little rest and relaxation.' He raised his head and looked around at the walls of his old family keep. 'Besides, cleaning up this place properly is going to take weeks.'

Dirk grinned at his brother. 'So you got it back in roughly the same condition as when you left it. As I recall, a mob of angry people ran through the place back then too, just like yesterday.'

Dunk nodded. 'It's too bad some of the Guterfiends got away. I suppose with the game being broadcast live it was bound to happen. They just weren't stupid enough to stick around after Khorne's team lost.'

'I don't think they'll be back to Altdorf any time soon,' Lästiges said with a carefree laugh.

'Why were you gone so long?' Spinne asked, motioning for Dunk to sit down next to her.

'I had something else to pick up,' Dunk said as he came over to stand in front of Spinne. He reached into his pocket, knelt down in front of her and gazed into her eyes.

'Blood Bowl has been great to me,' Dunk said. 'When I met Slick for the first time, I was just about ready to give up and let that chimera eat me. I was homeless, penniless, and friendless.

'Playing this game has changed all that.'

He nodded at Pegleg. 'It gave me money.'

He smiled at Dirk. 'It brought my brother back to me.'

He glanced around at the others. 'It made me many of the most loyal and trustworthy friends a man could wish for.'

He stared around at the four walls around them. 'It even restored me to my ancestral home.'

Dunk turned back to Spinne again. She was so beautiful he almost couldn't stand to look at her, but to turn away seemed far worse.

'There's only one thing I'd like to change,' Dunk said, as he presented the ring to Spinne. It had a wide band of gold and a diamond cut into the shape of a football.

'Yes!' Spinne said before Dunk could say another word. Her grin split her face and showed all her pearly teeth. 'I cannot wait to marry you!'

Dunk held her close for a long moment, and then kissed her, and she kissed him back like she wanted it to last forever. When their lips parted, they held each other still, and she wiped away the lone tear that had found its way onto his cheek.

'So, son,' Slick said. 'I hope this doesn't mean you're entertaining any silly notions of retiring from the game and settling down?'

Dunk cocked his head to one side. He heard something coming from outside the keep's walls. 'I don't think so,' he said as he leapt to his feet. 'Follow me.'

Taking Spinne's hand, he strode with her through the keep until they reached the balcony that overlooked the public square outside the small fortress's doors, which still lay smashed open from the night before.

As Dunk and Spinne stepped up to the balcony, the people of Altdorf in the square below erupted in cheers. When Pegleg, Slick, and the rest of the Hackers appeared behind them, the noise rose to a roar.

Dunk turned to kiss Spinne again, a grin on both their faces.

'What's that they're chanting?' she asked.

'Can't you make it out?'

'They may be wonderful fans, but they don't have the best rhythm. Tell me.'

Dunk leaned closer to her. 'Listen,' he said. '"Repeat! Repeat! Repeat!"'

'Oh,' Spinne said with a sly smile as she leaned in to kiss Dunk again. 'Don't mind if I do.'

ABOUT THE AUTHOR

Matt Forbeck has worked full-time in the adventure games industry for over 15 years. He has designed collectible card games, roleplaying games, miniatures games and board games, and has written short fiction, comic books and novels.

A GUIDE TO BLOOD BOWL

Being a volume of instruction for rookies and beginners of Nuffle's sacred game.

(Translated by Andreas Halle of Middenheim)

NUFFLE'S SACRED NUMBER

Let's start with the basics. To play Blood Bowl you need two warrior sects each led by a priest. In the more commonly used Blood Bowl terminology this means you need two teams of fearless psychotics (we also call them 'players') led by a coach, who is quite often a hoary old ex-player more psychotic than all of his players put together.

The teams face each other on a ritualised battlefield known as a pitch or field. The field is marked out in white chalk lines into several different areas. One line separates the pitch in two through the middle dividing the field into each team's 'half'. The line itself is known as the 'line of scrimmage' and is often the scene of some brutal fighting, especially at the beginning and halfway points of the game. At the back of each team's half of the field is a further dividing line that separates the backfield from the end zone. The end zone is where an opposing team can score a 'touchdown' - more on that later.

Teams generally consist of between twelve to sixteen players. However, as first extolled by Roze-el, Nuffle's sacred number is eleven, which means only a maximum of eleven players from each team may be on the field at the same time. It's worth noting that many teams have tried to break this sacred convention in the past, particularly goblin teams (orcs too, but that's usually because they can't count rather than any malevolent intent), but Nuffle has always seen fit to punish those who do.

TOUCHDOWNS AND ALL THAT MALARKEY

The aim of the game is to carry, throw, kick and generally move an inflated animal bladder coated in leather and – quite often – spikes, across the field into the opposing team's end zone. Of course, the other team is trying to do the same thing. Once the inflated bladder, also known as the ball, has been carried into or caught in the opposing team's end zone, a 'touchdown' has been scored. Traditionally the crowd then goes wild, though the reactions of the fans vary from celebration if it was their team that just scored to anger if their team have conceded. The player who has scored will also have his moment of jubilation and much celebratory hugging with fellow team-mates will ensue, although a bear hug from an Ogre, even if his intention is that of mutual happiness, is best avoided! The team that scores the most touchdowns within the allotted timeframe is deemed the winner.

The game lasts about two hours and is split into two segments unsurprisingly called 'the first half' and 'the second half'. The first half starts after both teams have walked onto the pitch and taken their positions, usually accompanied by much fanfare and cheering from the fans. The team captains meet in the centre of the pitch with the 'ref' (more on him later) to perform the start-of-the-game ritual known as 'the toss'. A coin is flipped in the air and one of the captains will call 'orcs' or 'eagles'. Whoever wins the toss gets the choice of 'kicking' or 'receiving'. Kicking teams will kick the ball to the receiving teams. Once the ball has been kicked the whistle is blown and the first half will begin. The second half begins in much the same way except that the kicking team at the beginning of the first half will now become the receiving team and vice-versa.

Violence is encouraged to gain possession, keep and move the ball, although different races and teams will try different methods and varying degrees of hostility. The fey elves, for instance, will often try pure speed to collect the ball and avoid the other team's players. Orc and Chaos teams will take a more direct route of overpowering the opposing team and trundling down the centre of the field almost daring their opponents to stop them.

Rookies reading this may be confused as to why I haven't mentioned the use of weapons yet. This is because in Blood Bowl Nuffle decreed that one's own body is the only weapon one needs to play the game. Over the years this hasn't stopped teams using this admittedly rather loose wording to maximum effect and is the reason why a player's armour is more likely than not covered in sharp protruding spikes with blades and large knuckle-dusters attached to gauntlets. Other races and teams often 'forget' about this basic principle and just ignore Roze-el's teachings on the matter. Dwarfs and goblins (yes, them again) are the usual suspects, although this is not exclusively their domain. The history of Blood Bowl is littered with the illegal use of weapons and the many devious contraptions brought forward by the dwarfs and goblins, ranging from monstrous machines such as the dwarf death-roller to the no-less-dangerous chainsaw.

THE PSYCHOS... I MEAN PLAYERS

As I've already mentioned, there are many ways to get the ball from one end of the field to the other. Equally, there are as many ways to stop the ball from moving towards a team's end zone. A Blood Bowl player, to an extent, needs to be a jack-of-all-trades – as equally quick on the offensive as well as being able to defend. This doesn't mean that there aren't any specialists in the sport, far from it – a Blood Bowl player needs to specialise in one of the many positions if he wishes to rise above the humble lineman. Let's look at the more common positions:

Blitzers: These highly-skilled players are usually the stars of the game, combining strength and skill with great speed and flexibility. All the most glamorous Blood Bowl players are blitzers, since they are always at the heart of the action and doing very impressive things! Their usual job is to burst a hole through their opponents' lines, and then run with the ball to score. Team captains are usually blitzers, and all of them, without exception, have egos the size of a halfling's appetite.

Throwers: There is more to Blood Bowl than just grabbing the ball and charging full tilt at the other side (though this has worked for most teams at one time or another). If you can get a player on the other side of your opponents' line, why not simply toss the ball to him and cut out all that unnecessary bloodshed? This, of course, is where the special thrower comes in! These guys are usually lightly armoured (preferring to dodge a tackle rather than be flattened by it).

Throwers of certain races have also been known to launch other things than just the ball. For decades now, an accepted tactic of orc, goblin and even halfling teams is to throw their team-mates down-field. This is usually done by the larger members of said teams such as ogres, trolls and in the case of the halflings, treemen. Of course this tactic is not without risk. Whilst the bigger players are strong it doesn't necessarily mean they are accurate. As regular fans know, goblins make a reassuring 'splat' sound as they hit the ground or stadium wall head-first - much to the joy of the crowd! Trolls are notoriously stupid with memory spans that would shame a goldfish. So a goblin or snotling about to be hurtled across the pitch by his troll-ish team mate will often find itself heading for the troll's gaping maw instead as the monster forgets what he's holding and decides to have a snack!

Catchers: And of course if you are throwing the ball, it would be nice if there was someone at the other end to catch it! This is where the specialist catcher comes in. Lightly armoured for speed, they are adept at dodging around slower opponents and heading for the open field ready for a long pass to arrive. The best catcher of all time is generally reckoned to be the legendary Tarsh Surehands of the otherwise fairly repulsive skaven team, the Skavenblight Scramblers. With his two heads and four arms, the mutant ratman plainly had something of an advantage.

Blockers: If one side is trying to bash its way through the opposing team's lines, you will often see the latter's blockers come into action to stop them. These lumbering giants are often slow and dim-witted, but they have the size and power to stop show-off blitzers from getting any further up the field! Black orcs, ogres and trolls make especially good blockers, but this fact has hampered the chances of teams like the Oldheim Ogres, who, with nothing but blockers and linemen in their team, have great trouble actually scoring a touchdown!

Linemen: While a good deal of attention is paid to the various specialist players, every true Blood Bowl fan would agree that the players who do most of the hard work are the ordinary linemen. These are the guys who get bashed out of the way while trying to stop a hulking great ogre from sacking their thrower, who are pushed out of the way when their flashy blitzer sets his sights on the end zone, or who get beaten and bruised by the linemen of the opposite side while the more gifted players skip about scoring touchdowns. 'Moaning like a lineman' is a common phrase in Blood Bowl circles for a bad complainer, but if it wasn't for the linemen whingeing about their flashier team-mates, the newspapers would often have nothing to fill their sports pages with!

DA REFS

Blood Bowl has often been described, as 'nearly-organised chaos' by its many critics. Blood Bowl's admirers emphatically agree with the critics then again they don't like to play up the 'nearly-organised' bit, in fact some quite happily just describe it as 'chaos'. However, it is widely accepted that you do need someone in charge of the game's proceedings and to enforce the games rules or else it wouldn't be Blood Bowl at all. Again, this point is often lost on some fans who would quite happily just come and spectate/participate in a big fight.

In any case, the person and/or creature in charge of a game is known as 'the ref'. The ref, in his traditional kit of zebra furs, has a very difficult job to do. You have to ask yourself what kind of mind accepts this sort of responsibility especially when the general Blood Bowl viewing public rate refs far below tax collectors, traffic wardens and sewer inspectors in their estimation.

Of course some refs revile in the notoriety and are as psychopathic as the players themselves. Max 'Kneecap' Mittleman would never issue a yellow or red card but simply disembowel the offending player. It is also fair to say that most (if not all) refs are not the bastions of honesty and independence they would have you believe. In fact the Referees and Allied Rulekeepers Guild has strict bribery procedures and union established rates. Although teams may not always want to bribe a ref – especially when sheer intimidation can be far cheaper.

THAT'S THE BASICS

Now I've covered the rudimentary points of how to play Blood Bowl it's worth going over some of the basic plays you'll see in most games of one variation or another. Remember, it's not just about the fighting; you have to score at some point as well!

The Cage: Probably the most basic play in the game yet it's the one halfling teams still can't get right. This involves surrounding the ball carrier with bodyguards and then moving the whole possession up field. Once within yards of the team's end zone the ball carrier will explode from his protective cocoon and sprint across the line. Not always good against elf teams who have an annoying knack of dodging into the cage and stealing the ball away, still you should see the crowd's rapture when an elf mis-steps and he's clothes-lined to the floor by a sneering orc.

The Chuck: The second most basic play, although it does require the use of a semi-competent thrower, which rules a large proportion of teams out from the start. Blockers on the 'line of scrimmage' will open a gap for the team's receivers to run through, and once they are in the opposing team's back field the thrower will lob the ball to them. Provided one of the catchers can catch it, all that remains is a short run into the opposing end zone for a touchdown. The survival rate of a lone catcher in the enemy's half is obviously not great so it's important to get as many catchers upfield as possible. The more catchers a team employs, the more chances at least one of them will remain standing to complete the pass.

The Chain: A particular favourite of blitzers everywhere. Players position themselves at different stages upfield. The ball is then quickly passed from player to player in a series of short passes until the blitzer on the end of the chain can wave to the crowd and gallop into the end zone. A broken link in the chain can balls this up (excuse the pun), giving the opposing team an opportunity to intercept the ball.

The Kill-em-all!: Favoured by dwarf teams and those that lack a certain finesse. It works on the principle that if there isn't anyone left in the opposing team, then who's going to stop you from scoring? The receiving team simply hides the ball in its half and proceeds to maul, break and kill the opposition. Chaos teams are particularly good at this. When there is less than a third of the opposing team left, the ball will slowly make its way upfield. The downside is that some teams can get so engrossed in the maiming they simply run out of time to score. Nevertheless it's a fan favourite and is here to stay.